A
Garland Series

VICTORIAN FICTION

NOVELS OF FAITH AND DOUBT

*A collection of 121 novels
in 92 volumes, selected by
Professor Robert Lee Wolff,
Harvard University,
with a separate introductory volume
written by him
especially for this series.*

USE AND ABUSE

HIDDEN DEPTHS

Felicia Skene

Garland Publishing, Inc., New York & London

1975

Copyright © 1975
by Garland Publishing, Inc.
All Rights Reserved

Library of Congress Cataloging in Publication Data

Skene, Felicia Mary Frances, 1821-1899.
  Use and abuse.

  (Victorian fiction : Novels of faith and doubt ;
no. 28)
  Reprint of the 1849 ed. of Use and abuse, published
by F. & J. Rivington, London, and of the 1866 ed. of
Hidden depths, published by Edmonston and Douglas, Edin-
burgh.
  I. Skene, Felicia Mary Frances, 1821-1899. Hidden
depths. 1975. II. Title. III. Series.
PZ3.S6277Us7   [PR5452.S7]   823'.8   75-474
ISBN 0-8240-1552-5

339079

Printed in the United States of America

USE AND ABUSE

Bibliographical note:

this facsimile has been made from a copy in the
British Museum
(12622.e.23)

USE AND ABUSE,

A Tale.

LONDON:
GILBERT & RIVINGTON, PRINTERS,
ST. JOHN'S SQUARE.

USE AND ABUSE,

A Tale.

BY THE AUTHOR OF
"WAYFARING SKETCHES AMONGST THE GREEKS AND TURKS,
AND ON THE SHORES OF THE DANUBE,
BY A SEVEN YEARS RESIDENT IN GREECE."

Post tenebras spero lucem.

London:
FRANCIS & JOHN RIVINGTON,
ST. PAUL'S CHURCH YARD, AND WATERLOO PLACE.

1849.

CONTENTS.

CHAPTER I.

                                            PAGE

The Philosopher in the desert:—" Requiescat in pace." 1

CHAPTER II.

The fire worshipper, Magus, and child of the sun 37

CHAPTER III.

The Greek Monk—he tells how the Serpent worship yet exists on earth 65

CHAPTER IV.

The servant of purity meets with the slave of iniquity 79

CHAPTER V.

Arabyn relates to Raymond the life of his mind 102

CHAPTER VI.

Arabyn details to Raymond in a letter how he designs to become master of his own destiny 134

CHAPTER VII.

Mr. Denham and his niece 142

CHAPTER VIII.

Arabyn enters on the execution of the plan whereby he designs to master his destiny 162

CHAPTER IX.

Arabyn prepares the snare successfully for the victim 181

CHAPTER X.

Arabyn casts the veil over the eyes of the victim 205

CHAPTER XI.

The victim blinded, follows on the path where Arabyn leads . . . 216

CHAPTER XII.

The first attempt of Arabyn to serve the power of evil is rendered abortive by Raymond 223

CHAPTER XIII.

Arabyn removes a human obstacle from his path 251

CHAPTER XIV.

Raymond and Arabyn meet face to face, and the victim for whom they contend is between them 270

CHAPTER XV.

The deeds of Arabyn bear such fruit as he looked not for 293

CHAPTER XVI.

Arabyn by the power of his words drives a soul to self-destruction 324

CHAPTER XVII.

The second attempt of Arabyn for the execution of his plan is thwarted by Raymond 340

CHAPTER XVIII.

Arabyn, baffled on all sides by an unattainable foe, continues the struggle with increasing energy 364

CHAPTER XIX.

Arabyn and his companion visit the Greek Bishops by night . . . 376

CHAPTER XX.

The last struggle of Arabyn and his victim 398

CHAPTER XXI.

The retribution commences for Arabyn 413

CHAPTER XXII.

The result of Arabyn's attempt to master destiny, and the work which he accomplished by the labour of his whole existence . 418

CHAPTER XXIII.

The return of the Philosopher to the desert 441

USE AND ABUSE.

CHAPTER I.

THE PHILOSOPHER IN THE DESERT:—"REQUIESCAT IN PACE."

NATURE, visible and glorious, is the priestess of the Incomprehensible Unseen. She ministereth (an holy vestal) in that temple of the Most High, whose walls are the blue unbounded ether, and whose ever-burning lamps are the eternal stars; there, through the veil of her eloquent beauty, she admits the soul of man to look into that Holy of Holies of which the shrine is infinity. Her incense, ascending for ever before the Invisible Throne, is wrung from the fragrance of ten thousand forests; her hymn of praise, which ceaseth not night or day, is chanted by the great voice of all inanimate creation; now, in the music of that deep rolling thunder, which sounds as though it were a dirge sung in the heavens, over some perishing world whose race is run; now, in the monotonous roaring of the ocean billows, that seem continually to lift up their crested heads towards the sky as they rage round these sin-polluted shores, and cry out, "Lord, how long?" Now, in the sweet wild melody of the unearthly winds, who visit the stars on their downward course to this world, and so can speak more feelingly of the Creator's never-ending glory! Her altar steps are the lofty mountains whence she offers up the spiritual sacrifice of mankind's instinctive adoration. Her admonitions are written in the various changes of her outward aspect; she tells of sin in the dark clouds which blot out the light of heaven,—of mercy in the healing dews that fall like repentant tears upon her breast—of divine love in her own loveliness! She writes the name of the great mystery, eternity, upon her midnight sky; with the finger of decay she has summed up the account of all life's vanities, and the annals of corruption are deeply graven in her bosom. But there is one lesson, more than any other, solemn and impressive, because it preaches of the eternal presence of God, which all men are not permitted to read—for it is given in the sunset of the desert.

This most sublime and gorgeous spectacle had just been displayed in the dreariest wilderness of Arabia Petræa, that magnificent pageant which nightly is shown forth to no mortal eyes in the breathless silence of that tremendous solitude.

How unlike the calm death agony of the pale sweet day of northern climes, is this most glorious sight! There, nature, teaching as ever by analogy, seems to represent in the gradual fading of the expiring twilight, the dying hours of some gentle being who has foreknown her doom, and seen the shadow of death lengthening on her life's pathway, long ere the night closed in. So like the lingering smile of mournful tenderness, is the last faint sunbeam that trembles on the earth's darkening bosom. So like the angel whispers that float around the dying couch of one who departs in peace, the soft winds stealing through the air, where silently the tears of evening fall, and like the delusive brightening of the flame of existence, just before it sinks and is extinguished, is the golden glory that illuminates the west for one short period, ere the prostrate sun is devoured by the darkness.—And then the faint stars, lit up one by one, are ranged all dim and flickering along the heavens, as though that world, so dark and still, deprived of light and heat, were dead, and themselves funeral lamps set round its mighty bier.

But in the Arabian desert there is no lengthened departure of light lingering sadly in the last decay,—rather the fierce night, black and cloudless, seems to murder the glowing day in the very height of its undiminished brightness; for in that great wilderness, that looks like a waveless sea of sand, there is not a single object which by casting forth a shadow can announce the fall of evening; there, at least, has time been impotent to leave a trace, the centuries have swept over that unchanging surface without the power to mark the print of their footsteps in the dust, and age after age, for thousands of years, the same scene has daily been visible there;—a desert without a shadow, a sky without a cloud, and the great sun rolling between them terrible and blazing!

Yet, this is no solitude! *God* is there! and no where does the consciousness of His awful omnipresence crush the soul with such a strong reality! There is but one real solitude upon this earth, and that is indeed the bitterest loneliness; the very abomination of desolation, for it dwells in that human heart where He reigneth not.

Thus, when the night comes down in this calm, changeless realm, nothing indicates its approach; the sun pursuing his path of fire, appears suddenly to hear some mysterious mandate summoning him to abandon his dominion, and, drunk with his own glory, he seems impelled to perish as he lived, in radiance unendurable, for, rushing headlong down the steep blue vault, he plunges suddenly below the dark horizon and is seen no more! One moment his beams stretch across the heaven, like the great bars of the golden gate of paradise, then he draws them after him and leaves the empire to his rival night. She meanwhile rises in her gloomy garments, as though to be his great chief mourner, and ascends with swiftest tread the ethereal vault, devouring as she moves along the ruins of the sunshine, whilst from her deepening shadows, brightest stars are born, in token that the Eternal can cause the darkness to bring forth light; then when like a queen she has taken her throne in heaven, she stretches out her heavy mourning veil and lets it fall upon the sunless earth, over whose shrouded beauty she sits brooding till the dawn.

This is the sunset of the desert; and when it is over, what words could describe, how lucid and how deeply pure do seem its dark unfathomable skies, where the great worlds hang, seeming in that clear atmosphere, more like globes of light than distant stars ? It is scarce possible to gaze upon these mighty spheres upheld in the thin ether solely by the unuttered will of their Maker, without fancying with a sort of fascinated awe that they await in such breathless stillness for some tremendous fiat, and that suddenly the Creator, unseen, shall breathe upon them and they disperse at once and die like sparks of fire upon the wind.

Beneath that cloudless heaven and in that shadowless desert two human beings were this night to be seen, and it was strange that in this wilderness they should be destined to appear as types of the two great mysteries of this world, for the one was living and the other dead. Life and death were represented there.

Life, burning, sentient, restless, that rushes up from the unknown infinity and hurries across this visible space, the isthmus between two dread eternities, bearing the infant immortal soul in its arms; causing it to ripen to maturity amid clouds, and tempests, and convulsions, till abruptly it makes it over to the mute stern implacable gloom of death.

Yes! These two great powers, to which we are in turn consigned, are mysteries indeed! And even revelation has willed they should remain so, though with strong hand and clear sweet voice and steady purpose, it leads all who will follow by its *via dolorosa*, and by that alone, through the mist and the shadows, over stones and thorns, a guide most faithful and unerring, to the far off unseen goal.

He, who alone was living in that vast wilderness, was one who for forty long years had dwelt in a world whose corruption and pollution we could in no wise comprehend, did we not bear in our own bosoms and co-existent with ourselves, the germ of that evil which there we behold in full fruition; this man had long since left far behind him the sweet and vain delusions of youth, which pierce not the greenness of the flowery earth, to behold the accumulated mass of dead corpses rotting beneath! His was not a face over which the storms of life had passed and left no sign, it sufficed but to look on Raymond's countenance, to read thereon the dark record of a tempestuous existence, an existence of which every moment had been felt, and had borne away its own weight of thought, of joy, and of sorrow; for there *are* beings on this earth, immortal beings, over whose tranquil heads the unruffled years glide smoothly as summer clouds over a serene sky; but these are they, who have allowed the power of the flesh to subdue and paralyze the spirit within, who live only in the present, in the actual occurrences passing before them every day—in the continual and unbounded gratification of sense. There was a deep and stern resolution on this man's thoughtful brow which told that no such degradation had been his. He looked as though bending under the weight of many more years than he could count; but the eternal life of thought, whilst it doubles each moment of actual time, gradually devours the existence it ennobles.

This was however no time to scan the features of the wanderer, or strive to read his character in his expression; there lay *that* beneath his awe-stricken gaze which cannot fail, for a time at least, to strike the human soul, whether it be that of an atheist, a sensualist, or a believer, with a spiritual paralysis which almost transforms the bodily frame to the likeness of the thing it dreads; the dead lay stretched out before him there, with the face, marble white in the pure starlight, upturned to the glorious sky.

The dead, not one of those ripe for the worm, whose worn-out body craves to be laid down that it may lose sensation in corruption; whose soul, fevered and wasted by the burning of the ceaseless passions which the ardour of youth would fan to flame, but the lassitude of old age could not quench, now pants to meet the cooling breath of eternity unveiled! Not one of those, but a woman young and beautiful. Young in the springtide of existence, when the eyes see only flowers, and the heart knows only hope; beautiful, with a countenance like the morning sky, all bright and fair, and masses of hair sweeping around it, golden as the sunshine. What the love had been which had bound those two to one another, linked as they were by the dearest and closest of human ties, not words could ever tell—but his present agony alone!

The history of Raymond previous to this awful hour, when he knelt in the lonely desert beside the corpse (how beautiful in death!) of the only being he had ever loved, may be given in very few words, for the actual life of his mind, the existence of his soul as worthy of its immortality, dated from that night only.

For the first few years of our sojourn in this mortal world, it seems to present the same aspect to us all, because for a time we live by the senses alone; we look out upon the beautiful and are glad, we feel our strength and vigour, our vast capacity for bliss, and rejoice as a giant refreshed; the future is before us as a golden land of promise, the present has pleasures for each moment, keen and vivid; to breathe the fresh air is delight, to plunge into the treasure-caves of our imagination, rapture; our mind and heart, our various faculties, in short, are all absorbed and satisfied in the mere animal enjoyments of life; in fact, to live is to enjoy; but the intellect meanwhile is in lethargy, the reasoning powers are untried.

We must have felt before we can reflect, and during this period we are utterly and altogether incapable of forming a just opinion of aught here below; because all life, our own existence, the whole world indeed, are falsely coloured by one radiant power within our own young heart, and that is the hope of happiness; the imperious hope which then is a belief of individual happiness for ourselves on earth.

This desire, which seems a part of our nature, is the first instinct of the soul—which it absorbs in one vast delusion; and that hope, which no fear can dim, is the syren voice promising long years of joy, that has power to drown the eternal wailing all around us, which else would startle us to the consciousness of a world full of misery ; it is the sunshine, so dazzling our eyes, that we behold not the corpses of our fellow-men whereon we walk—it is the ever-burning lamp within, fed with the sweet oil of fancy, that irradiates a magic circle all around us, wherein no gloomy truth, no terrified wonder, no maddening doubt may penetrate; for all the while the mighty, the awful gift of thought, lies dormant beneath our strong youthful passions craving to be satisfied, like an unsought treasure beneath the ocean's boiling waves; or rather, let us liken it to a devouring serpent lurking under flowers, ere it wake at last from sleep and sting us into madness.

During all this time we look not beyond the visible, palpable sphere of our daily existence, we do not speculate, we question not, we ask no explanation of death, we only feel that we live! We only live in the hope that we shall enjoy. But there is a crisis in the life of every one of us, an hour of disenchantment, of awakening, when this light of hope is extinguished, and we who in its false glare were blind, now, in the darkness, see. An hour, when we learn that a futile earthly happiness cannot be the aim and object for which we were placed here; that for the puerile and often unholy joys of a most brief space, no immortal soul was ever created by the Eternal God; that there is something more within us, than the capacity for earthly enjoyment; something more beyond, and around, than the possibility of its fulfilment!

In a thousand different shapes does this merciful disenchantment come. Often, very often, in that deep human sorrow, which shows us that never more in this world we can enjoy, and therefore must Immutable Goodness have formed us for higher purposes; in the violent rending of dear earthly ties, in the fierce quick stroke of death, in the failure of worldly prosperity, or the sudden blight of infirmity and sickness; like the thunderbolt, or like the rushing storm; and to some does it arrive on noiseless wings, unseen of other men; there is no outward change, no lack of seeming sunshine, but a dark shadow passes over the soul, and all is gloom for ever. To one it comes in satiety, to another in disappointment: but to some, apparently, only in the maturity of the intelligence, and it was thus with him of whom we speak.

It is a most awful moment when this dread awakening does take place, whether it be summoned by years or suffering. An invisible power suddenly shakes the spirit to its centre; the veil in which it walked enveloped is rent asunder, the last taint of delusion and blindness passes from its undying essence; it arises from the bed of flowers on which it lay dreaming the dream of youth, to find itself standing naked and shivering on the brink of eternity, and it quails before its own immortality, that assails it armed with the terrible scourge of unveiled truth. Then death, mysterious, inevitable death, starts up before it, so near that it seems almost at arm's length, and points with inexorable warning finger to the eternal shades beyond.

Like to an infant abandoned in the darkness is the soul in that tremendous hour; it looks around, it gropes in the gloom, it stretches out its feeble arms, menacing rocks may be all around, pit-falls beneath its feet; an awful abyss is there, and here are unknown terrors! It hears the roaring of the waves of mortal misery, on one side, threatening to engulf it, on the other, the deep tolling of funeral bells; there are clouds in heaven, and thunders in the air; there is the cursing of men, who rush wantonly to their destruction, and the weeping of babes who have not sinned, and shadows inexplicable are above, around, within! Yet, blessed is that hour; for it is then, that agonizing, dismayed, and trembling, the soul sends down into the depths of eternity that one most piteous and terrible cry, "Is there a God?" and never was that cry uttered in sincerity and truth, but straightway the echoes of the fathomless mystery have sent back the resistless answer, "God." Yes! God manifest in Revelation, this is the all-sufficient answer.

That one great mystery is the explanation of all that is mysterious: but not all men ask this question of eternity; and few, very few, receive the momentous answer; because it is scarce possible for human beings wrapped in clinging self-deceit, so to rid themselves of the trammels of the flesh, as to become without bias or prejudice, without the hope or the fear, such calm truth seekers. They dread the truth; if light be truth, then must they for ever abjure the darkness; and none can know till he has cut with a keen knife and unflinching hand, down to the very core of his dark human heart, how fervently we love the darkness rather than the light.

There are many, when thus brought to comprehend the nature and realities of life, to view it no more as the fairy land in whose long future they trust to reap the harvest of the bright hopes sown on the summer winds of youth—but as the visible and narrow space between the incomprehensible infinities, a breath, a vapour, sweeping them on towards the awful abyss, that lies beyond this world's contracted boundary, and on whose verge they already stand—there are many, who in puerile cowardice flee back from the fatal brink; and as fearful reflections rise out of it, and surround them, like spectres emerging from the innumerable tombs they have but just discovered beneath the flowery earth; terrified and horror stricken, seeking a means of escape and finding none, they plunge headlong into the dark stagnant waters of corrupting pleasure, paralysing the higher faculties by the indulgence of the carnal mind, drowning the soul as it were in the pollution that clings around it, subdues, corrodes it, till the hour when it is called upon to leave that flesh, which thus has the power in life's short day to work its ruin for eternity.

It was not thus with Raymond. Calmly he stood on the confines of time, when his eyes were opened to look beyond it, and gazed down into the fathomless gulf that girds this mortal world; he was ready to grapple with the truth, and face it, be it what it might; and, borne onward by the rushing wings of unshackled thoughts, he plunged into the dread eternity. He plunged not therein, following the wayward steps of that vain philosophy, which is bred from the arrogance of human reason, and the desire to gratify human corruption, but in deep humility, in the sincere search for truth, in the reasonable trepidation of a being who cannot die, and is responsible for his own immortality: and there arose for him, for the humble and earnest inquirer, amid these interminable shades, a star,—the same that once was seen in the East, whose pure and steady rays, with gradual, and, at last, most glorious light,—illumined all that dark infinity! The day-star itself dawned within his heart!

We must not now linger to speak of the many different shades of error into which men fall willingly or helplessly, at this critical period of their lives, which decides their whole future career, fixes their opinions, and gives them the distinctive character they are for evermore to bear; there are so many roads branching off from this turning point:—Rationalism, Atheism, Formalism; down these highways to destruction the great majority are sure to rush, when driven out of their stronghold in indifference, like the demons that ran violently down a steep place with the herd of swine into the sea when expelled from their human victims; any thing rather than Christianity,—that pure, immaculately holy, uncompromising religion, with its two-edged sword, quick, and sharp, and powerful, that cuts down into the natural man with such keen stroke, that it pierceth even to the dividing asunder of soul and spirit, of the joints, and of the marrow, separating the carnal from the spiritual with a struggle like that of death itself,—with its continual warfare between the earthly will and the holy law, its invincible purity claiming the sanctification of

THE PHILOSOPHER IN THE DESERT.

every moment—its uncomplaining surrender of the things that lie nearest the heart,—its silent, constant, bitter self-sacrifice.

Yes; most men will have any thing rather than this: scepticism, hypocrisy, or unblushing indulgence in open sin! But Raymond, when he came to demand the reason of his existence, sternly divested himself of all wish, or hope, or baser fear; he trampled under foot the cravings of his humanity, and presented his soul unbiassed, unhampered by the flesh, for the reception of the truth; as an unwritten scroll, whereon creation's Cause was to stamp His name: and he became a Christian.

He accepted Christianity from first to last; but not as the great mass of those professing it are wont to do, who with weak intellects and grovelling minds seek to drag down this all-holy and stupendous faith to the level of their own narrow capacity; detracting from the majesty of its doctrines, confining its aim and purpose to the destinies of mankind alone, profaning its awful names with words of weakness and folly, moulding it with self-satisfied presumption to suit their own bounded views and petty low opinions, till they have made of it a thing, at which we need not wonder, to see the sceptic scoff in willing blindness!

Raymond had a mind of no common powers; and, above all, he was, as we have said, altogether free from prejudice, from preconceived opinion, and from that unconscious slavery to the flesh, and the tendency to evil in the mental qualities, which influences men in their choice of a creed far more than they are aware of; and, therefore, when, with his forehead in the dust, and his hands outstretched into infinity, the

Sun of righteousness arose upon his soul, it was as the light of eternity itself, whose dawning and setting on this puny earth were but one passing phase in a tremendous everlasting purpose not yet fully accomplished,—even the overcoming of ancient darkness, the extermination of the unfathomable mystery of evil!

In the passing of these divine beams over the face of this world, he saw also the manifestation of that attribute of the Deity which pertaineth to Him alone—the power of so combining innumerable results with one operation, that the eternal happiness of every individual mortal was, if they chose it, ensured by the same act which involved the future entire destruction of the dread principle at enmity with the self-existent Himself. There seemed to open out before him, after much intense and anxious investigation, accompanied by unceasing thought, clear and well defined, an awful, a tremendous system, commencing long before the foundations of this narrow world were laid, embracing Christianity, as revealed in Holy Scripture, from its Alpha to its Omega, embodying the whole field of unfulfilled prophecy to the consummation of all things on this earthly stage, and extending on even to eternity, which is but another name for the existence of the Deity.

But Raymond must hereafter, in his own words, explain the nature of this vast sphere of divine action, into which his soul entered by faith, and was at rest. For the present, it is sufficient to look at the principles which he drew from it, to be the guides of his own existence.

He believed that the All Glorious had created man for perfect happiness: this end and purpose He permitted, or caused to be unaccomplished on earth by means of that evil, whose existence is His own unapproachable secret; but He ordained that it should be fulfilled in eternity by means of an awful atonement, which, at the same time, involved most stupendous results to all creation visible and invisible. Raymond, therefore, believed himself to belong altogether as a servant, or willing slave to the Atoner, who had bought him, to make him the recipient of eternal bliss. That bliss he felt to be,—communion with God, or (alluding to man's present state) restoration to Him; therefore, it is synonymous with holiness; and, in the same proportion as man advances to sanctity on earth, will he be capable hereafter of the happiness which consists in an union with the Father of his spirit.

For the space, more or less brief, during which Raymond believed he was to be prepared by mental discipline on earth for this glorious destiny,—two objects in life were set before him, which were to be at once his engrossing task and highest privilege, his difficult, constant, and severe labour, and his unspeakable delight. These were, inwardly, the purification of his own soul; outwardly, the attempt to aid in the advancement of the kingdom of the Holy One in this lower world. These two leading principles he placed before him to be the spring of every action, thought, and word; and, taking up his cross, he set forward on his earthly pilgrimage, marshalled by one bright, blessed, everlasting hope, that moved on before him through the gloom, shedding its serene light on the dark troubled waters all around.

But, as he began to walk through this world, and to meet with men upon his rough and thorny path, his soul grew faint within him; not at sight of the open vice rampant and unrebuked alike in the palaces of the rich, and the abject dwellings of the poor, but at the presence a thousand times more hideous of evil in the semblance of good: it was amongst his co-religionists that he met with that species of crime which caused him to feel that this guilty earth must long since have crumbled before the silent wrath of God, were it not upheld by the moral gravitation of ceaseless prayer, the continual lifting up of the hands of holy and humble men of heart!

That which first stirred his spirit with just indignation, was the degradation of Christianity to the capacity, and even the passions of man, instead of the elevation of man to its sublimity and holiness; but far more deadly was the ill, when he saw how hypocrisy arrayed itself in the white robes of pure religion, and walked abroad in these celestial garments, like the dark foul earth hidden beneath the spotless unsunned snow; often, nay, in most cases, this hypocrisy was unconscious of its own nature; for there is nothing that lies so deep at the heart, corroding it to ashes, as self-deceit.

But Raymond had probed with too sure a hand into the depths of his own soul's corruption, not to recognize the disease at a glance. He saw expediency come forth as heartfelt piety; an outward propriety, resulting from habit and education, as the determined practice of holy principles. Selfishness was termed prudence; coldness of heart was resignation; a want of sympathy with the feelings of others, abstraction from the world; and malice was called zeal. Men judged one another, (as Heaven forbid they should themselves at the last day be judged!) and said it was the performance of their duty. They chose out some one holy doctrine to be the instrument of their paltry enmity, or envy, and with it opposed and denounced their fellow-creatures; they cavilled at a word, and trod under foot the law of God; they fed their base vanity with choicest food, and declared they did but let their light shine before men; they indulged in excess of illiberality, saying they must needs be faithful to the cause of truth; and in those temples which penitence and faith can make the house of God, but else were truly dens of thieves, he saw priests ministering at the altar with stern rebuke and holy exhortation, whose souls the while were slaving to the lowest and meanest of human passions; while worshippers bowed down in pride and arrogance of heart, that men might see how very humbly they could kneel!

Raymond understood this matter; he saw that the god of this world, subtle and wary, perceiving how, in days of old, the faith of the Crucified flourished and prospered in persecution and torture, has, of late, manufactured in the deepest recesses of that depravity, which is his nature, a false Christianity, with which the world, (so sneering once, so softly smiling now,) can go all gently hand in hand; of whose followers men can speak well, forgetting that woe is denounced against such by those words which shall endure, when heaven and earth have passed away! Whilst the true faith, the faith of martyrs, whether their martyrdom be in body or in spirit, has taken refuge in the meek and contrite hearts of the unknown, unnoticed few, who labour so to keep themselves unspotted from the world that it knows them not at all!

When Raymond had seen all these things—when he

had breathed for a while that atmosphere of sophistry and deceit, of inconsistency and weakness; when he had watched how egotism and vanity were nourished carefully, while a fair show was made in the flesh, how meanness, and motives trivial and petty, lurked behind the lips that spoke most plausibly, how the meek hands were folded over the bosom swelling with pride, and eyes looked up to heaven, while the soul cleaved to the dust. Then was he seized with a fierce ungovernable desire to go forth and worship God in the desert; to meet Him in the wilderness alone, that by that solitude, full of His awful presence, he might test his own truth. For, amid so much falsity, surrounded by such inveterate self-deceivers, he came to doubt whether a perfect sincerity, or perfectly righteous purpose were not almost incompatible with human nature, and trembled lest himself should swell the list of unconscious hypocrites.

Of all those which surrounded him, how many there were, as he well knew, who, if they were torn away from their outward forms and ceremonies, their worship in common, their sanctity of words, their piety of imitation, their fashionable righteousness, (which like so many strong bands propped up the weak soul, that else would lie grovelling on the earth,) and were to be cast down unsupported and alone in a desert where none were present but the Most High God, would find themselves there stripped of their borrowed and hollow religion, bewildered and voiceless: they would cry out for human voices to aid them in singing His praise; for human guides to show them the path to His mercy-seat; they would demand what meant the terror, the awe, the agony they felt, little dreaming that for the first time the direct knowledge of the existence of the Infinite was piercing through the web of engrossing thoughts on minor doctrines and petty distinctions, which they had woven over their soul, and for the first time the conviction of sin was stirring within them, freed from the trammels laid upon it by their formal observance of trivial duties.

Raymond felt it would be thus with them, and he knew not how it might be with himself. He feared it was impossible that he should have preserved unsullied the vesture of purity he had sworn to wear amid such deep contamination. He longed to be where no whisper of flattery, no allurements of mankind should breathe upon his soul's latent corruption, and wake it into life and action, that he might search its inmost recesses, and cleanse it of every taint.

But there was another motive which drove him out to meet the undefiled wind of the desert. By his side, clinging to his hand as he walked over the difficult path of life, there went his fair young wife, whom he loved more than it is permitted to an immortal soul to love aught beneath the sky. She was of weak and gentle nature, with an unsuspecting guileless spirit, swayed by every breath that blew, and when he felt the reeling of his own strong soul, threatening to make shipwreck amid the delusive waters of the ocean of life, well might he tremble lest that frail bark went down, as it drifted to and fro among the dark clouds of a world's error and folly.

Therefore, he desired to bear her away from a baneful atmosphere, to tear from her hands the flowers whose scent was poisonous, to strip the gaudy wreath from her spotless forehead that she might bend it to the earth in humble adoration, to carry her where loving, heeding, hearing only him, he could preserve her scatheless, and where together they might fall down and worship in undeniable rectitude. Now, in all this, Raymond erred grievously,—what right had he to mould his own destiny and turn aside from his appointed path? Had he not seen two holy duties set before him, his soul's purification, and the advancement of religion? How did he dare to abandon the cause of the latter for the better fulfilment of the former? By what right did he desert his brethren on earth? Did he not know that the servant of Christ is the servant of the poor and needy—that the redeemed by suffering is the appointed guardian of all who suffer? Briefly, how did he not tremble to exclude himself from the prayer once uttered for those who are in the world, but not of it!

This for himself; and for her, where was his right thus to seek to temper the wind to the lamb with his weak earthly hand, when an heavenly had promised so to do? Where his right to divert from that young head the storms that might in wisdom have been sent to drive her the sooner and the safer into the blissful haven? Where his right to steal her away into that solitude, and cause her to live in his affection alone, till being thus all in all to one another, their mutual love deepened and strengthened till it grew to be idolatry in their hearts? For these things' sake judgment had overtaken him, merciful in that it met him on this side of the grave.

They had come to the desert, designing to fix their dwelling-place in the first green oasis, where a fountain murmured and palm trees grew, and caravans passing weekly could bring them food, but long before they found that place of refuge,—for one of them was another more secure provided. Thus far had they travelled with a merchant's caravan,—suddenly, so suddenly that Raymond for a time would feel no fear, the young wife drooped and languished, her cheek grew marble white, her eyes glared with unnatural brightness, her words came wild and incoherent from her pale lips. No sooner did the Arabs see her than they told him she must die—die within a day—one moment had she been exposed to the deadly burning heat of the noonday sun, and this had killed her, as it had killed thousands. Nothing could save her, they said, the deed was done, the fire was in her brain, and they counselled him to make her a death-bed in the sand, for she could go no further, and to leave her there without attempting to witness her last agony, for the caravan must proceed on its march, and he himself might perish if he remained alone in that vast wilderness.

In the midst of his agony, so bitter, so sudden, Raymond laughed them to scorn for such advice as this; he took her in his arms, for she shrieked out a prayer that she might rest in quiet, and laid her gently on the desert sand—he supported her burning head upon his knees, and with his hand shaded her fast glazing eyes from the murderous sun; so he remained, and bid them depart upon their way—the Arabs lingered to place food and water by their side, to promise that they would send some one soon to succour him, and resumed their trackless journey towards the far off mountains, whose outline in that clear atmosphere seemed traced by fairy hands upon the bright horizon. The tinkling camel bells sounded for a time on the clear warm air, the long train took the appearance of a dark serpent winding its way through the wilderness, gradually it vanished altogether; and they remained alone, those two—the one a prey to death, the other to despair—both were raving, the one in the delirium of fever, the other in the delirium of mental agony.

The mind of Raymond had for the time quite given way under the violence of the shock he had received; at least the power, the vitality of his intellect was gone, and his reason seemed altogether prostrate; the past, the future, heaven and hell, these great thoughts that so continually swayed his soul, had all passed from it, and one only idea possessed him entirely, and engrossed all the concentrated faculties of his spirit. This was the frantic effort and desire to forget the existence of death, to lose the knowledge of it as a thing actual and undoubted, whose presence was in the world; he had felt and understood that she was about to die, and from that conviction had arisen this mad wish to disbelieve in it altogether, and to disconnect her completely with the possibility of it as a truth from which there was no escape.

Here in the desert there were no graves, no passing bells, no crumbling skeletons, nothing that spoke of decay; he must, he would believe that it was but a dream, a delusion, this death; this boon companion of ours, this invisible unwearied attendant that walks for ever at our side, holds us by the hand, sits at our tables and watches our slumbers! He would not think of it at all, he would shut it from his mind altogether, and to this end, in the feverish excitement of his momentary madness he stooped over her, that was dying before his eyes, and began with sedulous care to arrange each golden curl of her waving hair, and smooth each fold of her white garments, whilst she, livid and agonizing, torn by the conflict of the life and the decay, writhed and moaned unheeded in his grasp.

So past the day, the last of their mortal union. Towards evening a strong convulsion suddenly shook the frame of the departing; a violent spasm distorted her features: it passed; and at once the delirium ceased; she sank into a state of complete stupor; the heavy lids half veiled the dim blue eyes that looked out with a strange fixed gaze; the breath came sluggish over the pale lips; the powerless hands, as she fell back upon the sand, dropped on the head of Raymond, which he had laid on the earth, that he might not look upon her agony, and seemed to give him a last unconscious blessing.

He lifted up his eyes, and fixed them on the sky; his senses returned to him; he saw that in an hour the sun would set, and he knew that at sunset she would die; for, however it may be in other countries, in the East, death from natural causes occurs only at the decline of day; and the dying seem to linger there till the last sunbeam shall open for their souls a golden path to heaven.

The thought, the certainty of death, which he had driven from him with such mad frenzy, rolled back upon him now with most tremendous power,—full, clear, unrevealed,—actually present with him there, with outstretched hands, brooding over its fair beloved victim. The complete consciousness of his misery, in its utmost extent, came over him; and the powerful frame of the strong man trembled and shivered as the storm of mortal agony drove through his soul, like a fragile leaf in the wintry blast;—the love he bore her, the deep idolizing love, rose up within him,—fierce, ungovernable, terrible!

With a cry of anguish, such as these deserts had never heard before, he flung himself down upon the sand, and writhed by her side like a crushed serpent; he dragged her close to him; he seized her in a grasp, from which nothing could have torn her; he groaned in very bitterness of heart. Could it be? Was it indeed possible, that the being to him so unutterably dear, the fair and fragile being he had shielded in his arms from every passing breath, and pillowed on his heart when weary, the sweet spring flower of his life, with her sunny smile and loving eyes, was she about to be delivered up to the curse of corruption, which is so horrible that man may not dare to look on it? One hour, one little brief inexorable hour, was this all that was left of life to his own, his only treasure? One hour, and the darling of his heart must for ever pass from his doating eyes! And vainly day by day would he seek her amid the gloom that now would shroud the world for him! She would no longer exist, a thing living and palpable, which he could hold in his arms and strain to his heart, but as an unreal image, a thought, an idea, haunting the treasure-caves of memory!

She was his wife, bone of his bone, and flesh of his flesh, and she must fade, and rot, and shrink into ashes. She must break this, the most sacred of human bonds, to go forth and say to corruption, "Thou art my father," and to the worm, "Thou art my mother and my sister!" No words can express the horror which he felt; but suddenly he started from his recumbent posture,—a new idea had risen up to torture him,—an hour! There remained but one hour for her to live; then, surely, he was losing time: they were passing, these fated moments that would not linger, though they were the last of a mortal's hope, and a woman's love; and must he not gaze upon her whilst still it was permitted him so to do? on those eyes of tender blue, about to close for ever? on those waving curls he had so often kissed? on those soft limbs about to moulder into dust?

He rose up; and calm, rigid, he fixed upon her a stony changeless look, which was most horrible to see: it followed her every movement, as she lay in her restless stupor, turning when she turned, drawing back if she rose up, always at the same distance from her. All that he had felt during the last few hours, all that he had suffered, had vanished away; and in his glazed and tearless eyes there was but one thought to be read,—the desire, the instinct, which made him scan, and scrutinize, and learn off by heart those features which were soon to be hidden beneath the damp black earth; to feed, as it were, while still it might meet the gaze of living eyes, on the sweet countenance, whose smile had been the sunshine of his days. This lasted till the final, the supreme hour had passed away, and at sunset she died.

So the glorious night of the desert looked down, as we have said, upon the living and the dead!

She lay with her fixed eyes wide open and looking upward, as though she were desirous of holding converse with some one in heaven, and her breathless lips were parted like those of a person who listens attentively.

Raymond, meanwhile, at some little distance from her, cowered down, crouching upon his knees, overwhelmed with inexplicable awe: he appeared to have undergone as great a change as that dead corpse, for all human feeling seemed to have passed from his face, giving place to this one awe-struck expression—his regret, his anguish, for the time were quelled, and his gaze, though fixed on her, gave no evidence that this was the being he had loved and lost. That which had so paralyzed him, so subdued his human nature, was the aspect of the sublime, unspeakable repose, that now was solemnly revealed on the face of the dead, filling that innocent countenance, those child-like features, with a majesty indescribable. A perfect repose, an inviolate rest, is the attribute of the Deity alone, therefore can no man living comprehend it; but when the soul departing returns to the bosom of the Father, in whose Incomprehensible Nature an eternal calm exists, she stamps upon the abandoned mortal clay the impress of her first thought in eternity; so that the last trace of spirit on the lifeless form betokens the new comprehension of this awful tranquillity.

For this cause, if any man doubt of his own immortality, of a God, or an eternity, let him go and look down upon a corpse, when the taint of humanity has been wiped from the stony brow, the last frown of its mortal sufferings effaced, and the indomitable calm—the seal of its new birth in infinity—set thereon; those livid, closed, and most eloquent lips shall read him such a lesson as shall cause his soul to shiver within him! they shall seem to wreathe in scorn when he asks if all be over; that stony vacant stare shall interrogate in sternest wonder, the meaning of his impious doubts;

in the very impotence and worthlessness of that leaden mass of corrupting clay, formed by an All Good Omnipotent—shall he receive the promise of a life, once given, renewed, but not destroyed: and finally, he shall quail before the deep things written in the awful beauty he shall witness there; for perfect beauty, like perfect rest, pertains to the Most High alone, and during the interval between death and corruption, it is permitted to the human frame to give evidence in Whose Image it was first created.

Therefore is there nothing, no nothing, upon this earth, so solemnly beautiful as the face of the dead who have departed in peace!—Their life may have been one of storms and gloom; up to the last hour of it, wretchedness and misery may have been around and within them; their hearts may have been broken, crushed, trampled on; their love betrayed, their friendship slighted, their truth misdoubted, their sympathy repelled;—but all is gone, vanished, past for ever, and there is nothing now but peace, peace ineffable, unearthly. Can those fixed, clear, rayless eyes have ever wept? Wept the hot burning tears that fall for the fading of fondest hopes? can that marble brow have ever glowed with the quick blood that resented a fellow-creature's contempt? that still, quiet breast, did it ever heave with the deep sobs that burst forth in the midnight hour, when there are none to heed or hear?

Oh! how do we seem struck with compassion for ourselves, as we gaze upon them resting there, with their meaning and indescribable smile—with compassion—forasmuch as *we* must still endure our living nature, and writhe, and struggle, and disquiet ourselves in vain, and still know what it is to torture ourselves with tenderness for beings that crumble from our arms into dust, or else grow cold and chill us, or false, so that they turn and rend us, and still prepare for ourselves a harvest of disappointment in the sowing of hope, and still above all, feel ever, with shrinking horror, the close and deadly contact of our indwelling sin, that twines around the soul like a serpent whose coils may widen but never break. We listen to the beating of our hearts, as they throb audibly in an hour like that, for we would fain count the moments till we too are summoned to lie in that ineffable slumber!—but again, we say—if a man would learn of immortality, let him look on death, and if of a future state, let him read of it in the ashes of the grave.

So Raymond knelt motionless and silent, gazing on the dead, and as he gazed, his soul arose up and went forth, following that enfranchised spirit in its joyous flight towards the unimagined Glory from star to star and world to world ; through the ranks of the veiled seraphim, that gird like wreaths of undying flowers the throne of Majesty ; on—even to the focus of eternal light, in whose first halo it was lost to his comprehension ; and as—beneath the flying feet of that departing liberated soul, this world, a dark and unclean mass heaving on the bosom of ether, grew less and less, decreasing, fading in the distance, till it was but a dim speck on the horizon; so did this mortal life recede beneath the soaring thoughts of Raymond, with all its burden of things temporal and finite, till it became a mere point on the great vista of his unending existence, a moment vain and valueless, on whose cares and hopes and sorrows it is folly to bestow a thought, and sin to waste a tear!

He beheld that soul entering in to the glory of her Creator, and he felt that this was the consummation of the destiny of man, the purpose of his creation as first conceived in the Eternal mind ; he felt that the presence of God could alone suffice to the creature He had made ; that a reunion with His most awful purity could alone satisfy the Being whose essence was from Him derived ; His eternity alone fill up the measure of the longing of that which He had made immortal! And with the conviction that this restoration of the soul to its Maker from whom it has been unlawfully severed by sin, is indeed the aim and end of its being—the full clear invincible hope of this eternal union with Eternal Perfection, seemed to enter living into the heart of Raymond, and flooded it with a rapturous delight.

Oh it is enough ! it is enough this hope ! what would a man have more, in that craving for happiness which he shares with all created things ? Let him be the most abject and the meanest wretch that ever trod the earth, his body corrupting before the time in foul disease, his heart crushed by the hate of those he loves, his soul scorched by the burning breath of present sin; on earth, friendless ; in misery, unpitied ; in pain, unaided ; in tenderness, scorned ; in constancy, unheeded ; alone, afflicted, tormented ; yet, amid the dreary darkness, and the howling tempests, and the bitter cold, let him but set this one great hope before him and look to it with faithful eyes,—and not the countless worlds rolling round him, with all their glory and their joys, could produce one being so highly, so supremely blest as he.

Raymond felt this, and he almost laughed within himself in childlike triumph, as he thought how brief, how very brief, was the space that intervened between him and the object of his immortality. Most brief indeed, most vapour-like, and having the nature of a dream ; yet even this life, sin-tainted, finite, and uncertain, was surely given for some purpose, some work must have been assigned to it, for nothing was ever formed to stagnate in inaction.

Yes ! there is a purpose, there is a work, and Raymond had long known it—and both are in this great task—*the overcoming of evil with good:* this is the tremendous work, the date of whose commencement and whose certain termination are hidden from us, but which is even now advancing throughout the interminable circles of the universe, and every human being that breathes upon the earth, is called upon, however weak and feeble, to be an agent and an instrument in its stupendous scheme. All things created, animate and inanimate, are moulded to the furtherance of this one object ; for this the Deity became Incarnate, and woe, alas ! to that man who leaves unaccomplished his portion of the labour. The flower, born at noon, to fade at eve, who by its beauty has drawn away a worldly eye from the contemplation of earth's vanities but one moment, has well and surely done its appointed task ; the babe, cradled and coffined on its mother's breast, in the selfsame day, if by its unconscious wail, it has awakened one spark of natural affection in the heart of a father, dead in sin, has lived to a noble purpose ; for there is nothing too great, and nothing too small, for the carrying on of this work, and the hastening of its consummation.

And Raymond,—had he performed his part ? What was he doing there in that desert, in the midst of beauty and solitude, when he ought rather to have been groping

THE PHILOSOPHER IN THE DESERT.

in the loathsome and crowded haunts of the most depraved of his fellow-creatures, to seek out the evil he was to combat in its vilest and darkest form? did he not know that the duty of advancing the cause of holiness in his own soul, and in the world, are both concentrated in this one mighty task, and that he had fallen into the sin of spiritual egotism (than which there is none more subtle) when he fled away from corruption into the wilderness? How did the Immaculate combat evil? by coming down out of the Light, to which no man can approach, into the very midst of it!

And Raymond in that solemn hour, alone with the dead and with his conscience, from which by these reflections he had torn the veil, acknowledged his sin, and took the holy vow to devote himself, with all the strength and power of his mind and heart, even from that hour to the last of his existence on earth, to this one great and glorious cause. Binding down his soul with the strong bands of faith, upon that Awful Cross which once was raised on Calvary, in hope immovable, that clinging thereunto he should drift safely over the ocean of Eternity to the adorable Presence, where existence would be joy—he solemnly determined in the mean season, for the period of his mortal life, to give himself up unreservedly to a warfare, constant, energetic, and laborious, with existent evil; fitting himself, as far as in him lay, for his future state, by driving it out of his own heart, and seeking for it in the world, in all the most loathsome shapes in which it can present itself, in order the more surely and effectually to wage war against it, with a stedfast purpose and an holy zeal.

To this should be given his whole intellect, his time, his energies, his powers of reason; as a stranger and a pilgrim he would wander over earth, hunting down the vice, slaying and destroying the crime, under whatever aspect it appeared.

Rest and peace, with which we of the hope Divine have nothing to do upon this earth, should be to him as things unknown, and from his heart would he cast out self; trampling it under foot with all its cravings, and desires, and fears, to be at once most gloriously free from the hopes and the ills that have power over man in this life, and a servant bound hand and foot to toil and to slave in the work of holiness.

When Raymond had taken this solemn resolution, by which he chained himself as it were to the stake, and delivered himself up to the fire of tribulation, as long as life should endure, there passed over him a deep serenity, and his soul became an apt transcript of those lucid skies above him, where the bright stars were floating silently; for like them it was cloudless and profoundly calm, and great lights were passing through it to and fro.

Raymond lay the whole night prostrate in the dust, absorbed in an awful contemplation; but when the first sunbeam shot a line of living light along the horizon, he rose up, calm and resolved, for he, the sworn servant, had no right to lose a single hour of the existence he had given away; at once must he quit this unfruitful desert, and hasten to a scene of profitable labour,—the night was coming in which no man could work.

Then his eye turned once again upon the unmoved corpse, and for the first time since his spirit had followed hers to drink such deep draughts from the fountains of living waters, his repulsed humanity awoke, and began with its serpent fangs to feed upon his heart; the blackness of darkness passed over the earth, and he beheld how unutterably drear the world was about to be for him! yet, though he did not altogether repress his suffering, because he knew Whose Will it was that he should suffer, not for one moment was his serenity disturbed; never did a juster judgment fall upon an erring soul than that which had attained him; never did a tenderer mercy labour to reclaim a sinner, than that which had removed his idol from between his eyes and heaven; for her he knew he might not mourn, for who dare weep for the holy dead, instead of rather praying when wearied and oppressed, to be spared the sin of envying their repose? And he well knew, also, that out of the graves of all believers, like the strange lights that rise over a dark morass, there ascends one bright and sacred hope; even that which teaches us, that if the Creator never assuredly made aught for destruction, that if His works, once called into being, cannot cease to exist, (however they may change,) so did He never inspire one feeling or medium of happiness to the mind, with the intent that it should be quenched for ever in the cold damps of death; therefore may we cherish our human affections, His sweetest gift, even when the object of them is gone from hence, fearing not that it is indeed His will they should outlive the world's overthrow, and become refined and purified, to our immortal being, what the fragrance is unto a flower.

But there remained one task for Raymond from which his very nature might well revolt,—a task which no human being could have undertaken, except their faith had been what his was;—he must bury his dead out of his sight before he went on his way; and with his strong arms crossed upon his heaving breast, he strove to master the fierce convulsion that shook his frame, at thought of such an awful duty! It seemed so horrible that his should be the hands to thrust down that beloved being, into the very midst of the darkness and horror, from which living she would have wildly shrunk and clung to him for succour. *His* hands must choke up with dust the lips that uttered such loving words, *his* hands must seal up with clay the eyes that never failed to smile upon him; *his* must be the hands to press down the heavy earth upon the gentle heart, so fond and true, that ever throbbed for him alone; his own grew faint and dead within him at the thought; but his life henceforward must be this—to obey, to labour, to endure! let him commence it even now.

He knelt down (for the attitude was fitting), and with his hands began to prepare a grave; it was an easy task, the light fine sand yielded at his touch, and very soon he had made ready the tomb wherein he was about to bury not only her, but all the hope, the joy, the love, that life was never more to have for him.

It was complete—he rose and approached the corpse with averted head—had he looked upon her face his dreadful task must have remained undone; he made her a shroud of the white veil with which he loved to hide her beauty from all eyes, and he raised her up. Then the thick dews of agony stood out upon his forehead, for the cold stiff body seemed to glide from his grasp, as though it shrunk unwilling to abide its doom! Yet a force invincible appeared to drive him to his work, and his palsied hands resumed their hold.

For the last time he took her in his arms, for the first time he repulsed her from them to give her up to the grave's most dread embrace! Then, when he had laid *her*

THE PHILOSOPHER IN THE DESERT.

down to dwell there, lonely, who had shared with him her every thought and hope, he began with feverish and rapid movement to gather in the dust and sand upon her; and as he did so, his memory seemed constrained to pass in review all that had been so tender and devoted in her affection for himself; he saw her true and unchanging, without a joy or wish on earth, save to minister to him; smiling when he smiled, and weeping when he wept, ever by his side in sickness or sorrow, to soothe, to cheer, to comfort him; welcoming pain if borne for his sake, mocking at fatigue if endured for him, through watchful nights, and days of heaviness tending him with a love unwearied to the last! And now all this he must shut in for ever into that closing grave; he must fill it up with all life's choicest blessings! he must himself scatter the last handful of dust upon the sepulchre of his earthly happiness; but his hands obedient, accomplished all that dreadful labour, and he, the ransomed by Agony most Sacred and most awful, could even in that hour rejoice that he was thus called on to pass through the fiery trial that was sent to purify his soul for everlasting holiness—he could welcome the biting flames that cleansed him from the taint of earth.

It was accomplished, and he rose up humble and chastened; but suddenly he shuddered violently,—he stretched out his hands to grasp the empty air,—and his eyes, dilating, fixed themselves upon the object which had moved him thus. With an indescribable horror he perceived that, when he had interred the uncoffined corpse, he had allowed one long lock of her sunny hair to escape from the shroud, and stream out from the grave over the sand, so that it had remained unburied when he threw in the earth, and still appeared from beneath the new-made heap! When Raymond beheld that long fair tress,—one of those with which he had so often played in hours of gaiety for ever gone,—a wild fancy thrilled through him that this was a token sent him by the hapless tenant of that tomb, in pledge of an affection which should live beyond it! He stooped down to press it to his lips; and, as he felt that soft curl twining round his fingers, tears such as that strong man never wept before burst scorching from his eyes. He severed this last offering of buried love, and thrust it in his bosom—with what agony of heart these weak words have' no power to tell!

And when all was thus concluded, that solitary and friendless man—who never more could be alone since God was with him—lifted up his eyes, and fixed them stedfastly on heaven, and so took his way over the dreary wilderness.

CHAPTER II.

THE FIRE WORSHIPPER, MAGUS, AND CHILD OF THE SUN.

On the confines of the Arabian desert, towards the east, a lofty and precipitous mountain separates that immense and burning waste from the more fertile regions of Mesopotamia. Over this it is necessary to pass, before the traveller can escape from the wilderness altogether; but its gushing streams and sheltering trees are so welcome, after the heat and thirst and weariness he has endured, that he is often disposed to linger thankfully among them. This had probably been the feeling which had induced one of the wandering tribes of the race of Kurds to encamp behind the chain of rocks which girt the mountain's base, and thus separated them from the desert. Their numerous tents, arranged systematically in groups of twenty or thirty, had quite the appearance of a little village, singularly defended against any attack from without by their camels, which lay in a circle round it, tied in couples, and perfectly motionless.

The nation of Kurds, though always remarkable for their wandering propensity, had, till within the last few years, remained comparatively stationary among the rich valleys which lie under the shadow of Mount Taurus. They were at that time divided into twelve tribes, each one governed by a bey, whose power was absolute. These princes, whose ambition and whose strength being equally proportioned, placed themselves too much on a level one with the other, were continually at war; and their internal strife soon reduced the population and the riches of the tribes to an extent which caused several of them to give themselves up to Persia or to Turkey, in order to escape from total ruin. A few of the strongest, however, disdaining a safety so ignominious, betook themselves to the mountains, where they could not only retain their independence, but also continue to indulge in the plundering excursions, which form the chief occupation and amusement of their lives. These expeditions were conducted on a very large scale, and generally comprised a journey of several months ; for they delight in travelling, and as they dwell habitually in tents, they carry their home with them wherever they go.

The Kurds, of whose encampment we have been speaking, were a party belonging to these last mentioned tribes, who had been leading a brigand life for some time, and were now leisurely returning to Kurdistan.

The tent of their chief, which occupied a central position, was formed of a sort of woollen stuff of a dark brown colour, which excluded the light, excepting when the loose curtain which formed the door was drawn aside. The interior was divided into five compartments; the first was the audience-chamber of the great man himself, where he passed the whole day in a strangely uncomfortable attitude, on his knees, boiling coffee for himself, and smoking in the interval. He was a fine-looking old man ; his rich oriental dress entirely covered by an enormous bernous of white cloth; his bronzed

THE FIRE WORSHIPPER. 39

complexion—so dark that he might almost have passed for an African—was relieved by a turban of various colours, from which five peacock's feathers floated ostentatiously,—being the sign that he had been five times a conqueror in as many battles; and his countenance wore the cunning ironical smile proverbial as being peculiar to his nation, it is in fact but the outward expression, denoting their inward treachery and craftiness; an extreme and habitual cruelty is also a very unpleasing trait in the Kurdish character, but they are often in the East compared to the lion for their courage and ferocity. The Kurds are Mussulmen, and scrupulous in their obedience to "The Book" (the Koran); but they belong to the sect of Omar, which places them precisely in the same position as schismatics in the Christian Church; they look upon a talent for cunning and intrigue as the most valuable a man can have; and perhaps their most undeniable virtue is the great generosity and scrupulous honour with which they perform the duties of hospitality.

The second apartment is the harem of the women,— where they cook, prepare the baths, and occupy themselves with other household matters. The third is the stable,—where the horses are ranged in a circle round the tent, their hind legs fastened to a stake, while the servants occupy the space they leave vacant in the centre. The remaining apartments are given up to the cattle and baggage mules.

In the first and principal room of the tent, the chief and several of his warriors were preparing to take their evening meal. They were seated in solemn silence, in the oriental manner, on the matting, which constituted the sole piece of furniture, surrounding a table not more than one foot high, on which several immense wooden spoons were laid. A number of cakes, thin as a wafer, and baked in the sun, were spread over it; and a dish stood in the centre, filled with balls made of goat's flesh mixed with rice. Without taking the trouble to change their attitude, the company dragged themselves on their knees close to the repast thus arranged for them. The chief elegantly insinuated two fingers of his right hand into the smoking dish, and drew out one of the little balls, which he swallowed without moving a muscle. He then invited his guests to imitate his example by addressing to each one, in the most majestic manner, the word "Bonyourum" (Let us eat): but just at this juncture, the loud barking of the sentinel dogs announced the approach of some one unknown to them.

Instantly, several of the younger men started up, and hurried out to ascertain the cause of their alarm; in a few minutes they returned and informed the chief that a stranger, who had apparently been wandering without food in the desert, was lying faint and exhausted beside the guardian camels.

"Bring him hither, that he may eat, drink, and be refreshed," said the chief,—and having given this laconic order, he resumed his pipe. His followers, however, seemed in this instance little disposed to render him their usual prompt obedience.

"This stranger is a Ghiaour," said one: "his dress is that of the children of Frangistan." "Shall a Ghiaour pollute our tents?" added another.

"Shall a stranger perish of hunger and weariness at our doors?" said the old chief, with great severity.— "Bring him hither,—I have spoken." The young men offered no further remonstrance; they went out, and

THE FIRE WORSHIPPER.

presently returned, bringing with them Raymond, who staggered on a few steps, and then fell to the ground, worn out with two days of fasting and misery. Notwithstanding his condition, the old Kurd ceremoniously gave him the usual salutation,—by laying his hand on his heart and saying " Marabat !" (Honey be with you !) he then made a sign that they should do what they could to revive him. This they effected by a very simple process,—merely rubbing his temples with the leaf of an odoriferous herb, common to those countries, and he was soon sufficiently restored to take a little nourishment ; after which he gladly accepted their offer of taking the repose he so much required on a couch they arranged for him with a carpet and a few cushions.

With the dawn next morning, all the inhabitants of the Kurdish tent were astir, and making their preparations for their departure, as they intended to proceed without further delay towards Kurdistan. The stranger however was not forgotten : according to their ideas of hospitality they were bound, for fifteen days at least, to give him food and lodging. When they found, therefore, that a night's rest had quite restored him, they proposed that he should accompany them on their journey if his route lay in the same direction. Raymond's sole object was now to reach Europe as soon as possible, and as it was absolutely necessary that he should travel with an escort, he willingly accepted their offer.

The old chief proposed, after passing through Kurdistan, to proceed on for purposes of traffic towards Ezyroum, in Armenia, whence Raymond knew he could easily travel to Constantinople ; he therefore exchanged a valuable ring which he wore for a horse—as the Kurds would by no means have been contented with a draft on a banker—and joined the cavalcade, when at sunrise they set out on their journey.

The men all travelled on horseback, the women in baskets slung on either side of a camel, and an immense number of dromedaries and baggage mules brought up the rear. They pitched their tents for a few hours during the heat of the day, and continued their course through the greater part of the night; so that it was not very long before they had reached the confines of Armenia. It was a strange thing to see the effect produced by Raymond's presence on these wild, fierce warriors: unconsciously to themselves, when he came near, the rude voices were hushed, and the cruel sports, in which they fought with one another, laid aside. Nor was this merely the effect of his civilized appearance and manners; he was destined now to cause a similar impression wherever he went, for from the hour when, in the desert, he offered up his soul and life to be a reasonable sacrifice on the altar of that grave, no one ever looked once upon his face without turning to gaze on it again. There was something so remarkable in the deep serenity, the stern passionless calm of that countenance, testifying boldly, and yet humbly, that nothing of this earth could henceforth have power over him. The words of his fellow-creatures' scorn and contumely (so bitter to humanity) might fall upon his ear, but they could bring no flush to that placid brow, where sat enthroned the faith of immortality. Cold looks, indifferent or unloving, might meet his gaze, but they could cause no tears to rise in those steady, up-looking eyes; nor yet could a world's applause and flattery make words of vanity or guile to pass over those lips, hallowed by the name of Him at the foot of Whose cross he had immolated self.

Oh! it is a glorious thing, this independence of soul, when a man, having grappled with his destiny, and forced that mysterious shapeless thing to stand before him in distinct and real form, has ascertained what it is given him to be, if he will, throughout the yet unborn ages of eternity; and sworn, whilst in the flesh, to work unceasing for that consummation of his being, as the noble, true-hearted, devoted servant of holiness. Yes, it is a glorious thing thus to lift up the cross, and go forth over the earth with the fixed eyes upraised to the sky (the starry veil which hides the eternal home), the hand stretched out to ward off the unclean; one firm purpose within, one holy hope before him; spurning earth, with all its joys and sorrows, beneath his feet; trampling down the mortal nature, with its propensities and cravings; having the name of the Prince of Peace set within his heart; so that powerless around him swell the waters of life's tempestuous sea, wave after wave dashing up against him, and falling back as from an adamantine wall; human love and hate, and hope and fear, contempt and fame, all raging round unheeded. Alike to him indifferent, man's condemnation or his praise, for neither can affect the one unchanging motive of his every action, even an unflinching obedience to the immaculate law of spiritual purity.

There are many different ways by which men attain to this noble liberty, this service of perfect freedom; but the surest and the swiftest is that which Raymond had trodden, even the path of agony; where the bleeding feet are dragged over the lacerating stones, and the thunders burst on the defenceless head. Therefore for this, also, men turned again to look upon his face, because it bore the holy impress of chastening, duely and meekly received.—And there could be on it no trace of human passion ; since, when his soul left one moment its post like a sentinel, at the gate of heaven, it was but to fly back, and nestle wearily within that desert grave, among the ashes of the imperishable image.

Raymond had travelled many days with the friendly Kurds, and they were now passing through the rich lands of Armenia. It was night ; but they designed to continue their march yet a few hours, when Raymond, who was riding silently beside the old chief, suddenly perceived, at a great distance from them, a luminous object of gigantic size, which shed a pale unearthly light on the vast plains around. He could distinguish that it was an immense mountain, but he gazed in wonder on the strange halo which it emitted.

"That," said the Kurd, answering to his look, "is the holy Mount Ararat: the mysterious light proceeding from it is caused by the huge masses of eternal snow that are heaped round its unapproachable brow: wherefore they should have the power to give forth this glare we know not, except it be by order of heaven ; that the sons of the faithful may have light to guide them over these dreary plains ; but this we do know by tradition, that ever since the foundation of the world it has glittered here by night, even as you see it now, so that it is called the Lamp of Asia."

Raymond was naturally much struck with this singular phenomenon, and he inquired from the chief if they were likely to reach it before morning. The Kurd answered, that they might certainly reach the mountain's base by daylight, were it not necessary that the cavalcade should halt for a few hours, as some of the horses were fatigued.

Raymond, who had often felt an earnest longing for a more perfect solitude than that which the society of the wandering Kurds might be said to afford, now proposed to the chief that he should proceed alone to an Armenian monastery at the foot of Mount Ararat, of which the position had been accurately described to him, and there await the arrival of his travelling companions. To this the old chief at once consented, as no danger was likely to befal him in those lonely regions; and Raymond soon after quitted them, when they encamped for the night, and proceeded alone towards the shining mountain.

Night, clothed in beauty and silence, was all around him; there was not a sound, save at times the hissing of a snake in the brushwood, or the faint shriek of a distant hyena; and the solitary man, bowing down his head upon his bosom, abandoned himself to profound and solemn reflections. He had need, in truth, so to do; for he had taken a holy vow, a momentous resolution—the hour was fast approaching when it must be put into execution, and he had not yet organized the process by which he was to work. He had sworn to combat evil, but how, where, when was he to begin? Not that there lacked opportunities; it was the very plenitude of the means afforded that bewildered him; for he well knew that no permanent good can ever be effected, except by the well-directed effort of the whole energies and talents, concentrated in some one channel; and he dreaded lest, from the very vastness of the field in which he designed to labour, he might neutralize his own endeavours, by dispersing them too much in various quarters.

It was evil which he had vowed to oppose,—and was not the world full of it, even to overflowing? Did he not seem to hear even then and there the great voice of blasphemy, of wailing, of impure mirth, of false unholy prayer,—the one mingled cry that for ever exhales from it, and ascends up in the face of the retributive heaven? When he sought to choose amongst and analyze the various aspects of the universal sin, it seemed to his oppressed and overwhelmed mind as though the earth's unnumbered crimes, in palpable shape, came rushing past him, over that midnight plain, calling on him to pursue and vanquish them ; each one equally horrible —and countless as the desert sands! There came the murderer, with averted eye and scowling brow,—and as he fled past he held up the bloody dagger before the eyes of Raymond. Then came the phantom of a being that once had been most fair in inward spirit and in outward form, that now, with blighted soul and haggard cheek, sped moaning on, and turned on him as she went unholy eyes, that formerly had been upraised in prayer. A slave crept feebly past, in abject terror, shaking his chains in Raymond's hearing: and next came one, with smiling face and soft mild eye, who hated his brother in his heart: then another rushed past, bearing in his arms the poisoned cup of this world's pleasures, whilst he trampled the cross beneath his feet: and then a rich man in his chariot, whose rolling wheels passed over the hearts of widows and of orphans: an atheist, howling out defiance to Him unto whom vengeance belongeth : a child grown old in sin : a rationalist, whispering impiety with gentlest smile: an old man gathering flowers on the wayside, with the grasp of death at his throat. One after another,—shape after shape,—each more hideous than the last,—seemed to career before him, all vile, polluted, and degraded,—yet each perhaps reclaimable of good: and how was he ever to choose amongst them? How must he commence on this mass of iniquity? Where first in this dreadful ocean of corruption must he plunge in the feeble arm with which he sought to stem its tide?

Raymond had passed days and nights in those bewildering thoughts, but as yet he found no solution to the problem they involved; yet he did not despair, nor did he for one moment abandon his resolution, because he had the firm faith that no man ever boldly and sincerely set forth as the servant of holiness, without finding a path opened out for him at the last, whatever might be the difficulties with which he had to contend.

Raymond continued buried in profound meditation, till, when the day began to dawn, he found that he was already ascending one of the steep and numerous hills which seem to cluster round the base of the great Ararat, but which do in fact form a part of that tremendous mountain. The sun, whose rising is there as rapid as his descent at night, had already sent forth a herald of his swift coming in one long glittering sunbeam, that shot up from beneath the horizon, and spread itself over the cloudless east like the unfurling of the banner of day. Raymond, seeing this, hurried on, in order that he might witness the magnificent pageant of an eastern sunrise from the summit of the declivity on which he stood; but scarcely had he reached this point, and dismounted, when his attention was irresistibly attracted by a figure standing motionless near him.

It was a stately, noble-looking man, in the prime of

life, whose dark countenance—of that peculiar caste which denoted him a Persian—was at this moment lit up with the wildest enthusiasm. His dress consisted of a long white robe, with a girdle of silver; on his head was a high conical cap of white beaver, from whence descended an ample veil of the same colour, which fell round him in heavy folds, and was crossed over his mouth, where it was fastened by a diamond clasp; his hair—parted on his forehead—flowed down over his shoulders; in one hand he held three small white wands, and with the other he restrained with a powerful grasp a splendid young horse, full of fire and impatience; it was without saddle or trappings, and was curbed only by a golden bit, whilst its neck and head were ornamented with wreaths of myrtle; close to them was a heap of stones, symmetrically arranged in the serpentine curve which is often to be found in druidical remains; on this sticks were laid, as though to light a fire, along with a bright two-edged knife. Raymond—much surprised at this strange sight—remained gazing on it like one fascinated, convinced that he was about to witness some singular ceremony.

The Persian continued immovable till—suddenly starting forth as it were from the dark earth itself, for there was not a cloud to be seen—the glorious sun rushed up into the heavens, and cast a perfect flood of light around him, as though with a rapturous smile he greeted the beautiful world that had lain so long like a pale flower on the bosom of night. In a moment, the snowy brow of Ararat was girt with a golden crown, and the sunbeams seemed to roll like the sparkling waves of a radiant sea over the plains and the valleys beneath.

No sooner did the white-robed Persian behold this

sight than he cast himself down with his face on the ground, and constrained the well-taught horse to kneel with him: then, with a loud voice, and every gesture of the most impassioned devotion, he called out,—"I adore thee, O Sun, source of light and glory,—O Fire, essence of all purity! Let thy beams, O Sun, being absorbed in all excellence, touch him who lives purely! May the brilliancy and grandeur of the Sun augment; he never dies, —he burns and rushes on like a vigorous steed, conquering and terrible,—may he succour me! There shall be neither life nor nourishment if we call not on him: may I adore him with purity of thought, of word, and of action; and may these be my aid in reaching the light, —may my prayer be pleasing to the Sun[1]."

He then rose, and having with a burning glass lit the fire, he flung into it what seemed to be an offering, composed of spices, amber, gold and silver coins, and a few precious stones; then, once more prostrating himself, he appeared to pray to the flames as they rose,—" O pure, O holy, O venerable fire, be favourable unto me! O fire, son of Hormazd,—benevolent and heaven-descended, I address to thee my vows; I desire to please thee. May the glory and the grandeur of the pure fire augment."

As the Persian continued muttering low through the thick veil which covered his mouth, seemingly in fervent prayer, the fire feeding on the dry wood soon burned fiercely, and began to wreathe itself over the circle of stones: perceiving this, he arose, and taking up the knife, retreated a few paces, while he still grasped the impatient horse by the mane: turning his eyes solemnly to the East he exclaimed loudly, " O Sun, bright and unextinguishable, accept this sacrifice;" and instantly plunged

---

[1] See " Zendavesta," sacred book of the Fire worshippers.

the sharp blade into the throat of the beautiful animal. With one bound it fell headlong to the ground, and whilst life was still agitating its limbs in a last convulsion, the Persian dragged the reeking body to the fire, and, with an exertion of strength which to Raymond seemed quite extraordinary, succeeded in placing it in the midst of the flames; they closed over the writhing victim, and as the smoke of the horrible sacrifice ascended, the worshipper once more fell down before the bright object of his strange idolatry in profound adoration. At length the ceremony seemed altogether terminated; and rising from his knees he turned round, when his eye fell for the first time on Raymond. A shriek burst from him as he beheld him, and rushing forwards he exclaimed,—" A Gùddin (Gentile) here at this hour! come, delay not an instant:" then seizing him by the arm, he would have dragged him from the spot,—but Raymond, shaking off his grasp, resisted him with a strength equal to his own: Then an expression almost of wild terror passed over the countenance of the Persian; he released his hold, but clasping his hands in the attitude of supplication, murmured hoarsely,—"Stranger, I beseech you only to depart from the presence of the holy fire,—your breath pollutes it; behold, even my lips are veiled, to save it from the contamination of a mortal's breathing."

Raymond then at once acceded, unwilling to do violence to the ideas of another, however strange they might be; and the Persian walked by his side till they had so far descended the declivity that the fire was no longer to be seen.

"And now," said Raymond, speaking in Persian to his strange companion, "tell me, I entreat you, who and what you are."

"I am a Magus and servant of the Sun," answered the Persian: "I am one of those who, from the heaven-sent book of the most wise Zoroaster, have learnt that Fire is the essence of purity,—the visible and only manifestation of our Deity: behold the glorious light which I adore!"

"You are then one of the Magi (priests) of the Fire worshippers," asked Raymond, with great interest,—for he had long been desirous of learning some particulars respecting this strange old creed.

In the course of his eventful life he had travelled much, and one result of his observations had been the conviction (to him truly blessed), that there is a glimmering of the truth in all false religions, however much it may be buried and overwhelmed in a mass of absurdity and error. In that great problem of a partial revelation, which has been a stumbling-block to many of the weak and narrow-minded, he thought he could perceive this ray of hope and consolation,—whilst, for high and mysterious purposes, (with which let no man dare to tamper,) it has been willed that the knowledge of truth should not at least as yet be universal,—still it seemed to him that the mind of no man was allowed to rest on that which is wholly false, unless by voluntary apostasy from the instinctive law of conscience, which, by inborn ideas, unconnected with external evidence, acknowledges the Supreme. In all, (save one idolatrous creed, which appears to be a distinct invention of the spirit of evil,—the worship of serpents,) he was convinced that the meek and purer souls might ever find some one principle among all their erroneous doctrines which would lead them—faint and struggling truly, and almost unconscious—towards the only true God, still

One and the Same, though He has not thought fit that they should be so marvellously blessed as to know Him revealed in His eternal Love Incarnate. The faith of Zoroaster had however always somewhat staggered him in this belief, as he found it difficult after much research to disconnect it with the worship of Baal,—undoubtedly the great serpent solar god; and he was now delighted to have an opportunity of gaining information on the subject, and ascertaining in what precise shape the power of evil was at work here also.

The Magus, he found, was, like himself, travelling to Ezyroum, and from thence to Constantinople,—probably on some mission connected with the support of the fire temple at Teheran, in which he served. He had left his horses and attendants below, whilst he ascended the hill to perform the sacrifice which Raymond had witnessed; and when they were joined by the Kurds, who soon after came up, the Persian willingly consented to accompany them for the rest of their journey.

In fact it was but natural that he should be greatly pleased with his new companion, for it was most rare indeed that one of his faith was even tolerated by a stranger. Everywhere in the East out of their own country, the Fire worshippers are treated with the utmost opprobrium, and even abhorrence, and nothing but the great influence which Raymond had acquired over the Kurds could have induced them to consent that the follower of Zoroaster should accompany them. At his request, however, they agreed, and the Magus was soon riding side by side with the Englishman, in the direction of Ezyroum.

Being desirous of making a convert, the Persian was most willing to enter into conversation, and Raymond had soon drawn from him a very sufficient analysis of his strange doctrines.

He found in it much to interest him: at first he thought he could perceive the confirmation of the opinion which he held, that a germ of truth lies at the root of every false creed, in the belief of the Fire worshippers in an Unseen, All Powerful Deity, whom they name Zaruana, or *Time without Bounds;* but again, this legitimate doctrine is entirely neutralized by their conviction, that this Almighty One is absorbed in his own being, that he is wholly unmindful of, nay unconscious of, the working of the universe. An error so great as this has compelled the Fire worshippers, so to speak, to create two other active gods, which thus renders them Polytheists. Idolaters they also certainly are, if we are to consider idolatry as the worship of any created thing, since from the very commencement Zoroaster has taught them in the Zendavesta, which he professes to have received from heaven, that fire is the manifestation, or, in fact, essence of the Deity; so that they adore it in whatever form it may appear, as the sun, moon, stars, and light or flame; they do indeed actually Deify all the elements, on what principle it is difficult to determine.

The Magus assured Raymond, that their certainly very ancient faith dated from the time of Enos, the son of Seth, long before it was brought into shape and form by the teaching of Zoroaster: he described to him in the most poetical and enthusiastic terms, the great Pyreum containing the unextinguishable Fire which they worship. This everlasting flame, he said, Zoroaster had brought down from the celestial dwellings, and that it contained intrinsic sanctity; it is a pure, gentle, soft, blue flame, springing spontaneously from the rock; it does not burn any substance applied to it, and appears to brighten in proportion to the fervour of adoration with which it is worshipped.

But there was one part of the creed of Zoroaster, to which Raymond listened with the most intense interest, because it was closely connected with the subject that engrossed his own thoughts. It is a doctrine which in the present day they have almost lost sight of, absorbed as they are in their worship of visible things, but which forms the essential groundwork of their faith, *viz.* Dualism, or the belief in the co-eternal principles of good and evil; each having its own author in whom they are existent and active, equal in power and in strength, for ever at war, swaying the destinies of this world, as it were, in regular rotation.

In order to obviate that mysterious difficulty of the origin of evil, which no man in this mortal life shall ever comprehend, by an impossible hypothesis they have supposed that Zaruana, the silent and all-good Deity, has caused the two subordinate gods, Hormazd and Arimanes, to become the creators and disseminators of good and ill; but that which struck Raymond most forcibly, was the description given by the Magus of the working of these two antagonist powers in the universe, always in opposition, and always on an equality, so that in the greatest event, as in the meanest trifle, they were matched against one another in the same proportion, to overcome or be conquered, as the revolving wheel of fate dictated.

Although, of course, Raymond rejected a theory so totally at variance with the belief of the One All-Perfect Supreme, yet the details of the doctrine suddenly conveyed to his mind a thought which appeared at once to dispel the difficulties which assailed him in his resolution to aid in the furtherance of good. It suddenly occurred to him, that whilst in his hopeless perplexity he had looked round on the fathomless abyss of sin, from which thick and interminable, dark volumes of smoke were for ever rolling up, to obscure the light of day; he had set aside altogether the simplest and most reasonable manner in which he could with his single arm make war against the foe of the Eternally Holy. He, an individual, with the means, opportunities, talents, and powers, which one man may possess, had undertaken to contend with evil, and how could he more advantageously and effectually do so, than in the person of another man, as completely the servant of sin, as himself was the follower of good? and whose power and opportunities of propagating iniquity should be equal to his own of advancing holiness! He was not alone in this great work; all creation was engaged in the tremendous combat; he was but one of countless agents, greater and less in their means and strength; and if he, one instrument of good combatted and overcame one instrument of evil, he had assuredly more fully done his work, than by disseminating his solitary and feeble efforts in quarters unconnected with one another.

The more this idea worked and became matured in the mind of Raymond, the more satisfactory it appeared to him, as the embodiment of his determination in palpable shape, on which he might at once and effectually work. He was well enough read in human nature to be thoroughly aware of the vast, almost incredible power which each individual possesses, of advancing the cause of one or the other of the two great contending powers ; how should we tremble, each one of us, if we knew how our present deeds and words shall work for good or ill on generations yet unborn ; for like circles widening on the water, our influence extends from mind to mind, far beyond what we can either imagine or control ; conveyed from the soul that has seen and heard us, to the souls of all in connexion with her, till it enters on spheres where even our fancy cannot follow it.

Raymond recollected in his past busy career, how often he had met with men of intellect and energy, equal if not superior to his own, who having in their contemptible arrogance rejected the truth of Revelation, had systematically given themselves up to the power of their inborn sin, till the dark spot which we all bear on our soul, had grown and spread ever theirs altogether ; so that the subtle venom of spiritual corruption pervaded their whole being, and emanated from them with every exertion of their faculties.

Such an one, thus slaving for and serving assiduously the power of evil, Raymond now solemnly determined to seek out—and having found, as he doubted not he would, as providentially as he had encountered the Magus, who had given him this idea, he resolved to attach himself to his steps. He would follow him over the world, wherever he went, shedding poison around him, as such men do, a very walking pestilence ; and he would concentrate his whole soul, he would bend the entire powers of his mind and capacity, to the one work of frustrating the evil which this man should accomplish, in every word or trifling action in which it appeared, and he would substitute for it the good which he might himself effect.

THE FIRE WORSHIPPER.

When Raymond had come to this decision he found his mind perfectly at rest; it seemed to him reasonable, and as soon as he should have chosen from amongst the countless slaves of iniquity, one against whom he might match himself with some hope of success, he would no longer be vaguely striving here and there, to gain some little advantage over the fatal power, but with a well-defined path before him, and a distinct purpose tending to a consummation equally clear, he would, as it were, enter the lists for single combat, and as the champion of purity, give away his life, not in one swift blow, which is indeed an easy martyrdom, but day by day, hour by hour, in unwearied self-denial.

And still side by side rode the Fire worshipper and the Englishman, through the gigantic forests which cover the whole country in the vicinity of Ezyroum,— forests interminable and sacred, inasmuch as, except on one narrow and intricate path, no foot of man has ever intruded on their deep recesses; no sigh wrung from a mortal's weak complaining heart polluted that pure air, or voice stirred the echoes in those fresh green bowers, less pleasing to that blue unsullied heaven than the wild bird's hymn of praise. And ever as they journeyed on their way, the Magus sought to exalt his false creed in the Christian's estimation. He told him how it had worked its mysterious way through the world, and that traces of it might be found, he was certain, from tradition, even in the northern land, which was the stranger's home; he described the peculiar symbol by which it might be recognized in ancient ruins of unexplained origin, as a triangular stone, emblematic of the Sun's rays, and Raymond well remembered that such are

D 5

almost invariably to be seen in Druidical remains, as well as in many of the most ancient relics of Greece, which do not bear, like the more recent, the signs of dedication to the heroes of mythology—at Mycenæ especially, and in the neighbouring plain of Argos, he distinctly recollected a similar emblem.

The Persian would have had him draw important conclusions from these facts, but Raymond was far more anxious to ascertain if there were any possibility of dispelling the thick clouds of error and falsehood, which obscured the mind of his intelligent companion, than to pursue the interesting field of research he had opened up before him. He found it, however, altogether in vain to attempt awakening him to a sense of the falsity of his creed. The shining gods of the Fire worshipper had so dazzled his eyes with their radiance and their brightness, that his soul had no longer power to comprehend that Eternal Glory, which dwelleth in the light that no man can approach unto.

So, when the stars came forth by night, glittering through the green vaulted roof of these never-ending forests, the Magus fell down and worshipped them, while Raymond felt a holy exultation in the purity and strength of the Christian's faith, when, like the sorrow-stricken man of old, he beheld the moon walking in her brightness, and turned aside from that visible light and beauty, to adore in hope the Unseen, Unheard, Incomprehensible, Who yet is known, believed, and loved!

Raymond found much to interest him at Ezyroum; it was the most important city of ancient Armenia in the time of Mithridates; the name signifies the " City of the

Romans," as it was at one time entirely occupied by them; and the ruins of a temple dedicated to Venus are still to be seen; but the Turks having long since taken possession of it, they have converted it quite into a Mahomedan town, with barely sufficient toleration towards the native Armenian population, to admit of their following their Christian worship unmolested; they are, however, unable to efface one marked line of distinction which exists between themselves and the people on whom they have so wantonly intruded, and this consists in the peculiar beauty and grace of the Armenians, both men and women. Their national character has also so far escaped the influence of the Mussulman control, that they retain all the gaiety and light-heartedness so natural to them, and throughout the long summer nights, the fountains of the countless gardens of Ezyroum are surrounded by the gay circles that dance round them with music and singing. Indeed, so constant are the festivities and mirth in this sunny town, that Raymond hastened his departure from it in consequence.

He had committed his spirit to the coldness and darkness assigned to him in this life, as men commit a body to the deep, in sure and certain hope of another and more blest existence; but it is the last stage of resignation for one whose mortal happiness is entombed, and its sepulchre sealed up, to listen, without shivering like a ghost in sunshine, to the voices of joy and gladness. And he could not yet endure to walk among scenes of revelry, with that pale, constant phantom gliding by his side, whose soft hair he ever felt sweeping over his arm, as her fainting head was laid upon it, and whose beseeching eyes he often fancied turned on him, imploring release from an abhorred shroud. Unconscious, many times, when these heart-sickening thoughts came over him, the strong man found his face all wet with tears; and then the Magus would tell him, if he mourned for one departed, in the name even of his love to refrain, for he knew, by the words of Zoroaster, that there is in the land of shadows a great river, ever rising, ever flowing, which is formed of all those tears of mankind which have been wept for the dead,—and because such lamentations are a crime, the souls of those for whom they weep must pay the penalty, and for this cause are tormented night and day upon the restless bosom of that bitter stream.

The Persian was still to proceed with Raymond as far as Constantinople, but the Kurds took leave of them at Ezyroum, and they continued their journey, accompanied only by a few Tartars, who were at once their escort and their guide.

It was night, and a night intensely dark, when Raymond and his companion reached Scutari. This picturesque little village lies in the centre of that strange land of the shadow of death, which occupies so many miles of the Asiatic side of the Bosphorus; formed by the one gigantic cemetery wherein, for more than a thousand years, the dead of Byzantium have been laid to rest. In the midnight gloom, however, Raymond could distinguish nothing but the black mass of cypresses, stretching out far into the darkness, with here and there, scarce discernible among the thick shades, a turbaned tombstone, gleaming white, like a sheeted ghost; nor did they pause to penetrate further into that sepulchral forest, but embarked at once in a caïque for Constantinople.

The strangely assorted companions were to part at sunrise; for the object which had brought the Fire

THE FIRE WORSHIPPER. 61

worshipper to this city was apparently of too secret a nature to be made known to the Englishman, and he had only twelve hours in which to accomplish his work, whatever it might be. This period was the utmost limit to which a Gheber could prolong his stay in any Mahomedan town, as the abhorrence in which they were held went so far, that they often were assailed and put to death without mercy. It was almost impossible for them to disguise themselves, being always at once distinguished by their long flowing hair, which their laws forbade them to cut off; and not long since an unfortunate and very innocent American missionary, who wore his hair combed straight down on either side of a very solemn face, was assaulted in an Asiatic town as a Fire worshipper in disguise, and narrowly escaped with his life.

Swift as an arrow, over the still waters which divide Europe from Asia, the light caïque flew on, bearing Raymond the Christian to a new and a holier era in his destiny. For a time he looked down on the clear, dark mirror over which they were gliding, and thought how many a fair young being, once loving and beloved, had gone down, with the warm blood yet gushing round her heart, to the vast, most crowded, and unhallowed grave, beneath that limpid wave, of which a despot holds the keys. Then, as they drew nigher, he strained his eyes to catch the outline of the queenly Byzantium against the pure, dark midnight sky; as it lay, like a spectre city, with its phantom minarets shooting up through the air, all dim and shadowy; and round him, every where, dropping softly like snow-flakes on the dark waters, were the restless birds, the weary "âmes damnées," toiling all night long, even as by day, in their never-ending, aimless flight. But to Raymond's fancy they did not present the idea of lost souls, wandering hopelessly in search of that rest which is the sure and sweetest promise of our paradise: rather they seemed to him apt emblems of those human hopes that wander over the glittering sea of this world's pleasures, and vainly seek repose on their deceitful waves.

The Magus, meanwhile, who abhorred the darkness, sat with his head bent down on his bosom, and his hands folded over the "kosti," or sacred silver girdle which he wore. Raymond could not look on this strange being without feelings of the deepest and most humble thankfulness; for he felt that nothing but the exposition of the peculiar principles of the Fire worshipper's creed could have led his mind into the train of ideas, whence he had deduced such important results to himself.

It seemed a strange, bold measure to have decided on, that of choosing out from amongst men one who should be delivered up to the power of evil, in order that he might fight that power, thus incorporate in a mortal like himself; but his mind rested more and more confidently on the idea, and when he thought on all the crimes one man might perpetrate in the term of his brief existence, he felt that his own would have an ample share of toil and labour, if he devoted it solely to the counteracting of that one baneful influence. For it is not in the gross and palpable vices, the visible sins, that man can most easily and direfully propagate iniquity, but in the influence of one mind upon another, in the power each individual possesses of moving, for good or ill, the soul of his fellow-creature, by word or example; of working on earth their bliss or misery.

There is a dark under-current in the stream of human life; it is not in the stir of politics, the fortunes of a nation, or the glaring horrors of war, that the most awful workings of Almighty will are to be traced out: nor is it there that the direst tragedies are enacted; but in some quiet and obscure home, in a little group of individuals, linked by the ties of blood, or thrown together by the course of events in the even tenor of domestic life. There are crimes which never see the light of day, conceived and brought forth in the silent breast of one mortal—working and accomplishing their fatal purpose in the uncomplaining heart of another. There is bitterest sorrow never acknowledged, never relieved; agony that finds no vent in tears, but saps the hidden springs of life: and these are around us every day, in the crowded streets we tread so carelessly, in our homes, and by our hearths.

It were enough to make the very angels weep to see how we, frail beings whose life is brief as summer's sunshine, do spend it in warring with one another; we depend so utterly upon each other—our sole capacity for bliss (purely of this earth) is in the sympathy of hearts that are human like our own—and yet, when driven by the winds of destiny across another's path, how wantonly do we often crush beneath our careless tread the few pale flowers, given to hide the piercing thorns! How many go down from an unblest life to an untimely grave, dragged thither by the remorseless hands of their fellow-men. Hate, envy, unrequited affection, faithlessness, deceit, who shall sum up the various tortures one mortal may inflict upon another?

Raymond thought on these things, and his strong heart burned with impatience to set his foot on European ground, that he might go forth to meet his destined adversary; but he would seek out no avowed criminal, for these are the least dangerous: he remembered how often he had seen the spirit of the stern commandments violated, and the violator walking over the earth with sweetly smiling lips and humbly folded hands, by all admired and revered. A man's hands may be pure from blood, but there is the far more deadly murderer of souls, or the assassination of another's happiness: he may not have bowed down to graven images, but he can set his own corrupt will on a royal throne, and there worship it with his whole being; and what robbery can be worse than that which steals the inestimable treasure of a heart's internal peace.

CHAPTER III.

THE GREEK MONK—HE TELLS HOW THE SERPENT WORSHIP
YET EXISTS ON EARTH.

It was about an hour before the dawn that the Magus and his companion arrived at the landing place of Stamboul. In that portion of this vast city, which is more properly so called, stands the tower of the Seraskier. It is of extraordinary height, and from the summit may be obtained a panoramic view of most surpassing beauty, unequalled probably in the world.

Thither the companions now bent their steps, for the Persian daily sought the most elevated position attainable, in whatever spot he found himself, in order to perform his devotions at the rising of the sun; and there Raymond was to take leave of him, that he might proceed on his secret mission.

Together they mounted the interminable flight of steps which led to the top of the tower, and when they looked down from it, they found that the shadows had grown so intense in this last hour of the empire of darkness, that nothing was to be distinguished except an indistinct mass of building, with here and there a gleaming light on the water, where the night caïques were passing to and fro.

Soon however they were amply compensated for their disappointment, when a soft beam of light stole down from heaven like a bright angel come to unlock the portals of day, and liberate the glad morning that came bounding forth with its smile of sunshine and voice of song. In a moment, like some glorious vision born from a midnight dream, beneath the feet of Raymond lay a golden city, more beautiful, in its rich oriental architecture, than any thing the hand of man has ever fashioned. Far as eye could reach, decking the sunny shores of that serene and limpid Bosphorus, lay pile on pile of fantastic buildings, with the arrowy minarets shooting up amongst them; and the fresh green gardens laden with the perfume of Eastern flowers; and, far off, the fairy sea of Marmora, in whose pure waters the light of heaven seemed to dwell, like Divine love reflected in the soul of an innocent child.

It was in truth a lovely sight—that of the sun rising over the gorgeous city of Constantinople, and Raymond was one of those who never failed to enhance any pure enjoyment it was given him to feel, by tracing it back to the source whence it sprung. As he gazed down on that magnificent scene, his heart filled with rapture at the thought that the exquisite delight which, by the very instinct of man's spirit, he must ever find in beholding the beauty of nature, results from the fact that the beautiful, in whatever shape it may appear, emanates from the Eternal Mind of that awful One who can alone satisfy the immortal soul; consequently, the deep joy we take in coming thus in contact with a visible trace of His Being, is a proof that we yet are linked in close union with Him here, though often we may seem to wander lonely, as in a wilderness.

Raymond loved also to mark the stamp of the One Omnipotent thought, ever the same, though varying in operation, in that analogy which is to be found in all the various phases of creation, and of which we ourselves unconsciously give the proof, by drawing comparisons—neither forced nor unnatural,—between objects altogether distinct in their nature.

We observe, with a strange sense of pleasure, the same soft shade of blue in the morning sky, and in the mild eyes of some gentle being :—in the still aspect of a quiet lake, within whose silent waters the pure moon sheds her beams, we see the image of a calm reposing child, on which a mother looks in love; we read in the last sunbeam the parting smile of one who dies in peace; and there is not a roseate leaf, tinged with the self-same hue that blushes on the sunset clouds, that fails to tell of a Creator, ever the same in glorious works as in His justice and His mercy.

Meanwhile the Fire worshipper, with his forehead on the ground, lay adoring the menial sun, as, in obedience to the unheard command, it walked its appointed path through the unresisting ether. Raymond had retired to the other end of the wooden gallery, and stood listening to the living voice that suddenly had arisen from every corner of that beautiful city, as though the first sun-ray had awakened it from lethargic slumber,—it was the call to prayers of the Muezzins from every one of all those thousand minarets, echoing a melodious mournful cry in one simultaneous peal through the still clear air. But his attention was suddenly withdrawn from it by a sound nearer at hand,—the measured tread of a slow heavy step ascending the stair, and passing along the gallery. Raymond turned to look on the intruder.

Standing by the side of the Gheber, too much absorbed in his devotions to observe him, was a tall, powerful man, wearing the dress of a Greek monk; the dark flowing robes that swept the ground on all sides gave an additional majesty to his figure,—while the black crape veil thrown over his high cap, and nearly shrouding his features, rendered the deadly paleness of his countenance almost startling.

As on the face of Raymond himself, there was in the expression of this man a strange serenity, which fascinated the eye of those who looked on him; it was the same inflexible, passionless calm, resulting in both cases from the one only cause which can set the seal of peace on the brow of a mortal man, while the living soul yet writhes within him: but though from both alike was effaced the stain of earthly passions, to be replaced by the light of an immortal hope, yet on the countenance of Raymond there lingered a soft shade of tenderness, reflected from the buried human love, that with its unforgotten joys had softened the man's hard nature, of which no trace appeared in the severe aspect of the Greek priest; the deep set lines of an implacable quietude which marked his features had been woven and imbedded there by the lapse of many years; and the darkness of some mortal agony now past, which had been akin to that worst pang, remorse, had flung over him a shadow never to be dispelled.

Both these men had attained the haven of spiritual rest; but dreary and mournful as had been the blast of sudden sorrow which had borne Raymond thither,—it was soft as summer zephyrs, compared to the tremendous storm which must have driven into port the soul of that stern monk; doubtless his strong heart had been scorched

THE GREEK MONK. 69

and withered by the fire of its needful trial ere it ceased to throb for earth, and the things of it.

But now, after gazing for a time on the Gheber with a look of concentrated indignation, which must have filled him with awe could he have seen it, the Greek priest lifted up the hands he had held crossed on his breast, and stretched them out over the prostrate Persian, while he spoke in a voice so deep and calm that it scarce stirred the lips through which it passed.

"What dost thou here, O thou false worshipper?—in hell-wrought madness adoring the visible things of the One Invisible, to whom alone adoration belongeth! Arise, Arise! thou follower of a falsehood,—thou servant of a lie! Turn thine idolatrous eyes from the weak orb that in servitude labours on the course commanded: and do thou adore the Sun of Righteousness, whose Light illuminates eternity, and yet disdains not to penetrate, with life-giving beam, the humblest soul among those worms which are called men."

At the sound of that solemn voice the Magus had started to his feet: but the priest had spoken in modern Greek, and he did not understand his words, though Raymond had well comprehended them: it was sufficient however for the Gheber, accustomed to be hunted down and persecuted wherever he went, to meet the menacing eye of the monk, flashing with the fire which age had failed to quench; he saw that he must at once endeavour to escape from his presence, or never perhaps be allowed to leave with life this beautiful but fatal city, whose streets are so often and so wantonly dyed in blood.

Gathering up with trembling hands the long locks of

his flowing hair, the Magus hid the sacred girdle beneath his robe, and resuming the slippers he had taken off while engaged in prayer, glided slowly from the gallery to the stair. The monk instantly snatched from his breast a small black cross, which he held out in one hand, while with the other he seemed about to arrest his flight; the very sight, however, of the holy symbol which he had taken out to enforce his authority appeared to awaken him to gentler and more forgiving thoughts; he stood back to let the Persian pass, and then, pressing the cross to his lips, turned to the window with a deep sigh.

As the Magus descended the stair Raymond approached to bid him farewell, but waving his hand with a look of terror, he signed to him not to advance, and almost instantly disappeared.

Meanwhile the monk had remained motionless, and when Raymond turned to look upon him, he was gazing down upon the lovely sunlit scene below; and still thrilling from the European shore, and echoed back again from that of Asia, rose and fell the last tones of the musical call to prayers. The soft cry ascended up, borne on the morning breeze, and it smote on the ears of the Greek priest, as it seemed, like a sound of horror. He flung back the thick black veil, and displayed a sternly marked forehead, with the long grey hair sweeping over his shoulders, whilst he lifted up to heaven his dark piercing eyes, and stretched out his arm over the Mahomedan city.

"Oh distichia!" (Oh misery) he exclaimed, "must these things be, in a world that yet bears upon its bosom the mount of the Crucifixion! here are mine eyes polluted with the sight of an idolatrous worship; there are mine ears defiled with the voice of a faith tenfold more dishonouring to man, more impious unto man's Creator; for if the Ghebers, in their mad folly, deify the elements, if of old my fathers sat in darkness, amid all the sunny light of our fair Greece, because they deified the attributes of the Omnipotent, how far more blasphemous the crime of those, who call indeed upon the name of God, but make that God a Licenser of evil, and swear that by following His laws, they do thus make themselves the slaves of their own basest passions! And thou, Oh most holy Cross, by whom was offered up the sacred Sacrifice of an incomprehensible Agony— sole path by which we may ascend unto the regions of Eternal Light, how art thou laid prostrate in the dust of earth! even of that earth by Thee redeemed, and bought! I know that there are lands where Thy holy banner waves triumphant; but I have seen and heard how, beneath its sheltering folds, there crouches, exulting in his secret victory, that most accursed of gods, the idol mammon; hiding with Christian emblems the mark of the beast upon his Cain-like brow, and holding the cup of spiritual corruption to the lips of the worshippers that kneel to kiss the ground before him! Oh Thou, in whose sight the stars are most impure, shall these things long endure within the world which Thou hast built?"

"Post tenebras, spero lucem," murmured Raymond, almost unconsciously, as the deep vibrating voice of the monk died away in prayer; but the sound caught the quick ear of the Greek, and he turned round hurriedly to see who had spoken. The Englishman came forward, and repeated his words in Greek. As the thought which these words embodied passed into the mind of the monk, his stern countenance become lit up with a passing gleam.

"Yes," he exclaimed, "stranger, you are right! for us to hope is a great and solemn duty; heaviness endureth for the night, but joy cometh in the morning. Let us hope—be ours the patient abiding of the meek." Then, looking with a keen earnest glance on Raymond, he said,—

"You heard, then, the words which burst from me, moved by this morning's sights and sounds, but are you a Christian? whence do you come?"

Raymond answered by making the holy sign, which he knew would best give the desired assurance, and the monk, seeming in the dark thoughts that were crowding in that moment on his soul to forget how completely they were strangers, at once continued to speak on the subject which so engrossed him.

"Then can you understand with what bitterness of heart I turned from the worshipper of Fire here, to the idolaters of sense that grovel there, in systematic depravity? for am I not one of those sent forth as a labourer to gather in the harvest of souls to the garner-house of the King? and my cry, with the cry of those that have reaped, has entered into the ears of the Lord of Sabaoth; and am I not one of those who, with a baptism of blood, bestowed the name of a Christian land once more upon that fair lost Greece, defiled with the yoke of the infidel? and am I not destined to see that the regeneration of that sacramental war has but awakened it to a new life of a more subtle and more perilous corruption?

"But, stranger, would you know the secret of it all? would you know what is the dark religion that does in

THE GREEK MONK.

deed and truth bind, as in bonds of iron, the race of man, enslaving them under a thousand specious names? Look here!"—he grasped Raymond by the arm, and drew him to the window, whence they could look down on every part of the city.

"Behold!" continued the monk, "do you see that open square, over which towers the gorgeous mosque of Achmet? It is the At-Mehdan—the ancient Hippodrome—the stony death-couch of a thousand Janissaries. Do you perceive there a conical column, formed by the encircling folds of the body of a brazen triple-headed serpent? That is the tripod of the Pythian priestess, the serpentine pillar brought by Constantine from Delphi to this city; and it is the symbol of that most demoniacal worship of the "Ophiolatriea," which at one period, in visible, palpable form, reigned triumphant over every quarter of the globe. Various were the shades and gradations it assumed, many the names and titles given to it; but the revolting, fiendish creed was the same.

"The Egyptians taught, with subtle sophistry, that divinity must be symbolized by serpents, and the fallen world obeyed their teaching well, for the divinity they symbolized and worshipped was the Spirit of Evil.

"The sign of the Caduceus, which first took rise in Egypt, became, in actual fact, the emblem of earth's religion in that ancient time. It was formed by two serpents, male and female, representatives of the sun and moon; objects then as now of senseless man's idolatry; and their bodies intertwined depicted the solar circle and the lunar crescent[1]. And now, behold,

---

[1] Symbol of the Caduceus ∪ Lunar Crescent.
○ Solar Circle.
+ Four Elements.

although that visible sign no longer is acknowledged, although in outward palpable form man no longer bows to the idol snake, yet the religion of this world is the worship of the serpent still, even the adoration of the power of evil.

"Yes; that dark mysterious power, who first in this revolting form allured the woman to conceive sin in her heart, and bring forth death, has but one object in his hidden labours—to be adored of God's created; and from one Immaculate alone he claimed that worship altogether vainly; for strange as it does seem, when in every human breast there is an instinctive horror for the creeping thing whose shape he took, yet under that very form, as I have shown, he caused himself to be revered in idolatry most awful; and now, I tell you, even as heretofore, do men fall down and worship him, though he has veiled himself in robes of purest white.

"It matters not what be their outward faith—the snake, the snake is coiling round their hearts—he is there, gliding over the miser's heap of gold—he is there, entwined with the laurel wreath of fame; look for him beneath the pillow of the child of luxury; lift up the veil that hides that woman's beauty, and seek him in her bosom; in the palace of the hard rich man; in the hovel of the discontented poor; in the gorgeous tomb-vaults of a noble house; in the offerings of ostentatious charity; going up with the haughty priest to the altar; with the egotist to his pleasures; with the lover to his slumbers, to dream of mortal clay beloved too well—the snake! the snake! yes, seek him, find him every where."

The monk paused, apparently overpowered with the

intensity of his feelings; and Raymond answered him in his own language.

"I can indeed well understand the sorrow of a soul like yours, Pater mou (my father); for I too, wandering through this pleasant world, have seen the serpent coiled amongst the flowers, and I too have learnt that men can madly lift on high and worship the accursed thing which was condemned to cleave unto the dust for ever! Truly the night is very dark,—yet have we not the sure promise of the rising of that Eternal Sun, which never more shall set? and who can say but even unto us it may be given to hasten the coming of that triumphant Light?

"Remember, Patera, how, like yours, that cry went up from the souls beneath the altar of the Omnipresent: 'How long, O Lord, holy and true?' and to them were given the white robes, as earnest of their eternal purity; but it was told them that they must wait a little season, till their brethren, which must suffer for the Word's sake, should be fulfilled; and now, surely, by the martyrdom, whether in heart or blood, of every one who is content to live in desolation or to die in anguish for the cause of truth, the probation of these expectant spirits shall be shortened; and for every life offered up in sacrifice a moment shall be struck off from that dim, dreary interval, ere the glorious fiat is pronounced: 'There shall be no more night,'—and darkness, fleeing away before the unveiled glory, shall make him wings to wander over the repulsing spheres, powerless for evermore.

"But if this be so, Christian priest, shall we not too perform our part, and find therein the needful solace? Have we not lives to be delivered up to many sorrows, and bodies to be bruised and crushed with endless labour? Can we not find a funeral pyre for our earthly hopes and joys, and a sword keen and sharp, wherewith to cut deep into the heart that fain would throb for them alone? Say, what hindereth us to be martyrs?"

"My son, you have well spoken," exclaimed the monk: "ours must indeed be the faith of deeds, not words; thrice blessed is he who, by the shedding of his heart's best blood, can cleanse one inch of that ground, accursed for man's sake. Often, when gazing up into that lucid sky, it seems to me as though there sat in the dim ether a mighty shadowy figure (even the spirit of the human race), weeping and making lamentation, and brooding with clasped hands over the dark earth, as it sends up, with self-accusing voice, the cry, 'Unclean, unclean.' But you have well said; let us labour, and, if need be, die; rather than live thus idly, to dream and to lament."

The priest folded his black veil over his face for a few minutes, seemingly in prayer; and then, turning round, looked with much interest on the stranger, to whom, almost unconsciously, he had been imparting his thoughts. Suddenly, as he looked on him, an expression of great pleasure passed over his countenance. "Tell me," he said, "are you an Englishman, as your dress bespeaks?"

Raymond answered in the affirmative.

"Then heaven, yes, heaven has sent you here! for it is in your power even now to be of incalculable service to one of your own countrymen; and if I mistake not, you are of those who with thankfulness accept the means of doing good."

Raymond started involuntarily at these words of the

monk: he remembered that when he had taken the resolution by which he believed he could best render his life useful to the cause he served, he had, with determined faith, trusted that his destined human adversary would speedily be sent across his path, in order that he might track his course through life, and destroy, as far as possible, the traces of his baneful influence; and now, scarce had he set his foot on the shores of Europe, where he designed to seek out some servant of iniquity, than he is told of one who required his services. Was it superstitious to imagine that this might be the man in whose person he was to combat the power of evil? With great eagerness he assured the monk of his willingness to serve him, or any other, and begged to be made acquainted with the details of the matter.

"My son," said the priest, "I thank you for your confidence, which you shall assuredly not repent. I would have asked you to accompany me at once to the dwelling of that most unhappy man of whom I speak, and told you, by the way, the details of his history, but it grows late, and you must not brave this burning sun. Trust me, stranger as I am, till evening, then will I come for you, and together will we go, to bring light, if it may be, into a soul darkened by sin and sorrow."

Every word which the Greek monk uttered only strengthened Raymond's hopes that his heaven-directed path was about to open out, even now, clear and distinct before him; and he readily entered into this arrangement.

They agreed to meet at the hotel in Pera, to which the Englishman was going, about the hour of sunset;

and the priest then took his leave of him,—saluting him after the manner of his country, by laying his hand on his lips and his forehead; whilst Raymond left the tower, and proceeded through the narrow, tortuous streets of this city of pleasure, towards the European quarter.

CHAPTER IV.

THE SERVANT OF PURITY MEETS WITH THE SLAVE OF INIQUITY.

THE Greek monk was true to his appointment. The sinking sun's last beams came stealing over the pure waters of the Bosphorus, like the light of an immortal hope over a meek and quiet soul; the sounds of life and activity, that during the day's intense heat had all been hushed, now woke anew: in the crowded bazars on all sides were to be seen the gay arabas, drawn by oxen adorned with silver bells, which were conveying the jewelled slaves to the gardens of the "Sweet Waters," where they love to spend their summer evenings; while their haughty masters rode along the streets at a majestic pace, followed by negroes running on foot, who carried their pipes or perfumed beads.

Silently, through the groups of picturesque oriental figures, Raymond followed his guide, who walked before him with slow and stately step, his arms folded, and his face hid in the long dark veil; he led him down to the landing-place of Tophana, and there embarking in one of the light swift caïques, they were soon gliding over the still water towards Scutari on the Asiatic shore, where the person they were about to see at present resided. As soon as they were established side by side in the boat, the monk proceeded to give the desired explanation.

He said it was but due to the trust his companion had reposed in him, that he should dwell for a few minutes briefly on his own previous history. His name was Neophytus, and the early part of his life had been spent in the beautiful monastery, now so lonely and deserted, of Daoud in Attica ; there he had remained, leading a life of stern contemplation, in which earth had no part, till the outbreak of the Greek revolution, which had shown him that men's energies and intellect are not given for prayer and meditation only. In that noble war of independence he had taken an active part, not because it was in truth a dauntless struggle for liberty, but for the cause of Christianity which it involved. One only joy of this earth had been permitted to him during his long monastic life, and that was the care of a gentle young brother of his own, whose guileless soul was given him to nurture and to lead—and he loved him with a passionate affection, which had no place within the cold still convent walls ; but when the hour for action in the good cause came, he offered up this one only treasure to be the first martyr among the sons of Greece, and that under circumstances of peculiar horror[1]: from that period, when by his own order his brother was sacrificed for the "Cross and Victory" which was the motto of the insurgent Greeks, his heart was, as it were, sealed up to this world, and earth be-

---

[1] A record of the life of Neophytus, the Monk, has been given in the Dublin University Magazine.

came but the battle-field whereon he was to fight for
an immortal crown. He shared in all the most striking
events of the long protracted war, and when at length
it was terminated, and the monarchy established in
Greece, he had come to devote the last years of his
declining life to the interests of the Greek church at
Constantinople, which the severance of this Apostolic
branch from the government of the Patriarch resident
there, had somewhat endangered. He then proceeded
to detail his first meeting with the Englishman whom
they were about to visit.

About a month previous to this time, Neophytus
had been returning late one night to the village of
Scutari, where he was then residing, and his course lay
of necessity through the boundless cemetery which
surrounded it on all sides. As he took his way among
the tombs, he suddenly perceived the figure of a man
lying prostrate at the foot of a cypress tree, and hastened
to the spot, fearing that some new case of assassination
had occurred. This, however, was not the fact; the
stranger, who wore the European dress, was only insensible, from what cause Neophytus had never yet discovered, and he soon revived; the monk procured assistance to convey him to his own dwelling in the village,
as he was evidently extremely ill. It proved, indeed,
that he was in the first stage of a brain fever, and from
that day Neophytus had tended him with unremitting
care. He found that this stranger had been for several
months inhabiting one of the houses in Scutari, and
from his servants, who were much astonished at his
sudden illness, the monk obtained some little information respecting him.

It appeared that he was an Englishman, who had

been travelling for a considerable period on the Continent and in the East. He had for some time led a most dissipated life, but of late he had fallen into a state of profound melancholy, and of utter indifference and apathy, from which nothing could rouse him. It was evident from what the monk was told, that he was a man of no principle, and at the same time of extraordinary talent: his servants said they knew he was not a Christian, but could not tell what creed he professed; he had apparently fixed on Scutari as a residence, because it afforded him the means of perfect solitude, and had spent his days chiefly in wandering alone through the vast tract of land there consecrated to the dead. They could give no explanation as to the cause of his sudden illness; and the monk having gathered these particulars, betook himself, in the true spirit of charity, to the care of this unhappy man, though well aware that he was not of the brotherhood of the faith. He recovered slowly from his fever, but Neophytus became seriously alarmed at the state of mind into which he fell, even whilst still weak and languid from illness; he seemed absolutely torn asunder in the conflict of his soul, between an utter abhorrence of life, and a most unspeakable dread of death: at times, so uncontrollable seemed his horror of existence, that the monk dreaded he would have recourse to self-destruction; and again, when a Turkish funeral passed beneath his windows, a sight occurring daily and almost hourly in that town, he never failed to fall into a perfect paroxysm of terror and disgust at thought of the shroud, the worm, and the grave.

It was the more painful to the monk to witness this mental agony, that he could have little or no communication with the sufferer; he was not acquainted with the Greek language, and Neophytus could not speak Italian, though he understood it sufficiently to have gathered the substance of the bitter speeches in which the Englishman sometimes sought to lay bare to him the torture of his spirit.

He told Raymond, that he could by no means account for the species of fascination which this unfortunate man exercised over him, and which constrained him, little as he was apt to be moved by external influences, to feel for him the very deepest interest.

After having detailed these circumstances, the request of the Greek monk to Raymond scarce required an explanation. In this emergency nothing could be more fortunate than his meeting with one, whose noble self-devoted heart, and sound judgment, had very speedily been discovered by his shrewd penetration, and who, being the countryman of the object of his anxiety, could easily as well as ably minister to that mind diseased.

Raymond entered with the warmest interest into the feelings of the monk respecting his unhappy charge, and promised to spare no pains to win his confidence, and guide him, if possible, out of the abyss of despondency into which he seemed to have sunk.

The bright moonlight, which had followed rapidly on the decline of day, was streaming down on the oriental village as they disembarked, and passed through it to the dwelling of Neophytus, from which the stranger had not yet been removed. It was one of those low Turkish houses, whose flat roof is intended as a place of refuge after the heat of the day. Nor could the most splendid apartment afford half the enjoyment which is to be found in that strange resting-place, with the starlit canopy above, the soft wind of evening sighing round, and the nightingales making sweet music among the cypress groves. Thither the monk now conducted the Englishman to meet his countryman.

Raymond paused to look on him whilst yet unperceived.

Reclining on a heap of cushions with an air of extreme languor, he saw a tall striking-looking man, of some thirty years of age, or rather more; and, as he looked, he felt that it would be impossible to conceive a face more perfectly beautiful than that which was now before him, illuminated by the moon's full radiance. It was not so much, however, the symmetrical perfection of feature which gave that countenance so inexpressible a charm, as the stamp of a noble intellect that lit up the deep large eyes, and might be traced in the pale expansive forehead, shrouded by heavy masses of dark flowing hair. And yet there was a something on that fair face from which the soul recoiled, as though, when looking down on the pure bosom of the sea, its hideous, monster-filled depths had been suddenly revealed; in that full dark eye there was an evil glance; on that chiselled lip a bitter sneer; the face was angelic, but by those who looked closely, the mark of the demon might have been seen. To most men, however, it was a countenance fatally, nay, fearfully, attractive, and to Raymond it was not unknown; already had he seen Philip Arabyn, and he had seen him as one whose name was coupled with that of an infidel. It was many years since they had met, and their acquaintance had been but slight; yet as Raymond recalled to memory all that he had heard connected with this man, he bowed his head in mute

THE SLAVE OF INIQUITY. 85

submission, for he felt convinced that his destiny was before him.

Arabyn was very young when his path had crossed that of Raymond; but he was even then a marked man, noted for the peculiar manner in which he had been, as it were, loaded with the choicest gifts of nature. He seemed to possess every advantage which could enable a man most powerfully to exercise an influence over the mind of others; strikingly attractive in appearance, with an intellect of extraordinary powers—gifted with singular eloquence, by which he gave utterance to thoughts both profound and startling, and with a rare combination of talents, readily turned by him to any purpose.—And this man, with his voice low and sweet as that of a woman, and his face of haunting beauty, was the bold propagator of the most determined infidel opinions.

Well might Raymond feel almost with awe, that the being he sought, the slave to the power of evil, was indeed before him even then, armed with all that is most fascinating to the human mind, like the master spirit himself arrayed as an angel of light! Could any character be more utterly dangerous in a world like this, than that which has been described above? every power given him, and those powers turned systematically to evil! Yet Raymond would not judge too hastily; as he looked upon the face of Arabyn, still unconscious of his presence, it wore an expression of such deep thought, that it was possible he yet might become a sincere inquirer, and receive the reward which is ensured to all who are such, even the conviction of truth. At all events, the monk had spoken of a mental conflict, of some mysterious irresolution; and Raymond, rousing himself from the recollections which had crowded on him, prepared rather to make acquaintance with the person into whose presence he had so strangely been brought, than longer to speculate on his character.

Signing to the monk to precede him, he advanced, and stood face to face with Arabyn. A faint expression of pleasure stole over the beautiful face of the infidel as Neophytus announced, that having accidentally met with an Englishman, he had brought him to visit him; but when he lifted up his languid eyes to look on the new comer, he recognized Raymond, as he himself had been recognized: nor had he been more prominent as the professed atheist, than his visitor as the enlightened and devoted Christian, at the period when they had met formerly. This recollection had evidently its full weight; he could scarcely expect that a meeting between persons of such opposite opinions should be agreeable to either party, and he at once drew back with the utmost coldness and reserve.

Raymond readily understood his feelings; he saw at a glance that the greatest caution would be necessary if he wished to win the confidence of the remarkable man before him, but he determined to spare neither time nor trouble in becoming acquainted with his character; and sitting down beside him, he alluded very briefly to their former acquaintance, and then began to talk of Arabyn's illness and present state of health, with a look of kindness and interest which could not fail to be agreeable to him. He found him, however, little disposed to give any explanation of the cause of his fever; and Raymond soon passed from this topic, and began to converse on subjects which he thought likely to please the strong intellect of his companion.

Arabyn could not but take some pleasure in a species of intellectual enjoyment of which he had so long been deprived, and though he continued to entrench himself in a cold indifference, he owned, as the hours passed on, that it was many months since he had spent so agreeable an evening; and he seemed rather willingly to accept Raymond's offer of visiting him often, as a relief from the distracting thoughts which evidently persecuted him.

After this first evening Raymond gradually acquired the habit of coming every day to spend a few hours with his countryman, for the intense heat of the weather greatly retarded Arabyn's recovery, and he continued too weak and languid to admit of any change for the present.

It was with the utmost skill and prudence that Raymond carried on his intercourse with the infidel. Arabyn had adopted a system of implacable reserve, from which nothing could allure him; he openly acknowledged that he took great pleasure in Raymond's society, but he never gave him the slightest clue to the state of his mind, beyond the tranquil and sneering avowal of a total scepticism; he could not, however, conceal the dark depravity which had blighted his soul, and perverted as noble and powerful a mind as ever was given to man: and Raymond might have thought it unnecessary to pursue the examination further, but for a certain mysterious irresolution which it was evident was fiercely agitating the spirit of the sceptic; he more than once, indeed, hinted vaguely, that a dreadful hesitation seemed to place him on the rack, but that he was about to escape from it by coming to some decision on his future destiny; and Raymond had little doubt that he was balancing between life and death, from the manner in which he spoke of his abhorrence of existence, and his shrinking hatred for the silent ever-working corruption of the black mysterious grave. Moreover, if he chose to live, it was clear, from his custom of reasoning upon all points, that it would only be on some organized system,—even as Raymond himself had fixed and defined the principles which were to guide his own future years in this world ; and if the law of his mortal life, prophetic of the purpose of his immortality, was a willing servitude to purity, what more likely, from all he knew of him, that Arabyn's would be a systematic abandonment of himself and his rare talents to the power of evil ?

Raymond shuddered as he thought of this too probable consummation. It was impossible for him to be so constantly in the society of the infidel without perceiving, even from experience, the singular fascination which he exercised irresistibly on all who approached him. Every thing which could render a human being attractive to others seemed combined in this man, and not the least remarkable of his gifts was the power he possessed of practising the most extraordinary deception on those he sought to allure; he could assume, beyond the power of mortal eye to detect, whatever character he chose,—even the most pure, the most holy: the sweet voice, the sweet smile, the mournful supplicating eye, were ever ready to hide most winningly the black stain that lay upon his soul ; and Raymond felt that if his decision were indeed to take to his embrace in fearful love the accursed thing, for himself had in truth been provided a most powerful adversary ! He dwelt, however, with hope on some circumstances in Arabyn's

THE SLAVE OF INIQUITY. 89

life which he trusted might tend to lessen his evil influence.

The infidel was the son of an Englishman, who had left him almost for sole inheritance a name disgraced by many crimes. His mother had been a slave by birth and by education, the property of a Russian nobleman of high rank, resident at Moscow; and from him she had been literally stolen by the father of Arabyn, who conveyed her to Italy, where he married her, and continued to reside, not choosing to brave the rigid exactions of English society.

It was with difficulty that the slave was concealed from her master, who made unremitting search for her; but finally she died, leaving one son, and a daughter many years younger. The father was also soon after killed in a duel, under circumstances the most dishonourable; and Philip Arabyn then came to England, to take possession of the small property to which he succeeded, and which was burthened with debt nearly to its full value.

It may be imagined what reception Arabyn was likely to meet with in a world which does right heavily visit the sins of the fathers on the children; and much of the fatal tendency of his mind may be attributed to the stinging pangs he endured while reaping this bitter harvest of another's crimes. It was one good trait in his character that he never brought his young sister to England, not wishing to expose her to all that he himself was forced to meet with; and she remained in Italy, under the care of a respectable Englishwoman.

Raymond trusted that the opprobrium thus attached to the name of Arabyn might lessen his power of spreading evil, at least in his own country; but meanwhile he continued with care and perseverance his endeavours to penetrate into a character whose influence for good or for ill must, even with these disadvantages, still be incalculably great. In his conversations with Arabyn, he carefully avoided bringing forward too prominently his own deep-rooted opinions: not that he concealed in the slightest degree what was the pure faith he professed; there was no possible contingency in which he could have thought it right so to do; but he avoided that very common and grievous mistake, which is often committed by persons as injudicious as they are zealous, when they strive to thrust pure principles upon a mind unprepared for their reception, and seek to enforce a holy practice where the spirit is too dark to admit the fundamental truth.

Cold and apathetic as Arabyn ever seemed, it was, however, soon evident that there was one peculiarity in Raymond with which he was greatly struck. It was the contrast between that deep and unchanging serenity, and his own agonizing restlessness; once, indeed, he was moved even to ask what could be the secret of this unspeakable peace of the soul; and when Raymond calmly answered, that it sprung solely from the faith and the hope that lay deep at his heart, the sceptic writhed on his uneasy couch, and muttered that it was then most unattainable for him.

The question had been called forth by an accidental circumstance. Arabyn recollected that the Christian had not always stood alone upon the earth as now, and he casually asked one day, where was that beautiful young wife, from him whose tortured fancy was for ever following her gentle form through the various stages of its necessary corruption! For one instant Raymond's convulsed features told what depths of agony had been raked up by those few words, and the next a deep calm had settled on his face; he lifted up his grateful eyes to Heaven, and, with a radiant smile, told tranquilly how he had delivered up that sweet companion to a care more tender and more watchful far than his, and to a love more pure than that with which he cherished her on earth: and from that hour Arabyn often looked with wondering upon the countenance of his companion, which never for a moment lost the impress of a solemn ineffable rest.

One evening, when their acquaintance had already continued some weeks, Raymond went with Neophytus, the monk, to attend Vespers at a small Greek chapel; the service was very simple,—for ceremony there was none; and beautiful as was the architecture of this old Byzantine church, there was little in the interior to attract the eye. The two side aisles were occupied by the men and women, thus separated from one another; the nave was reserved for the priests alone. Through the deep narrow windows the sunbeams came stealing, and lit up the few quaint pictures of the blessed saints and martyrs, all, without exception, depicting the moment when they had bartered their death-agony for an everlasting crown. A low door, on which the cross was emblazoned, hid the altar from the eyes of all but the consecrated priest, where the light of the tapers, contrasting with that of day, seemed to form an atmosphere apart.

The service commenced by the solemn declaration, uttered by one voice alone, that "God is Holy—Holy and Omnipotent—Holy and Eternal!" And then, whilst the people bowed themselves at the announcement, the prayers for mercy were offered up, being for the most part the still living echoes of the voice of him, who in the days of old was for his eloquence surnamed "The Saint of the Golden Mouth!" (Chrysostom.) Next, the Psalms and Lessons for the day were read in ancient Greek ; and when they were concluded, the priest came forward with his silver censer, and offered the smoking incense to each individual in turn ; after this he retired within the altar, and was heard through the closed doors chanting in a low solemn tone : in a few minutes he re-appeared, holding the consecrated elements on his head, which is considered by the Eastern Church the profoundest mark of reverence ; having stood silently exhibiting them for a few minutes, he made the sign of the cross over the people, and returned whence he came (for the Holy Communion is administered only at dawn of day), nor did he again appear amongst them, though for about half an hour the worshippers remained absorbed in secret prayer.

Raymond knelt with the rest; he was not one to require any external aid to devotion : yet they do err most assuredly who despise the power of those outward things, which the men of old, holier and wiser than we are, deemed advisable for rousing and moving the luke-warm, earth-drawn soul. The sacred stillness of that ancient church lulled the man of thought and energy to a tranquillity like that of a child at rest. The shadows of evening deepened while they prayed, as though the earth were darkening, that heaven might brighten on their view ; and, dimly seen, the faces of the agonizing saints seemed to gleam pale and solemn from the walls: only the steady lights on the unseen altar shed a glow on the mosaics of the roof, and the columns

THE SLAVE OF INIQUITY.

which supported it. And in that quiet hour, thoughts of eternal love fell soft on Raymond's heart, as dews of evening; his soul rose up, unclogged by an earthly wish or hope, and ascended into the paradise of God.

At length the worshippers arose, and went forth one by one, repeating on the threshold the sign of the cross, which they had made as they entered the church, —on entering, in token that by this hope alone they dared to penetrate within its sacred walls,—on quitting it, because in that strength only they could brave the world's contamination.

Raymond then at once proceeded to pay his accustomed visit to Arabyn. These meetings were still always held on the terrace which was formed by the flat roof; and when Raymond sat down beside the infidel, and gazed up into the solemn sky, the mighty treasure-house of those unnumbered worlds of light, he found it impossible for some time to rouse himself from that abstraction, full of the profoundest joy, which had taken possession of him in the quiet darkened church.

And the sceptic lay looking on him with his weary, restless eyes, feeling at his heart the gnawing of the immortal soul's unsatisfied desire, and inquiring of himself whence came that aching pain; till at last, almost unconsciously, deep mournful words came bursting from his lips.

"How calm, how peaceful is that face!" he murmured, as he fixed his gaze on Raymond; "and yet he bears the weight of forty years of this most vain and hopeless existence, and he has passed through suffering which I would not have borne alive. And this is not the calm of listless apathy, or the peace of one who can revel recklessly in oblivious and debasing pleasures. It is, I well can see, the intellectual repose of a mind, satisfied and convinced, for ever freed from doubt. Can this be the result of thought, when thought, for me, is the fiend that drags me over the dark infinity, as over a vast tempestuous ocean, tossed from wave to wave, and rock to rock, for ever unquiet, for ever unsatisfied; till I could long to sink within the unfathomed waters that gird this visible life, and ask for mercy from annihilation?"

These last words were uttered so loud that they aroused the soul of Raymond from his calm contemplation, as the sighing of a passing breeze troubles the surface of a tranquil lake. He turned round.

"I have disturbed you," said Arabyn, bitterly; "and I regret it; for *you* need not to break the silence which if no human voice dispel, lies heavy on my soul as molten lead. Oh, wherefore is that solitude, which is to me so horrible, to you a source of calm enjoyment?"

"It is but natural," said Raymond soothingly; "you are at that age when the impetuous passions and keen sensations crave for society and excitement, and I must soon enter into the dark shadows which border this side of eternity."

"Society!" echoed Arabyn; "I tell you it is more terrible to me than solitude itself. There seems a spell hanging round me now. A dark power of prophecy has long since fallen upon me; my mind is as it were condemned to forestall the inevitable destiny of that on which my eyes must rest. I look on all that is fairest and brightest; and, cursed with a horrible foresight, I behold it in the state of corruption to which its inherent decay is even now leading it. When I stand amid the young and gay, seeking to join in the revelry which has for them such intoxicating power, they are to me but as the fragile insects we see disporting themselves an instant in some bright sunbeam, till the first light summer breeze pass by, and disperse them to the elements. Even when the glad eyes smile the brightest, and the ringing voices echo with words of sweetest hope, and the hot blood dancing in their veins warms the beating hearts that never throbbed with pain, even then I can distinctly hear the swift-approaching wail of that awful blast of destiny, which shall soon rush past, to sweep them away with the wreck of all things perishing—and whither?" The infidel paused; then lifting up his eyes, he exclaimed, "Raymond, again I demand from you the secret of your peace!"

"I can give no other answer than that which I have made already," said Raymond, calmly. "I am a Christian; and in the one immortal glorious hope of that most holy faith, I find enough to satisfy for ever the undying spiritual essence, which tortures you, because you offer it no aliment for its immortality."

"Tell me not it is your Christianity which makes you what you are," said Arabyn, with a sort of impatient resentment; "your mind is as capable of appreciating truth as mine, and to me this creed is, and ever will be, nothing. No, some secret lies hid beneath that false delusive name: some mysterious system of philosophy, which I have sought in vain. Raymond, hear me; we are about to part, for I must soon go hence; and then, doubtless, we shall meet no more. Oh, depart not from me, to enter, when your hour comes, fearless and calm, into the abyss of impenetrable night, till I have learnt to share your marvellous repose! I tell you, that tomb, which seems to be for you the parent of immortality, bearing within it the life-germ of unnumbered ashes, that tomb has no voice for me. I have questioned it unwearied in every shape; I have penetrated into the horror of its corruption with unshrinking eyes, and with steady hands have rifled the depths of the charnel-house; but all was mute—mute for me. Nor ever one of all that countless and corrupting dead returned to say, 'We live and love, as we have lived and loved!' Oh, if for your strong unyielding mind the silence of the sepulchre is broken—if but one whisper have reached you from the dark and infinite Unknown— speak! and destroy for me this thought which tortures me, the thought of so horrible a paradox, that a being, with the capacity of imagining eternity, should have been created capable of existing only for time!"

Raymond listened with intense interest to the words of the infidel; but when he answered, it was without reverting to the distinct profession of faith which he had just made.

"Arabyn," he said, "you would have me minister to your mental unrest; but you forget that your mind is a sealed book for me: unless you explain to me what your opinions are in their distinct, decisive form, I do not see how I am to answer your question satisfactorily."

"You are right," exclaimed Arabyn, starting from his pillow, with more of energy than he had yet displayed. "I will detail to you the burning thoughts which have rushed through my brain from the first dim uncertainty of my awakening intellect, to the deep blank void in which I now exist. Not that I hope for aid from you; I was grasping at a shadow when I spoke of it. Not you nor any mortal man could ever give that which my own reason failed to find; but I feel that it would be a strange relief to me to reveal the history of my mind to you, who are capable of comprehending it; to drag up to the light all the shapeless phantoms that crowd around me, when I seek to penetrate beyond the visible narrow circle of my actual life. Though it can avail me nothing to hear your answers, the answers of a Christian," he added with a sneer, "yet it may avail myself much, thus to define my own belief, and organize my own ideas; for I am resolved that I will no longer drag on an aimless existence, in careless and confused uncertainty. I will either now at once die, and deliver myself up, without further anticipation, to the horror of that inevitable evil; or I will find some means of so moulding life to my will, that I shall be able to endure it while it lasts out its natural term."

This was exactly what Raymond had felt convinced the infidel was balancing in his mind: it seemed to him to tally strongly with his own resolutions; and however ungracious the manner in which Arabyn had offered his confidence, he was too anxious to ascertain what his views really were, not to accept it at once.

"But tell me," he said, "before proceeding further, have you ever at any time accepted the Christian religion as truth in earlier years?"

"Doubtless," replied Arabyn, with his taunting laugh, "it was duly inculcated on me in my childhood; but my mind rose above it as soon as its powers became developed. This creed, like all other shadows without a substance, on which enthusiasts and bigots have built their hopes, soon seemed to me unworthy of that reason, whose light and whose existence in my own

F

breast I admit, though whence it comes, or wherefore given for a brief space to animate this body, heir to corruption, I know not."

"If I mistake not," said Raymond, "you have never in your mature years examined into the doctrines of Christianity."

"I have not, in truth," said Arabyn: "even at that early age it seemed to me that the idea which the Bible itself gives of the Deity was perfectly incompatible with the belief that His proceedings on earth could have been such as I was taught, and it became a matter of astonishment to me to hear my teachers so assiduously instructing me in views of the Being they represented as Creator—not of this world only, but of sphere upon sphere, of universe on universe,—in views, I say, of Him, and in accounts of His mode of Government amongst men, which appeared to me altogether derogatory to the character of the Supreme ; and I own I marvelled much that, century after century, so many able men, of strong and vigorous mind, of genius, and of judgment, should have passed through life—ay, and gone down to the grave, in the full and firm belief of a system which thus to me appeared untenable."

"And did this not induce you later to inquire more deeply into that faith which to them proved satisfactory ?" asked Raymond.

"Never," replied Arabyn: "the lessons of my childhood were not forgotten, and they sufficed me."

"Then," exclaimed Raymond solemnly, "if this be all you know, I, the servant of the Most High God, and of His Christ, declare unto you that you no more know what is that religion by Him revealed, than your unassisted eyes can discern, in those far-off gleaming stars, the stupendous worlds, filled with life and beauty, which your reason has long since acknowledged them to be. Yes," he continued, "your case is but another proof to me of what I have long and painfully felt to be a deep-seated and most corroding evil in the English system of religious instruction: an evil far more extensive and important than is generally supposed, and to which I attribute almost entirely the spread of infidelity amongst us of late years; I mean that mode by which, both in public and private tuition, injudicious persons, whose own intellect is too often of a very low order, endeavour to bring down to the comprehension of children those high and holy mysteries,—nay, the very highest and holiest which the Spirit of God alone can convey to the soul in all the strength of its maturity; and even then only in the exercise of faith unto salvation,—a faith which knoweth not what the Lord doeth now, but shall know hereafter; and they,—those teachers, blind leaders of the blind,—forgetting that first impressions are never lost, seek to explain in their own weak words the most abstruse doctrines of Christianity,—lowering, degrading, profaning them; detracting from their vast importance, where they do not pervert the sense; passing over the hidden meaning; and daring to give the most awful truths to the pliant mind clothed in some low and earth-born imagery, from which it never again can separate it. For the time they are of course successful; the weak capacity of the child imbibes with ease and satisfaction the narrow doctrines and familiar illustrations wherein the Most Holy and Dreadful Names are fearfully tampered with; but the result is inevitable,—you have yourself described it. As the mind expands, it revolts from the feeble and shallow ideas with which its unripe powers were satisfied; and the soul, craving for that hope which her immortality imperiously demands, too often seeks it in vain, even in that immaculate truth which was first presented to her so garbled and distorted. Nor is the evil always remedied, even where there is afterwards a candid endeavour to investigate personally and thoroughly into the religion of revelation; we are more hopelessly the slaves of early impressions and preconceived ideas than we can imagine; and with however much of impartiality we may intend to read the Scriptures, there are portions of them which will always continue to appear to us inadmissible and contradictory, as they were originally known, which, had they been received in the first instance by the judgment, unprejudiced and mature, would in their awful sublimity and simplicity have brought conviction on the soul, clear and strong as the unobstructed light of day."

"There may be truth in what you say," observed Arabyn; "but for me, Raymond, it is too late! As soon could you restore to the withered flower the peculiar colouring and hue which the influence of the burning sun has blighted and effaced, as reproduce on my mind the conviction of truth in a faith my reason has once rejected."

Raymond had no time to answer this admission which the infidel had perhaps made unawares, that in his puny arrogance he had turned from the light, because his finite mind could not grasp the mysteries of the Infinite. Neophytus the monk entered, and the conversation ceased,—but not before Arabyn had once more promised Raymond that he would acquaint him with the whole of his history next day, adding sneeringly,—" and then we shall part, and the Christian and the infidel shall go forth each with his separate belief, to consummate his separate destiny."

Raymond heard the words with awe, for he saw that unconsciously the sceptic had uttered a prophecy.

CHAPTER V.

ARABYN RELATES TO RAYMOND THE LIFE OF HIS MIND.

Raymond could not help entertaining some fears that the infidel would draw back from his promise of entire confidence when the moment for its fulfilment came, accustomed as he was to the impenetrable reserve he knew so well how to assume, and it would have been a serious disappointment to the Christian. He was now thoroughly convinced that when he had made acquaintance with Arabyn, he had, in actual fact, been led into the presence of him who was chosen to be his especial and personal adversary in the universal combat of good and ill.

It was Raymond's principle to acknowledge the Ruling Power in the most casual event, as in the most important; he admitted no right in man to limit the superintending government of Him for whom the relative importance of all things is null; because to the Infinite nothing can be great and nothing small; he therefore,—believing that Arabyn had been given to him as the servant of sin whom he sought,—was deeply anxious to become acquainted with the peculiar bent of his mind, that he might the better destroy its influence.

Raymond entertained no hope, as others in his place might have done, of restoring the sceptic to Christianity;

he knew too well (and it is a bitter truth to every one of us) that the inherent principle of man's nature, before any external influence has opposed it, is the love of evil; and this deadly affection, if resisted by no rule of faith or light of hope, grows with his growth, and strengthens with his strength, till he is so completely delivered up to its intoxicating, fascinating power, that he would sooner let the life be torn from his body than the iniquity from his soul!

Pride, the arrogance of intellect; that is the iron chain which binds men to the Power of Evil! to bow down their will, to lay their reason prostrate before inexplicable mysteries, to receive commands from an unheard voice: these are no easy lessons, to be learnt by those who have throughout life indulged themselves in the fatal seduction of independence of mind! Raymond felt that Arabyn would never name the Name of Christ, unless he could do so without departing from iniquity.

"I am glad you are come," said Arabyn to the Christian, as he took his usual place by his side. "I feel anxious to give you the account you have wished for of the life of my mind, for I find that illness has weakened my faculties, and that a systematic definition of my views at this time will be quite necessary for the decision I desire to make respecting my future destiny."

Raymond begged he would proceed at once.

"You do not require that I should speak to you of my birth or parentage," commenced the infidel. "You well know that I was born heir to a curse; nor did my father and mother ever seek to compensate by affection for the irreparable injury they had done me in giving me life.

I was sent to England for my education when still a mere infant, and they died without seeing me again: thus I commenced life, as I shall end it, alone. I passed from a studious, dreaming boyhood to a fiery, tempestuous youth ; full of vigour, of health, and of strength, I thirsted for excitement and pleasure, longing madly to taste every varied feeling of which humanity is capable, and finding a wild enjoyment in each one of my own keen sensations, even when they were painfnl ; contradictory as it may seem to say so. Action was my life, and I took a wondering interest and delight in feeling and watching the development of my own powers and passions, as each new circumstance in my eager busy existence called them forth.

"Hurried on from day to day, unthinking and uncaring, by the stream of events—some of which were created by my own adventurous spirit, and others by a wayward fate—I was guided by no principle or settled opinion whatever. I had long before, as I told you, discarded all the doctrines and tenets of my early belief— if belief it can be called, which was merely the mechanical acceptance with which a child receives the theory inculcated before he is of an age to appreciate its merits. I was too vividly engrossed by the material pleasures of the present, the actual occurrences of each passing day, to pause in my rapid energetic career for wonder or reflection. I never dreamt of inquiring even into the cause of my own existence, its meaning and end, or, to be brief, into the origin and purpose of all creation. I did not believe in any one of the received theories on these points, and I admit my knowledge of all to have been superficial ; but I felt no anxiety, no wish to collect materials on which to found an opinion of my own. I lived, I felt, I enjoyed, yes, and suffered! These actual internal sensations seemed enough for my ardent and excited mind : the future was to me but a fair field for hope and ambition ; and death, that one unconquerable fact, that wonderful consummation to our destiny, which stands immoveable before us, testifying, when we would deem our existence natural, the mere effect of chance, that there is a *something* which we cannot grasp ; an immutable power that suddenly, for no visible cause, checks the healthy functions of the body, and in one moment can reduce the thinking, speaking, reasoning being, animated by a power which is undoubtedly spirit, though of what nature we know not, to a dead mass of insensate clay, —even that death and its certainty could not recall me from my life of movement and excitement to ponder over my destiny : it was but for me a mysterious evil, which I delighted to brave every day, along with a thousand other dangers.

"During this period, when I thus gave free scope to my ungoverned passions, I never however fell into the vile debasement of low dissipation ; not that I refrained from any principle of good in myself, but because, while I was intoxicated by that which you call vice, when it was bold, energetic, and enterprising, I found it revolting whenever it was degraded or mean ; I strove, in short, to bring refinement into my very crimes.

"Intense was the enjoyment I derived from my cultivation of the fine arts, and still more that which I found in my study of the abstruse sciences. Of these astronomy occupied a large share of my time and attention, and I pursued it with an ardour with which nothing now could inspire me ; indeed, to this study I attribute much of my inability to admit the doctrines of Christianity, or of any other revealed religion. The faint, unspeakably faint insight which I thus obtained into the stupendous wonders of the universe—million worlds on million worlds, rising inexhaustible on my weak sight, ever beginning, never ending, and they but the heralds to all that peopled infinity which none shall ever explore—this glimmering of knowledge sufficed to convince me that the tremendous Author of so awful a creation could not be known in any of these revelations."

He paused, as though anxious to know what answer the Christian would make; and Raymond, interpreting his look, said with a quiet smile, "You will think it a strange contradiction, Arabyn, when I tell you that I believe this conviction on your mind to be produced solely by your low and narrow views of the Deity; but I do not now wish to attempt refuting any of your opinions: the recital of the progress of your ideas, as they grew and changed, is as interesting as it is necessary to me, for a due appreciation of your present state."

"I come now," said Arabyn, "to a period in my history, when it will be painful to rake up the thoughts and feelings I never dreamt to have disclosed to any, but which have so completely influenced my destiny, that, except you hear them in full detail, you can never know me as I am."

He pressed his hand to his forehead, as though to drive back a tide of recollections, and his convulsive breathing told how each one was armed with a sting. After a momentary effort he regained his composure, and went on.

"There is a crisis in every man's fate—a turning point in his life—which decides his whole future career. All do alike live a bright internal life of hope and fancy, till something comes to destroy their unconscious belief in an individual and earthly bliss, and then they wake up amazed, and ask wherefore they live, if it be not to enjoy? But I have no need to tell you, Raymond, of this inevitable change; you have well known what it is to be torn away from the stronghold of hope, and cast out on the deep waters of despair; I must try to tell you calmly of the stroke which aroused me to perceive what a bitter, mocking mystery is this existence. You must now listen, calm and passionless as you are, to the wild beating of a heart that never has belied the dust from whence it sprung, and has clung, how madly, to a perishing child of clay.

"You know that I was more than an orphan, and friendless as few have been upon this earth; thus from infancy to youth my natural feelings were never called forth, and I guessed not how there lay within my breast, as in that of every human being, a power of affection which is almost omnipotent, binding the strongest and the proudest as a very slave. I never learnt the lesson of love from a mother's eyes, or heard it in a father's voice; and living solely for myself, I never dreamt how life itself can be bound up in the ties of nature, how the sentiment of individuality may almost seem lost, and our whole existence merge into that of another. But the strong necessity of attachment, which nature plants within us, and all the deep unfathomable tenderness which, had I been differently placed, might have flowed in many channels, all was reserved for one alone.

"Over my wild tempestuous career, like a star,

serene and bright, arising on the ocean's stormy wave, there appeared a being, fair and pure as ever dream of unseen seraph; yes, fair in form, and pure in soul like unsunned snow. By some strange fatality she was ever thrown on my path; for months I saw her every day, almost every hour, thus beautiful in body and in mind. Raymond, of what avail to tell you how her image grew within my soul, and there became enshrined, its idol and its sun.

"I had no religion to offer me more enduring joys, no friend to bind me with the resistless tie of blood, and therefore unto her were given the first fresh burst of youthful feeling, the longing affections of nature claiming an object, and the clinging passionate tenderness with which one mortal's heart yearns to another. All these combined to form the mighty love with which I worshipped her, till she became my all, all of hope and joy, whose presence was my life.

"I tell you this tale simply, Raymond, though it may seem to rival the exaggeration of a poet's dream. You have not lived so long, nor scrutinized men's hearts so closely, to learn now how awful and how actual is the power one strong affection may possess.

"During the period when I saw her daily, and this attachment grew upon me till it enveloped my whole soul, as the sweet sunrise breaks on the dull dark sky, and spreads over it one unchanging light, I never asked myself if I loved her, or in what hope I did so. It seemed a thing so natural, so necessary to my whole existence, my soul demanded her presence as my body required the air it breathed,—I loved her as I lived. At length there chanced an event, simple, natural, a thing of every-day occurrence: circumstances called her away from the city where she had dwelt as well as myself, and necessitated our separation. Raymond, in the same hour that I awoke to the full consciousness of the unfathomable, unchangeable affection I bore her, I remembered that she was about to become the wife of another; and before I could arouse myself to the stunning misery of this certainty, it was done, and she already bore his name. I had known that this would be from the first moment in which I saw her, and it may seem to you unnatural that I should never have thought on this inevitable result; but I tell you there had been neither fear nor hope in my love, because it was my existence; and from that hour I knew (and it was no fancy, for so it has been), I knew that the hope and the power of happiness had for ever departed from me. Life was one vast, sunless, miserable blank; all was colourless, vacant, dead; and I was alone, without one hope, or wish, or desire, without the power of enjoyment in things I once appreciated, or pleasures yet unknown; without an aim in life, or an object in living; haunted by one image, from which, day and night, waking and sleeping, alone or in a crowd, I could not escape—the fair image of her I never more was to behold, for whom I longed—Oh, with how inexpressible a longing! Then, Raymond, when I found myself thus, by no will or power of my own, existing in the dreary wilderness of this earth, I asked myself what I was? whence I came? wherefore and by whom created? To find an answer to these questions I turned round, and beheld the world as it is."

Arabyn paused for a moment in astonishment at the emotion with which Raymond listened to him; for the

Christian could not perceive, without agitation, the strong parallel between his own case and that of the infidel ; and how exactly they stood on the same footing as to external circumstances. Each had been deprived of the same treasure ; each by the same blow had been dragged out from their first unconscious delusions ; each, awakened to the mysterious realities of existence, had turned round to look upon the world, and ask what was to be the object of their lives. The paths—the two only paths in which mortal feet may tread—were before them, which to take, the evil or the good. The one had chosen, the other was about to choose.

Raymond earnestly entreated Arabyn to proceed, and he continued.

"With unveiled eyes, from the dark and vacant chambers of her own despair, my soul looked forth, first, on the visible globe ; and there she beheld in truth a fair and glorious creation, with the spirit of beauty living in the face of nature, in all her varied aspects. And she beheld a harmony in this creation, harmony in the very loveliness which smiled in softest hues of sunlit radiance on the green and flowery vale, or awed the spirit with its solemn grandeur on the lofty mountain, and in the boundless desert. And she beheld a Power, invisible, indefinable, incomprehensible, pervading, penetrating all ; and that power was, life—the name we give unto a mystery which seems the principle of the universe ; animating every iota, every particle, from the air, instinct, as it were, with the viewless animalculæ, to the whole peopled earth, pierced through and through with this power, existent a million of times in every inch of ground, till I have often wondered if it were not in itself the creative power, which, if withdrawn, would leave the whole world to crumble into dust.

"This harmony of beauty, this animating principle, seemed to me to announce a Creator; but I looked more closely into the visible globe, and lo! I beheld this earth, where consummate wisdom seemed to have been employed to produce the wonderful effects of mere outward loveliness; where, in the very most trivial operation of the routine of nature, was ever to be found such a marvellous adaptation to the purpose intended. I beheld this earth refuse, niggard-like, to yield the fruits by which her children sustained existence, except at the price of their most painful toil; thus bringing before me, in its first stage, that awful mystery on which every living soul has rung the changes from the beginning— the mystery of suffering.

"The fair and glorious creation, the harmony of the vivifying principle, these things had seemed natural unto my soul: even if she understood not their nature, she assented voluntarily to them as though she could. They were a part of one most beautiful and perfect whole; but at the first-fruits of suffering she was staggered, like a man when the unsteady ground, shaken of the earthquake, trembles beneath his feet. The first doubt, the first misgiving, the first question, rose within her: if there be a Creator, if this be His work, is He not good, or could He not make His creation faultless?

"Then I turned to look on man that I might kno' more. I beheld a rational and reasonable being, exist? by no act of volition of his own, consisting of inward ritual powers which have been named 'the soul,' ·

wonderful in their nature, extent, and capacity, and of a body at once admirably formed and adapted to his necessities, and at the same time liable to, and inheritor of every conceivable infirmity! To this being, brought into the world unconsciously, and moulded from first to last by a power over which he has no control, are given, first—the mighty illimitable gift of thought, and reason, along with the capacity for the enjoyment of the most perfect happiness, and for the endurance of the most exquisite suffering! I tell you, when I look on him as he is placed on this earth, he seems to me to be but a bewildering incarnation of contradictions; as though he had been formed in the sport of some awful being, author (inconceivable thought!) of good and ill at one and the same time.

"Man—capable in the strength of his intellect of embracing eternity in a thought, and measuring from his puny dwelling the career of the worlds that plough their fiery paths in the boundless gloom of infinity, incapable of comprehending who or what he is, how or wherefore existent here; capable, by his reasoning powers, of forming the most wonderful and abstruse combinations in science, incapable of comprehending by what invisible means his secret thought acts on his powerless limbs, and moves them at pleasure; independent in will; slave to every trifling circumstance which the veriest chance may throw in his way; formed to adore the good in whatever shape it present itself, his own natural passions for ever prompting him to evil; worshipping virtue, practising vice; shrinking from crime, himself producing it; a free agent, ruled by an invisible, immutable fate; left blind and unaided to use the means he deems best for his welfare, those very means becoming the instrument of his misery, the knife with which he would carve out a fair destiny, turning in his hand and stabbing himself; haunted with a fierce, self-existent desire for immortality, perishing into dust; noble in thought, vile in action; fed by hope, reserved for despair; formed for life, destroyed by death; man, man, is a living paradox!

"And when I had looked on this creature, of whom, to sum up the description in few words, I would say, that it is a weak yet wonderful body, formed from clay, containing in itself no life, and solely animated by the contending principles of good and ill, I further sought to read his destiny, to understand the end and meaning of his creation. Oh vain searching! Oh bitter toil! As well seek to know why the falling star shoots across the midnight sky, aimless and unnecessary, causing a momentary light, then expiring in darkness, leaving no trace behind! As well ask why billow after billow rolls wailing up, to dash itself to destruction on the rocky shore, and be succeeded by another as mournful and as lost?

"I behold this living creature, formed with every sense, every fibre, every nerve, adapted, as I have said, to the most exquisite capacity for enjoyment; ere he is conscious of existence, I behold him suffering: ere his eyes have well opened to the light, they are dimmed with tears; the tyrannical power which men call nature, has given the infant wants, imperious wants, which in a thousand cases to one are not, and cannot be supplied. How often does the innocent babe come into the world, to reap in the first hour of its unwilling existence the bitter fruits of that which it hath not sown: to be the prey of cold griping poverty—cursed by the father who gave it life and cannot give it food, and wringing the heart, tender to the last, of the famishing mother, because her emaciated frame cannot supply the nourishment it demands. If born in another sphere—and wherefore should one unconscious child, of the same human flesh and blood as the other, come into the world to find it a hell, whilst to his fellow babe they seek to make it a paradise? by what law, by whom is it decreed, that one shall be heir to wealth and blessings, the other to misery and curses; but if, I say, the mortal be born in another sphere, can all the luxury with which it is surrounded, and the doating love of high-born relations, secure it one hour from the pain with which the subtle frame is often racked, ere the natural functions, so well suited to give it the sensation of pleasure, have well acquired their sway; and again, how many are there, who, with the unasked gift of life, receive also that of an incurable infirmity; stamped as sufferers from the first breath they draw; their sentence written in some hideous deformity; that the curse of their body shall be continual pain; the curse of their spirit, men's contumely.

"Let us pass on, and taking it for granted that the child has escaped the thousand dangers which surround him—for I would suppose to the man the utmost length of an earthly life," continued Arabyn with a bitter sneer, "we now behold him a man, already one quarter of his existence, taken at the longest computation, has been devoted to fitting him, by the acquirement of knowledge, for that which is to come: at that brightest, because most reckless and ignorant period of life, when the young healthy frame might find so much enjoyment in sport and freedom, though it were but in wantoning with the fresh sweet air; he must abandon the woods and the sunshine, and the poor joy of exercising his pliant limbs, to toil in premature slavery at the vain labour of endless study, storing, perhaps, his mind, and cultivating his talents, but to afford a richer morsel to the eternal hunger of the tomb ; or if he lives, having only learnt enough to know, that, surrounded as we are with contradictory, inexplicable mysteries, we can in fact know nothing.

"And now the first wild fire of youth is spent, the pleasures of the senses satisfy no more, the man feels within, the one insatiable longing for happiness, and in his soul, abhorrent of vacancy, a craving restlessness which seeks an aim and object in existence. To satisfy these, which if unallayed gnaw like ravening wolves, he grasps at one or other of the fair shadows without a substance which invite him on.

"There is ambition: and if he be not deterred by the sight of the laurel-crowned skeleton whose living heart was broken by neglect, he may deliver up his life to the pursuit of earthly fame, a thing not tangible, never acquired till men have learned utterly to despise the fellow-creatures who bestow it, and find that it is in fact but another name for envy without, and bitter disappointment within. There is wealth to be obtained, a goodly prospect truly, for it would seem to promise all that earth can offer, and men do toil, and sap the springs of life, and waste their every energy, and then suddenly the end comes, and lo! they have given their life to buy themselves a costly tomb ; or if they are allowed to count their gold around them for a few short years, so withered is their frame, so dim their eyes, the sense and sight of pleasure all are gone ; and mark the issue, the riches for which the miserable old man has toiled, becomes the heritage of some young voluptuary, the very abundance of whose pleasures pall upon his senses, and he turns away in loathing weariness. And there is love; for in our natural affections we find the best capacity for happiness, and, oh ingenious tortures! in how many different ways do they make themselves our curse. He loves, and the being he clasps with such clinging tenderness unto his heart, stricken by an unseen blight, fades, droops, and crumbles into loathsome dust in his very arms. He loves, and the fair form which meets his doating eyes, veils the traitor heart beneath the fond sweet smile. He loves, his whole soul bounds forth to one sweet being; her presence is a joy too great for words, aching the void, dark and dreary the vacancy of her absence; he loves, till his heart swells to bursting—Raymond, and she is the wife of another.

"But it avails little to trace out the various dreams with which men give a distinctive colour to an uniformly vain existence. Let the path they choose be what it will, in smiles or tears, blessing or cursing, hoping or despairing, in agony, in disappointment, in love, in hate, in solitude, in woe, in base ingratitude, in poverty, in wealth, on, on, rushes the living palpitating man, with his glorious intellect, and his weak heart, his calm deliberate reason, and his torturing affections, than him more strong—on, blind and captive does he rush, over a narrow space in this strange wilderness, when lo! unforeseen, invisible, incomprehensible, the unknown Power checks his brief career: suddenly, by no law which man may understand or see, for no reason which our nature can comprehend, the living creature ceases to exist;

the wondrous powers of his mind, the subtle faculties in their prime, and in their strength, when imagination can people fair worlds it hath created, when memory can paint the past in living hues, and reason fix the laws that rule an universe, and hopes are teeming high— all these depart, vanish, expire ; the spirit becomes extinct, and the body, so marvellously formed, which human love hath cherished with a futile care, the body corrupts and perishes in vile decay, feeding with its rotting flesh the generating earth, till in the process of complete destruction, the ashes are sown upon some whirlwind ; and now, servant of the Creator, wherefore was this thing created—to suffer ?"

Arabyn paused, and raised his eyes to ask an answer. Raymond replied to him calmly.

"Your description of life," he said, " as it appeared to you, is exactly similar to that which a man would give of the outward face of nature, who had refused to look on it in the light of day, and went forth to judge of it for the first time, when the great darkness was abroad and spread over it; truly he would return and tell what a strange world it was, and how the vast shadows lay impenetrable over it, and how the mountains in the deceptive gloom looked a hundredfold more high and heavy, and the precipices yawned fathomless, and there was no light save the traitor glare of the ignis-fatuus, or the passing gleam of a meteor, flashing into existence but to expire ; and he would tell how the very stars were hid by clouds that swept the flying rack of heaven, and how he heard the wild beasts prowling about, and the hissing of snakes among the rustling bushes ; and though his words were true, and his description all exact, would he not tell a different tale if suddenly the sun arose and brought to light the living beauties of this world. Arabyn, even as that man, you have walked forth with darkness round you; but this is not the moment to enter into a discussion with you, you have promised to trace out the career of your mind even to the present day, and I must hear all before I speak."

"As you will," said the infidel, and at once proceeded: "I had looked on life, and it was to me as a scroll written in unknown mysterious characters; I saw that I could not understand it. I would not believe that a Power all evil ruled this world, still less could I deem this wonderful universe the offspring of a misguided chance; yet, if not, what meant that mystery of woe, which, unarrested, dragged its desolating steps wherever there was a man with a soul capable of feeling, and a body of enduring agony: nay, what meant my own actual existence? As I stood there in the prime of life, of energy, of strength, mental and physical, by a power over which I had no control, blasted within like the stalwart tree scathed and blackened by the sudden lightning, so utterly dead to all hope or joy that I could not even wish, and all was drearily the same to me. I had not one desire; I looked over the blank, dismal, vacant life that might stretch on unasked for, through long joyless years, and there was no light, earth could bestow that could inspire one faint wish within me; except, perhaps, to be one moment free from the undying gnawing pain which preyed upon my soul, for ever yearning to behold one face I might not see, to hear one voice I never more might hear;—Oh! truly this creation was to me an interminable mystery. I no longer sought to comprehend it, and I sunk into a deadly apathy. I wandered an outcast, branded with misery, from land to land, and found every where the same inexplicable discord, the jarring elements of good and evil. As for me, though I sought the brightest climes, treading the burning desert, and roaming over all the glowing East, still wherever I went, the day for me was sunless, and starless the night, because the sun and star of my own existence were for ever set! Then there did at length arise one fierce desire within my soul, or rather a strong necessity, imperious and urgent, 'to be at rest;' how or by what means I knew not; but never captive craved for light and liberty, or wanderer beneath the flaming sun of Africa to slake his thirst at some cool stream, as my whole soul demanded, longed for rest.

"One day I was passing beneath the gateway of an old castellated mansion in Hungary, and as I chanced to raise my eyes, they fell on the words of the family motto, which were inscribed over the door, they were these, 'Mors æterna quies.' A promise of eternal rest, however it was to be obtained, fell soft upon my soul, corroded with a sleepless pain, as cooling dews upon a parched and burning ground; but over death there hung the same uncertainty which curses the inquiring mind on every point, and I felt that this sweet promise might but be like the rest, delusive. Although I saw and see no grounds whereon to build the doctrine of the soul's immortality, yet no eye HATH pierced the secret of that sullen tomb; and whilst my own conviction has ever been that we perish utterly in that awful change, for ever dispersed unto the elements, by the same wayward breath that called us into being; still there were times when I felt so instinct with spiritual life, that I shuddered as the thought presented itself before me, that in the very grave I might find a last deception.

"Raymond, you will think what I am about to tell you but the sickly fancies of a diseased mind; yet I would fain show you how my soul was beaten back from the last refuge to which it had flown, how tossed, rudderless, on an interminable ocean of doubt, the strong waves hurled her from the last rock whereon she sought to rest, and left me the being I am to day. 'Mors æterna quies,' those glad words haunted me wherever I went, from land to land, from city to city— in the crowded scenes of gaiety and mirth, where I took a strange interest in watching how the fever of unconquerable passions wasted men's brief lives, nursing in their own breasts the seeds that must inevitably bear such bitter fruit; how awful is the power one mortal may have over the destiny of another; how wantonly they will abuse it; how calmly they inflict on their fellow-creatures mental tortures, from which themselves would shrink; how a single word may be a deathblow, and a friendship betrayed, or a love despised, be like canker on the soul; how many a silent martyr smiles, and smiles in hopeless misery; how the bold spirit of evil is crowned with success, and the timid gleam of virtue quenched by ridicule or misconception; how deceit and hypocrisy are the atmosphere wherein they walk most naturally, for truth were to them like the keen sharp air of the mountain-top, so difficult to breathe.

"In scenes where I was called to witness things like these, how sweetly sounded then the promise, 'Mors æterna quies!' and when I fled to seek for solitude, and found it not—when in the midst of some desolate

THE LIFE OF HIS MIND. 121

and savage scene, where never voice of man was heard, from out the treasure-caves of memory, the sleepless spirits of the past, of joys departed, and of hopes untrue, came stealing forth together, mourning round me, peopling the desert with images of bliss, I might have known, and never was to know; with scenes of happiness, where for ever one fair shape with mocking smile allured me on and fled at my approach, causing the sunshine of bygone hours to gleam upon the dreary landscape, and filling the silent air with strains of remembered music; then with what impetuous yearning I exclaimed, ' O mors, mors, æterna quies!'

"Gradually these words assumed over me a magic power, till they bred a monomania, which altogether absorbed my disordered fancy; they ever brought before me images of death, quite disconnected with the theories or speculations of metaphysics, as to the separation of mind and matter, and yet more, with the sure and horrible mystery of corruption which must follow it; but as the labourer when the toilsome day is over stretches his limbs in some cool shade—as the tired child lays down its head upon its mother's breast—a sweet lassitude, a blessed sinking into forgetfulness, a delicious apathy of repose,—with thoughts such as these did the false words feed me, till I came to think on death,—yes, and to believe it to be only a deep, serene, eternal sleep, of which both body and spirit, whatever it may be, should partake—and of the loathsome grave as a green and quiet couch no dreams could haunt, where I would sleep—sleep with the long grass waving over the breast aching no more, and the dewdrops falling, and the lulling winds sighing round me, and all the while an instinctive consciousness of most unutterable

G

rest! Vain folly! for assuredly if death be not annihilation, if there be aught of man which outlives the loathsome process of decay, it is not in the grave! It was a delusion of the mind, and it required but the evidence of the senses, in a circumstance which might otherwise have made little impression, to overthrow this last, sweet, visionary hope for ever, even when it was so alluring to my madness that I had unconsciously formed the determination of terminating my existence.

"I had been living for some time in this town of Scutari, and had strayed one evening into the cemetery which lies beneath us there, stretching far beyond the limits where our eyes can reach. You know well, Raymond, how vast and how beautiful is that immense domain of silent calm corruption, that mighty cypress forest, where every dark and sullen tree keeps watch over a dark and sullen tomb; a very kingdom in fact, where the dead have established themselves, and the extent of whose still population no thought can realize. I threw myself down on the ground amongst them, half believing that something of their universal rest must have an influence even on my living frame; but, like the smouldering fires of a volcano, the demon thought was burning at my heart, and soon it woke to rack me with ever-revolving speculations, bewildering and vain.

"The very sight of all the ruined life that was around me plunged me into an abyss of mystery, holding up before me the awful Spirit Life of the universe at once, as Maker and Destroyer; employing the eternal void of His never-ending existence in creating glorious systems, which, ere they started into being, He destined to destruction! I groaned aloud, and knew not how to escape from myself, foreseeing the tortures which these speculations never failed to bring me, for my mind would not be controlled, and ever flew to grapple with the mystery, though the struggle was one of hopeless agony; but I thought on the charmed words of 'Mors, æterna quies,' and turned to look on a new-made grave, that had been prepared for one already relieved from the load of this living sleepless spirit.

"Oh! how inviting seemed that quiet couch! it merited not the appellation of the "deep dark grave," for according to the custom of this country, it was wide and shallow: beneath the eternal shade of those mighty cypresses, the rich grass and the wild flowers grew luxuriantly, and a few green sods merely had been lifted up, which would press but lightly on the heart no longer throbbing painfully, while the whole air was redolent with the sweet breath of the violets that had been disturbed, but soon would take root again, when the sleeper should have laid him down.

"Mechanically I drew from my sleeve the small dagger which had been my companion for some time, and scarce knowing what I did, with my eyes still fixed on that alluring bed, and my lips murmuring the 'Mors, æterna quies,' I bared my throat, and felt if the edge were sharp, when suddenly the solemn stillness was broken by the measured tramp of many steps, and ere I had time for thought, I saw winding amid the trees the funeral train of him who was my rival for that grave. I felt a bitter jealousy at the sight, as though he had robbed me of my birth-right, and then I smiled to think how speedily another such green and quiet couch should be prepared for me! My hand (the hand of a suicide in will) fell from my throat, and dreamily I lay watching the interment.

"Quietly and silently the procession moved on; but there was none of that solemn paraphernalia with which in other countries men seek to make the horror of death more horrible. In an open coffin strewn with flowers lay the sleeper of that dreamless sleep; he was young, and had been beautiful; his long hair was bound with a garland, like one who had conquered, and oh! what a glorious expression of unutterable repose was on that marble face! I scarce looked on those who accompanied him, save one veiled figure of a woman, from whom were heard suppressed groans, full of anguish: the ceremony was soon over—gently they lifted that unresisting form from the coffin, and laid him in his grave; the Koran was placed for his head to rest on, the wine was poured on the earth, the corn and the vase of water were set at his feet, and then the green sods were replaced, and earth had gathered to her breast her weary child,—and deep should be his rest.

"They now prepared to depart, but the veiled woman struggled in the arms of those who supported her, and bursting from them, flew to the green mound, where he whom she had loved had fled for a sweeter rest than even her care could provide him: she threw herself down on the fresh earth, the veil fell back from her head, and I beheld a fair young face convulsed with the most dreadful despair.

"Is it not a strange mockery that affection should outlive the object of its worship? With what bitterness in her vain tenderness did she kiss the jealous mould that hid him from her sight, and threw her arms (powerless to hold him here) across the precious mound! The despairing tone of her lamentations was frightful in one so young; shriek followed shriek till she fell down senseless; and then they bore her away, and the solemn silence of death re-entered on its empire.

"The conviction that over my tomb no wailing from loving lips should sound, but made me long more passionately to enter on its oblivious sleep; and I determined that I would use that power which the most wretched of captives, oppressed or fettered, yet may wield, and deliver myself up to annihilation, as soon as I should have made such arrangements as would ensure my being permitted to repose in this beautiful spot, a very Garden of Eden for the dead. Meanwhile, the quick transition from day to night of an Eastern clime had taken place; but the twilight darkness seemed almost the same, for the full moon had risen in a cloudless sky, and her light, though soft, was powerful from its brilliancy; and it was now that I was witness to a sight so dreadful that I shudder even to think on it [1].

"I still lay at the foot of a cypress tree, when a low, suppressed howl sounded near me; it was repeated in other directions, and when I looked up, I saw on all sides troops of dogs stealing through the trees towards the newly-made grave, which seemed for them the centre of attraction.

"I knew that these wretched animals, whose life, you are aware, is held sacred in this country, swarmed in thousands in the streets, famished and savage; but it was with utter amazement that I now saw them, in bands of twenty and thirty, creeping noiselessly up to the tomb round which they collected in vast numbers.

---

[1] The circumstances, of which the account follows, are of *nightly* occurrence in many Asiatic towns.

A doubt as to the hateful instinct which brought those starving creatures to this spot suddenly froze the blood in my veins with horror, and ere the idea was well formed in my mind it was realized. Even now I feel the chill pass through my limbs which then seemed to turn me into stone, when, with one simultaneous rush, those ferocious dogs attacked the grave, and with their digging claws tore asunder the newly-placed sods: in a moment the corpse was disclosed to view. They gaped with their ravenous jaws over their rich repast, and then,—O horror unutterable!—they pounced upon their prey, digging their sharp teeth into the defenceless form, which they devoured before my very eyes! For a moment I was paralysed with sickening disgust; my limbs refused to move; but when I heard the grating of their teeth on the bones they had stripped bare, when they raised their smoking and distended jaws,—with a cry of horror I staggered in amongst them, and sought to drive them away: as well might I have tried to dispel a cloud of locusts; I would have let them tear me into pieces to defend that helpless corpse,—like me, living yesterday,—like whom I might be dead to-morrow, so loved, so cherished one half-hour before; but the wolfish animals found the dead a richer feast than the living; as long as one inch of flesh yet clothed the skeleton they heeded me not; and while I killed two or three a hundred were at work, and they ceased not till they had gnawed the very bones in their insatiable hunger.

"I stood like one fascinated. Where was now my mad delusion of the perfect rest,—the dreamless sleep,—the weary head laid down upon the green earth's breast? My disordered imagination had altogether overlooked the process of decay, and now it was not enough that I was destined to stand and look upon the desecration of that envied corpse: but the ravenous animals—their craving whetted by the taste—had dug yet deeper into the grave, which seemed to me so sweet a couch, and proved it to be but a nest of living corruption! Body after body did they drag forth, in all the various stages of decay; but I spare you a further description; I will but tell you how in that hour I comprehended for the first time that the certain doom which awaits us helpless victims when life is over is indeed most awful, most degrading, more than tongue can tell! Now my fantastic mania of eternal rest for body and spirit was replaced by an invincible sleepless horror for the dismal results of death, which, sooner or later,—it maddens me to know it,—must be my lot. I pressed my hands to my eyes, to shut out the dreadful sight which had too surely done its work, in robbing me of my last hope; and I fled from that deceptive garden of delights, knowing how beneath my feet the living worms were preying on the helpless dead; my brain reeled under the strong revulsion of feeling, my sight grew dark, I felt myself falling, and strove with a last effort to avoid the contact of a grave on which I stumbled,—then I remember no more.

"You know the rest; Neophytus the monk brought me hither, and tended me with constant care. After many days I woke again to life and thought; but I also awoke to that which seems to be a new principle in my nature,—irresistible, because it is a part of my very being,—an unconquerable dread,—a shrinking from the inevitable corruption that awaits me, which has power to make me resume unresisting the load of a joyless existence, dragging it on in misery from day to day, yet shuddering, as every hour brings it nearer to a close;

bearing with—yes, clinging to—a life which is without a faith, without a joy, and without a hope!"

The infidel's voice died away, his head sunk on his breast, his tale was told. Could he have said a word to add to the fearful picture he had drawn? Had he not disclosed most fully in his long narrative, even to minute details, that state so awfully, so comprehensively described in these words—" without God in the world?"

Raymond breathed a long sigh of relief, when at length the deep despairing accents of the sceptic ceased to fall upon his ear,—like one who on a gloomy winter's night sits listening with a sort of fascination to the moaning of the wind, that seems to wail in bitterest lamentation; a sound more full of hopeless melancholy than any nature can produce, he had sat there, while the infidel laid bare before him the desolation of his soul; stripping the veil from every delusive joy this earth can offer, and giving not even the shadow of a hope to fill the vacancy they left. Now, overcome with the ghastly images he himself had conjured up, Arabyn sunk into a state of utter exhaustion, and he had turned away his face from his companion as though he desired never more to look on any human being.

Raymond spoke very gently: "Arabyn," he said, "you know not how deeply I feel for you; if there can indeed exist upon this earth that thing of which we often lightly talk—despair,—to you it is assuredly given to know its bitterness. I feel as though you had taken me by the hand, and led me forth into a dismal wilderness,—a black, a dreary, boundless waste; no light in heaven, but only thick, portentous clouds; no flowers on earth, but only thorny labyrinths, and pitfalls deadly and unseen. But, O wanderer, most helpless and benighted, wherefore is it that you cannot see how your own words rise up in judgment against you? You have said you will not believe a power all evil formed and rules this world; nor yet that it is the spontaneous effect of chance: see you not, then, that if the Creator, whatever be His awful attributes, had never given a hope to man, your existence—even yours only, one of unnumbered millions of His creatures—would be a blot upon His gorgeous and sublime creation, which could obscure and tarnish all the glory of His hundred thousand worlds?

"Well have you shown what this life is; how ephemeral, deceptive, and corrupt; and can you suppose that generation after generation, age after age, the helpless race of man would have been cast forth upon this desert world, to wander to and fro, bewildered and weeping, till driven to the tomb like cattle to the slaughter,—whilst, throughout His serene eternity, the Universal Father never once sent up through the echoing realms of infinite space, the one all-sufficient word—consummation of every soul's desire—the awful 'I AM?' No; it is an impious thought; there was, there is a revelation!

"You have shown what a horrible mocking sport would have been the creation of man, if he were destined never to know an existence holier and happier than this brief feverish strife; but is there nothing sublime in the idea, worthy even of the Deity, that the Omnipotent called forth from the womb of vacancy by the mere power of His will this whole stupendous universe in all its wonderful details, with myriads on myriads of living creatures, exquisitely formed, for the one and only purpose of giving them the sensation of happiness? Not here, for here He hath permitted that a power should work, of which we can and may know nothing; and there was never madness like to that which would seek to penetrate the mystery of evil; for it is self-evident that to comprehend the Infinite and His mysteries the mind must in itself be infinite, and His own created soar to a level with the Supreme, the Unapproachable even in thought! O folly most presumptuous!"

Raymond paused, and lifted up his eyes in deep thought to that weak, faint reflection of the Eternal's glory which the skies by night display; while Arabyn, burying his head in the pillows, seemed determined not to hear him. The Christian observed this with a heavy sigh, and when he spoke again he made no attempt to address his companion, but continued to pursue the train of his own reflections.

"There is a thought," he said, "one awful thought, beneath whose power the soul shrinks, cowering as a stricken bird beneath the lightning's flash—the thought of that tremendous solitude enduring from all eternity, when the First Cause, the one only Self-Existent—did alone exist—ere yet from His inscrutable will the universe had sprung, bearing aloft into space the principle of life; and infinity, knowing His presence only, was replete. It is thus that the spirit, rising up to acknowledge and to know the Father, must first behold Him; then came the rush of the worlds through the air, as, born from the Omnipotent Thought, they fled into existence through the realms of ether: star after star brightened into life, and marshalled themselves in glittering ranks, like soldiers at the war-cry; system after system, majestically complete and perfect in each minute detail, rose up from void, and ranged themselves in order. Like a wind rife with fragrant odours stealing over the sea, a life-giving breath swept through the vibrating air, and speedily whole myriads of sentient and seraphic beings awoke to purity and joy; and the first cry of their new being was the sweet melody of adoring praise. Hand in hand did life and beauty walk abroad to penetrate the young creation.

"Then, and with awe-struck reverence, let us approach this mystery: slowly from unfathomable depths a mighty shadow rose. Darkness in visible shape passed over the shrinking universe; but in that same hour it was decreed that by the light it should be combated and conquered. And so it was, and is; the war doth yet endure, the triumph is to come; and every event, the least as well as greatest, which occurs in the vast regions of unknown space, bears reference to this decree: not a helpless babe is born of human parents, or mighty world extinguished and driven a wreck from sphere to sphere, but to this end! Our sight is limited, our minds are finite; we can only look around and see it working here.

"Troubled and heavy laden, our earth hung powerless in its appointed place; confused and blind, her children staggered over her breast, mournfully wondering why they existed and why they suffered. Those who sat by the dead sorrowed without hope; those who by sin could gratify their evil passions, sinned and repented not; those who, being deceived, were tortured, in their turn used deceit and smiled again; virtuous names were given to unholy deeds; revenge was called honour; cruelty was termed justice; oppression was said to be necessity; there was a chaos in every soul, and a blight on the sweet flowers of innocent love and faithful friendship, which had strayed from Paradise to blossom here.

"But the revelation came: not in the whirlwind—not in the fire—but in the still small voice, in the first low murmur from the Sinless Lips of the Child Divine. The declaration sent from the high and lofty One that inhabiteth eternity, to His creatures on this puny earth, was simply this, 'God is love!' At His command the words made themselves wings and passed over the world, penetrating every corner. The deep shadow had been there, but they dispelled it; as of old the outer darkness fled, when it was uttered, 'Let there be light.' They passed over the earth, and her children ceased to wonder mournfully why they suffered; but, looking upward, adored Him who chastens where He loves: they who sat by the dead, sorrowing without hope, arose and sung hymns of thanksgiving, of which the burden was ever immortality. Men ceased from iniquity, repented them of sin, and plucked the unclean thing from their breasts, through self-inflicted wounds: the deceived forgave and prayed for the deceivers; meekness was exalted, pride and arrogance laid low. There was a new creation, bright and pure in every soul, when the Spirit of God moved over the chaos of the mind. The blight was taken from the flowers which love or friendship scatter on our path, and hues to them were given which should be able to endure throughout the light of everlasting day. From those blest realms, where good will is cherished towards men, the Spirit of Peace descended upon earth, and passed with pitying steps from land to land. Beneath her soft and pure white wings she gathered all who mourned and were oppressed, the weary and the penitent, the desolate and lonely, the outcast from the world, and chilled in heart, the rejected and betrayed; to her they came, and nestled closely by her side, and from their eyes the tears were wiped away, and the throbbing of their hearts was stilled ; for there they rested in hope."

"Raymond !" exclaimed Arabyn, starting up, with a flushed cheek and glaring eye, and with something almost of madness in his feverish excitement; "I tell you I cannot bear such words to-night ; they mock me with their whispers of peace. Go, leave me, I entreat you; the sound of a human voice is hateful to me: I have fulfilled my promise; I have told you all. Now why do you stand to triumph over me with your unattainable calm ? why do you speak to me of joys I cannot share ? To-morrow—another day—we may talk again, but now,—now you torture me with your serenity. I will not lie here to see you looking out from the paradise of your soul's deep rest upon my miserable strife. Release me from that quiet gaze,—leave me to-night."

Raymond saw that it would be both cruel and injudicious not to comply at once with the request of the unhappy man ; he therefore rose, and would have given him his hand, but Arabyn turned away impatiently, and hid his face on the cushion; it was evident that his envy of the Christian had turned to positive hate.

CHAPTER VI.

ARABYN DETAILS TO RAYMOND IN A LETTER HOW HE DESIGNS TO BECOME MASTER OF HIS OWN DESTINY.

RAYMOND left the presence of the infidel with many sad forebodings: he could see not the slightest hope of a change being effected by his means, or at least at the present time. There was in Arabyn a sort of impatient resistance, not only to all discussion, but even to all mention of that faith which he imagined he had thoroughly examined, and certainly had determinately rejected. He had cherished the darkness too long in his wilful heart not to shrink with dislike and dread from the light. He believed himself open to conviction, and yet he clung so tenaciously to what he called his independence of mind, that it would have been impossible for him to have judged impartially of any creed which came before him, proposing to shackle him with moral duties, or bind him down to peculiar laws.

Raymond saw, in short, that he would not, if he could, believe. Nevertheless, however thankless the task might be, he was preparing to go to him the next evening as usual, when the door opened, and Neophytus the monk appeared. Habitually stern as was the expression of his countenance, it was to-night even more so than usual; and he was very pale.

Raymond, who was thoroughly conversant with modern Greek, had never failed to communicate to this upright and zealous man all that took place during the visits he had made to Arabyn, for a period now of some weeks; and he had found him ever ready to share to the full in all his fears and feelings on the subject. Often had they talked, almost with dismay, of the incalculable ill this man might diffuse through the world, if he went forth with all his singular attractions, bound by the chains of his own will to the service of evil. Only the night before they had conversed long on this matter, after Raymond had left the infidel; and now he saw at once that something had occurred. From the folds of his dark robe the monk took out a letter, and put it in Raymond's hand.

"All is over," he said; "he is gone."

"Gone!" exclaimed Raymond; "who? Arabyn?"

"Yes," replied Neophytus. "How, when, or where, I know not; but he is gone, to work his will upon the earth; and another link is added to that chain of iniquity, dragged on from soul to soul, and guided by a master hand, that seeks therewith to draw this unhappy world into his bonds."

"But give me some particulars," said Raymond earnestly.

"This is all I know; I left my house at dawn this morning on my usual duties, I returned to it according to custom at sunset, and found that the Englishman was gone; I was told that shortly after sunrise he had quitted Scutari, taking with him his servants and all he possessed; one of my men who followed them from curiosity, had ascertained that after crossing over to Pera, they had embarked in an European steamer and sailed past the Golden Horn before noon, my servants were duly recompensed, and this letter was left for you, further I know not." To the letter Raymond now anxiously referred, and read as follows :—

"Raymond, between us two there must be no paltry cavilling, no veiling of stern thoughts in specious language, let us cast aside the set and hollow phrases received in society, and talk together as man with man. I will tell you the truth. I can no longer endure the torture of your presence, the pure cool limpid lake and the hot hissing stream of lava that rushes into it from some burning mountain are more congenial than your soul and mine. I know not how you feel when by my side, but I am maddened by your words; last night I felt fierce passions working in me; I will not restrain them, for now have I decreed that henceforward I will in all things gratify and never subdue my propensities; but I go hence without again seeing you, lest I return with insult and injury the kindness you bestowed on me, and which I acknowledge. I told you I was about to come to a resolution respecting my future destiny; it is taken, and you shall hear it, for I feel a certain triumph in rising up even yet, from the abyss of doubt and misery in which I lay unnerved, and standing alone, firm, undaunted, and independent, both of all the world, and of all powers, visible or invisible, true or false. You know that I designed to die; you know by what fearful process the horror of death replaced the wish for it, so that now I am constrained to foster and cherish the flame of life within this grave-doomed body, as anxiously, as tremblingly, as though each moment were delight, and every thought a rapture; but the abhorred hour will come. Oh! destiny dreadful and inevitable! I, even I, shall be the toy of this wayward and inexorable fate; I cannot escape; the wheel will turn in its senseless course, and I shall sink into the blackness of darkness for ever.

"But now, Raymond, mark this. If I am slave to this one power,—if I can neither resist nor conquer death, at least I am master of this life; this brief period is mine, and mine alone. I have pondered well on the capacities of this fleeting existence, and I have learnt as I reasoned on it a lesson on which I now will act.

"There are pleasures—pleasures of the sight, the senses, and the intellect, which earth can offer man, and which may be wrung and extracted from the hours of his mortal life, as they sweep over him; but of this I am very certain, they are only to be obtained in satisfying fulness, if he eject and expunge from his own internal being all sentiment or principle which oppose his pursuing his own will on all occasions, and by every means. Yes, I am convinced that man may enjoy; he may accomplish his own enjoyment, but *not* if there be in his own mind one feeling which shall ever at any time prevent him destroying the obstacles that will arise upon his path to thwart him, both in his lesser and his greater pleasures; if he ever give way to a scruple, though it be one which would prevent him driving a knife into the heart of an innocent babe, he cannot accomplish his purpose; if he admit that justice is due from himself to others, he cannot accomplish it; if he allow that his fellow-creatures have a claim on him, even for the negative good of being left by him uninjured, he cannot accomplish it; if he hesitate to inflict on them the greatest pain for the attainment to himself of the smallest gratification, he cannot accomplish it; if he indulge in one human affection which shall prevent him removing from his path, if they obstruct it, those most closely allied to him by blood, he cannot accomplish it ; but if he go forth, setting before him as a sole and undivided object his own gratification, and deal with this fair world and all its living inhabitants as though it were one huge senseless mass given him to be material whereon to work, then I believe that he may obtain the fulfilment of his own will. And this will I do. I did not ask for existence; but since it is mine I will force it to minister to my pleasure, and I recognize no law—natural, moral, or revealed—which shall prevent me attaining to this—by the deepest crimes, if necessary; rather, in fact, will I mould crime to be the subtlest instrument of my will, and, were it worth my while to give a reason for my intentions more than that it is my wish, I might call upon you to prove that crime has any existence at all; it is impalpable, it has no being except in connexion with some well-defined law, reverse that law, vice becomes virtue, and virtue vice. In your principles my scepticism and its present fruits are deadly sins; in mine they are a noble independence, a virtuous casting off of prejudices. I have no God to fear, no cold religion to shackle me with stern duties, no heaven to gain, no hell to escape, and she is lost to me who alone could move me with touch of human love or human sorrow.

" Now, therefore, will I go, strong and calm in my own inflexible and unbending mind, insensible to love, to hope, to fear, to ambition, except when I can bend them to my purpose, walking out into this world among its weak inhabitants, whom I will make the unconscious agents of my will; wearing the resemblance of their fancied virtue when I will; and, when I will, sinking into their reality of vice. I will not torture them unnecessarily; but whenever by their misery the least of my pleasures can be enhanced, they must suffer. Nay, you talk of justice, look well and you will find it here; did not I suffer? why or by whom? If there are powers invisible, one of them must have caused this my torture for their delight. It is my turn now. I feel my nerves braced, my energies aroused, when I look forward to this wrestling match with life and man. I feel that I shall grow intoxicated with the exciting strife, like men when they play a difficult and subtle game. There will be for me a strange fascination in deceiving with a thousand different deceptions, in masking myself in goodness in order to lead others to evil, in counterfeiting despair that I may ensure success.

"Thus will I walk on from this day, plucking the fruit from every tree, and crushing them beneath my feet, to extract the fragrant juice, no obstruction shall arise even to a momentary pleasure that I will not trample down, overmastering life by despising its pain and sorrow, and using every joy it can bestow, unshackled by one of those iron chains of duty, faith, affection, hope, or fear, which make of man as much a slave to this existence as he is to death itself.

"This shall be my course, and, Raymond, yours will be to go forth a martyr in heart and soul, devoting yourself to incessant and most irksome labour, depriving yourself voluntarily of every pleasurable sensation your nature is capable of appreciating, for the sake of one unseen hope beyond the dark portals of the dungeon-like eternity, on whose threshold it may dissolve into despair. Go then, give your tangible life for a dream, I will give the untangible dream for a life; follow your path, I depart on mine; fulfil your work, I will work my enjoyment, and let the unrevealing tomb judge between us.

"PHILIP ARABYN."

Raymond read to the last word of this letter, and then letting it fall from his hands, buried his face on his folded arms; his first feeling was one of bitter self-reproach. This strange communication needed no comment to show how ably the infidel was about to fight for the evil, in that great combat in which both were now engaged, and he was gone; and Raymond had, from motives of what he believed to be necessary prudence, delayed until too late the efforts he purposed making for his conversion. However hopeless he might have been of the result, it was an awful thing to think that he had let him depart, to go like a living active curse over the world, shedding poison wherever he went, without ever having uttered a word to drag back that wandering soul from the wilderness into the presence of the light, and there force it to look up and see.

That very night had he purposed to bring before the sceptic the full weight of that complete and incontestable evidence in favour of revelation which none can resist, except by predeterminate and blind opposition; but it was too late.

Raymond felt that in the cause of good, the present only is available. The infidel had embarked on his career of crime, and nothing now remained to him but to follow after him, and destroy as far as in him lay all the work that Arabyn would assuredly perform for the power of evil, counteracting every where the influence he knew would be so baneful.

It was some consolation to Raymond to feel that the hand of his destiny was upon him; too surely had the human adversary he sought been set before him; no where could there have been found a man more capable, by his personal and intellectual advantages, of propagating iniquity than Philip Arabyn.

The Christian folded up this fatal letter, wherein the infidel, by giving a distinct form and colour to his intentions and opinions, had but confirmed himself in his premeditated and deadly servitude to evil, and then prepared to follow on his track.

CHAPTER VII.

MR. DENHAM AND HIS NIECE.

SEVERAL months had elapsed since the period last referred to, and the scene had altogether changed; it was no longer the splendid Oriental city, wrapt in the evening shadows like an Eastern beauty in her veil, that sat on the Byzantine shores, and bathed her feet in the most limpid and bluest of waters: no deep funereal grove was here, no gilded mosque, no gay bazar,—but, fair and peaceful, lay a quiet English village, in the sunny light of a fresh spring morning. The sky that canopied this humble spot had none of the glory of the Eastern heaven, when the gorgeous sunrise fills it with magnificence; but the pale delicate blue was so pure and so transparent, that the longing eye half sought to pierce into the Paradise beyond; and feathery white clouds were passing lightly over it, like the snowy wings of angels floating upwards.

Sweeter far than the nightingales in the myrtle groves were the wild bursts of melody that rose so thrilling and joyous from the heart of the old oak trees; and pleasant was the rustling of their leaves, as the cool free breeze swept through their waving branches, so rich with the green luxuriance of early spring; beneath their shade gushed a clear, bright stream, singing and dancing along like a child at play.

Instead of the fairy palaces of the Eastern city,

whose marble floors were stained with blood, and worn by the feet of captives; whose walls, all decked with silk and gold, rung daily with unheeded shrieks,—here were only lowly rough-built cottages, from whose latticed windows came the merry shout of the laughing children full of life and health within: and yet greater was the contrast between the splendid mosque—temple of an abhorrent worship—and the quaint old parish church, so completely buried among the trees that nothing was to be seen but the grey tower, the most ancient part of the building.

It stood on a gentle elevation, and a winding path led up to the gate of its green churchyard: so that, although forming the most conspicuous object in the village, it was yet sufficiently apart to have gathered round it as it were an atmosphere of its own, a stillness deep and sacred, which, except at stated periods, was never disturbed by sounds less congenial than the sighs of those who came to mingle their tears with the purer dews that lay so thick on the grass-grown graves.

On a nearer inspection there was much to attract and please the eye in this quiet humble sanctuary. The old Gothic porch, surmounted by the rough stone cross, that stood out against the clear sky in strong relief, was full of picturesque beauty; and the dark hue of the ivy-covered walls was pleasantly contrasted with the brightness which at this hour always illuminated the deep-set arched windows, as they caught the rays of the early sun.

And now, from the time-worn tower the sweet-toned chimes were ringing loudly, calling on all who could appreciate the privilege to join in the daily morning prayer. Along the winding path, and through the green churchyard, the worshippers were coming slowly,— they were few, very few in number,—and yet, perhaps, the church was better and more completely filled when they were within it, than with its numerous Sunday congregation,—for it might reasonably be hoped of them that almost every one was accompanied by these unseen friends who minister only to such as shall be heirs of salvation; the poor, the maimed, the blind, the infirm, and afflicted,—those who, being in necessity and tribulation, required help and comfort, were amongst the number; the widow, whose treasure lay hid beneath that drooping willow tree, could not afford to lose a day without hearing "that she might hope at the last to come to His eternal joy;" nor could that aged man, whose feeble steps showed that he must soon glide from the altar to the grave, let another night come down ere he had prayed that he might "have in this world knowledge of the truth, and in the world to come life everlasting."

There was one, however, among the assembling congregation, to whom none of these cases applied. The quiet and unpretending appearance of Ruth Vincent might almost have led a bystander to confound her for a moment with her poorer neighbours, but for a certain indefinable grace, which never fails to give evidence of the perfect refinement that is allied to gentle blood alone. Her noiseless step, the gentle courtesy with which she recognized even the humblest as she passed them, and the low sweet voice with which she thanked the old man who opened the gate for her, were alone indications sufficiently strong to show that she belonged to a class totally distinct from all those

MR. DENHAM AND HIS NIECE. 145

who surrounded her; and they made way for her, seemingly with a species of reverence, mingled with affection. She passed on into the churchyard, and turned to look down on the green sunny landscape below.

Ruth Vincent was not beautiful; hers was not a face to attract the eye at a first glance, but none could have been more calculated to rivet the attention if once arrested; there was in her expression a purity, a repose, an air of abstraction from the world, that was very remarkable, added to a gravity and a thoughtfulness perhaps ill suited to her years; yet there was nothing of melancholy or of morbid feeling. The smile that came so readily to her lips was full of peculiar sweetness, and her whole aspect betokened a quiet and deep-seated happiness; still, the weight of thought that seemed to hang on that pale forehead, and darkened as with a shadow her earnest eyes, was both intense and powerful; and greatly as she was calculated to inspire an idea of purity and holiness, it seemed not to arise so much from the first fresh innocence of youth as from that resolute and nobler guilelessness of one, who, having seen the evil, has chosen the good with calm deliberation.

Yet it was not only the incontestable stamp of intellect —the impress of a noble and energetic mind—which gave to the face of Ruth Vincent so great a charm; but rather the extreme gentleness and softness, and, above all, the unfathomable tenderness, that filled her eyes at all times; though most especially when they turned on any suffering being. Any one well versed in the human heart might easily have read on that countenance how hers was full of love to all mankind, full of that rare and beautiful quality—an uncontrollable sympathy for all who were afflicted; which, though it made her a minister of peace

H

and joy wherever she went, never fails, in this hard cruel world, to bring great misery on all who are possessed of it.

It was evident that Ruth Vincent could suffer, even to the death, to save another from a single pang, whilst at the sight of misery she could not relieve she would shrink, and pine, and wither, like a flower in some unseen and causeless blight.

Her gaze was full of gladness now, as she looked down on the sunshine and the waving trees, and then raised her eyes with a fond lingering look to the clear blue sky. Soon the chimes began to ring faster, as the hour for service approached, and she turned to enter the church; as she passed along she paused occasionally to remove the stones and weeds which had gathered on the neglected graves around, and then, stooping lowly, crossed the sacred threshold, and took her accustomed place. She had chosen it among the seats reserved for the humblest and poorest of the congregation, side by side with a wretched infirm old man, whose palsied hands could no longer uphold his book, and who now, from long habit, looked upon it as his right and privilege to have this gentle attendant, ever ready there to give him the support of her arm, that he might rise from his knees; and who day after day patiently traced out before his dim eyes the holy words which he could not without her aid discern. By the side of this poor aged beggar Ruth knelt at once, sinking down upon her knees with a sigh of relief, as a bird falls wearily into his sheltering nest.

The manner in which the service was conducted might have served as a proof to the villagers of L—— that they were fortunate in their clergyman. There must in truth be a certain degree of difficulty in performing this duty day after day with an equal fervour of devotion; yet in this, Mr. Grey perfectly succeeded, and the propriety of his proceeding on other points may be better rendered by instancing what he did *not* do than by describing what he *did*. He did *not* commence a solemn service by rushing hurriedly into the reading-desk, as though he were taking refuge there from some unpleasant pursuit; nor did he afterwards retire from the same with a degree of nervous haste which indicated a gnawing anxiety to find himself in his own dwelling at breakfast; he did not regulate the propriety of his priestly costume by the numbers of his congregation, or the ceremonials of the Church by the wishes of the inhabitants of the large square pew which blocked up the chancel, and which he had found required only a moat and a drawbridge to be an impregnable fortress. He did not glibly swallow down the prayers, with his face eagerly turned to the people, seeming to give them merely a little casual information, while he reserved his energies for the important sermon,—offspring of his own ideas; nor did he in his general conduct so assiduously study the feelings and want of feeling of the weak brethren, that he became unconsciously included in their number himself. No; decidedly the village of L—— was fortunate in its clergyman.

The service was over, and Ruth Vincent passed from the quiet gloom of the little church, so favourable to concentration of ideas, into the gladness and sunshine of that bright spring morning. She went and sat down on the trunk of an old tree, that the last storm had blown down from its post, as guardian of those humble graves; and scarcely was she seated when there came stealing towards her from all sides a number of ragged, miserable-looking children; who, with a timid look of joy on their wan faces, gathered round her knees. They were the wretched little troop destined from their birth to thankless toil and untimely cares; who in another half hour must be hard at work in the adjoining manufactory; and who, by weary days of unceasing labour, scarce reconciled their poverty-stricken parents to the misery of having given them life.

For each and all Ruth had a sweet smile and a gentle word of kindness, and then she took from her basket the food she had brought for them, and distributed it among them.

When they had finished they all sat down at her feet, and gradually the little hands were slipped into hers, and the wearied heads rested against her knee. Then she began to speak to them in a low sweet voice, using simple words which they could readily understand, and telling them things brighter than all the fairy tales with which the children of luxury beguile their listless hours.

She spoke to them of a fair land that is very far off; and yet not unattainable, even to their infant feet and feeble steps; where, by still waters and among green pastures, they should lie down to rest, and where their little trembling hearts should grow light again for ever, as children's hearts should be. She said that they would rest; no more to hunger and to faint, no more to toil; that from their aching limbs the pain would pass away, and from their eyes the tears, wiped off by a Hand that never comforted in vain. No more would they remember harsh reproach or heavy blow, when wandering with their angel friends through realms of light, hearing their loving voices, and the melodious strains of joy ineffable. No more should they think upon their hopeless, changeless labour, when sporting in celestial bowers, gathering flowers that never fade. No grief, no darkness, and no fear: only the eternal shining of a Light Divine, and bliss unspeakable, and deathless love. Love!—then the voice of Ruth Vincent deepened, and her eyes were full of solemn tears, and she told them of a Love that was around, above, about them even now. Inconceivable and tender, deeper than that the mother bore them when she took from her own lips the last morsel of food to give to them; deeper than all that human heart can dream. A love that watched them while they slept, and warded off, with outstretched arms, the fiendish things they feared; that moved ever by their side unseen; that lit up that dazzling morning sun to gladden their eyes, and warm their frames, and spread out the soft grass beneath their tender feet. A little trial, a little patience, and this same Love would bear them away, on wings of everlasting pity, to that lovely shore which was their own dear home.

She showed them how the slanting beams of the morning sun streamed clear and distinct over the clouds, like so many golden roads from earth to heaven; and told them there were paths unseen, and yet direct and sure like these, which would lead them from their dark world of penury and want, straight to the radiant door of that celestial dwelling, more glorious far than the shining gate of day before their eyes, through which the sun had entered from the east.

Carefully did Ruth Vincent abstain from bringing before them mysteries for which their minds were most unripe, or from attempting any explanation of those which human words can only profane ; but she strove to inculcate that first great lesson which every soul must learn, of unquestioning faith, and to fill their thoughts with bright images, which should for ever prevent their religion being made to them as it were a gloomy shadow, obscuring all that is bright in life; instead of a most glorious sun, giving immortal lustre even unto mortal joys.

Then, when the hour struck which called them from this their only and daily pleasure to their weary labour, they rose and left her with smiles on their haggard faces, and a sweet hope stirring at their childish hearts; while Ruth, quitting the churchyard, walked homeward through the village.

Her home was a large and antiquated house, standing in the centre of an extensive park ; but the whole place wore an aspect of gloom and desolation, which must have made it a dreary residence. As Ruth paused at the gate, an expression of suffering stole over her features, and she gave a deep sigh, with an upward look of calm resolution, like one who takes up the burden of a heavy cross. Not a human being was visible in the long avenue, or in the vast pleasure-grounds ; and Ruth walked slowly on towards the house. She entered it by a glass door opening into the breakfast-room, where a scene presented itself which contrasted singularly with the fresh sunny nature she had left.

The apartment was large, and luxuriously furnished; every comfort which could be imagined to make life agreeable seemed to be collected within its walls, and on all sides were many tokens of abundant wealth. It contained, however, one object which was by no means picturesque, or in any respect pleasing to contemplate:

this was an old gentleman, who was seated in an immense arm-chair, drawn close to a blazing fire. He was evidently a great invalid; and his countenance was expressive of the utmost disgust at the world in general, while the most intense fretfulness and irritability was clearly marked on every hue of his harsh features. His small grey eyes glanced round continually with a look of angry impatience, as though he firmly believed that all things, animate and inanimate, were in league to torment him; and his whole appearance plainly denoted that he considered himself a most highly injured and persecuted individual.

This unfortunate old man was in actual fact a victim and a martyr—victim to prosperity, and martyr to unwearied good fortune. The unlimited command of money, and the possession from his infancy upward of almost every advantage which the world could offer, had fostered, to a fearful extent, the two worst propensities of his nature, a profound selfishness, and an extreme irritability of temper.

Mr. Denham had been an only child, sole object of interest to himself and his parents. He had thus been deprived of that early discipline of care which is usually awarded to the member of a large family, and which is so inestimable a benefit; so that, in the absence of these ordinary claims on his affections, they had centred entirely on his own person. Accustomed to find every thing prepared to meet his wishes, and to the gratification of all his desires, he learned to look upon the continual enjoyment of perfect ease and pleasure as his undoubted and lawful right, whilst pain or suffering of any kind he held to be a most unjust and intolerable persecution. Unconsciously, perhaps, to himself, he practically considered the whole world as a pageant, got up for his express gratification; and had he ever analyzed his own feelings, he would have discovered that mankind was to him as a race created solely to minister to his convenience.

Weak in intellect, and swayed entirely by the inclination of the moment, he had no fixed law of action, and a long systematic course of self-indulgence seemed to have deadened within him all soaring thoughts of another and purer existence, all wish for holier joys than those which this world can offer.

Thus, when late in life Mr. Denham was assailed by an incurable malady, resulting chiefly from his luxurious mode of living, his temper became so violent, and his disposition so tyrannical, that he soon scared from his side all the acquaintances he had ever made. So great was the dislike he inspired in all who approached him, that he could not, with the most munificent offers, induce any, except the mere hired servants, to remain with him,—even those could never be persuaded to endure his irritability and exactions above a month or two; and he at last found himself abandoned to a solitude which was quite insupportable to him. Harassed by disease, that often kept him prisoner for weeks together in a darkened room, and without a single person from whom he could exact that attention to his unreasonable caprices, which had become so necessary to him.

In this emergency he suddenly remembered one, who alone, whenever an opportunity occurred, still never failed to show him the utmost kindness and consideration. This was Ruth Vincent, a connexion of his own. She was an orphan, heiress to an extremely large fortune, and, like himself, without any of the ordinary and more engrossing ties of relationship. He knew that she was quite independent, having attained her majority; and Mr. Denham, utterly unable to endure the miserable situation into which his own violent temper had driven him, finally determined on entreating her to come and live with him.

He did so without a hope that she could ever consent to so selfish and unreasonable a request; for even he, accustomed as he was to think only of himself, could not but perceive the extent of the sacrifice which he asked of her. When he besought her, in the summer of her days, to give up her pleasant home with her guardian, and all the prospects of happiness this world could offer, in order to devote herself, in a solitude complete and hopeless, to the care of a fretful invalid. And yet, to his own utter amazement, as well as to the surprise of all who knew him, Ruth Vincent consented to his strange request: she agreed to come into his dreary abode, there to shut herself up, as a voluntary exile, from all the joys of life; spending her days, from morning till night, in ministering to his comfort, and submitting herself with the most patient meekness to his innumerable caprices.

Certainly, to the worldly wise, this seemed a strange resolution; but Ruth Vincent was no ordinary person: her mind had early reached its maturity, and she had unconsciously reversed the process by which the intellect usually ripens, for she had *thought* long and deeply before she had ever *felt*, instead of being forced to reflection by disappointment. The prevailing feature in her character, from the moment that she could discern between good and evil, was a most intense and unspeakable longing after purity. Even in material things it affected her, causing her to gaze with extraordinary joy on an unspotted, cloudless sky, a lake, serene and mirror-like, or a lily in its robe of stainless white. But this was only the outward demonstration of the deep yearning within, which drove her soul from attempting to harbour itself in this world, and sent it, winged by strong desire, on its upward path. It was to her as a talisman, worn in her breast against the serpent fangs of evil. She had, as it were, an instinctive worship for the principle of good; and irresistible horror for every thing that was low, mean, and polluting. Her spirit flew forth to that which was pure and noble, as the lark to the first rays of the sun; but, like that lark who falls disconsolate to earth, when heavy clouds obscure the light it loves, so, when the mists of human error, the darkness of human depravity, dimmed the faint rays of struggling virtue amid her fellow-creatures, she fell back upon her own self, not in hate or in morbid misanthropy, for she was gentle and tender as a guileless child, but in voiceless sorrow, in deep and wondering regret.

Ruth possessed in common with most minds of a high order a singular degree of penetration, and a strange foreknowledge of those stern realities of life which, for a time, are hidden by the delusive brightness of its spring. Earth seemed never to have had a delusion for her, nor worn that dazzling robe of sunshine with which youth ever decks it. That calm young soul stood forth alone and independent, unallured and undeluded; and looked down, beholding the world in its true colours, till she turned sickening from the sight. That knowledge which men acquire in their own bitter experience, when the radiance of the first unquestioning hope is gone, and the heart is poisoned, and the spirit broken, seemed to be hers from the first. She tried all things by the fire of her own sin-abhorring mind, and they passed not unscathed: she weighed earth in the balance of the immaculate law, and it was found wanting. Then, turning away from this world the eyes that could but weep to look upon it, she raised them upward, and fixed them stedfastly on heaven. Straightway her lofty aspirations after the good and excellent, her longing for the pure and holy, her adoration for even the faintest gleam of virtue, like so many winged steeds, bore her soul away, nor rested till they flung it down prostrate before the eternal throne.

It were in vain to attempt to describe the joy, too holy and too deep to be expressed in human words, which lifted Ruth Vincent far above this world, and all it has to offer, when she attained to the actual perception of an existent All Pure, to whom in purity she would one day be reunited.

There is a vast difference between the knowledge of the understanding, and the perception of the spirit: that truth which contains a full and eternal satisfaction for the wants and desires of our immortal nature may be known and valued long before it appears to us, in so comprehensive a view that we seem to sink into its glorious hope as into a sea of light, and are engulphed; never more to know the horror of darkness, though at times passing shadows may flit over us, and the grave look gloomy to the bystander's sight as we go down to it.

It is not until the dweller on this earth, by the subtle power of suffering, or by premature and bitter wisdom, is constrained to cry out, "Who will show us any good?"

that the answer comes up from the depths of his own inner being, yearning after his Original, with those words of deepest meaning, "Lift Thou up the light of Thy Countenance upon us."

Very different were the paths by which Ruth Vincent and Raymond attained to the spirit's resting-place, but the result could not but be the same. Even as he had done, so did she now deliver up her soul to that one hope, and to the fitting herself for its fulfilment, overstepping, with firm resolve in every thought, the boundaries of time and space.

Simple, though severe, were the laws she laid down for herself, to purify herself even as He is pure, and to love the brethren whom His universal love had given to her on earth, with an active and a faithful tenderness, which should minister to them in this mortal life, retaining ever the distinct perception of time only as the germ of eternity.

Ruth believed that sin and suffering, holiness and happiness, were actually synonymous. To combat the first, and promote the second, wherever and in whatever shape she found them, was, she knew, to accomplish that part of her work which was to be performed outwardly on the earth, whilst it unconsciously aided in that severer labour which was to be carried on inwardly in her spirit.

In contradistinction to Arabyn, the self-bound slave to evil—who, as we have seen, had determined to procure the smallest gratification to himself even by the most inadequate proportion of suffering in others—Ruth Vincent steadily resolved that she would ever purchase, when necessary, the least amount of happiness for those around her, by the greatest of sorrow to herself.

Nerving herself to a calm and noble independence of all things earthly, she set forward on her rough and narrow path, immortal purity her goal, the cross her burden and her hope, self-sacrifice her chosen portion. As yet though weak and erring, she had kept her high resolve amid many and strong temptations; not passionless, not dead to human feelings or affections, but moving through the world with quiet and serene aspect, mixing with it as much as was necessary for the performance of all the duties of her station in life, hearing but heeding not the voices of its manifold allurements, living outwardly the life of those who surrounded her, whilst inwardly, in the hidden world of the spiritual existence, her soul revolved for ever round its one immortal hope, like the earth round the sun.

For this cause, as she had no other ties to claim her attention, she agreed to reside with Mr. Denham, for it seemed to her, that by this request, a means was offered to her of serving the Sufferer Divine in daily suffering, which she had no right to refuse. She knew how precious in the sight of Him, whose Silent Will can draw a million worlds out of void, was one immortal soul. And across her path, even now, a soul seemed cast, as dead to God in the corruption of sin, as the body to which it was wedded must soon be in the decay of mortality.

Mr. Denham was an instance of that strange phenomenon often exhibited in this world, of a man who goes on through a long life, with the certain knowledge of death at its close, without ever pausing to inquire if there is aught beyond it; who sees how all the love and hate, the joys and hopes, which bear us like swift waves over the sea of life, must come to be dashed against a coffin at the last, and yet never seeks to know whether that coffin shall contain but senseless ashes, or the seeds of a life that shall cope with eternity; who hear for ever echoing around them the words of immortality and judgment, of death and destruction, yet seem to conclude that they bear no reference to themselves, who perceive that others devote every hour of their existence to the great struggle for salvation, and never dream that their own lives can have any other end or aim but the attainment of their present happiness.

Mr. Denham was a materialist, not from conviction, but because he believed what he saw, and nothing more; because he would have laughed to scorn any one who proposed to him to give up but one of the attainable pleasures of this world for the sake of a hope unseen. He served the power of evil, not from a bold and extraordinary resolution like that which Arabyn in the perversion of his soul had taken, but because the unconscious rule of his existence was to follow unquestioning and unthinking the bent of his own inclination, wheresoever it might lead him. Nothing could have arrested him in this contemptible slavery to his own vile nature; and though he thought with an indefinite terror of the approaching termination of his earthly career, as yet not a ray of penitence or belief had shone in upon his self-darkened soul.

Ruth Vincent knew this; she knew that, impenitent and unbelieving, for every day and hour of his life he had incurred the pure uncompromising wrath of God. She knew that he was dying by slow degrees, a year or two must terminate the period of his mortal probation. It was an awful thing to think of him speeding on to that grave which must be for him as the condemned cell to one ordered for execution, without an effort being made to break open his heart of stone, for the reception of repentance and faith: awful to think of him reaching in his wilful blindness the last and darkest hour of his existence, that hour when the bolts and bars of the spirit are withdrawn, the veil of the flesh rent asunder, and the first terrible ray of the light, which is Truth, shoots in upon it, and to know in so fearful a moment there would not be one voice to utter in his dying ears the *Name* that often is as the cry of land to the drowning mariner perishing in the tempest.

Yet so, she felt, it must be with him if she refused to remain with him; she well knew that human agents are generally chosen in such cases, and though she never would have dared to have imposed upon herself so responsible a task, yet she saw that no choice was left her, since to none other would it ever be offered. Ruth was sincerely humble, she had no confidence whatever in herself, and had there been but one little child whose stammering lips could have murmured to the dying man the one word which embodies an eternal hope, she would rather have trusted the arduous duty to that innocent teacher than to herself.

But there could be none such, for it was to her a source of the deepest distress, that Mr. Denham had the most violent repugnance to the mere idea of admitting into his house any one of the ministers of God, to whom alone the care of his wandering soul could with propriety be given. Her path, therefore, appeared to her clearly marked out, and at once she calmly bartered all the enjoyment of life in its best and brightest hours for the remote chance that she might in his hour of agony comfort and sustain this selfish and degraded man.

Perhaps the bitterest drop in the cup of suffering which Ruth thus voluntarily raised to her lips, was her quiet and uncomplaining endurance of the hatred which Mr. Denham bore to her, for he did in fact dislike her with all the bitterness which a man of his character could not but feel for one so superior to himself. Not all his selfishness and worldly-mindedness could quite deaden within him the perception of good and evil, and with the instinctive conviction which he could not quell, that the holy life and self-devotion of Ruth would one day meet its reward, there often came a vague terror as to the result of his own life-long egotism and sin; so that he hated her in fact as his living conscience, for ever condemning by her quiet and unobtrusive goodness his own corrupt existence.

Very bitter and dreary then was the life she had thus accepted, for whilst he implored her presence as his chiefest good, he scrupled not to show her by harshness and unkindness that she was only less distasteful to him than the solitude which none other would dispel. Ruth had a mind of uncommon power, and a reason strong and unbiassed; but there was a feature yet more prominent in her character, and that was a clinging tenderness, a total want of self-confidence, and a power of deep devoted affection, which made her ever lean on others, ever seek some guiding fostering hand to lead her through the desert of this life. She was diffident and timid, except when strengthened by her own determinate resolution, and was not by any means one of those bold independent spirits, who can embark with a stout heart on their destiny, ready to battle with the winds and waves alone. Independently of the principles which would have tended to produce a similar feeling, her own warm heart had taught her to seek and find no other enjoyment than that which was always hers when ministering to others, and she would have bartered years of incessant labour and self-sacrifice, for the certainty that she had ever soothed or comforted one suffering being.

She submitted, however, without a murmur, to all Mr. Denham's cruel treatment, and to the still more distasteful expression of a false attachment when he was occasionally terrified by the idea that his unkindness might drive her from him, for he could by no means appreciate the motives which had actuated her, nor understand that the more heavy grew the burden which her obedience had laid upon her, the more meekly and unreservedly would she give herself up to its endurance. To her it seemed but a reasonable duty that she, the servant of the Crucified, should give her life for a soul which He had bought, and therefore gladly and unsparingly she delivered it up, knowing that He loveth a cheerful giver.

CHAPTER VIII.

ARABYN ENTERS ON THE EXECUTION OF THE PLAN WHEREBY HE DESIGNS TO MASTER HIS DESTINY.

Mr. Denham was this morning more than usually irritable. Two long years, during which Ruth Vincent had resided with him, made him feel as though he had a sort of right over her, and as she had never during the whole of that time given him the slightest reason to fear that she would abandon him, however harshly he might treat her, he now felt quite sure of her, and made no attempt to restrain the violence of his temper.

She, meanwhile, had purposely rendered herself necessary to him by her tender and unceasing care, soothing him in pain, comforting him in weariness, and amusing him in his moments of ease.

As yet she had seen no fruits of the sacrifice she had made, for he never would allow her even to approach the subject nearest to her heart, but she waited patiently, trusting that some unforeseen circumstance, or an increase of illness, might so far subdue the rebellious spirit, that she might whisper to him the words of the glorious hope; but even if she never reaped this blessed recompence of her toil, she would not murmur, for she knew that no duties should ever be performed with a view to the result, but solely for His sake Who enjoined them, and in Whose hands alone is the issue.

There was certainly a singular contrast between those two strangely-assorted companions; as Ruth stood there so pale and still, with her meek thoughtful eyes fixed on him, whilst he, every line of his sullen countenance telling of a fretfulness which a word would have roused to a burst of passion, poured out his ill humour unsparingly upon her. She tried in vain to soothe him, but she could not succeed in pleasing him; her coming in was an offence, and her having delayed to come so long, a still greater; a stray sunbeam which dazzled his eyes, he treated as a premeditated insult; and Ruth was condemned for the barking of a discontented dog, as though she had purposely instructed the animal to torment him.

She felt thankful when the arrival of a letter addressed to himself, turned his thoughts in a new direction. It was very seldom that Mr. Denham received a communication from any one, his acquaintances had long since forgotten him, and friendship (that true friendship whose light brightens with the darkness of adversity, and strengthens with each new claim on its endurance,) he had never felt, and consequently had never inspired. He became, therefore, at once ferociously impatient to know who had written to him. Ruth always read to him, as his increasing blindness rendered him incapable of distinguishing the letters, and he now called out to her to turn quickly to the signature, that he might learn instantly from whom the letter came; she read the name of Arabyn—Philip Arabyn.

"Arabyn!" exclaimed Mr. Denham, "my wife's nephew; why! it is years since I have heard of him, I thought he had been dead long ago, and so he ought to have been.—I tell you he ought to have been dead," he continued, looking at Ruth as angrily as though she had violently contradicted him. "Why so?" she asked timidly, shrinking from the sound of his harsh grating voice. "Why? because he is a miserable outcast, whose name is a disgrace. His father was outlawed for forging a deed, and would have been executed had he not escaped. He was brother to my wife, and it broke her heart, as well it might, for it brought dishonour on all his relations, and on me amongst the rest; but I was not the man to submit tamely to it. The matter might have been forgotten now, if this son had not existed; but there he is, carrying through the world the stain of his father's infamy; so I say again, he ought to have died."

Ruth felt a strange pity rise in her heart for one so severely visited with the weight of another's crime.

"But if he has done no evil himself," she said gently, "surely no one would make him suffer for that over which he had no control."

"And how do I know that he has done no evil?" said Mr. Denham. "He is a dutiful son, no doubt he will follow in his father's steps; I know that when he was in England some years since, strange stories were told of him, he was not well received then at all events; but why do you not tell me the reason of his writing to me? What does he want?"

Ruth took the letter and read it aloud, and it seemed to her the most touching and beautiful piece of eloquence she had ever read. It was dated from London, stating that after many years Arabyn had returned to England, and that he felt very anxious to see Mr. Denham, his last remaining relative once again: he mentioned the species of moral persecution to which he had so often been subjected by the disgraced name he bore; but he spoke of it, as a Christian would speak, with the most humble resignation to the will of Heaven, and with a calm forgiveness of the injustice from which he suffered. He touched slightly, but evidently with deep feeling, on certain great and bitter misfortunes which had of late fallen upon him; and concluded by saying, that weary and heavily burdened with much care and sorrow, as he was, it would be a source of great thankfulness to him, if he might hope to find an asylum with his uncle.

It was a letter which Ruth believed could only have been written by one whose soul was in all truth and earnestness delivered up to the pure faith, it seemed to her so full of the holy and humble spirit which that faith alone can give; she looked up wistfully to Mr. Denham, dreading that he would refuse the reasonable request of a being seemingly so unfortunate, and for whom even the few words she had read had filled her with compassion. Greatly to her astonishment, however, Mr. Denham desired her to write to Arabyn, to inform him that he was willing to receive him at once, and to beg that he would come immediately, and remain with him as long as he pleased.

The fact was that Mr. Denham disliked exceedingly the dull monotony of the life he led; any prospect of change or excitement was exceedingly agreeable to him, and he had no fear now that a new arrangement could induce his patient companion to leave him.

Mr. Denham was in many respects like an overgrown child, and no sooner was the letter written and dispatched, as he desired, than he began to fret and complain because Arabyn was not yet arrived; he was so accustomed to exact an unquestioning submission to his will on all points, that he would even have had time and space subservient to it.

It seemed to Ruth that she had never had to endure so much from him as during the long day which succeeded; hour after hour she strove unwearied to amuse and comfort him, now reading to him, and now singing soft low songs which would have soothed any spirit, save one so determined to be unquiet as his. The evening came at last, however, and when she saw that he had fallen into the slumber in which he usually indulged at that hour, she gladly left his side to avail herself of this brief period of freedom; it was the only time she could call her own, as Mr. Denham merely awoke to be removed to his room, so that she was always released from her charge during the whole evening.

In a few minutes she had left the house, and walking quickly on, she felt that she breathed more freely when she had passed the gate of the park; she turned her eyes wistfully in the direction of the country, thinking how much she would have enjoyed a walk through the green woods and by the murmuring streams on that still mild evening. Then she could have gazed on the first sweet star that comes forth (so pale with looking on this dreary world), to be as a beacon of hope, telling of holier lands, till she had dispelled the chilling sense of loneliness that crept over her at times with thoughts of the bright true friends that ever walked with her unseen; and so learned to feel grateful, that since no broken reed was given her on which to lean, she need not fear the sure piercing of the hand that might too much have trusted to it.

But Ruth turned resolutely from the quiet fields, and

the waving trees, where the cool dew-drops were glistening in the last bright rays; she remembered that there were many around her in disease and wretchedness, whose only sunshine was the smile of human kindness, and the brightness of the day became an unlawful joy to her, when she knew that her presence could be as a light in the house of mourning.

Thankless is in truth the task of ministering to those whose very nature seems perverted and debased by sin and ignorance, whose hearts are hardened and dead to all kindly feelings. Yet Ruth Vincent would not have bartered the inexpressible joy she felt in tending and waiting on the most abject and degraded of the poor around her, for all the fondest care and tenderness that could have been bestowed upon herself. To her it seemed an unsatisfactory and earthly pleasure only to love those who loved her, but to minister with gentlest and most devoted kindness to some diseased and wretched being, from whom all others turned with loathing, to brave the pestilential air which scared the lawful attendants from many a bed of agony, to draw close to her own fond heart the neglected infant whom infirmity had cast out even from a mother's love, to clasp with a warm friendly pressure the withered hand of some aged and forsaken pauper, who had lingered so long in this world, that all the love which brightened it had died out round him,—these were the works which made Ruth Vincent often feel as if her sum of earthly happiness were all too great.

After visiting several houses she entered one which stood somewhat apart from the rest; it was inhabited by a paralytic old woman, who had for years lain in the same posture on her miserable couch. She was an unsightly object to look upon, and the atmosphere of the room was painfully oppressive; but Ruth sat down beside her lovingly, as though she were a tender friend, and took the cold stiff hand in hers; she gave her some fresh dewy flowers which she had gathered for her, that the remembrance of her Father's beautiful works might not altogether pass from the memory of this her afflicted sister, and then she listened with the gentlest sympathy to the long and wearisome detail of all her sufferings; finally, at the poor old woman's request she began to read to her. Whilst she continued thus employed, it suddenly appeared to her that the pages before her were darkened, as though some one had stood for a moment at the open window, but on looking up she saw nothing, and thought no more of the circumstance.

On returning home she spent the remainder of the evening in reading quietly as usual, and it was late before she retired to her own room; she went up to the window, and throwing it wide open to admit the soft star light, and the sweet breath of the flowers in the pleasure-grounds immediately below her, remained for a long time gazing out on the quiet landscape with her earnest thoughtful eyes; gradually, although almost unconsciously, she sunk upon her knees, and burying her face in her hands remained motionless.

Now, throughout the whole of this day,—to Ruth seemingly so uneventful, but which nevertheless was the crisis of her destiny,—a dark shadow had followed on her path wherever she went. In the morning it had been with her as she passed to the church, that she might within its holy walls sanctify her first waking thoughts; when she knelt beside the aged beggar, a face of peculiar beauty, and of dark and meaning glance, gazed in upon her through the low narrow window, and watched every movement of her lips, and the tightening of her clasped hands, when the prayer for the confession of sins was commenced; when she sat in the churchyard, gathering to her bosom the squalid and wretched children, who, but for her love, would have found existence so unlovely, a figure had been concealed behind a massive tombstone, and an attentive ear had drunk in every word which she had uttered; and her steps had been tracked as she walked homewards, and it had been carefully noted how often she unconsciously trod the flowers of earth beneath her feet, because of the intensity with which her gaze was turned to heaven.

When she sat by the side of Mr. Denham, and read from the letter the name of "Arabyn, Philip Arabyn," a voice from among the bushes at the window echoed the word with taunting accents, and prophesied, by its peculiar intonation, of the varied manner with which she would one day repeat that name,—now in supplication, now in agony, now in vainest tenderness!

Throughout the whole day every movement and look was observed: it was seen with what patient meekness she endured the open manifestation of her companion's hatred; it was remarked how the melody of her voice was heightened when she sung, by the deep and concentrated feeling which thrilled in every tone; when she went out in the evening, it had been noted how longingly she looked upon the quiet woods, and how resolutely she turned from them to enter into the close infected atmosphere of the house of sickness and poverty. The shadow that had darkened her page as she read to the deformed cripple had followed her homeward, and was even now among the trees below her window; but when she sunk down in voiceless prayer, the sight of that kneeling figure, with its folded hands and gently heaving breast, so perfectly in harmony with the quiet midnight scene, seemed to have scared him who watched her as though it had been some dreadful vision, for instantly there might have been heard through the brushwood the rush of the footsteps of one who fled from the presence of that soul in communion with the Eternally Pure.

Philip Arabyn entered the room which he had now occupied for two days in the little inn of the village of L——. Like her, on whose bowed head and prostrate form the starlight still was falling, he buried his face in his hands, and gave himself up to deep and quiet meditation; and as his thoughts wove their dark web over his mind, a fanciful ear might have seemed to detect in that deep silence the clanking of the chains which he was forging by his own will for the binding down of his soul irrevocably to the power of evil.

When Arabyn left Constantinople to embark on the career in which he designed to master destiny, and compel life to minister to him, with his own will for his god, and for his handmaid's crime and pleasure, his first endeavour was to arrange systematically the plan he was to pursue, in order to wring from out his fleeting existence every possible enjoyment of which his nature was capable,—his intention being to attain to the power of an organized and unfailing gratification of every desire, instinct, and propensity.

A first great obstacle to this egotism, embodied in a life, arose up before him at the very onset, claiming the exertion of all his energy and talent for its destruction.

He saw at a glance that the pleasures of this world must be bought, there is no free gift with the god mammon; and that unbounded luxury, with which he proposed to cover as a gorgeous veil the bitter realities of life, would never be his, without the unlimited possession of wealth —countless, inexhaustible wealth! To the attainment (as complete and speedy as possible) of this,—which was in fact but the foundation of his proposed enjoyment,—he therefore determined, in the first instance, to devote himself entirely, as his primary object.

It was a strange thing, how, from the hour when Philip Arabyn had taken the corruption of his own human nature, and set it within his soul, as an idol in a temple, there to be worshipped, he became as it were intoxicated with evil. It was necessary to the strong powers of his mind, to his energetic intellect, to have some aliment on which to feed; his powerful faculties could not endure to lie inactive,—they must have something on which to work, to exercise themselves; and for this cause, having once conceived the extraordinary scheme we have detailed, he seemed to have thrown himself into the struggle with his destiny with a degree of ardour and keen delight hardly proportionate to the value he himself attributed to the end he had in view.

But, especially, Arabyn felt that he took a strange pleasure in exercising all those peculiarities of his character which gave him a greater facility in the use of crime as his instrument than in any other; his subtle mind entered readily into the mazes of a refinement of iniquity; he anticipated with a deep enjoyment the crafty silent working of the dark and skilful machinations by which he was to accomplish his purpose; with the smile of a fiend on his lips, he traced out the tortuous paths wherein he was to glide, wearing the semblance of virtue, that he might allure men to vice.

He had all the sensations of fierce delight of a wary gambler, playing a deep and difficult game; all the bracing excitement of one who loves the chase,—only that he fled after his prey with noiseless steps, and sought to hunt down living men. With the deep spirit of intrigue which has for some minds such allurements, he thought how he would spread his nets, and fabricate unhallowed snares, wherein his victims—entering unawares—should only wake to struggle as they perished. But chiefly he dwelt with complacency on all the opportunities he should have of exercising his extraordinary power of deception, in walking about as an angel of light, with the guile of a demon at his heart.

It was not that Arabyn had naturally a stronger propensity to evil than other men; this was but the craving of his mental faculties to be employed; had he not sealed up his soul against the light, he would have nerved himself with equal delight to the strong exertion of his powers for good: but now he was like to a fierce, strong horse, that has broken loose from all restraint, and, maddened by his own fiery ardour, rushes on, trampling down all things on his path with a reckless, frantic desire to deal destruction round him.

Arabyn had asserted a complete independence, moral and actual; he had sworn to have the mastery by working out his purposes in perfect freedom, and by so doing he had caused his own will to become his executioner, and had made of his passions so many powerful fiends, to drag him down with strong hands into the abyss. Let a man become his own creator before he talks of liberty.

The attainment, then, of boundless wealth became his first object. It is certain that in this world no end is to be gained, either for good or evil, without a firm concentration of the energies and faculties on its accomplishment; and Arabyn, therefore, for the present determined to devote himself exclusively to the most needful acquirement of riches, reserving the further moulding out of his destiny for pleasure, till he should be possessed of this necessary instrument. His first attempt for the fulfilment of this purpose Raymond was even now occupied in rendering abortive; and when this plan failed, (the details of which must be given hereafter,) his thoughts naturally reverted to his uncle, and to his companion, Ruth Vincent, who was the possessor to an unlimited amount of the thing he coveted. No sooner had he recollected this circumstance than he resolved, with that prompt decision which is a sure characteristic of genius, that this desirable wealth should be his.

What more simple than to marry her, make himself master of her fortune, and then abandon her? It was precisely the scheme to foster his base vanity, which exulted in the idea of using his fellow-creatures as his instruments so long as he required their services, and then flinging them aside, or trampling them under foot, when his object was attained. He therefore at once adopted this plan, and determined to proceed without delay in working out its accomplishment.

He never entertained the slightest doubt of his success; he well knew what were his own powers of fascination, and it was with a keen relish that he thought of feigning with subtle art the affection it was perfectly impossible he should ever feel; for there lay deep buried in his heart, like a corpse in its grave, the one fair image which alone had ever made him know what subtle and enduring chains must, in some one shape or other, link us human beings close together; dust clinging to dust, and clay to clay, each with the germ of death within us! But, independently of this, he had laid it down as his first principle, and one perfectly indispensable to the development of his system of life, that he should root out and utterly destroy within him all human affections; for if ever any thing had power to turn him for one single instant from his sole and undivided love of self,—if ever he was moved by the faintest sentiment of pity or of tenderness,—he was no longer his own master, he was no longer independent; in fact, there is no slavery more complete than that of a true and profound affection, inasmuch as it renders even the will altogether subservient to that of another.

Arabyn, however, had no cause to doubt his powers of dissembling and alluring, and he would have thought it unnecessary to take any precautionary measures for ascertaining the character of his destined victim had he not heard that Ruth Vincent, either on account of her large fortune or her personal qualities, had already had many opportunities of repulsing, with singular determination, all persons whose intentions were similar to his own. Whilst, in all other matters, she yielded systematically to the wishes of others, on this one point he was told she had evidently resolved on keeping her own will inviolate; therefore he had thought it prudent to ascertain, by studying her peculiar disposition, in what guise he must present himself before her, in order the more speedily to allure her to become his tool.

Philip Arabyn was a quick and a keen observer; in the course of that one quiet and uneventful day, when

Ruth Vincent believed that no human eye was upon her, he had gained all the information he desired ; it is by far the surest way of rightly estimating a character, to scrutinize those words and actions which are too trivial and unimportant to have been influenced by previous calculation ; and he had seen quite enough to point out most clearly to him the disguise he must assume before that upright and unworldly being, so strong in her deep tranquillity, could become his prey. It was perfectly evident to him that Ruth Vincent would never be induced to lower her heaven-drawn gaze on any earthly friend, except he appeared before her as a rare example of that goodness and holiness for which her own soul longed, as a devoted follower (infinitely more advanced than herself) of the faith to which she was devoted ; who—as he ascended more speedily than she could do towards that awful union with Perfection which is hereafter to be our life—might stretch forth a hand to guide her tottering steps upon that difficult ascent, and cause her to enter in with him, where alone she might have lain trembling and weeping at the door !

Arabyn hated Christianity and its followers with a deadly hate. How he exulted now, as he thought on the cunning vengeance he was about to take upon them all, by assuming as his disguise their own vesture of the beauty of holiness, and outdoing them, seemingly, in all truth and faithfulness, that he might further the vice they abhorred, crown with success the iniquity against which they were in arms, and draw down one of their own band into the abyss of misery he had prepared for her !

Arabyn felt, however, that even in the semblance of the most devoted virtue he might have failed to win back to earth one who had learned to contemplate that Purity which alone is Infinite and Perfect, but for another weapon, which the very noblest trait in her character had placed in his hand. He must appear before her as a suffering being,—if goodness failed to attract her uplifted eyes, the aspect of misery would have that power; he must go to her as one lonely, friendless, despairing,— victim of the world's cruel sentence, that cast him out, because his father sinned before he gave him birth; as having been doomed to seek, and never find, one unprejudiced, unworldly friend, who would have taught him how, though dark and drear, and like to a wilderness, this earth may seem to one who walks on it alone, yet flowers can spring up, and sunbeams gather round, when two are treading in the self-same path, leaning on one another. He must seem to her as one who suffered, and none mourned; who was in pain, and no one comforted. If once her sympathy was roused the game was his.

Then must he seem never to imagine that she, more than others, could sorrow for his sorrowing, or long to befriend one so friendless; he must shrink back as though for him to hope was a lesson too difficult to learn; that she, tortured by compassion, might be constrained to advance, and so would he lead her on; and she, unable to endure the sight of his suffering, longing to bear his anguish, to take upon herself his burden, must follow after him till he had as it were allured her out alone with him into the wilderness, and then would he turn round and fasten his hold upon her, with a grasp like that of a fierce eagle, when he fixes his claws in the tender breast of a gentle dove.

Thus Philip Arabyn sat musing, while Ruth Vincent, afar off, prayed; and the dark thoughts kept stealing out and in his soul like so many lurking, subtle demons; whilst, as an angel of light, one holy conviction of a Love, that was revealed in agony, kept the portals of her pure, regenerate spirit, and admitted none other to enter there.

And the same soft starlight was around them both, and the same sweet flowers sent up to each their fragrant breath, freely bestowing all they had to give, for the comfort and the solace of the creatures God had made; and the same fair tranquil sky that told of Him in its spotlessness was spread above their head. And yet they heard not and saw not the same things, for the aspect of this world is altogether different to those whose eyes have been opened by the same Touch that once caused the blind man to see as he sat by the wayside begging; and to such it is given to perceive in the beauty of nature a closely-written book, where they may read, in fair and distinct characters, a record of the secrets of eternity.

At the same moment, the Christian rose from her prayers and the infidel from his meditations; and there was a smile upon the face of each: on the countenance of Ruth Vincent it was beautiful and joyous, and like that which sometimes lingers on the lips of the dead when their death has been dear in the sight of the Lord; and on the face of Philip Arabyn it was full of wild triumph, and ominous as the lightning's flash which precedes a dark and portentous storm. He smiled, because, as his quick thoughts glided on through the intricate path he had traced out, and rested with complacency on the final accomplisnment of his purpose, a new idea had suddenly struck him, which filled him with a keen sense of pleasure.

Arabyn had never been able to account to himself for the imperious desire that seemed to exist within him, to destroy, at all times, the faith of other men, and induce them to adopt his own infidel opinions. It was not certainly that he felt for them such love as should constrain him to seek to release them from the bondage of a delusion; nor yet did he hate them sufficiently (being altogether indifferent to them, and absorbed in self,) to make him undergo any labour for their destruction. But we read of drowning men, who, when sinking, moved by some strange madness, fling their arms around those who would attempt to save them, and drag them down along with them into the whelming waters; and some such senseless frenzy seemed to move him in this matter beyond his power to control. Nay; according to his present principles, why should he control it?

His desire and resolution were to indulge in every impulse of his diseased and deformed soul, which, by its gratification, could procure him the smallest pleasure. The idea, then, that had brought so triumphant a smile to the lips of the infidel, was simply this: he resolved (with the blood thrilling strangely through his veins at the thought of so consummate and artful a scheme of iniquity) that when, by appearing before Ruth Vincent as the most pure and holy follower of the faith she adored, he had won her altogether to himself,—when, by his hand had been for the first time unsealed the deep fount of tenderness that dwelt within her,—when the love he had created could not be rooted out of her without the breaking up of the heart itself, or his image torn from her breast, except by the rending of the bonds of life,— when he should so have taught her soul to turn to him as a flower to the sun, that she should live only in his life, think with his thoughts, love that which he loved, and hate that which he hated,—then would he turn round exultingly, and destroy within her the very faith by which he won her; that all men might see how the belief on which they founded an eternity could fade and dissolve, and pass away, beneath the sweet power of human love! And because, from the lips she loved, all words should seem as truth,—because she should have learned to look up to him with that deepest reverence which is, in an affection, founded on the belief of the goodness and holiness of the object which inspires it,—he, the intellectual philosopher, doubted not that he would be able to subdue the weak woman, to the destruction of her soul's guiding principle, and, by his sophistry, kill the spiritual life within her.

Miserable schemer! Did he not know that to no mortal hand shall it ever be given to dim the lustre of the jewels wherewith the King shall make up His crown? Human agents may, indeed, be chosen to be the instruments of their needful chastening; to pierce them through, if ever they are beguiled into seeking a rest in this world, with their indifference, hollowness, or treachery; till, like the stricken deer, with the arrow in their heart, they fly moaning to the covert from the tempest, to the shadow of the great rock in the weary land. But to each one of those (whose arm is guided where to strike,—blind workers of a Love Unseen,) it is said, " Thus far shalt thou go, but no farther!" For there is a holy and peculiar atmosphere around *His* own, impenetrable as an adamantine wall; and they have each one of them, deep-set within their hearts as a pearl of great price, a joy which is unapproachable; with which no human woe can tamper, nor human disappointment blight.

And now they both slumbered, and the still solemn night, walking with the dark hours as in a funeral march, led them both, while they slept oblivious, closer and closer to the retributive grave, till that sun, which rises obedient on the just and on the unjust, gave light to the day which was to witness the first meeting of the infidel and his victim.

CHAPTER IX.

ARABYN PREPARES THE SNARE SUCCESSFULLY FOR THE VICTIM.

At a late hour the next evening, Ruth and Mr. Denham sat together in their large desolate room, into which no other light was admitted than that of the moonbeams streaming through the windows.

Ruth was placed at the open window, and she sat motionless, gazing out into the still night, with the moonlight falling on her pale quiet face; whilst the two bloodhounds pressed close to her side, as though with the consciousness that something evil was near her.

Slowly and silently, through the glass door, Philip Arabyn passed from the garden into the room. Even as Raymond had paused to look on him, believing that he saw his destiny before him, so did he now stand unperceived, and look upon Ruth Vincent; and as he gazed, he felt his heart recoil from her, prophetic of the hate which he would be constrained to bear her; for there was an indescribable expression on her countenance, which told more plainly than words could have done, that even whilst still chained to the mortal body, her soul had already returned to the God who gave it. And never did the midnight darkness fly from the morning light with such deep abhorrence, as the gloomy, restless spirit of the infidel from a fellow mortal, on whom was stamped the seal of the Unearthly Peace.

Like unto one who goes forth to look upon a still and lovely landscape, with some dark human grief, untold and unpitied, curdling round his heart; over whose soul, with a roar unheard to other ears, the bitter waters of despair are sweeping, quenching for ever the unuttered hope; and who finds so cruel a want of sympathy in the universal calm of nature, that he turns aside with a yet deeper despondency, hating the sunshine because of the dark clouds that lie so heavy on him; and unable to endure the tranquil sky, because of the tempest howling mournfully within; even so did Philip Arabyn turn with loathing from all in whom was revealed the surpassing majesty of pure and undefiled religion.

He could associate, with a mocking satisfaction, with those who, assuming that name, content themselves in the midst of their luxurious dwellings with uttering a few pompous sentiments of cold morality, maintain a strict propriety of word and gesture, and, without ever curtailing even one of their superfluous pleasures, in the name of Christ, thank God that they are not as other men are. But when he came in contact with the religion of the days of old, when its enmity with the world was open and declared, when self-devotion and uncomplaining sufferings were its sure companions, when those who took up the Cross to follow the Man of Sorrows, through fire and blood, rested not except it crushed them beneath its weight,—then he felt himself bound, as it were, to take vengeance upon all such; and it seemed to him at that moment a task full of fierce delight, to hunt down that triumphant Christian as his prey; to murder that pure soul; to slay and destroy the peace he could never know.

Arabyn advanced and presented himself to Mr. Denham, who received him with an almost childish delight; for he was too thankful to enliven his miserable existence by any means.

And now Mr. Denham called to Ruth; and she, turning round, looked for the first time on that face of melancholy beauty, which was never more to pass from her memory—whose image was henceforward to stand between her and all other human beings—whose remembrance was to accompany her through the various stages of life, even to the threshold of eternity, and only pass from before her eyes with the light of day itself.

Mr. Denham eagerly inquired of Arabyn where he had been and what were his future plans. He answered, that he had been wandering for some time in different parts of the world, and now had no wish save to find some quiet resting-place, some peaceful solitude, where he might live unmolested for a time. With some curiosity, Mr. Denham asked the reason of such a wish; and the infidel replied that, owing to recent misfortunes, the details of which he could not endure to give, he had been plunged into a state of such profound despondency, that he felt anxious at least to retire where he should cast no shadow on the life of another, from the gloom of his own spirit.

Mr. Denham then anxiously proposed to him that he should take up his residence with them for some time to come; adding bitterly, that the solitude would be as complete as he could desire, and that there was no one there whose life he could make darker than it was already. After some apparent hesitation, Arabyn consented to remain with him, at least for the summer, unless any unforeseen event caused him to change his purpose. He then commenced talking on indifferent subjects, seeming unconsciously to cast over all he said the sombre hue of his own mournful feelings; till, when they retired for the night, Ruth Vincent, of whose presence he had seemed scarcely aware, felt herself saddened by a sort of vague conviction that it had never yet been given her to conceive the amount of suffering which one human being may endure.

All feelings of sadness, however, had passed entirely from her mind when, early the next morning, the sweet fresh breeze came rushing to meet her, over the green fields sparkling with dew, as she once more took her way to the church, with the light of the cloudless spring day all around her, and the sunshine of joy in her heart.

It was one of those bright and sunny days when instinctively we sympathize with rejoicing nature: and Ruth felt within her soul the rising of the imperious and prophetic hope of happiness which at such times assails us; being, in fact, but a pledge given to us by our immortal nature of immortal joys; but which we, yielding to the irresistible yearning that draws us to our mother earth, too often shape out into dreams of earthly bliss. And she yielded to-day to this alluring and deceitful pleasure (notwithstanding the constant effort she made to tear away her heart from the dust out of which it was formed). The future appeared to her brighter than ever it had done before; for she had been struck with the idea that the arrival of Arabyn might ultimately be the means of her release from the bondage in which she dwelt, as the sole companion of the selfish old man. It was possible that he might decide on remaining altogether with his uncle; and if he did so, and were in truth one of the brotherhood of faith, how gladly would she give into his stronger hands the difficult task of dragging back that blind bewildered soul from the brink of the terrible abyss! Then would she go forth among the friends and relations who loved her well; and to her should be given that joy, than which there is none of this earth more dear, even the hearing of her own name uttered by lips that lingered on the sound with tender accent, and a friendly arm should uphold her when wearied or in sorrow, and she should no more shiver and shrink in the chill of the stern loneliness from which her nature revolted.

These were gay dreams for her; and her step grew light, and her heart beat high, and gaily she laughed with the merry village children, that clung so fearlessly to her hand, and there was a smile on her lips like that of an innocent child that has never known care.

Most bright and buoyant are those hours, indeed, thus winged by an invisible hope, that sometimes pass over this mortal life like sunshine over a cloud. Surely, never did the saddest wanderer on earth fail at times to know their blessed influence, when the light on the green woods is faint to the light in the heart, and the song of the gay spring birds is unheard, because, from the realms of a radiant future sweet voices are calling to us with soft promises of friendship or sympathy, and the fond ties that bind us to our fellow-creatures gild every thought and gladden every dream. And yet, weep not, thou wearied mortal, from whom this brightness has departed, leaving but the sadness of remembered hope—weep not; for thou art saved from loving earth too much, to long for heaven the more. Yes; those short hours of deep, anticipated joy, are given us as the earnest of divinest hopes: but better they should pass—better that the cold breath of winter should dim the greenness of the valleys, and the chill of disappointment sweep, piercing and keen, through our breasts; for then we walk as strangers and pilgrims on the earth, waiting with earnest expectation for the consummation of our bliss, and gladly we lay down our heads in the grave, because it is the portal of that home of rest which we have learned to ask from this world no more. It is a bitter thing when life has been too bright; when its mortal ties have twined themselves too much round an immortal being; when we can look around on watchful eyes and loving smiles, in the happy home where we have dwelt so long, the object of care and of affection: yes, then it is a bitter thing to leave them all for the lone, cold grave. But to die when the course of gradual suffering has weaned our hearts from earth, pang after pang; joy after joy vanishing away, each day a hope the less, a wound the more; when the indifference of some, the falsehood of others, oblivion or absence, time or change, have left us lonely and desolate, unthought of and unloved; then, after the long struggle for a holy patience, the fierce battle for submission and faith, how gladly do we grasp the friendly hand of death when he comes unto us, and saluting us, says, "Peace be with you," after the manner of all Divine messengers!

But meanwhile, in fearless gladness, Ruth Vincent walked on with a gay smile and a light heart to meet the sharp arrow that even then was winged to pierce her breast with the keenest stroke of human sorrow. The first object which met her eyes on entering the church was the form of Arabyn, kneeling at a short distance from the seat she occupied; and never had she imagined a greater fervour of devotion than that displayed in the uplifted countenance of the infidel.

One less guileless than Ruth Vincent might have seen, in the uncovered face and studied grace of his attitude, rather the likeness of a beautiful statue kneeling on a tomb, as the actual presence of a penitent sinner, stammering forth, with bowed head and sinking heart, his confession of guilt: but she fell into the common error of all frank and unsuspecting minds; that of judging others by herself; and she went to her place with a feeling of deep thankfulness, convinced that Arabyn was all and more than she could have hoped to find the nephew of Mr. Denham; and that on his heart was written, "Holiness to the Lord," even as upon her own.

She left the church, after service, before he had moved, and went as usual to attend to the wants of the poor little children of the manufactory. When they left her she walked slowly through the churchyard, and perceived that Arabyn was lingering still among the graves. She went towards him, but he did not observe her, and as she stood for a moment unnoticed at his side, she looked for the first time attentively on his countenance.

As she gazed upon him, gradually her very heart seemed to die within her; for never could she have imagined an expression of such unutterable melancholy as that which cast its shadow over him. His face was calm, even beautifully serene, but to her it appeared to be only the calm of a settled despair, so deep was the mournful sadness of the eyes, and the fixed stillness of the lips, which seemed incapable even of forming a smile. Another might not have been so painfully impressed as was Ruth Vincent, by this evidence of the deep despondency to which her companion was a victim; but, as we have said, her whole soul seemed at all times to revolt against the sufferings of others, and it was utterly insupportable to her to see the misery she could not alleviate, whilst she would ever have made light of pain, sickness, or sorrow, so long as they fell only on herself.

Arabyn seemed so absorbed in thought, that she did not venture to speak to him, but passed slowly from the churchyard, unobserved, as she thought, by him. Throughout the whole day the expression of his face haunted her, and when he was present the quiet cheerfulness which usually never failed her seemed to her almost unfeeling. He spoke but little to her, and his manner was singularly reserved and retiring, but he devoted himself assiduously to his uncle.

Mr. Denham, though imperious and exacting as usual, seemed nevertheless highly pleased with his nephew: the variety and amusement which his presence afforded him, caused him actually to experience the novel sensation of a transitory fit of good humour; and there was a quiet firmness and dignity in Arabyn's manner which appeared to exercise a strange influence over him. He did not, however, allow the new-comer to interfere with any of his ordinary arrangements. He went out as usual to walk slowly and painfully for a few minutes on the gravel-walk, leaning as heavily as he could on Ruth

Vincent's arm, whilst she carefully and gently guided his feeble steps. In the evening he followed his invariable custom of going to sleep for several hours in his chair; and when Ruth had arranged his cushions, and made all her usual preparations for his comfort, she went quietly out, as she was accustomed to do. She saw that Arabyn was walking in the shrubbery; but she did not join him, for she had imagined that he had avoided her throughout the day, and she was besides so singularly humble, that she never supposed it possible that any one could wish for her society.

The dim quiet hours of the lengthened twilight were always devoted by Ruth Vincent to one particular duty which she had imposed upon herself, and which fully occupied her during the evening. Occasionally she was detained too long at home, as it had chanced the day before; but whenever she could escape from Mr. Denham in time, she invariably proceeded at once to the house of the only neighbours of her own rank in life with whom they were acquainted.

It was a fine old English manor-house, more remarkable for the comfort of its internal arrangements than for the beauty of the exterior. The grounds were extensive, tastefully laid out, and carefully kept: the garden was abundantly stocked, and the fruit well preserved. Terrific warnings of man-traps and spring-guns defaced the trees, figurative, no doubt, but at the same time highly expressive of the substantial reality of the strong measures taken against the village children or unwary beggars, if they ventured beyond the gate.

There is always something in the appearance of a place which indicates to a certain degree the character of the proprietor; and in this gentlemanlike and pleasant residence there was a solidity of comfort which told very eloquently that the inhabitants thereof had found their rest in this world.

Mr. and Mrs. Harcourt, to whom this well-regulated abode belonged, had for many years enjoyed the substantial respect and approbation of all who knew them. They were first cousins, and with that attention to propriety and prudence which they ever afterwards displayed, they had married in order to unite two estates which had always been in the family. They appeared to have inherited, by lineal descent, all those virtues which, in tombstone phraseology, had been accorded to their ancestors. On the family monument, held up by two triumphant-looking cherubim to the admiring gaze of the humble worshippers in the parish church, it was recorded that the gentlemen of the Harcourt race had ever been of good parts and affable manners, especially to be revered of succeeding generations for their parliamentary discourses; whilst the ladies had invariably been condescending to their inferiors, and remarkably attached to their children.

It was clear that Mr. and Mrs. Harcourt were pursuing a course of life which would infallibly entitle them to the full numerical list of those peculiar graces of the respectable dead. They were at once the most inveterate and the most unconscious of self-deceivers. They had always lived in an atmosphere of very decent and very moderate piety; and the outward observances and general rules of religion formed a conspicuous part of their manners and customs. Having deliberately accepted Christianity, they firmly believed that the whole system was embodied in their own lives; nothing doubting that their every action was directed by religious principles, and never dreaming of inquiring, during their long course of systematic self-indulgence, how it chanced that their duties should so invariably agree with their inclination.

This well-intentioned couple did, in fact, perform the part of godparents to their own souls, professing the faith and holding the vow of obedience with a conscientious exactitude, which, being altogether external from the inward spirit, could in no degree influence it. There were none of the feelings and effects of a devotedly religious life, which they did not believe themselves to share. Often, surrounded by every luxury, they talked complacently of their beautiful resignation to the will of Heaven in all things, and with family and friends around them, they would bid some child of sorrow mark how *they* never repined.

Sunday after Sunday they garrisoned with their household the fortified pew of which we have spoken; and, strange to say, they never failed to gather from the sermon some additional aliment to their mysterious self-satisfaction; for if it spoke of warnings, they looked back on their respectable lives, and rejoiced to think they had nothing to do with them; and if of promises, they felt, with an innocent humility, that these were their own.

With heroic constancy they endured prosperity, and often, drowsily reclining in their arm-chairs, they spoke with a heartfelt experience of the Christian conflict. Duly and at full length their names appeared in certain subscription lists; but they would be scrupulously careful never to encourage idleness and poverty (to them synonymous terms), and much—very much—they had of that charity which begins at home.

With all this, Mr. and Mrs. Harcourt were kind-hearted and hospitable in the extreme, but according to their own account it was all done on principle. On principle they mixed largely and at no small expense with the world, because they desired to show in cheerful society that their religion was not one of gloom: whilst they were careful to exclude from their acquaintance all but the wealthy and fortunate, because they believed it their duty to maintain their proper station in life.

Their children were like them. They had two daughters: one was in her own estimation a domestic martyr, a visionary state which she endured with the most conspicuous meekness, and which resulted solely from her inordinate vanity. She believed herself unappreciated, and not loved so much as her merits deserved —but who (let us put the question fairly) ever looked down honestly into the depths of their corrupt heart, and found therein any reason why they should be loved at all? Let us tear aside the veil of self-esteem, and see of what materials our virtues are composed, and we shall find that it is enough for our own deserts if we were permitted only to minister in patience and lowliness to our fellow-creatures, for whose sake the cross stood on Calvary, without so much as asking a return of our affections.

Her sister, who was handsome and accomplished, had adopted a line of conduct which is generally singularly successful with the world; she was extremely exclusive, silent, and reserved; she admitted very few to the privilege of her acquaintance, and none to her friendship; the habitual expression of her fine features was a graceful contempt. She seemed to consider herself extremely fortunate in having no duties whatever to perform towards those whom she removed so far from her by her cold dignity and most forbidding politeness. Whether they had any feelings which might be wounded by her unexpressed rejection of their intimacy, any sufferings which her sympathy might have relieved, any distress which her efforts might have removed; whether, amongst them there might not have been some whose inward holiness would have made their very presence a blessing to herself, was a matter apparently quite indifferent to her. Yet she was as scrupulous as her parents in fulfilling the outward claims of religion; carefully she went to that church, where the solemn admonitions concerning love to the brethren, rung for ever in her ears; and then she went home, entrenching herself in her cold, proud demeanour; and so passed the lilies of the field and the Lazarus at her gate.

In short, this whole family skated comfortably over the surface of life, never seeking to look down into the depths of the mysteries that lay beneath.

It was not to visit any of these that Ruth Vincent went every evening to the Manor House; although she was warmly welcomed by them all, both on account of the advantageous position which her large fortune gave her in the eyes of the world, and also because her manner—so gentle and courteous to the poorest, as well as the highest, endeared her inexpressibly even to those who knew her but slightly.

They were all assembled in the drawing-room, with a few of their friends, when she arrived this evening; but she soon disengaged herself from them, and passed into the recess formed by the large oriel window, where she knew she should find the object of her visit. Extended on a sofa, lay a deformed and sickly-looking young man, of some nineteen or twenty years of age. He was hopelessly and fearfully crippled, and had been so from his birth; but his face had none of that strange beauty which is a very general characteristic of persons so afflicted; his eyes were dim, his features sharp, and his face wan and wasted; a malformation of the neck and shoulders rendered it impossible for him to turn his head; and it was with difficulty that he could walk a few steps. Yet, though his appearance was in many respects painfully unpleasant, he was, beyond measure, lovely to look upon, for those who could appreciate him; for there was in that thin haggard face an expression of the most holy and humble resignation to an accumulation of this world's ill,—sickness, deformity, friendlessness, and poverty; whilst in those sunken eyes there dwelt the evidence of a spiritual purity, which was of a nature very rare on earth.

Edmund was an orphan, desolate and destitute; and it might almost have seemed strange that one so helpless and infirm should have been thus cast forlorn on the world; but, doubtless, because no earthly father could have looked with sufficient love on the poor deformed boy, he was reserved for the tender care of Him only Who carrieth the lambs in His bosom. He was a distant relation of Mr. Harcourt's, who had most unwillingly received him on the death of his father. They had intended, however, long since, to send him to some asylum, where they would have satisfied themselves with knowing that his bodily wants were attended to, without ever recollecting that he would be deprived of all those intellectual advantages from which he derived so much enjoyment.

But this determination had been overruled by Ruth

Vincent, whose character and position in the world had given her great influence in this house, at least. She felt a sympathy and an affection for this poor cripple, proportionable to his sufferings and trials, and she well knew that by this means she had rendered her own presence the one only joy which this world had for him. She therefore out of her own fortune settled upon him an income amply adequate to supply him with every comfort, on the express condition that he should remain in Mr. Harcourt's family as long as he lived; a period which his increasing weakness seemed to indicate would not be greatly prolonged. She also stipulated that he should never know from whom his little fortune came, and from that hour she endeavoured assiduously to counteract, by her own tenderness and unfailing kindness, the coldness and neglect of the Harcourt family.

Ruth gave him the dear name of brother, and she promised to be a loving sister to him even unto his life's end. Soon her sweet voice and her beaming smile became the music and the sunshine of his life; all the happiness which earth could give him was centered in her generous affection, and all that the tenderest sympathy could do she did for him; but there was a Care more precious than hers around him, and he possessed a full assurance of peace, which she would have laid her head in the dust to pray for.

This poor deformed boy was one of those beautiful instances of the power of the hope Divine to lighten the darkest existence, before which we can only bow in adoring gratitude. He had been a prisoner, like to him who of old lay sleeping between two soldiers, for he languished in the dungeon of that unsightly frame bound with the double chains of bodily deformity and mental misery, and when as to the blessed saint so to his soul did the angel of the Lord come down, and a light shined in the prison, and to his fettered spirit it was said, "Arise up quickly," then speedily the chains fell from his hands, and though he had been cast into the burning furnace of affliction, yet now he walked loose in the midst of the fire and had no hurt, for there walked with him One whose form was like to the Son of God.

Great was the measure of the faith which it was given to this son of misery to know—a faith strong and beautiful as that of a little child, most guileless and unquestioning; his mental powers were weak, his intellect of no high order, and yet to that patient, humble soul, the Divine Presence was revealed with a radiance and a power which many a noble-hearted Christian would have perished to obtain. *He* Who on earth went about doing good amongst the sick, the halt, the maimed, still visits them in secret even now, and to them He makes Himself known, as often in His Adorable Wisdom He sees not fit to manifest Himself to the more gifted in mind and talent, who lie low at His sacred feet, although He is not the less near that their dim eyes see Him not.

It was extraordinary to what a clearness of spiritual perception Edmund at last attained; he was by his infirmity an outcast from all the common affections and ties of life, an exile from earth and its joys, even while dwelling on it; there was nothing to weaken his soul or dull his sight from gazing on the glorious Beauty of the Unseen; those awful realities of truth which for us are obscured by the mists of earthly things, for him were strangely near and palpable.

The eternal and the temporal can never hold a place

together in the mind of one individual; according as we teach our soul to look upon them, the one will ever be a warm, vivid, and beloved reality, and the other a far-off shadowy vision. With Edmund it was the fleeting dream of life which was so vapour-like and unsubstantial, whilst eternity, with its unending future of unutterable bliss, was so true, so near to him, that his soul for ever floated as it were in an atmosphere of its own, far above the world and the things of it.

Ruth Vincent looked with wonder, and almost with awe, upon this innocent and happy faith. Edmund seemed to have little temptation to sin. The powers of the world to come had such a hold over him, that he appeared to live already in the future of the grave; he was for ever looking with a glad smile into the vacant air, as though he discerned the angels carrying away the souls of the faithful departed, and often he seemed to hear a voice saying to his spirit, "Lo, I come quickly," so that he was fully occupied in answering constantly his "Even so," with earnest and imploring tone.

Ruth wondered to see so little of a struggle in this calm spirit's following of its Lord, for in her experience the good fight was a great and terrible combat; it was to her such grievous misery to sin, and night after night in the sad retrospection of the day for ever gone, she shed those tears,—the bitterest that human beings can know!—the weeping of a soul for its stained purity. It seemed to her on looking round upon the earth, that even now the coming of the Son of Man might be expected, because already He shall find small faith upon it. We *imagine* we believe, but surely if we could but for one moment realize the actual meaning of those doctrines we profess, it could not be that we should go on living as we do. If a man really *felt* in his inmost soul that there is an eternity to-morrow, whose perfect bliss or perfect woe depends upon his work to-day, he could not go and spend the brief hours in plucking flowers by the way-side; or, if he really comprehended that it is possible for him even now to have a holy, mystical, but actual union with the High and Lofty One, it must needs be, that with unsparing anguish to himself, he would hew down whatever barriers arose before him.

Oh! when for one instant there comes, as come it will at times, the actual awful thought of the tremendous "for ever," rending aside the veil of the flesh, rushing in, like a flood on the overwhelmed soul, how does he turn with a sad scorn of himself from these creations of dust, the creatures of his love, to which he has so madly clung!

Edmund was gazing from the open window on the green lawn and pleasant woods where his powerless limbs had never carried him, when Ruth Vincent approached him; as he turned to meet her look of gentle kindness, a flush of the most rapturous enjoyment passed over his sickly countenance. The brightness which her daily visit cast over one hour of his long solitary day, was sufficient to give a lustre to all the rest, for his mind was perfectly capable of appreciating the purity and elevation of her character, and in conversation with her he enjoyed that intellectual gratification of which he was at all other times deprived.

Ruth sat down by his side, she saw that the pain he constantly suffered was more than usually acute this evening, and she spoke to him for a time soothingly and with hopeful accents of the cold and dreary path by which he was advancing to the unimagined rest, measuring its length and its darkness by the light and the glory of one moment in eternity, and reminding him how the faintest moan that ever mortal breathed has never been unheard by Him Who once looked up to heaven and *sighed deeply*, even although in the same moment that the faint human breath of sadness goes forth through the unfathomable ether towards His throne, some mighty world may be hurled past it, crashing down to its destruction.

The sound of Ruth's low voice, so full of deepest feeling, seemed to act like a charm on Edmund, he was too exhausted to talk much himself, but he laid his pale cheek down upon her hand, and sunk into the state of quiet repose which the mere sense of her presence seemed always to give him; for Heaven has willed that there should be for us a strange fascination in human sympathy, in order, doubtless, that when ofttimes we are deprived of it, we may turn the more thankfully to that which shall not fail us, when earth itself is swept from its place within the universe.

Ruth remained silent, that she might not disturb this needful rest, and her attention was speedily attracted by an animated conversation which was passing in the room around. All present seemed to be joining in it; but the chief speakers were Mrs. Harcourt and her nephew, Mr. Parker. This last-named gentleman was a person who rejoiced in a universal reputation of being a most excellent man; his conduct from his infancy upwards had been quite exemplary, his sentiments tremendously honourable, and his whole robust person seemed enveloped in an atmosphere of proper feeling and good principle; no one had ever found a word to say against him; at the very mention of his name his acquaintances elevated their hands and eyebrows with the most expressive tokens of approbation, and yet in their secret hearts they all disliked him most thoroughly. There were various reasons for this; first, Mr. Parker gave out that he always spoke exactly as he thought, and that frankness and plain dealing were a part of his character. There are many people who go on this system, but it is in fact merely taking out a special licence for unwarantable interference and ill-natured remarks.

Mr. Parker, however, went through the world very well with it, always telling people he did not doubt they thought him very rough and disagreeable, but that they would find out in the end that he was the best friend they had ever had; and really he bore such a character for rectitude and honesty, that no one dared to disbelieve him. Moreover, having apparently no sins of his own to burden him, Mr. Parker had established himself conscience-keeper-general to all his acquaintance, and liberally dispensed his reproofs, persuasion, and stern disapprobation to all around him. He loved to tell people, that if they did not take his advice they would infallibly be lost; and the worst of the matter was, that he would *then* be unable to help them, as he would be in heaven himself. Composedly as he was wont to make these and similar remarks, it was singular to see how perfectly incapable he was of enduring the smallest retaliation upon himself, for he was particularly tenacious of his dignity as an estimable right-thinking man, and a very slight blow fell heavily on the broad basis of his respectable vanity.

Mr. Parker's voice was loud in discussion, when Ruth paused to listen, and she perceived at once that he was vehemently combating the resolution which Mrs. Harcourt had just informed her daughters she had taken, of inviting Arabyn to accompany Ruth to her house whenever she came there in the evening. This decision seemed to be the result of some very private and subtle calculations of her own, as she had already questioned Ruth very closely respecting Mr. Denham's nephew; but these she did not make public, merely informing Mr. Parker that whenever she determined on any thing, he might be assured that she had her own reason for doing so, than which no statement could have been more true, for Mrs. Harcourt was not a person to act upon impulse. Vainly Mr. Parker informed her, with all the exaggeration which a few years had wrought, of the disgraceful circumstances connected with Arabyn's father, and enlarged on the extreme probability, amounting, in his opinion—owing to his extraordinary knowledge of human nature—to a certainty, that the son would, in all respects, prove himself an equally worthless character. This he conceived it his peculiar and painful duty to tell her; but Mrs. Harcourt was immovable. It was clear that some mysterious quality, designated by herself as firmness of character, was now enlisted on behalf of the criminal's son; and every word uttered by Mr. Parker only served to strengthen her purpose. She, however, appealed, with the most dignified and stern submission, to Mr. Harcourt, and demanded if he had any objection to her admitting whom she pleased into their house? He answered, that he could have none whatever; and requested her at all times to act exactly as it suited her convenience.

This gentleman habitually resigned himself to his wife's wishes on all minor points, not because he was indisposed to assert his authority, but simply because he was saved much annoyance by this quiescent line of conduct, and also because it afforded him a fair and legitimate excuse for charging Mrs. Harcourt with all the guilt of those little misfortunes which occasionally shadowed over, in the faintest degree, his sunny prosperity,—such as the failure of the crops, or the loss of a favourite horse. He found it comforting, when such events took place, to be able to exclaim, "So, Mrs. Harcourt, I trust all to you, and here is the result!" In this instance his approbation settled the matter; Arabyn was appointed an eligible acquaintance; Mrs. Harcourt triumphed; and Mr. Parker retired—defeated, but not abashed. One of the young ladies gave various manifestations of resignation under the trial she had undergone when her opinion was not asked; and the other looked forward with some satisfaction to the introduction of a new friend, with whom she could avoid all appearance of friendliness.

Ruth Vincent, however, reverted painfully to the conversation as she went home that evening. Not only did she commiserate profoundly him who, unoffending, was thus subjected to the rigour of systematic prejudice; but she had heard that which at all times was strangely repugnant to her—she had heard one man arrogate to himself the right to judge another. This always appeared to her one of the strangest anomalies in our strange world—that human beings, all alike frail, erring, and fallen, should so bitterly accuse one another of the very failings of which themselves are, or at least may be, guilty. It seems so grievous a thing that we, all partakers of the common suffering and the common death, should yet find such cruel judges and accusers amongst our very brethren. Who, in truth, should have pity on us, weak and sorely tempted as we are, if not those who share in the weakness and temptation? If we must needs set ourselves upon a height, and look around us to scrutinize and to condemn, as though we had no part in this world's guilt, let us endeavour in thought to separate ourselves from them so completely that we may look impartially, and see if there be nought in them which shall plead for mercy from us. Let us see them labouring under the great misery of their sin, and the great guilt that is often in the things whereby they suffer; hoping, till disappointment comes, then weeping for the vanished dream; loving, till change comes, then mourning for the lost affection; living, till death comes, then agonizing for the misspent existence, often so desolate, often so weary and forlorn, often so full of bitterness, which their own heart knoweth only. And when we have looked upon them thus, as a race apart from ourselves, surely we could not bear to let one harsh thought rise in our hearts against them, still less, by a single depreciating word or unkind look, to add to the burden of those already so heavy laden.

Men say that they must condemn the erring, that they may show their hatred for the error. But if they find it necessary to have some tangible substance whereon to lay the proof of their righteous love of virtue, let them seek it in their own persons, where they shall find it most abundantly. Let them drag out and freely confess the sins they have themselves committed, and then show forth their loyal indignation and just abhorrence in a deep repentance. But for the fellow-men, of whose hidden motives, whose secret trials, whose whole internal history, they know nothing, let them be left to the One that judgeth, and let us have but one feeling towards them,—even that of loving sympathy.

Ruth knew enough of that plausible reasoning by which many endeavour to convert their failings into virtues—like the false alchemy that seems to change dross into gold—to feel very certain that most of the party at Mrs. Harcourt's would consider it their bounden duty to treat Arabyn in a manner which it would greatly pain her to witness; for there is something fatally pleasant to human nature in the self-superiority which we feel when animadverting on the sins of our neighbours, whether personal or imputed. She could only trust that Arabyn would decline the acquaintance; and she thought it indeed most probable that he would do so, for he appeared too sad and dejected to find any pleasure in society.

CHAPTER X.

ARABYN CASTS THE VEIL OVER THE EYES OF
THE VICTIM.

ARABYN was again at church the next morning, apparently fervent and absorbed in devotion; but he hurried home immediately after service, and Ruth found him sitting with his uncle when she entered the breakfast-room. She started and trembled a little when Mr. Denham turned towards her, for his countenance was this morning singularly tempestuous. She saw at once that a storm of anger was preparing to burst from his lips, and that it was certainly not directed against Arabyn, who was advancing in the old man's favour with extraordinary rapidity. She herself was clearly the culprit; nor did he leave her long in ignorance of her crime.

The cause of his displeasure (which had been most ably fostered) was simply the want of proper attention which he declared she had shown to his guest the evening before, when she had gone to Mrs. Harcourt's without begging Arabyn to accompany her. Mr. Denham demanded if she were ashamed to introduce his nephew to her friends? and seeming to grow more irritable with the sound of his own voice, he loudly reproached her in the bitterest terms. Ruth ventured to say, timidly, that, as the Harcourt family were total strangers to Arabyn, she had imagined it would not be agreeable to him to visit them; but this seemed only to increase Mr. Denham's rage. Did she suppose that *his* acquaintances would not be charmed to receive his nephew? He triumphantly produced a note from Mrs. Harcourt to himself, the purport of which was her anxious desire to become acquainted with his relation, and her request that Arabyn would, without ceremony, come and visit her.

By this time Mr. Denham was convinced that he could not possibly feel so angry unless he had some good cause for it, and he therefore proceeded to enlarge on the subject in a manner most painful to Ruth. She made no attempt, however, to defend herself, but listened patiently and without murmuring.

Arabyn, meanwhile, had manifested the utmost distress at the harsh and unjust reproaches of Mr. Denham. He assured his uncle he had no desire to visit Mrs. Harcourt, but that, on the contrary, he wished to avoid all society; but the old man angrily refused to believe him, declaring it was only an attempt to excuse Ruth.

Finding there was no other means of pacifying him, Arabyn at last, with what seemed to Ruth a generous forgetfulness of self, promised to go to Mrs. Harcourt's that evening, and as often as Mr. Denham pleased, provided he would let the matter rest, and say no more on the subject. Mr. Denham agreed, and so it was arranged; but Ruth felt touched at the readiness with which Arabyn had given up his own wishes to save her from a little uneasiness. She could not guess the truth—that he had purposely raised this storm (though Mr. Denham was wholly unconscious of the subtle means by which he had suddenly found himself so angry), in order that his allaying it might be a merit in the eyes of Ruth herself, and also that he might seem to her forced into the society where he most desired to go, that he might gain a more accurate knowledge of all her proceedings.

The result of his successful manœuvre was, that Arabyn appeared in Mrs. Harcourt's drawing-room that same evening about half an hour after she had gone there herself. His reception was exactly what Ruth had anticipated; Mrs. Harcourt was ostentatiously benign, and her husband, acting on private instructions, peculiarly polite; so also was the suffering young lady, who seemed anxious to prove that she had found a companion in her invisible martyrdom. But the rest of the party, headed by Mr. Parker, like a body of troops under an able commander, performed all those ingenious evolutions by which a man is, in the politest manner, silently constituted a Paria of society.

It was one of the principles of Ruth Vincent's life invariably to choose out those who were despised and neglected of others, to be by her most honoured and cared for; and on this occasion she treated Arabyn with a quiet deference and respect which could not fail to be singularly soothing to him. He showed her quite distinctly that he had understood and appreciated her kindness, but he manifested at the same time a degree of dignified indifference to the rest of the party, which seemed to intimate that he was not much moved by their coldness; and gradually this very composure, as well as the great talent displayed in his conversation, created a considerable diversion in his favour. Arabyn appeared to be greatly interested in Edmund; he spoke much to him, with a manner almost as kind and gentle as that of Ruth herself; and soon a little circle had collected round the sofa where the deformed boy was laid, consisting of Ruth and Arabyn, Mr. Parker, and Mr. Grey, the clergyman of the parish.

There could not be a more conscientious or devoted parish priest than this really excellent man; but he was an instance of a character by no means rare, where innumerable good and estimable qualities are neutralized by one comparatively unimportant. Kind-hearted, generous, and self-denying, Mr. Grey had made one great mistake in his clerical career;—he had forgotten that cordiality is a Christian virtue. Whilst by the poor he was beloved and respected, amongst the richer portion of his flock—for whom he was surely equally responsible—he had entirely lost that influence which he might and ought so beneficially to have exercised, by a reserved coldness of manner, which, to many of the timid and sensitive, was positively repelling.

It is not enough for a clergyman to *permit* confidence on the part of his parishioners; he must *invite* it, and foster every disposition to intimate intercourse, in order that they may not shrink from turning to him in their hours of mental conflict or distress. The duty of courtesy, though so distinctly and positively enjoined upon us all, is often strangely overlooked by persons most conscientious in other respects. We know not how many opportunities we may lose of doing good, by consoling the afflicted, succouring the erring, and sustaining the weak, when we refrain from showing our brethren, be they whom and what they may, that warm kindliness of manner which is so attractive in this cold, selfish world.

On Edmund, the effect of Mr. Grey's habitual silence

and reserve had been most pernicious. The painful consciousness of his infirmities rendered him morbidly sensitive and timid; and though he knew that the clergyman was his appointed guide and adviser, he yet shrunk with such unconquerable distaste from his coldness and distant manner, that he positively refused all intercourse with him beyond that of ordinary civility, so that on Ruth Vincent alone devolved the task of consoling and supporting him. The conversation had naturally turned on higher subjects than the ordinary most unmeaning and frivolous topics of the day, for in the presence of Edmund the thoughts could take but one direction.

Ruth had been reading to him from the life of one of the early martyrs, and they began to talk of the marvellous change which had taken place since then, when the holy Christian faith went forth, like one clad in sackcloth and laden with chains, and had her dwelling in dungeons and caves of the earth, whilst now she wears such gorgeous robes and bears a crown upon her head, and sits in the palaces of kings.

Mr. Grey said he doubted not that the faith of many who now seemed most earnest and devoted, would have waxed cold indeed, had they lived in those days of fiery trial.

Ruth answered "that she had long been haunted with a terrible dread, amounting almost to a conviction, that the greater part of the Christian world were now labouring under a fearful mistake, respecting the nature of that service, that taking up of the Cross and following of the Crucified, without which we have no part in Him. There were certain words in Scripture, words intended to be taken literally and in their fullest extent, which would seem to imply that the sufferings wherewith we are to be made like unto Him, are very different from the trifling and easy amount of self-denial which we are apt to be contented with laying upon ourselves." She gave as an instance that awful announcement, that they "who are Christ's have crucified the flesh with the affections and lusts." If those are His who have done so, none are His who have not. We know what is the nature of crucifixion ; it is the most inconceivable torture which the human body can endure. Was there any thing, she asked, in the suffering to which any one of us subjected themselves for His sake, which could be thought at all equivalent to the extreme agony intimated in that term?

Ruth spoke forcibly, for it was a subject on which she felt most deeply, and as she concluded Mr. Grey let his head fall on his hand, and sighed heavily.

Mr. Parker, who had looked exceedingly uncomfortable while she was speaking, now coughed once or twice to attract attention, and prepared to answer: he informed Ruth, that in his opinion these over-strained and absurdly-exalted ideas were quite out of place in the present day, persecution had ceased, and the necessity for any violent suffering had altogether passed away; a man's sphere of duty now was in his own home, he might almost say in his own person; he would also take the liberty of remonstrating with her against any such sweeping condemnations as that in which she had just indulged ; it was, he must tell her frankly, quite unjustifiable on her part, considering how many pious and sincere Christians she could find in her own small circle of acquaintance, and he must caution her to recollect, that it was precisely those persons who said the least about it, who were in actual fact possessed of the greatest amount of true religion, honest, heartfelt piety, and genuine self-denial.

Mr. Parker concluded by assuming that peculiar look of most modest vanity, which an individual seems unconsciously to wear when covertly making mention of his own merits; but if that unfortunate gentleman were in fact alluding to himself in the latter part of his speech, he had but succeeded in proving most clearly on his own principles, that he could not possibly be in possession of any one of those qualities, whose existence was to be proved by the silence respecting them of their possessor, for no one could more assiduously or devotedly talk of himself and his merits, than did Mr. Parker.

There was a pause; and then Arabyn took up the subject in answer to Ruth, as though quite unaware that Mr. Parker had been speaking. In a voice low and sweet, with the most beautiful language and the most startling eloquence, he drew a picture of what the life of a true and devoted Christian ought to be; he spoke of what the holy burden of the daily Cross was in truth, with a thrilling power that pierced the very hearts of his hearers, and filled them with the most bitter and painful sense of their own lax and unworthy service. Seemingly quite unconsciously, Arabyn displayed an intensity of feeling and a depth of experience, which carried to the minds of all present the complete conviction, that he was himself one who had attained to a most unusual excellence in the difficult and sacred course of which he spoke, but who, thirsting after an immaculate holiness with that thirst never satisfied on earth, still yearned for more and more of the noble devotedness to which he had already so largely attained.

So extraordinary and so subtle was the eloquence of

the infidel, that before he concluded he had succeeded in establishing this belief in the mind of Ruth Vincent, with a strength which he knew would not easily be overcome. This was the aim he had in view; but he was well pleased to see that the others shared entirely in the reverence and admiration which she could not but feel for him; and even Mr. Parker, who with all his failings had many redeeming qualities, was moved to express his approbation, tacitly to withdraw all his former prophetic declamations respecting Arabyn, and openly to declare that he considered his acquaintance a decided privilege.

Arabyn received this public testimony politely, but evidently with some little repugnance; he immediately rose and went to converse with Mr. Harcourt, followed by Mr. Parker, who had a vision passing through his mind of a meritorious friendship felt by himself for this estimable man. Mr. Grey went home, innocently wondering that Arabyn had not taken holy orders, when he could preach so well in private; and Ruth remained in deep thought at the side of Edmund.

The only remark which Edmund had made at the close of Arabyn's striking burst of eloquence, was one which had appeared to her rather singular; he had been intently watching the infidel while he spoke, and when he had risen he remarked in a low voice, "It is a strange countenance;" he now seemed a good deal agitated, once or twice he attempted to speak, and then paused.

Ruth asked him soothingly if any thing distressed him; for a few minutes he did not answer, then suddenly grasping her hand he said, there was something he had long wished to say to her, and he felt that he must say it to-night ; but she must come close to him, for none must hear it but herself. Ruth knelt down beside him and raised his heavy head on her arm, for he breathed painfully, and seemed greatly oppressed ; gently she laid her cool hand on his burning forehead, and encouraged him to tell her all he felt.

Still Edmund hesitated, then seizing her hand with a feverish energy he suddenly exclaimed, that he had a request, a prayer, to make to her, which he implored her not to refuse ;—he wished her to give him her promise that she would be with him when he died.

Ruth started, and hurriedly asked if he felt worse.

"Yes," he said, "I am worse to-night, I am dying faster than you think ; but this is a thought which has weighed upon me for many months, and I never dared to utter it because it seemed to me so selfish; but to-night I feel that I can have no peace till you have promised me my last, my only earthly wish. Dear Ruth, listen to me," he continued imploringly, "do not look sad when I talk of dying soon, you well know how bright, how glorious, is for me that grave which is the portal of my home; I have had little part in this world, I have sought to have none; but I have been blest beyond what words could never express, in the sure promise of that which is to come ; I have not missed the human ties, the sweet affections, for whose loss men weep so sorely, because of the close links that have knit me to the angel brotherhood above, *they* have been with me when none knew of it. I have often fancied I heard their voices on the breeze, and felt their soft wings fan my face ; often have I seen them in my dreams, in all their holiness and purity, whispering to me to have a little patience, and soon I shall be with them.

"Ruth, my gentle sister, my only earthly friend, I have loved you more than all the world beside, but *less* than the least of these bright seraphim in heaven; therefore rejoice with me when I go hence, sing hallelujahs over my dead body; but it is for this that I must have you with me, you whose affection has been the sunshine of my world below, must be ready there to consign me to the care of those whose love shall brighten my eternity, from the arms of my earthly sister the angel brethren must take me; with the echo of your last blessing lingering in my ears, let me hear the first sweet words of their welcome. Oh! Ruth, promise that your hand shall close my eyes. I feel as though all that is left in me of human affection had gathered itself into one deep wish, that the light of human love might be around me in that dark hour, when this mortal is struggling to put on immortality; all the hopes and dreams and desires for earthly bliss, which men stretch over a long course of years, for me are centered in this one longing, that the last of human touch for me may be the warm grasp of your kind hand, the last look from mortal eyes as mine are closing, be your own sweet pitying gaze."

"Dear Edmund," said Ruth, struggling with the emotion which his words had caused her, "can you doubt that I will be with you if possible, I have never forgotten or neglected you in life, I will not surely in your dying hour."

"But you must promise more," said Edmund earnestly, "you must promise that wherever you are you will try to come to me, that you will count it a duty, a sacred duty, that nothing but the most unavoidable circumstances shall keep you from me."

OVER THE EYES OF THE VICTIM. 215

"I do promise," said Ruth; "the most absolute impossibility shall alone prevent me if I am myself alive."

Edmund thanked her by a look of eloquent gratitude, and then sunk back on the cushions quite exhausted, and Ruth soon after left him and returned home.

Every word of the above conversation had been heard by Arabyn; he had that faculty, peculiar to some persons, of being able to hear distinctly what was passing in another part of the room, even whilst to all appearance listening to the person with whom he was conversing; every word had been heard and carefully noted, for nothing was unimportant now which concerned Ruth, and there was much in the promise she had just made which was highly displeasing to him.

CHAPTER XI.

THE VICTIM BLINDED, FOLLOWS ON THE PATH WHERE ARABYN LEADS.

As Ruth left the churchyard the next morning after service, she perceived that Arabyn was still lingering among the graves apparently in deep thought—he turned towards her as she approached, but he seemed so absorbed in his reflections that his words were but an echo from his thoughts as stretching out his hand over the narrow dwellings of the dead, he murmured sadly, "They rest!" Ruth was surprised and yet touched by his solemn mournful tone.

"Doubtless there is a rest," she answered, unconsciously applying to the word a very different meaning to that which he had given, "assuredly there remaineth a rest."

"From which a life-time divides us," said Arabyn with a faint sad smile.

"And that life, what is it?" continued Ruth,—"a shadow, a vapour, a dream."

"Most true," said the low voice of the hypocrite; "but that shadow may be so cold and black, that it may chill and darken even an immortal soul; that vapour can send up a pestilential breath that blights with unseen poison, and in that dream so torturing, restless, and yet implacable in its decrees, the man may be persecuted with misery, driven to and fro by buffeting winds, from pang to pang, till he is hunted down by death, and entrapped into his horrible snare, which is the grave; and as in all visions of midnight slumber there are most strange deceptions and unexpected changes, so in this dream he labours to attain some bright and sunny spot that allures him to its verdant pastures, and when with pain and toil he has struggled to come near, it is transformed into a howling wilderness; and fair shapes rise around him with syren voice and tender smile, and when he flies to them for comfort or compassion, they change into taunting fiends that mock him in his agony."

"Yet even if these things be," said Ruth, "the life is not the less brief for him, even if the wisdom of Love have ordained that the angel of mercy should walk by his side clad in mourning garments, offering to his lips, when parched, only the bitter draught of human sorrow, still the distance he must tread shall speedily be accomplished, and from beneath the sable robes the angel shall spread out most radiant wings, and bear him away where streams of living waters shall replace the cup of misery." As she spoke they turned from the churchyard and proceeded together through the village.

"You say the life is brief," continued Arabyn, "and it may be so by the common rate of computation, but rest assured that the soul holds no account with time; she reckons by suffering alone; by the dull heavy beating of the heart in despondency, she measures out years in a day; in the one sharp pang of a moment's duration, which a word or a look may cause, can be concentrated the anguish of months; our life is in fact twofold, as the poet well expressed it; there is the outward mechanical, almost involuntary existence, influenced entirely by circumstances, and coloured by the events of each passing moment; and there is the hidden inward life of thought, sentiment, and idea, the under-current as it were, that flows on silent and unseen, bearing the spirit on its deep waters. Notwithstanding the mysterious yearning of human nature for human sympathy, we dwell each one of us in a world of our own, utterly distinct and apart from that in whose outward pageant we must all bear a part as members of society. We walk among our fellow-creatures with smiling lips and weeping eyes, according as the shadows of sorrow, or the sunshine of hope, seem to be upon us; but who amongst those who surround us, has the most remote idea of all that the invisible soul is in fact doing and suffering in that vast wilderness of thought, wherein she walks alone? Oh! the dark tide of passion, hope and joy, anguish and despair, that sweep over us unknown to others, while in outward aspect we are smiling and serene! and in that inner world we reckon not by years,—I am competent to judge," he added, with the most melancholy smile, "for to me centuries of misery have been meted out."

"But were we true to ourselves," said Ruth Vincent very gently, "and to our most noble hope, no human grief could ever have the power to lengthen to our souls one of those days which are our stepping-stones to eternity. It is because we are so weak (and of this weakness I can speak with bitter knowledge), that we do not overcome the strong power of the clay, the inborn sympathy which binds us to this earth, and darkens even the light of reason, causing us in youth to place therein all our hopes, our dreams, our energy, and still in riper years to cling to it, in face of our own dark experience. Even whilst our understanding acknowledges the glory and excellence of all that revelation has taught us, we yearn for the mortal tie, made to be broken; for the mortal joys, given to be taken away: even while despising earth, we cling to it; while adoring heaven, we turn from it. And for these things' sake we should suffer ages of remorse indeed; but as for human suffering—oh! if the radiance of a Light Divine be in the heaven above us, let us not stoop to count the thorns that pierce our feet as we walk on upon our earthly road."

"Your words are invigorating to my soul, as a draught of pure water to a fainting man," said Arabyn; "and truly this firm and noble courage is only what is due to our immortality; but the mind too often sinks below itself when left, alone and uncheered, to wrestle with misery."

Ruth turned her eyes with a look of the profoundest compassion on the infidel.

"I cannot admit that life is so dismal as you would represent it," she continued, trying to speak more cheerfully: "surely, though many a needful pang is sent, though we are often made to walk over the grave of a buried hope, in order to draw us a step nearer heaven, yet earth is full of bright and beautiful things, and there are many sunny days for the saddest here, many holy and innocent joys for all. Oh, look there! even before us now is an endless source of pleasure; look at that glorious nature—a Father's work; and the power to enjoy it which we possess—a Father's gift. Think of all the gay beauty that is preparing to gladden our eyes when the summer comes, the merry summer time, rich in those long glad days when the sunshine wantons with the green woods and sparkling streams, when the mornings are so radiant and fresh, the evenings so calm and holy, and man, full of faith in the joys to come, sees the whole earth sympathizing with him!"

"The merry summer time!" said Arabyn; "alas! there is nothing, perhaps, more sad than this season of the year to those from whose own soul the inward sunshine has departed; the weary and the broken-hearted; the neglected and forgotten; the disappointed and despised; those who are draining the cup of life without a hope to sweeten the draught—who are treading the painful path without an arm to sustain them—how dreary to them is the merry summer time! They are outcasts, as it were, from their own race; and when they turn for sympathy to nature, she has donned her gayest smiles, and is mocking their wretchedness. How can they bear the sweet songs of the birds, when they may never more hear the music of the voice they love? how can they look upon a clear and smiling sky, when their own path is through eternal clouds? must they not turn mournfully from the glowing sunbeams, which cannot warm the sepulchral coldness of their heart, now but the urn where lie the ashes of departed joys? Perhaps beneath the green breast of that smiling earth is laid the mouldering form they still adore; and shall they not shrink with bitter hate from the flowers which have sprung from the dust of those they loved? And is not the very air redolent with recollections, speaking to them of summer days like these, which were brightened by a happiness long perished, and of those who shared the sunny hours with them, and now lost, changed, or perhaps, unmasked in all their cold hypocrisy, have fled from their arms for ever, and left them to the winter of their own soul?"

Arabyn paused, and then said in a yet lower tone, "I pray that you may never know what it is to shudder at thought of the merry summer time."

Ruth felt chilled and saddened by the words of the infidel to a degree which rendered her incapable of finding an immediate answer. So hopeless a despondency was quite contrary to the manner in which she conceived that suffering should be accepted by a follower of the Sufferer Divine; yet she was unable to divest herself of the idea that Arabyn was far more deeply versed than herself in the wisdom of the eternal hope.

He seemed to read her thoughts, for he continued, in a tone less despairing,—

"I must endeavour to forego this habit of viewing all things through the sable veil which sorrow has, as it were, placed between my soul and this fair world. Assuredly I have no reason to complain, for we know that when the earth is dark and in mourning for the death of the day, it is then that the stars in heaven shine brightest."

"Yes," exclaimed Ruth, turning to him with a joyous smile, "and these glorious stars are in fact ever present with us; it is only because the earthly sunshine dazzles our eyes too much by day that we see them not."

"Then let me thank Heaven that it is so long since a sunbeam has touched my heart," said Arabyn.

Ruth would have answered, and told him how the Incomprehensible Pity never leaves even this world altogether dark too long; how, ever sooner or later, some sweet ray of earth's permitted joys comes stealing forth from the heavy clouds, to strengthen the sinking spirit,—but they had reached the house.

Arabyn stood aside to let her enter first; and as she passed he caught the expression of her face, and a wild smile of triumph lit up his own. He followed her quickly into the dwelling, which was hers, and had become his; and the door closed on the deceived and the deceiver.

CHAPTER XII.

THE FIRST ATTEMPT OF ARABYN TO SERVE THE POWER OF EVIL IS RENDERED ABORTIVE BY RAYMOND.

RAYMOND left Constantinople the day following the departure of his destined antagonist, but it was some weeks before he could trace out the course Arabyn had taken. His pursuit, however, was at last successful, and he discovered him at Trieste.

The Christian was now quite aware that the power which the antagonist principles of good and evil can possess in the person of individuals, must henceforward, as far as regarded Arabyn and himself, be developed in action, and no longer merely in words. He had readily perceived in the infidel that imperious activity of mind of which we have spoken, and he doubted not that he was even now engaged in carving out the tortuous path by which he was to attain the uncontrolled gratification of his independent will; and Raymond shuddered as he thought how many human victims must fill up the chasms in that terrible career, how every step of the hypocrite would be tracked, if not in blood, at least in tears. These thoughts nerved him with strength and perseverance to enter on his resolute opposition, bringing with him to counteract the superior advantages and singular fascination of the infidel, a most holy self-devotion and an invincible rectitude.

Raymond did not know that Arabyn was at Trieste

when he arrived at that bright Italian city, that lies surrounded by its circle of vine-clad hills, like a jewel well set. He believed, from the information he had obtained, that he should find him at Verona, where his young sister resided; and designed proceeding thither himself next day, had he not met him that same evening as he was walking along the road leading to the Boschetto, which is the name given by the gay Triestines to their public promenade.

Raymond had paused under the shade of a large tree, from whence could be obtained an extensive and beautiful view, when suddenly the infidel was sent across his path. He recognized the remarkable figure of his opponent at a considerable distance, but it was so dark that he was himself unperceived by Arabyn, who came and stood directly before him without observing him.

Raymond saw that he was greatly changed since they had met at Constantinople: his renewed energy of mind had restored his vigour of body; he seemed now in all the strength and beauty of his life's best days. His countenance was full of animation, his voice clear and distinct, and singularly melodious: for Arabyn was not alone; he was talking with impassioned eloquence to a young man who leant on his arm.

Raymond had, in a remarkable degree, the faculty, which some possess, of gaining an intuitive perception of a person's character by the first glance at their countenance; and he bent his searching gaze eagerly on the companion of the infidel, nothing doubting that he beheld in him a destined victim; for he was well assured that Arabyn would not bestow a single moment on any who were not to be instruments in his strange undertaking.

DEFEATS ARABYN.

The stranger was evidently an Englishman, and his appearance was very prepossessing; he had a fine face, with a frank, open expression, though without the evidence of any very great talent; but there was a certain indecision in the lines of the mouth, and a restlessness in the eye, which convinced Raymond that he would be most easily influenced by others; and that his character, from being vacillating, was in fact weak. On scrutinizing him more closely, however, he saw that the expression actually on his countenance at that moment could by no means be habitual to it. He was haggard and careworn to the last degree, and was evidently suffering from intense anxiety of mind. He listened with the most absorbed attention to all that Arabyn was saying, and seemed to feel quite a frantic eagerness to catch every word.

Arabyn, meanwhile, whose eloquence was at all times most remarkable, was clearly exerting his whole powers, as, with his eye fixed on the listener, he appeared to vary his arguments according to the changes on his countenance. They were so close to Raymond, that he could hear every word they uttered; nor did the infidel appear to wish that their conversation should be secret, as many others were standing near; but with what feelings the Christian listened may be imagined, when he heard Arabyn, with an ability, a power, a talent, far exceeding even what he expected from him, carefully instructing his companion in the most seductive doctrines of a profound scepticism!

With the most subtle arguments, the most beautiful language, and poetic imagery, he advocated the false, unholy creed, while, with the fiercest sarcasm, the boldest daring, and a fearful cunning, he assailed the Christian faith. And he who listened to him,—that pale, remorseful-looking young man,—seemed to long and pine to find truth in these startling words; he brought forward a few weak, unsound arguments against the doctrines of the infidel, which he evidently passionately desired to hear refuted; and Raymond could plainly see that something lay brooding on his heart, which made it for him a very necessity to disbelieve.

Arabyn had paused, almost unconsciously, from the earnestness with which he was talking; and after a few minutes they walked on, and were lost in the crowd.

To Raymond, it seemed as though the infidel and his victim had thus been driven past him, in order that it might be clearly shown him what was the duty and the work prepared for him; and then he was left, as we ever are and ought to be, to refuse or accept the burden, according as he had the heart and the courage for it. He turned at once, and followed them; they entered the immense hotel which stands by the sea-shore, and where he himself had apartments; and he immediately went to his own room, to decide on his future movements.

Raymond's first care was to send for the *commissionaire* of the hotel, in order to obtain what information he could respecting his two countrymen. That Arabyn had some deep purpose in thus undermining the principles of his young companion was very certain, and Raymond hoped to be able to penetrate it, in hearing some account of their late proceedings; in this, however, he was disappointed. The *commissionaire*, quick-sighted and clever, as such functionaries generally are, could give him many details concerning Arabyn and his companion, but they were such as to astonish Raymond considerably, and render him quite incapable of fathoming the secret motives of the infidel.

He found that Arabyn had been at Trieste some weeks, and he had come accompanied by the young Englishman, whose name was Stanley. He had apparently acquired the greatest influence over this young man; they were always together, and had for some time past been almost constantly night and day in the gambling-houses.

This Raymond would readily have understood, as it was natural to suppose that wealth, lawfully or unlawfully acquired, would be Arabyn's first object; but, to his surprise, he heard that he himself never touched a card, and that Stanley was altogether without fortune. Still, the *commissionaire* could vouch for the fact that he encouraged and urged the young Englishman to play; and the result had been that the latter had contracted enormous debts, which it seemed wholly impossible he should acquit. These had, however, all been bought up by a certain Corfiote merchant, named Vellio, well-known in Trieste as the greatest *birbante* which even the Ionian Islands could produce; and whose fortune had been chiefly made by transactions of that nature. Stanley was therefore altogether in his power; and should he prove, as the *commissionaire* fully expected, finally unable to pay him, he would not be the first whom Vellio had, for a similar inability, consigned to a prison for life.

Having heard these particulars, Raymond directed the *commissionaire* to ascertain from Vellio the exact amount of the claim he possessed on Stanley, of which it appeared he publicly boasted, and was about to dismiss him,—when the Italian, suddenly drawing him to the window, pointed out to him the figure of Arabyn, in earnest conversation with the merchant himself. They turned down a dark and narrow street, and appeared anxious to avoid observation; and Raymond became more and more convinced that some most iniquitous scheme was in progress against the unhappy young man he had seen.

The *commissionaire* then left him, assuring him that next day he could, without difficulty, obtain from Vellio the information he desired; and Raymond, feeling that he could do no more that night, went out on the balcony to enjoy the soft evening air. This was the hour of amusement for the Triestines, and the wide streets were filled with merry groups, whilst sounds of music were heard in all directions, but principally from the countless boats that glided over the Adriatic, whose waters looked so blue and sparkling, as the moonbeams glittered on the foam of its dancing waves.

It was a gay sight, but Raymond saw it not, nor did he hear the melodious sounds. That is a strange faculty which we possess, of being present in soul in a scene totally different from that in which the mortal body moves. The fair city and its joyous revellers were before him; the blue Adriatic heaved and sparkled at his feet; but, *in spirit*, he was slowly passing through a desert, in whose vastness solitude seemed to dilate: distinctly he heard the hollow rush of the wind through the vacant realms of the unresisting air, and overhead great stars were flashing with extraordinary brightness; but his eyes were earthward turned; he moved on till he stood by a small heap of sand, which the strength of the fierce simoom had nearly levelled with the ground; then a bitter cry burst from his lips,—he bowed himself, and fell prostrate; then the grave opened, and a form arose from it, pale and pure, calm, as no living mortal ever was; and she extended to him her arms, and looked upon him with eyes full of mournful love; and with her wan hand she pointed upward, and detaching herself from earth, rose slowly through the air; but he, clinging to her, rose also, and so they ascended together to the heaven above.

And nightly thus, through the desert, the spirit of Raymond passed; and nightly the grave opened, by which he cast himself down bitterly mourning; and the form arose, which had been too much beloved, and turned upon him eyes of sorrowful tenderness, and ascended upward, and he followed after: therefore, surely, it was a blessed thing for him that she no longer stood a living treasure by his side,—with her hand clasped in his, and her warm heart beating at the sound of his voice, and her quiet look, telling all that was too deeply felt to be expressed in words!

Raymond acknowledged that it was, and gave thanks for his great misery, even while the deep sobs shook his breast.

The next morning, almost the first thing that met the eyes of Raymond was the same ominous sight which had filled him with apprehension the night before. Arabyn stood at a corner of the street, in close conversation with Vellio, the merchant. Even from that distance he could perceive that there was an expression of great satisfaction on the countenances of both. They seemed perfectly to understand one another; but Raymond did not stay to watch them; he went down at once to the public room, where he hoped to find Stanley, as it was the custom for all the inmates of the hotel to breakfast there together. In this he was not disappointed; the young Englishman was walking to and fro through the long room in a most restless and agitated manner. He was alone; and when Raymond entered he looked round, as though well pleased to be relieved from his solitude. It is certainly very rarely that an Englishman addresses a stranger, but Stanley at once entered into conversation with the new-comer, seeming very glad to have a companion. Raymond met his advances with the greatest cordiality, and exerted himself to interest and amuse him. Fortunately they soon found they had many mutual acquaintances, and this preserved them from the restraint they would have felt had they been total strangers. No one interrupted them, and they remained together some time.

Unhappy and agitated as Stanley evidently was, he was insensibly led away by the peculiar charm of Raymond's conversation. Its chief characteristic was its perfect freedom from conventional insipidity and established fallacies. Every subject on which he talked was brought at once to its proper level, and analyzed with a degree of energetic truth which admitted of no compromise. He never accommodated himself to received opinions, being perfectly aware with what high and noble names society has dignified many of its own unsound and hollow principles. No man could more warmly appreciate whatever was intrinsically good; but none could more quickly detect, and more ably uncloak, the whitewashed evil.

Raymond had that most valuable faculty, the power of discerning between right and wrong, without which, if a man goes forth into this temporizing, inconsistent world, his reason must become bewildered and his judgment perverted. He chose to see things as they were, and not as he was expected to see them, in quiet defiance of a world's opinion. He felt a profound contempt, and spoke with a stern reprobation, of the hero, worshipped as a demi-god, who had marched to fame over the bodies of his fellow-creatures, and worn an imperial crown whose lustre was obliterated by the tears of the widowed and fatherless. He refused his admiration to the poet who, from vanity, had abused and perverted an intellect by whose powers he might have won many a soul from perdition. Raymond would give no approbation to the wily statesman that, like a spider weaving his subtle web, from a corner of the realm directed his plots and counter-plots; to the orator, fattening on his own praises; to the rich man, to whom public acclamation and self-endowment had awarded the kingdom of heaven; to the wholesale patriotism that made a virtue of war, and required to be gratified by individual murder; to the success of high-born men in those trades and callings which they seem to think most suited to their rank, such as political intrigue or diplomacy, whose basis and primary principle is falsehood; for Raymond, in looking on all these things, had ever before him the image of a little child set in the midst by a Hand Divine.

He conversed for a considerable time with Stanley; and the young man, though often startled by the bold and uncompromising truths which were uttered by the Christian, evidently took the greatest pleasure in listening to him. Suddenly, however, Raymond observed that he became deadly pale, and that his eyes turned with a terrified expression to the door. He looked round, and saw that Vellio, the Corfiote, had entered.

Raymond instantly rose, and taking up a book, went over to the other side of the room, which was sufficiently vast to make it impossible that he should hear what they said to one another. He could perceive, however, by their gestures that Vellio was talking in the most peremptory manner, whilst Stanley feebly and incoherently attempted to pacify him. Just as the Corfiote seemed to have assumed almost a threatening manner, the door softly opened, and Arabyn glided in between them. He did not perceive Raymond, and Stanley turned to him with a look of inexpressible entreaty. Vellio greeted him, as though they had met for the first time that day. Arabyn asked a few questions of Stanley, and then, turning to the merchant, appeared to talk persuasively and earnestly with him for some time. With the greatest difficulty he evidently induced him to relent, for the Corfiote finally took his leave of them, only saying, as he passed Stanley, in a tone so authoritative that Raymond could hear his words, "Remember, then, one week, but not a day beyond it!" As he left the room, the young Englishman sunk down on a chair, and buried his face in his hands. Arabyn, stooping over him, spoke to him soothingly for a little time, and at last, taking him by the arm, they left the room together.

Raymond felt thankful that he had escaped the observation of the infidel, and sent immediately for the *commissionaire*. This active person arrived, already furnished with the desired information; and Raymond found that the sum by which Stanley was in the Corfiote's power was so great, that it would require the sacrifice of nearly half his own fortune before he could attempt to free him from the claim. The Christian nevertheless proceeded at once to his banker's, and made such arrangements as should place this sum at his command on a moment's notice.

It was late before he returned to the hotel, and just as he was approaching the gateway he perceived Arabyn and Stanley, arm in arm, pass through it, and walk down the street together. Turning instantly, he followed them at a little distance. The young Englishman seemed passive in the hands of his companion; his cheek was flushed and his step uncertain. The infidel meanwhile was perfectly calm and collected; his eye piercingly bright, and his features composed to a mild and soft expression. He led Stanley wherever he would, who seemed too utterly prostrated in mind to care whither he went.

Arabyn conducted him through various streets, till they reached a building brilliantly illuminated, from whence the sound of music was proceeding—it was the Opera-house. They entered, and Raymond followed: he sat down near them in the *plateo*.

It would have been difficult to have conceived a scene of greater enchantment than that in which they found themselves—not so much from the stage effect as from the brilliant appearance of the audience. Nothing can be more gay and attractive than an Italian crowd, composed of the best society, pleasantly occupied in enjoying their favourite amusement; there is so much beauty, and grace, and animation; such vivacity, such melodious voices and impassioned words, such eloquence in every face, and brightness in every smile; such a thorough enjoyment of life and its luxuries: besides all this, the music was admirable, the *prima donna* a first-rate actress, and her voice sweet and thrilling.

Harmony has a strange power over the human mind;

there are few of the minor gifts of nature which may so effectually serve the cause of holiness and purity, as a voice full of touching melody, when its powers are given to swell the high and solemn strains that draw the soul to realms where eternal music breathes through undefiled ether: but few certainly of the powers given to man have been used for more ignoble and debasing purposes.

To-night those bursts of song, so wild and beautiful, were calculated, in every word to which they gave utterance, only to enhance and magnify the joys of this world, and to raise a tumult of earthly passion in the breasts of those who heard them. Just when the effect was most powerful, and the whole audience seemed to have given themselves up to a delirious excitement—when even Stanley, forgetful of all but the charm of the moment, luxuriated in the life and the youth that promised him both the capacity and the time for much enjoyment, Arabyn seized him by the arm, and whispered, "You promised to let me show you life in its various aspects to-night: this is a scene from the life of pleasure; come now, and we will go elsewhere."

Stanley seemed unwilling to move, but the infidel possessed an influence over him which he could not resist,—he rose. Raymond did the same; and all three left the gay theatre, and went out into the dark street; the wavering soul moving on unconsciously between the evil and the good.

Arabyn led them out of the town altogether; the illuminated streets and the noise of human voices were soon left far behind them. The night was chill and dark; fierce gusts of wind came sweeping up from the Adriatic, and went on, moaning and howling, towards the distant plains of Styria. A steep ascent, rough and difficult, strewn purposely with the sharpest stones, led them up to a gloomy and isolated building.

Arabyn drew back the curtain that hung before the door, and it fell again behind them. As they entered, a cold rush of damp air, as though from a sepulchre, caused a shiver to pass through the frames of each. A single taper, burning faint and dim, scarce penetrated the deep shadows, and disclosed long vaulted aisles, and black recesses, and a rough stone pavement, on which lay prostrate a number of shrouded figures, like so many corpses.

It was a church opened for midnight service; and the congregation consisted of a company of penitents, in their strange black dresses and hoods, which give them so unearthly an appearance, who were holding a vigil of humiliation. Every thing had been done to render the scene sombre and impressive: the glass-cases had been opened, in order to expose to view the wasted and shrivelled bodies they contained; and there was something very horrible in the sight of these poor blackened relics, to whom the sacred seclusion of burial had been denied, and who are thus unnaturally preserved, all decked in tinsel and flowers; when, perhaps, no faithful memory ever embalmed them in a living heart. The solitary taper on the altar revealed a dark figure standing near it, and cast a sickly glow on a pale, stern face, lit up by a fierce enthusiasm. It was a priest, thundering out most fearful denunciations against the pleasures of the world, which had brought too many of those before him to their present bitter penitence. He called upon them, by self-inflicted tortures, to forestall the sure punishment to come; and, wrought up to an almost frantic excitement, he condemned even the most innocent joys, and denounced those sacred human ties from which he was himself cut off, as too engrossing for a grave-doomed body and an undying soul; whilst, by the holier laws of our regenerate nature, these bonds of mortal love are in truth but destined to be riveted by death, and by immortality rendered indestructible! And ever as his voice rose and fell in melancholy threatening accents, the penitents beat their breasts and groaned aloud, whilst the wind, howling and muttering through the dark aisles, seemed to join in their lamentations.

Stanley was powerfully affected by this scene, it was so strange a contrast to that which they had just quitted. Arabyn stood close to him, and whispered in his ear with low, soft words, while Raymond, who never entered a Christian church, of whatever denomination, without remembering that he was treading on holy ground, was kneeling silently at a little distance. It was an apt representation of the powers of good and evil contending for a human soul; for thus on the one side the deadly insinuations of the infidel assailed Stanley, and on the other, winged by the irresistible Name, arose the prayers of the soldier of the cross for his preservation.

Again Arabyn took him by the arm, and led him forth, murmuring with taunting voice as they quitted the church, "This is a scene from the life of religion!" and Raymond followed after.

The infidel led them once more through the town, but no longer among the gay, well-frequented streets. Along close and narrow lanes, where the ruinous-looking houses, densely crowded together, seemed the abodes of vice and wretchedness: by the sea-shore, whose waters, unseen in the darkness, murmured hoarsely; till they stood before the massive door of a dark building, which Raymond knew to be the common prison. Not a light was to be seen through the closely-barred windows; not a sound was heard, save the clanking of the convicts' chains within.

"And this," exclaimed Arabyn, with a wild laugh of exultation, "shall be the scene of your future life, if, for the most false and most austere religion, whose practical working you have but now seen, you abandon those real and palpable pleasures, which may become your own from this day forward, to the utmost extent of luxury!"

Stanley clasped his hands, and looked round with a restless, despairing glance, as though his spirit were actually torn by the conflict he was enduring.

"And remember," continued Arabyn, "that unto that stern and frightful faith, that binds the free-born in intellectual bonds more firm than iron chains, the soul must be all or nothing; here is the alternative they offer you," and he laughed bitterly; "a living death in this world, or a death eternal in the next. They will have no half measures: they will say that the scanty joys of your past youth were crimes, and bid you expiate them by a life of self-created torture. Stanley, it is the lingering delusion of the creed that was given as an aliment to your childish questionings, but from which I should have looked to see your manhood turn with scorn; which alone prevents your adopting the measure I propose. I have shown you how, by the nobler law of your reason, you are positively called upon to do this petty, insignificant deed, not worth a moment's deliberation, this writing of two words, by which you shall purchase to yourself a lifetime of enjoyment, unless for the sake of a chilling deception which each crumbling skeleton might refute, you consign yourself, in the summer time of life and strength, unto that living tomb."

"No, no!" exclaimed Stanley. "Arabyn, it is enough: your unwearied efforts to save me shall not all be in vain. I will rise victorious over destiny and delusion. I go to sign the deed,—I go."

"Go!" echoed the infidel, in mocking and triumphant tones, as the young man broke from him and rushed impetuously through the streets in the direction of the hotel. Arabyn turned down another street; and Raymond, who had with difficulty refrained from confronting the sophist, when he had so glaringly falsified the truth of the unfathomable mercy, followed quickly after Stanley, feeling that the moment of the struggle for the possession of that tottering soul was come.

On arriving at the hotel, he was told that Stanley was in the public *salle*, and thither he went immediately. The young man was seated at a table at the furthest corner of the dimly-lighted room; he was alone: writing materials were placed before him; and with one hand he held the pen, whilst with the other he hid his eyes, and seemed in extreme agitation. The sound of Raymond's step startled him; he dashed the hair from his forehead, as though he would have effaced some bitter thought,—thrust the pen into the ink, and was about to write.

Raymond rushed forward, and seized his hand.

"Beware," he exclaimed; "if what you are about to do is at the instigation of Philip Arabyn, I charge you, at your peril, do it not!"

Stanley let the pen fall from his hand, and gazed at him in stupified amazement.

"I entreat you to forgive me," continued Raymond, earnestly; "doubtless I have no possible right thus to address you, and to interfere with your proceedings; but I have come to save you from utter ruin, and I had no other means."

"From ruin," exclaimed Stanley, as though that word alone conveyed any idea to his mind; "I am ruined already; and if all be true in which I once believed, I am so both in soul and body!"

"Not so," said Raymond; "it is not yet too late. I know you stand on the brink of a precipice, but trust to me, I implore of you—little as you know me,—for I am come to save you, and I both can and will; at least, do not refuse to hear me before you consummate that act. By your whole future life, which the crisis of this hour shall make one of anguish and remorse, or else of joy and peace, I entreat of you, deliberate before you write this word, and listen to what I have to tell you."

"I will, I am ready to hear you," said Stanley, looking up with involuntary trust into the noble face of the Christian. And Raymond, instantly taking out the letter which Arabyn had written to him at Constantinople, begged the young man to read it through.

Stanley took it,—he knew the handwriting well; and, as he read, an expression of indescribable horror and bewilderment passed over his countenance. When he had concluded it, his trembling hands could scarce restore it to Raymond. "What means this," he said; "do I dream, or am I the victim of a demon? Is this man then a fiend with whom I have had to deal?"

"In purpose and in power he might well be called

so," answered Raymond ; "and that he thought to make you his victim there is no doubt. But now that he is, by his own words, unmasked before you,—now that you see for what deadly aim and end he tempted you to crime,—trust yourself from this hour to my guidance, and I will draw you out of the snare into which he has allured you."

"You cannot," said Stanley, despairingly ; "willingly would I trust you, but you cannot save me. Let him— let Arabyn be what he will, this cannot change my fate. In this at least he spoke the truth, when he said that the dungeon awaits me,—a dungeon for life ; and that nothing can save me from it except this act, which I yet must perpetrate. It is iniquitous, I know, at least in a Christian's eyes ; but better this than to let my soul moulder with my body in a hideous tomb, which death has not prepared."

"Doubt not that I can save you," said Raymond ; "how should I ever have proposed it, had I not known the full extent of the danger in which you stand, and pondered well the means of assisting you. You are in the power of Vellio, the Corfiote merchant, are you not ?—and this is the amount of his claim upon you."

He put a note of the sum into Stanley's hand ; without waiting for his answer, he then placed before him a cheque to the full extent of the debt.

"And now listen," Raymond said, calmly and simply, as though this act of generosity towards a perfect stranger were a natural and ordinary occurrence ; "there is no time to be lost ; let us go at once without delay to the bankers, to draw the money ; we will then drive together to Vellio's, and pay him to the last shilling ; so that in one half hour you shall be released altogether from this unhappy debt,—and that, by no deed which shall defile your soul, and wither your whole existence with remorse! One thing only do I ask you in return, and I entreat of you not to refuse me; when you have concluded this matter, promise me that you will leave Trieste with me this very night, without again seeing Arabyn, or attempting to take leave of him."

"Oh! I would do what you will," stammered the young man, quite bewildered and confused at this unexpected assistance; "but how is it possible,—how can I abuse your kindness? What right have I, a stranger, —besides, I know not if I ever could repay."—

"You shall repay me when you will," said Raymond, gently interrupting him; "sooner perhaps than you expect in friendship and affection. But you are exhausted and prostrated in mind and body by all you have undergone; you are indeed incapable of thought to-night; therefore must you quietly submit to give yourself up to me; let me for a few hours guide and lead you where I will, and do you forget all but that you are about to leave this city and your miseries behind you, to fly where peace and happiness I trust await you."

Stanley looked up at the Christian with a glance of the most speechless gratitude, but he was now quite unable to express his feelings. With something of the trusting confidence with which a child submits itself to a father's guidance, he suffered the noble and strong-minded man to lead him away; and all things seemed to swim before his eyes as he felt the fierce bounding of his heart at thought of his unexpected release.

A carriage, which Raymond had ordered as he passed into the hotel, stood ready at the door, and within an hour's time the money was paid,—the acknowledgment placed in Stanley's hand,—and he himself, seated by Raymond's side, was travelling at a rapid pace on the road to Germany.

At midnight Arabyn returned to the hotel, ready with his soft voice to breathe poison into the soul that trusted him; ready with his friendly hand, that could give so warm a pressure, to grasp more tightly the throat of his victim; and he returned to find his purpose defeated,—his able and deeply-laid calculations utterly overthrown,—his subtle machinations, on which so much intellect and genius had been expended, altogether destroyed; and that by no other means than the devotion and self-sacrifice of a Christian.

He stood alone in the centre of his room, where he had entered, bearing with him the knowledge of his defeat; and his beautiful countenance became transformed by the fierce passions raging in his breast, till his look might have drawn the fiends out of hell for very sympathy. Then the fire, which opposition had kindled within him, seemed to diffuse itself in deadliest energy through his veins; the power, the will rose up within his soul—tremendous, indomitable; his teeth were clenched, —his eye dilated,—he walked out on the open balcony, that in the face of heaven he might defy it; and stretching out his hand, he swore a deep oath, that he yet would triumph, he yet would conquer, by the force of his own resolution, though he rifled the depths of all the iniquity that earth had ever witnessed, to sustain it; though, in order to attain the fulfilment of his will, each step that he took was bought by a human life; and each hour that he lived marked by the destruction of a human soul.

Raymond and Stanley travelled on for some days, till

they reached the quaint old town of Innspruck; and here they decided on remaining together for a few weeks. By this time the fullest confidence subsisted between them, and Stanley had detailed to his newly-made friend his whole previous history, but more especially the particulars of the plot by which Arabyn had sought to entangle him.

Stanley was of good family, and though at present altogether without fortune, would ultimately succeed to the enormous property of his cousin, who bore the same Christian and surname as himself,—that of Richard Stanley. This wealthy relation, although little older than himself, was not likely to stand many months between him and the family estates. He had a short time previously received a mortal wound in a duel, from the effects of which it was perfectly impossible he could recover; and which, having already disabled him altogether, was slowly and surely destroying him. Some family quarrel had estranged the cousins completely, and they had not met since their childhood.

Such was Stanley's position when he met with Arabyn at Smyrna, two days after the infidel had quitted Constantinople. It appeared evident to Raymond that Arabyn, who had some previous knowledge of the family, had mistaken the young man for his wealthier cousin. The efforts he had made to become intimate with him, the care he had taken to arrange that they should travel together, clearly proved that he had some plan in view for profiting by his fortune.

He allowed no sign of vexation, however, to appear when he discovered his mistake. Not choosing, probably, his labour to be lost, or any obstacle to foil him in his wishes, he speedily fabricated a scheme by which he was ultimately to attain the same result as that which he had first projected. Arabyn's powers of fascination were not likely to fail with any one, much less with a man of so amiable and yielding a disposition as Stanley, who soon became warmly attached to him ; he admired, trusted, and revered him ; yes, he revered his extraordinary intellect and superior talents ; and being himself diffident and retiring, was abundantly willing to be guided by him in all things.

It was clear that the plot which Arabyn had attempted to carry out was simply this: He had warily and cautiously initiated Stanley into the maddening and seductive excitement of gambling; he led him on, he stood ever at his side and prompted him ; he drove him into it ; then, when the debts which the unhappy young man had incurred were sufficient for his purpose, he caused Vellio to buy them up, and opened out to the eyes of his wretched victim the gulf of ruin and misery on whose brink he stood. He descanted, with all the eloquence of which he was master, on the infamy, the disgrace for life, the utter wretchedness, that awaited him in the debtor's prison, the contempt, the abandonment of all the gay companions he had gathered round him at Trieste, the destruction of his youth, the bitter exile from all the joys of life ; then, when he had plunged him into the most helpless agony of mind, Arabyn suggested a remedy.

He reminded Stanley that in a very short time he would be in possession of an immense fortune, nay, according to the infidel's reasoning, it was virtually his already, for his unhappy cousin dying by inches, palsied and speechless, could assuredly never more profit by it ; what then was to prevent him making use of this his future wealth in the present terrible emergency, by simply signing his own name for that of his cousin,—committing in short a forgery, (though Arabyn glossed over this palpable crime with many specious representations,)—in order to raise money on his relation's supposed signature. Most artfully did the sophist clothe this scheme in fairest colours, declaring even with a glaring openness of falsehood, which any one less perfectly confiding than Stanley would easily have detected, that the forgery might never be known, if his cousin died as soon as it seemed probable he would; and even were it discovered, there were many fair lands and glowing climes to which he might escape in time, where even his name was quite unknown, and he would, unmolested, revel in the fruitful results of his successful enterprise.

It is almost needless to state, that Arabyn's design for his own advantage in this matter was to obtain possession himself (by abuse of Stanley's trust in him) of the forged deed, and consequently of the fortune which was to be obtained by it, and then to fly with the money, leaving Stanley to bear the weight of the crime and its punishment.

So powerful was the eloquence of the infidel, who day after day unweariedly assailed him, seemingly with no motive but to save a dear friend from misery, that every barrier was overthrown in Stanley's mind against this crime except one, and that was the principles of the Christian faith, which, though neglected in youth had been accepted and believed in earlier and brighter years.

We have seen how Arabyn, knowing that it was hopeless to attempt reconciling crime with that most pure belief, had, with a horrible delight, destroyed it in the soul of his young victim, rejoicing that in the person of one man at least, he had murdered the faith which was his enemy, from which he shrunk, as the devils in possession of human beings from the contact of aught that was holy; and we have seen how on the very verge of destruction, the servant of Purity snatched back that falling soul, receiving power so to do, doubtless, because for that poor wavering child of sin a prayer was once breathed upon a night the universe remembers, and the victim was safe at the crowning moment of his peril; saved not only from great anguish here, but in all human probability from a yet more awful doom; for it is but too likely that Stanley never hereafter could have returned to the light, because of that most evil deed.

Stanley was free therefore; he had been delivered from the bonds which the infidel had woven round his soul, and his gratitude to Raymond knew no bounds, his affection and esteem for him daily increased, and he took greater pleasure in his society than he had ever before experienced in that of any other person, yet he could not conceal from himself or his friend that he was extremely unhappy. This was exactly what Raymond had expected, he knew well that his work was not yet done.

Stanley had been a Christian—careless, thoughtless, negligent, certainly, otherwise he never would have fallen as he had done, having his sight so weakened by the lustre of the bright things here, that he had not strength to pierce the veil of the flesh and look into eternity, and his ears so full of the music of human voices that he heard not the celestial strains;—but still, though shackled and earth-bound he was yet a believer, through whose soul when sorrow or disappointment paved the way, came swelling up the sweet and rapturous conviction of a pure immortality.

There can be no mental agony on this earth comparable to that experienced by one who has rested on this Hope, (albeit, almost unconsciously amid the allurements of the world without, and the din of the raging passions within,) when for the first time a doubt is driven into his soul by Satan, as though a murderous hand suddenly smote a nail into his brain. No feeling can be like unto it, except that which appals a man in the hour of death, when through the awful eternity opening before him, this paltry perishable world flits away like a vapour, which the rising sun disperses; for in the hour when the Immortal Hope appears about to quit the spirit that too long, perhaps, has neglected and well-nigh forgotten it, it appears to it in its true aspect, in its full immeasurable value, and before its glory and its splendour, all things temporal shrink back into their own insignificance. He looks upon the friends he has loved, and behold they are dust; on the hopes that were his life, and in their failure he beholds despair, in their fulfilment disappointment; yes, earth itself passes from him, recedes, dissolves, bearing with it the all in which he lived, and he remains alone, in a dark, a tremendous, a mysterious vacancy.

There is no instrument which the spirit of evil can use for man's destruction so potent as the introduction of scepticism into the mind; none which he employs more frequently and more subtlely; but when the soul, clad in the whole armour of God, has long been marching steadily beneath the banner of the Cross, it has a shield wherewith it can withstand all those fiery darts, and fighting manfully, doth conquer. It is only when the pure faith has lain fallow in the heart, and the flesh and the world have triumphed already, that this device of the last and worst enemy becomes successful.

Such had been the case with Stanley, and for his greater jeopardy, that agent of evil who first planted the germ of doubt in his breast, remained by his side to foster and cherish its poisonous growth, till ripening, it bore its accursed fruit in deadliest sin. And now, though removed from the power of the infidel, his influence yet worked in the mind of Stanley; the faith and the hope had passed from his soul, and departing had so revealed their glory, that all earth had darkened before them, and now they were gone, as he thought, never to return, but the shadow remained. In the same moment that life became worthless, he was told there was nothing beyond it, therefore he was miserable, but a keen and watchful eye scrutinized the workings of his mind.

Raymond would not quit him till he had perfected his work ; it would have availed little that he had saved him from dishonour, and from the consequences of the meditated sin, whose guilt was already his, if he had left him to this worst despair. Carefully and judiciously he rekindled a spark among the ashes of that extinguished faith, slowly but surely he fanned it into flame.

It is not necessary to detail the process by which, day after day, week after week, with watchful and unwearied care, the devoted Christian gradually dispersed the blighting mists which the infidel's unhallowed words had breathed over the soul of his victim, till clear and distinct the unobstructed truth passed before him once more, leading the way to eternity, and, like the man who was healed at the gate of the temple which was called beautiful, his feet received strength, and he was given a perfect soundness through faith in that Name, and entering on the sacred and narrow path, he walked therein praising God.

It was not many weeks before Stanley, restored to vigour of mind and body, with a free and joyous aspect, and a voice of deep emotion, looking upon Raymond with unspeakable gratitude, called him his father and more than father, for if from his natural parent he had received the mortal existence and the day's sweet light, through his instrumentality he had been restored to that life which should endure, when the huge world beneath his feet had crumbled into ashes, and to the glorious undying radiance that should beam for him when earthly suns were all extinguished.

Raymond did not at all regret that the young man had passed through this fiery trial, he had been taught the unspeakable value of the treasure he once had lightly esteemed, by the peril in which he stood of losing it for ever; and the Christian now saw clearly that Stanley would henceforward cling to the faith as to life itself, nor ever allow the most seductive of all earth's joys to induce him one instant to relax his hold.

One piece of advice Raymond strongly impressed on Stanley, before they parted at Innspruck; it was, that during the whole of his future career, he should carefully and scrupulously avoid the remotest intercourse with persons professing sceptical opinions. He told him openly and honestly that the contact which would be altogether without danger to a more mature and stronger mind, might not be so for him; both on account of his naturally yielding and pliant disposition, and also from the circumstance of his having been already shaken, which would always lead him to meet a similar temptation with too much of fear, and too little of hope.

Stanley promised to look upon it as a positive duty in his peculiar position, and after a residence of some months at Innspruck they parted; the young man to explore some parts of Italy yet unknown to him—Raymond to follow once more on the path of the infidel.

CHAPTER XIII.

ARABYN REMOVES A HUMAN OBSTACLE FROM HIS PATH.

ONCE more Ruth Vincent held her solitary vigil in the silence of the night, and again the moonlight streamed through the window on her pale face and kneeling figure; but the aspect of the world without was altogether changed. The spring that bloomed upon it then had perished, like all bright things of earth, on which the eyes that shall be sealed in death must never look too long ; and the merry summer time had passed away, whose glowing brightness Arabyn had told her could never dry the dew of human tears, or warm the heart that had grown chill and dead for very loneliness. It was autumn now, whose voice and whose smile are like those of a dying friend, speaking low and faint of that decay in which is the germ of a life renewed. The wind rushed and shrieked through the skeleton trees, as though it were laden with the souls that shall not enter His rest ; and through a wild, tempestuous sky, the moon was sailing on, like a stately and glorious vessel speeding to ethereal climes, unmindful of the storms and gloom around it. At times it was altogether obscured by black and angry clouds ; then suddenly it burst forth amongst them, like hope in affliction, or receded again, like a joy too engrossing. But still, whether hid or revealed, it was ever there, and its beautiful radiance shone steadily behind all that darkness, and its soft rays went stealing to and fro, visiting even the most threatening clouds.

It was even thus in the soul of Ruth Vincent. Dark and unwonted clouds were there, heavy and portentous; chill winds were sweeping over her, prophetic of a coming winter; but there was a light that beamed within steady and serene, which no mortal darkness could overshadow long; for the soul of a Christian is a deep clear water, wherein dwelleth the smile of Christ; the waters may be troubled for a while, but soon they settle again, and the smile is reflected as before.

Ruth had extinguished her lamp, that, in the darkness, she might feel more perfectly alone with Him in whom there is none at all; but the struggling beams of the moon showed with sufficient distinctness the words written in large characters on the paper she held in her hand; they were these: " Blessed are the pure in heart, for they shall see God." By that most solemn and awful declaration, which she sought to engrave, as it were, upon her life, in every thought and action of her daily conduct, she had been in the habit nightly of trying and examining her own soul; and when she had looked upon the well-known words, she laid them aside with a most bitter sigh, and let her head fall lowly on her clasped hands. Could she dare to believe that she should ever now attain to that purity of heart which might enable her, without annihilation, to see God, when she had allowed a human affection to intertwine itself with her very existence? when often she was weighed down with a deep sense of happiness, which sprung from an earthly joy alone? when, to purchase peace or comfort to one fellow-creature, she would fain have received permission to lay down the life given her for higher purposes? Unconsciously she had commenced by revering and admiring in the mortal the reflection of that holiness which she worshipped at its Source; but Ruth was no self-deceiver, and she knew well that it was the human being now to whom she clung with such unconquerable sympathy, for whom to gain one blessing she would gladly have seen her own existence made a curse.

Very bitter was that moment, in which she clearly felt and understood that, while great and indestructible was her treasure in the heavens, she now had one on earth which might too powerfully draw down her soul towards it; that no longer could she return thanks because no human love had been allowed her to deaden her keen sense of that which is eternal. But she had become (as she believed) the object of a true and most profound affection, and should she, who could not bear to crush a little senseless flower beneath her feet, cast from her the solitary and hopeless being, who had flown to her side for refuge against a cold, a dreary, and a lonely life?

There was nothing morbid or overstrained in Ruth Vincent's ideas. Although it had long been her fondest wish that she might be enabled, in the spring-time of her youth, to offer up to the Most High a life in which no other sentiment save love to Him should have a share; a heart free, pure, and undivided, unshackled by an earthly bond, unsullied by an earthly wish; yet she well knew that human ties are perfectly compatible with the holiest and most unlimited devotion to Him, and that often, indeed, they are made the means whereby we may most truly serve Him in self-denial and spiritual martyrdom. She felt, indeed, that there was something most touchingly beautiful in that arrangement of His tender care, which causes us mortals, all weak and erring and helpless alike, to lean so trustingly on one another. The frail arm, that has no strength to ward off a single blow that falls upon itself, can yet securely shield another from many a heavy stroke, and courageously uphold him when the way is rough as he journeys graveward; and the heart that has no power over its own destiny, save that of turning curses into blessings by a holy endurance of its anguish, can still, by its dear love, so brighten and beautify a fellow-creature's path, that life is like a dream of man's first Eden. The sensitive retiring being, who shrinks from a rough word or a chilling breath, can, in another's stead, stand forth undaunted and serene to brave a world or meet a tempest's shock; and the pang, the torture, or the fierce unrest, that would crush us to the earth alone, are gladly met and thankfully received, if by our suffering a friend is spared.

Ruth Vincent, therefore, believing herself by Him appointed as guardian most devoted and tender of one of His weary and heavy-laden on the earth, attempted not to restrain the profound and powerful attachment, destined by its very nature to end with life alone, which she now experienced for Philip Arabyn; although she could not choose but mourn over the ruins of the pure hope which had brightened many a year for her, even that of making her soul like unto one of those vast solitudes of nature, in which the presence of God alone existeth.

And now, accustomed as Ruth Vincent was most rigidly to examine and sound the secret springs of her own actions, she almost trembled as she felt how inexpressibly dear to her would be the task of devoting herself on earth to this sad, friendless wanderer; of so girding him about, and encircling him, as it were, with her affection, that the storms and the strife without should have no power to touch him; that lonely, outcast, wretched, as he said he was, the love of one might shield him from the hate of all. She felt that willingly she would give up her whole existence to smooth his path and cheer his life, and chase from his soul the remembrance of those mysterious sorrows, whose effect she saw, while their origin remained unknown. And not without terror did she contemplate the depth and deathlessness of the attachment with which he had inspired her; for it is indeed an awful thing thus utterly to deliver up the all of earthly happiness into the hands of a fellow-creature, investing him with power to trouble it by a look, or destroy it by a single word. But it was done. His image was stamped within her heart, never more to be effaced; there to be waited on and attended by her every earthly wish and thought, that ranged around it ever, like the constant waves upon the same bright shore. Well, and ably, and artfully, had the infidel carried on and accomplished his work!

"But, lo! now is the hour of watchfulness, my soul!" said Ruth Vincent as she rose at last, to seek what rest she might in slumber. "Cursed is he who letteth the love of the creature surpass the love of the Creator; cursed is that idolatry of heart that bows down and worships the perishing child of clay. Now, by the promised strength, do I solemnly resolve, if I find that this love does draw me one hair's-breadth from my allegiance, at once to tear it from my heart, and cast it out like deadly poison, though myself should perish in the struggle. But rather shall he lead me on more swiftly in the path of holiness; for he is unworldly and pure, and looks already as though he were not of this earth, but sorrow had won him up to heaven. Oh, joy unspeakable! to walk with him through this world as through the gateway of the eternal paradise, and so pass on and enter there together!"

And whilst she spoke, at the self-same hour, Philip Arabyn was cursing the necessity which made him seek to link himself with one whose constant reference, in action if not in word, to the religion he abhorred, caused him to shrink from it as a most hateful and unnatural union; and he was feeding himself with the hope that he might have power to blight and taint that pure soul before he bound it to his own, and that at least he would not let one day elapse after that in which he vowed to love and cherish her till death, before he abandoned her to the poverty and despair he had created for her.

There was as yet no engagement between Ruth and Arabyn, but he had left no means unemployed to show her most distinctly that she had become the only and most beloved hope of his existence, the sweet and solitary star that had risen on his path when all was dark and cheerless. Week after week, month after month, had he remained by her side, never for one single moment, or in the most trivial action, losing sight of the object he had in view; and unless she could, with her cloudless eyes, have looked down into the depths of that most refined depravity in which his soul was steeped, it was indeed impossible that she should have mistrusted him.

At all times it was strangely difficult for Ruth Vincent to doubt the sincerity of another; and to have suspected Arabyn, the eloquent supporter of the cause she served, the resigned and devoted servant of the Cross, of one single unholy thought or untrue word, would have been to her almost like a doubt of the power of the faith itself; and she therefore believed in the love of the hypocrite, as having no right or power to do otherwise, since he had convinced her of it: whilst he did so mortally hate her for the uncompromising holiness of her principles, that he had delayed as yet bringing the matter altogether to a conclusion, till he should be able in some degree to overcome his repugnance to the union.

Thus far, then, the infidel had succeeded in his iniquitous project; but it had been at a fearful cost to one most unoffending, and for Ruth, the chief victim, the seeds of a most unspeakable anguish were already sown, in that affection which had entwined itself with her very life. An obstacle had risen up before Arabyn in the prosecution of his plan, an obstacle rather in the future than in the present, but which not the less must be speedily overcome; he had found it in the person of the meek and suffering Edmund.

One of Arabyn's first objects in the minor details of his plan, had been to acquire the greatest influence over all those who surrounded Ruth, and in this he had amply succeeded. He was, as we have said, singularly attractive in every respect, and when he chose to exert his talents in gaining a moral ascendancy over minds less gifted than his own, his success was invariable.

Mr. Denham was his first and most important object, and so artfully did he work on the capricious and violent old man, that he at last exercised an influence over him which amounted to a species of fascination. Instinctively, he seemed to obey the slightest word or look of his nephew's; and although he was quite unaware of it himself, his own proceedings both of word and deed, were constantly dictated to him by Arabyn's subtle spirit of intrigue. With the Harcourt family the infidel had rapidly gained ground, and he now held a high place in their friendship and esteem, he was received as their most favoured guest, and their party never seemed complete without him; even Mr. Parker patronized him, and continually enhanced his merits by informing all strangers in a very plain-spoken manner of his father's disgrace, and of the extreme probability there had been of Arabyn himself following a similar course.

Edmund alone had never been able to overcome his silent shrinking from all contact with the infidel, or the strange and nameless dread with which Arabyn had inspired him from the very first day he beheld him. He could by no means account for this, as he fully believed in all that Ruth and others had told him of the hypocrite's exalted faith and holy life; but, although for this cause he tolerated his society, and listened with humility to his conversation, he yet could not in the slightest degree conceal his feelings towards him, for the thoughts of his pure mind were at all times transparent, as the clear waters of a limpid stream.

It is not a vain superstition to assert, that when a soul has, like that of Edmund, been drawn out of the thick foul atmosphere of this world and admitted to the far off faint reflection of the Glorious Purity that inhabiteth eternity, it acquires a marvellously acute perception of evil, and seems to be warned by some internal shrinking of the approach of any unholy thing, like the mysterious instinct of the sensitive mimosa. Whilst all around him were captivated with Arabyn, and looked upon him as a most uncompromising follower of the faith, and when even the powerful and imaginative mind of Ruth Vincent was utterly subdued to his, it was given to the child-like purity and innocent simplicity of Edmund only, to discern the guile of the demon under the form of the angel.

Arabyn was perfectly aware of this, and he dreaded unspeakably the effect of it on Ruth. He knew how she reverenced the holy guilelessness of the deformed boy, and how she bowed in spirit before his wisdom which was not with the excellency of that of man; he felt convinced that even the unconscious distaste and mistrust which Edmund felt for him would have a most powerful influence upon her, for she saw more clearly into the feelings of the simple-minded Christian than he could himself. In addition to this difficulty, which Edmund had unknowingly raised up before Arabyn, there was another which was equally annoying to him. He had, as we have said, overheard the urgent request made to Ruth Vincent, that she would promise to be in attendance at the death-bed of her adopted brother; she had herself often alluded to it in conversing with him, and observed, that, if possible, nothing should deter her from complying with this wish; and it now seemed likely that very few months would elapse, before she was called upon to fulfil her engagement.

Arabyn foresaw that this would greatly interfere with his plans, as it might detain Ruth in this place after the period had arrived when he would wish to remove her, and his failure with Stanley at Trieste had made him fully determined that in this matter he would have no delay, so soon as his scheme was ripe for execution. These considerations decided him, that it was absolutely necessary that the intercourse between Ruth and Edmund should cease altogether.

Having come to this determination, at once, with that strength and energy of will, which rightly directed might have been to him an inestimable treasure, he bent the whole powers of his mind to accomplish it. The first idea which suggested itself to his mind as the simplest means he could adopt was to destroy the faith of Edmund. Could he make of this unhappy boy an open and avowed infidel, he knew that he would place a gulf between those two, which neither would ever seek to pass again; what recked he, if by so doing he cast out that poor, infirm, friendless creature, from the repose of hope, of most celestial hope, in which his quiet spirit had so long lain cradled! Arabyn soon found a favourable opportunity for making this attempt; Ruth was detained at home for nearly a fortnight, in close attendance on Mr. Denham, who was suffering from an attack of illness, and during that period Edmund did not see her at all.

It was now that with the most consummate art, Arabyn endeavoured to insinuate into the mind of his victim, the most subtle doubts respecting that faith which was the star of his eternity, and this he did, whilst seeming to converse as a Christian on the marvellous nature of their mysterious religion; to the very uttermost he exerted his remarkable talents and his rare eloquence; but both fell powerless on that guileless soul, so strong in its deep trust and unquestioning submission, as the speculations of human reason would fall on the ears of an infant that in slumber smiles to the viewless angels round it,—like deadly vapours over the surface of a still pure lake, or a foul breath over a clear mirror, the wily, poisonous words of the infidel passed over that serene spirit, leaving it calm and spotless as before.

Edmund could not have answered a single argument, open or concealed, against his religion; he could not even have reasoned upon it, but he could say "I believe," for *He* hath said, "if it were not so I would have told you." Truly the weak things of this earth are chosen to confound the mighty!

Arabyn speedily found that this effort would be altogether hopeless; yet it had not been entirely useless.

When Mr. Harcourt had told Ruth how constantly and assiduously Arabyn had supplied her place, in reading to Edmund and amusing him by his conversation, during her absence, he saw a bright smile pass over her expressive face, at this new proof of the goodness in which she believed so trustingly; for there was to her a singular enjoyment in feeling and acknowledging the great superiority which she imagined Arabyn to possess over herself.

But the infidel had another plan in view for detaching Edmund from his only friend, which he well knew would not fail. Although the faith implanted in that meek spirit by a Power Divine was unattainable by him, yet the affection which was of this earth only lay open and undefended against the wounds he could so skilfully inflict. Edmund was sensitive to the last degree; he was keenly and morbidly susceptible, and he carried the painful consciousness of his infirmity to such a painful extent, that he had always believed himself to be a miserable burden to those around him, and that it was nothing less than a penance to any one to approach him. This idea had eaten like a canker into his heart, till Ruth Vincent came to him with her pitying love and warm friendship. She saw what was the envenomed wound that lurked in his breast, and with tenderest care she healed it. She made it her study to convince him, that it was not compassion, or a holy charity alone which brought her to his side; but her true and actual affection for himself: this was a difficult task, but she at last succeeded, and heaven was none the less bright for him, that from that hour earth had its sunshine also.

It was this charitable work, the labour of months, which Arabyn was now about to destroy: this was the light he was to quench in Edmund's cheerless existence.

He found the task was easier even than he had hoped. Edmund had retained the painfully morbid feelings we have described, with respect to all, excepting Ruth herself. She had forced him to look upon her as an exception, though he often wondered how it could be so; for it was scarce unnatural that he should think, with such morbid sensibility, that it was hard for others to bear with his sad infirmities, as he was subject to periodical attacks of convulsion, which were indeed most frightful to witness. Ruth had been with him many times on these occasions (though her natural timidity made it a severe trial to her), for the sole purpose of convincing him that nothing could deter her from attending upon him; and still, often, when he saw how pale she grew if he seemed threatened with an attack, a bitter fear shot through him, that she had, after all, undertaken a task too painful for her strength. His mind was, therefore, in a very fit state for Arabyn to work on.

Although he had never yet doubted her affection, Arabyn's object was to convince him that any such feeling on the part of Ruth for himself was wholly impossible, and that the sole motive of her conduct was the noble resolution to perform the arduous duty she had imposed upon herself,—a duty which, from first to last, could only be performed at the cost of a most severe self-sacrifice. He determined to effect this, if possible, in one single conversation, so as to make Edmund himself avoid seeing Ruth again; for he knew that if they met she would speedily detect any change; and he feared that the candour and truthfulness for which she was so remarkable would counteract all his wily endeavours.

It was on a dull, sad autumn day that Arabyn came into the room where Edmund generally spent the mornings alone, and where he was lying, exhausted by pain, and unusually dispirited; for his weak frame was very susceptible to the variations of the weather, and he felt severely the loss of Ruth's cheerful society. He felt glad to see Arabyn, despite of his instinctive repugnance to him, as he seldom came without some message from her, and he could at least hear what she was doing.

Arabyn looked very grave and sad when Edmund inquired after Ruth, and answered, that she was far from well—that she had never been well since the last day she had spent at Mrs. Harcourt's. On that occasion Edmund had been seized very suddenly with a spasm more than usually violent; and, in the sort of delirium into which he was flung by it, refused to let any one but Ruth support him. This recollection now sent a flush across his pallid face as the infidel spoke.

Arabyn then began to talk, in the most exalted terms, of the extraordinary absence of all selfishness in Ruth Vincent's character, and of her continual self-denial; saying openly, that it was inconceivable to him how those to whom she devoted herself could, with so little consideration, take advantage of her generosity, and overtax without scruple her powers of endurance.

Edmund looked deeply pained and uneasy, and said that he had often dreaded beyond measure that he might himself be one of those.

Arabyn seemed to hesitate for a moment, and replied, that he had long wished to speak frankly to him on this subject, as he knew him to be in ignorance of many things which he thought it but right he should know. They might pain him, but where the health and interest of Ruth Vincent were concerned, he knew that Edmund would himself be the first to feel anxious.

The unfortunate young man clasped his hand anxiously, and implored him to proceed.

With a very few words Arabyn produced to the uttermost the effect he desired. He began by telling Edmund, what had always been carefully concealed from him, that his little income was the gift of Ruth Vincent; and he so successfully falsified his statement, as to make it appear quite evident that she had impoverished herself to the last degree in order to provide for him.

These tidings fell like a thunderbolt on the very heart of the sensitive cripple, whose delicacy of feeling was quite remarkable. Arabyn continued to say, that the noble self-sacrifice with which Ruth had imposed upon herself the task of attending on him, was now proving too much for her health and strength. The reason of her present absence was not Mr. Denham's illness, but the absolute necessity she felt of giving some repose to her shattered nerves, after the last terrible scene she had witnessed with him. The constant recurrence, indeed, of these painful trials had rendered the care of her adopted brother a burden too heavy to be borne.

Further, Arabyn said that the promise she had given of being with him in his last hour had become a source of serious annoyance to her now. Mr. Denham was anxious to go abroad for his health (this was true), and she herself had many reasons of the first importance for wishing that they should go immediately. She was only detained by her generous wish to gratify Edmund's desire: but Arabyn thought it but an act of kindness to tell him these facts, as he felt sure that any little pleasure he might find in Ruth's society could never compensate for all the pain and distress which her attention to him had caused her from first to last.

He paused, for Edmund lay gasping before him, as though his very heart were bursting. He tried in vain to speak several times, and at last a few words came faintly and tremulously to his lips, gathered from the lingering strength of the hope that was expiring within him. He murmured that Ruth had ever said she rejoiced to come to him, because she loved him truly as a brother.

"Doubtless she would tell you so," said Arabyn, sneeringly; "hers is the refinement of generous kindness; she would ever strive to hide the beauty of her own devotedness. Even now she is trying to regain her strength, that she may come to you again, although she knows how injurious it is to her health; and you see she makes you believe it is on Mr. Denham's account that she is absent. She has often, I assure you, explained to me all her feelings with regard to you; they are what I have told you. As for affection——"

Arabyn paused: he left the torturing fancy of the cripple to complete the sentence, and he did well; for no words of his could ever have given to the idea he wished to convey, all the bitterness which Edmund's own wounded spirit gave it.

"It is most true," he said, as he writhed upon the sofa where he lay; "too deeply true: how could I be so blind? I see it all—it could not have been otherwise; and now there is but one remedy. She must not come to me again—I will never more be a burden to her—I will not see her: tell her this—tell her that I will not see her. Do not give the reason, it would only bring her back to me more pitying and kind. Let her think me ungrateful, or what you will; only let me never see her more, that not another hour of her life may be saddened by me."

Edmund fell back, exhausted by the vehemence with which he had spoken; and Arabyn quietly promised to say all he wished, praised the wisdom and propriety of the resolution he had taken, and affected to believe that the loss of Ruth's society, which it involved, was but a small privation for him, surrounded as he was by so many friends.

Edmund made no answer, except to gasp out a faint entreaty that he would desire the servants to carry him to his room, and he was in a few minutes laid fainting on the couch—from which he never rose again.

Of all the miseries with which this world is rife, there is none more piteous or more cruel than the desolation of him whose repulsed affection has been sent back curdling on his heart, there to lie like a leaden weight, from which there is no escape. He has loved some one human being—be it brother, friend, or lover—with the love that passeth not away—in all truth and faithfulness; and his warm affection has been like the sunbeam falling on the cold, hard rock; and he only learns to know the riches of the treasure he has vainly proffered, in the agony which its rejection causes him. Then does the peopled world become a wilderness for him, because of the one friend that is not: and who shall describe the passionate longing for death, of the spirit driven out so lonely into that unutterable solitude, which is the absence of one most dear—the vague dreariness that is all around it, and to which there is no limit; the deep shadows that encompass it, shutting out all earthly hope, and light, and joy; enclosing it, as it were, alone in one vast desert!

For a time Edmund felt as though he must have sunk under it: this was the first *actual* misfortune he had ever known. Much of trial and sorrow he had borne, but it had always been a part of his existence— his inheritance from his birth; and the power to endure it had grown with his growth, and strengthened with his strength. Now this heavy blow was no longer merely the absence of good: it was an actual evil, full of bitterness to him, and it crushed him to the dust.

But *the Voice*, which, amidst this world of strife and

turmoil, had held his soul steeped in celestial music with the melody of its whispers of mercy, was not silent now. Through the cold sad wilderness, which now the peopled earth was made for him; through the chilling regions of that solitude, where one alone was absent, dispelling the illimitable dreariness, and piercing all the dark thick shadows—that Voice most blessed came, uttering those words, that to many a sinking heart has brought again the warmth of life: "Be of good cheer, it is I."

Then speedily from his fainting spirit the desolation passed away, and Edmund felt that he would have endured a lifetime of that bitter loneliness for one hour of that ineffable consolation. Then he became calm and cheerful as before, though he strictly adhered to his resolution of not allowing Ruth to come to him again. But the stroke of this unexpected misfortune had given so violent a shock to his enfeebled frame, that it burst the bonds of the life which he held with so frail a tenure; and from that hour he sunk with a rapidity which proved that the term of his mortal trial was well nigh over.

Ruth Vincent was naturally extremely astonished, and also much distressed, when she was told of Edmund's apparently inexplicable resolution. It was, however, from Arabyn that she heard it, and he explained the matter in a manner which somewhat diminished her astonishment, although it grieved her still more. He told her that Edmund had been seized with an attack so frightfully violent that it had actually affected his mind; and that his sudden repugnance to see her whom precisely he had most cherished formerly, was the species of monomania on which his insanity had settled; a peculiar form of aberration of intellect by no means unusual in such cases.

The Harcourt family readily adopted this explanation of a change in their unfortunate relation, which could not otherwise be accounted for; and even the physician who attended him said it was by no means impossible, whilst he strictly forbade them to force his inclination in any way.

Ruth was therefore obliged to submit patiently to what was really a great trial to her; and it pained her especially to hear that Edmund continually repeated that he would not allow her to be near him in his last hour, and that he constantly begged his attendants to tell her so. She still, however, cherished the confident hope that his natural affection would return upon him at the last, and she determined at least that nothing should induce her to leave the place, whilst there was a possibility that his former urgent wish should resume its ascendancy.

CHAPTER XIV.

RAYMOND AND ARABYN MEET FACE TO FACE, AND THE VICTIM FOR WHOM THEY CONTEND IS BETWEEN THEM.

The bell was ringing for evening prayer a few days after the fatal visit of Arabyn to Edmund, and Ruth Vincent was slowly walking towards the church. It was a mild afternoon, though the country already had the appearance almost of winter. The faint light was dying away over the melancholy woods, where the withered leaves were falling thick and fast; not a breath was stirring, and no sound was heard save the distant chimes pealing through the still air. To Ruth they sounded strangely sweet in that hour, when all was redolent of decay, coming so softly on the ear, like a whispered promise of immortality.

As she walked through the park she saw Arabyn waiting for her; he was leaning against a tree, and seemed in profound meditation; but a sudden smile brightened his countenance when he joined her, and they walked on together.

"You were very deep in thought," said Ruth, after a moment's silence.

"Yes," said the infidel; "and true to your office of good angel to all who are afflicted, you come just in time to release me from the spell. Thought is a subtle instrument, wherewith we can inflict upon ourselves most insupportable torments, or else conjure up visions of such exceeding brightness, that the actual world looks cold and dim when we return to it. But I was occupied just now in wondering at my own self, that, after having been so roughly handled by destiny, I should not yet have learned wisdom, but have allowed myself once more to be tied and bound with the bright golden fetters of hope."

"And why not?" said Ruth. "It is not compatible with our human nature that we should ever cease from hope. Man hopes from the cradle to the grave, and Heaven forbid it should be otherwise: for this undying longing is, even from the dawn of our existence, the seal set on our souls by the truth of Eternity! The last most awful hour of life is the first in which hope leaves us, for then it becomes merged into perception and enjoyment."

"But by all this you mean only those aspirations of the spirit, which have no connection with this world," said Arabyn, almost impatiently; "and I was speaking of those bright day-dreams whereby we weave that glittering veil over this world, which the first breath of cold reality disperses, to show the howling waste beneath. It is a strange thing, truly, how men will thus incessantly shape out to themselves the materials of future disappointment, and toil, like very slaves, for the accomplishment of their own despair. Alas! why will they hope,—why wish,—why dream,—why seek to relieve the dull monotony of the present by forming rainbow hues, in which to deck the future, that may never dawn for them? I tell you, Ruth, it is most horrible to see some great mind give up to toil a whole long life, with all his energy and intellect for the attainment at a distant period of the fair object that for him has the aspect of happiness; and when at length weary and way-worn,—his youth, his strength, his innocence departed never to return,— he claims the harvest from the seed he has sown, fruit from the land he has tilled, in the sweat of his brow,— then the serpent hope he has nourished in his bosom turns round and stings him; and he finds that he has been struggling and labouring for his own misery!"

"You know this is a point on which we never quite agree," said Ruth smiling gaily; "I cannot take so dark a view of life as you do; but this, doubtless, is because I have not suffered as you have done. But certainly it is no reflection from my own inward happiness which makes me feel so sure that there is much calm enjoyment for us here, in the society of those we esteem, in generous friendship, and mutual affection. Oh! rest assured, amid all the coldness and hypocrisy of this world, there is much that is good and true."

"As yet I have known most of its coldness," said Arabyn; "it were well, perhaps, if I could still teach myself to ask for nothing else."

"I think you have too low an opinion of your fellow-creatures," said Ruth; "their sympathy could enable us to bear the heaviest burden. With the consolations of the blessed human ties, and the certainty of eternal peace before us, life may surely be something more than supportable."

"You shall teach me how to make it so," said the low voice of the hypocrite; "remember that till I met you I stood alone and helpless in the darkest night."

Ruth turned towards him with so bright and noble an expression, that any less hardened than Philip Arabyn into a total unbelief of all that is good would have shuddered at thought of deceiving one so upright and so true.

"Courage!" she said; "you are yet as a man stunned from a heavy blow by the keen stroke of your misfortunes; and to your eyes, because of the dimness of many tears, the blessed Light that irradiates even this world seems to burn faint; but we must remember this: there can be no victory without a battle,—no peace in eternity without a struggle in life,—no rest by the still waters except, weary and foot-sore, many a toilsome journey is made over the storm-swept paths of earth. Yet take courage; and doubt not that the kind hand of your fellow-creatures shall smooth your way as you struggle on, all rough and rugged as it now may seem."

They had reached the church door when she finished speaking, and she passed in without waiting for an answer. And Arabyn knew not as he followed her—with such a smile upon her lips as would have chilled her to the soul could she have seen it—how, behind him, at that hour, walked as it were his living retribution! For even as he had once tracked the footsteps of Ruth Vincent, that he might learn from the knowledge of her great unworldliness, how best to make her the slave of his hideous egotism, and out of the very tenderness of her disposition, and intensity of sympathy with suffering, to weave the bonds that were to bind her down upon the rack he was preparing for her,—so now did another follow after him, watching his every word and look, and ready to arrest his iniquitous arm when it should be too daringly upraised against a servant of the Lord.

Ruth still retained her seat by the side of the old beggar, whose wistful eyes were ever wandering round in search of her, whilst Arabyn advanced to his place near the altar. The fading light of the autumn day came dim and faint through the narrow windows of the little church, seeming to fill it with a mysterious sanctity; and one pale gleam, that lingered at the sun's departing, caught the bright hue of the stained glass through which it passed, and fell with a warm glow on the grey stone of the altar steps.

To Ruth Vincent there was always something inexpressibly soothing in this one half-hour, spent every evening in the still atmosphere of that holy place, where the quiet shadows seemed so utterly to shut out all earthly things, and the deep silence was broken only by the one solemn voice that went echoing through the dim aisles with its message from the realm unseen.

She felt—as all must feel who acquire this habit of daily withdrawal from their earthly occupations,—as though she had been drawn out for a little time from the troubled, restless world, where she dwelt a pilgrim, and placed at the portal of the promised rest, whence a vision of her own true home came to overshadow her soul, and recal her to the recollection of the glorious destiny for which she was created.

The heart may beat thick and heavy in its passionate struggle with life, the spirit be never so faint and weary with the sickening pangs of disappointment; still, at that sacred threshold the burden is laid down involuntarily; the majesty of immortality and incorruption arises before the mortal and corruptible, who shall hereafter be invested with its glory; and when he goes forth again into the world, it is with a calm strength, against which its tempests shall beat in vain.

Ruth Vincent had arisen from her knees; the service

had not yet begun, and suddenly her attention was irresistibly attracted by a strange scene which presented itself before her. Arabyn was standing upright, apparently transfixed by some sudden emotion, and gazing, like one paralyzed, on a man of imposing appearance who stood a few paces apart, and with stern countenance returned his look. As Arabyn arose from the spot where he had knelt in mockery, suddenly his eyes had encountered those of Raymond, and he knew by their glance whom it was he sought.

For the first time, the infidel had a clear and distinct perception of the moral duel in which he was in fact engaged. He had readily discovered, when Raymond and Stanley left Trieste, by whom and in what manner the young man had been liberated from his snares. The fact that the devoted Christian had followed him to this place, added to his recollection of the letter he had written, and his knowledge of Raymond's holy and self-denying principles, enabled his acute mind to grasp the truth at once, and show him that the most formidable obstacle to his plans would, in fact, be this determined antagonist.

Raymond, meanwhile, was not deceived by the presence of the infidel within these holy walls. He well knew that he still was, and too probably would ever be, in bondage, absolute and determined, to the cause of iniquity. The letter, which Arabyn at this moment was so full of rage for having written, was, in truth, a tremendous instrument in the hands of his antagonist; and that, along with the recollection of his proceedings at Trieste, was sufficient to convince Raymond of the truth, while he pondered within himself on the motive of the peculiar line of deception which he saw the infidel had adopted in thus presenting himself as a Christian within that church.

So they stood face to face, these mortal enemies, and gazed silently upon each other. Both were overpowered at that moment with the full consciousness of the tremendous nature of the struggle in which they were engaged. It was not the wrestling of man with man; it was the good and the evil, far more clearly defined, more equally matched, in the persons of these two individuals, than as they are generally to be seen, vaguely swaying the great mass of mankind, who are so bewildered by the mutual indwelling of these antagónistic principles in each human heart.

Raymond and Arabyn felt themselves in that hour to be but weak and fragile instruments, that well might be shivered into atoms in the clash of the two mighty principles incorporate within them. In many respects, how unequal was the combat! The infidel, with all his advantages, intellectual and physical; and the fearful power which his attempted spiritual independence secured him, in the mean time, of using all means, even the most iniquitous, for the accomplishment of his purpose. The Christian, bound not only by the general law of unflinching rectitude, but by the most minute command of the written word; having for earthly weapon none save his solemn self-sacrifice—his calm determination that, if need be, his whole life should be spent in washing out the stain of this man's crimes.

So they looked on one another, each with his settled purpose graven on his heart; for already the mind of Arabyn, fired with a fierce ardour, was braced for the encounter. His iron will was strengthened by opposition; and since a struggle was forced upon him, he was resolved it should be a war unto the death. At a little distance, Ruth Vincent gazed upon them both with an innocent wonder in her eyes, little dreaming that she was herself the unconscious prize for which these two men were about to play so deep and terrible a game.

In the midst of this turmoil of contending feelings, suddenly the quiet voice of the clergyman arose, breathing out the whispers of peace and mercy, and all three assumed at once the attitude of devotion. Two of them knelt down to implore a blessing, and the third hid his face while he invoked a curse. And the prayer of each one was answered; for the blessing and the curse rested on the heads of those who asked them.

When Ruth Vincent left the church, she looked round eagerly for Arabyn, but he had disappeared, and Raymond almost instantly passed her, evidently in pursuit of him, and with so severe an expression of countenance, that she trembled as she looked on him. She walked on towards Mrs. Harcourt's, where she was going to inquire for Edmund, and where she doubted not Arabyn had preceded her. Ruth felt strangely oppressed and uneasy, for she was convinced that it was no common meeting she had witnessed. She was quite unable to comprehend the meaning of the stern look which had passed between those two men, but it was sufficiently plain that Raymond was an enemy, and not a friend; while Arabyn's most unusual agitation convinced her that his sudden appearance boded no good.

We are apt to be speedily alarmed when the faintest shadow of evil comes nigh to those whom we have, as it were, surrounded with an atmosphere of affection; and

Ruth Vincent, who had borne many a heavy trial with the most cheerful resignation, now trembled and shook with a vague indefinite fear. That any one should look with other than a friendly gaze on him she believed so noble and so good, seemed to her most unnatural and strange; she could only account for it by remembering what Arabyn had so often told her, of the ignominy attached to his name, and of all he had already suffered from the power of conventional laws, and systematically developed prejudice.

Ruth thought with generous pleasure, how, by the utmost deference, the most delicate respect and consideration towards Arabyn, she would show this stranger that she, at least, treated him as one to be honoured and revered; and as in imagination she glanced on into future years, her heart beat high, at thought how boldly she would take her stand at his side in face of all the world, smiling at the contempt that might attach to herself as his wife, increasing in her respect and devotion in proportion as others shunned and slighted him, and sharing in his sorrows with a deeper joy than if all the happiness this world can offer had been given to herself.

Arabyn was not at Mrs. Harcourt's when Ruth arrived there, and she felt a chill of disappointment, for the instinct of her true affection told her that he was suffering at that hour, and these were the moments when she most desired to be with him. She trusted he would still come, as she knew he fully intended doing so; but he did not appear, and her uneasiness became excessive. Edmund refused to see her as usual, and she heard that he was now daily more weak and exhausted, for his life was fading fast away. Mrs. Harcourt told her, that Edmund had that morning had a note from a gentleman, who it appeared had been an old friend of his father's, saying, that as he had long been absent from England, he had never known that his former acquaintance had left a son, till he had heard him accidentally mentioned in the village, and that he would come to see him the next day. Edmund was pleased, he said, at the idea of seeing his newly found friend; but Mrs. Harcourt herself wondered much what could have brought this gentleman to their dull neighbourhood.

Ruth was instantly struck by the idea that this might be the person she had seen; but her anxiety continued undiminished, as she could only conclude that he had come to this place in search of Arabyn; a thousand nameless fears assailed her; and she watched vainly, in the idea that he might still arrive, till the increasing darkness made it necessary for her to return home.

Ruth was thankful to go at last, in order to escape from Mr. Parker's admonitions, so emphatically qualified by himself as humane remarks prompted by a judicious kindness. It was the custom of this worthy gentleman, who was always remarkably happy and comfortable himself, to assure any of his friends who were sorrowful, that they were in a morbid state of mind; he had speedily observed, that on this occasion Ruth had lost her usual cheerfulness, and he therefore thought it his duty to tell her that health was the greatest of all blessings, and as he perceived she was still in full possession of it, he did not suppose there was any other cause of annoyance which could justify her desponding appearance; at all events, consideration for the feelings of others was ever a sufficient motive, with strong-minded persons, to induce them to look gay upon every occasion,

—merely as an illustration, he would beg her to remember that no one had ever known *his* sufferings (this was strictly true, for he had never even known them himself). Poor Ruth listened patiently to all he had to say, but it was with a feeling of intense relief that she at last found herself alone in the quiet lanes.

It was not late but already quite dark, and a few pale stars were gleaming tremulously in the clear grey sky, whilst far on the shadowy horizon, just where the day so lately had expired, there lingered still a soft bright light, like to that golden radiance that hangs for ever benignly over man's universal tomb. Ruth took no heed at first of the calm beauty of this scene; there was a dark foreboding busy at her heart, a strong conviction that the human sorrow, for which she had ever looked with such serene courage, was stealing towards her now, armed with a power it never could have had before, since it was about to wound her in the person of another; and for herself too there was a shrinking dread of coming evil, a terror that she was about to lose some of the brightness and the beauty which had of late been given to her mortal life. Long since, when praying hourly that her earthly career might be so directed that each event should be the means of bringing her more humbly unto Him, it had ever seemed to her as though a prophetic voice had whispered to her soul, "Thou shalt come to Him through thy desolation," and she had looked forward with a calm enjoyment to a lonely exile from all the joys of this human existence, in the bright hope that it was His Hand which should lead her into the wilderness of her life, to commune with her there alone; and to-day for the first time, the thought of this desolation came to her with a sharp and bitter pang.

Ruth Vincent was suffering now the penalty of that which men do not usually hold to be a sin; she had indulged in a hope of earthly happiness, she had permitted a sweet dream of mortal joys to pass before her immortal spirit, in all the fascination of its brightness; it was a pure and lawful hope which she had admitted into her heart, far less for herself than for another, a quiet, happy vision of the time when she should give new joy to a life she believed most joyless, and be a friend to one unjustly friendless; yet it was a dream of earth, it had its root and spring in the dust of the ground, and to dust it should have returned, trampled beneath her feet, if for one moment it retarded their progress on the steep ascent that leads to Calvary.

We say that there is no sin in the innocent joys of earth, and in earth's innocent sorrows; and for others so let it be, we may not condemn our brethren; but for ourselves?—Is there any one to whom at times the doctrine of the Cross has not arisen in a light most new, distinct, and piercing? When we behold it terrible in its surpassing purity, its awful dominion over our whole entire being, its boundless demands on each individual soul, are we not then suddenly lost in horror, to think that so many centuries should have rolled around that Cross Divine, bringing each one a freight of adoring spirits to its foot, and that still we should have such low and narrow views of the service required of those who are bound to it by the holy tie of their regenerate life? What mean these words which we all profess so openly, "I am determined to know *nothing*, save Him crucified?" If ever we are acquainted with any joy or sorrow out of Him; if ever one thought, or hope, or feeling, or desire, that is not His alone, is admitted to our souls, now made the temple of that too awfully holy to be mentioned here? Are we not deceiving ourselves when, not content with thanking our Father for the fair aspect and pleasant fragrance of the flowers He has scattered in our path, we pluck them in our hands and press them to our breasts, till their intoxicating sweetness passes into our very souls, and still we say, "these are but lawful joys;" or, when He in His mercy hath rent away the links that chained our feet in our heavenward path, and sorrow hath come upon us, is there no mockery in professing to endure our afflictions with a holy resignation, because we are His people? Are they then borne for His sake? have we found a martyrdom of flesh or spirit in labouring for the glory of His name? If not, what have we to do with them, wherefore are we weeping, if we have still the promise of His great redemption? If we are His, should we rejoice in aught save our salvation, or in the advancement of His kingdom, or over the repenting of a sinner, and should we ever mourn, except for that one fearful misery, the bitter woe of sin?

These thoughts suddenly assailed Ruth Vincent with a stinging power, when unconsciously lifting up her eyes, she met the solemn gaze of the pure stars that were brightening rapidly in the lucid sky; those stars! how often had she looked upon them with unspeakable joy, because she held them to be the glorious types of those immortal hopes, which were attainable even to her weak, helpless spirit; and were the stars less radiant now, or the celestial hopes withholden from her grasp, that she walked thus sorrowful and anxious, full of terror and despondency? No! it was for the shadows or the sunshine of her mortal life that she was so troubled and careful;

and as she confessed to herself that it was so, she bowed her head on her hands, stricken to the heart with a passionate remorse, to think that it should be so full of human hopes and fears; her soul had never for one moment quitted its allegiance; but she felt that the earth-stain was upon it, and they who have struggled as she had done for the perfection of the *puri corde*, alone can know how sore is the conflict, how bitter the consciousness of repeated failure: then came upon her that unutterable longing after Him Who is the Life, the Light of man, with which the soul is at times so awfully overwhelmed; and as she thought how the afflictions, whose vague prospect had so terrified her, might be the appointed discipline of His great mercy, she felt that not only would she willingly welcome them in all their sharpness to her heart; but that she would pray for them, plead for them, as the sweetest gifts His bounty could bestow.

With renewed strength, though sorely humbled, Ruth Vincent now walked on, thinking how, to win the blessing of the mourners, she would gladly become chief among them. A letter was put into her hand as she entered the house, and a faint smile passed over her lips as she thought on the timely lesson which the stars had taught her, for the trial was come, it was from Arabyn; and announced his departure. He began by saying in words, what he had so long taught her to feel, that to her alone he now looked for happiness on earth; he was forced to leave her thus suddenly, he said, by an occurrence to him most disastrous; but he entreated her to agree to Mr. Denham's wish of going abroad immediately, where he would join them without delay. For the time she remained in England he had a most urgent request to make to her, with which he besought her to comply. The cause of his sudden departure was the arrival of a man who was his mortal enemy, and who had come hither in pursuit of him; there was a secret between him and this man Raymond which he could not now disclose to her; but which she should one day know. Meanwhile he hoped and believed that she would trust in him, that he had some important reason for what he asked, when he besought of her to avoid all intercourse with him; and if they met (as Raymond would certainly seek her society) he implored her never to let the name of Arabyn be mentioned between them: he concluded by saying that this request must seem to her strange, and almost suspicious, especially as Raymond was not only a devoted, but a most eminent Christian; but hereafter all should be satisfactorily explained; and meanwhile, he trusted implicitly to her own generous faith in himself.

Arabyn had judged wisely when he calculated so composedly on the trusting simplicity of Ruth Vincent's character. She had once for all judged him worthy of her highest esteem and affection, and from that hour she held herself bound to believe in the rectitude and purity of his motives at all times, however mysterious his actions might seem to herself. She never dreamt of inquiring into the reason of any thing he did, but quietly trusted to his superior goodness and wisdom.

Ruth was not one to repose confidence in friends, and then cast them off as soon as there seemed any ground to mistrust them: she felt no wonder, no suspicion, respecting this request of Arabyn's. She never doubted that he had some excellent reason for making it; but with that she had nothing to do—it was her part merely to obey it implicitly.

Arabyn had also been very prudent when he took care himself to bear testimony to Raymond's high character, whose true devotion to Christianity he knew Ruth could not fail to learn ; while he trusted that, by the silence he had imposed upon her, he had rendered it impossible for Raymond to discover what the object of his sojourn in this place had really been. Of course his immediate departure was absolutely necessary to effect this : but it was only the delay of a few weeks, as Mr. Denham had decided on going abroad before the winter set in, and would, in fact, already have started but for Ruth's earnest petition that he would not take her away from Edmund's vicinity just at this period.

Arabyn's scheme, devised and executed in the space of a few hours, proved perfectly successful. There remained, in fact, no means by which Raymond could have discovered the truth, as the infidel had been known to none but the Harcourt family, and they were in complete ignorance of Ruth Vincent's position with regard to him. She had been at their house very seldom of late, and besides, they would have found it very difficult to believe that the wealthy heiress, the last of an ancient race, could ever have looked on Philip Arabyn with any other feeling but the most condescending compassion.

Of Ruth herself Raymond heard but little, and never saw her until he had been so completely deceived with respect to Arabyn's plans and intentions, that it never occurred to him to imagine her implicated in them. He had very speedily found traces of the infidel's influence on the mind of Edmund, in whom he soon became deeply interested. Raymond saw that his faith had been tampered with, and though it burned all the brighter for the vain shadows with which Arabyn had sought to darken it, still, in the excitement of fever, or the exhaustion of weakness, these dark insinuations and subtle doubts haunted his memory, and harassed him, from the very horror with which his whole soul repulsed them.

Still more evident was the work of the infidel in the morbid terror which the deformed boy seemed to feel lest he should be a burden to those around him; in his strange anxiety to be left in solitude, unwatched and untended; above all, in the vehement desire he expressed that he might die alone, when none were near to be saddened by his last agonies. Raymond knew well that these unnatural feelings must have had a cause; and when his kindness had at last completely won Edmund's confidence, he obtained from him the recital of Arabyn's cruel statement respecting Ruth Vincent.

Raymond was at first unable to imagine the probable motive of this proceeding; but when Edmund went on to tell him of all the misery he had endured when he discovered that he was actually a dependant on her generosity, he was naturally struck with the idea that Arabyn had entertained some plan for possessing himself of the income thus secured to Edmund. Raymond could not doubt, however, that whatever the infidel's project had been, his own arrival had frustrated it; and he now devoted himself to the task of soothing and consoling the dying sufferer, whose peace of mind had been so wantonly assailed. Much he effected in cheering his last hours, and effacing from his mind the poisonous effects of his contact with Arabyn. He overruled his sensitive desire for solitude during these the awful hours of his last conflict, and persuaded him to admit his friends, especially Mr. Grey. From him Edmund derived much benefit and comfort; for his unfortunate coldness of manner invariably melted away at sight of the bed of death. But Raymond failed completely in effecting what he most wished—in restoring Edmund to the care and tenderness of his adopted sister. He could not be persuaded to see Ruth Vincent: the blow had sunk too deep—his affection for her was so profound, and at the same time so perfectly unselfish, that he could not endure the idea of trespassing on her generous kindness. He sent her messages breathing the most heartfelt gratitude, and he wrote to her daily, so long as his weak hand could hold a pen; but his resolution not to see her became at last what Arabyn had represented it from the first—a species of monomania, which it was in vain to combat.

Raymond only saw Ruth Vincent once at Mr. Harcourt's, and then he was singularly interested by her appearance. He was prepossessed in her favour by all that Edmund and Mr. Grey had told him of her: he had heard from them how rare and unworldly was her character; how truly she sought to worship only in the beauty of holiness; how, day by day, her young life glided away, so pure and spotless; her eyes ever turning instinctively from all unhallowed things, to look up unto heaven with such meek faith; and when he saw her he felt that she was one of those indeed who, walking through a most corrupt and sin-defiled world, calmly gather their white garments round them, that no stain of earth-dust may pollute them.

Ruth, on her part, felt an irresistible reverence for Raymond, even although she knew him to be the enemy of Arabyn. She could only feel convinced that he was strangely deceived respecting the infidel, for of the rectitude and purity of his own character it was impossible to entertain a doubt.

Mr. Denham, meanwhile, like a child with the prospect of a new toy, was frantically impatient to put in execution his scheme of going abroad. Ruth was every day laden with reproaches for the delay she had occasioned; to which he had consented not in the least out of regard to her, but from the dread that if he refused she might leave him to go alone. He had every thing prepared, however, to start at a moment's notice, and Ruth remained resolute in lingering, with the faint hope that Edmund might at the last feel a wish to see her once again: but her suspense was soon removed.

One evening, when the old man lay reposing in his chair, and she was singing a low soft song to lull him into slumber, it suddenly seemed to her as though a solemn echo had mingled with the melody, like a mysterious answer to her own sweet voice. Her hands fell powerless from the instrument, and she listened, almost breathless, while there came to her, distinct upon the still night air, the deep slow tolling of the passing bell.

It is a sound that none can hear unmoved; for it is an awful thing to think how, through the mighty shadows which encompass the terrible Unseen, a soul is going forth alone—a soul that a few hours since was one of us; living our life, sharing in our weakness and our ignorance, and now passing from us like a breath, as though it had but sighed itself out of a world of which it was weary, and wandering away we see not where; never to weep again; to struggle and to hope no more! As the knell of its departure rolls towards us, they whose lives are brightened by earth's blessed ties, grasp with a sudden terror the hands of those most dear to them; and through the chilled heart of those to whom it is given, desolate to bear their cross, there steals a feeling so like to envy that they dare not dwell upon it.

Ruth knew well what was the message brought to her by that sound, and she would not grieve that the orphan and the sufferer had gone to his home: she knew that death was to Edmund but release to a prisoner.

Mr. Denham decided that they were to start the day after Edmund's funeral. They were to go to Switzerland, where Arabyn was to join them immediately.

On the morning of their departure, Ruth stole out to visit the new-made grave of him whose last hours she had not been permitted to attend. The heap of fresh damp mould, beneath which poor Edmund lay, looked chill and black on that cold wintry morning, and Ruth remembered with a pang how the head, now laid so low, had been pillowed on her arm the last time she had seen him. And yet that deep rest seemed to her more than ever sweet just at that moment, for she had a strong conviction that for herself the storms and tribulations of this life were but commencing. She thought on the cheerless existence of the helpless being thus stretched so calmly at her feet, and blessed heaven for the glorious atmosphere of love into which he had entered now, whilst the quiet tears gathered unconsciously in her eyes, and fell upon his resting-place. Suddenly she was startled by a voice close to her, whose tone was full of reproach.

"No tears should be shed for him who lies here,

taking his patient repose, save those of deepest gratitude and joy."

Ruth looked up, and met the gaze of Raymond fixed upon her, with an expression stern yet kind.

"I was wrong indeed," she answered meekly, "but I was not with him at the last; had I seen him in his hour of triumph, doubtless I could not have felt even sad; you were with him, were you not?"

"Yes," said Raymond, "but the last words with which he spoke of any earthly thing, were uttered for you; he bade me tell you that henceforward he would remember all your love and kindness, with the memory of eternity itself;—you do well, indeed, to call that last hour one of triumph."

"His death was happy then, as I knew it must be?"

"So happy, that even to the bystanders it seemed as though they had obtained a glimpse of the glory to come; the departing of his soul was like the rushing forth of a child to its mother's embrace: he had lain still for some time, unconscious of all that was passing round him, but evidently alive to much of which we knew nothing; for often his eyes opened suddenly with a bright glance of recognition, and at times when they were closed, there flashed across his pale lips a smile of the most rapturous joy, like a glowing sunbeam sparkling on serenest waters,—when at last the summons came, for it seemed actually audible to him, though we heard nothing but the sighing of the breeze past the windows, he raised his head from the pillow, and looked up with such a glorious expression of intense ecstatic happiness as I never before saw on the face of mortal man; he stretched out his arms like one about to meet a beloved friend, and with that gaze of deepest bliss, his life on earth was consummated; the light faded from his eyes, the hands fell gently folded, and the passing of his spirit was like the setting of a star into the golden glory of the sunrise."

"Dear Edmund!" said Ruth, "how that one moment must have repaid his life-long suffering! now, indeed, I can leave his grave without a sigh."

"Yet the last few weeks of his life were strangely saddened," said Raymond, "the influence of Philip Arabyn,"—he stopped, for Ruth suddenly started so visibly, that he could scarce believe it was the effect of his own words; but the sound of that forbidden name had reminded her that she had promised to avoid all intercourse with him, and hurriedly saying that she could stay no longer, she thanked him earnestly for his kindness to Edmund, and left the churchyard before he had time to add another word.

Raymond remained motionless for a few minutes, paralyzed by a sudden doubt which seemed to shoot through his mind, that Ruth knew more of Arabyn than he had imagined; could it be possible that she also had been a victim of the infidel?—perhaps the chief object of his sojourn there? The idea was beyond measure dreadful to him, and he determined that very day to go to Mr. Denham's, and ask to see Ruth herself, that he might speak openly, and ascertain the truth in a matter which might be of such fearful importance to her.

Raymond did not know that she was to leave England within an hour of the time when their interview had taken place, and she was already many miles distant when he reached the house; he found it entirely shut up, and from the Harcourts he could only learn their ultimate destination, but not the route they had taken. It was impossible therefore for the Christian to follow them, and he thought it best at all events, that he should follow his original plan, and proceed at once in search of Arabyn.

CHAPTER XV.

THE DEEDS OF ARABYN BEAR SUCH FRUIT AS HE LOOKED NOT FOR.

On one of the richest and most fertile plains of Lombardy, stands a very beautiful little village; amongst its picturesque, but humble buildings, a small Italian villa stands out conspicuous, for it is built with considerable taste and elegance, and is surrounded by a large garden filled with stately poplar trees.

In one of the pleasantest rooms of this pleasant little abode, sat Richard Stanley, one bright Autumn day, when the Italian sky was still glowing with warm sunshine, though in more northern climates it was already almost winter.

It would have been scarce possible to have recognised in the young man the same person who stood shuddering beside the prison-house of Trieste, on that dark night; then his haggard and anxious face told but too plainly of the fierce disquietude within; now his eye was clear and joyous, his smile frank and ready, and his step firm; he had escaped from the most powerful of all spells, the influence of a superior mind,—and that mind at once most gifted and most perverted.

Stanley had, throughout the period of his temptation, been sinning against his own better judgment in adopting the fatal opinions of Arabyn.; but it would have required a faith far more rooted and firm, more living and active, than his had ever been, to have resisted the singular eloquence of the infidel, or the powerful fascination of his fine intellect. Now, however, the months of prayer and reflection, which he had passed since he parted with Raymond, had been sufficient thoroughly to confirm and strengthen those principles with which the Christian had given new life to his soul, and, although his hope and confidence were tempered by the recollection of his fall, yet a submissive and unquestioning faith was grounded and settled within him, with a strength and vitality which nothing could overthrow. Never, certainly, had life been so joyous or so bright to Richard Stanley, as it was since he had finally turned his gaze from earth to heaven, and openly taken his stand as a follower of things spiritual, an heir of immortal life.

There are many things in this our world, whose cause and purpose are altogether hid from our darkened eyes, and before whose bitter and mournful consequences we can but bow down in blind submission. Of these, perhaps the most universal and the most inexorable is our unconquerable longing for human sympathy; doubtless the sweetest and the best feelings of our nature are connected with the natural course of our affections, for they call forth much that is noble, generous, and devoted; but it is equally undeniable, that if our only earthly happiness is derived from them, they are also the source of all our misery; all may be bright and cheering in the exercise of filial love, or in fraternal intercourse; and there may be something of unimagined joy in the mother's fond look upon her first-born child: and yet even there, how often are ingratitude and cutting indifference manifested! and if, in the absence of these ties of blood, men go further, and seek to lavish somewhat of that mysterious tenderness for our brethren of the dust, which dwells within each one of us, on the friend they have chosen, or the being they have loved ; how often, how almost inevitably does it happen, that they do but work out thereby a degree of wretchedness, which otherwise they never would have known ! But notwithstanding the experience of almost every life that struggles through its little day, so burdened and weary, because it will for ever forge chains to bind itself to the earth ; it is strange to see how we do rouse up our latent affections, and wantonly, as it were, twine ourselves with clinging affection around some perishing mortal like ourselves ;—yet better thus, better in deepest sorrow to mourn the defection of those to whom our hearts have warmed, than, in the stoical indifference of the egotist, to wrap ourselves round in cold security, and leave those about us to smile or suffer as they may.

And now, at the very time when life seemed to him most radiant and smiling,—when all was serenity and bliss within, Richard Stanley was madly giving up his every hope and dream to one frail being, seeking to make to himself new ties, to win to his side a gentle child of clay, over whom to watch, and pray, and weep! Was there no passing thought to bid him pause ere he raised a new obstacle between himself and Heaven? No ; gay and light-hearted, Stanley daily followed the path which led him to the presence of his new-found treasure, and often pondering, as he walked from his own dwelling to the villa, on the high and glorious destinies that open out before the Christian in his earthly pilgrimage, he little thought that the severest trial to his faith would be in the love he was now cherishing.

Richard Stanley was not alone in that sunny little room, through whose open windows the soft Italian air was breathing warm and fragrant. By his side sat a young girl, whom, although he had been acquainted with her for months, he only knew by the name of "Nadine ;" a name which she told him expressed, in the Russian language, the word "hope," and which had been given her by her mother, who was a native of that country; while that of her father, who was an Englishman, had been carefully concealed from her by her brother, her only surviving relation, because, he said, it was in Italy so disgracefully notorious that it would be injurious to her to bear it.

Stanley, however, cared very little for her birth and parentage as he gazed upon her; she seemed to him the sweetest and most attractive being he had ever seen. She was evidently very young, and looked almost too fair and fragile for this rough world; her colour came and went with every changing thought; and there was something almost wild in the fitful glancing of her large hazel eyes; her soft hair, so long and silken that it could scarce be confined, hung round her face like light clouds round some fair star. She seemed sensitive to the highest degree, a breath of wind passing over her made her shudder; and she was evidently of enthusiastic temperament, and full of imaginative thought. Her manners were perfectly artless, and showed more of her feelings towards Stanley than one less innocent and natural would have ventured to display.

At some distance from Nadine and her companion sat a lady whose appearance was rather singular: she was extremely tall, and certain angular proportions, as well as her being slightly bent, seemed to render it probable that she was somewhat advanced in years; but there was something very juvenile in the arrangement of her headdress, which, in connexion with her person, was positively startling; her hair was cut short, and curled round her neck; and a set of very unmeaning features were gathered up into an expression of sweet simplicity and most prime innocence; her voice was screwed up to a gentle soprano, and it was her invariable rule to speak with her eyes half shut, and her head on one side. This lady was occupied in dissecting the leg of a fly, the fragments of which she then examined with the microscope.

Stanley's first acquaintance with these ladies, the solitary inhabitants of the villa, had been quite accidental, but it soon ripened into a pleasant intimacy, and he had speedily learned all of their history which there was to tell.

Nadine was an orphan; she had no recollection of either father or mother; and Miss Goodwin had been her governess for many years. The young girl had been left to the care of her only brother, and had from her infancy resided in this little villa, with the respectable Englishwoman described above for her sole companion and friend; the monotony of her existence being only varied by an occasional visit from her brother. Stanley very soon saw that Miss Goodwin was the last person who should have had the charge of a young mind; she was a well-meaning woman, but without either sense or judgment; she had vast pretensions to being a "religious person," as she herself expressed it, and was in fact quite sincere, and in general honestly influenced by her principles; but she had set out on a totally mistaken system, and the line of conduct she pursued in accordance with her ideas would inevitably be repugnant to an unprepared mind or an unyielding temper.

She affected—for in a woman of fifty it could only be affectation—a childish innocence of ideas, and an extreme simplicity of tastes; and instead of reproving or resisting the universal evil which forced itself before her eyes, she endeavoured to appear unaware of it. She attempted—what is utterly impossible in a world like this—to retain, in the present ripe stage of her existence, all that ignorance of evil and love of unsophisticated joys which are so pleasing in childhood. She did not seek to separate the good from the ill, which is to be found in the pleasures and occupations of maturer life, but entrenched herself in an ardent passion for pastoral amusements and innocent frivolities without either aim or substance. Doubtless, all this was the result of a weak mind, for it is in the very nature of a strong and sound judgment to extract the good from the mass of this world's sin and weakness, and use it without abusing it. But by this means her natural energies, such as they were, were frittered away on unmeaning trifles, and the real power of usefulness, which she had in common with the lowest and meanest of this earth, were expended on devoted attentions to bees, butterflies, and flowers.

Such a representation of religion (if we dare so profane the name) was most pernicious to a person of Nadine's character; there was nothing remarkable in her talents or her intellect, but she was quite capable of reflecting on cause and effect, which perhaps Miss Goodwin was not; and for her own great misfortune, she was of singularly imaginative mind. A vivid and susceptible fancy can scarce fail to be a dangerous gift, when there is so much of real and certainly providential darkness round us, that, except we do, in child-like confidence, walk only by the light that is given us, the soul plunges hopelessly among the clouds which veil our life, and we become unfit for the duties and the trials of our daily existence.

Nadine's reasoning powers were not strong, and her mind was easily led away. She had a physical dread of suffering, and shrank hopelessly from the mere thought of life's actual trials, from the positive and palpable misfortunes which are our heritage here below. She had never known what it was to endure pain, mental or bodily; and her peculiar mode of existence had spared her the knowledge of the daily disappointments and difficulties which are sooner or later inseparable from our mortal state. She lived, in fact, in a world of her own creating, built on the wildest fancies, and brightened by the most impossible dreams.

Singularly sweet and amiable in her temper and disposition, she might have been moulded to a character of great excellence in many respects; but, left to the tender mercies of Miss Goodwin, she had become timid and visionary, with a weak and ill-regulated mind.

Miss Goodwin had received orders to keep her young pupil in strict seclusion, and to these directions she had as yet adhered; but Miss Goodwin possessed some ideas of her own, and, though singularly few in number, not altogether to be despised. She was perfectly aware of Stanley's position and prospects in life, (as a single lady of fifty, could she be otherwise?) and she considered it highly advantageous to Nadine, that she should encourage the attachment which she had perceived before the young man was at all aware of it himself; nothing doubting, in her well-meaning officiousness, that the brother of the orphan girl would thank her for having settled his young sister comfortably in life, and so relieved him of a heavy responsibility,—and perhaps she was not far wrong in her conclusions.

As for Stanley, he had, from the commencement of his intimacy with Nadine, determined upon marrying her, if, on a longer acquaintance, she appeared to him still as gentle and lovely a being as she now seemed to his admiring eyes. It mattered nothing to him that she had inherited only a name, so disgraced that she could not even acknowledge it,—he was now perfectly independent, no one had a right to ask a reason for his actions; the death of his cousin had put him in possession of a large fortune—his debt to Raymond was long since acquitted, and he might have concluded this matter when he pleased, for the young Nadine made no attempt to conceal how very dear had become to her the pleasant companion of the last few months;—but there was one circumstance which had caused him as yet to make a delay most painful to himself.

As may readily be supposed, one of the most determined resolutions which he had taken when he openly enlisted under the banner of the cross, was, that not only he never would take, for the companion of his life, one who was not like himself an open and sincere Christian, but that he would avoid with care the slightest intimacy with any who were not so. This was in accordance with the advice of Raymond, for whom he felt so profound a reverence; and he was also too painfully aware of his own weakness and instability of disposition, not to feel that it was his distinct duty to abstain from entering into those temptations, which it might be equally incumbent on another to brave. Now he could not but own to himself, that there was much in the tone of Nadine's mind to cause him the deepest anxiety. She was certainly neither thoughtless nor unreflecting, and he felt it to be most natural, that she should show a decided disinclination to join in such outward manifestations of religion as Miss Goodwin was pleased to exhibit; but there were times when Nadine had, seemingly quite unconsciously, given out sentiments and opinions which sounded strangely from the lips of a young girl, and even so nearly approached to atheism as to make him shudder; nothing pleased her more than a metaphysical discussion, which she handled in a manner almost worthy of a disciple of Kant.

It was at first a source of wonder to Stanley, how she had ever acquired such ideas, for it was easy to see that neither Miss Goodwin's conversations, nor yet her own private reading, could have produced them; but it very soon ceased to be a matter of astonishment when she began to talk to him of her brother, and of the delight she had taken in learning from him the doctrines, apparently to her so fascinating, of a most false philosophy. Stanley could never exactly ascertain from what she said, whether this brother, who had so unfortunately been her teacher, were actually an infidel. Nadine's ideas on the subject were too confused and vague to admit of a clear definition; but it was sufficiently evident, as it seemed to Stanley, that he was a person of singular talent, with, at the very least, a strong tendency to scepticism, and that she had not escaped the fatal taint altogether; but she was very young, and of a pliant disposition; and at times, after a conversation with himself, she would speak as though she had a due appreciation of the great truths he urged upon her.

It is very easy in most cases, to make our reason subservient to our inclinations, and Stanley argued himself into the belief, that her mind, having been perverted by the influence of another, might equally be led to sounder doctrines by his own endeavours. With this hope he quieted his conscience; and, giving way to a weakness peculiar to some minds, never allowed himself to contemplate a different result from that which he so ardently desired. Still he never for a moment wavered in his firm determination, that, if he failed in his efforts, he would tear this fatal love from his heart, let it cost what it might.

There were times when Stanley asked himself if, in such an emergency, Nadine would not have a right to accuse him of having destroyed her happiness, perhaps for ever; but he loved well and truly, his heart beat high with hope, he would not even think that this could be the case, and so went on from day to day, luxuriating in the sweet present, with that instinctive dread of the future which haunts each child of clay.

Thus, then, undisturbed and unreproved, they had passed together that brief and happy summer; in Nadine it was perhaps excusable, that she should forget all save her present deep enjoyment; but in Stanley it was assuredly a criminal self-indulgence, which he expiated with long years of remorse, and for which even then his heart rebuked him. Yet he too might be forgiven for clinging to a happiness so rare on earth, as day after day they went out wandering together through the waving woods, and beneath that bright blue sky, with no other companion than their own glad thoughts, which scarcely required to be expressed in words, seeing the brightness of the summer reflected in each other's eyes, while earth seemed to give forth her sweetest flowers and her softest light, as though in joy to see her children thus rejoicing.

During hours such as these Stanley was lost to all but the actual presence of Nadine; but of late, when alone in the stillness of the night, whose stern solitude tears back inexorably the veil we draw around our souls by day, his mind had frequently become the prey to a most painful conflict. He could not conceal from himself, that while he became each day more passionately attached to Nadine, he was not aware of having made any progress whatever, in implanting the principles of Divine truth in her soul; yet he still flattered himself that she was not altogether devoid of them; there was but as it were a vein of poison running through her whole mind, which pervaded every thought and sentiment; he well knew how strong is the power of early impressions, more especially when, before the judgment is mature, sceptical ideas have been introduced into an active mind. Sometimes his words so evidently produced an effect upon her, that, after much restless and painful thought, he invariably arrived at the conclusion, that he must not yet despair, that it was a work of time, but that all would still be well. He had sufficient self-command over himself, never openly to avow to her either his attachment, or the obstacle which forced him to conceal it, dreading that the knowledge of it might influence her in any change of opinion; but Nadine was far too guileless and confiding ever to look beyond the present day.

Meanwhile the sunny hours had made themselves wings and flown away; that summer (to which Stanley long looked back through the vista of departed years, when old and broken down, tottering to the grave, as the one green spot in the desert of his life), had faded into autumn, and autumn again had deepened to winter; the country had assumed that peculiar appearance, which gives to the gay and happy so painful an impression of universal decay, and to many an aching heart so sweet an assurance, that, since all things fade and die, it too shall rest at last.

On the morning of which we speak, Nadine had met Stanley, on his arrival at the villa, with an announcement which he felt to be of the first importance to them both, and which must in fact bring matters at once to a crisis. She informed him that her brother was to arrive the next day, to pay her a passing visit.

Stanley was well aware that her brother would undoubtedly object to the uncertain position in which they had as yet remained towards each other; nor did he himself think it right that this state of things should continue any longer. But it was from him—it was from this her only relation that Nadine had learned those insidious and dangerous principles; and he deemed it absolutely necessary that he should become acquainted with him, in order that he might judge if his influence over his sister was likely to be permanent.

Stanley was also fully determined that she should only become his wife on the positive condition that she was to give up all intercourse with her brother; and he could not of course feel certain that he would obtain the consent of either of them to what must appear so unjustifiable a request, though it seemed to him quite necessary that he should make it, as he dared not run the risk of seeing her who would be united to him in ties so close, drawn away by the arguments of another from the faith of which he was the chosen servant.

Stanley at length came to the conclusion, that, after seeing the brother of his Nadine, he would decide finally and permanently whether a union with her would be justifiable in him, as a follower of the cross; and though he had a confident hope that it might be so, he was yet solemnly resolved not to deceive himself, and to act according to the law of obedience, though by so doing he involved the perishing of his whole earthly happiness.

It was now for the first time that Stanley felt and understood, how greatly he had erred in the temporizing and inconsistent course he had hitherto pursued. With a heavy sigh he at last raised his head and met the large wondering eyes of Nadine fixed upon him, eloquent of her unuttered anxiety; for it was very unusual for him to seem so forgetful of her presence. He made no other answer to the question which she asked him in that earnest look, than by proposing that they should go together to take their accustomed walk.

Miss Goodwin, one of whose most favourite amusements was ill health, refused to accompany them, on account of the cold; and they proceeded alone through one of the interminable avenues of poplar trees so common in that part of the country. It was one of those fitful days of an Italian winter, when the sky is one moment bright with sunshine, and the next covered with clouds that flit swiftly over it: the wind sighed with a melancholy sound among the trees, and swept the withered leaves to their feet.

Stanley walked on in silence, for there was a dark

presentiment busy at his heart He felt that, whatever might be the issue, this was at least the last day of this long period of undisturbed enjoyment; and there is something in the uncertainty of human life which makes us shrink from the prospect of a change, even though we look forward to better days. It is so rare (and there are few of our earthly blessings more valuable than the certainty of this fact), so very rare that we are permitted to enjoy a season of peace and joy in this life, that we may well tremble to look back on it, even though no audible voice have announced the rising of the coming storm on the far horizon.

How did Stanley cling to this last walk, these last hours of a long period which had been rendered so bright by that fair precarious dream! The very uncertainty had been attractive to him;—the secrecy, the poetry of their attachment. There had been nothing in it of this world, of every-day matter of fact life; it had been a silent affection, enshrined in their own breasts, and never unhallowed by being expressed in words. None knew of it; they scarce knew it themselves; only they had felt day after day the gradual strengthening of the invisible link which bound them together—the silent drawing of soul to soul, of heart to heart. But Stanley felt sadly that all this at least was over; and, depressed as he was by the strange chill which seemed to envelope him, he dared not at that moment admit even the possibility that Nadine might yet be lost to him for ever. Independently of his own utter misery should this be the result, there had arisen this day before him a terrible remorse, at thought of all that she would suffer if he were forced to leave her.

Alas! Stanley felt, as he thought on this, that there are none of our evil propensities so difficult to root out as selfishness. It had seemed to him impossible, in the earlier days of their intimacy, to abandon at once the tempting and dangerous hope that he should at last obtain her to be his gentle friend through life, as heavenly wisdom would have prompted in those emphatic words, "Come ye out and be ye separate;" but he should have remembered, that it was too great a risk for her to run, who might have been happy with another.

And slowly Stanley walked on in silence, while Nadine seemed to have caught the infection of his sadness, and walked quietly at his side, occasionally glancing towards him with an anxious look. They came at length to a spot where they generally paused to look at a fine view, displayed to great advantage by an opening in the trees; and now, by the mere force of habit, they paused to look upon it.

Long afterwards, when Stanley had passed through a lengthened and cheerless life, and had reached the extreme verge of old age, when his soul was already, as it were, on the wing for another world, that scene, as it was now before him—that hour, never to be forgotten—revisited him in his dreams. The far distant hills crowned with fleecy clouds, the nearer country, rich in its variegated colouring, the tall trees round them, and the slight form at his side of his sweet Nadine, with her soft eyes raised to his face with that pleading look of anxious inquiry. Yes, often in his heavy slumbers did his soul turn from the awful realm to which it was hastening, to behold once more this scene of earthly joys; and the old man would stretch out his withered hands to clasp again the form that had mouldered into dust, and when they only fell in empty air, he would wake to beat his breast and weep for the vanished dream of his early days.

At length Nadine spoke, half trembling, for Stanley's manner had alarmed her, she knew not why.

"You are very silent! perhaps it is the melancholy beauty of this landscape which saddens you. I feel it also—this wind chills me: our bright summer days have indeed passed away."

"They have passed away for ever!" echoed Stanley; for her voice sounded to him almost prophetic.

"Oh, not for ever!" said Nadine, earnestly. "Spring will soon come again, and we are young: we have surely many years yet to live." Poor child of clay! and the flowers of that expected spring were to blossom on her grave!

"Let us hope it may be as you say," said Stanley, in a low voice. Nadine pressed closer to his side, and they once more walked away, slowly and silently; whilst the wind howled sadly round them, and there came a darkness over the clear sunshine, as though nature were mourning now for her hapless children.

They parted at the gate of the villa; and Nadine, tormented by a vague disquietude, entreated him to come very early next day,—it was possible that her brother might arrive that same night.

Stanley promised to do so; then he lingered long, and gazed upon her face, and held her hand, as though he could not bear to part from her: but the last walk was ended, the last day was drawing to a close, and he could stay no longer. He turned at length, and walked slowly to his own house, which was a mile or two distant from the village. Nadine watched him till he was out of sight, and wondered, as he disappeared, how she had ever believed that she had known happiness before she met with him.

Stanley continued the whole of the evening feverish and anxious, and he passed the long hours wandering about in utter restlessness of mind; night came at last, but without repose for him; he lay revolving in his mind again and again his present position, and his future prospects, with that self-torture which we cannot avoid during the dark silent hours when there is nothing to distract our thoughts from self; and, when at last he slept, he was pursued with dreams far worse than his waking reflections.

He rose in the morning weary and unrefreshed, and sought for some occupations which would employ his time until it was a suitable hour for proceeding to the villa, where he doubted not Nadine's brother was already arrived.

On the table before him lay a packet of letters, and mechanically he took them up, and commenced reading them; they were those which Raymond had written to him since they parted at Innspruck; they were written with a view to confirm and strengthen him in the pure creed from which he once had fallen; and Stanley grew more restless as he read them, for they recalled to him most painfully the influence, so singularly powerful, which Philip Arabyn had exercised over him; and he pondered long on the strange power which this man seemed to possess over the minds of all who approached him, resulting alike from the extraordinary fascination of his manner, and the might of his strong intellect, and most rare eloquence.

Stanley felt also, as he read the words of noble counsel, stern and uncompromising, which Raymond had addressed to him, how far he had come short of the high standard which his friend had encouraged him to take; how perfectly incompatible with our faith, severe in its unearthly purity, are half measures, inconsistency, or self-indulgence. When he remembered the gulf of misery from which he had been rescued, Stanley saw, with a tardy and vain repentance, that he had of late been most unworthily weak. He could not redeem the past, but he could preserve the future from the stains which never could be effaced from the vanished days; and he took his way to the villa in deep thought.

He was met at once with indications of the arrival of the expected guest; the door of the sitting-room was open, and he entered unobserved; the brother and sister were standing together at the window; Nadine's hands were clasped on his arm, and she was looking up to him, talking earnestly, whilst he seemed listening with calm and cold attention. A sudden pang shot through Stanley's heart as he caught sight of that tall commanding figure; his breath came short and quick,—he moved forward; slowly the brother of Nadine turned towards him; the clear dark eyes met his,—the well-known smile of bitter scorn rose on the curved lip; there was no mistaking that face of intellectual beauty,—that piercing glance of proud defiance!

Stanley clasped his hands over his eyes, and uttered a cry of anguish; it was the face of Philip Arabyn! The truth flashed upon him; he remembered that he had often spoken of his young sister, on whom, as he expressed it, had been inflicted, as on himself, that conventional ostracism with which the world punishes the sin of another's reflected crime. And he, Stanley,—the sworn Christian,—*he* had learnt to love, had chosen for the wife of his bosom, the sister—the pupil of Philip Arabyn!

He reeled as though his senses were abandoning him, and leaned gasping against the wall. The dark thoughts came rushing like a torrent through his soul, sweeping away for ever his hopes, his dreams, his all of life. Philip Arabyn, Philip Arabyn, the scoffer, the infidel, the hypocrite, the traitor, the murderer!—for surely he was so in thought and will when he wrote that fearful letter—the fiend in the form of an angel, that walked over the world, withering every soul that came in contact with his own; seeking to pollute the pure in heart, to lead the young astray, to shake the firm faith, to cause the tottering to fall, and hurl the fallen into deeper darkness; to dispel the immortal hope of the imprisoned spirit, feeding with consummate art the appetite of those who hunger and thirst after vice and degradation. The fiend who had so nearly ruined his undying soul, instilling with his syren voice the darkest principles into his mind, working on his weakness to lead him into crimes which he now shuddered to think of; the fiend whose intellect was unequalled, whose fascination was irresistible, whose extraordinary hypocrisy could deceive the strongest reason.

Too surely all was over now; he dared not place himself once more within the thrall of him whose power could destroy his soul, for whom he felt the horror with which an evil spirit might inspire him. And Nadine, he knew, he felt, that she must be her brother's victim; how could she, the ignorant enthusiastic girl, escape the influence which had overcome many a strong mind? and how could he, so weak, susceptible, and yielding, even attempt to save her?—it would be but to involve himself, his own immortal spirit in her utter ruin. What company dared he to have with unbelievers,—what had the follower of Christ to do with Belial?

It seemed to him at that moment as though unknown and hideous spectres came crowding round him,—the spectres of those whom Arabyn had perverted, all pointing with horror to the certain tomb whence the infidel had torn the immortal hope for them! Oh! the horrible remorse which laid waste his soul as he thought on Nadine; yet he must leave her, he must fly from her, bearing with him but one hope, that she would soon forget him. Oh! that he could with his own life-blood blot out from her heart the memory of the last few months; it might be that he had no strong hold in her affection,—and he earnestly trusted that so it was.

These thoughts passed over him like lightning, while Arabyn and Nadine stood looking on him; she with a painful wonder, not unmixed with a dark indefinite fear; he with the cold contempt which was the habitual expression of his face in the presence of his fellow-creatures, unless he purposely disguised it.

Arabyn was the first to speak; he turned calmly to Nadine:—

"This, then, my sister, is the friend of whom you have talked so much; the person whom you have chosen to believe a demi-god, till you are about to discover that he is of baser clay than your own self! Poor child; you are to be early initiated into the established ways of this pleasant world. You know not that he was once my friend also; yet look upon him now, with what a glance of hate he gazes on me!"

"Oh! what means this?" exclaimed Nadine, as she broke from him, and advanced with timid steps towards

Stanley; "I entreat of you, tell me what this means,—what has happened? Why do you look upon me thus?"

His breast heaved, he wrung his hands as though in torture, he turned from her with an agonized effort.

"Nadine, Nadine," he murmured, "you are lost to me for ever! O agony! for ever!—You are *his* sister, and in these words my sentence is sealed, and we must meet upon this earth no more; you have taught me what human happiness may be,—and now it is gone from me, and for ever. Yes, all is over for us both perhaps; but do not curse me: if I have darkened your life, believe how horrible will be my own. Oh! pray that I may die, that I may never see the light of day again. I would have bought one hour of joy for you with my own life; and yet it is I who have blighted your young existence! It is vain to linger here, to seek to utter what I feel. I do not ask you to forgive me; it is better you should hate me; it were but scanty justice to my sinful folly. Nadine, Nadine, forget that ever I have crossed your path; a little while since, you knew me not, and you were happy; think of me no more, and be so yet again. And now farewell! for ever in this life farewell!"

He gazed upon her one moment, as though he sought to stamp every feature on his memory; then, with one despairing moan, rushed from the room. Nadine stood for a moment mute with astonishment and dismay; and then, with a piercing shriek, she called his name, and would have darted after him, but Arabyn seized her by the arm.

"What! would you degrade yourself by following him?—let him go, base, cold-hearted bigot!"

"I cannot, I cannot," shrieked Nadine, falling back

upon the arm that prevented her sinking to the ground, "Oh! Philip! you do not know what we have been to one another, and he said farewell!—did you not hear him, he said *farewell!*"

"He said it, and he meant it;" answered the cold stern voice of Arabyn,—"would you know why he deserts you thus? come, I will tell you; his letter to me, when he left me at Trieste, sufficiently explains his present conduct: listen, wretched child, and take your first lesson in human life. This man dreams that he has a soul—know you what he means by that?—a something invisible, impalpable, a spark, an empty sound, a name to which men in very wantonness have prefixed an idea; and not only does he imagine this rare conception to be existent now within his body, (though he awards not the same honour to the animals, whose intelligence is but a little lower than our own,) but he believes it will exist, long after his flesh has mouldered into dust, exist to suffer, or to enjoy: to recollect the petty crimes, (if that be crime, which is the involuntary submission to our resistless destiny,) the petty crimes of his unasked for life, and bear their penalty throughout eternity! and now, to keep this visionary spark immaculate in its temple of clay, weak wretch! he dares not come in contact with me, because my eyes are no longer blinded by bigotry, or false enthusiasm, and he leaves you whom he loves as well as such a being can love, and abandons all earthly happiness to grasp at the shadow of a future life—which is not."

"Alas!" groaned Nadine, as she sank despairing at his feet, "if it is the power of his religion which has torn him from me, then is he indeed gone for ever! yet say not that it is so. Philip, you cannot dream what it is to me to lose him! I shall not live to bear such agony! tell me he will yet return!"

"He will never return," said Arabyn, in his calm melodious tone; "I know him and the power of his unnatural creed; resign yourself, my sister, he will never return; yet mourn him not too deeply,—know you not those eyes wherewith you weep must one day be sealed in death? why dim their fleeting brightness with most unavailing tears?—do not cling to me so wildly, I go to avenge you!" He disengaged himself from her as he spoke, and left the room.

Nadine had thrown herself down, her face convulsed, her bosom heaving, her long hair sweeping over her to the ground; but her senses had not deserted her, this momentary relief was denied to her,—the power of thought, which in such a moment is torture, was still in full force, and drove her almost to madness; what a fearful revolution had taken place in her feelings since that morning! Then she had risen bright and gay, and full of hope, scarce knowing what was the power which, within the last few months, had so brightened the world for her, only feeling it was the deepest happiness when Stanley was with her, the most weary vacancy when he was not; but, alas in the same hour that he had bidden her farewell for ever, she learned how completely every thought, every hope, every wish, had been centered in him,—how utter was the void, how dismal the chaos of life without him. Then she had never felt a fear for the future, or looked beyond the happy morrow, which was sure to bring him to her side; and now the mere thought of a long and miserable existence passed without him, was an agony she could not, would not bear.

The shock had been so sudden, that she felt like one

beneath whose feet the earth itself has crumbled away and hurled her to the depths of darkness and despair; all was confusion and dismay within her mind, and she knew not where to turn for help or hope. Perhaps with the natural instinct of the creature, her soul might have flown in its agony to the Mercy Seat above; but the principles and teaching of the infidel had quenched the spark of spiritual life within her, and the bitter contempt with which he had just spoken of Stanley's religion had influenced her unconsciously; there was still within her mind a hope, vague and dim, but still a hope, that the latter would yet return. She could not think that all was indeed over, that he had left her never to see her again; but, amid the tumult of distracting thoughts that raged within her, there was one that rose mighty, irresistible, decisive,—and this was the instinctive determination, that if she did indeed find that a fate so terrible was hers, that all which made life supportable was gone, that she would—she must—find some remedy, some means of deliverance from a torture which she would not bear.

She knew nothing of that Power of Love, most sweet, most irresistible, which constrains the Christian to fold the meek hands upon the aching breast, and smile with gratitude upon his misery. A human affection is an awful thing when governed by no holier law than that of natural impulse.

It has been said that Nadine had neither strength of mind nor faith; and without this it is not to be wondered at, that her strong feelings and vivid imagination should have rendered her, who had not yet known what it was to suffer, incapable of supporting a sorrow she had never dreamt of. Had there been some one near at that time to hold up the glory of a Hope Divine before that immortal soul, just torn from the earthly dreams in which it dwelt enshrined, how far different might have been the wretched being's fate!—but there were none to counsel or direct her. She was all alone with her wretchedness, and with the dark and horrible fancies which assailed her.

When Philip Arabyn returned several hours later, he found his miserable sister in the very same attitude in which he had left her; as he approached, she raised to him a face so awfully changed, that even his cold heart was moved as he looked on her ghastly paleness, her dim and sunken eye. Slowly he stooped and raised her in his arms, she tottered and could not speak; but she fixed on him a gaze so earnest, so imploring, so eloquent, that he answered her at once.

"Nadine, I have not seen him, but if there has remained one lingering hope within your heart, let it now be rooted out; for ever forget, despise him;—he is a coward as well as base;—there, read this, and blot his hateful name for ever from your memory;" he put a note into her trembling hands; she tried to read it; but the letters swam before her eyes, and she could not. Arabyn took it from her, and passing one arm round her, he read it calmly aloud; it was scarcely legible, and showed from its incoherence that it had been written under violent agitation.

"You will seek me, I know you will, to avenge *her* with my life; but in vain! How willingly, O Arabyn! how thankfully, would I surrender to you the intolerable burden of my existence!—but it cannot be, my life is not my own; it may be, that I must expiate, with years of utter agony, this one most fatal error; it is all in vain!

in vain ! and for me, I will shed no man's blood, far less that of *her* brother. I go this very hour! I leave this place for ever! to hide in some far distant land my remorse and my deep anguish. Call me what you will, coward !—villain !—I have caused *her* misery, and I merit all."

"And he is gone," continued Arabyn, as he concluded this fragment, which did not even bear a signature, "he is already gone, with the impossibility of discovering what road he has taken, or what is his destination."

Gone !—it was her death knell, the last lingering hope gave way, her destiny stared her in the face, She gave one long groan, and fell back on the floor. Arabyn raised her up, but she lay quite motionless in his arms. At this moment, Miss Goodwin, who had been out all day, rushed into the room filled with curiosity and horror, and giving vent to both in incoherent nonsense; Arabyn sternly bade her help him to convey Nadine to her room, and when this was done, he told her he chose to be alone with his sister, and quietly shut and locked the door.

It was from a strange motive that Arabyn wished to be the only person to witness the return to life and misery of his unhappy sister. His most favourite study was that of human nature, as displayed in the inner workings of the human mind. He loved to dissect, as it were, men's passions, to scrutinize their secret thoughts, to see them at times when the restraints of society, of habit, of education, or of expediency, were destroyed by imperious circumstances, and the real character shone forth He loved to be with them in their wretchedness, their rage, or their remorse, that he might learn how these took effect on different characters; diving down into the most hidden springs of men's motives; witnessing the triumph of their bad passions, and the struggle of humanity with destiny.

Arabyn was now himself hardened, by his own dark principles, into a cold and scornful indifference to all mankind; but he was not originally devoid of those natural affections which usually strengthen with our strength, and grow with our growth. His scepticism had raised a spring of bitterness within his soul, which gradually had spread itself over every thing—stifling every tender feeling, and checking every better impulse of his nature. Some degree of affection for Nadine alone retained its place in his heart, along with a bitter and despairing recollection of another; but he depreciated even his sister, and believed her, with all other women, frivolous, artful, and unstable. He could not fail to be convinced that her attachment to Stanley was at least for the present sincere, but he had no idea of the strength of it; and never doubted that time, or absence, or the yet more efficacious remedy of a new fancy, would soon dispel this first deceitful dream.

Meanwhile Nadine lay still and motionless, as though the springs of life had been dried up; and Arabyn scanned, with a painter's eye, her fixed and delicate features. To him she was but as a spring flower, withering in beauty, and it was a dark confirmation to his opinions to see her thus—so young and so wretched. But gradually there came a faint tinge of colour in the marble cheeks, and a fluttering of the eyelids: once or twice she raised her hands feebly, and then let them fall with that utter listlessness which follows violent grief. But the restlessness of self torture was returning upon her, and she opened her eyes with the fixed, calm look of despair. She sat up, and leant her head on her hands: it was evident that the full sense of her misery was upon her. But she could weep no more; the violence of her agitation had exhausted her, and she was perfectly still.

There is a vigour in the human mind, which is quite wonderful, and which renders it when strongly affected, whether by grief or joy, incapable of repose; when the body is worn out, and the tortured spirit would fain seek rest in apathy, it yet so revolts against suffering, which would seem almost unnatural to it, that it must work—revolving again and again its prospects, and plunging into the darkness all around, in the agonized endeavour to find a hope—a consolation—a something to relieve it from the presence of despair.

At length Nadine turned towards her brother, who sat with folded arms, gazing on her.

"Philip, you do not believe there is a God?" A bitter smile passed over his lips

"Of what avail to you even if there were, since He has created you only to destroy you?"

Her head sank again upon her hands. "He spoke to me," she murmured, "of life beyond the grave; of a heaven, where all is joy and peace; where they who have loved on earth may meet to part no more; of One Who bought for us a blessed eternity by unimagined sufferings. Oh! could I believe this, I might live to do His will, and trust to be reunited to him who is gone from me, when this most bitter life is over. Philip, tell me, can the dead rise again, as he told me?—shall we yet live once more in a purer world? Oh, speak! for this life I will not bear. Is there another?—is there a heaven, a hope, an existence after death?"

"There is no heaven, no hope, no existence after death;" was the stern answer. "Child! child! be not like to those weak, superstitious wretches, who dare not analyze their own destiny, and foster themselves with vainest dreams, which are but shadows. Had you frequented, as I have done, the charnel-house, and watched the dead in their corruption become a handful of dust, scattered to the four winds of heaven, you would have known and felt, they live no more."

"No more!" she echoed, with a feeble moan; "they live no more! this, *this* is the all of life; and, oh! wretched being as I am! how horrible is now *my* life!"

She fell back, in an agony of passionate weeping; and, in a voice half choked with sobs, she begged of him to leave her: for there is a sacredness in real grief, which makes the sufferer revolt from any witness to his agony.

Arabyn bent over her, and kissed her burning forehead, and then quietly left the room. Nadine was left alone to the most terrible of human pangs—sorrow, unsustained by faith. What the anguish of that pang may be, no mortal words can tell; though it were easy to speak feelingly of that strange, sweet pleasure, with which one stricken and bruised in heart can, with a meek faith, deliver himself up into the Everlasting Arms, nothing doubting that the sore trial is all too light for his necessity; and feeling that in the contemplation of His love all earthly misery shall melt away, like dark clouds when the sun shineth in its strength.

Arabyn flung himself down on a sofa in his lonely room, and gazed with his keen, restless eyes out into the far night. It was now quite dark, and through the large windows he could see the wide expanse of cloudless sky shrouded in a deep gloom, through which the mighty worlds ploughed their way in glory unquenchable. And as he looked, the soul of the infidel flew forth into a night yet more dark and unbounded; plunging into the depths of scepticism and doubt; losing itself among all those wild fallacious fancies with which, from age to age, man has sought to replace the pure light so repugnant to his carnal mind. But since the hour when he had finally chosen out his path, Arabyn had always resolutely turned from these maddening thoughts; and, burying his head in the cushions, he sought rest in slumber.

He fell into a light and broken sleep, which lasted for some hours. Suddenly he was awakened, he knew not how; and raising himself upon his arm, he looked around.

A strange sight presented itself, which caused an involuntary shudder to pass through his frame. The moon, which had now arisen, shed a faint but clear light through the room; and there came, slowly gliding from among the shadows, a slight figure, that looked, with her white garments and flowing hair, like a being from some unearthly sphere. Her face was deadly pale, and her large eyes glared with an unnatural brightness. Noiselessly she came towards him, with a strange uncertain step, and laid her hand upon his arm: it was so deadly cold that it sent a shiver through his frame with that slight touch; while her voice sounded hollow and deep on the still night air.

"Philip, is death forgetfulness?"

He looked calmly on her fixed and marble face, and answered; "It is annihilation!"

She bowed her head upon her breast, and, passing from his side, glided slowly from him, mournful and silent as she came. He watched her as she retreated; the moonlight gleaming on her white dress and pale loveliness, which resembled the marble beauty of the dead. Then she vanished like a wandering spirit from his sight.

CHAPTER XVI.

ARABYN BY THE POWER OF HIS WORDS DRIVES A SOUL TO
SELF-DESTRUCTION.

THERE are times when the unvarying revolutions of day and night,—the passing away of darkness, and the coming of the sunbeams,—seem to us a strange and unnatural thing; when some great change has taken place in our own mind; when all is restlessness and misery within, we scarce understand how the quiet stars can fade so calmly into light, or how the joyous morning can greet us with its glad rays as it was wont in our days of happiness. And yet, not only is it frenzy to ask for sympathy from nature, but folly to claim it from our fellow-creatures.

What is so common in this world as sorrow? As men mourn yesterday we mourn to-day; as men die to-day we die to-morrow! and, too surely, no morning dawns that beams not on a breaking heart, on some fainting spirit newly awakened into misery.

Once more the bright day rose over the green woods, and the birds sang out in their careless glee; but the voice of poor Nadine joined them not in their wild melody, nor was her light step heard among the fallen leaves. She did not leave her room, where Arabyn in vain endeavoured to gain admittance; she begged to be left alone in a manner which checked all remonstrance, and

ARABYN DRIVES A SOUL TO SELF-DESTRUCTION.

he did not urge her, thinking she might benefit by a few hours of quiet.

Cold and unnatural as Arabyn most certainly was, he had not witnessed the sufferings of his sister unmoved; and now, anxious to relieve the oppression of his spirits, he ordered his horse, and rode out.

In a different direction from the wood, which had been the favourite walk of Stanley and Nadine, lay a wide and desolate plain, extending to a considerable distance; and over its dull expanse Arabyn, harassed with gloomy thoughts, urged his horse to its utmost speed. The sky was dark with clouds, and there was a cold and angry wind sweeping in gusts across the moor. These symptoms of stormy weather increased every moment; and at length the indications of an approaching tempest became so evident, that Arabyn checked his horse with the intention of returning at once to the villa; but he had been riding hard for more than an hour, and had already left the plain far behind him. He now found himself in a broken country, amongst tangled brushwood, where he could not ride fast; and although he turned immediately, by the time he reached the open heath the black clouds seemed almost touching the earth, the thunder was heard growling ominously in the distance, and his horse broke at once into a fast gallop.

Suddenly it seemed to him as though a loud wailing cry was borne towards him by a fitful gust of wind which now flew over his head; he concluded it to be but the howling of the mournful breeze, whose sound is so often like the wail of a human voice; and he continued his rapid course undisturbed. But again that cry arose, nearer, more distinctly than before; and with so horrible, so unearthly a sound, that Arabyn involuntarily arrested his horse, and listened with a strange, indefinite fear. It almost seemed as though the animal partook of his sudden terror, for he stood perfectly still, his fore-feet stretched out, his ears laid back, and his limbs trembling. Again and again it arose—that awful cry, and nothing could be more dreadful than the sound, for it was that of a human voice, stretched far beyond its natural pitch, and uttering shriek on shriek, expressive of the utmost agony.

Arabyn shuddered violently; his whole frame trembled, and his heart throbbed painfully; but in a moment more the cold drops stood out on his forehead, when it seemed to him as though in the inarticulate words which the wind bore towards him, he could distinguish the incessant repetition of his own name! And now his straining eyes fell on a distant object which made his very blood run cold; he could distinguish a white figure flying with incredible swiftness across the desolate plain, and advancing rapidly towards him with outstretched arms and agonizing screams! Arabyn became incapable of movement, he could not articulate a word, his hands fell by his side, his whole body shook. On and onward it came, that ghost-like figure, with unearthly speed; and as it drew close, he beheld with his fascinated eyes the face and form of Nadine,—but changed, how fearfully changed!

The quivering hands were twined in the long hair in a manner which evinced great bodily torture; the features were dreadfully convulsed by some intolerable suffering, and the face of so livid a colour that it could only be caused by the near approach of death! And there was foam round her blue lips, and the eyes glared as though starting from their sockets, and that voice —that horrid voice, which had not ceased for a single moment,—how it rang on his ears : " Philip, Philip Arabyn ! brother ! save me, save me ; I burn, I die !"

She rushed towards him, she fell beneath his horse's feet ; he threw himself to the ground ; with a wild snort the frightened animal fled from the sight which had scared him ; and Arabyn, flinging himself down beside his sister, tried to raise her.

" Save me, save me !" she screamed, as she writhed in his arms ; " save me, brother !" and her shriek rang wildly over the plain. He tried with trembling hands to lift up her head, but she resisted him with a frantic and convulsive strength, and rolled on the ground.

" Oh these tortures!—have mercy, I cannot bear them ! You told me death was forgetfulness ; and I took poison, and I perish ; but it is *not* annihilation; I know, I feel it *now*. I have destroyed this body, but my soul is unchanged, and lives as strong and clear, and will live for ever. Save me, Philip, save me ; give me life—life ! I ask not joy or peace, but life ; to repent, to find a God. Oh ! the horror of this eternity is worse than the horror of these tortures." And again the froth flew from her lips, and she rolled her fair young head in the dust : but worse than all was the agonized glare of her eyes to Heaven ; for she had said truly, that the horror of the unknown doom was more awful than the agonies of the deadly poison.

And her miserable brother knelt by her side, with emotions wholly indescribable : stretching out to her the shaking hands that had not strength to hold her writhing frame ; whilst ever when she felt his touch she screamed out, " False words ! false words !—it is *not* annihilation !"

He was altogether unable to help or succour her; he would have flown for assistance, but he dared not leave her there alone to die; he felt, he knew, that she was dying, for it was evident that she had taken poison to a most fatal amount; but it was not even in his power to alleviate the sufferings which were destroying her under his very eyes. Oh! for one human being at that moment —for one of the race he so despised—to bring him some assistance; as much of aid as mortals could bestow!

But her strength was becoming exhausted, and her words were quite inarticulate. Once he distinctly heard her say, "The curse of the knowledge of eternity is upon me;" and then she continued to shriek piteously, whilst the incessant movement with which she tried to deaden her physical agony was horrible to look upon.

Suddenly, to Arabyn's unspeakable relief, the quick gallop of a horse was heard approaching; he started up, and saw an Austrian soldier approaching at a rapid pace, attracted probably by the screams of the unhappy suicide. Arabyn threw himself across his path, and seizing his horse by the bridle, checked him with a suddenness which made him rear violently.

"For Heaven's sake help us,—my only sister, she is dying; she has poisoned herself; in mercy fly to the village for a physician."

The soldier listened with compassion to that voice of passionate entreaty; he saw the prostrate form within a few paces of him, and rode up to her; but starting back, he hurriedly made the sign of the Cross, when he looked upon the horrible expression of her face, and the dreadful convulsions which agitated her.

"It is better that she should be taken to the village at once," he exclaimed to Arabyn; "there is a peasant's cart passing on the road, close at hand, which can convey her there; I will bring it in a moment." He set spurs to his horse and gallopped off, but returned almost immediately, followed by the cart. It was fortunately full of mulberry-leaves, which they were conveying to the silk manufactory; and, when they were arranged into a heap, Nadine was gently laid upon them by her brother and the soldier. Arabyn then took his place beside her, and they drove slowly on, while the Austrian hurried to the village, in order to have the physician in readiness at the villa.

Nadine was now quite exhausted, and gave no sign of life, save by deep and continual groans, and a gurgling in her throat which seemed to intimate a speedy dissolution. She lay there like a tired child; it was evident that the pain was gradually ceasing, and that she had fallen into the brief calm which generally precedes death in such cases. Arabyn felt the soft hand which he held in his own become cold and stiff, with that chill which can alone still the restless beating of the human heart, and which even the voice of one long-loved cannot dispel. Arabyn seemed to listen spell-bound to her faint irregular breathing, and turned shuddering away when the veined eyelids slowly rose, and showed that awful look within, which is only known to those who have beheld men die. He expected each moment to see her expire, for the heaving of her breast was now scarcely perceptible, and but for a slight tremulousness at the mouth, he might have believed she had already ceased to exist.

At length the heavy minutes passed away, and they reached the gate of the villa, where the soldier stood waiting to receive them with the physician. They carried Nadine into the room where she had parted from Stanley, and laid her on the sofa. The physician gazed silently upon her for a few minutes; he was aware of the cause of her illness, and saw at once that those eyes would never more open on the light they had so loved. He attempted to bleed her, but quite in vain, and finally desisted from any endeavours which were so utterly hopeless.

The three men stood silently round her, as utterly impotent, ignorant, and helpless, in all the pride of their strength, as the living must ever be in presence of the dying. For some moments there was a deep silence, and then each one felt as it were a cold shiver creep through his frame, and the consciousness of a something awful seemed to rise from some fearful instinct within him; the physician went forward, and gently lifted up the long hair which hid poor Nadine's once smiling face; for an instant he looked at her, and then replaced the soft waving curls with a sort of solemn respect; and, turning to Arabyn and the soldier, he folded his hands with all the fervour of a true son of the Church of Rome, and said in Italian, "Let us pray for the soul of the departed." The soldier at once took from within his cap a little silver image, and knelt quietly down beside the dead body; but Arabyn, muttering hurriedly to the physician an entreaty that he would make what arrangements were necessary, rushed from the room, and was heard to lock and bolt the door of his own with great vehemence.

The house was soon one scene of horror and confusion; but the Italian was a good and sensible man, and deeply compassionating the unfortunate brother, he took the entire charge of the investigation which necessarily followed a suicide of so extraordinary a nature, although such an act created far less astonishment in Italy than it would have done in England.

Miss Goodwin was the only person who could give any information as to the circumstances preceding the death of Nadine; and from what she said, the physician concluded at once, that Arabyn had communicated the news of some great misfortune to his sister on his arrival, and that she, unable to bear the sorrow that had come upon her, had, as many of his countrymen would have done in like manner, sought a refuge from despair in death.

Miss Goodwin said, that she had been out during the whole of the previous day, and knew nothing of what had occurred until late in the afternoon, when she had returned, and found Nadine insensible in her brother's arms. She had assisted in conveying her to her room, where she had left her at Arabyn's request, nor had she attempted to see her again till this morning, when she had been refused admittance by Nadine herself. She had seen Arabyn ride out, and some time after he was gone she was startled by the sound of prolonged groans proceeding from his sister's room. She had gone up, accompanied by the servants, and had vainly endeavoured to open the door; Nadine seemed to be in a state which rendered her incapable of attending to their entreaties that she would admit them; and they remained listening to screams which filled them with horror. These at last became so dreadful, and seemed to intimate that she was in such agony, (in the agonies of death as it afterwards proved,) that Miss Goodwin gave orders that the door should be broken open; before this could be accomplished, however, Nadine suddenly burst from the room herself, seemingly in a state of frenzy, and cleared her way through the horror-stricken spectators with the quickness of lightning.

They attempted to follow her; but when they reached the gates, she had already disappeared; and, though her screams were audible for some time, they could not distinguish which way she had gone, nor knew any further, till they saw her brought home lifeless.

It was quite clear to the physician, that, after Nadine had committed the fatal act, she had been seized with a panic of terror, and, maddened by suffering, had flown to her brother (whom she had probably observed as he left the house), in the vain hope that he would save her, not only from the actual torture which the poison produced, but from the yet more overwhelming fear of approaching death.

No further information could be obtained, or was indeed requisite; and after all due inquiry had been made, there remained nothing more to be done than to consign to the quiet earth that sweet spring flower, that gay, light-hearted being, whose one short day of suffering had swallowed up the brightness and the promise of a life.

It was the night before the funeral, and the brother and sister were alone once more—yet not together. Arabyn had never dared to look upon her since that hour, when she had in his presence delivered up the young life he had destroyed by his words, as surely and certainly as though with the knife of an assassin he had severed her soul from her body.

Alone, stiff and cold in her ghastly shroud, waiting for the stated hour when she should be given to the worm and to darkness, lay that fragile being, for whom the winds of summer seemed to blow too roughly, beneath whose light and buoyant feet the kindred flowers were wont to spring. She lay there, stiff and cold, her young existence closed for ever. That beautiful form, so wonderfully created to be the holy temple of spiritual religion, the shrine of a future immortality, was about to return to the dust without having fulfilled the purpose for which it sprang from thence. That voice, destined as the voice of a responsible creature, of an active servant of the Creator, to soothe the mourners, to rebuke the sinner, to instruct the ignorant, and speak comfort to the weary;—that voice was hushed for ever, and who had gathered from it hope, or consolation, or reproof? And that immortal soul, sent down on earth to become the heir of eternal life, commanded to live its hour of mortal probation for the glorifying of God and the purification of itself—that soul had deserted its post uncalled, and none dare surmise its awful doom!

She lay there stiff and cold; and she had lived, but she had lived in vain: she had died, but there was no hope in her death. And whose was the power that had thus destroyed the creature made in God's own image, for His own purposes—the destined servant of His Almighty will? Who had thus brought her down to the grave, ere she had fulfilled the work He had given her to do, or lived to the end for which she was created? —It was the power of her own fellow-creature; of a being subject, like herself, to sorrow and to misery; requiring, as she did, the sympathy of others; doomed, like her, to ills from which there was no escape; like her, depending on those natural affections which can sweeten the bitter draught of human life. Oh! when will men cease to prey the one upon the other? when will these fellow-heirs to a most sad inheritance desist from warring with each other? Is it then but a Utopian dream to look forward to the hour, when each individual member of this great human colony shall cease to stand isolated, occupied in defending himself against those from whom it was ordained that he should seek for consolation and happiness; when man shall no longer be the curse of man, or slave of slave; nor the step to the joys of earth—a brother's grave!

She lay in her ghastly shroud; and Stanley, for whose unhappy love she perished, was flying, ignorant of her fate, over the restless waves; seeking peace for his yet more restless soul. And Arabyn, who, one day before, might have given an aim to her existence, and a hope to her most weary spirit, but with the cold sophistry of his atheism had driven her from the despair of life to the despair of eternity—he sat in stern tranquillity, resolutely subduing the natural feelings of humanity, that he might, in his arrogant independence of soul, grapple with the bitter thoughts that well nigh mastered him. Since the hour of her death he had been stunned, powerless, subdued; and he had felt as though his strong energy was giving way—his strong will sinking before the power of destiny—but this must not be: he would not retreat one inch in his battle with existence; he was to be the conqueror, and not the conquered. He would collect his thoughts; he would look into his position; he would stare in the face this evil, which seemed to be overshadowing him; he would trample it down; he would nerve himself to the contest once more; then he would speed on, through obstacles, over graves, among shrieks and cries, with his servants, crime and deception: meeting innocent men, and talking with them, passing on, and leaving them felons; meeting happy and gladsome beings, smiling on them, and passing on, leaving them broken-hearted:—on, on, to the consummation of his resolution, till he had forced life to yield up to him its pleasure.

Arabyn rose: he folded his arms; he bent down his head; and pacing to and fro through the room, commenced the analysis of his actual condition.

He perceived that already two of the stepping-stones which he had passed over in his career of independence were tombs. The one, that of Edmund, driven prematurely to death by his wanton cruelty—the other, that of his only friend, so constituted by the ties of blood. And now, deeply pondering, Arabyn walked to and fro. The feeling, which had for the last day almost overwhelmed him, was the conviction that he was himself the cause of his sister's fearful death, and in order the better to do battle with this pang, and destroy it out of his breast, he admitted to himself that such was the fact—by his hand, first the soul, then the body, had been poisoned—he was doubly her assassin. By his abortive attempt upon Stanley he had rendered their union impossible; and she had seen her mortal happiness expire before her eyes: by his words he had torn from her misery its sole refuge and hope, and she herself had expired before him.

Well, he thought, and if it were so; had he in actual fact done her an injury? No doubt it would have been better for her never to have been born into this miserable world, but, since she had existed, surely it was well that she was dead—that she could feel no more. Not words of hate from lips beloved could have caused her a moment's anguish now; rivers of tears might have flowed from the eyes she loved to look upon, and failed to stir her heart with a throb of painful sympathy. It was well that she was a dull, dead mass of clay, which might have been trodden down beneath the feet of him for whom she died, without giving forth a moan or a shudder. True, she had perished in her youth and her loveliness; the bright morning had passed into night, and where was the promise of the brilliant day? She was stretched in her coffin with youth on her brow, and a world of hope lay prostrate there: she had baulked the grave of its sweetest privilege,—the giving of rest to the weary and footsore, when the way has been long and toilsome: she had gone to it without the store of memories, of gay dreams grown to stern realities; of dear hopes changed to bitter pangs; of sorrows concealed; and of half-closed wounds which are buried with men's bodies, when age has made them ripe for death. And yet sooner or later it must have come to this, and the sooner the better. That one day of suffering, wherewith she had done homage to the sovereign Woe, that sits enthroned as ruler of this world, was surely as small a tribute as ever mortal paid: had she lived a little longer, the monarch of human sorrows would have exacted more. She was come to her strength and maturity now, fit for his service, and he would have levied a tax on each year of her life. No! it was good for her that she had died; that she was past feeling now; and Arabyn had done well to kill her. But he should do ill by himself if he ever let a thought of her stir him to a painful emotion: it was a false pang, a vain, a childish, a most weak pang, that had thrilled through him, with the certainty that he himself had destroyed her; but he had mastered it now; he had put it from him; he had replaced it with the conviction that he had done well to kill her; and henceforth he would crush her remembrance within his soul, as they had crushed her body in its coffin.

Now he began to look on the progress he had made in his predeterminate career. Though he still felt certain of success, and that soon, he yet felt he had been strangely thwarted; he remembered his own simile when conversing with Raymond: he said, that the knife wherewith a man sought to carve out his destiny, turned in his hand and pierced himself; it seemed very apposite to his own case now—he had been working, hewing, and hacking his way with his keen weapon, crime; and when he looked that it should bring forth success and prosperity, it had but produced death and destruction.

What was this thing which baffled him, this invisible thing, untangible and silent, that rose before him as a thwarter and an enemy, in every shape, at every turn?

Arabyn was a deep thinker, he looked close into the matter, he examined into it; he saw, it was the Christian faith; for this Raymond struggled with him, for this Ruth delayed her coming, by that delay his sister perished.

Philip Arabyn lifted up his eyes, they were filled with the most frightful expression,—his soul rose up within him, strong with the most deadly loathing for this unattainable and exalted foe; he loathed it all the more, that once he had almost yielded up his spirit to its holy influence; once on the terrace at Scutari, in presence of Raymond,—it had passed before him fair and glorious, it had come to him like a strain of ineffable music, of winning sweetness, and most touching melody, that had sought as it were to envelope his whole soul, and bear it away,—away, floating up through the blue ether, thrilling with an unutterable hope, that was the purest rapture,—on, on, he knew not whither! he had but heard in that hour what all men hear once, at some one period of their lives; and for those who listen and yield to the divine and softly-thrilling melody, it deepens and strengthens, till their spirit has no power to hear aught save those ravishing sounds. First, the loud voices of this world are deadened and die away, the voice of its allurements, of the roaring of its ever-restless strife, of the lamenting of its people, and the swift recurring death shriek of its hopes; then as the glorious strains swell louder and louder, though still of a sweetness ineffable, in like manner the voices within are deadened and die away, the voice of the passions, of the earthly desires, of the human affections, of the flesh bemoaning itself for its exile from the world and the lust thereof, and the swift recurring death-shriek of the heart's cherished hopes; and so deepening, deepening ever, louder, clearer, stronger, swells on that celestial music, till as in a flood of sound, divine and exquisite, the soul glides out into the ocean of eternal harmony. But he had closed his ears, he had hardened his heart, he had sealed up his soul; the sweet strain had floated on, elsewhere to sound over the wide world; in every land, from every corner, some spirit thrills responsive to the sound; but for him—no more.

Arabyn arose from his meditation as though his soul had been steeped anew in strength, more than ever was he ready to combat and to conquer. In the ardour and fury which opposition had instilled into him, losing sight almost of the ultimate end and aim of his present endeavours, he bent himself with the most desperate energy to that which he had looked upon merely as the primary step; but its accomplishment he believed near at hand. Soon would he stand at the side of Ruth, and make her the slave of his will, and her wealth the tool of his fixed resolve. Soon would he revenge himself in her person on the immaculate faith,—the unseen and untangible foe that had thwarted him hitherto.

Quick! let them make ready the grave, and thrust in the coffin, and shovel in the damp black earth on the form so lovely and beloved; let them seal it up, and tread down the mould, that the place of her rest may be effaced from earth, as her memory from his own heart! Yes! since the last link was severed that bound him to his fellow-creatures,—since the last chord was shattered wherewith his soul could vibrate to human love; yet more dauntless, more free, unshackled by earth or by heaven, would he go to lay hold on this life as a man grasps a snake by the neck to extract its venom, and tame it down, till, powerless to hurt him, but obedient to his will, it works out his pleasure from day to day.

In vain, in vain, most miserable infidel; you may choke up, with the cold clay, the lips that demanded, "Is death forgetfulness?" but the voice unsilenced shall ring in your ears, when yourself are about to prove by eternal experience, that the words of your answer were falsehood!

CHAPTER XVII.

THE SECOND ATTEMPT OF ARABYN FOR THE EXECUTION OF HIS PLAN IS THWARTED BY RAYMOND.

PROFOUND was the solitude and deep the silence that reigned over these mighty Alps,—yet most unlike the solitude and silence of the desert. Here nature is like to a strong man sleeping,—all things bear token of convulsions past, and of fierce agitation, and the spirit of the storm is only laid for a season; soon, whenever the mysterious command is uttered, unheard by the quick ear of man, but audible to the rocks and the torrents, the winds and the avalanche, down the chasms and ravines, shall the blast come roaring as though pursued by fiends, and the thunder shall howl among the mountain echoes, like a great voice sounding the dirge of some perishing world, and the lightning shall flash like the gleam of the swords of the armies of heaven; even now the fresh breeze blows keen and swift, like the breathing of the tempest that pants for release. There is none of the lifelessness of the desert, the intensity of solemn repose, whose type is only in that peace to all living incomprehensible, since not till the quick subtle spirit departs, can it enter into the human frame.

The lofty mountains stood dark and stern, rising far above the clouds, and displaying the stainlessness of their eternal snows only to the gaze of the sun in heaven, like saints that stand aloof, with their feet chained to earth, and yet soaring far over the clouds of mortal sorrow, and mortal joy, or care, with their purity of soul and blamelessness of life, shining only in the light that cometh from above; and the bright torrents leapt and sparkled in the morning beams, and the mists rolled away from the cliffs and the crags before the smile of day.

Ruth Vincent stood on a height and looked down on the little hamlet where Mr. Denham had fixed their abode for the present; but she quickly turned her eyes away from it, not to fix them on the majestic scene around her, nor yet to look up into the glory of the pure blue sky; but to gaze on the far distant spire of a church, for there, in a very little time, she was to hear the words which secured to her an amount of earthly happiness beyond what she had ever before imagined; and there was she to be constituted, by heaven's own ordinance, the friend, the comfort, the solace, the support, of one with whom in his sorrow she would rather have wept, than rejoiced with all the world beside. There would she acquire the right, by watchfulness unceasing, by care unwearied, by tenderness unexacting, by constancy unfailing, to make this life as bright for him as it may be for mortal man; and there was a smile on her lips such as never sparkled there before, and a light in her eyes, through which gazing on this world, it seemed to her like Eden; for he had come to her so weary, wretched, and despairing, his head had drooped so mournfully on his breast, he had stretched out his hands to her, almost as a child in sorrow to a tender mother, and told her how, since she left him all had grown dark and cold, and the shadows had deepened round him, and how the hour of his loneliness and her desertion had been chosen for the infliction of the bitterest pang he yet had borne, the stern and sudden severing of the last earthly tie that death had left unbroken, the cruel and fearful perishing in the springtime of her days, of his fair young sister, his only remaining relative ; he had laid her in her grave, and assuredly he would have lain down beside her in that hour of anguish (not dying by self-murder, but for his very loneliness and misery would life have relaxed its hold upon him, and the power to live have expired within him), but that he remembered Ruth, his sweet link to existence, his solitary hope, his one and only joy ; he had seemed to hear her soft low voice, and the painful throbbing of his heart was stilled ; he seemed to see her gentle, pitying look, and it was as though a light had shone in upon the darkness of his sorrow, and he had come to her, he had come back to her, to give into her hands the power which none but herself could have on earth, even that of making his life blessed, of breathing into his existence, so chill, so lonely, and so cheerless, the warmth and the sunshine of a true affection.

And Ruth had listened to that voice of mournful pleading, as she would not have listened had he come in all the pomp and the glory of earth ; and she, who would have turned from him coldly perhaps, had he offered her all the luxury and grandeur which the world can bestow, looked on him, now so desolate, so afflicted, so wayworn, and thanked him with meekness and fervour for the privilege he gave her of so compassing him about with her devoted care ; so hedging him in, as it were, with her unremitting tenderness, that not a sorrow should have room to enter on his life, not a toil or a pang should have power to attain to him, when she was at hand to bear them all.

And the hour was fast approaching when they would kneel side by side in that church, to part no more till they lay side by side in one grave. And she believed that hour would be the first of a life of joy,—while he designed it should be the last of a hypocrite's treacherous delusion, the first of her awakening into misery.

Ruth stood there with a heart full of joy, the sweet power of fancy weaving many a golden dream for the years to come; but the vision of her hopes was ever the same; her anxious labour, her earnest and faithful service, ever tending, comforting, and cheering him; and day by day, beneath her gentle influence, the shadow passing from his countenance, and the sorrow from his heart. Now, whilst she lingered, with that sweet hope nestling in her breast, to which she clung far more fondly than she was herself aware of, there was one coming slowly up that mountain-path towards her by whose hand it was appointed that her present happiness should be for ever wrung from her heart.

Raymond now knew all the truth; he had been with Stanley; he had stood by the grave of the unhappy Nadine; and he had tracked the author of all that misery and sin to this spot, where he found him about to bring his schemes to a successful conclusion by his union with Ruth Vincent.

Raymond now wondered at his own blindness in not having seen clearly what had been Arabyn's design from the commencement: perhaps he had found it the more difficult to believe that Arabyn could ever feign a new affection, from his vivid recollection of the true and intense feeling with which the infidel had spoken of the buried love that lay for him interred in the great sepulchre of the past. Raymond judged him in this respect by his own feelings; for to him, in whose ears even then the desert blast was ringing, revolting was the supposition that the sacred affection with which, according to God's holy ordinance, he had cherished that sleeper in the wilderness, could ever fade from his immortal soul; rather would that soul pass through this world, keeping its solitary love undivided and undiminished,—that, meeting on the radiant and eternal shores, she should recognise him by that token.

But now he thoroughly understood the whole dark plot, which he must at once frustrate. It was perfectly plain to him what was Arabyn's motive in attempting to marry Ruth Vincent: it was but the following up of the same desire of wealth which had moved him to Stanley's destruction at Trieste. Raymond had read, in the actions and in the countenance of Ruth, the evidence of her pure, self-devoted, resolute Christianity, as clearly as though the cross once traced on her forehead yet shone there with unearthly light; and he knew that towards such an one as she was, Philip Arabyn could feel nothing but a shrinking hate: he might link himself to her in name, for the accomplishment of his designs, but never could he intend to retain, as his companion, one in whom was incorporate that faith unto salvation, wherein was his own greater condemnation. Doubtless, he sought but to lure her on till he could with safety rob her, not of fortune only, but of joy and hope, and faith itself if possible, and then to deliver her up to a base desertion, and a dismal solitude, thickly strewn with the crumbling ruins of her own destroyed happiness.

She must be saved from such a fate, and Raymond

would save her, but he must pierce her to the heart in so doing. He had not watched the noble trusting expression of her countenance, nor looked into her deep earnest eyes, so full of tenderness and sympathy, without knowing very certainly that the love wherewith she loved would be no common sentiment. He saw that beneath that quiet exterior there lay hid a depth and strength of feeling which, if thrown back upon herself, would turn to inconceivable torture. He felt convinced, (knowing how the glorious faith casts its pure lustre round every thought and feeling) that she held the affection which now bound her to Arabyn as a thing sacred, which, once given, she could never more recal; which should pass from her breast only with the mortal life itself.

Raymond did not doubt, that, when the solemn fiat was announced to her, commanding her in the name of the Most Holy to depart from him who walked disorderly, she would at once and for ever separate from him, denying to her breaking heart its light of life, the only treasure for which it ever longed or beat; to her whole existence its sole earthly joy; and that without a murmur. But when it was done, he felt that she would be like to one who is haunted by a spectre, making the day abhorrent, and the night most terrible; for by her side would ever move one great misery,—a misery that would enter into her soul to quit it no more, from the hour when she first learned that the being she believed pure, sincere, favoured of Heaven, was lost, and worthless, and degraded. Far more bitter for her than the betrayal of her affection would be the destruction of her esteem for him who had inspired it.

Raymond felt, as he went in search of her, thinking

of these things, that it required all the power of the inflexible law of obedience to nerve him to his present task; he had fully anticipated, on undertaking the arduous duty of this moral combat, that he would bring upon himself much toil and suffering; but he had never looked to the necessity of inflicting pain upon another. Ruth Vincent had passed before him in her holy contentment, her thoughtful serenity, as one on whom the eyes might well love to rest in this fierce world of turmoil and defilement; and to him it was given to cause the convulsion of mental anguish to pass over that calm, mild countenance; he must change the gentle tones of her voice to cries of bitter wailing, and for ever banish from those lips, that loved to speak joy and peace to all, the sweet gay smile that told so brightly of her own internal happiness. He knew how intense and devoted her attachment must be, and he felt that not without a rending asunder, like to that of soul and body, could it be torn from her. His heart smote him to think how he was about at a single blow to shatter the fair fabric of her whole earthly happiness, and leave her (as he doubted not she would) to kneel down in unquestioning submission among the melancholy fragments: it was a cruel and a stern duty, but it must be done, even at the price of all this anguish to the unoffending victim; he must rescue her, before Arabyn had advanced another step in his frightful hypocrisy.

Raymond remembered that for her eternal satisfaction might be necessary here that sharp chastening, which is our sure and sweetest proof of His great love; and calmly he resigned himself to be the instrument of her affliction.

Ruth still stood on the mountain path, enjoying the

freshness of the keen Alpine breeze, when she was startled by hearing steps approaching towards her; she looked round as they came close, and uttered an exclamation of surprise when she found herself face to face with Raymond; a vague sensation of terror took possession of her at his unexpected appearance, for she remembered how, once before, his coming had been the herald of misfortune. She was about to bid him welcome, however, when she was arrested by the strange manner in which he seemed to look upon her.

Pale, stern, and silent, he stood before her,—uttering no word, only gazing at her with eyes full of a severe, yet mournful determination. She shrank back terrified, she scarce knew why, and for a moment neither spoke; at last she faltered out,—

"Has any misfortune happened? why are you here?"

"I am here," said Raymond, with a voice full of melancholy, "in order that I may accomplish a work to which I am called;—a task difficult and painful, and yet most needful."

"Whatever your task and duty is," said Ruth, "doubtless it is a righteous and a pure one; for I know *Whose* servant you are."

"I am here," continued Raymond, increasing in sadness as he looked upon her innocent face, so candid with its meek, trusting expression; "to perform in truth a bitter labour, and yet it must be done; for the work I have to accomplish, Ruth Vincent, is to save you."

She started, and looked at him in utter amazement.

"Do you remember when we last met?" he said. "It was beside a grave; and now, would—oh! would that you could listen to the words of my lips as though they were uttered by one who had arisen out of that tomb—who had come from the dead to speak them! Yes; would that you could give to the disclosure I now must make to you the full belief, the implicit reliance, which you would assuredly award to a messenger from the world of spirits!"

"Oh! what is it you have to tell me?" exclaimed Ruth; "what is it that could require so terrible an affirmation? You are almost a stranger to me; and yet you look on me with pity, as though I were your child—oh! surely some sorrow is coming upon me!"

Raymond took her by the hand. "You tremble," he said; "let us sit down; I have much to say."

They placed themselves together on the bank; and after a few minutes Ruth spoke more calmly.

"You are little known to me," she said; "and I cannot even imagine what nature of communication you are about to make to me; but I know, I feel within me, that I must—I will believe you, be your words what they may. Yes; even as though you spoke with the voice of one from the dead, who truly cannot lie! I must believe you, Raymond, for I know Whom you serve; I have read it in your countenance; I have heard it in your words; and I know that you serve Him in spirit and in truth. Therefore say what you will: doubt not that I will give your words the fullest credit."

Raymond thanked her warmly, and then, turning to look on her, he said, "But are you prepared for all that I may have to tell? are you prepared to hear that which must cause you unexpected and most bitter suffering?"

Ruth's voice was sweet and clear as she answered, "The human nature shrinks from suffering, and the spirit faints at thought of it; but it is a good and holy thing, for it comes from the Source of all goodness and holiness: in meekness and in gratitude let it be accepted."

"You are strong," said Raymond: "calm, gentle soul, your strength is very great. But I—oh! how shall I ever have courage to inflict on you so terrible a pang? I know in part what is the agony you are about to feel, but not all: I know what it is to lose all that you have ever loved on earth. This unutterable anguish I can understand; I have proved it; I have grappled with it; I have carried it home to my bosom, and enshrined it there—a living flame that feeds upon me, tended by the vestals, thought and memory, who will not let it die. But though at first, in my weakness and my torture, it seemed to me as though from all heaven's wealth of angels one might have been spared to me, and that amongst the countless ranks of glorious seraphs they would not have missed the gentle smile that was the brightness of my life; still, when I found they could not be without her in that radiant host, I was content to let her go. I would not ask her back again; and therefore there was a hope in my great misery which yours, alas! can never know."

"Do not keep me in suspense," said Ruth, tremulously; "tell me what it is that I must bear."

"How will you bear," said Raymond, "to hear that one, whom you have believed most holy, pure, and true, is vile, and worthless, and a hypocrite, beyond what you have ever imagined of worthlessness or hypocrisy? that one, in whose affection you have reposed with a joy unspeakable, hates you even now with a bitter and a deadly hate? that one you have believed, more than any other, the faithful and devoted servant of the Cross, is the sworn and willing bondsman to iniquity? that the being you have looked upon as most exalted, most noble, most worthy to be loved and honoured—has practised on you a mean and horrible deception, and that for the lowest and basest motives? Ruth Vincent, how will you bear to hear, that the friend you have revered as you would a saint in heaven, is stained with crimes from which your whole soul would revolt?—and now, even at this hour, meditates others which would cause you to seek rather the society of a fiend from hell, as the companionship of a mortal so depraved. How will you bear to hear—oh! climax of agony!—that the friend in whom each thought and hope is centered is of those who trample beneath their sacrilegious feet the Cross adorable? who dare disown the Name at which every knee shall bow, of things in heaven, and things in earth, and things under the earth; who, because the awful thunderbolt is yet suspended in the unoblivious heaven, walk on to death and judgment—making themselves, by a most foul, and impious, and ever-working unbelief, as a living blasphemy on Him Who once redeemed them?"

Ruth Vincent had listened to him; she had heard every word which he had uttered in that solemn, stern voice, even to the very last; but she did not speak or move; and for a few minutes the silence was so intense, that Raymond could hear her quick convulsive breathing. All around them was most calm and peaceful: the clouds hung so motionless and still on the rough breast of the gigantic mountains, the winds were hushed and laid to rest in their mysterious caverns, the pine forests stirred not, and spread like immoveable shadows over the cliffs: only two human beings were there, fragile, perishing, and helpless; and the sublime repose of nature was marred by the strife of the mortal passions, as though an echo had been borne in upon that vast solitude from the far off world of turmoil and sorrow.

At length she turned slowly round and gazed upon him: her eyes, full, clear, and dilated, were riveted on his; and from her face every shade of colour departed, leaving it pale as ashes; her lips, deadly white, were parted, and trembled, and twice she endeavoured to speak, and could not; then, making a violent effort, she forced herself to utter the sentence, "It is of Philip Arabyn you speak."

Raymond, sick at heart with intense compassion, laid his hand upon hers.

"Ruth, you love him well?"

Her whole frame shook at the question, her breast heaved, and a cold chill seemed to pass over her: again, with the utmost difficulty, she uttered distinctly, "More than my life."

"Alas! alas!" murmured Raymond, letting his head fall on his clasped hands, for he could not bear to see her present misery, knowing how much was yet to come: but Ruth grasped his arm, and this time her voice was clear and vehement.

"Speak! tell me all; let me know the worst at once; let me know the truth, be it what it may; tell me all, even to the uttermost extent of its horror, to the full extremity of my prepared misery."

Raymond shook off his momentary weakness: he raised his head.

"Nerve yourself, then," he said, "to listen to that which I solemnly believe, were you not a Christian, you would not hear and live. Clothe yourself with strength; put on the armour of the saints."

She moved her lips once more, but not addressing him; again she lifted up the eyes so clear and dilated, but not to look on earth; she leant back her head on the rock, she crossed her hands on her breast, and then said calmly, "I am ready; say on."

And he spoke,—he told her all from the very commencement. Clearly, distinctly, with a truth and a power which were not to be set aside or resisted, he displayed before her, even to the most minute detail, the actual character of Arabyn, his past career, his present deception, and his future intentions. He told her of his first acquaintance with him, when even in his youth he was known as a most determined infidel; of his own solemn vow taken in the temple of the desert, kneeling on the dead ashes of his mortal happiness, of his resolution to seek out him, whom in all the earth he should judge to be the most bitter and determined enemy of the Lord of their adoration, who most resolutely should walk by the law of evil, who most zealously and willingly should do homage and service to iniquity, that he might destroy his influence and counteract his crimes, and how he had found all this and more in Philip Arabyn. He described their meeting at Scutari, when he seemed borne by a mysterious power into the presence of the enemy he sought; he could repeat to her almost word for word, (it was so deeply graven on his memory,) the long account which the infidel had given of his opinions, of his hesitation at that time between life and death,—death, with a desperate, a compulsory resignation to destiny; or life, with an arrogant defiance of heaven and hell, of all laws Divine or human, save that one of full and unlimited indulgence of his own most utterly depraved will. Then Raymond told her of the fearful decision to which Arabyn had come; of the resolution he had taken, to which he had so firmly adhered up to this hour, and so frightfully worked out; of the letter he had written; of his first attempt on Stanley for the acquisition of wealth, and its defeat; of his second attempt on Ruth herself for the same purpose; and of his destroying poor Edmund's earthly happiness, because he interfered with his plans.

Lastly, Raymond told her how Stanley had come to him, heart-broken, penitent, almost despairing, to confess to him his error, and to tell him that he had placed his whole mortal happiness upon one hope, and how that hope had been crushed, destroyed, effaced from his existence, by the fatal power of the infidel; and how the soul of her he loved, that should have been in her youth and innocence, fresh and pure, and like to a flower that opens only to receive the dews and the light of heaven, had been marked by a brother's hand with a foul and blackening stain, that might grow and spread, till it enveloped her in a darkness eternal; and when Raymond, (doubting much, whether Stanley had indeed acted consistently with a Christian's principles, in leaving Nadine after he had won her affections, though he well understood, that, from the very magnitude of the sacrifice, he should have conceived it his duty to make it,) had returned with him to Italy, in order to see her, they found that already the grass was green over the grave of the suicide, and they gathered but too surely from all they were told, that she had been driven to that unhallowed refuge by the dark influence of Arabyn himself.

Finally, Raymond placed in the hands of Ruth Vincent the letter, whereby the infidel had unconsciously furnished him with so sure and infallible a weapon against himself; and she took it, because, even in that hour of mortal agony, almost instinctively she submitted to the law of obedience, which constrained her to drain even to the last drop the most bitter draught, which, by her Father's will, was now offered to her lips; but it needed not—it needed not this last and incontestable proof, this well-known hand writing, this clear and distinct statement, in his own peculiar style, of an organized apostacy from God, to convince Ruth Vincent of that which half an hour before would have seemed to her wholly impossible and inconceivable, and to carry every syllable which Raymond had uttered, with a deep conviction to her soul.

There is that in truth, simply and forcibly expressed, which is and must be at all times irresistible, and there is also that in hypocrisy, however artful, complete, and refined, which sooner or later must betray itself. There were many things both uttered unconsciously by Arabyn in conversation, and conveyed indirectly in his garbled account of his past life, which had ever been quite inexplicable to Ruth, because so inconsistent with the opinion she entertained of him; but, with the trusting simplicity of a loving child, she believed that she did not understand him, because his intellect was of a higher order than her own; over these a light not to be mistaken was now cast by the narrative of Raymond, and in his account, strange as it was, the events rose too naturally one from another, and the chain of cause and effect was too complete, not to bear the stamp of an undeniable accuracy,—moreover, pure and gentle as she was, it was singularly easy for Ruth Vincent to imagine a character as completely iniquitous as that of Arabyn; and for this simple reason, that, although she ever sought to preserve her soul even from a thought of sin, yet as she had deeply studied to what a height of perfection man may ascend in this life, by the resistless power of a holy faith, she could readily comprehend to what a depth of depravity he must fall without it. No! all was distinct, palpably evident, undoubted, and certain, before her now,—so thick a veil had fallen from her eyes, that it seemed as though she had never seen clearly before; so far from having a doubt upon her mind, she only wondered that she had ever been deceived.

She took, then, that letter, with hands cold as death, and Raymond dared not look upon her face, as he gave it to her: she read every word slowly, deliberately, as it appeared to him, till she fixed her eyes on the name of Arabyn traced by his own hand, whereby he, whom she loved best on earth, had affixed his signature to his distinct and positive declaration of his own depravity; when she had looked upon it long, Raymond gently withdrew it from her passive hold; then a low deep indescribable groan burst from her lips, as though the very soul were struggling within her to escape to some better home, before the full sense of her misery came upon her; and when the firm bonds of clay held it fast chained down till the ordeal was undergone, again instinctively she submitted, her head fell down upon her clasped hands as they lay on her knee, one long fit of shuddering shook her frame, and then she lay still. In the calm which succeeded, nature seemed to have re-entered into her sublime repose, notwithstanding the presence of two human beings, living, feeling, struggling before her, for both were motionless, locking within their own breasts the whirlwind and the storm.

Raymond was agitated by the most painful emotion; not so much with sympathy for the suffering of her who crouched before him, gathered into a heap, convulsed with anguish, as with a longing anxiety to know whether this servant of the Crucified would pass unscathed through the fiery furnace into which she had been thrown; that she was to suffer, was clear; that she was to be one of those who should come out of great tribulation in robes white and clean, he felt convinced; but by the manner in which that suffering came before her now, by the shape it assumed for her, would be tested whether that meek head was ever to wear the martyr's crown.

There were many characters in which Ruth Vincent was now called upon to endure bitter misery,—as the woman weeping for the breaking of her heart, whose deep affection, though altogether vain and hopeless now, could not and would not die,—as the betrayed, complaining, in mournful resentment, of the sharp and cruel piercing of her breast by the hand she had leant upon so trustingly,—of the wanton blackening and destroying of her life by him, for whom she would have died,—or as the Christian bewailing in holy sorrow the perishing of an immortal soul;—how was it then with her, as she sat there shivering so still and silently? to which of these tortures had she delivered up her soul, from which the bright hopes were falling away one by one, like the withered leaves from off the blasted tree? it was hard to say; he had not gathered, from the lips of those who had known it in its practical working, the details of the holiness of her life, nor witnessed himself in her a calm strength of mind, altogether foreign to her naturally yielding disposition, without being fully aware that the pure principle which guided her was deeply rooted and settled within her; but yet he had not met her earnest thoughtful gaze without learning, that there was in her a depth of feeling which would render the sorrow he had brought upon her unspeakably acute. How he longed for her to look up and speak! he could not but own as he pondered on the circumstances of the case, that many would have thought it a most natural result, if, like to the counselling of Job's unworthy companion of old, the human nature to which it was wedded had called upon her spirit " to curse God and die;" and he trembled for her as he wondered sadly, where in all the wide ocean of misery into which he had flung her, the soul of that unoffending victim was drifting now; it seemed to him an interminable interval before she looked up; but when she did so, he shrank back almost with an exclamation of horror.

The sight of her face was to him perfectly appalling, so dreadfully was it changed since he had first seen it that morning full of joyous animation, and bright with contentment and hope; now it was ghastly, livid, and rigid as marble, the mouth convulsed, the forehead contracted, the eyes dim, sunken, and heavy; terrible must have been the anguish which during that long silence had passed over her spirit, before its evidence could thus be stamped upon her countenance; and when she spoke in a voice of piteous entreaty, the broken accents seemed to convey to him a sense of the most unutterable dreariness and desolation.

Lifting up her hands with the imploring gesture of

an infant whose tottering feet can no longer support it, she cried out, "Have mercy—have mercy upon me, O Thou Most Merciful;" and then, slowly looking round upon the scene before her with a dim bewildered gaze, as though all to her eyes was changed, she murmured, like one who speaks in troubled slumber, "Surely a star has fallen from heaven, and all the world is dark, —darkness for evermore!" Then, having thus spoken, again the helpless head fell down, and the trembling hands, unable to support it, hung feebly by her side: and Raymond saw and knew that the sorrow which possessed her soul was such as no human words could ever describe; but he was well content,—for that one sentence had revealed the state of her mind, and he knew that, bitter as was her mourning, it was of that nature on which a blessing once was solemnly pronounced.

Yes; not for her breaking heart did Ruth Vincent weep; though it was no light affection which had lived within it, and no light pain which now rankled at its core, never to suspend its wearied aching till the beating ceased with life itself. She knew that there are certain flowers which, except they be bruised and crushed, give forth no fragrance. The fragrance of a human heart is the love of God, and she was willing even to pray that hers be crushed and bruised, if thereby alone it was to breathe forth and exhale that heavenly perfume: not for the base betrayal of her true and faithful love did she grieve in bitterness, for she felt no resentment; she knew she had received an injury, but she had too lowly an opinion of herself to feel aggrieved; and as for the destruction and ruin of her life by him to whom she was willing to devote it, she well knew he was but the instrument, and calmly she could say, "Father, Thou didst give to me this mortal life ; take it now, and deal with it and me as seemeth best unto Thy mighty love." But for the exile of a living spirit from the life eternal; for the everlasting degradation of the being designed to live throughout eternity in God—the everlasting distortion of that which in His image was formed—Ruth Vincent endured at that moment an anguish which may be felt but not expressed.

A vision of the glory to come passed before her spirit, —the cherubim and seraphim were there, and the countless hosts of the redeemed ; the spirits of just men made perfect ; the lowly and the meek ; they who, having been abased, were now exalted ; they who, having been last, were now first; all who from the heart had uttered the cry of the publican when he smote upon his breast, or who with the thief had uttered the prayer that, spoken from a cross, from The Cross was answered; those who had given a cup of water to a little one in His Name; those who in all generations have gone very early in the morning to the sepulchre to seek Him, who, having crucified the flesh and buried it with Him, with Him are risen ; those who, since the hour when the holy women first sat on Calvary, have, century after century, gathered round that same Cross, weeping. All these were there ; but one place was vacant—the place of him who was dearer than human words could tell, and for whom the awful price was paid in vain : one voice was silent when the eternal hallelujahs, eloquent of an eternal joy, thrilled through the responsive spheres ; and that voice was sweeter to her than all the music of earth, but it was the voice of one of those in whom the Love Incarnate shall not see the travail of His soul, nor be satisfied. And when she had thought upon these things, it seemed to her that her burden became insupportable; and there rose from her very heart an exceeding bitter cry, like unto that of him whose blessing was stolen from him, and she raised her hands, joined convulsively, and fell down prostrate, and laid her head in the dust.

"O thou afflicted, tossed with the tempest, and not comforted!" murmured Raymond, as he rose and approached her; "truly has it been said that 'vain is the help of man!'"

He bent over her, and smoothed with a father's tenderness the long hair, matted and dripping now with burning tears, and then gently spoke her name.

She turned her head, and taking his hand, said in a broken voice, while the words seemed to choke her, "I thank you—I *can* thank you—but, oh! in pity leave me! No one must be with me now, lest in mine agony I fall, —lest by my weakness I fail to show forth the glory of the faith which is my life. My flesh is weak, my spirit faints within me, there is a sound like to the roar of many waters in my ears, urging me to despair: no human eyes must see this conflict. O! leave me till I can stand forth with a holy strength, or perish in the effort."

Instantly Raymond gently released his hand from her grasp, and turned to leave her; for he felt that she was right.

In those hours, known doubtless to many, when the soul struggles with the humanity that would force it to stand upright and rave in lawless agony, whilst itself is sternly determined to fall down prostrate before the judgment-seat and say, "Thy will be done,"—in hours like these, when perhaps a watcher and a holy one come down from heaven to take their stand beside the martyr, no unhallowed human footsteps should be nigh; and the Christian, who remembered how he had himself in the lonely wilderness heard sweet counsellings, and from the barren desert reaped consolation, and from the burning sands gathered refreshing dews—now left her alone in that savage and majestic solitude.

She remained alone with the certainty that he whom she had cherished with an indestructible affection was the open, determined, and active enemy of the God by Whose agonizing death and passion she was redeemed; and with this conviction a palpable and thick darkness spread over her soul, and she sank, subdued and annihilated, beneath the misery whose term was the term of her earthly existence.

Very sudden had been the stroke whereby she was severed, in one instant and for ever, from him in whose presence alone she would have wished to live, and the solitary hope she had given to this earth, round which every thought and wish revolved, changed into uttermost despair!—whereby, in short, she was hurled from the height of a great and heartfelt happiness, to the depths of a most bitter suffering; yet the unexpected shock, instead of bringing unconsciousness, seemed to have endowed her threefold with life and feeling—she was all energy, all misery, every nerve quickened, every fibre strained.

How long she lay there she could not tell; for all was complete confusion and bewilderment in her mind. All that she had thought, and hoped, and wished before, she could no longer think, or hope, or wish; for she was separated, as by a gulf impassable, from her whole former existence, and in the chill and dismal region into which she had been cast, all full of shadows and blackness, she knew not where to turn for light, or hope, or succour: the very words of prayer seemed taken out of her mouth; over the glory even of immortal joys it seemed to her that a cloud had passed, for it was not her own suffering that caused her this exquisite pain, but his sin. Calmly she could resign herself to the overthrow of her own happiness, but not to his eternal perdition. She could have seen him die, and turned from his grave with hands crossed in submission on her breast, thanking heaven for his rest. She could have heard from his own lips that he hated her, and bowed her head in meekness; believing that in truth she were little worthy of his love. But to know that he was lost! she could perceive no law by which she was bound to submit to this: and yet to feel within herself an opposition to the will of God was a fearful thought, and reason almost gave way in the conflict.

She looked up, and when she saw that twilight had commenced, she was glad to think that one day of her wretchedness was gone; then, repelling the unworthy feeling, felt that, if by a Father's hand she were afflicted, in thankfulness she desired to suffer.

She looked around, but it seemed to her as though some convulsion of nature had taken place, and that all was chaos where order and beauty had reigned before. She knew not where to fly to escape the leaden weight that lay upon her heart; she knew not what was to become of her: her soul was shaken as though its anchor had been wrenched away; it could not exist thus crippled, helpless, and alone; it could not see, because of the great darkness of its despondency; nor hear, for the roaring of the billows on the ocean of sorrow in which it was steeped.

She looked up, and her dim eyes fixed themselves on a cross, roughly hewn in wood, placed on the summit of a cliff, as is customary in some mountainous regions; and the sight of that outward and holy symbol seemed to lure back her tortured and wandering spirit to its haven. She stretched forth her arms towards it: "O refuge of the desolate,—home of the weary,—hope of the soul!" she murmured faintly; and like the stricken deer, when the refuge is nigh, with one bound she flew forth to attain that spot:—over rocks and stones, up the steep mountain-side, by cliff and ravine, she darted on, heedless that her feet on the rough path were wounded and bleeding, that the fierce wind drove against her, and the spray of the torrents drenched her garments with foam; on—on she flew, as the stag would have flown with the arrow in its breast, till she reached that haven of rest; and then twining her arms round the rough wood of the cross, she fell down at its foot, like a suffering child on the breast of its mother.

Throughout that long night, in the mountain solitude, while the pine-forests lay still and breathless, and the wind swept noiselessly over the trackless snow, there ascended a voice, a human voice, going up hour by hour with weeping and prayer.

CHAPTER XVIII.

ARABYN, BAFFLED ON ALL SIDES BY AN UNATTAINABLE FOE, CONTINUES THE STRUGGLE WITH INCREASING ENERGY.

When morning dawned, Ruth Vincent still lay at the foot of that cross, pale and exhausted, but perfectly calm: not in vain had she passed that night alone with her God, surrounded only by the mountains which held the tremendous avalanche suspended, till, at the silent intimation of His will, they hurled it down the valley; by the storms that dared not breathe till, at His Word, they unlocked their fury; by the torrents that followed on the course marked out; by the stars that walked each in its appointed path; by the worlds that revolved obedient; by a whole universe working in the silent spirit of submission.

His Omnipotence, His Might, Dominion, and Power, had risen up before her so awful, so inscrutable, that, had she not clung to the cross, she felt as though she must have dissolved into dust before Him! Into the Everlasting Arms she had resigned herself once more; into the infinity of His Eternal Love her soul glided, like a bark from storms and whirlwinds on to a waveless ocean. And as for Arabyn, she had given him back to his Maker as she would have delivered the clay into the hands of the potter: what had she to do, coming between that soul and his Creator? Did she doubt that

ARABYN CONTINUES THE STRUGGLE.

he had been and would be dealt with according to a mercy of which she could form no conceivable idea; that an eternity of the love which she had given him was lost in one moment of that which the Being had bestowed upon him; Whose officers were peace, and Whose exactors righteousness?

When morning dawned, her spirit was altogether at rest, though sorely bruised and crushed within her; but when the sun rose, calling the world to labour, she rose also, for she knew that they who follow on the path which she had chosen, and which One wearing a crown of thorns had trodden before her, must never think of rest; it must ever be action, and energy, a struggling and a wrestling to do His will. And she knew well what she had to do, it was clear and distinct before her eyes: she could not surmise the consequences, she could not see how it would be her duty to act one hour beyond the present; not one inch beyond the point at which she now stood was visible to her in the light of His Commandments. But it is ever thus with those whose life is hid with Him: He lightens only the ground whereon their feet obedient are now about to tread, and bids them not look beyond that narrow circle, trusting all to Him.

Ruth Vincent rose: she wrung the cold dew from the hair that hung so wet and clammy over her face; she dashed away the last tears from her eyes, and began to descend the mountain path. She was very weak; her feet tottered, her strength seemed failing at every step; never had existence been to her so weary or so painful a burden. As she descended, she met a mountain shepherd leading his flock to pasture; struck by her aspect, as fainting and wayworn she drew near him, he offered her a draught of milk; and she gratefully and meekly took it, although she knew she was thereby binding to herself again the life which Arabyn had sought to make a curse, and which, unsustained, would so easily have slipt away with all its subtle powers of torturing.

Thus strengthened and refreshed, she took her way to that which yesterday had been a happy home. It seemed designed that she should in every way be tried; as she approached the door, Arabyn stood upon the threshold; she stopped, shaking as though she had seen a grave give up its dead: as he saw her, he called out, and the sweet mournful tones of his voice reached her ear,—"Ruth, my Ruth, where have you been so long?—how have I longed for you!"

To her it was as though thunders rolled over her head; she felt in that hour as if soul and body were being rent asunder! with an effort—such an effort as can be made but once in a lifetime; she gathered up her strength, and rushed past him into her room, where she fell on the ground panting and convulsed: for as she looked upon that face, and heard that voice, the maddening conviction rushed in upon her, that, base, degraded, lost as he was, she who once had loved him must love him still, even to the last day of her existence. Yet this thought, though it seemed the very climax of her trial, the bitterest drop of all her bitter portion, did not cause her to swerve one moment from her obedience, or shrink from the task allotted to her.

She rose at once to accomplish it,—even the separation, complete, final, and irrevocable, between herself and Arabyn. She determined to write to him, for she dared not trust herself to speak; although to some it might have seemed that her mental strength and resolution were very great at this dark crisis in her life, she yet well knew her own weakness and insufficiency.

This was her letter:—

"God is just! That God, in whom you do not believe, and before whom throughout eternity you shall bow down, is just! *Raymond is here*, and I know all! But God is also merciful; may He have mercy upon you!

"Arabyn,—that one prayer which my soul shall breathe for yours by day and night through every hour of existence unto my life's end, must henceforth be the only link between us; you know that it must be so. Were you bound to me by the ties that should have linked us, you were like unto the galley-slave who was chained with an iron chain to his most hated enemy. And for me, my lips have named the name of Christ, and never shall they utter the vow of love and allegiance to one who dares disown Him!

"Arabyn,—when standing by my side, in the face of Heaven, you swore that I alone was dear to you in all the world: your oath was false! But when I, answering, said that to you my whole and undivided love was given in all its strength, I spoke the truth. And I rejoice that it is so; I bless and praise Heaven, that from the beginning you have hated me; for if I only loved, I alone shall suffer. This might have made the Cross, which I to-day have lifted up, too heavy for my weakness, too sharp for my vile humanity, had I known that even as I shall mourn, you must have mourned also. You may doubt this my affection and my suffering, because I now do utterly renounce you, and for ever: yet doubt not; for if the hour should ever come when your proud spirit fails, and your self-confidence gives way, then it may soothe you to remember, that you, who from mankind have severed yourself in hate, were, above all mankind, beloved.

"My words must be few, for they are of those, 'weighty and momentous,' which, once uttered, shall never be recalled; they must seal up and conclude for ever that portion of our destiny which we have accomplished side by side; they must evoke and create the vast impassable gulf that shall lie between us from this hour till the tomb supplies its place. They must pronounce the fiat of our separation immutable, irrevocable, complete; even though still you should constrain me to look upon your face and hear your voice.

"Yet one word would I say before that last is written; one word, lest for me you should yet be stricken with remorse, if, ere your body turn to dust, your soul should turn to God. Arabyn, if that change come—as I, on bended knees seven times a day, shall supplicate it may —then do you thank Heaven for my present sorrow, as I now thank it for your bitter hate, whereby you are exempt from pain. I do myself adore Him for the heavy blow, the heavy, overwhelming blow, with which I have this day been smitten; since thereby has been shattered for ever the chain that was binding me all too powerfully unto earth. Now, from this hour, and for evermore, there is nothing between me and Him; now can I think of His awful agony upon that night when the angel strengthened Him, without the mournful remorse of feeling, that not every thought, not every hope and wish, to Him exclusively are given. Now free, free and unshackled, I can lay me down at the foot of that Cross, to rest in a peace ineffable, which there only on this earth it is given us to feel.

"Oh! He only is Holy, He only is Pure, He is the only

and all-sufficient Life of this immortal soul. I adore Him for the sharp severing of the one link that drew me from Him: I bless Him for the destruction of the mortal joy, for the shaking of the earth beneath my feet, for the piercing of my soul with that fierce pang. I abhor myself that ever for one hour I turned from the contemplation of His love. He knoweth that although dimmed and weakened by the earthly affection, the earthly rapture, and the earthly care, still my whole being longed for Him, and cried out after Him, and struggled with its baser nature to be with Him.

"But now I come, now I return, now I lie down at the Sacred Feet, pierced for my sake: Oh! let Him take me—let Him take me to be all His own. I am weak, but henceforward I am His; His alone on earth— His only in eternity: therefore farewell. Arabyn, even though we daily meet, these words are spoken, and they shall be true; Farewell for ever!

"RUTH VINCENT."

She folded this letter, she rose, she called the servant and bade her give it Arabyn; as she was about to put it into her hand she paused, she drew it back, it seemed impossible to consummate the sacrifice,—then she murmured to herself, "Do I mock Him, that I cling to the outward symbol of His cross, and will not drive it into my heart?" quietly she gave it away and closed the door. She went and laid herself down upon the couch where she had so often slept the calm sweet sleep she never more must know, and calmly said as she closed her eyes upon the light she fain would have beheld no more, "Surely the bitterness of death is past!"

Arabyn had remained petrified with astonishment

when Ruth Vincent fled past him in this extraordinary manner, looking, with deathlike face and dripping hair, almost like some risen ghost shrinking from the contact of a mortal yet in the flesh. That some marvellous change had taken place in her was most evident, but he could by no means surmise what had caused it; it was indeed impossible for him to have any clue to the truth, as he still believed that Raymond was in England, and he well knew that there was no other who could have unmasked him. Yet for the first time Ruth had taken no heed of his pleading voice; for the first time she had passed him without a look of sympathy, or a word of kindness uttered.

Arabyn sent message after message to entreat that she would see him, but the servant could gain no admittance to her room; at length the letter was brought to him, he seized it, tore it open, and when he had read it, it is not possible to describe the fierce rage that rose up within him. What! was he thwarted again? was there opposition again? and opposition from her whom he believed he had thoroughly subdued, by the most powerful of all methods, that of affection!—her on whom he had expended all his powers of fascination for so many months: to gain whom he had exercised his talents to the uttermost! Oh! how he hated her! how he hated Raymond!—Raymond, who at every turn stood up to baffle him; by whose power Ruth, but yesterday obedient to his slightest wish, to-day renounced him, and for ever!

He threw down her letter, he set his heel upon it, he clenched his hands, and nerved himself to think; then he laughed out with a loud scornful laugh, when he reflected that he had for a moment believed Ruth Vincent could escape him, his tool, his victim, the weak, gentle, timid woman, round whose very existence he twined himself;—did she think by a few words like these, to break the iron bonds wherein he had bound her? he dismissed the idea altogether from his mind; but there was a more urgent matter to be arranged,—Raymond was near, his active, powerful, determined enemy; it was ruin and destruction to him, if Ruth, if even Mr. Denham, remained in this man's vicinity another day; what was to be done? in ten minutes his inventive genius had suggested and arranged a plan suitable to the present emergency; but not a moment was to be lost, and he did not lose a moment. He despatched one servant to the village inn for a carriage and horses, he sent another to make all preparation for an instant departure, and went himself into Mr. Denham's room.

We have already described the extent of the infidel's extraordinary influence over this weak and capricious old man; it is a case of very common occurrence, that a person habitually violent and overbearing to all, should at last yield himself, with an abject submission, to the ascendancy of some one superior mind. The power of Arabyn over his uncle was now complete; he had succeeded in inspiring him with the most ungovernable and absorbing affection for himself, and he was never content except when his nephew was by his side; at the same time, Ruth was still quite necessary to his comfort, and it was therefore with the utmost satisfaction that he heard of their proposed marriage, as Arabyn had taken care to assure him, that both would then remain with him entirely.

Arabyn now informed Mr. Denham of all that had passed, for in this instance it so chanced that the truth (though distorted) served his purposes better than any story he could have invented; he told him that Raymond, a personal enemy of his own, had come in search of Ruth, and had made to her such a false statement respecting his own character, that she had suddenly written to tell him she renounced her engagement, and would see him no more.

Mr. Denham's rage at this announcement was unbounded. That Ruth should dare to thwart his views in any thing, seemed to him incredible; he declared to his nephew, that he would at once force her into renewing her consent to the union he deemed so desirable.

Arabyn replied, that he believed any means he might use would be justifiable in such a case, as he knew that it was solely from a mistaken idea, and at the cost of much misery to herself, that Ruth had adopted this strange resolution,—if his uncle would follow the plan he would recommend, all might yet be well.

Mr. Denham undertook readily to do whatever he pleased.

Arabyn then proposed, that they should leave this place that very day, taking Ruth with them, and using such precautions as should render it impossible for Raymond to follow them—for so long as she remained within reach of his enemy's influence, all their efforts would be vain; but they might take her to some remote spot, where no one would interfere with them; he would then undertake to convince her very soon of the folly of her present proceedings.

Mr. Denham thought this an excellent project; he became impatient to put it into execution without delay; it mattered not to him on what part of the continent he resided, and any thing was better than to

CONTINUES THE STRUGGLE WITH ENERGY.

allow Ruth to adhere to her absurd determination; he started up to go to her at once, and bid her prepare for an immediate departure.

Arabyn detained him; he said he believed there would be some difficulty in persuading her to accompany them; it would be necessary to resort to an innocent stratagem, which his uncle certainly would not object to adopt, as it would tend to promote Ruth's own happiness hereafter.

Mr. Denham assured him he had no objection to any thing which could further his own wishes.

His nephew then suggested that the old man should appear to think her resolution irrevocable; but that he should tell her, if she designed to give up her engagement, she must at once quit the place with him, before Arabyn discovered their intention, as he would never voluntarily consent to quit her; thus she would be induced herself to hurry their departure, and would never discover the truth till she was too completely in their power to escape. This subtle plan having been duly arranged, Mr. Denham proceeded at once to carry it into effect.

Ruth Vincent still lay exhausted and faint, oppressed with a sadness more intense than any she had ever imagined a mortal could endure, but perfectly submissive and tranquil. She had so irrevocably and completely determined on her separation from Arabyn, that she scarce thought of speculating on the manner in which he would receive the announcement of her resolution. It might disappoint his schemes for the acquisition of wealth, but it would not otherwise cause him a moment's pang. She well remembered now many an unguarded word and look of his, unthought of at the time of her delusion, which to her unveiled eyes most plainly proved how he had hated her whilst counterfeiting a very different sentiment.

Drearily was she looking into her future life, whose great occupation was to be the supplicating of heaven for his sake, when the door opened, and Mr. Denham entered.

It is needless to detail how successful he was in the stratagem Arabyn had so artfully prepared. He began by reproaching her, with all the anger which he really felt, for the letter she had written; and then, finding her resolute in adhering to her new resolution, he appeared to relent and take compassion on her for her evident suffering. He then told her, if she must abandon her engagement, it could only be done by their immediate departure; otherwise Arabyn, frantic with grief, would never consent to part with her.

Ruth at once gratefully agreed to go immediately. Thanking Mr. Denham for what she believed to be an act of unwonted kindness, she promised to be quite ready to start in a very short time. Two hours afterwards she sent to tell him that her preparations were complete; and Mr. Denham came to conduct her to the carriage. She had entered it, the old man had followed her, and the door was shut, before she perceived that Arabyn sat opposite to her, gazing at her with a look of scornful exultation. A scream of horror burst from her lips—the truth flashed upon her at once: she saw how she had been purposely deceived, in order to withdraw her from Raymond's protection. She felt that Arabyn would never let her escape from his grasp: an agonizing terror seized her that they were about to take her to some desert place, where they would force her to be hour by hour in contact with him whom she had renounced for ever, and who must be for ever dear!

Half frantic at the idea, she endeavoured to throw herself out of the carriage, but Arabyn held her back with a firm hand. Then she shrank from him as she would from the touch of a snake, and, flinging herself into a corner, buried her face in her hands. She felt as if her senses were abandoning her, when the carriage rolled off, and she was borne down the mountain road at a furious pace.

CHAPTER XIX.

ARABYN AND HIS COMPANION VISIT THE GREEK BISHOPS
BY NIGHT.

To one of the most remote and desolate spots on the sunny shores of Greece, Ruth Vincent was now conveyed by the two men with whom she was so strangely associated; yet, wild and solitary as was their retreat, it possessed much of the peculiar beauty, all brightness, softness, and tranquillity, which characterizes the scenery of that fair land.

Their dwelling was an old Turkish tower, standing on the sea-shore. On one side, almost overhanging it, rose a lofty hill, rocky and precipitous, near the summit of which a little chapel was picturesquely situated; on the other, a wide plain, covered with olive trees, extended to a more distant range of mountains, whose delicate outline seemed pencilled with a singularly graceful curve against the clear bright sky.

To one whose mind was at rest, and whose footsteps no sorrow haunted, it would have been a pleasant thing to wander on these golden sands, watching the light waves of the blue Ægean, as they danced and sparkled all day; showing how, even as we can judge of the glory and power of the sun only by the shedding of its light on outward objects, so the goodness of the Deity is visibly revealed in the world's external beauty:

or by night to walk there, and note how that deep clear sea, not content with beholding the splendour of the midnight stars, wore the transcript of them in her bosom; even as one who long contemplates the brightness and purity that is above, till the reflection of them enters into his own soul. But Ruth Vincent was destined in this calm and beautiful spot to pass through a probation, under which, had it continued any length of time, she must utterly have sunk.

Arabyn more than ever fiercely, almost frantically determined, that he would accomplish his designs in spite of all opposition, whether from earth or heaven, imposed his presence upon her continually, and left no means untried to subdue her to his will. He well knew the power he had acquired over her, by the sympathy he had caused her to feel for him; and it was impossible for the infidel to imagine, that the earthly affection should weigh nothing in the balance with her, when by the keeping of holy commandments she was called upon to show forth a holier love. From a perfect confidence of ultimate success he passed, therefore, to great astonishment, and finally indescribable rage, at finding her altogether immovable in her determination to separate entirely from him who was to have been her husband.

It was quite impossible for her to conceal from herself, that the attachment she had borne him continued, and must continue, inviolate and undiminished, as long as life lasted, although the esteem from which it had originally sprung was altogether destroyed: and thus it was positive torture to her to be continually in contact with him towards whom it was necessary she should act as though she hated him as truly as he detested her,—to be thus for ever, over and over again, destroying by her firm refusal her sole hope of happiness on earth. She endeavoured to avoid, and hide herself from him as much as possible; but it was a fruitless attempt, as he persisted in inhabiting the same dwelling; and to have left the country altogether (as she would have believed herself justified in doing, notwithstanding Mr. Denham's claims on her) was completely out of her power, as both the old man and Arabyn took effectual means to prevent her escape. She was, in fact, their captive and slave, and nothing but the firm belief that their agency in thus torturing her was both permitted and commanded, could have enabled her to live on in such meek and humble endurance.

It was a bitter thing for her to be thus constrained, almost hourly, to renew the tremendous sacrifice she once had made when she resigned him; for the strength which we can find wherewith to perform one great and solemn act of duty almost seems to fail us, when we are called upon, day after day, to persist in the offering up of self.

Weeks passed away, during which Ruth Vincent underwent a degree of persecution and misery which it is difficult to describe. All the talent, ingenuity, and eloquence of the infidel were exercised in every different way to induce her to become his wife. Now he loaded her with the most bitter and cutting reproaches, accusing her of having blighted and cursed his existence, and leagued herself with his enemies to snatch from him the only joy he asked on earth; and fiercely upbraided her with falsehood and hypocrisy, in having ever said she felt any compassion for him. And she would stand meekly before him, whilst with cruel eloquence he poured out his anger upon her, pale as death, with large tears falling slowly on her folded hands, thinking only how good a thing it was to suffer for well-doing! Or again, he would use another method (to her far more terrible), and speaking softly, in accents so like those of affection that it seemed almost madness not to believe him, he would implore her, whose heart had ever melted to the least tone of sorrow in a stranger's voice, not to abandon him to his loneliness and misery, but yet— even yet—to have compassion on him.

Fortunately for Ruth, Arabyn now made not the slightest attempt to conceal from her the infidel opinions of which she was so fully aware. It had become an insupportable burden to him, the necessity of masking himself in the religion he so abhorred; and so far from endeavouring to do so, he took a savage pleasure in showing his contempt of the faith she cherished, hoping by his powerful eloquence to induce her to abandon it.

He little knew how the soul he assaulted was surrounded with invisible strength, against which all the powers of darkness could not prevail; but in the mean time it was an agony almost unendurable for her to hear the words of blasphemy and fearful impiety uttered by lips so beloved. Often it seemed to her as though her reason would fail her in this sore trial, and many a dark temptation assailed her, offering the means of deliverance from her constant and harassing misery. If she walked on the sea-shore, and gazed out on the tranquil deep, when the calm moonbeams were cradled there, and the storm lay sleeping on its breast, like a tigress hushed in her lair; again and again wily fiends seemed to stand by her side, and whisper to her that a rest and a refuge was there for one hunted down and pursued of men. The roll of the wave seemed so cool to her ear, when fevered and tortured with grief, and the voices ever told her how calm she could lie, with the clear waters rushing over her weary head! and that to one so friendless and lonely it was permitted to die, since the winds and the waves would alone sing her dirge, and none but the dews of the sky weep over her. From suggestions so horrible, so unnatural for her, there was but one escape, and Ruth Vincent would fly from the seductive waves to the chapel on the hill, there to gain new strength for her ceaseless struggle.

Temptations such as these, however, led her to fear that her mind might give way at last; and after a time, depriving herself of the air and exercise which were her only pleasures, she shut herself up in her own room, and positively refused to see Arabyn at all. He then wrote to her a letter, to which it was quite necessary that she should pay attention.

He said, that he now desired to make her one last solemn appeal, and if this failed he pledged himself to molest her no more. She had told him, (and he could indeed well perceive,) that her faith was the sole obstacle between them; were this but overcome, both might be saved from misery. She knew in what light esteem he held the priestcraft which deluded her, and he had it in his power to give her such a proof that it was a delusion, as should utterly and for ever destroy her belief; he summoned her therefore, as she valued the peace of his whole life, and of her own, to grant him an interview that same evening, when he would bring before her the proof of which he spoke, incontestable and palpable: if she refused to meet him, and to face the undoubted warrant he could show her, that Christianity was a falsehood, he would, he must, attribute her refusal to her consciousness of the weakness of her cause; and her present seclusion, to the fact that she in her blindness was panic-struck, because his arguments had already so far caused her to waver, that she was obliged to fly the temptation.

This was the substance of Arabyn's letter, and it seemed to Ruth that she had no choice but to accede to his request. That no such proof as that of which he so mysteriously spoke, could in fact exist against the truth, she well knew; but that he believed himself in possession of some irresistible argument she did not doubt, as he had often of late, when forcing her to listen to his own views, spoken of a tangible demonstration which in the last emergency he would make to her, in order to convince her that the faith, to which her soul was bound, was a false and vain delusion. She could readily perceive that the threat, with which he concluded, was made solely to constrain her to compliance with his wishes; but she felt herself not the less bound to show that there was no possible weapon he could think fit to use against Christianity, which she was not ready to face and to destroy. She would, moreover, by this last encounter, force him to terminate a strife that was killing her; as he promised after this to desist from further discussion, she could without any appearance of vacillation refuse to hear him again; the very fact that Ruth Vincent shrank from another meeting, another struggle with Arabyn, as she would have done from the tortures of the rack, was a reason why she decided on undergoing it. She felt she could never be mistaken in accepting the largest measure of trial and suffering which could be received by her. She agreed to meet

Arabyn that evening on the sea-shore, as he had appointed, and when she had despatched a message to that effect, she laid down her head upon her folded arms, and murmured, "Spare not, spare not, stay not Thine Hand, strike on, strike deep; cut into the very core of this sinful heart, till its corruption is rooted out of it."

Wearily, wildly, to and fro in his lonely room, Philip Arabyn meanwhile paced the floor; there had passed over him of late a mental change, for which he could not account, and of which he was not always quite aware himself. Solitude had become insupportable to him, sleep had fled him, and a thousand ideas of which he had no control, crowded on his mind when no external objects attracted his attention; he knew not how it was, but it seemed to him as though gradually the struggle he had established with his own fate, were growing more unequal. He felt that "the spirits he had raised abandoned him;" and when his soul, in its restlessness of unattained desire, flew forth to plunge into the mysteries of futurity, his mind became confused, his thoughts wandered, and nothing remained distinct save the insupportable misery of a dread which had no defined object; the powerful intellect he had worked so fiercely, and curbed so sternly, that it might be the submissive instrument of his will, now often seemed like a restive steed, to bound beneath his hand, and carry him he knew not whither.

But that which was worst and most unaccountable to him, who, like the Sadducees of old, believed neither in angel nor spirit, was a horrible delusion which at times came over him, especially in the dark and silent night, making his very flesh to creep; he, who had stood over his dead sister in her shroud, making himself by a resolute and systematic calm, almost as insensible to human feeling as the corpse before him, was now often constrained, in the midnight gloom and solitude, to shrink back pale and trembling, shivering and quailing, his limbs bending beneath him, as it seemed to him that her avenging spirit rose up into his presence, close beside him, her icy breath upon his face, forcing herself back into his sight, robed in all the ghastly horror of the tomb; night after night she appeared before him, as if for a most awful purpose; for that voice, whose sound chilled him to the bone, never failed to wail out its unceasing question, "Is death forgetfulness?" and night after night was he forced to answer, "It is annihilation!" and then ever rose the shrieks he once had heard upon the plain, but now they seemed to come from the lowermost depths of the abyss, and he clung frantically to the walls, lest she should draw him down after her.

These horrible fancies recurred continually when alone, and though with the return of light and of the means of intercourse with his fellow-creatures, they speedily vanished, and left him despising himself that he should be thus influenced by a disordered fancy; yet they seemed to be beyond his control, and no exercise of reason could destroy the horror with which they inspired him. Wearily and wildly, therefore, he paced to and fro, waiting for the hour of his appointed meeting with Ruth Vincent; and when with the deepening twilight, dark shadows seemed to gather in the room around him, he gladly fled down to the sea-shore to join her and escape them.

They met, these two, the torturer and the victim, at that soft evening hour when all on earth was peace and beauty, and from the clear and lucid sky, the golden sepulchre of day, the pure pale stars, were starting like drops of liquid light, most glorious tears shed for the perished sunshine: they met, to bring the elements of discord and of strife into that scene, whose quiet loveliness made it seem like a sketch of Paradise, taken by an angelic hand; to cause that wind that went so softly murmuring by, reviving the weary with its fresh and perfumed breath, to bear away their bitter sighs, and to mar the melody with which the sea was singing a lullaby to earth, with the voice of misery, and the whisperings of sin.

They met: Ruth Vincent raised her eyes, so dim and sunken now, to meet the bitter and reproachful gaze of Arabyn, and her face, already so pale and wan, grew whiter than before, and she clasped her hands tightly together.

"Will you consent to follow me," said Arabyn, "to the ruined monastery in the olive grove?—it is only there that I can give to you that proof of the falsity of your most false religion, which shall cause your soul to fill with rage, at thought how nearly you had bartered all the joys of earth for a deceitful name,—will you trust to me—one hour to me? who once hoped to protect and cherish you till life itself should terminate."

Ruth bowed her head, for she dared not trust herself to speak when he addressed her thus softly and pleadingly.

"You think yourself most strong," said Arabyn, with difficulty mastering the anger which her calmness always caused him, "you believe you can resist me and the most infallible of proofs?"

"In my own strength," said Ruth, "I can resist

nothing, and can accomplish nothing; in that which is given to me, I can resist and accomplish all."

Arabyn angrily turned and led the way to the olive grove; and she followed him, treading in his shadow, and thinking how that same shadow had fallen darkly on the whole extent of her life's path, and lay even now shrouding her soul in gloom.

It was very beautiful, that olive wood, so sombre, and so still, with the moon's rays shooting here and there through its deep shades, like the smile of a friend in a season of darkness; but when they reached the deserted monastery, the whole place was full of a dreariness and desolation which sent a strange chill to the heart; it was completely ruined, having been burned down during the revolution, and the fragments of the bare blackened walls had assumed many distorted and fantastic shapes: it was now night, and the snakes that hide themselves from the light, like the black thoughts of men, came stealing out with their cold grey rings glistening in the moonshine.

Arabyn and Ruth passed through the roofless passages, and entered the church; it was the only part of the building which was yet entire, and a faint smile passed over the face of Ruth, as she thought how the infidel was weakening his own cause when he brought her into that holy place, there to strive to undermine her faith.

She looked round on the pictures of the martyrs, still visible on the walls;—the blessed martyrs who had been faithful truly unto death;—and she remembered how they were waiting now in their white robes till the number of their brethren should be complete on earth. Dear friends and companions, they seemed to her so

s

lonely and persecuted; and she could fancy that their mild gaze exhorted her to constancy; while the lamp before the altar, which some good peasant failed not to trim and to replenish weekly, was to her an apt emblem, as it burned there so brightly amid all that gloom and desolation, of the holy flame of faith, that abides so clear and steady when most the soul's horizon is dismal and lowering.

With a firmer step, and a brighter eye, Ruth Vincent followed her companion along one of the aisles. At a particular spot, with which he seemed well acquainted, he stooped and lifted up one of the broad stones with which it was paved, by means of an iron ring; a wide aperture remained, through which might be dimly seen a flight of steps descending into a dark cavity. Arabyn took one of the tapers which lay on the altar, lighted it at the lamp, and then holding it so as to cast a faint glow on the stair, desired Ruth to descend into the vault. Quietly she prepared to obey him; and as she placed her foot on the first step, that seemed to lead down into a complete darkness, from which a chill damp air rushed up, causing a strange and peculiar sensation, he involuntarily gazed at her with the utmost surprise.

"Have you no fear," he asked, "thus to descend by night into a dark sepulchral vault?"

"Fear," said Ruth, her voice sounding sweet and clear, "whether of danger or of misfortune, is a selfish and unholy thing; being the preference of our own will not to suffer, to that of God that we should do so. I desire to be ready this night, as ever, to meet whatever He may choose to send me, however menacing the shape in which it come."

"Go on, then!" exclaimed Arabyn, fiercely; for he

felt himself, with all his talent and powers, actually humbled in presence of one who could speak thus.

She descended a long winding stair which brought her to a closed door; Arabyn then passed before her, and flinging it open, entered first into the vault; he held the taper high above his head, and turned to look on Ruth, as she passed the threshold of this subterranean chamber, with a glance of exulting triumph. He seemed to have no doubt of the effect of the scene which was to meet her eyes; nor was he mistaken; for no sooner had she looked around than she uttered an exclamation of horror, and fell back trembling against the wall.

"So I have at last found means to move you," said Arabyn, with a savage joy.

"You have found means to startle and to horrify me," said Ruth faintly; "it was cruel to bring me here."

The scene into which the infidel had thus abruptly introduced her was certainly calculated to strike terror into the most dauntless heart. They had left the solitude and desolation of the ruins, to enter into a well-peopled chamber;—and a still and solemn company they were, in truth, who sat before them there, surrounded by all the pomp and splendour to which their rank entitled them. This vast dim vault was the sepulchre of the Bishops of Western Greece, and, in accordance with a very ancient custom, the last mark of honour which is paid to these dignitaries of the Church is by means of a very singular mode of burial.

The first sight which met the eyes of Ruth Vincent so fascinated her with its strange horror that she could not withdraw them. On three large chairs, decorated in a costly manner with velvet and gilding, sat three dead men, each with his mitre on his head, and the gorgeous sacerdotal robes falling round him; the right hand of each one was uplifted, as if in the act of giving the priestly blessing, the three fingers being raised in the peculiar manner which is used in that ceremony as a sign of the Most Holy Trinity: and so earnest and devout did they seem in the performance of this solemn act, that it was scarce possible not to imagine that the souls of those whom they blessed on earth were gathered at their knees even then to receive the benediction, now thrice hallowed. In the other hand they held a volume of the Holy Scriptures, which lay upon their lap, and the open page of which they appeared to read with deep attention.

The rush of air from without, sweeping through the vault, stirred their dried and withered bones, and caused them to shake their heads, as though in deprecation of the intrusion which disturbed them at their awful study.

These stately Bishops, fearful to look upon in their grim splendour, had been consigned at different periods to this their tomb; and the process of embalming by which they are prepared thus, with hideous mimicry, to imitate the actions of their living bodies, being very incomplete in Greece, all were more or less in decay. One, who for many years had zealously played his part in that sepulchral drama, was now nothing but a bare and crumbling skeleton; and the fleshless skull seemed to grin in horrible mockery over the pages of the book he still conned so attentively. The second, to whose bones some remnant of the human form still clung, was in a state of working corruption too dreadful for description. And the third, who had been there but a few months, had stiffened into an incarnation (so to speak) of the most perfect soullessness, the most dead and vacant imbecility, which conveyed a strange and fearful impression to the mind.

Scattered all around, in addition to these, were fragments of similar seats, heaped up with ashes and crawling dust, which an instinctive thrill and creeping of the flesh convinced Ruth Vincent had once been human beings like herself. In short, that which Arabyn had brought her here to witness, was a revelation full and complete of the corruption of mortality in all its various stages; such as usually is religiously buried from the profanation of a living gaze beneath the earth. And now, seizing her by the hand, he dragged her forward into the very midst of it.

"I said that I would give you a tangible proof of the falsity of your delusive faith," he cried, "and I demand of you, is it not here? The whole foundations of the Christian creed on which it is built up, from first to last, are the doctrines of the soul's immortality, and of the resurrection of the body,—and now look here, look here; bend down, I tell you, and look into this loathsome creeping dust,—these are the doctrines; but here is the fact, the actual, tangible, palpable fact; this—this is the all of man; in your fancy, in the chimeras of superstition, he may have another existence; but this is in very deed, and in substantial truth, the man; the man who lived, who died, who is here and no where else. The soul! that name, that idea, that falsehood, that untangible delusion, you say has gone to some unreal abode. I tell you I have seen men die by scores, and as I live I swear to you, that nothing passes from them save the breath, dying away full often in a curse that ever they existed; their spiritual essence, be it what it may, is extinct as the flame that perishes in air; but let that pass, for it admits of no palpable demonstration as does this grosser delusion. You admit that if I disprove the resurrection of the body, the Christian faith is abolished and untrue. Look then, and judge by your own eyes: here is the body, the precious, wonderful body, that is to rival, with its life, eternity! This is it; these ashes light and feathery, which, behold, I breathe upon, and with my breath they are dispersed. Kneel down, you who love to prostrate yourself before divinity," he forced her to fall on her knees, "kneel down, I say, and worship immortality here present before you, and in this devotional act you will the better see the process of its working: truly you have spoken well and wisely; man does indeed live again, we distinctly see it here; he is regenerate in the worm:—see, it lives, it moves, it crawls, this was man's flesh—certainly the body shall rise again, it is risen even now in this creeping vermin. Oh! glorious regeneration! Oh! desirable resurrection!"

Arabyn paused, almost exhausted by the vehemence with which he had spoken, and Ruth, whom he still held down amongst these dreadful remains, could not for a few minutes overcome the deadly faintness and horror which the sight of them caused her; soon, however, the immortal soul within her,—the very soul of whose existence he doubted,—rose up and mastered the weak humanity that shrank from the presence of itself in corruption; she remembered for what purpose the infidel had brought her into this strange charnel-house, and in what hope, and she trembled lest, by a moment's delay, she gave him reason to think her faith was failing her; gently she displaced the hand that kept her kneeling there, and stood up calm and collected.

"This then," she said, "is the means by which you thought to assail and conquer the Holy Truth! This is the proof of which you spoke! even the revelation, awful and entire, of that mystery of corruption, which it is doubtless sacrilege to search into. Since, however, you have believed that this could be an argument against Christianity, I, a Christian, will now look quietly and dispassionately on it, that you may judge impartially, how far it is available as a weapon against that which, immaculate and indestructible, is enshrined in eternity."

As she spoke, she turned and slowly looked around, till she had examined the whole scene in complete detail; then she walked across the vault with a step as steady, and a countenance as calm, as though she were still in the olive grove, and taking up her station by the side of the dead bishop, who yet retained most of the semblance of humanity, composedly laid her hand on his shoulder, and remaining motionless for a few minutes looked fixedly upwards.

In spite of himself, Arabyn was awe-struck and subdued, as he gazed upon the still, strange group, which the light of the taper rendered dimly visible,—that corpse sitting there in his splendid robes, the ghastliness of his appearance singularly enhanced by the extraordinary length to which his beard and the nails of his fingers had grown after death, and appearing, with his sullen eyes staring wide open, to wait impatiently for the first words which were to be uttered by the living being at his side, whilst she stood close to him, so pale, so perfectly serene, handling the dead flesh, and seeming wrapt in some beautiful dream. She turned at last, as if there was a mysterious affinity between herself and the dead man, which caused her to hold converse with him, as he seemed earnestly to expect she should.

"O thou mute witness," she said, every word sounding clear and distinct through the echoing vault, "possessor of the secrets of eternity, which thou dost keep locked within thy silent breast, and dead, cold heart, how far better than I, couldst thou speak to this man of immortality; for I yet struggle beneath the veil of the flesh, and thou dost now behold it in the open face of everlasting day; but lo! thou, being dead, yet speakest! for there is a mighty eloquence in thy decay; there is a noble defence of the pure revealed Faith in every atom of thy flesh as it turns to dust: in thy very corruption dost thou prove its truth, by the worms that feed on thee dost thou show it forth; for therein thou tellest, plain as written words, that He who made the tremendous universe altogether glorious and beautiful, and created complete perfection in every most minute detail of all His works, formed *not* man, His highest, noblest, and most divine creation, for the sole purpose of delivering him up, in awful and wanton cruelty, in an impossible mockery of His own attributes, to this slow, fearful, loathsome annihilation: thou showest in thy sullen vacancy, how the soul, His breath, the breath of God, hath straightway on its release flown back to its originator, to the Eternal Spirit, which is the mighty, awful Magnet of all spiritual essences; and by thy present humiliation, Oh! thou redeemed of spotless holiness and innocent blood, by thy present acceptance of the wages of sin, thou speakest to this infidel of the one inscrutable mystery of evil, which lies at the root of all things incomprehensible—which is the reason of all dimness, bewilderment, and difficulty, in the reception

VISIT THE GREEK BISHOPS BY NIGHT.

of the true revelation; but which being the secret of the Infinite, we must to comprehend be infinite ourselves—gods, having the knowledge of good and evil. Tell him, that for this cause the tomb has been ordained to be the mighty crucible, wherein the human body is melted down and purged, to come forth refined and pure, like gold from the dross; demand of him, by the sins which stain his own soul, if he have no need of such a purifier as this corruption, wherein the foul taint that blackens every mortal man exhales and is dispersed, for those who rise to eternal righteousness." She paused a moment, and then turned to the infidel.

"You brought me here to overthrow my faith in Christianity; and now I tell you, by the immortal joys of those putrefying ashes, that none but a Christian could stand forth,—as I am ready now to do, in this awful place,—and sing over the grave a Hallelujah of triumph; to which these dead men, though you hear them not, respond 'Amen!' For none but a Christian could stand there, having by his side *One* Whose words are eternal truth; and Who can say, 'O Death, I am thy plague!'

"Bring hither all others,—unbelievers, or believers in falsehoods,—and see how they will fare in presence of these worms! Bring here the deist, who believes in a God all good, but not in immortality; show him these miserable wrecks of beings, who, throughout their brief life, were tortured and harassed with many sorrows, and now are here without a hope; and he shall fly hence, shrieking out that his was a devil-worship, though he knew it not!

"Bring here the worldly man, and show him the world's pomp and glory, clad in this ghastly dress; till, with a horror unspeakable, he finds he has lived in a delusion, of which this is the sole reality. Bring here an idolater, who has made himself an idol of a fellow-creature, and show him the clay he adored instead of God, till he falls down and curses his own great madness: bring here an infidel, and he knows what you now feel gnawing at your heart,—despair."

She paused, seemingly overwhelmed with the thoughts which rushed on her soul; and then proceeded, lifting up her eyes to Heaven.

"Despair! O ye Seraphim, who, in the presence of the Living God, know perfect bliss, if ever from your radiant home you have looked down, and wondered what means that cry, which, generation after generation, men have sent up to you—ever the same word, repeated in such varied accents; hear me, and I will tell you what it is. Think not that you see it in the bitter mourning of the widow over the corpse of her only child; for there is One, at Whose command women have received their dead raised to life again; and shall receive them all at the last great day. Believe not that it is present with you, when, lonely and joyless, a helpless wanderer walks the earth, excluded as yet from the common grave, where the beloved of brighter days have gone to rest; for there is One who to the desolate is Father, Brother, and unchanging Friend. Or dream not you have found it in the torn breast of one from whom the sole and most dear hope of earthly happiness has been rent, with a pang like to that of death; for there shall be a sweet and profound peace in that broken heart, when the cry ascends from it, as now from mine, 'Thy will be done.' But I will show you what is this fearful thing—despair.

"It is for the soul to be *alone*, as that of this infidel here present; the immortal, invisible soul, who can hold perfect communion with none save the Eternal and Unseen Spirit, alone, in a solitude, utter and abhorrent, because it knows Him not.

"Oh! this solitude is indeed an unspeakable despair, for the Creator is the Life of the Spirit,—the One only, All-satisfying, Infinite Perfection, for which it pines and yearns with a longing and desire which seems as though it had the power to cause even that soul's immortality to waste and wither away, if unsatisfied. It may for a time lend itself to the joys or the hopes of the humanity to which it is wedded; and seem outwardly to hold intercourse with its fellow-souls; but there is a wall of flesh between them, and sooner or later it will be driven out into the desert of infinity, there to wail and to cry out with anguish inexpressible for the Eternal; and if it find him not, like a feather tossed in the air, the helpless, incomplete spirit flits aimless through the eternity, now rising, now sinking, without hold, or stay, or support,—without foundation or anchor,—without hope, in void and in darkness;—a victim *then*, and *only* then, O Seraphim, to a perfect and true despair.

"Therefore it is, that the Christian alone can stand amongst this human dust with the song of rejoicing on his lips; for this place is the antechamber of heaven, where these redeemed must wait awhile ere they are ushered into the presence of the King; and to them— to me—O corruption! how sweet thou art! how dear art thou, O death! We open to thee our arms, as to a loving friend; take us to thy beneficent embrace, and lay us to rest with a kiss, as a mother cradles her infant. Like unto the wakening again of a tender parent shall be the Voice that calls us from thine arms to everlasting day: meanwhile purge us, thou merciful corruption! and so shall we be ready against that hour. And now, my brethren in Christ, departed as I trust in Him, I thank you for the renewed and sweet assurance of immortality which you have given me, by your sad aspect here. I leave you strong in the hope and faith which for you have turned to certainty and bliss."

Ruth Vincent lifted her hand from the dead man's shoulder, and quitting his side with a quiet parting look, as though she bade him farewell only for a season, she walked towards the infidel.

"Are you satisfied now," she said, "that from the aspect of unveiled mortality, and the horrors of the tomb—even as from the existence of life, and beauty, and the glory of the universe—the Christian faith (opened to us by the golden path of revelation) acquires but a deeper and stronger confirmation, if confirmation can be desired, for that whose *basis is eternal truth? Are you content to let me go, and rather bear not only the anguish of separation from you, but, if it were possible, all the sorrow of this whole world, as abandon even for a moment the adorable belief of a life in God— into which I hope to merge from this dim and incomplete existence?"

"Go!" said Arabyn: "I detain you not; for I see that this at least has been in vain."

She bowed her head, passed him, and went out; and this time it was he who followed her. She did not linger in the church, but passed on into the olive grove, and went her way homewards; and as she wandered on before him, her white dress glancing among the sombre trees, whilst the peculiar expression of purity and repose seemed to have deepened on her pale countenance, even to him she looked like a blessed spirit leading the way to some holier sphere.

But he came after, with a face over which the blackness of rebellious passions was darkening fiercely; and now he looked with menacing gesture upon her, and now shook his clenched hand in the face of the moonlit heaven, with a wild and impious defiance. And so through the solemn, peaceful night, holding no converse with one another, they took their way to their dwelling.

CHAPTER XX.

THE LAST STRUGGLE OF ARABYN AND HIS VICTIM.

The sun was setting on a sweet, calm summer's evening, and Ruth Vincent sat alone by a rock on the sea-shore. Her face was pale as marble, and her sad eyes perfectly tearless, though filled with the most piteous expression of utter misery: she sat motionless, taking no heed of the spray that drenched her long hair, and wet the cold hands she held folded on her bosom. There was a settled anguish at her heart now, from which she could not escape. She sorrowed not for herself, but for another; and she sorrowed almost as one who had no hope.

She had not seen Arabyn since the night when they had visited the monastery together, and the intervening days had been spent by her in the bitter effort to overcome the yearning of her soul towards him. What was there she would not have endured to procure him one moment's happiness even on this earth?—and yet she had no power to give the shadow of a hope to his tremendous eternity.

She heard, too, from the servants, and from Mr. Denham (whose rage at her obstinate refusal of Arabyn continued undiminished), that the infidel was fearfully changed since that dreadful night. They knew not

THE LAST STRUGGLE OF ARABYN AND HIS VICTIM.

what it was that had fallen upon him; but he seemed at times plunged into the lowest depths of a hopeless, sullen despondency; and often he appeared like one delirious with the working of some hidden passion. Sometimes they saw him rushing through the woods with a face of horror, as though an unseen enemy pursued him; and at night such groans and cries issued from his room, as terrified all within hearing. These Ruth Vincent had heard herself—alone, prostrated in agonizing supplication—she heard the moans, evidently in anguish, of him for whom her unhappy affection seemed but to deepen and strengthen every day, and she dared not comfort—she dared not soothe him—she must not bestow on him the tenderness and care she would have given to the most abject beggar at her door.

Often Ruth was seized with that strange pity for herself, which we feel at times when oppressed with some hidden grief unknown to all. To-night, as she leaned her aching head upon the cold rock, and felt the chill from the wet stone send a shiver through her frame, the sense of her great and bitter loneliness came upon her with the most overpowering misery. Over that bright sea far away how many happy homes there were! where the kindred in name and blood were linked in soul by the common hope of the One Salvation; where they who loved on earth knelt side by side, praying that they might meet in heaven; where the absent of an hour were greeted with the fond smile of welcome, and sorrows shared were almost joys. And for her there had been but one affection on this earth; and that had turned to poison, pervading all her life! What had been the sufferings of the lost Nadine to those which Ruth Vincent now endured? what was the attachment of that young, untried spirit to the deep undying constancy of this noble-hearted Christian? Yet a grave, alluring as that to which the suicide had flown, lay sweet and tempting even now beneath her feet: but *she* turned to it no sinful, wistful eye. Patient and meek, she lifted up her head and resorted to that expedient which had never failed her in her darkest hours: she drew her thoughts determinately into contemplation of the scene that once took place without the gate of the Holy City between the sixth and ninth hours; and then the great Calm passed into her soul.

She did not spurn the sweet consolation of death, only she was content to abide her appointed time; for the hope of death is in truth the legitimate comfort of all who suffer here: and who has not known how gently it often comes to us in the still, silent night, with its light step, like to that of one accustomed to tread near the bed of the dying—with its cool hand, that stills the pulse's throbbing—and its soft voice, reminding us that the time is short?

Suddenly, while Ruth sat there, she heard a rustling in the brushwood, and looking round, she saw that Arabyn was standing near, though he evidently did not see her. She would have risen to hurry from the spot, but her attention was irresistibly attracted by the singular expression of his countenance. A strange chill passed through her as she gazed upon him: the infidel and hypocrite had at that moment an aspect serene and innocently joyous as that of an infant, unconscious of its own happiness. On his calm and beautiful face there was not a trace of fierce or unholy passions, and a smile played on his lips that seemed to denote an almost childish pleasure, as he watched the movements of a bright green lizard that was darting to and fro on the rocks.

It was perfectly clear to Ruth that he was at that instant completely oblivious of all the thoughts, feelings, and desires which influenced him at other times; though by what means he had become so she could not understand, and a wild doubt and dread, she scarce knew of what, passed through her mind.

She rose to move away, but his quick ear heard the sound: he turned and perceived her; then the placid and beautiful expression passed away from his face, like a fleeting sunbeam from a threatening cloud, and it was replaced by the darkness of all the fierce unhallowed thoughts that blackened his miserable soul. It was thus that Ruth had been accustomed to see him; and she almost fancied she had dreamt of some quiet and lovely vision, when she thought she beheld him otherwise.

Arabyn sprang towards her to prevent her leaving him; and exclaimed, with a wild laugh of exultation: "Have I found you again?"

She shuddered, and stood motionless in his grasp: the continual exertion which she had undergone in resisting the infidel's persecution had overtaxed her mental strength, and for a moment she felt almost incapable of continuing this combat, so unutterably dreadful to her. She looked up to meet his stern, inexorable gaze, and her voice was faint and broken when she spoke.

"Arabyn, have you come to torture me once more? Oh! is it not enough?"

"No, it shall never be enough till I have succeeded

in that which I have undertaken. I am here again, to demand of you to pause and reflect before you seal your own fate and mine—before, for a false and childish scruple, you condemn us both to misery. By the years which we must live each in our own desolate course, lonely and wretched—who together might be so blest— I entreat of you to pause. In the name of all the days and hours we yet have to exist, which for me shall be accursed, and for you most dark and dreary; by my loneliness and my despair; by the agony which is written at this moment on your brow; by your dim eye and hollow cheek; by your wan face and wasted form ; which all attest to the sufferings you have undergone in your mad struggle with me ; I call upon you even yet to relent. Is there no argument, no means by which it is possible to move you?"

"None," said Ruth: "Arabyn, this is all in vain— most vain. Oh! let me go in peace; I cannot and will not revoke what I have solemnly and truly spoken: you have set your foot upon the Cross of Christ, and I will never on this earth hold fellowship with you."

"And you dare to say that you have felt some affection for me," said Arabyn, fiercely; "for me, whom to-day you trample as it were beneath your feet; whom you deliver up to solitude and misery; whose whole existence you destroy and ruin; whose condemnation to a life most joyless and abhorrent you seal without remorse."

"I have so loved you," said Ruth, her voice trembling with emotion, "that I have shuddered lest for your sake I was an idolater. I have so loved you, that since the hour when I was constrained to abandon you, because you are the enemy of my Lord, this whole world has grown so dark, and cheerless, and dismal, that, did I not keep my eyes for ever fixed on heaven, I could not endure my life."

There was a misery so bitter and intense in Ruth's voice and aspect as she said this, that Arabyn could not believe it possible that she should have courage to condemn herself to such a deep affliction.

"Oh, Ruth!" he cried, "be not so mad, as thus to destroy your own happiness! say but one word, and you shall make an Eden of this world for yourself and me."

"I would sooner die at your feet!" Ruth uttered these words with inconceivable effort.

"Would you?" said Arabyn, with a strange and horrible smile. He remained silent for a moment, whilst his countenance underwent a startling change. A wild gleam seemed to light up his eyes: her speech had evidently inspired him with some singular idea.

"And what if I take you at your word?" he exclaimed, with a burst of vehemence which filled her with terror; "what if I give you your choice, of death before you have time to ask for mercy, or instant submission to my will? It is a noble idea; now will I test your constancy to your false and hateful faith."

He darted towards her—he seized by the shoulder, with a grasp which seemed full of the most unnatural strength.

"Look!" he said, pointing down to the clear waters beneath them. "Look how easy it were; with one effort I can hurl you from this rock into that remorseless sea: you will fight in vain with those waves, though with me you have struggled so boldly. Speak! which will you choose, submission or death?"

It had suddenly occurred to Arabyn, that, by using

this terrible threat, he might at last overcome, in Ruth Vincent, the dauntless resolution which had so baffled him ;—he who dreaded death with that dread of annihilation which the instinct of our immortality constrains us all alike to feel, could not believe that the frail and helpless being shivering in his grasp would prefer, rather, to be driven to an untimely grave by the violent hand of him she loved, than consent to the union in which alone she would have looked for a life of happiness, but which she had renounced for ever, (albeit with agony), because of the Cross which stood between him and her.

By the terror of the death-pang, of the rending asunder of soul and body, by the horror of the young life quenched in the noisome corruption, the infidel imagined he yet might triumph over the Christian—he dragged her close to the brink of the precipice, he held her down over the foaming waves, and awaited her decision.

A spasm of the most deadly fear passed over the face of Ruth Vincent; she believed that her last hour was come; in that first terrible moment she was but the weak and timid woman, shuddering at thought of the violent death, and the horror of the choking breath, striving with her feeble hands to ward off her enemy; but when this instinctive tribute to her humanity was paid, the undying spirit within her resumed its supremacy; the spirit for whom a price was paid, strong in its glorious faith and hope, compelled her in that hour to act as beseemed a servant of the Crucified; again the infidel shouted in her ears the question, "submission or death?"—and she answered "death!" then meekly she lifted up her soft mild eyes to his face.

"Take this mortal life," she said, "if so it must be—

kill and destroy this miserable body: with the life eternal you cannot tamper, unto the soul immortal you cannot reach,"—gently, even whilst he still held her, she sank upon her knees, and raising up her unstained hands to heaven began to murmur a prayer for the remission of sins.

Slowly Arabyn released his grasp, he staggered back a few paces, and stood gazing upon her as she knelt there at his feet, prostrate in supplication:—but not to him ; she asked not life from the mortal foe, but only forgiveness from the Righteous Judge. A bright beam of moonlight rested upon her flowing hair and fair spotless brow, whilst in her uplifted earnest eyes there was, in this her hour of agony and death, an expression of holy calm, such as he in his least guilty hours had never known ; and as he gazed, the unhappy infidel buried his face in his hands, as though to shut out that sight, and muttered,—"Oh! this unconquerable holiness, this indomitable strength; it baffles me with a mysterious power which I cannot overcome." He withdrew his hands and looked upon her once again ; then, folding his arms tightly across his heaving breast, he bent his face towards her, filled with an expression fearful to look upon, and said in a voice hoarse from concentrated rage: " Ruth Vincent, you know not how mortally I hate you, for the holy dignity of this your invincible faith, that has risen superior to earthly love and earthly anguish, and now to death itself;" these words seemed driven out of his lips, by a power he could not control, and she distinctly heard that bitter declaration—he hated her! Nothing which Ruth Vincent had yet endured had brought her such a pang as these words—this assurance given to her by his own lips; she shrank back, she cowered down almost to the ground. "It is too much," she groaned out.

"Not too much, but enough; He suffers us not to be tempted above that we are able," said a deep and solemn voice behind her; she turned and saw that Raymond stood by her side, having approached unperceived in their agitation by Arabyn and herself. "Ruth Vincent," continued the Christian, "know you not that every hair of your head is numbered by Him who hath made you His own, and He hath sent me here that not one of them may be injured by this wretched infidel?"—he turned towards Arabyn as he spoke, and he saw that he had arrived but just in time to stand once more between the infidel and his last victim; for there was a something fearful in the look he had fixed on Ruth, which seemed to intimate, that he might speedily have been goaded on, by his revengeful rage, to put in actual execution that which he had but used as an unmeaning threat; then Raymond stretched out his hand, and laid it on the head of Ruth, in order that his antagonist might see and understand, how a servant of the Most High had been sent to save, and guard, and release for ever from his power, this lamb of the blessed fold, whom he had persecuted and hunted down till she lay helpless and exhausted at his feet,—by that gesture, wherein he silently promised Ruth his strong protection, he knew that Arabyn must comprehend, that he was at last most utterly baffled and overthrown in his strife for the unholy mastery, and then he spoke.

"Arabyn, most awfully, in truth, have you kept the impious resolution whose record you sent to me; you have kept it, that is, to your own soul's destruction, for as to the victory you sought to gain in your presumptuous combat with destiny, your repeated failures, and now your complete defeat, must have proved to you, that, in spite of your blasphemous arrogance, and impossible independence, you do at this moment lie a worm, impotent and degraded, paralyzed before the bulwarks of your God's omnipotence."

Raymond paused, for he was horror-stricken at the convulsion that was passing over the face of the infidel; it had changed to an expression so unnatural that it seemed scarcely human, the eyes glared fearfully, and foam was starting from the lips; suddenly he lifted up his hands above his head, and in a hoarse discordant voice, such as they had never heard from him before, burst into a frenzy of delirious raving, as wild and incoherent as ever passed a madman's lips, and which a madman alone could have uttered; the terrible truth, that he had become such indeed, flashed upon Raymond at once; but he had only time to seize hold of Ruth that he might shield her from the maniac; and then both stood rooted to the spot, gazing on the fearful spectacle before them.

Arabyn—the proud, the independent, the master of himself and his fate,—stood raging and foaming, unconscious of what he was uttering; he was calling down maledictions, fierce and terrible, on the heads of Ruth and Raymond; shrieking out that he abhorred them, that he longed to see them perish, both on earth, and in the eternity in which they believed, with imprecations too dreadful to be repeated. Suddenly he stopped, he looked at them with his wild senseless eye, his jaw fell, and he moaned and gibbered; then they could distinguish that he said,—"It is in vain, in vain for me to heap curses upon them; they have a blessing which devours them all; I see it, I see a glory round the heads of both. I alone am accursed—I alone, alone!" And before they could anticipate his purpose, he had uttered one long shriek, and, darting from the spot, fled through the woods, and disappeared.

Raymond stood transfixed, perfectly appalled at this frightful and unexpected occurrence; he felt that what he had now witnessed was the inexorable execution of a righteous and awful sentence; to his soul's hearing had assuredly been made audible the terrible voice of a most just judgment. The punishment of Philip Arabyn was as it were embodied in his crime; by his mental powers he had sinned, and by them he fell; by his intellect had he dared to brave Omnipotence, and in the very act it was self-destroyed,—for never did a human soul presume to quit the posture of adoration and submission before the presence of the Eternal Spirit, but straightway, by the very laws of its own nature and existence, it falls blasted and withered, even as the clay of the body must perish when the life goes from it.

By his intellect he had said, "There is no God!" and his intellect, distorted and destroyed, turned upon him now in its very destruction and distortion, to roar out, "There is a God!" He who had said he would have no Deity for his master, no faith for his law, no virtue for his duty, was now—slave to himself, constrained to do deeds and utter words in his delirious madness, from which, sane, he would have shrunk; his law, ruling him with invincible power, was his own diseased fancy, which governed, in every word and look, the man who would have been independent of the universe; his duty was now to follow every imbecile impulse of his unconscious ravings.

He, who was to have trampled the world under his feet, now whined and gibbered like a frightened child at the shadows his own disordered imagination created. He, who was to have overcome all obstacles for the accomplishment of his will, was swayed by every external circumstance, and by himself deluded into actions he wished not to perform. In his presumptuous attempt to attain to an impossible liberty, he had bound himself to the direst tyrant that is ever on earth permitted to possess the soul of man;—for henceforward he was the bondsman of madness, and the captive of delirium.

But Raymond dared not linger to think of these things; he felt that it was absolutely necessary that he should at once follow the wretched maniac, lest the paroxysm in which he had burst from the spot should drive him to self-destruction. The Christian looked with intense compassion on Ruth Vincent, who had flown to the remotest corner among the rocks, where she was crouching down bewildered, and overcome with horror and fear; he would fain have remained by her side, to soothe and comfort her; but his duty to Arabyn was too urgent to be set aside for any reason whatever; and having conducted her home, and seen that she was attended to by the servants, he left the house on horseback, in search of the infidel.

It was not until noon the next day that Raymond returned to the tower; he had traced Arabyn in his flight without much difficulty, as he had been seen by several peasants, and he ascertained that he had been seized by some of them, when in the act of flinging himself over a precipice, and conveyed to the nearest village; thence he had that same morning been taken to Athens, by the dimarch (or magistrate) of the place, who very naturally took this course, in order to deliver him up to the proper authorities; as he was altogether ignorant of Arabyn's name or abode, and only perceived that he was a helpless madman, who must be watched and cared for.

Raymond instantly determined upon following his miserable enemy, that he might see him suitably provided for; but he would not do so without returning for a few hours to Ruth Vincent; his anxiety was extreme to know the effect of this awful visitation upon her; and he found, as he had expected, that she was dreadfully shaken by the shock she had received; but he also felt that he might leave her in perfect safety; for, although heavily smitten and bowed to the very earth with a load of misery,—though all the world was to her a most weary land,—he saw that she herself abode beneath the shadow of the Great Rock.

As Raymond came into the room where she was, and bent kindly over her, her first words—whispered low, for she was feeble and exhausted,—were these:

"I thank Heaven that it is thus,—that he is mad,—for he is no longer responsible for these tremendous crimes. Oh! who can tell how long he has been deprived of reason?—he may yet be forgiven." But she said nothing of the cruel treatment she had met with from him; for Ruth would rather have died than have deepened by her disclosure the stain that already blackened the character of the infidel. The Christian was, however, thankful that there were any means by which she could find comfort in that hour; and he could not refuse her the promise she required of him, that he would acquaint her with every particular respecting Arabyn, as soon as he had rejoined him, and give her even the most minute details of his mental condition. She was herself the first to urge him to leave her at once, and proceed on his search; and he made no attempt to induce her to break the silence she maintained respecting all that had occurred since they parted.

He had little doubt that it had been a period of unmitigated suffering to herself, for her countenance wore the deep traces of a profound anguish; and he regretted still more that the wily precautions taken by Arabyn to hide their place of retreat should have prevented him joining her sooner.

Raymond remained only a few hours at the tower, but he was enabled in that time to perceive that one faint gleam of sunshine had sprung up in the midst of all that great darkness.

Mr. Denham had been deeply struck and awed by the terrible retribution which had stricken his unhappy nephew; even he, wilfully careless as he had ever been, could not but perceive therein the righteous judgment of Heaven. He had in fact been greatly changed of late: conscious, from his increasing infirmities, that his days were rapidly drawing to a close, and moved by Ruth's unwearied efforts far more than he was aware of, his heart had been gradually softening for the reception of the Truth; now terrified by that awful fact, which the fate of Arabyn so clearly proved, that His Spirit will not always strive with man, he trembled, lest he should in like manner be cut off, without time for repentance. It was now that Ruth was destined to reap a rich reward from her seemingly fruitless labour for the salvation of this man's soul: stretching out his hands at last to her, who had so long stood as a ministering angel at his side, he implored of her to lead him to the Mercy Seat!

Raymond was doubly rejoiced at this occurrence,—both for the old man's sake, and on Ruth's account,—as it afforded her an occupation, which, being at the same time an imperative duty, would have power to prevent her sinking altogether under her affliction.

It is a fact, which may be very clearly noted by those who watch the workings of Almighty Will, that when, by some strong stroke, which has cut its way more keenly than any other into the very depth of our heart, we lie prostrate and subdued,—disposed only to turn aside from the world, and close our aching eyes on the light, it is then, precisely, that some imperious claim of our religion rises up before us, and forces us out of that sinful paralysis of mind into labour and activity.

The bearers of the Cross have no time here to sit down and count their tears as they flow; or read the record of their sorrows as graven in their hearts; the whole world lieth around them in wickedness. Few as yet are the stars in that firmament, where they are to shine who turn many to righteousness,—and what have they to do with selfish mourning, or listless despondency?

CHAPTER XXI.

THE RETRIBUTION COMMENCES FOR ARABYN.

RAYMOND was gone, and Ruth Vincent was left to a desolation of which she had never before formed a conception; it was now that she felt the reaction of the great agony and struggle of her soul during the persecution of Arabyn,—the excitement was over, the constant exertion and over-straining of her mind had subsided,—the separation between them seemed eternal and irrevocable, and for the first time it appeared to her as though she understood how insupportable it would make her existence; unconsciously to herself there had been for her a strange enjoyment even in his occasional presence, though it had ever caused her most bitter suffering, and now she could scarcely find strength even to think of the long days, and weeks, and years, that yet might bind themselves up into a most dismal life for her. She felt this world to be a chill and comfortless abode, for her loneliness was very great. She was an outcast from all the sympathies of earth, an exile from that sweetest home of humanity, which is in the common affections of our nature; she must never find rest for her tired head on a friendly arm, nor repose for her weary spirit in human sympathy.

But sorrows, which touched herself only, were for

Ruth Vincent light indeed; it was not trials such as these which made her life each day seem more difficult of endurance; there was one thought from which she shrank with inconceivable horror, because it contained a most fearful temptation to repining against the will of God, a thought that seemed to stand up behind her night and day, like a haunting fiend, that tracked her footsteps when she wandered by the bright sea-shore, and hung over her when she sought to rest in slumber;—it was the dread that Philip Arabyn, dying in his madness, would be lost for ever; that he, who had once abused his intellect and reason, would never again be allowed to use them. There was no boundary to the abyss of misery which this one reflection opened up for her, and her whole existence became as it were one long prayer for him; hour after hour her wan hands were lifted up, her aching eyes were raised, and the deep earnest pleading of the pure and noble heart he had betrayed rose unceasing for the perishing infidel to heaven.

As the days and even weeks wore on, her anxiety to hear from Raymond became almost intolerable, and when at last one morning she was told that a messenger had arrived with a letter from him, it was with difficulty she could find courage to read the contents.

The Christian wrote, that, but for the positive promise he had given her, that she should be made acquainted with all particulars respecting Arabyn, he would certainly have withheld from her the communication of facts which could only give her great pain; but she had a right to know, and heavy as were her trials, it was not for man to limit the strength that might be given for their endurance. He then stated, simply, that Arabyn had been conveyed to Athens, where he remained a short time, while arrangements were being made for his admission into the lunatic asylum in the island of Tenos, which is distant but a day's journey from the capital; during this interval he seemed in a state of imbecile apathy, and his keepers often took him down to the sea-shore, at the Phalerium, that he might enjoy a comparative liberty in walking about; on one occasion when they had done so, he had wandered, followed by the two men, among the rocks which there overhang the sea, and suddenly, when apparently quite calm, he had started and sprung to the side, uttering the most fearful shrieks, and holding out his arms as though to ward off something invisible, imploring them to take *her* away, the spirit of his dead sister, who, he said, was haunting him and torturing him with her shrieks, which he was obliged to imitate; then he had commenced running with extraordinary swiftness, and precipitated himself over the rocks into the sea; the water was at this point too shallow to drown him, but when they drew him out, it was found that he had received very serious injuries; he had at once been carried over to Tenos, in a sailing-vessel; and, on examination at the asylum, it was found that not only his madness was clearly quite incurable, but that it was impossible he could long survive the effects of his fall; he was therefore now lying there, the inmate of a madhouse, and not expected to live many days.

Raymond concluded by saying, that it was a source of the deepest regret to him, that he could only watch over the fallen infidel at a distance, for Arabyn, even in his madness, had retained so extraordinary a hatred to him, that the very sound of his voice threw him into the most frightful paroxysms, and the physician had declared it to be quite necessary that he should not approach him.

Ruth Vincent read all this letter, and when she had finished it, she cried out in a tone of passionate agony, "My last hope gone! my last hope gone!"—And what was this hope, this dream, to which she had clung unconsciously ever since Raymond left her, which she had cherished and longed for, as men cherish and long for some fair vision of happiness?—it was, that when she had ascertained the retreat they had chosen for Arabyn, she would go to him, and take the place of the hired attendant that would be necessary, and from that hour leave him no more, till death should release one or both; and so devote her whole life to tend, and soothe, and serve the wretched madman, who had deceived, betrayed, hated, and well nigh murdered her; and she mourned now for this hope destroyed, with the mourning that is given to the ruin of the fairest dreams of bliss; but she did not sit long to weep over it; it seemed to her that a duty was before her now, clear and evident, which left no time for the wringing of hands, or the bursting forth of the deep sobs that were rising from her very heart,—Arabyn was alone, the infidel was alone, Raymond could not be with him, and he was dying, having loaded himself with a weight of sin, which would carry him down to the abyss as surely as the mill-stone hung around the neck of the man would have sunk him to the depths of the sea.

Ruth Vincent knew, that, immediately before death, there is often a lucid interval, even for maniacs whose insanity has been long confirmed; such a breathing space might be granted unto him, and let the consequences to herself be what they might, in that hour she was resolved that she would stand by his side, and teach the feeble, newly awakened soul, its first cry for mercy, tenderly as a mother guides her infant in the half formed accents of its earliest prayer.

CHAPTER XXII.

THE RESULT OF ARABYN'S ATTEMPT TO MASTER DESTINY, AND THE WORK WHICH HE ACCOMPLISHED BY THE LABOUR OF HIS WHOLE EXISTENCE.

RAYMOND sat at the window of the house he inhabited in Tenos; he was waiting till it should be the hour for admittance into the asylum, where he went every day to watch beside Arabyn, when he could succeed in entering unperceived by him, into his room. It was now evident that the infidel had not above a very few days to live; the violent fever, which had been the consequence of the injuries he had received in his fall, had left him in a state of utter exhaustion, and the little strength which remained to him was rapidly failing under the constant recurrence of his fierce paroxysms of insanity.

It was a beautiful view which was spread out beneath the eyes of Raymond, as he sat there; the gay picturesque little town of Tenos with its bright vineyards and green orange groves, the quiet sea beyond like a vast field of sunshine, cradling on its breast the fair islands of the Cyclades, and very far distant, a low range of beautiful hills, so dim, and blending in their rose-coloured hue so softly into the sunny sky, that they seemed to belong almost to the realms of Dream Land.

Raymond turned his face to the east, where lay that

desert, for him the only peopled spot in the great wilderness of the earth; and straightway, obedient to the call of his spirit, *her* spirit came—rising like a pale star from that shadowy line of mountains, floating on over the purple islands, gliding along the sea, passing pure and fair through the crowded town; on, ever to his side, where she stood unseen, and whispered to his soul—telling him ever of the marvellous bloom on the flowers of Paradise, and of the Glorious Light which was not of sun or moon, that shone in the abode of the blessed.

Raymond was so intent in listening to her, that he did not hear the step of one yet of this earth, who, weary and wayworn, with heavy heart and weeping eyes, came stealing to his side. But a hand was laid upon his shoulder, and a voice whose tone was one of heart-breaking misery, murmured faintly, "Take me to him!"

Raymond turned.

"Ruth Vincent! Alas! why are you here?"

"Because he is dying; because he is alone; because he has cursed me, and I must come to bless him. Oh! take me to him."

"Ruth, what do you ask? this is impossible."

"Impossible? impossible for one who believes in eternity to go and stand by the side of a man on the brink of eternal condemnation, and be ready, if reason returns in the last hour, to whisper to the infidel—who in the agony of conviction reads the name of 'God' on the banner in the hand of the conqueror death—that ' God is love?' This is—this must be possible. If you could speak to him, I would not ask it; but he will not hear you, and the task is mine. Oh! it is not enough that I will wing every moment of his now brief existence with my humble supplications: while he lives, while the day of grace yet lingers in its setting, I must—I will be with him."

"Would that you were in a position with regard to him which could sanction such a step," said Raymond.

She turned on him a look of mournful reproach.

"Are you thinking of what the world might say?" she asked. "Oh! what is all the world to me now—its praise, its blame, its scorn? what are youth and hope, and friends, and name? what is life itself, but one long hour of probation—one sore and needful trial? Fear not that the world will ever more think of me; for I am dead to it altogether. As long as my Father shall bid me dwell on earth, without a murmur I will live; but not to mingle with mankind, whose vain joys I would not share: I will live for my Master, and for Him alone; to do His will; to walk in holiness before Him, in submission and in love. And, oh! Raymond, if it be His will that I should labour long upon this earth, would you have me make this life one long remorse, tortured with the undying thought that he perished in his sins, in misery and in neglect; struggling perhaps for repentance, and I not near to point out the way? that, when his unbelief departed from him, I was not there to say, 'Behold the truth,' or dispel his horror of eternal death with the knowledge of the life? Oh! could I ever lie down in peace to take my rest, and think that I was not there to raise his dying head, or close his weary eyes? that none knelt down beside him in his last agonies, to speed the parting soul with prayer? There may yet be time; while there is life there is hope. I will tell him of repentance and salvation, and at the eleventh hour he may repent and be saved. Raymond, I have a right to be with him which none can gainsay, for he has wronged me! he is my enemy! and therefore it is mine to soothe and bless him in this lást tremendous hour: he has deceived, betrayed, abandoned me; and who would forbid that I should watch, and tend, and comfort him? Let me go to him, and when all has been done that man can do, I will surrender him in unquestioning submission to the justice of his God. Let me go to him, and with his last breath shall pass from me all earthly things, and the immortal hope alone remain."

"Ruth, it is enough," said Raymond; "I will take you to him."

He saw that if he refused her it would embitter her whole life; and he knew that she would brood with a tenacity of remorse over the thought, that she had neglected to make a last effort for the perishing soul of her cruel enemy.

"Now, then," she said, grasping his arm; "let us go now without delay."

"But you are exhausted and overcome: will you not first rest awhile?"

"And what if he should have no rest throughout eternity?" she whispered, shuddering.

"We will go at once," said Raymond. He led the way, and she followed him.

They soon reached the asylum, and he left her alone while he went to obtain the physician's leave for her to enter into attendance on the madman. This was easily procured; but Raymond was at the same time informed that Arabyn had become rapidly worse during the night, and could not survive beyond a day or two at most. It was thought that he would expire during one of the paroxysms of delirium which still seized him at intervals.

In answer to Raymond's inquiry, the physician said, it was just possible that the patient might have a lucid interval immediately before death, as this very often occurred in similar cases: but the Christian could not draw much comfort from such an idea; he had not at any time great hope of a death-bed repentance, and still less of such a death-bed as Philip Arabyn's was likely to be; who, after a life of utter defiance of the truth, would have required little short of a miracle to enable him in the last hour of weakness and agony to receive the faith he had so long rejected. Yet he felt glad that he had acceded to Ruth's request, since he found that the closing scene was at hand. He foresaw that it would ever be a solace to her, to think that she had done her utmost for her dying persecutor.

When he returned to the room where he had left her, she was walking to and fro with a quick and restless step, sustained by the false strength which results from nervous excitement; and, clasping her hands passionately, kept murmuring continually,

"Eternity! eternity! a soul perishing for eternity! Did ever any mortal man realize so awful a thought? and yet such things have been and may be!"

As Raymond entered, she turned round to him, trembling so violently that she could scarcely stand. The physician, who accompanied him, offered to conduct her at once to the madman's apartment. Raymond asked if such was her wish, and her lips moved, but he could hear no sound; for her agitation had become incontrollable. She looked at him imploringly, and he understood her: she desired to proceed at once into the awful presence of him who stood so close to the brink of the world unknown, that he had already lost the consciousness of existence here; whose body, forestalling its doom, had become the grave of the soul.

They walked on through the long dark passage in silence; the physician going before, and occasionally giving a side glance at the death-like face of Ruth Vincent. Raymond became very uneasy as he heard her deep breathing growing every moment more laboured, and saw the convulsive shudderings which she could not control.

They reached the door—it was opened; Ruth leant against the wall for a moment, gasping and faint, then made one strong effort, and they passed the threshold. At the first glance which Raymond obtained of the prostrate form stretched out before them, he suddenly drew Ruth behind him, and endeavoured to intercept her view, but it was too late. She also had seen that sight, and in the power of a strength he could not resist, she broke from his hold, and, flying to the side of the dying maniac, hung over him with a gaze that was awful in its intensity.

Yes, it was a fearful spectacle! He lay there before her, whom she had so lately seen in all the pride of intellect, of beauty, and of hope—now the mere spectre of humanity, the wasted victim of disease, dreadful to behold; an emaciated wreck, bearing on that face, once so beautiful, the mysterious horror which characterizes the madman, and from which all others shrink with loathing. He lay there before her—the betrayer, persecutor, and murderer—but where were now her wrongs, and his great cruelty?

She was on her knees beside him; never more to quit

him whilst mortal sympathy could soothe him, or mortal tenderness avail. She grasped within her own the hand that had been raised against her life; she alone would henceforward hold the cooling draught to the lips whose words had often tortured her, or bathe the fevered eyes that had so often glanced at her in hate; for those dim glassy eyes, glaring with the vacant gaze of idiotcy, were the same whose light had once been dear to her as the sunshine of the heavens; and that wretched maniac, —that dying infidel,—accursed of God and man,—was he in whose every joy she had rejoiced,—whose every sorrow she had shared; whom she had encircled with one undying thought wherever he went; for whom she had striven, and wept, and prayed; for whom she would have sacrificed all, save her eternal hope; for whom too much she lived; for whom she all but died. Yes, it was he—the lost, the mourned,—he had crushed, and wounded, and tortured her; and she returned to him unchanged in his hour of darkness, forgetting all, save his affliction.

Long was her fixed and agonized gaze upon his ghastly face, and deep the groan that burst at last from her pale lips; but slowly she rose from her knees, and seated herself beside him—calm and collected; for at that moment she had lost the sentiment of individuality, and only knew that he lay there perishing; and that she was come, if such were Heaven's will, to save at least the never dying soul. She thought not of her own sorrow, nor remembered that she had undertaken to watch the fading of all that was hope to her on earth; her affection had conquered her anguish, and she had taken her place there to watch and guard him till he should be beyond the reach of human aid.

Raymond was greatly moved as he looked upon her;

for there is nothing more beautiful than that depth of affection, which, in the hour of trial, rises superior even to its own uttermost sorrow; driving back the overwhelming tide of its misery, in order to have nerve and strength to be the ministering angel of the being to whom it clings as unto life; checking its convulsive sob, lest it break too harshly on the dying ear; and repressing all such outward demonstrations of grief as could give a last pang to the departing child of sorrow.

Ruth Vincent did not lay her down to weep and writhe in unresisted agony; she scarcely knew that she was suffering, or that she must suffer; she only felt that he was there to be cared for, and she was there to care for him.

Philip Arabyn had lain all day in a state of restless stupor, having had the night before a violent fit of delirium. Life was fast ebbing away; he could take no nourishment, and he clearly suffered much, though unable to express it; his vacant eyes rolled carelessly from side to side, and it seemed impossible for him to find one moment's real repose. His attendants until now had been the physician, who saw him once for a few minutes during his daily round, and a hired nurse, whose treatment of him was such as might have been expected from a sordid woman, caring only for her own comfort and interest.

But now Ruth paused not a moment before she took her position by his side, to minister to every want, and alleviate every pang; and throughout the long hours of that miserable day, his aching heavy head reposed on the bosom his cruelty had wrung; and the hand of her whose bitter enemy he was, wiped the death-dews from his brow with the tenderest care.

When Raymond would have urged her not to exhaust her strength, and besought her to take a few hours' rest, she told him quietly, that she would quit Arabyn no more; for that the day for him was far spent, and the night at hand, and she must work for him while it was called to-day.

Raymond looked on the horrible and ghastly face of the madman, and shuddered to think of her brooding over him through the long hours of darkness with such ceaseless anxiety, but he could not remonstrate; the traitor and his victim were face to face, and who dared interfere between them?

It was a strange sight to see them there; all trace of his former beauty had vanished from the face of Philip Arabyn, and had given place to the mournful traces of wasting disease; while the indescribable expression of his countenance, which so horribly betokened madness, was rendered yet more dreadful by the evidence of an internal and awful unrest. Over this repulsive form bent Ruth Vincent, with her pure calm brow, and deep tender eyes; the high and holy resolution, which constrained her thus to bless him who had cursed her, and do good to him who had despitefully used her, giving to her mournful face a serenity not of this world.

"Shall I watch with you to-night?" said Raymond; "I fear your strength will fail."

"It were better not," she answered; "they say that if he recognized you in his delirium, it might be fatal. And as for me, fear not,—I have yet much strength wherewith to suffer, if need be."

As she spoke, Philip Arabyn suddenly opened his dull eyes; a wild glare of insanity passed through them; he started, and, sitting upright, tossed his arms wildly over his head, uttering shriek on shriek. The nurse, evidently aware of what was to follow, ran to the door, and called for assistance. Raymond was not less prompt in dragging Ruth from the madman's reach. The keepers rushed in just in time to hold him down, as, in the strong convulsions of delirium, he raved and screamed. Raymond would have conveyed her from the room, but he found it impossible to move her; she stood gazing on the maniac with dilated eyes, fixed and rigid as a statue.

The attack continued with increasing violence.— Arabyn uttered shriek on shriek, and at last commenced, with singular rapidity of utterance, pouring forth his incoherent ravings; yet there was a strange distinctness in all he said, and horrible was indeed the picture he thus unconsciously drew of his own polluted soul; the names of Stanley and Nadine were repeated again and again, mingled with imprecations and curses; then he called out for Ruth Vincent, with a wild fiendish laugh; and asked where she was, that he might crush her beneath his feet, because she had injured him,—he knew not how, or where, but surely she had injured him. Suddenly his screams changed to a low wailing cry; he no longer resisted his keepers, and sinking back on the pillows, he held up his hands in supplication, and breathed forth the name of her whom he had loved in youth, with every expression of the most passionate affection; and Ruth Vincent, standing uncomplaining by his side, from his own lips received the assurance, that, even on the brink of the grave he mourned for another.

She listened to each word,—but as soon as the frenzy had passed, and he fell back fainting, she went quietly to resume her place at his side; and without a murmur raised his head on her arm, and bathed his livid brow and burning hands.

The physician now declared that he would continue in a state of stupor through the night, and added, that another such attack would infallibly terminate his sufferings; he then retired, and Raymond, seating himself in a distant part of the room, where the madman could not perceive him, determined to remain there all night; in order that he might be at hand to assist Ruth in her painful task, if necessary.

And now Philip Arabyn and Ruth Vincent were alone once more; he lay motionless, the livid hue of his face, and the leaden veil that had spread itself over the once radiant eyes, seeming to announce that death had already glided, serpent-like, into his breast, but for the ceaseless moving of his fevered lips, which spoke so awfully his weariness of unrest; while Ruth, as the redeemless hours wore on, fixed her mournful eyes with unrelaxing earnestness upon his face, watching for the faintest ray of returning reason, that she might utter one word of faith and hope wherewith to wing that spirit over the dark passage of the valley of the shadow of death; and though every faculty was alive to profit by the slightest symptom of a change in his state, this one pre-eminent anxiety rendered her almost forgetful alike of his suffering and her own sorrow.

It was a high and noble office which she had undertaken, and, even had it lasted so long that her strength had sunk under the task, Raymond would not have bidden her relinquish it, though he himself entertained not a hope that any satisfactory change would take place, even should Arabyn recover his senses.

Doubtless many a sinner, redeemed at the very gates

of hell, shall stand forth at the last day, to attest that there is no limit to the mercy of our God; but Raymond felt as though it would be almost incompatible with the immutable justice of Him in whom is no variableness nor shadow of turning, that, after a life of such hardened unbelief, such determined rejection of the August Revelation, Philip Arabyn should, at the last hour of a detestable career, receive the power of faith from that Holy Spirit, whom he had blasphemed so often.

And solemnly did the midnight darkness walk over the face of the earth, and the silent hours rolled slowly along, while death sat brooding over the livid brow of Philip Arabyn; and at that awful moment, perhaps more awful for the watchers than for him whose death-warrant trembled even now on the lips of the destroying Angel, how unworthy of a moment's thought or care became the whole world, and all things that therein are, before the advancing, incomprehensible eternity—hope, and love, and joy, and pain, and woe, all which makes the human heart to beat, and break, and the human soul to strive, and yearn, and pine, all had vanished before this one thought—*death*, and after death, the judgment!—life, for him, the life that once seemed almost without end, was shrivelling up like a burning scroll; the past, whose every hour had been fraught with joy, and desire, and sorrow, with care, and effort, and energy, had shrunk into a vain and hollow dream, and the future of death, whose home is mystery, whose hope is mercy, whose fear is justice, whose duration is eternity, alone remained for the imperishable impenitent soul!

Beneath this one terrible certainty which alone existed for Philip Arabyn, Ruth bent trembling and agonized, every thought a prayer, every look an eloquent entreaty, that ere the subtle spirit escaped, and left but the senseless clay in her hands, she might have time to breathe the words, "believe and live;" and yet, even while with bitter agony of soul she contemplated the probability that he would die in unbelief, she never one moment swerved from her deep submission to her Father, her earnest desire that His will should be done and not her own.

Thus passed the night, and soon the sunny morning came blushing over the green earth, and smiled in the glad blue sky, the sweet flowers rose beneath her feet from their dewy beds, and opened their petals to her reviving light, the gay birds sang in their careless glee, and the bright rays sparkled on the white sea waves, for what recked they of that man's perdition, or that woman's long regret? But as the first gleam of sunshine streamed over the ghastly form of the infidel, and the face, scarcely less ghastly, of the mourner by his side, she turned, and said in a voice of ineffable sadness, "Close the windows and let the room be darkened, for there is no light here;"—truly there was no light,—the hope that had so long sustained her was fading away, for the dying maniac whose features were dreadfully distorted by the convulsions which precede death, seemed indeed, little likely to regain, even for a moment, the power of thought. The horrible simile of idiocy, which at times passed over his livid face, showed but too plainly that his reason still lay prostrate.

As the glorious sun of that radiant land rises above the horizon, it becomes evident to all present that Arabyn has entered into his last hour; the delirium returns on the feeble sufferer, he foams and writhes in the last power of his expiring strength, and utters faint curses with the gasping breath which death was devouring on his lips; then the fit passes, and he sinks back convulsed in the last agonies—his features are singularly changed, he holds the hand of Ruth Vincent in his, and she feels it grow chill and clammy—he opens his eyes—she bends over him—surely there is reason and animation in their light; he raises them, full, clear, bright as ever in the days of his intellect's pride, and looks stedfastly up to heaven, there they remain fixed, and dilate into a gaze of horror, so intense, that she gasps aloud; she strives to utter that Name Mighty to save, but her contracted lips refuse to give it utterance, and her heart ceases almost to beat, so dreadful, so unutterably dreadful, is the silent eloquence of those upturned eyes, where all that remains of life seems gathered, where the immortal soul beams in clearest light ere it depart for ever!

What does he see? O heaven! O *hell!* what does he see? Wider, wider, open the eyes; they distend, they glare out, as though drawn almost from their sockets by some tremendous sight; the bystanders fall back appalled, the jaw falls, the mouth opens, and thereby the face assumes an expression of the most fearful wonder, the most thrilling awe, the most terrible amazement—it remains rigid, immovable, with that look, that awe, that wonder, that amazement,—expressing in its dreadful eloquence how the whole spirit of the infidel would in that moment breathe forth and cry out, "O God!" were it not paralyzed by that on which it looks. It seemed to those who stood around, as though an age passed while that stony gaze remained riveted, then suddenly the heavy eyelids fell over these awful eyes, one gasp of mortal breath went out into the mortal world,—and the soul departed into the unknown.

Ruth Vincent had felt the grasp of his cold fingers tighten on her hand; she had seen the indescribable shadow flit over his face; his head had fallen on her shoulder; she knew that he was dead. Then a cry like to that of a perishing crew when they feel the ship founder beneath them burst from her lips, "He is gone! he is gone!" she cried, "the spirit hath departed, and whither!—not one hour was given him for repentance, is he *lost?* Oh eternity! is he lost? inexorable justice, is there no hope, no mercy?"

"Ruth, what words are these?" said the stern voice of Raymond; "shall mortal man be more just than his God? shall man be more pure than his Maker?"

As he spoke she shuddered, and sank down on her knees on the floor, whilst through her gasping sobs he heard her murmuring, "Forgive, forgive; O Merciful, forgive!"

Raymond lifted her up, that he might carry her from the room; but the hand of Arabyn, which in the last convulsion had seized her in his grasp, was locked in hers, and he could not force the stiffening fingers to relax their hold.

"Look! look!" exclaimed Ruth, wildly; "look how he clings to me, his only friend! he knows how I was faithful to the last!" She flung herself down upon the corpse. "Oh! return, return, poor erring wanderer! but one hour—but one moment; and I will so pray for thee, that all thy sins shall yet be washed away. Return, return! repent, and thou shalt live: yet shall we walk together through the bowers of Eden, and drink the sweet waters of eternal life: yet may the voice of pardoning love redeem thee at the gate of hell, and the holy angels shall come forth with me to welcome the sinner that repenteth !"

This scene was becoming more than Raymond could endure: the piteous and imploring tones of Ruth Vincent's voice thrilled to his very heart, and he stood shaking with deep emotion. The physician, meanwhile, more callous, had unlocked the cold fingers of the corpse from her hand, and tore the living from the arms of the dead.

Ruth offered no opposition when he lifted her up; and, passive as a child, she suffered Raymond to lead her away. Suddenly, however, when they reached the door, she stopped—she raised herself upright—she seemed to gather together all her strength,—then she said distinctly, "It is not thus, with words of wild and sinful raving on my lips, that I must leave the presence of one on whom the judgment of the Most High hath fallen, though that one was dearer to me than tongue can tell."

She quitted the supporting arm of Raymond, and walked alone to the bedside; with her own hand she closed the eyes of the corpse—then she knelt down, and bowing her head, said, "It is written, 'Be still, and know that I am God.'"

The colour fled from her lips; the hands, crossed on her breast, fell down; and she sank gently on the floor. Raymond lifted her up, and carried her away.

That same night Raymond entered alone into the room where lay the corpse of Philip Arabyn. It had been made ready for interment, and all that mortal men could do for him had been done; now they had retired from it, leaving the worms to do their office, for themselves must tamper with it no more. Very quiet now lay that man of terrible passions and resistless energy; the face inexorably fixed in its sullen despair, revealed by the faint light of the midnight sky, where the pale moon seemed to stand still in contemplation of that dead body. It is not till we actually look on such that we realize the separation of spirit and matter: although through the long dim aisles of the future, all who listen for them may hear the footsteps of the approaching death—that awful shrouded figure, that, ever beckoning from the gloom, causes men in the midst of their busy cares and engrossing occupations to turn aside, and rush into its mysterious embrace. But those who remain behind take no heed till their own hour comes, and then they follow with a swift and unwilling obedience.

Raymond had come hither, that, looking down on that cold and senseless mass, he might realize the fact, that for the infidel the end was indeed come, the probation over; and in order to inquire of those mute and sealed lips—those dead and vacant eyes—what this man, so highly gifted, so richly endowed, had succeeded in accomplishing during his earthly career? what was the work which he had effected? what the harvest of the seed he had sown? There is no labour without its fruit. The splendid intellect, the noble intelligence, whose destroyed temple lay breathless there, had toiled and wrought for their tyrannical taskmaster (his own indomitable will) like galley-slaves—and what had they performed, worked out, and accomplished by their efforts?

As Raymond asked this question, he set himself, with all the powers of his mind, to examine into it, and his very intensity of thought seemed to create an answer to it in palpable shape. It seemed to him, that he beheld, as it were, a vast company of phantoms, dark and shadowy, stealing in from all sides, that came and grouped themselves in mute and solemn array round the dead man's bier, who lay in the midst of them, unresisting and impassible. They uttered no word, but gazed upon the corpse with reproaching, mournful eyes; and Raymond knew that they were all those upon whom this man had wrought evil or injury by his one individual power. They seemed to marshal themselves according to the extent of their wrongs; and they on whom he had worked the deepest woe took their stand nearest him, as in the place of honour.

At the head of the coffin stood Nadine, with her fair face livid from the deadly poison, and her young soul blackened by the deadly taint; and by her side was Stanley, with the strength and beauty of his manhood withering away beneath an unavailing regret. At the foot stood Ruth Vincent, wounded, crushed, and weary; bearing life as a heavy burden, with a never-dying pang rankling in her gentle bosom: and close to her bent the deformed cripple, care-worn and anxious, shivering and gasping in continual terror, lest his faith, sole treasure of his immortal soul, should fail him, ruined by the same power which destroyed his earthly joy.

Behind these were all whom the infidel had corrupted by his example, perverted by his counsels, shaken by his words, deceived by his sophistry, tortured for his own purposes, bent to his own will; and behind them came the innumerable company of all who, never having seen his face, or heard his voice, had been in contact with others on whom his influence was working, and from them had caught the infection of his iniquity, soul by soul, and link by link, forming an electric chain, whereby the power of evil was conveyed on into the unseen ages of the future, from the one focus or centre of this dead body.—Stealing in, crowding in, came the shadows, dim and vapour-like, for they were from the yet unborn generations, whose parents or friends, by him defiled and perverted, had received the taint he gave as an heritage, and in their turn communicated it to their children ; by thousands, by myriads, they came floating in, for it is inconceivable how one man may propagate iniquity, and to Raymond it was as though the whole air were full of these mute accusing witnesses; the moments which composed the life of Arabyn, were not more numerous than the human beings he had injured, —far and wide had he spread the taint, far and wide had he diffused the evil; his deeds and his words had gone forth from him for his own purposes, but no sooner had they left him than he lost all control over them, and they wrought and performed such things as he had not dreamt of; it is so with all human actions and words ; but his being evil, and springing from evil sources, had worked according to their nature, and therefore every item of woe or iniquity, from them proceeding, was as a crime charged upon his own head, and although his power over others was limited, because each one had a Father, and each one had a Saviour ; though he was permitted to work tribulation upon them, only so far as Immutable Wisdom and Love saw fit, yet since that same Wisdom and Love judges of men's actions by their motives and not their effects, against him was the accusation made to the uttermost.

But now, through the midst of this solemn crowd,

who all give way before it, comes a dark and shapeless thing, more than any other demanding vengeance on the dead ; who, not content to stand with the other accusers round the bier, arose, and lay down on the breast of the corpse ;—it was his own immortal soul! and truly it had a right to come forth pre-eminent, as witness against him, and chief condemner ; for no limit had been set to his power over it, and the wounds, gaping open, self-inflicted there,—the stains self-impressed upon it,—neither God nor man shall now ever heal or take away!

Raymond beheld,—and the years passed on ; and the ashes of the infidel mouldered into dust and his name was forgotten amongst men ; and they whom he had injured went one by one to their rest ; but that immortal soul remained unchanged, immutably fixed, with the self-inflicted wounds, and the self-impressed stains : and that generation passed away, and other generations rose, and lived, and loved, and died ;—and the end of all things came at last ; the antichrist, and his destruction by the brightness of the Lord's coming ; and the new heavens and the new earth appeared : but that soul remained fixed, with its wounds and its stains. Then time was no longer, and the cycles of eternity were only marked by new creations, each more fair and glorious than the last ; but on, far as human thought can speed unto, the incomprehensible "For Ever," that soul remained unchanged, with its wounds and its stains.

What, then, had this man accomplished? What work had he effected with his toil and his labour? He had demanded freedom, he had asserted independence, he had usurped liberty ; and freedom and liberty *had* been given him, to murder, ruin, and destroy his own soul!

—this was what he effected, this was what he had done,
—and this alone ! He had worked in the sweat of his
brow, he had wrought, he had laboured, he had strained
every nerve, he had roused every energy, he had exerted
every talent,—day and night, taking no rest, labouring
ever; and he had at length accomplished his task,—he
effected his own eternal destruction !

When Raymond had understood and ascertained this
thing, he rose, and went forth ; for if the infidel's work
was done, his labour and toil concluded, the Christian
yet lived to do and to suffer; his task was all around
and before him still ; for, as he goes from the presence
of the dead, to enter the world again, evil shall meet
him at every turn, and iniquity shall tread upon his
heels.

But Raymond felt that the corpse of that dead man
had been to him as a stepping-stone, whereby he had
ascended to a yet clearer comprehension of the Divine
Truth. Truly the dead are teachers, terrible and eloquent !

There had been to him a volume of most awful
instruction in the last faint sigh which passed from
the cold lips of her who died in the desert. Thereby
had he learnt, that, for the soul of man, there does
in actual reality exist but one great fact,—which can
alone be true, all-sufficient, available to it; namely,
that GOD IS! that He, the All Pure, is Existent.
Yes, this alone is truth to the spirit; there alone can
its burning immortality repose ; but it recognises it
only when stripped of the thick clouds that press
upon it here, obscuring, defiling, stifling it; the legion
of human feelings, the one great power of human love ;
the world is around it as a vast world of phantoms ;

the joys of earth encompass it about with armies of delusions, intoxicating, paralyzing; but let some keen sword clear away that outer crust, leprous and tainted; let it pierce down—down into the one necessary principle of its unquenchable life, and it shall feel and know that each individual soul is ALONE in the universe with its Creator.

There are many who can never, on this side of eternity, so far thrust back the earthly shadows that crowd upon them, as to realize that He is in truth the sole object of all their undefined desires; their Life, without which they pine and consume away; but Raymond had learnt it from the death of the being who loved him best on earth; and in obedience to the knowledge thus obtained, he had given his life to be, by its devoted purity, the outward illustration of his inward aspiration after the All Holy.

And now, by the death of the man who hated him the most on earth, another weighty lesson had been given: he had learnt, by the ardour and devotion with which that lifeless corpse had served the power of evil, what may be the ardour and devotion with which a Christian may serve his Master. There was an awful thought that long had haunted Raymond, and now, more than ever, seemed to rise distinct and overpowering before him; it was the dreadful doubt, that scarce even yet hath mankind understood what is, in truth, that surrender of the soul to God, required of those who shall walk with Him in white, for they are worthy!

These are terrible words: "If any man serve Me, him will my Father honour." Oh! what manner of service must that be, for which the Holy Omnipotent shall honour the sinful human worm? Raymond thought, with a shudder, of the thousands who day by day knelt down, and said, "Thy will be done on earth, as it is in heaven." Are they not deceived? Though God is not mocked! *His* will done by *them* on earth as it is in heaven, where nothing that defileth can in any wise enter in! None dare say, "this is too hard for me," even when the commandment is, "Be ye perfect;" for who shall limit the promised help? Was it ever said to a mortal man, striving to approach his Maker in holiness, "Come not too nigh?"

Raymond would judge no man; many there might be who long had seen the truth as he saw it now; the Lord only knoweth those that are His; often do we entertain angels unawares. But for himself, nobly as he had striven, truly and fervently as he had devoted himself, he felt that the strife might yet be nobler; the prostration of his spirit to his Redeemer,—in every word and thought and deed, in every day and hour and moment,—yet more complete. His course was not yet run; time still remained for him to struggle after a more exalted holiness, to be the germ of a more exalted bliss. Again he renewed his vow, and set out to embody in his life these words, "Thy will be done."

CHAPTER XXIII.

THE RETURN OF THE PHILOSOPHER TO THE DESERT.

And Ruth Vincent lived ; she lived a long, a patient, and an active life, who would so gladly have gone, with her youth and her strength upon her, to lie down in the infidel's grave, at that solemn hour, when, with a spasm at her heart, she heard going past her door the tramp of the pall-bearers, as Arabyn was borne to the dust and to darkness. She lived,—having set before herself, as type of what the life of Christ's followers ought to be, that pale evening star, that comes forth so regularly and constantly into the wide waste of ether, all alone ; and still and silent night after night, by its pure and steady light, shows forth the glory of its Maker.

Mr. Denham died a penitent, and then she quitted the station she had hitherto occupied ; that, by reserving of her fortune only what was strictly requisite for the necessaries of life, she might devote it and herself entirely to the ministry of the suffering and afflicted. She had not a friend on earth ; but if any man, having read these words, " Abide in Me, and I in you," dares to say that a Christian can ever be alone, he is a blasphemer and an unbeliever. She belonged to Him of Whom the whole family in heaven and earth is named, and therefore she walked out amongst mankind—not motherless, because, wherever an aged woman, having outlived all natural ties, wasted and pined in solitude, Ruth Vincent came, and was to her a daughter;—not childless, for, wherever an orphan shivered in the chill blasts of this cold hard world, she gathered it to her bosom, and bade it nestle warm and happy in her gentle arms;—not without brothers and sisters, for all who mourned were such to her; all who had erred, and sought, repenting, to return to the fold; all who wandered and strayed afar, looking about as though they sought a God on earth.

Nor was she without affection to soften the rugged path of her pilgrimage; for wherever a dying beggar lay, with aching head pillowed on her breast, sweet words of love were lavished on her, and fond eyes grew bright at her approach.

Ruth Vincent lived, and became the rich inheritor of that peace, which, being the Bequest of Him Whose kingdom is not of this world, the world can neither give nor take away.

*　　　　*　　　　*　　　　*

Many years had passed away,—years, during which millions had lived and hoped, despaired and died; empires had risen and fallen, monarchs had bowed their crowned heads to the majesty of death, and the busy, ever-moving world had worked and fretted itself so far nearer to its mysterious doom; but in the silent, sterile, lonely desert, time had been powerless to leave a trace, the rushing of his dark wings in their ceaseless flight, laden with the burden of the vanished years, had not even ruffled those smooth barren sands, and still the serene and changeless skies were spread over the changeless empire of desolation; here was no crime to ripen to remorse, no hope to grow to despair, no misguided longings to turn into madness, no bright dream to be the soul's chastener in its non-fulfilment, no sweet and blooming infant to become the man of scowling brow and angry passions, no child of hope to waste into the weary and desponding being weeping for an unfound repose; all in that immutable nature, sacred from human strife, was the same as it had been centuries before, and fancy might have sought, on that wilderness of golden sand, for the footsteps of the kindly angels who walked this world in its infancy.

It was sunset once again, and the only trace of the existence of man that ever appeared in the desert, was passing through it now; the tinkling camel bells were ringing on the soft still air, and the long picturesque train of the caravan was winding gracefully along, similar in all respects to the procession that once brought hither two pilgrims, who came to seek a resting-place in the desert, and found, both of them in truth, a rest,—but such as they little dreamt of; the one in a grave, the other in submission.

The caravan halted; for an aged and feeble man, who formed one of the company, had pointed to a small hillock scarcely perceptible on the sand, and signed to them to stop; two young Arabs, who seemed to have received their orders previously, dismounted and approached him; he was a man of serene and noble aspect, but his face was as the face of a corpse, for he had reached the last hour of his existence, worn down more by toil and suffering than by years or disease; they lifted him in their arms, and carried him to that low mound, where they laid him down; then he bade them depart in peace, and they, well content to be rid of a dying stranger, obeyed him instantly;—as once before, so now did the caravan resume its march, and passing away, grew to the likeness of a dark gliding serpent, and disappeared from his view, leaving him once more alone with her beloved in youth, and unforgotten in decaying age. Then the old man breathed a long sigh of intense relief, he lifted up his feeble, withered hands, and murmured, "May all men look to the Cross and live, but they who would live by looking to it, must also take it up; here where mine was raised, I now return in joy and thankfulness to lay it down, for the burden and heat of the day is spent and gone, and the soft cool night is come."

With that he stretched out his arms across the grave, pillowed his head upon it, and, closing his eyes, so took his rest.

The ashes of Raymond and Arabyn have long since mingled with the common dust; but from their graves a voice yet speaks to those who will to hear it,—a voice that tells, how in the lives of those two men was shown forth what may be the use, and what the abuse, of the one awful gift, which to each living soul is given at its entrance into this world.

That gift, O mortal! is thine immortality!

To thee, as a human being dwelling in the flesh, this most tremendous treasure is committed, and power is given thee to make of it what thou wilt,—thine it is to glorify or to defile, with a glory indestructible, or a defilement ineffaceable; from the cradle to the grave thou dost hold it in possession,—to thee—the fragile and helpless, compacted of dust and ashes,—eternity submits itself, and awaits the form which thou shalt constrain it to assume.

There is no limit to the unutterable rapture with

which thou mayest invest it, by ascending now, in the days of thy flesh, through the way opened for thee by the Sinless Humanity of the Incarnate God, even unto the Bosom of the Father ; but there is no bound to the redeemless horror in which thou mayest envelope it, by descending through the way opened for thee by the world, the flesh, and the devil, into the unholiness which is a hopeless exile from Him.

From this power over thy never-ending existence, thou canst not escape,—neglectful, oblivious of it, thou mayest be ; yet shall thy weak hands of clay mould out an infinite futurity, building up therein an everlasting habitation, or digging out an unfathomable abyss.

Thus shall it be till the death hour comes, and thy soul is stripped of the flesh that masked it, and then is thy dominion over—the treasure taken from thee.

Thou shalt no longer possess eternity, but eternity shall possess thee ; that which thou hast made it, it shall remain ; but thou shalt be its slave : in the form with which thou hast invested it, of glory inconceivable, or darkness most implacable, it shall rule over thee for ever.

Take heed, then, O mortal! that thine immortality curse thee not hereafter, for thine abuse of the fearful gift. Rather so use it, O corruptible! that thou mayest be eternally blessed by thine incorruption.

THE END.

HIDDEN DEPTHS

Bibliographical note:

this facsimile has been made from a copy in the
Yale University Library
(Ip.Sk267.866)

HIDDEN DEPTHS.

EDINBURGH: PRINTED BY THOMAS CONSTABLE,

FOR

EDMONSTON AND DOUGLAS.

LONDON, . . .	HAMILTON, ADAMS, AND CO.
CAMBRIDGE, . .	MACMILLAN AND CO.
DUBLIN, . . .	M'GLASHAN AND GILL.
GLASGOW, . . .	JAMES MACLEHOSE.

HIDDEN DEPTHS

'VERITAS EST MAJOR CHARITAS'

VOLUME FIRST

EDINBURGH
EDMONSTON AND DOUGLAS
1866.

PREFACE.

This book is not a work of fiction, in the ordinary acceptation of the term. If it were, it would be worse than useless; for the hidden depths, of which it reveals a glimpse, are no fit subjects for a romance, nor ought they to be opened up to the light of day for purposes of mere amusement. But truth must always have a certain power, in whatever shape it may appear; and though all did not occur precisely as here narrated, it is nevertheless actual truth which speaks in these records.

CONTENTS OF VOL. I.

I.
THE DEPOT, ... 1

II.
COLONEL COURTENAY, ... 20

III.
ON BOARD THE 'HERO,' 33

IV.
THE LAST NIGHT, ... 53

V.
THE TRUTH REVEALED, ... 77

VI.
THE PROMISE TO THE DEAD, ... 97

VII.
THE LAST RESTING-PLACE, ... 113

VIII.
THE OPINION OF THE WORLD, ... 131

IX.
THE SEARCH AT CARLETON HALL, ... 144

X.
LADY CARLETON'S DECISION, ... 163

XI.
GREYBURGH, ... 170

XII.
DR. GRANBY, ... 185

XIII.
REGINALD, ... 214

CHAPTER I.

THE DEPÔT.

THERE must be a something remarkable, generally speaking, in the appearance of an individual who attracts attention in the crowded thoroughfares of a large city. Yet it is a noticeable fact, that if, amongst the numbers hurrying to and fro, there is one person whose mind is fixed with a determined concentration of the will on any given object, that energy of purpose, silent and secret as it is, will make itself felt on the passers-by with a power of which they are themselves unconscious. Such was the case one bright spring day in a wide street in Seamouth, where a young woman, walking rapidly along, was observed with a vague curiosity by all who approached her. There was nothing in her dress or appearance to justify the attention she excited. She was handsome, certainly, but her beauty was evidently dependent on that evanescent brilliancy of youth and health, which our neighbours term '*la beauté du diable;*' and there were already indications on her strongly-marked features of the coarseness which usually takes the place of these transitory charms amongst women of the lower orders. Her dress was chiefly remarkable for its costly material, which ill befitted the station in life to which she clearly belonged, but its elaborate display of colours was arranged with a certain picturesque adjustment, which heightened the effect of her dark eyes and bright complexion. It was, however, the expression of her face which caused every one to gaze at her as they passed along; for it must have been some desperate purpose which had drawn her forehead into such a frown of stern resolution, and lit up that lurid fire in her eyes, while the set teeth and quivering nostril told unmistakably of a fierce internal struggle. So strong was the impression of passionate energy which seemed to flash from her convulsed yet rigid countenance, that several persons stopped to watch her as she hastened on, clearing the way before her, as if determined not to allow anything to turn her from her course either to the right hand or to the left.

To her it evidently mattered nothing whether she were observed or not, and she only noticed the numbers passing round her by grasping more tightly some papers which she held in her clenched hand. A child came across her path, but she would not stay her impetuous course one moment to let it pass, and appeared not even to hear its sharp cry as it fell on the pavement; then a carriage came at full speed down the street she was crossing, but she paid no attention whatever to the shouts of the coachman, who called to her to stand back till he passed, and he could only save her from being trampled under the horses' feet by throwing them on their haunches just as the pole touched her shoulder; other obstructions met her in the crowded way, but still she never so much as turned her head, and held on her course, breathless and determined, till she reached the gate of the court-yard in which the Emigrant Depôt is placed.

This building is used for various purposes, and amongst other, for the shelter of the soldiers' wives who are sent to their husbands in India at the expense of the Government, and who generally remain at the depôt for a few days previous to their embarkation. It was occupied, at the time of which we speak, by the women belonging to two regiments stationed at Lucknow, and they were to sail the following day in the 'Hero,' which was also to take out Colonel Courtenay of the —-th Regiment, returning from leave, and a few other officers and men.

The principal door stood open, and the young woman

walked straight in, and advanced into the first room on the ground-floor which presented itself before her. It proved to be the kitchen, where a little man with a merry, comical face was presiding over various caldrons, and brandishing a huge ladle in his hand. She went up to him, and laid her hand on his shoulder so suddenly that he started violently.

'I want to go to India!' she said, in a voice harsh from suppressed agitation.

'Well! and if you do, you need not make a fellow jump sky-high for that,' said the aggrieved cook.

'Here are my papers,' she continued, in the same hoarse tone.

'I don't want them, bless you! There, you go up these stairs'—he pointed to the right—'and you will find some one to take them.'

Instantly she turned and was gone, almost before he had finished his sentence. He looked after her for a moment, then shrugged his shoulders, and turned round with an air of paternal tenderness to a huge piece of beef, which had been occupying his attention when she interrupted him.

Meantime, up the creaking wooden stair went that determined step, and on into a small room on the first landing, of which the door stood wide open. Here a non-commissioned officer was seated behind a small table covered with papers; a large book lay open before him, and he was engaged in entering into it the name of a soldier's wife, who had just arrived with her two children to embark next day. A private was in attendance at the door, and as he saw the young woman draw near, he signed to her to wait till the other was disposed of. She did so, standing rigid as a statue. On her right hand was an immense room, the temporary abode of some hundreds of women and children, whose voices were coming from it in shrill confusion; but she did not seem even to be conscious of their vicinity, and remained with her eyes fixed on vacancy till her turn came for inspection. At length the certificates of the soldier's wife were pronounced 'All right,' and she was passed on to join the others. Then the girl went forward, and laid her papers silently on the table before the sergeant. He took up the printed form authorizing embarkation, which he knew so well, and glanced at the place where the names of the women and their absent husbands were inserted. Those marked on the girl's paper were 'Mary Anne Reed,' wife of 'James Reed,' private of the —-th Regiment, stationed at Lucknow. The sergeant read them two or three times, then looked up keenly at the young woman.

' Are you sure this is your certificate?' he asked.

' Quite sure,' she answered doggedly.

' In that case,' he said coolly, 'Jim Reed has two wives, which is one too many for a living man, let alone a dead one, as he is at this present time.'

A visible tremor shook the girl from head to foot, yet she stood firm.

' These are my papers, and they are right,' she said, articulating with difficulty.

The sergeant turned to the private—' Smith, did I not send you to the station yesterday to meet James Reed's wife, and tell her that the last mail brought the news of his death?'

' You did, sir.'

' Is this the woman?'

' No more like her than I am, sir! She was a thin little woman, with a pale face, and this here '—he paused and looked at the girl; ' why, this here is a stunner!'

' She passed herself off for his wife, but she was not so really,' said the young woman.

' Not his wife!' exclaimed Smith, with a burst of indignation; ' I should like to see any one venture to say that who saw her face yesterday when I told her he was gone. She looked at me as if she thought the world was come to an end. Then all of a sudden she gave such a shriek—I can hear it now. "My Jim! my Jim!" she cried out, and after a minute she said, quite low, "O Lord, I wish I were dead!" and down she dropped on the ground as if she were shot. I shan't forget it in a hurry. She had friends with her who knew right well she was his wife; and they took her back, poor creature, the way she came.'

The girl's hands worked convulsively, but still she did not move.

'Come, come, my girl, this is no use,' said the sergeant; 'if you could prove you were his wife it would do no good: the man's dead and gone,—you can't go out to him.'

'There are two James Reeds,' she said in her hoarse voice.

'Now, look here,' he answered angrily, 'there is not the least use in your attempting to gammon me, my girl. Do you suppose I don't know the name of every man in the regiment rather better than you do? There is but one James Reed, and he died of cholera two months ago. You were not his wife, and what is more, I don't believe you ever called any honest man husband.'

'And I can tell you how she came by these papers,' exclaimed a woman, rushing triumphantly into the room with all that satisfaction beaming on her face which it affords some of us in this world to hunt down our fellow-creatures. She had been on her way to the kitchen from the other room when the altercation commenced, and, true to her sex, she had remained listening to it with eager curiosity. 'I was at the station when Mrs. Reed was told of her poor man's death,—you remember me helping you, no doubt, Mr. Smith?' she continued, appealing to the private, who nodded, with a look which seemed to imply that the recollection was not particularly agreeable, and she went on giving her evidence after the manner of women. 'I helped to carry her out into the air, poor woman. I could feel for her, sir, for I am a wife and a mother myself, and a widow too,—leastways I buried my first, eight years come Michaelmas; and a great brute he was to me, and seven children I've had—'

'Well, well, what do you know about the papers, Mrs. Miller?' said the sergeant, cutting her short.

'I knows this, sir. Mrs. Reed had them in her hand when she fell in a faint in the waiting-room, and when she came to herself on the platform she had not got them, and says she to me, says she, "Would you please to look for my papers, ma'am; perhaps they will be wanted?" and I went, sir, for she could no more have walked than a new-born babe; and I know what the 'sterics are myself: I am very subject to them, sir, and a drop of peppermint—'

'But the papers, Mrs. Miller?'

'Well, sir, you do flurry me so, sir. Well, I went back and looked for them everywhere. I looked in the gentlemen's hats as was standing on the table, and in the coal-scuttle, and everywhere I could think of, and nothing could I see of them; but this here young woman was stooping down at one of the seats when I came in, and I saw her stuff something into her pocket, and off she went out of the station, and I thought no harm,—bless you, I thinks no evil of no one; never,— but she had them safe enough, I'll warrant—a hussy!'

'What answer have you to make to that charge, young woman?' said the sergeant, looking sternly at her. Her lips moved, but she did not speak, and she remained gazing in his face with such a look of wild misery in her eyes, that he was touched in spite of himself. He turned to her accuser—

'Well, Mrs. Miller, I have no doubt you are right, and I am much obliged to you; and now, will you please to go down? I see some other persons waiting to give in their papers.'

She opened her mouth, but the proposed remark was

lost to this record by the silent eloquence of Smith, who put his hand to her elbow and quietly turned her out of the room. She muttered a protest against this summary ejectment, and then hastened down stairs to enlighten the cook on the extent of the young woman's iniquity, and her own sagacity.

The sergeant then turned to the unhappy girl, and said, not unkindly, 'Now, my girl, you see this won't do. I have no doubt you have a sweetheart in India, and it is natural you should wish to go to him, but we can't let you cheat Her Majesty's Government. You must find some other way to go out—'

'Or get another sweetheart,' said Smith, in an oracular tone, and, at a sign from the sergeant, he drew her from the room with much more gentleness than he had shown to the acute Mrs. Miller. He then turned from her and proceeded to usher in some other women who had arrived in the meantime, leaving her standing close to the door of the large room where the women and children were assembled.

The girl looked in upon the noisy crowd with a wistful, longing gaze, and saw that, from their numbers and the size of the room, an interloper might easily remain undetected, and with a sudden determination she walked in quietly and took her way to the farther corner of the apartment. The sole furniture it contained was a long row of tables placed near the wall, with a bench on either side, and, at meal-times, when a certain amount of regularity prevailed, it might have been seen that each of these tables was allotted to a fixed number of women, who were not allowed to interfere with their neighbours. She went on to the most remote corner, where two women were engaged in clearing away the remains of their dinner, while several others were sitting round, with their children scrambling at their feet and fighting for the fragments that had fallen down. Stealing in amongst them, the girl took her seat in the darkest place without uttering a word; but of course she had not been there a moment before the sharp eyes of the women spied her out. One of those, who was cleaning the table, a tall, bold-faced woman, who might, from her appearance, have been to India half-a-dozen times with as many husbands, laid down the plate she held in her hand, placed herself in an attitude of interrogation of a very marked character, and said, ' Are you come to visit any one ?'

' No,' said the girl; ' I am going to India.'

' And do you mean to say that you have been ordered to mess with us ?'

' Yes,' she answered in a low tone hardly understanding the meaning of the question. Thereupon the soldier's wife struck the table vigorously with her fist, and exclaimed, 'I declare it is too bad! Here we are at No. 60, twelve of us already, besides the children, and they send us a new-comer, while down there, at No. 52, there are only ten of them. But I won't be put upon, whatever the rest of you may do; I'll go to the sergeant and complain—I will. Why, we've only just victuals for ourselves as it is. I'll go at once.'

The young woman seized her by the arm with a suppressed shriek. 'O no, no!' she cried; 'pray don't say anything about me. I won't trouble you—indeed I won't. I don't want anything to eat, and, besides, I can buy it, I have money;' and she pulled out a well-filled purse, and held it up before the woman.

'Well, to be sure! you have a sight of money there,' said the other, evidently mollified by the discovery of such unusual riches; 'there's not many of us has such a purse as that, and you have no children that I can see. You are a lucky one, that's certain."

'Still I don't see why she should not go to No. 52, where they have plenty of room,' said another woman; 'there are quite enough of us here, and I am sure our quarters at night are crammed full already; I don't know where she could find a hole to put her mattress in.'

'Oh, never mind,' said the girl, 'I don't want to sleep, I'll lie at the door; I won't disturb you, only let me stay here. Don't go to the sergeant.'

'Let her be, Mrs. Hardy,' said a quiet little woman from the other end of the table; 'she is in sore trouble, poor thing, or I'm much mistaken. Don't let us worry her. She can sleep by me.'

'Very well, you must please yourself, Mrs. Clement; and if you should be stifled by the heat at night, you have yourself to blame.'

'And *I* think these are very smart clothes for a soldier's wife,' added the other, looking significantly at the girl's gaudy silk dress. All the heads nodded in acquiescence at this remark, except that of the gentle Mrs. Clement, who quietly moved away a large box, in order to make room for the girl in the dark corner she had chosen, and then sat down silently to her work. Gradually the other women subsided also to their usual employments, which consisted in worrying their children to the last pitch of endurance, and then scolding them for the inevitable result. One little girl, however, who belonged to the redoubtable Mrs. Hardy herself, crept towards the stranger, and began to look up into the dark eyes that were so deeply sorrowful, with an unconscious expression of sympathy stealing over her sweet childish face. After a moment, she drew nearer, and softly stroked the girl's cheek with her little hand. The young woman's attention being thus attracted, she turned to look at her; and as she met that gaze of innocent, half-wondering pity fixed upon her, a choking sob escaped her. She threw her arms round the child with a sort of passionate tenderness, and lifting her on her knee, she clasped her close in her embrace, and leant her weary head against her. The little girl nestled into her bosom, and remained motionless, till gradually her eyes closed, and she fell asleep on the aching heart that never again assuredly would know the blessed rest of peaceful innocence. After a time, Mrs. Hardy looked round for her child, but, termagant as she was, she had a woman's heart; and as she saw how that countenance darkened by hidden anguish, seemed to grow more gently mournful as it dropped over the calm face of the slumbering little one, she made no attempt to remove the child from her arms, and even ceased to look with malevolent eyes on the gay dress that contrasted so forcibly with the homely attire worn by herself and the other women.

Some hours passed away undisturbed, except by the unceasing din which was created all day long by the assemblage of so many women and children in one place. At last it so chanced that the acute Mrs. Miller, who was placed at the other end of the room, had occasion to borrow a pair of scissors from Mrs. Clement, and she suddenly made her appearance in the group which surrounded the stranger. For a moment she did not perceive her, and the girl, trembling from head to foot, buried her face among the fair curls of her little companion. But the attempt at concealment was quite in vain. Mrs. Miller bent forward to inspect Mrs. Clement's work, and her eye fell on the crouching figure in the corner. She uttered a loud exclamation, which attracted the attention of all who were near her, and then stood staring at the girl, while she gave vent to her indignant astonishment in a series of fragmentary remarks that were not very intelligible.

'Well I never! Well! to be sure, here is imperence. Who could have believed it? A brazen-faced hussy!' and so on, for some minutes.

'What is it, Mrs. Miller?' exclaimed all the women eagerly, while Mrs. Hardy especially requested to be informed if she had not shown great wisdom in pronouncing 'this here young woman to be a bad 'un.'

'A bad 'un ain't no word for it, Mrs. Hardy, I can assure you,' said Mrs. Miller, looking as if she possessed a State secret. 'Just call Mr. Smith, if *you* please,' and forthwith she began to call him herself in tones resembling those of an agitated peacock. The cry, taken up by half the women in the room, who crowded round in the delightful anticipation of a scene, soon brought the warlike Smith to the field of action, where he was immediately collared by Mrs. Miller. She dragged him forward, and, with much unconscious stage effect, pointed out the delinquent.

The unhappy girl, forced to leave her seat by the women crowding to the spot, had risen, and now stood like some wild animal at bay, with her merciless pursuers closing round her. With one hand she still held the little child, and pressed her close to her side, while in the clenched fingers of the other she seemed to expend some of the strength with which she would gladly have fought her way out of that crowd of enemies. Her face, meantime, seemed to grow dark with the despair that was settling on her heart, and her eyes, unnaturally dilated, gazed out upon the excited women with a look of savage agony, which was much more the expression of a hunted beast than of a human being. Smith did not look at her face, however, in his virtuous indignation at this breach of military discipline. Setting the women aside, he walked straight up to her, and seized her by the wrist in an iron grasp.

'Now, you deceitful young woman, you will please to walk out of this, or I'll know the reason why.'

She only answered by wrenching her arm from his hold, with a violence which caused the mark of his fingers to remain in a livid streak upon her wrist; then, gathering her cloak round her, she crouched close to the wall, as if resolved that no human power should uproot her from the spot.

Smith's face flushed with anger, and he was advancing somewhat fiercely towards her, when he suddenly met the gaze of her despairing eyes fixed upon him with such a look of hopeless desolation, that it went straight to his honest heart. He paused, rubbed his forehead, glanced uneasily at Mrs. Miller, as if he felt he was about to sink in her estimation for ever, and then, his better feelings mastering him, he laid his hand kindly on the girl's shoulder, and said, 'I'll tell you what it is, my poor girl, I am sorry for you, I am, for I can see that you are hard put to it, somehow or other; but I wish you would believe me when I tell you it is no manner of use going on like this; you are playing a losing game, you may depend upon it. Why, your papers would have to be seen half-a-dozen times before you could sail. Your luggage must be overhauled, the doctor must see to your health, and the matron to your outfit. You would be found out over and over again before ever you got on board.'

'And serve her right too! a-setting *her*self up for a soldier's wife,' exclaimed Mrs. Miller. 'I wonder at your meekness, Mr. Smith, I do!'

'You take my advice,' said Smith, nothing moved by this cutting remark; 'just take yourself quietly off, and don't oblige me to report you to the sergeant; for if I do, it's ten chances to one but you go to gaol for coming here on false pretences; and you don't look to me like one of a sort to stand locking-up.'

'Locking-up! O no!' she gave almost a scream; 'anything but that just now. I will go—I will go,' and hurrying nervously from her place, she began to move through the crowd. The little girl still clung to her, upon which Mrs. Hardy seized hold of her and administered a violent shaking, according to the approved mode of punishment adopted by mothers of her description. The child cried out, and at the sound the young woman suddenly turned, stooped down and kissed her, in spite of Mrs. Hardy's resistance, then, thrusting aside all who impeded her progress, she made her way from the room, and finally disappeared.

'There! that's a precious riddance, if ever there was one,' said Mrs. Miller triumphantly.

'Well, Mrs. Clement, I hope you are satisfied now?' said Mrs. Hardy. 'So sure as I am alive, that wench is no better than she should be!'

'Then she is the more to be pitied,' said Mrs. Clement, with a gentle sigh. And would to Heaven that all who may read these words would not only agree with her opinion, but act as though they did.

CHAPTER II.

COLONEL COURTENAY.

AT noon next day the 'Hero' was to sail with its human freight, and from the first dawn of morning all was bustle and confusion on deck, whilst a constant succession of boats plied between the ship and the shore, bringing the soldiers' wives and children from the Depôt. Their friends and acquaintances were allowed to see them on board, which added in no small degree to the bewildering noise and confusion; and it certainly seemed as if nothing could reduce the motley crowd to anything like order or quiet.

The principal passenger, however, Colonel Courtenay, took the matter very composedly, and had evidently no intention of risking his comfort by appearing on the scene till everything was ready for immediate departure. At ten o'clock he was still seated at breakfast in one of the most luxurious rooms of the hotel, with apparently no greater anxiety on his mind than the final accomplishment of that repast to his own satisfaction. It would not have been easy to have found a more comfortable picture of *bien-être* than he exhibited as he sat in the light of the morning sun, laughing and talking gaily with the beautiful woman whom, within the last fortnight, he had made his wife, and caressing with easy good-nature a rough little terrier frolicking round him.

George Courtenay was a man universally envied, and almost as universally liked; and certainly, in the whole outward aspect of his life and being, appeared to be possessed of all that on this earth is held most good and valuable. He had good birth and a good fortune, unshackled by the duties of a landowner, which to a man of his temperament would have been exceedingly irksome. His father, the younger son of a wealthy peer, had left him an excellent income, which gave him no cause to regret that the family estates had passed to his uncle, Lord Beaufort. In person he was strikingly handsome,—too much so, an artist would have said; for it was a beauty entirely dependent on the regularity of his features, the rich brown of his hair and beard, and the massive proportions of his tall muscular figure. There was no ray from the divine fire of intellect, or spirituality, to glorify the fine face and relieve its earthliness. A painter would have found it easy to make a correct likeness, but he would have had no scope for the exercise of his genius in the play of thought or expression. In character he was indisputably brave, of which he had given abundant proof in the Indian Mutiny—full of energy and decision,—the sort of energy which carried him at the head of a handful of men amongst a swarm of revolted native soldiers; and the kind of decision which, when the victory was gained, made him only wait to smoke a cigar before he had half-a-dozen of the rebels shot. He was further characterized by two qualities of so very opposite a description, that they might seem to form an impossible combination, though in truth a very common one, and these were deliberate cruelty and careless good-nature; both, in fact, being the development of that which was his ruling passion—an intense self-love. Thus, for instance, in India his black servants found that he never intimated his wishes to them by means of blows, as our freeborn Englishmen are in the habit of doing in that land of their tender adoption, but at the same time they found that he made them work for the gratification of the very smallest of his pleasures till they fainted from exhaustion. He would spend hours feeding and caressing his favourite dogs, but if it suited him to ride a certain distance on a certain horse, he would ride that horse to death without the smallest compunction. Of course, in general society, while his good nature and lavish generosity were extremely prominent, his cold-blooded selfishness and cruelty were quite in the background, and thus, by the world in general, Colonel Courtenay was considered perfectly charming. It is not to be denied that he was a most agreeable companion, a thorough gentleman in manner, with a full share of the light graceful wit which is so attractive in society; and, as he possessed the additional advantage of a brilliant talent for music, he was welcomed and flattered wherever he went. As to his private life, the refined ladies and gentlemen with whom he associated never gave themselves any concern about it. Not that they were at all deceived on the subject. Every man's secret character somehow makes itself felt in the air that surrounds him, and certain facts had transpired with regard to George Courtenay which laws divine and human have qualified by very ugly names. But the world has a marvellously convenient way of settling such matters. People solemnly accept and believe (chiefly on Sundays) in the eternal truths revealed by the Holy God, and then they go and systematically act as if those truths were lies. How would the brilliant crowd in some ball-room have been startled had a voice proclaimed in their midst, that the noble-looking man whose frank gaiety charmed them, and whose soft tones echoed on their ears in gentle love-songs, would one day be a condemned soul,—the denizen of hell, the companion of devils! Yet, according to the belief they openly professed, he could be nothing else,—unless he repented, which they knew well he would be exceedingly sorry to do.

It would seem as if in the world it was sufficient that a vice should be fashionable and almost universal to transfigure it into a virtue, or at least into a mild weakness; and crime well-dressed and aristocratic is received with flattering warmth, which, when it appears clad in tatters and vulgarity, is denounced according to the laws of eternal righteousness. Devout old ladies, who were extremely rigid as to the morals of their servants, watched in a flutter of anticipation the attentions of Colonel Courtenay to their unmarried daughters, earnestly hoping that they would ripen into a substantial proposal; whilst worthy gentlemen who spoke loudly at county meetings on pauper dissoluteness, eagerly invited him down to their country houses, and were delighted to see their sons in close fellowship with this fine dashing officer.

Of such were Sir John and Lady Talbot,—' excellent people,' as every one said when their names were mentioned; so amiable and benevolent, so ready always to further schemes for the suppression of vice, under whatever form they appeared; so solicitous for the moral improvement of their tenantry, and the mental culture of the pauper children; so rigid in dismissing every one from their employment whose conduct failed in being irreproachable, and yet, with the most entire complacency and self-satisfaction, they handed over their young daughter to be the wife of Colonel Courtenay. From her infancy upward they had hired nurses and governesses of the most immaculate description to guard her from the faintest breath of evil; and now, in her riper youth, they called on a bishop to sanction, with much religious fervour, her union with a man whose inner life they well knew no pure eye could dare to look upon. Yet they were not conscious hypocrites; the sense of their inconsistencies never struck them; no voice in the silent night thrilled on their conscience and bade them give account of the soul of the child they had linked to unblushing and unrepented sin. Surely they had done their best for her? They had given her a good position, a luxurious life, and a husband possessed of every attraction earth could offer. Nothing more could be desired in their theology, which consisted in taking with them through life just as much religion as they could carry, without inconvenience, on the easy-going paths of this world. As to the beautiful Julia herself, she never thought of inquiring into the private character of her husband, simply because she was as much in love with his handsome face as it was possible for her shallow nature to be.

Humanity is full of strange phenomena, at least it seems so to our veiled eyes, and few perhaps appear more inexplicable than the existence of such a character as Mrs. Courtenay's. If this world and all it contains were to last for ever, it would be sufficiently comprehensible; but she seemed to possess no element of mind or spirit which one could imagine expanding into a solemn immortality. A soul for ever blessed, it is, thank Heaven, easy to believe in; a state of everlasting wickedness, it is, alas! not more difficult to conceive; but a soul *eternally frivolous,* how can such a thing be— what possible position can it hold in the grand infinity of holiness which shall hereafter be made manifest?

There was one other person in the room with Colonel Courtenay and his wife, who had been sitting silent at a little distance while they finished breakfasting. It was his only sister, Ernestine Courtenay, who had come to witness his embarkation, in order that she might take leave of him at the very last moment. She was exceedingly like her brother in appearance, save in two particulars. She had his face and features, but not so great a share of beauty; while she did possess the spirituality of expression which he so entirely lacked. Thus, though no one would have called her remarkably handsome, there was something in the hidden soul within which gave her an indescribable charm, felt by all who approached her.

She had a peculiar look of gentleness, and her voice, even at its gayest, had a pathetic tone which was singularly touching; yet the prevailing expression of her face was not mere sweetness only; there were lines of intense thought, making a shadow below the clear eyes, and there was a sensitive tremor about the mouth, which spoke of feelings too deep to be tranquil, while the whole mobile countenance was the instantaneous interpreter of every thought that passed through her mind. It was curious to watch the play of her features when animated: the changes of her ever-varying expression were rapid as the alternations of light and shade on a landscape over which the summer clouds are flying. Even then, as she sat motionless, the thoughts of her heart might be read unmistakably in her eyes. Her gaze was fixed on her brother with a look of intense affection, which showed that to him had been given in largest measure that peculiar trusting love which an orphan girl so naturally lavishes on her eldest brother.

Ernestine had never known father or mother; and George, her natural protector and guide, had been her dearest upon earth, until the day came, a few months before, when the man who was to be her future husband had won from her a yet more absorbing love.

She had always looked up to her brother with thorough admiration and respect; to her innocent faith he was all that the world, better informed, pretended to consider him. She alone, perhaps of all who knew him, was in ignorance of his real character. That man must be base indeed who can let the poison of his own life taint a sister's mind; and one strong motive for the warmth with which he returned her affection was the consciousness of her misplaced trust in him. He knew that she did but love an ideal, yet it was pleasant in her presence to fancy himself for a time the noble high-souled man she imagined him; and there was a sense of rest and security, knowing the world as he did, in the sure possession of this guileless love, which had never failed him.

All her life long, then, Ernestine had met with nothing but kindness from her brother. When he first went to India, now seven years ago, and left her, a sensitive girl of eighteen, to the care of her aunt, Lady Beaufort, she nearly broke her heart, and pined for many months, till her thoughts were diverted by the severe illness of her only other brother, Reginald, who was younger than herself, and whom she had known but little till she was called to nurse him. When he recovered, however, after two or three years spent in Italy to ward off his rather ominous delicacy of chest, he left her to go to college, and again she began to long for George's return, till, as we have said, a love stronger even than that which she felt for him, came to lure her soul into that species of idolatry, which a woman is so sorely tempted to bestow on the one who can alone take the first place in her heart. Her marriage with Hugh Lingard, however, could not take place for some time. His father had left him an old manor-house, and an estate so heavily burdened with debt, that his present income was entirely swallowed up by the claims he had to meet; so that he could not afford to lose a fellowship he had at one of the colleges in Grey-burgh, of which his marriage would deprive him; but he held a small office under Government, with the certainty of obtaining a more lucrative one in the course of two or three years, which would then enable them, with the addition of Ernestine's fortune, to settle comfortably.

Ernestine's great desire had been to spend this interval

with her brother George, with whom she had lived since his return from India, and who had seemed not unwilling to agree to her wish that he should exchange into another regiment and remain in England. All these plans were, however, completely overthrown by the passionate attachment he suddenly conceived for Julia Talbot, and the marriage in which it speedily resulted. There was no longer any reason why he should remain in England, and all thought of keeping her place near him vanished from Ernestine's mind. She had too much good sense to think of living with him even if he had not returned to India, and she felt that he was lost to her as the friend and companion he had been. In her simplicity, however, she believed that his fierce love for the beautiful Julia would last for ever; and if he were happy, her unselfish affection was satisfied, even though finally separated from him. Her only request was that she might be with him to the last, and she had joined him the day before at Sir John Talbot's, whither he had returned with his wife from their brief wedding tour.

Breakfast was over at last, and Colonel Courtenay looked at his watch.

'It is later than I thought,' he said; 'Julia, love, we have only half-an-hour before the time when we must be on board. Are all your preparations made?'

'No, indeed! I have a great deal to do; yet I must change my dress, and settle what hat I shall wear. Can you not send and tell them to wait for an hour or two?'

He smiled and shook his head. 'No, I am afraid you must try to get ready; but I daresay, with the help of your maid, you will manage it.'

She answered that she would try, and left the room to spend the last moments of sojourn in her own country, the home of her girlhood, gone for ever, in discussing with her maid the most becoming costume for her appearance on board.

'One half-hour,' said Ernestine, as the door closed on her sister-in-law, 'only one half-hour more.' She rose and took a low seat at her brother's side,—'Oh, dear George, when shall I see you again?'

'Who can tell, Ernie? It is not my present intention to stay many years in India. I only want to get my promotion, and then I shall retire. I don't think Julia will like the life out there, though she fancies she will.'

'Well, so far as I am concerned, a few years is the same as a lifetime; in the uncertainty of the future, I must count on you no more as a part of my happiness, when once you have left me for an indefinite period.'

He did not deny this; but after a moment's silence, he said, 'You have never told me what your plans are, Ernestine. How are you going to dispose of yourself when we are gone? I suppose you will return to Lady Beaufort's till Lingard carries you off.'

'I do not know what else I can do at present; but you cannot think how I dread returning to the hollow objectless life I lived with Aunt Beaufort before you came home. I do so want to try and be of some use in the world.'

'Why, Ernestine, you alarm me! You are not going to turn out a strong-minded female, I hope, and raise a regiment of riflewomen, or establish a printing-press for the publication of pamphlets on the rights of women?'

'I don't think I show symptoms of being very strong-minded just now,' said Ernestine, laughing, 'when I am half breaking my heart at parting from a brother who cares very little about me. And as to the sect who want to raise women out of their natural position, I utterly detest and abjure their opinions; they are contrary to laws both human and divine, in my opinion.'

'I am relieved to hear you say so. I confess to having a great horror of the ladies who are benefactresses of mankind.'

She lifted up her sweet serious face towards him:

'George, I can quite understand your laughing at this sort of thing; but, after all, it cannot be meant that women should spend their lives in dressing and visiting, and working at their embroidery. It must be possible for them to be useful to others, without going beyond their own province.'

'But what then do you mean to do?'

'I have no defined idea as yet. Till now, you know, George, I have thought of nothing but the happiness of being with you, and I have a bright future to look forward to in hope; but the two or three years I have to pass first, are too long a time to waste in amusements which weary me beyond expression; and I am sure of one thing,—there must be in this great suffering world some work even for me, weak and ignorant as I am.'

He respected her earnestness, and did not wish to vex her; but all such ideas were very repugnant to him.

'Lady Beaufort will not countenance your philanthropic schemes, Ernie. Do you mean to act without her chaperonage in your future plans?'

'I do not think there is any reason why I should not. I am five and-twenty, and I have an independent fortune. Hugh Lingard is really the only person who has a right to control my actions now; and although I would not do anything to distress Aunt Beaufort, I do not see why I should not quietly go my own way without consulting her.'

'My dear Ernestine, I am afraid it is a dreary prospect. I can conceive nothing much duller, or more oppressive, than a life of general benevolence.'

'But it will be life with a purpose, and that will make up for everything,' exclaimed Ernestine, her eyes lighting up with enthusiasm.

It was a specimen of Colonel Courtenay's selfishness, that he had never inquired into his sister's plans till this moment; and his heart smote him somewhat as he felt that, if he had spoken to her earlier, he might have advised her against those schemes which appeared to him so absurd and unsatisfactory, and which, he believed, would only end in disappointment and annoyance when the realities of the world came to dispel her visionary dreams. To make any serious attempt now, however, to alter her intentions, was more trouble than he could inflict on his indolence.

'I wish I had known what an eccentric career you were planning for yourself, Ernie, as I should have tried to dissuade you from anything of the kind; and I am afraid Lingard will not, he is so strong on letting every one follow the bent of their own inclinations. I ought to have asked you what your plans were before now; but the truth is, that little witch Julia has occupied my thoughts entirely for some time past. I am seriously afraid, Ernestine, that you will find these new fancies very impracticable.'

'They are not new fancies, dearest George. The life of mere society has never satisfied me, and I brooded over these thoughts long before you came home; only I did not think of putting them into execution, because I was looking forward to living with you; they have revived with double force, however, since I knew of your marriage, and I only want to find some way of giving them shape and reality, for the next two or three years at least.'

'But in the meantime, when you leave us to-day, where are you going? Do you return to the Beauforts at once?'

'No; I have almost made up my mind to go down to Greyburgh to see Reginald. His letters, which are very rare, have made me anxious for some time past. He admits that his bodily health is weak and failing, and he seems to me to be depressed and unsettled in mind.'

Colonel Courtenay shrugged his shoulders. 'As to Reginald, he is a perfect enigma to me. I saw one of the undergraduates of his college the other day, who was telling me about him. It is incredible that a young man of one-and-twenty should spend his life dreaming over theories which have no more connexion with this world than the man in the moon. I hear he sits up half the night, perplexing his brain with all manner of theological inquiries: *à son age je m'occupais de bien autre chose!*'

'Reginald was always thoughtful and quiet,' said Ernestine, 'but so reserved that I never could thoroughly penetrate into his mind.'

'Well, I must go and see what Julia is doing, or we shall really be too late. We may not meet for a long time to come, Ernie. I think I shall give you a substitute for myself in the shape of Fury, if you like to have him,' and he pointed to the wise-looking terrier, who sat with his speaking brown eyes fixed on his master.

'Oh, I should indeed,' said Ernestine, her face brightening with pleasure. 'I have taken care of him in your absence, and he has been such a friend to me—so intelligent and affectionate. I assure you he comforted me in the wisest manner the night after your marriage, when I was feeling rather dreary.'

'Well, I herewith present him to you,' said Colonel

Courtenay, lifting the dog by the neck and swinging him into his sister's lap. 'Fury, be faithful to your new mistress. I daresay he would have died in India, so you and he will be mutually benefited.' And stooping down he kissed her affectionately, and left the room.

CHAPTER III.

ON BOARD THE 'HERO.'

THEY stood at last on the deck of the 'Hero,' which in ten minutes more was to weigh anchor. The soldiers' wives had been stowed away in the narrow limits they were to occupy for some time to come, and their friends had all been sent on shore. None but the passengers remained, with the exception of Miss Courtenay, who was allowed to wait till the last moment, but the boat which was to take her on shore danced on the waters at the side of the ship, along with several others containing persons anxious to watch the final departure. Colonel Courtenay was standing on the poop talking to the captain, whose quick eye all the while was glancing everywhere to see that his orders were being obeyed. Ernestine leant on her brother's arm, clinging to these last moments when she could still see his face and hear his voice. Mrs. Courtenay, seated at a little distance, was playing the coquette in the most refined and lady-like manner possible with some of the officers of her husband's regiment. Ernestine remembered the scene long afterwards; everything looked so bright and prosperous, with the sunshine sparkling on the blue waters and on the white sails of the ship.

Suddenly a great noise and confusion was heard at the lower end of the vessel. There was a scuffling of feet, a clamour of voices, and an occasional volley of oaths. A struggle of some kind was evidently going on, and the captain called out angrily to know what was the matter. One of the ship's officers came up to him at once—

'A woman, sir, who was found secreted in the hold, and refuses to go on shore.'

'Is she not on the War Office List, then?'

'No, sir, she is not a soldier's wife at all. Sergeant Dale and Private Smith say they know her for an impostor. She tried yesterday to get herself passed among the women at the Depôt with false papers.'

'Send the jade ashore at once, then, we have no time to lose; we must be off in five minutes.'

'They are trying to get her into the boat, sir, but she won't go. She is like a wild cat, and clings to every thing she can lay hold of. It took three men to get her up from the hold.'

'Oh, bother! Hoist her overboard with a rope, then. Threaten her with a ducking for her pains, there are plenty of boats to drop her into. I can't have the hands hindered from their work.'

The officer touched his cap and went off to obey orders. In another moment a shriek so wild and thrilling that it startled every one on board, rang through the air. A figure was seen to burst from the crowd of sailors, with streaming hair and outstretched arms, dashing them aside with a force which seemed almost superhuman. With one bound she broke away, and leapt from the forecastle, flying rather than running along the deck, up the steps to the poop, and on till she flung herself down at Colonel Courtenay's feet, and clasped his knees with power which he could not resist. She threw back her head, showing a face, once beautiful, but now distorted by an intensity of agony and passion that smote the bystanders with a sense of terrible mental pain; her long black hair, wet with the dews of anguish that stood on her forehead, fell back in masses from her flushed face; her dark eyes were full of wildness; her whole frame quivered, and her dress, torn and disordered, was stained with blood, from the injuries she had received in her struggle with the men.

It was a pitiable spectacle, but it was left to the tone of her wild mournful voice to convey to the bystanders a conviction of the utter misery that was desolating the soul of the unhappy girl.

Her flight from the one end of the vessel to the other had been so instantaneous, that the breathless impassioned words she now spoke seemed but the prolongation of the shriek that still appeared to echo in their ears. Clinging to Courtenay as if her life depended on the tenacity of her grasp; looking at him, speaking to him only, she gasped out, 'George, George, my own George, save me, save me!—don't let them send me away; I must go with you, I will go with you; I cannot live without you—indeed I cannot: I have tried it, and I cannot; I must be with you—nothing shall tear me from you!'

At this unexpected address, spoken loud enough to be heard by all present, a look of significant meaning passed among the officers of Colonel Courtenay's regiment, and from them to the captain and the men who stood round; while Courtenay himself looked down on the girl at his feet with an expression of absolute fury.

'Is the woman mad or drunk!' he exclaimed, struggling with a cruel violence to disengage himself from her convulsive grasp; 'how dare you attack me in this way? Here, men, drag this woman off, some of you.'

At these words a cry more appalling than that which had startled them before burst from the poor girl's lips. She lifted up her eyes to his face, piteous with their expression of sorrowful dismay,—

'O George, my dear George, don't you know me? I am Lois, your own poor Lois, that you said you would love for ever and ever. Am I so changed? I daresay I am, for I have cried my heart out after you pretty near; but look, it is me myself—here is the ring you gave me, and the locket with your own hair in it, and the bracelet—look!' And the unhappy girl strove with her trembling hands to show him the trinkets, which she thought might convince him of the identity he knew too well. Courtenay literally stamped with rage and impatience, especially as he saw the smile which was appearing on the face of every man round him, to whom the scene was sufficiently intelligible.

'The woman is raving mad;' and he made another futile attempt to shake her off. 'Leave hold, I tell you, or I'll have you sent to gaol for a month.'

'Me! me sent to gaol! O George, it is you that are mad, not to know me; you can't have forgotten me;

you took me from my home; you took my good name; you made father curse me; but I don't care for that— I'd do it all again, I love you so; and you kept me six months—such a happy time; don't you remember? It is but three months since you left me. You sent me to a gay house, and said you'd come to fetch me, and I've waited and waited, and longed for you so; then I heard you were going to India, and I knew I must come. I can't live without you—I can't, and I won't; and oh! George, you will take me with you, won't you? I'll be your servant, or anything you please, only don't drive me away. I love you, I love you so, dear, dear George!' and she burst into tears, laying her face against him, and kissing the fierce hands with which, all the time she spoke, he had been trying to loosen her hold. Not one of the men moved a step to help him; their sympathies were evidently with the girl.

But now Mrs. Courtenay, who had been engaged in a lively conversation at a little distance, began to be attracted by the noise and excitement, and when looking round she saw a woman clinging to her husband, a sudden colour flushed her face, and she came forward, saying, 'Colonel Courtenay, what is the meaning of this?'

'Only a drunken woman, my love, who mistakes me

for some one else.' Then suddenly stooping down over the girl, he said to her in an energetic whisper,—

'Lois, you fool, I do know you, but that lady is my wife. You can never be with me again; you might have known I had done with you for ever when I sent you away. Go on shore quietly, and I'll give you some money; but if you dare to say another word to me now, I'll have you taken up by the police as sure as I live.'

He knew her! That beautiful lady was his wife! He had done with her for ever. She must not *dare* to speak to him. He would give her in charge. As sentence after sentence revealed to the wretched girl her true position, a stillness as of death seemed to settle down upon her; the passion of her manner died away; the irrepressible burst of feeling ceased with a sudden gasp; the crimson flush on her face faded to an ashy paleness; her hands relaxed their hold on Courtenay; her arms fell by her side; her lips parted, but no breath appeared to stir upon them; and she scarcely seemed to live, but that her eyes, alive with agony, were fixed wide open with a strange fascinated stare on his face.

He saw at once that she was finally subdued, and made a sign to some of the men to take her away. Two sailors came forward, they raised her gently, and

set her on her feet. She made no resistance; it
was as though they were dealing with a corpse, but
for the staring mournful eyes. Some money which
Colonel Courtenay had secretly thrust into her hand
fell from her powerless fingers and rolled on the deck.
A young naval officer standing near, with an unmistakable expression of disgust at the scene, kicked it
away with his foot into the water, and then went to
help the men in taking the poor stricken girl as carefully as possible to the boat. They half carried, half
supported her along the deck, and she neither spoke nor
struggled, only, as they moved her, her head turned mechanically, so that her eyes with their look of anguish
left not the face of him who was her best beloved on
earth, and her bitterest enemy.

They took her down the gangway and placed her in
a boat. Then the officer and sailors came on deck again
and stood watching her; the boat shot out from the
vessel's side. She was seen seated in the stern, upright,
her head turned back to the ship, the haggard gaze
still seeking the figure of Courtenay, who stood conspicuous on the poop. Rapidly she was borne to the
shore, soon did her form become lost among many
others; but so long as it was visible, however indis-
tinctly, those eyes, tortured, despairing, glared back

through the sunlight on the face that had charmed her to destruction. And when he lies an expiring man upon his deathbed, or on the battle-field, shall not these eyes look back upon him still with their remembered agony?

She was gone, and Colonel Courtenay breathed freely again. He was too entirely a man of the world to feel in the least seriously embarrassed at the situation in which he found himself placed; his *savoir faire* would have brought him through worse difficulties than this. The beautiful Julia was no deep thinker, and a whispered regret that her delicate nerves should have been pained by so disagreeable an object as a drunken woman, accompanied by one of his charming smiles, was quite sufficient to restore her self-satisfied equanimity; and in another moment the incident had almost passed from her memory, as she glanced her bright eyes from side to sidé to see if the grace of her attitude was observed as she leant over the ship's side, and took a sentimental leave of her native country.

As to the captain of the ship and his own officers, Courtenay knew well that they perfectly understood the whole affair; but he also knew that they would offer no open criticism on the private conduct of a man in his official position. So he merely said a few easy words, which showed that he assumed them to be imperturbably dense on the subject, and then let the matter drop as completely as if it had never occurred. But there was one with whom Courtenay attempted neither palliation nor deceit. Some instinct withheld him from trying any such means with his pure-hearted sister. His hope was that she had neither understood the scene, nor heard the words he spoke to Lois when his wife drew near. He was mistaken. Ernestine had heard every syllable, and she would have understood it all, if she could have brought herself to believe in the wickedness of the brother she so loved and trusted; but such lessons are amongst the hardest we have to learn in this hard life; and she stood there, her cheek now flushed, now deadly pale, with a crowd of bewildering thoughts careering through her mind, and one maddening doubt lying underneath them all, which she felt, if realized, would banish all happiness from her intercourse with her brother for ever. Her brother! beloved, admired all her life long, could it be that he was wicked, cruel, heartless? Her childhood's idol, to whom the incense of such true affection had been offered; had he fallen—fallen into the ashes of the worst corruption? And that poor girl! How her whole soul burned with compassion for the utter misery which her woman's heart could understand so well; even while the mere thought of its probable cause sent the vivid flush so painfully to her very forehead. Some one had been that hapless woman's curse. It could not be her own dear brother. Yet—what if it were? She shivered from head to foot at the bare thought. So well had she loved him, that the girl's agony seemed to fall like heavy guilt on her own soul; and she felt that if it were so indeed, his victim must become her own most sacred charge. She must know the truth; she could not rest in so hateful a doubt, and the moments were flying fast; already it was time she left the ship. She tried to raise her eyes to her brother; she tried to whisper a few hesitating words, but the nature of the subject checked even the faintest effort. To a stranger she could have spoken better than to him, and already the opportunity was gone. The captain came forward, raised his cap, and, with a regret for hurrying Miss Courtenay, said that 'time was up,' the men were weighing the anchor, and the boat that waited for her could no longer stay alongside. Colonel Courtenay felt that fortune favoured him, for he had read the meaning of her half-averted face, her quivering lip, and crimsoned downcast face; and now he put his arm round his sister, kissed her affectionately, and bade her a tender farewell.

'Take care of yourself, dearest Ernestine, and write soon; we shall long to hear from you.'

He spoke in his own winning, open manner, and her heart bounded up to him once more. She laid her head fondly on his shoulder, and tried, in a choked voice, to say good-bye; then he gave place to Julia, who lightly kissed her on both cheeks à la Française, and murmured some pretty meaningless speech, and in another moment Ernestine was parted from them both, and seated in the boat to which the captain had conducted her. One vigorous stroke of the oars, and it bounded from the vessel's side. She looked up, and saw through her tear-dimmed eyes her brother and his wife standing at the gangway that they might watch her to the last. As they caught sight of her, Courtenay lifted his hat in a parting salute. She saw the sunlight falling on the rich masses of his dark-brown hair, and his fine face lighted up with the bright smile that had won him many a heart, and, leaning on his strong arm, was the delicate, graceful figure of his wife, stooping down to look at Ernestine, with her fair hair escaping from her hat, and half hiding her lovely radiant countenance. Ernestine looked up eagerly at them as they thus appeared before her in their beauty and happiness, seeking to learn by heart, as it were, and print upon her memory that fair bright picture that she might carry it away with her, to cherish its remembrance in the long years of absence. But suddenly a shudder passed over her. What if, instead of the charming countenance that shone so bright by her brother's side, there ought to have been, by all Divine laws, by all that is truth, and honour, and equity, that face, pale, haggard, and sorrow-smitten, which she had seen fade from its look of passionate love and entreaty to the fixed, hopeless stare of utter bewilderment, as the low whisper hissed upon her ear, ' Lois, you fool.'

Little, indeed, do we know in what state of feeling an hour may find us. If any one had told Ernestine Courtenay that she would see the figure of her brother lessening in the distance as she was being borne away from him, to meet perhaps no more, and that her thoughts would not be with him, but with another—a stranger in name and history,—she could not have believed it; and yet to that unhappy one, known only by the common power of suffering, her heart was turning now with pain and grief, in which her brother's departure had no share; and her first eager glance when she stepped on shore was not to the ship, already gliding fast away, but to the motley crowd on the pier, in the hope that she might see amongst them the poor girl whom she was resolved at all hazards to find. She looked, however, in vain.

ON BOARD THE 'HERO.'

Many faces were there, and many sorrowful enough, but the one living aspect of despair which had so riveted her attention was not amongst them. Ernestine inquired of the bystanders if any had seen her, and she was met with the contradictory accounts which invariably follow a question addressed to a crowd. Several persons had seen her, but all differed as to the direction she had taken on landing from the boat. Ernestine's servant, who had been with her on board, stood with an expression of intense disgust on his face as his mistress thus demeaned herself (in his estimation) by asking questions about a person whose existence he conceived she ought to ignore. At last, seeing that she was actually going to start in search of the girl, his superior wisdom could stand it no longer, and advancing, he ventured to suggest that Miss Courtenay should allow him to engage a policeman to carry on the pursuit, which he felt certain she herself would find utterly impracticable.

Ernestine could not but admit that he was right, much as she disliked using such an agent under the circumstances. The chances of her own search being successful in such a place as Seamouth were certainly small enough, and she trusted that it might be possible to discover the poor girl's abode without letting her find out that the police had been in any way employed in the search. Ernestine, therefore, herself gave orders, with many minute directions, to the man whom her servant brought to her; and having received his assurance that she should know every particular of the girl's position by the next morning at latest, she left the matter in his hands, and returned slowly to her desolate rooms at the hotel.

CHAPTER IV.

THE LAST NIGHT.

THAT day was drawing to a close. Within the streets there were all the usual tokens of approaching night: the shopmen were lighting their lamps for the later customers, the labourers were hurrying home, the diners-out were arriving at the houses of their friends,—all things were as they had been the day before, and as they would be when the next day came. Yet strange it is to feel, as the weeks pass over us unmarked and uneventful, that there is no one day of all those that make up our years that is not to some human being the most awful and portentous that can be for them in time and in eternity,—the climax of their sufferings, or the very crisis of their doom. How often is the soft air, as it passes over our cheek, laden with the last sigh of a ruined soul gone to its dread account, or vibrating with the bullet-shot which has made some wretch a murderer. No day—no hour rather—that is not burdened with some fearful struggle, some great crime, some deep despair. We think we know enough of this world's teeming sorrows, and that we hear too often the many mingled cry that ever rises from the suffering heart of all humanity; but how awful must be the sight on which the Omniscient Eyes look down, to which no tear is hid, no pang unknown of all the weltering mass of this earth's agony! How awful that tremendous sight—fruit of the ancient curse—atoning Calvary alone can tell. For us, we may well give thanks that we know not even all the sorrows that may be gathered in the narrow limits of a single human heart; and that perhaps the one most near our own.

The evening was closing in, and through the busy streets there went a figure,—the same that had hastened the day before so rapidly towards the emigrant Depôt. The same, yet not the same: gone was the quick elastic tread, the energy of purpose, the strong, passionate life gleaming in the dark eye and flushing on the fevered cheek, which then had been so marked. Now all was languid, hopeless, apathetic, in the feeble creeping steps, the nerveless arms and drooping head. The tall figure seemed to have collapsed, and was now the form of a woman broken down,—it might be with age, or it might be with sorrow. She seemed to have a definite object, and to be guiding her steps towards some settled goal;

THE LAST NIGHT. 55

but so feebly, so wearily, that none but a close observer would have thought her course was anything but aimless wandering. This time there was no impetus to carry her through the crowded streets, and she was jostled from side to side without appearing conscious of it. Once a rough carter passing by threw her against the iron railings of an area, and she would have fallen had not his companion caught her on his arm.

'Why, girl, you don't seem to know where you are going,' he said, as he steadied her on her feet. She looked at him for a moment with a dreamy, unconscious gaze; then, as she seemed to understand his meaning, she shook her head, and said in a faint voice, 'O yes, I do; I know where I am going too well—too well.' He left her, and she wandered on, and presently she came to a brilliantly lighted shop, where the windows were filled with children's toys of every description. At one of the huge squares of plate-glass stood two little girls, their arms round each other's necks, gazing in ecstasy at some of the glittering treasures displayed before them. Just as Lois was passing them, the one said to the other,—

'O Mary, shouldn't we be happy if we had those beautiful dolls!' She stopped and looked at them: 'Happy, would you be?—then you shall have them.'

She went into the shop, pulled out a gay purse, and bought the coveted toys, with a lavish carelessness as to the price which astonished the shopman. Then she went and thrust them into the hands of the children, who looked at her, and then at their new possessions, in utter amazement.

'Shall you be happy now?' she said to them, with a sad sweetness in her tone.

'O yes, yes!' exclaimed the children, almost shouting with delight.

'I am very glad of it,' she said, 'for I shall never be happy any more;' and then she walked away, wiping the tears from her eyes with her hand. Soon she had left the principal streets and entered on the outskirts of the town. Still she held on, taking the direction of the beach, and soon the houses grew fewer, the lights scarce, and the eye could see beyond the town out into the desolate night. When she had nearly passed all the streets she stopped, looked at the purse which she still held in her hand, and then glanced all round as if in search of some one on whom to bestow it. Presently an old man came out of a wretched house and tottered along, guiding himself with a stick, and evidently very feeble. She went up to him and touched him on the shoulder, 'You are very poor, are you not?'

THE LAST NIGHT.

'I should think so!' he exclaimed with an angry exclamation; 'none poorer, though many makes more cry.'

'Take this then,' she said, dropping the purse into his hand. He started, felt its weight, then, struggling feebly to take off his hat, exclaimed, ' God bless you, my dear lady; you be a good one, you be!'

She left him and went on, then suddenly turned back and came up to him.

'Say that again,' she said.

'Say what, my dear?' said the old man, who was fastening up the purse with his shaking hands. 'I'll say anything you like, for there's meat, and drink, and baccy for me in this here purse for a month to come. What be I to say?'

'Say that—that which you said about a blessing.'

'Was it "God bless you," I said, my dear? I'll say it as often as ever you please, and good reason too, for it is little enough I get most days for the asking, let alone such a present as this when I had said never a word. God bless you a thousand times over, and I hope He will.'

She listened eagerly, then cast a wistful glance up to heaven, as though she would fain know if there was any chance of the prayer being heard; but the sight of the darkening sky seemed to bring no thought of comfort to her, for she drooped her head again and sighed heavily.

'Anyhow, they are good words to hear for the last,' she murmured, as she once more took her solitary way along the water's edge.

And now all human habitations were left far behind, and she had entered on a solitude as complete, at that late hour, as if she were many miles from any town. The scene was cheerless in the extreme: the waning twilight half revealed, half hid the long low beach, with its black masses of dank seaweed and the slimy reptiles creeping to and fro among them; the dark restless waters moaning heavily as they beat upon the unyielding sands; the lowering clouds rolling in heaving masses over the leaden sky. Far away on the horizon there gleamed one ghastly streak of light, where all that remained of the dying day was gathered, while over all the dreary landscape the rising wind went sighing in fitful gusts, rendering the damp air more bleak and chill. Well was this scene in keeping with the forlorn figure that now went stealing with dejected steps along the shore of that dark sea, shivering in the cold blast, and weeping hopeless tears, which brought no relief to the dead weight at her heart. She went on till she

THE LAST NIGHT.

came to a spot where a high rock rose abruptly out of the waves, and shelved back, forming a sort of little promontory, of which the farthest extremity was in deep water.

Up the steep ascent which led to the part overhanging the sea the poor girl toiled with painful steps till she stood on the summit, with nothing around her but the dark expanse of sullen heaving waters. She looked down upon them as they beat with heavy monotonous sound against the rock, and an expression of strange calmness passed over her wan face; then she cast a glance on all sides, and saw that no human being was in sight. She was alone with that leaden sky—that deep black sea—that sighing, mournful wind. Night was falling fast, no one would pass there now till the sun should rise again; that sun which she had watched in its setting as we look upon the face of a dying friend whom we shall see no more. She had time before her yet, and with a long weary sigh she sunk down upon the rock, folded her arms on her knees, and laid her head upon them, whilst in a low calm voice she murmured, 'Here, then, it must end.'

Her own heart seemed to answer back and ask—'What must end?' Even her life!—her life of twenty years—her young strong life, with all its promise for this world, and all its responsibility for that which is to come. It must end; there was no question as to that, nor had there been any for the last few hours; but as she pronounced the sentence, the existence thus condemned seemed to pass in review before her, and drag her back in spite of herself to live it over again in thought from the first day of remembered infancy to this the last—the unendurable!

Her earliest recollection was very sweet and bright. The morning sunlight of a summer day shining on the cottage that had been her home, and was still her father's; the good old grandmother, who supplied the place of her dead mother, standing at the door, kissing her and stroking her curls as she sent her off to school; and herself an innocent little child bounding away over the dewy grass, singing and laughing in her careless glee with the merry birds that carolled from bush and bough.

That summer morning, and life all before her—oh, the anguish of the contrast with this dreary night, and death beneath her feet! She literally groaned as she thought of it, and cried out,—

'O that I were a little maid once more, playing at my father's door!' In vain—in vain! What power could turn the tide of time, and bring the sin-stained woman back to childhood's innocence? God help those who know the utter agony of the burdened conscience,

THE LAST NIGHT.

longing with that vain longing to recall the guileless days for ever gone!

The next scene that came upon the rack of memory was one of sadness; yet, contrasted with her present bitter wretchedness, it seemed only to breathe of peace and love. This was the death of her old grandmother. It was from her that Lois had gained all the good that had come to her from external influences. Ever since the day when that good old woman had given the unconscious babe a 'Bible name,' in the hope that she might be as faithful as the Lois of St. Paul, to the night when on her deathbed she solemnly charged her to 'attend her church, and keep from all bad ways,' she had done her utmost to make the child as true a Christian as herself. Nor had the heavenly light she sought to kindle ever quite died out of the fallen girl's life. It was that which now burnt up as with an ardent flame her poor guilt-laden soul.

Lois remembered how they laid her grandmother in the green churchyard on a calm spring day. 'And O that I were lying by her!' burst from her lips, as again the hopeless yearning for the purer past rose madly within her. She remembered the touching Burial Service, and how it stilled her little heart, and dried her childish tears, she knew not how. Alas! what

words of blessed hope would ever sound over her
unhallowed grave? Then that scene passed away, and
she saw her daily life as it went on for years; her
father married again; the stepmother was not unkind.
Poor Lois had not that excuse, as too many have who
share her evil deeds; but she was a weak, timid woman,
wholly occupied with the children who were born to
her, and quite unequal to coping with a proud, high
spirit like that of Lois. She had scarce a place in the
girl's remembrance, where two figures stood forth at first
with equal prominence—her father, a hard, stern man,
whose religion was his respectability, as it is that of
nine-tenths of the better class of English peasants, and
it was a *cultus* which he found well received by the
divinity whom he most delighted to honour—the great
lord whose park-gate he kept, and in whose lodge he
lived rent-free. He had but one code for his children,
which from infancy they learned to understand: so
long as they did well, and brought him to honour, they
should share the best he had; but in the day they
brought disgrace upon him, they might go seek a home
and a father where they would, for they should have
none under his roof-tree. Far brighter was the other
face that looked in upon her from the relentless past—
the sunny face and blue eyes of her own sister Annie.

Annie! She started as the name came to her; she had not thought of her since this day had wrought a total change within her; but now, when face to face with death, all things wore their true aspect. The remembrance of her sister was the worst pang that had touched her yet, for she knew that her own ruin had induced that of the child she should have guarded with a mother's care.

She turned sickening from the thought, and welcomed with avidity in its place the glowing recollection which rushed over her of that day, the most beautiful and the most disastrous of her life, whose memory even in that dark hour still thrilled her with a mournful semblance of delight. Well had it been for her if she had died ere ever that day dawned upon her. Yet how little was there in its outward aspect to lead any to suppose that it had been to her indeed a day of doom, pregnant with the accursed seeds of sin, despair, and death. It had been like other days; she rose at early morn, went through her household duties singing like a bird, with light step and lighter heart, and then flew to deck herself for that part of her daily business which specially pleased her girlish vanity. It was her duty to open the gate for the visitors at the Hall, and many a time had she heard them remark upon the beauty which she well knew she possessed. On that day, as she looked at her face in the glass, she smiled with pleasure, for she saw it was fresh and blooming as the rose, which she had coquettishly placed at her waist; and though she longed in vain for a costly dress like those worn by the ladies at the Hall, she could console herself triumphantly with the reflection that none of them had such masses of glossy black hair as those she had just dressed with elaborate care.

She remembered how she went and sat down with some work in her hand, on which she would have it supposed she was engaged; but really her dark eyes were glancing hither and thither, noticing every one who passed, and seeking an aliment for the excitement her passionate nature craved.

At length she heard on the still summer air the quick ringing gallop of a horse, and soon on the winding road horse and rider appeared. She watched them as they came along; was there ever such a beautiful sight!—that noble gentleman—for so he seemed to her, with his fine face and his haughty bearing, holding in his fiery black mare as it champed the bit, and sent the foam in snow-white flakes on its glossy mane. She knew who he was, though she had never seen him before. He was coming as a visitor of some weeks to the Hall, and his servant had arrived that day with his luggage. He had been at the lodge, and had spoken of his master. Such a brave colonel, just come from India, where he had killed at least a score of blacks in the mutiny with his own right hand. So in Lois's eyes he was a hero.

She was ready waiting at the gate as he came up. She flung it wide open, and as he rode slowly in she looked up at him with an expression of undisguised admiration on her bright blushing face. Something in her glance attracted him; he looked down at her, and remained struck with some surprise at the brilliancy of her fresh youthful beauty. He made a trifling remark, which brought light into her eyes and a gay smile over all her face. She answered him, glancing up with a look, half coy, half admiring; and when at last he rode slowly on towards the house, he gazed back more than once at the pretty figure leaning against the gate and watching him.

Next day he sauntered up to the lodge, and stood talking in the little garden with Lois,—and the next, and the next; why linger over the sickening details? Soon they walked together daily in a wood at some little distance, where she went to meet him. Colonel Courtenay stayed through the whole shooting season at the Hall. By the time the day of his departure came, Lois loved him with her whole heart and soul, and desired nothing so much as that he should know it; her ears were closed for ever to all voices in heaven or on earth alike save his; and his least word alone governed her will. She saw no more the far-off glory resting on the delectable hills, of which her dead teacher had told her; only the sight of his dear face was light and life to her; and all things that pertained to peace, and honour, and a quiet conscience were torn from her soul in the whirlwind of passion.

It was to this that he had willed to bring her, working thereunto with calm, deliberate forethought. So when he left the Hall he rode away on his beautiful black mare which was to take him to the station, some miles distant; and his host came to the door with him, and took leave of this brave, honourable man with the highest esteem, and Lois's father held the gate open for him, as his daughter somehow was not at home; and this noble colonel smiled as the man touched his hat, and threw him a guinea, which he thought a very handsome gratuity, and then he galloped away to the station, and walked in amongst passengers and porters with an air of lordly ease. His servant met him, grave and respectful, of whom he asked the question, 'Which carriage?' and he was conducted to one where sat a woman closely veiled. He sprang in, the train darted off, and never more, in all the retributive ages of eternity, can that wretched man undo the fearful ruin he has worked on that poor lost soul.

Three months of intoxicating delight—the recollection of them rushed over her like a delirious dream. A villa at Richmond, servants at her command, beautiful dresses, a fine horse to ride,—these were as nothing compared to the wild joy of being with the object of her idolatry.

But in the course of that brief fever of pleasure she was pierced with one sharp pang, which seemed for a moment to tear the veil from her eyes and show her what she was, and whither tending. A friend of Colonel Courtenay's, who had been staying at the Hall, had seen and admired her sister Annie; but lacking that indomitable determination to minister to his own gratification at all times which characterized Courtenay, he had regretted that she was a girl of good character, and thought of her no more. Now, the sight of Lois, and his friend's superior villany recalled the wicked thought, and ripened it to crime.

At his suggestion, Courtenay told Lois to write and invite Annie to come and visit her. Annie! At the very thought her proud wayward heart sank within her. Anything but that. She saw her again, the little child, so sweet, so innocent, kneeling at her grandmother's knee to say her evening prayer, 'Pray, God, bless my sister Lois.' Oh, whatever she was herself, whatever she might be hereafter, she could not betray that innocent child! For the first time she resisted; she clung to Courtenay, kissed his hands, and told him she could not obey. What! his bought slave dared to dispute his will? One word such as he could speak, one frown such as he could give, and she was at his feet in a moment; she would do whatever he pleased. She wrote and told her sister she was married—married to a gentleman, and she must come and join her; that a like brilliant fate might be hers; and with that she sent her money for her journey, more than Annie had ever seen in her life before. The poor child was unhappy at home since her sister's disappearance. She asked no leave of the stern father, but stole away to join the companion of her happy childhood in the home Lois had described to her; and she knew not 'that the dead were there, and that her guests were in the depths of hell!'

One single day little Annie dwelt in that house of splendid infamy, bringing with her as it were an atmosphere of freshness and innocence which recalled to Lois the dewy fragrance of the early mornings when they gathered wild-flowers in the woods, and the pure serenity of the starlit nights when they slept on their little bed clasped in each other's arms. One day, and the next Annie's father summoned her home, and the gentleman whose admiring eyes had met her at every turn, when he was staying at the Hall a few months before, offered to drive her to the station; but Lois heard the laughing communication to Courtenay of his real plans in taking the girl with him to the railway. Annie went, well pleased with the novel excitement of the rapid motion, and with the opportunity of displaying the hat and feathers which this same gentleman had given her that morning; but thinking no evil beyond the indulgence of her coquettish vanity. As the horses bounded forwards at their master's touch, she turned her laughing face, and kissed her hand to Lois, and from that hour her sister never saw her more, nor did her light step ever again cross the threshold of her father's home.

And, alas! Lois soon ceased to think of her; for the first shadows of the night of sorrow, whose total darkness had now overtaken her, were deepening round her even then. She lived but in one, and that one was beginning to neglect, or rather to forsake her. Days and weeks he left her now alone, and the look of calm contempt with which he met her reproaches froze into her very soul. Then there came a day after his absence had been longer than it had ever been before, when a letter was brought to her from him, worded almost as tenderly as in the first rapturous days of their acquaintance; he told her he must be absent some time, and he could no longer keep her in the villa she now inhabited. She must go to a 'boarding-house' in London, which he indicated, and remain there till she heard from him. He bade her enjoy herself, and follow in all things the example of the companions she would find leading a merry life there.

This letter was brought by Courtenay's confidential servant, who had orders to remove her; and Lois, so soon as she had read it, began with tears of passionate agony to ask when she should see his master, and implored of the man to let her go to him at once. He answered, with an insolent sneer, that her only chance was to do as the Colonel desired; the gay house was the place for her, and doubtless she would see Colonel Courtenay there, 'or half-a-dozen others as good,' he muttered audibly. Lois felt to the innermost depths of her heart, that the time was come when she must drink the bitter dregs of the intoxicating cup of pleasure, which the cruel hand of this very honourable gentleman had held to her lips; but she never guessed the full extent of her calamity. She had ever believed his lightest word, and she believed the mocking promise he made her now. She was to remain there till she heard from him; therefore she did not hesitate to go to this place at once, clinging desperately to the only hope that remained to her of seeing him, without whom she knew she could not live. She went, and she remained there waiting; waiting for the fulfilment of his word as men wait a reprieve from execution. Lost as she was, dead to the voice of conscience and the sense of moral right, she yet loathed the place, the life, and herself, who perforce lived in it. One thought alone sustained her: day and night one face was before her eyes, one voice in her ears; and the cry of her longing agony went out, hour after hour, to him who had taken her from her home and her God, imploring him to come and give her back at least the treasure for which she had paid that tremendous price. In vain! She might as well have called upon the vanished past to give her back the guilelessness of childhood. But still she trusted him, until one day she heard two men who frequented the house talking of Colonel Courtenay. They knew him, and she listened with a terrible anxiety which seemed to exhaust her very life. They spoke of his approaching departure for India, and mentioned that he was to sail in the 'Hero' two days from that time. Five minutes later, Lois had crossed the threshold of that accursed house, and the night of Courtenay's departure found her on the lonely rock, the dank night dews falling on her unprotected head, the sullen waters chafing and moaning at her feet.

Yes; she had retraced her whole life to this hour; and now unto this hour she had come, and here, she echoed back as she began—here it must end. One stinging thought remained to her, however, from that sad retrospect,—the thought of her sister Annie, lost— lost through her means! She dashed her head on the ground, and literally groaned when she thought of it. 'O Annie, Annie! poor mother's darling, she must not come to an end like this.' Suddenly she lifted up her head, raised herself on her knees, and prayed:

'Our Father which art in heaven, I dare not pray for myself—but for Annie—for Annie, oh let me pray! She did not know what she was doing, and I did. Oh save her, save her for the dear Lord's sake. Amen.'

The prayer seemed to calm her anguish. 'Perhaps God will let me do something for Annie,' she murmured. 'What was it grandmother used to say? "He is full of compassion and of great goodness;" at least I will try.

THE LAST NIGHT. 73

I shall die the easier for the chance that it may help her.'

She took from her bosom a little ornamental pocket-book, cherished there because Courtenay had given it to her, and wrote on the page prepared for indelible writing these words:—

'To COLONEL COURTENAY.

'MY DEAR, DEAR GEORGE,—When you get this I shall be dead—dead and cold in the grave, where I'll never trouble you more; so I've nothing to ask you for myself. It is all over with me. You have forsaken and deceived me, and I can't live; that's all. I must die. Don't think I am blaming you, my dearest; for I love you still. Oh, how I love you! But I do want you to do one thing for pity's sake. I want you to save Annie—my poor little sister Annie. George—George, don't let her come to a death like mine. I tell you it is terrible. No one but you can save her; for you only know who took her away. I don't know his name myself. Oh, find her out, I beseech you, and send her home to father. It is the last thing I ask you. I can't write any longer. George, good-bye; I want to die quick, for I can't bear this misery; so no more for ever. —From your loving LOIS.'

The fact of writing to him had brought as it were his presence before her, and stirred the depths of her anguish till it was unbearable. With trembling haste she closed the pocket-book, wrapt it in many folds of her handkerchief, and placed it far within her bosom, where she thought the water could not reach it; then she started to her feet, looked wistfully all round, and saw, far off on the eastern horizon, the first faint streak of dawn; at the sight she uttered a shriek: 'Oh! I never will see daylight more,—my own dear George; good-bye!'

She clasped her hands above her head, and bounded from the rock, the dark cold waters opened to receive her; one moment of convulsive struggling in the horror of the death agony, one despairing glance of the wild terrified eyes to heaven, one glance of the dawning day upon the white distorted face, and the dark deed was done, the wondrous human life gave way; the soul violently wrenched from its earthly dwelling-place went forth to its account; and the beautiful form, so fair in its youth, and health, and strength, fashioned for long life and work in the service of its God, went down a dead mass of senseless clay to swell the vast corruption of the grave.

Our ideas of a murderer mostly carry us to the condemned cell at Newgate, or, more fitly, to the ghastly scaffold and the sea of human faces round it waiting to behold justice done on the destroyer of life, and blood given for blood; yet there are other aspects of a murderer in the sight of the Great God, who sees not as man sees, and here is one of them:—A handsome, smiling gentleman, seated in the luxurious saloon of a fine vessel among a merry group of passengers, the gayest of the gay, delighting all present by his charming manners, his exquisite voice, and his sparkling wit; admired by every woman, envied by every man, a favourite with all. How courteous he is, how gentle, how softly he speaks, how sweetly he smiles; how lightly he passes over his own great merit when they speak of the Victoria Cross, with which his sovereign had decorated him a few days before, as the reward of his distinguished bravery, and in recognition of the great advantages he had given up for a punctilious point of honour. What affinity could that favoured individual have with the lonely figure, which at that very hour was crouching in mortal agony upon a dark rock overhanging turbid waters, in which she was about to quench her life?

By the side of this brave officer sits his beautiful wife, to whom he has sworn a hundred times that she is his first, his only love; and now as night advances he retires to rest, and lays himself down in dreamless sleep, such as men should know whose hearts are free from care, and whose conscience is unstained by sin; and in dreamless sleep he still was lying when the first streak of dawn flashed on the eastern heaven, and touched with rosy light his slumbering eyes. That same first ray of dawn, which on the lone rock by the sea drew from the white lips of her for whom he had made the sight of God's fair sun accursed, the despairing cry, ' Oh! I never will see daylight more, my own dear George, good-bye!' And as he slumbers on, the moaning waters close over her whom he has murdered, and the life he has blasted is extinguished in that most fearful of all deaths, which leaves to the undying soul no time for a tardy repentance. And for this man, this murderer, shall there be no condemned cell, no scaffold, no avenging justice and consenting crowd? Who is it that has said, ' Vengeance is mine, I will repay?'

Little shall it avail him that he sleeps securely now. Vengeance, too, may sleep a while, but yet a little, and his condemned cell shall be the grave, his day of doom that resurrection morning, when the Judge of all the earth shall execute justice on him, and the witnessing crowd shall be the mighty multitude of quick and dead assembled before the great white throne, to hear for every soul that ever lived the sentence of the Eternal Truth.

CHAPTER V.

THE TRUTH REVEALED.

ERNESTINE COURTENAY returned to the hotel after the departure of the 'Hero' with some dread of the dreary evening before her. In general she was only too fond of solitude, but on this day she would gladly have escaped by any means from the uneasy thoughts that rankled in her mind. Feeling thus, it was with no small pleasure that she welcomed the companionship of the little terrier, Fury, whose speaking eyes beamed with delight from under the overhanging shaggy hair as she approached him. She had tested his powers of consolation before, and there is a very real comfort to be derived from the friendship of a dog. Those who have experienced it will know that this is true; and if they wish to analyse the elements of the satisfaction to be derived from this cause, they will find it in the fact that the affection of a dog is so generous and confiding as regards the person he loves, and so unexacting as regards himself. A dog has none of that self-consciousness which our human friend invariably has, more or less, and to which we are obliged to minister, whilst he believes so implicitly in the perfection and goodness of his master or mistress, that we need never fear to be doubted or misunderstood by him.

In the future history of Ernestine and Fury, it will be seen that she at least did well to trust to his almost human comprehension of her feelings, and sympathy with them. He took up his position now at her feet, as she sat by the window while the shadows of evening deepened round her, preferring the aspect of the sky, dull and lowering as it was, to the flaring of the gaslights within. There was nothing to be gained by letting her mind rest on the subject uppermost in her thoughts, for she could come to no conclusion respecting the unhappy girl whose despairing look still haunted her, till she had seen her next day, as she hoped to do; and therefore she turned herself resolutely to the contemplation of her own plans of usefulness for the uncertain period which must elapse, before her marriage would bring definite duties and occupations to fill her ardent mind.

Ernestine Courtenay had of late been greatly influenced by one of the most striking characteristics of the age in which we live—the spirit of inquiry now agitating the whole length and breadth of the land as to the real condition of the lower classes, and the responsibility of the upper ranks with regard to them. In a thousand different shapes, in details unnumbered, each one more perplexing than another, has the same great question arisen. The wisest and most learned amongst us have given it their deepest attention. Many who have greater gifts than wisdom or learning have given their lives to it, and even the worldly and indifferent have it thrust before them whether they will or not; but as yet the result of this living recognition of a mighty universe of suffering and evil lying at our very doors, is the conviction, that of all social problems the most perplexing, the most mysterious, and we may say the most awful, is the condition of the poor, who are never to cease out of the land, and the true nature of their claims upon us; for this is what hitherto the activity and enterprise of the nineteenth century have discovered on the subject, that in this wealthy, enlightened, and Christian country a portion, fearfully large, of the population are heathens in religion, worn down by the bitter pain of abject want, and brutish from the uncontrolled abandonment of themselves to evil.

We know that round all the luxury, the comfort, and the domestic happiness of our country there is a vast surging mass of suffering and wrong, where the souls and bodies of God's creatures, untaught, unpitied, and unsuccoured, are drifting day by day from a life unblest to a death without hope. We know this. We know, moreover, that it is our duty to remedy these startling evils; and, for the most part, there is in the upper ranks a willingness, and even an anxiety, to perform this duty, but how, in the name of all that is practical, how is it to be done? Those who have never tried to learn by their own personal experience how the misery and degradation of the poor is to be relieved, can have no idea of the gigantic difficulties that stand in the way of the plain precepts, to feed the hungry, to instruct the ignorant, to loose the bands of sin and let the oppressed go free.

We hear of men and women dying of starvation on the workhouse steps; of the constant recurrence at Waterloo Bridge of suicides such as that of Lois; of children educated in vice; and we know that for things such as these, we, living amongst them in social and intellectual luxury, shall surely be brought to judgment by the Father of the poor. Yet when we would seek to succour or to christianize them, we find ourselves encouraging drunkenness and imposture,—idleness, which prefers a trade of lucrative infamy to a life of honest

THE TRUTH REVEALED.

labour,—and that deliberate wickedness which has discovered that certain evil qualities have their market value in this world, and therefore are to be cherished and ripened by every means available. In speaking thus, of course, we do but touch, as it were, the outermost edge of that great ocean of darkness and difficulty in which this question is steeped; but these were some of the reflections which passed through the mind of Ernestine Courtenay as she sat gazing out that night upon the dim gray sky. She thought on this subject with perplexity, it is true, and yet with calmness; for there was peace for her in the fixed resolution she had taken, that at least in the narrow circle of her individual existence, not only before her marriage, but always, so far as other claims permitted, she would work out this problem with all the energy, power, and devotion of which her life was capable.

Her life—one little, feeble life, how impotent a gift it seemed wherewith to meet the terrible vastness of the evils which lay even within the sphere of her own vision; yet it was a life which, like that of every other human being on this earth, had its special mission for the furtherance of God's glory, and if even it accomplished but a small amount of actual good, it yet might clear a little space for the labours of more efficient workers, and sound at least some of the unknown depths of that infinite suffering which was heaving and moaning around her. For Ernestine Courtenay believed in the immortality of the soul, unlike the great majority of those who call themselves by the name of the religion which is founded on that doctrine; unlike them, for if that wonderful belief had really fallen upon their spirits in the greatness of its glory and calm, they could neither have fretted and pined over the passing troubles of their little day on earth, nor looked with such dismay on the manifold evils in the world. To believe in the soul's immortality as Ernestine did, is to know that for the whole mass of this earth's misery there is an infinite compensation, a perfect solution, in that grand eternal Love into which all of the human race who seek it, shall be drawn up to find, in perfect union with the will of God, for the past as well as the present, a thankful acceptance of that which in the darkness of earth's night seemed to be evil, but in the pure light of the unending day shines forth as heavenly good.

This was her faith, and therefore it was that, with a quiet resolution of enduring constancy, she prepared to give herself, so far as she might, to advance, were it but a hair's-breadth, that glorious consummation. As yet she did not see one step before her as to the means by which she was to carry out this resolution; not because there was any lack of opportunities, but because the field was so vast, the evils so manifold, the channels of usefulness for her and for all so numerous and so urgent, that she believed to each one on earth must be given some special work to do on behalf of their fellow-creatures, if only they have the heart to undertake it; and believing this, she did not doubt that her own portion of the universal labour would be made known to her when a fit time came. She knew who had said, 'He that followeth ME shall not walk in darkness;' and she felt that amid all the dimness and perplexity of the world in which He went about doing good, the trace of His steps shines forth ever as a luminous path, whereon the feet of all may safely tread, who follow Him in sincerity and truth.

And while Ernestine sat there thinking thus, the darkness deepened round her, even as the night which never was to lighten into day was deepening in the soul of her who was keeping her death vigil on the lonely rock by the cold sea shore; and Ernestine little dreamt that, in the silent tragedy which was being enacted there beneath the eye of God alone, she was to find the token her faith so wisely sought to show her the work appointed to her on earth for the glory of God and the good of His suffering creatures.

Ernestine's first thought next morning was for the poor girl of whom she hoped to hear some tidings, and when her early breakfast was over, she sat waiting anxiously for the arrival of the policeman, who had promised to come as soon as possible to tell her the result of his search. Hour after hour passed away, however, without his appearance, and Ernestine began to grow very impatient. She did not wish to remain in Seamouth longer than she could help, and the idea that he might after all fail in obtaining any trace of the unhappy girl, gave her more pain than she could well account for. She waited some time without making any inquiry, for the dread that her brother might indeed be only too deeply implicated in the matter, made her shrink from mentioning the subject; but at last, as the day wore on, she could no longer delay, and having sent for her servant, she told him to go and find the policeman she had seen the day before, as she wished to speak to him. The man looked perplexed, and at last said, with some hesitation, that the policeman had been there already.

' And why was I not told?' exclaimed Ernestine, much

THE TRUTH REVEALED.

vexed. The servant shifted uneasily from one foot to the other.

'The policeman found Fenton still here,' he said, 'and he took him out with him.'

Fenton was Colonel Courtenay's confidential servant, whom he had left behind.

'What had he to do with Fenton?' said Ernestine, colouring; 'you knew that I had told him to come and speak to myself this morning.'

'He found that Fenton could give him some information he required.'

Ernestine turned away to hide her burning cheeks. 'The man has made a great mistake,' she said; 'I wished him simply to ascertain where that young woman had gone. You will go, if you please, and call Fenton back, there is no occasion for his interference; and tell the policeman to come to me.'

'He said he would return in the evening, ma'am; but I think I ought to let you know there has been an accident.'

'An accident! What do you mean?'

'That young girl, ma'am, it is no use looking after her any more,—she was found this morning drowned!'

Ernestine started to her feet and stood transfixed; the pallid face of the girl as she had last seen her, with her despairing look fixed on George Courtenay, rose up before her, and a horror beyond words took possession of her as to the manner of her death; but the man had said an accident. Oh! that it might, indeed, be only an accident which had quenched that forlorn life! She clasped her hands tightly together that her agitation might not appear, and said, 'How did it happen?' Is it known how she was drowned—quick—tell me?'

'There is no doubt, ma'am, that she made away with herself. Two men in a fishing-boat saw her throw herself into the water, and they went to her as quick as they could, but before they could get her out she was quite dead.'

Ernestine buried her face in her hands with almost a groan of anguish. The man went on hurriedly, as if there were something which must be said, and the sooner the better.

'The policeman came here, ma'am, to ask you to attend the coroner's inquest on the body; but Fenton told him he could give more information than you could, and he said the coroner would be glad not to have to ask a lady to attend; but the policeman told me to beg you to be so good as not to leave Seamouth till he had seen you, for there was some kind of a paper addressed to Colonel Courtenay found on the body, and they wished to deliver it to you, as the Colonel has sailed. The policeman said he would come when he was off duty to-night.'

'That will do,' said Ernestine in a low voice; 'I will see the man when he comes;' and the servant left the room. Then, when she saw that she was alone, she flung herself upon her knees, and sent as it were her whole soul to heaven in the one imploring cry: 'My God, forgive, forgive him;' but the very words which thus came spontaneously to her lips brought with them a revulsion of feeling. 'Why should I judge him?' she exclaimed, starting to her feet; 'my poor brother, he may be wholly guiltless of this dreadful death; he may have erred through thoughtlessness, or even through compassion for the lost. I have heard of such things; at least I will wait till I know the whole truth.' And unable to endure the restlessness of suspense, and the dull aching at her heart which showed that she strove in vain to deceive herself, she walked to and fro through the miserable hours of that long afternoon, seeking vainly to lose, were it but for a moment, the consciousness of the terrible certainty from which there was no escape, that the unhappy girl she had seen the day before living, breathing, suffering, now lay cold and rigid in the irrevocable silence of that death which to her had been no heaven-sent rest, but a self-wrought crime;

and why—why had she died? This was the fearful question that racked poor Ernestine through that dark troubled day.

At a late hour she was disturbed by the entrance of a waiter with the evening paper, which he laid on the table before her. 'Latest edition, ma'am, just out; thought you might like to see it;' and having lighted the gas he left the room.

Ernestine continued to walk to and fro restlessly, taking no notice of the newspaper, till, as she passed the table, her eye accidentally caught the heading of a column in the 'Latest Intelligence,' 'Inquest on the body of a young woman found drowned this morning.'

She had not thought of this, and a sickening dread as to what she might learn came over her as she seized the paper in her trembling hands and sat down to read it.

The account of the inquest and the depositions of the witnesses were given at length; for such events were much less common in Seamouth than they would have been in London.

First there was the testimony of the two men who had witnessed the suicide. They described how they had been out all night with their nets, and were

THE TRUTH REVEALED.   89

coming slowly homewards as the dawn approached, when suddenly they saw the figure of a woman standing on a rock; one moment only they saw her stand, and then with a cry, whose mournful echo reached them even where they were, they saw her fling herself with one bound into the sea. She sank, then rose for a moment, and sank again. They rowed with all possible speed to the place, which they had carefully noted, and found the water sufficiently shallow to give them a chance of reaching the body with their boat-hook. Nearly half-an-hour elapsed, however, before they succeeded in finding it, and when they were at last enabled to bring her on shore, they were convinced that she must be quite dead. Nevertheless they carried her to the nearest house, a fisherman's cottage, and one of the men went at once for the doctor.

The doctor's evidence was then given very briefly, to the effect that he had endeavoured for upwards of an hour to restore animation, without success, and that he had no doubt the young woman had been dead some time before he saw her. On examining the body, he had found a pocket-book within her dress, which had been placed in the hands of the coroner.

The coroner here stated that the pocket-book contained only a letter addressed to Colonel Courtenay, of the —th Regiment, which he would lay before the jury when the witnesses had been examined.

Policeman X next stated that he had been requested the day before by Miss Courtenay to find out the abode of a girl she had seen on board the 'Hero;' that he had traced the individual in question to a lodging-house which he had reached in the evening, and found from the woman who kept it that she had just gone out. He had followed in the direction she had taken, and he found that the last person who had seen her was an old man, to whom she had given money; and he then lost all trace of her, till hearing in the morning of the suicide, he suspected it might be the same person, and took the lodging-house keeper to see her, who at once identified the body.

This woman now appeared, and said that the girl had been for two days at her house. She had seemed very energetic and animated when she first came, and stated that she was going to India in the 'Hero.' At first she had said she was going with the soldiers' wives, but on returning from the emigrant depôt announced that she had changed her plans. The next day she had been out all morning, the woman did not know where, but after the 'Hero' had sailed she came back so altered that she seemed no longer like the same person. She had sat down in a corner with her face buried in her hands till evening, then she rose, paid what she owed without speaking a word, and went out. The woman never saw her again till the policeman took her to look at her dead body.

An old man then described his meeting with her near the beach; her giving him a purse containing money, and her coming back to ask him to pray God to bless her.

Fenton, Colonel Courtenay's servant, was then called to state what he knew of the deceased. His evidence was given in such a manner as to display the peculiar characteristics of that phase of human nature which develops itself in the fashionable servant of a fashionable man. It was very evident that Mr. Fenton found the public revelation he was called upon to make, a favourable opportunity for paying off his late master for the various occasions in which his selfishness had interfered with his servant's pleasures or vices—the terms being in this case synonymous.

He deposed that he knew the deceased very well. Her name was Lois Brook. She was the daughter of the gate-keeper at Carleton Hall. Colonel Courtenay had seen her there. She was a fine-looking girl then, and he had taken her away with him, as gentlemen will. He kept her three months at Richmond, longer than Fenton had ever known the Colonel keep a girl. By that time he was courting Miss Julia Talbot, his present wife, so he sent Lois Brook to a gay house, and never troubled his head about her again; but the girl was wild about the Colonel, and was fool enough to fancy he would come to see her. Fenton had no doubt, from what he had heard, that she was determined, by hook or by crook, to go to India with him. He had been on board the 'Hero' the day before when she was found in the hold. He heard her begging the Colonel to take her to India with him. The Colonel swore at her, he believed. Anyhow, he settled her somehow; and Fenton would really have been sorry for the girl, if he had not been so used to that sort of thing in Colonel Courtenay's service. He saw the girl taken ashore, and he was not surprised to find that she had made away with herself. The Colonel could make himself very pleasant to those who only saw him occasionally, and Fenton knew he had promised the girl half a hundred times he would never forsake her; and he had often heard her tell him she would die if he did, so she kept her word to him sure enough; but, bless you! the Colonel would not have cared if she had made a hole in the water before his very eyes.

Here Fenton's evidence terminated, and the letter

THE TRUTH REVEALED.

poor Lois wrote in her death agony was handed round by the jury. It was given entire in the paper, and Earnestine read it word for word. Finally the jury consulted, and gave in their verdict, the usual conventionalism,—' That the deceased destroyed herself in a fit of temporary insanity;' a sentence which they recorded with as much pomposity as if it had been a striking novelty. Just as they were about to separate, however, a juror started up, a butcher, as it happened, by trade, but an honest, true-hearted man by right of nature, and demanded that a resolution should be passed, expressive of the jury's extreme disapproval of Colonel Courtenay's conduct to the unfortunate girl. The coroner, a man of higher 'cultivation' than the sensitive butcher, was quite shocked at such an unheard-of proposal. Most unbecoming, most improper. They were not there to try Colonel Courtenay, a gentleman of position and high family; a very distinguished officer, the coroner believed, decorated by her Majesty. Of course gentlemen would indulge their little fancies, but it was highly creditable to Colonel Courtenay that he had dismissed this young woman before his marriage. The coroner had no doubt the gallant gentleman would have amply provided for her, if she had not placed herself out of his reach in this very culpable manner. The coroner trusted he should never again have to comment upon such an improper proposal from a juror.

With this the inquest terminated. Ernestine Courtenay let the paper fall from her grasp, and sat with her hands clasped on her knees, and her eyes wide open, gazing into vacancy, while a sensation of horror and dismay chilled her to the heart. Gradually, as she sat there, an expression of grave determination, such as never before had settled over that fair sweet face, grew dark and rigid upon it. There are moments in this life which come to us with such tremendous power, that they can actually petrify, as it were, the subtle human spirit into one peculiar mould, in which it remains fixed and unchanged for life. Such a moment there was for Ernestine when she learnt the truth of her brother's guilt and his victim's death, and her soul was sealed in that hour with an impress which it would carry with it into eternity.

She had, however, little time for reflection; the policeman was ushered in, and she turned round calm, though deadly pale, to meet him. He brought the pocket-book containing the letter to Colonel Courtenay, and said he was desired by the coroner to place it in her hands. She shivered as she took it, discoloured by the water which had blotted out a human life. The

THE TRUTH REVEALED.

policeman was about to enlarge on the inquest, but she stopped him hastily.

'I have seen the newspaper; I know it all; but I wish to ask you one question, Where is the body?'

'It is still at the fisherman's cottage, ma'am; but it will be removed to the workhouse to-night, and buried to-morrow by the parish authorities. If they had brought in *felo de se*, you know, ma'am, it could not have been—'

'I know, I know,' exclaimed Ernestine, hastily interrupting him; 'but can you tell me if there would be any objection to my undertaking the funeral expenses?'

'Well, ma'am, I should say not, by no means; they would be glad enough to save their pockets, I make no doubt.'

'But in that case could the body be allowed to remain where it is till proper arrangements could be made? I should not like it to be moved.'

'That depends on the fisherman and his wife; if they don't object, no one else would; and if you were to make it worth their while, I should think you might do as you pleased. They seemed poor folk enough.'

'It must be settled now though. I suppose orders were given to remove the body to-night?'

'Yes, the workhouse cart was to be sent for it; but I

can stop that, if you wish me to tell the master of the workhouse that you will bear all expenses.'

'I should be obliged to you to do so.'

'And some one must go to the fisherman,' continued the policeman. 'I should not have time myself.'

'I will settle that, if you will tell me precisely where the cottage is.'

'It is easily found; it is the first cottage you come to on the beach after you leave the town. Hill is the fisherman's name; any one could show it.'

'That will be sufficient.' She dismissed him; and then went to the window and looked out. The twilight was deepening, but it was not yet quite dark, and in another moment Ernestine, with her face veiled, and her cloak wrapped round her, was taking her way in the direction the policeman had indicated.

CHAPTER VI.

THE PROMISE TO THE DEAD.

AND again the long low beach lay dim in the twilight, and the rising wind swept in fitful gusts across it, and all things were as they had been the night before when Lois Brook still held the awful gift of life within her power,—the seed of immortality which she had madly flung upon the barren waste of waters, when even then it might have ripened under the gracious dews of heaven-sent penitence to bear rich fruit in the eternal harvest, and be for ever stored in the garner-house of God.

And now, as then, a woman walked with sorrow-laden steps along the sands; for the horror Ernestine felt for her brother's sin produced an anguish as near akin to remorse as one actually innocent could feel.

A low-roofed cottage, with nets spread out to dry, appeared in the shadows before her, a light twinkling in one window, the other looking black in the white wall. Ernestine knocked softly at the door; a rough-looking woman opened it, and seeing a lady, drew back and asked her to walk in. She entered a little kitchen, scantily furnished, with a few cinders burning on the hearth, over which a man was crouching, spreading out his hands to catch the faint heat. A little girl sat on the ground near him, and two younger children were asleep on a wretched bed spread on the floor. On the table some empty cups and plates revealed that a meal of some sort had taken place, of which not a vestige remained.

The woman wiped a chair with her apron, and asked Ernestine to sit down, with much more civility than might have been expected from her appearance. But amongst our English poor, the one idea which presents itself to their mind when they are brought in contact with a person above them in station, is that of gain, for which purpose they are ready with all possible servility; and this is the case even with those who are not in needy circumstances. It is a disagreeable fact, but a true one; and in this book the truth must be told about the poor, instead of their being represented in ideal colours, as they generally are in novels and religious works of fiction. The fisherman merely looked round and touched an imaginary cap upon his head without speaking. Ernestine sat down, begging the woman to do the same, and then remained for a moment silent, during which time the man and his wife speculated as to the purpose of the lady's visit, and the woman resolved that whatever it might be, she and her children should be the better of it. At last Ernestine spoke—

'It was to your house, was it not, that the body of the poor young girl was brought?'

The woman took her cue at once.

'That it was, and pretty sight of trouble it has cost us all, and not a penny have we had give us to help us through with it. Why, it has put the place all of a muddle. I never was so upset in my life.'

Ernestine looked at her in amazement. Heart-sick as she was herself with the unavailing pity that oppressed her, it seemed to her marvellous that any one should connect the presence of that forlorn corpse with thoughts of self and of petty discomfort.

'Well, ma'am,' said the woman, answering her look, 'just look at them children turned out of their beds and left to sleep on a bit of a quilt, all along of that corpse. I could not get them to sleep in the room with it not nohow. Me and my husband we made shift to stop beside it, for we have not another hole to put ourselves in but they two rooms.'

'I am very sorry you have been inconvenienced,' said

Ernestine, fearing it would be quite in vain to ask them to keep their silent guest.

'Ah, little them crowners and juries cared for our convenience. They crowded into this room, if you'll believe me, ma'am, till there was not a corner left for me to stand in. They just gives a look at the corpse, then off they goes to the public-house to sit upon it comfortable, and never so much as offers us a farthing for our trouble; not but what I told them as me and my husband we works hard for our living, and I've lost a day's work by it, and mayhap two.'

'Then I am afraid,' said Ernestine, 'you could not be induced to let the body remain here another night. I would willingly pay you well,' she added hastily, seeking to anticipate a refusal, which the woman had not the least intention of giving.

'Well, ma'am, I don't know but what I would be willing to do a kind action by the poor thing. It will be a world of trouble, to be sure, but I has a feeling heart, ma'am, and it 'ud hurt me to see her took off by the work'us cart. One of the children's ailing, sure enough, and it is a sin and a shame to keep him out of his own bed, still I'd wish to do as I'd be done by. I'll keep her, if you asks me, only it'll need a good bit of money to make up for all as it costises us one way or another.'

'Will this be sufficient?' said Ernestine, putting into her hand a sum of money, so far beyond what the woman expected, that she at once began to exclaim that she would keep the body in her house three or four nights if the lady wished it; but Ernestine, little as she knew of the poor, could not be blind to the woman's selfishness, and answered quietly that one night was all she asked, the body would be buried next day.

'Did you know this poor wench, ma'am?' said the fisherman, for the first time looking round—the financial department being evidently entirely in the hands of his strong-minded wife.

'I only saw her once,' said Ernestine, her voice trembling, 'but I know her history, and I wish to do what I can for her still.'

'Ah, friend and foe is all alike to her now!' said the man, shaking his head. 'Poor wench! poor wench!'

'My husband 'tended the 'quest to-day, and he's quite upset by it; he's been a-moaning and groaning over the girl ever since; but I tells him he has no call to trouble hisself for such a one as she were.'

'And I say,' said the man, suddenly striking the table with his clenched fist, 'that that 'ere fine gentleman as took her out of her father's house and ruined her, and then broke her heart, and let her go and drownded herself, is as big a scoundrel as walks the earth, and I'd tell him so to his face if I seed him here now.'

Ernestine sat motionless for a moment, and then said, in her low sweet voice,—

'You are quite right, he is most guilty; but are there any on earth so much to be pitied as the wicked? Should we not pray for him, that he may repent of his deadly sin?'

'Pray for him! If ever any rascal were to serve my Katie here as he has served that poor dead corpse, I'd have the life out of him once for all, though I had to swing for it the same day;' and he drew his little daughter to his side with an impassioned violence.

Ernestine hid her face in her hands without speaking.

'Law! John, you frightens the lady with your tantrums; ha' done, I tell you. Would you like to see the corpse, ma'am?' she added, as if offering a soothing palliative.

'Yes,' said Ernestine, rising; 'I do wish to see it, but if you have no objection, I should prefer to go in alone.'

'Just as you please, ma'am; I've no objections, if you are not scared; and she's a very pleasant corpse, I must say that.' She gave Ernestine the rushlight which burned on the table, opened the door of the room, then closed it after her, and George Courtenay's sister stood alone in the presence of his victim.

In one corner of the room stood a bed, in the other, a board placed on two chairs, on which lay the body of Lois Brook. A sheet was spread over it, on which the dim light cast shadows that made it seem to move as Ernestine came near. She could have fancied that the dead corpse writhed beneath its covering when she approached; and in spite of herself, she shook from head to foot as she placed the candle on the table and uncovered the face. Then, as she gazed on it, she ceased to tremble; for when she had last looked upon that countenance it had been terrible from the bitter anguish with which it had been convulsed; and now, wheresoever the soul of Lois Brook might be, at least the stamp of agony had passed from her dead face—cold, white, and rigid it was, but fixed into such stillness as no living heart could ever dream of. Not only were the despairing eyes which had so haunted Ernestine now closed as in gentle sleep, and the mute lips sealed for ever from whence that dreadful shriek had rung, but there had passed over the countenance that peculiar change which is often seen, even in cases where death has taken place at an advanced age, when the features seem to return to the mould in which they were first cast, and grow childlike again, as if the cold hand of death had wiped out all trace of the life they have passed through, and smoothed away the furrows left by this world's care and suffering.

In the present instance, it seemed as if it were actually the face of a child that shone out so white from the dark masses of hair that hung around it; and as Ernestine bent sorrowfully over it, these touching words came vividly to her mind:—

'Weep not for the dead, neither bemoan them, for they are at rest; but weep sore for him that goeth away, for he shall return no more, nor see his native country.'

She knew that, according to the spiritual interpretation of an old writer, he that went away, went from holiness and innocence to serve the world, the flesh, and the devil, never more to return to God, or see in heaven the native land of His elect. Well might the case apply to Lois and George Courtenay. The girl had fearfully erred, but she had been the tempted, not the tempter; and as for the deed that destroyed her life, she might well be supposed to ignore, with the majority of the poor, that it was a crime. For her, at least, it might be that there remained a refuge in the Infinite compassion, which still, through the long vista of centuries, echoes in our ears those tenderest words: 'Neither do I condemn thee.' But for him, the educated gentleman, the clever, clear-sighted man of the day, what excuse could be found in heaven or in earth? The tempter, the betrayer, with deliberate forethought, and now the murderer,—who shall remove the blood-guilt from his head? For a passing self-indulgence he had trampled under foot the innocence, the happiness, the life of one of God's creatures, and steeped in deadly sin a soul that could never cease to live through all eternity; and where could the annals of crime record a blacker deed than this?

Ernestine was aware that in giving this judgment out of the determined truth of her nature, she was reversing the sentence of the world in such matters; but not the less she felt in the depths of her true spiritual instinct that it was thus the comparative guilt in such cases was balanced before the righteous God of all. And she was right. In vain will be all efforts to stem the 'social evil' in this land, so long as this, the most odious of the world's hypocrisies, is allowed to hold the place of justice and equity with regard to it. It is a marvel which can only be accounted for by the power of self-deception, inherent in human nature, that any who profess the principles of truth and honour, much less of religion, should dare truckle to so mean a sham as that which pretends to uphold the interests of morality by trampling under foot the fallen woman, and holding out the right hand of fellowship to the man who dragged her into sin, and shared it with her.

No amount of contumely, of degradation, and of abhorrence, can be too much for the weak, ignorant girl who has listened to the voice of the tempter and believed his lies; but as for the experienced man, with every advantage of position and education, who knowingly, wilfully, has chosen vice for his pleasure, and the ruin of an imperishable soul for his amusement, by all means let him be received by the most immaculate society, and honoured with all such homage as his worldly advantages command. He might be appointed inspector of the public morals, if such a post happened to exist in England; for on him there is no disgrace, no stain. That which, in the feeble and thoughtless, is a crime, to be punished with a severity from which there is no escape but in death, is in the strong and experienced but a natural weakness, bearing round it, in the eyes of younger men, a certain *prestige* of manliness which attracts their imitation. Nor is the world ashamed of its code of morality. No one ever questions the social law which protects the sin in the one case, and hunts it down in the other. The public journals lately gave a notable instance of effrontery in this respect.

At a recent trial, which involved a question as to a young man's moral conduct, his counsel openly announced his belief that there was not a statesman, or a bishop, or a judge on the bench, who had not committed similar 'follies' in his youth; and if there were one, he added, he should think the worse of him for it!

Who cares what dead men's bones fill the whited sepulchre, if only it be garnished with the appliances of wealth and station! Let the pale wasted girl be driven from your door; suffer her not to contaminate with her presence so much as the pavement under your foot; but take my Lord, her betrayer, by the hand, and seat him at your table, heap honours and friendship upon him, and give an indulgent smile to the rumour of his deeds of darkness.

So judges the world in its well-varnished complacency; so does not the Most High God judge in the clear light of His perfect justice.

But Ernestine Courtenay had not come there simply to look on her brother's victim from curiosity. She had come to renew, in presence of that mute witness, the resolution she had taken as she sat for the first few moments motionless, with the record of her brother's guilt lying at her feet. The knowledge of his crime had entered into her soul with an anguish only less bitter to her than the unavailing pity with which she thought of the lost girl, dead by her own hand. Yet for neither of them could she do aught now; both were beyond her reach: the one in his independence, his luxury, his determined freedom of will, to make his whole life black with sin, if he chose it; the other in the stern coldness of that inanimation over which the words 'Too late, too late,' could alone be spoken.

Still there was one way in which it seemed to her she might even yet serve both. She might try to save that other lost one, the guilt of whose ruin lay on both their heads alike. The dying appeal of Lois Brook on behalf of her sister Annie must not fall to the ground unheeded; and Ernestine had learnt in that day's revelation to know her brother too well to hope that he would ever respond to the last prayer of his unhappy victim. The man who could deal with such selfish cruelty by the soul which he himself had ruined, was little likely to give a single moment from his luxurious ease to seek the deliverance of one who was only the victim of his friend.

But Ernestine could feel that in this she was surely appointed to be the representative of her brother. To her had been brought that letter, with its half-obliterated words; and to her heart, heavy with the weight of that dreadful suicide, had come the piteous cry of the dying girl, when, in the last agony of life, she had called upon her Father in heaven, and upon her best beloved on earth, to save her sister Annie. God—how far more merciful than man—had heard the prayer, and sent to the rescue a brave true-hearted messenger, who had resolved that she would never cease her efforts to seek and save that one lost child.

And now, as Ernestine stood and looked upon the marble face which she had seen but once living, and once dead, and which she never more would see till, at the voice of the archangel, she should rise and behold life quivering through those fixed lineaments, and Lois standing by George Courtenay's side, to hear their sentence from the lips of the One All Pure;—as she looked on the cold corpse and thought upon these things, her heart burned within her, and she felt that life itself were cheaply given, and with life all she might have to sacrifice, in the search on which she was about to enter, if only in that tremendous hour she might bring this one soul, rescued from the enemy and the avenger, to the dear feet of Him whose infinite compassion flowed forth in His very heart's blood for the wandering and the lost.

Yes, all that she must sacrifice. Ernestine did not deceive herself; she knew that for a young lady of her rank in life to go out alone into the very haunts of sin to seek one of the fallen and degraded of her own sex, would be considered a very reprehensible departure from the usages of the society in which she had always lived. She must break down the barriers that hedged her in from so much as a knowledge of the existence of the deadly vice, with which she had now to grapple face to face. She must overcome the shrinking horror which she felt for even the slightest contact with this hateful evil. She must lay aside the natural reserve which on such a subject sealed not only her lips, but her inmost thoughts. To do all this would be a sore trial for a pure-minded Englishwoman; and yet, for that very self-sacrifice, she knew she would meet with unmitigated censure from all her acquaintances. She would be told that her conduct was improper, unbecoming in a lady, and incompatible with womanly delicacy. She would hear that it was contamination to breathe the same air with the degraded and the lost; that the scenes she would witness, the words she would hear, would seem to herself so corrupting, that she would feel unable to pass from that atmosphere of vice to the polished society where sin is ignored, and men and women, by common consent, agree to hold each other immaculate. To all this Ernestine had an answer

THE PROMISE TO THE DEAD. 111

ready in her heart from the memory of these words, 'They shall walk with Him in white.' If with Him who passed unscathed and spotless through this world she walked amid the scenes of infamy where undefiled charity might lead her, she knew that she might keep the garments of her soul as white and stainless as the mountain snow; and the presence of the deadliest evils that ever cursed the earth, would be to her as harmless as the hot breath of that fiery furnace in which the three children walked unhurt, because of One who was with them in the fire.

'If they drink any deadly thing, it shall not hurt them.' This promise, made to those who first carried the Gospel of Peace to the people who sat in darkness and the shadow of death, would not fail her who was about to carry the Evangel of Mercy to the fallen, and she would be as safe from harm by touch of evil as they were from the poisoned cup or venomous snake.

'Oh, who could live to seek their own happiness alone!' said Ernestine, as she laid her hand on the cold forehead of the dead girl, 'while sights like these are common on the earth, and each day adds to the wreck of souls that have gone to their destruction, without a hand stretched out to save them! Lois, I go to seek your sister Annie, and I will never rest, or cease to labour with my whole life's strength, if need be, till I have found her, and can hope to yield her up to you, at our next awful meeting, a penitent and pardoned soul; and you, Lois, forgive, forgive my cruel brother.'

She stooped down as she spoke and kissed the cold white face, then reverently covered it, and with a few words of thanks to the fisherman and his wife, went out once more into the dark silent night.

CHAPTER VII.

THE LAST RESTING-PLACE.

THE very first step which Ernestine felt she must take in her self-imposed mission for the rescue of Annie Brook, was one which jarred upon her natural sensitiveness to the utmost degree. She knew of but one means of obtaining immediate information concerning her, and that was through her brother's servant, Fenton. She was aware that he must leave Seamouth next morning, therefore her first act on returning from the fisherman's cottage was to send for this man, whose true character she instinctively understood, in order to speak to him on the very last subject she would ever have wished to mention to him.

Most thoroughly astonished assuredly was Fenton, when, having appeared in the lady's presence, he found himself called upon to state what he knew of Lois Brook's sister. How it came to pass that the refined, gentle Miss Courtenay touched on such a subject, was a mystery to him; but he could not if he would have avoided her calm, grave questions. He told her all he knew; how he had seen Annie Brook, a girl of seventeen, at Colonel Courtenay's villa at Richmond for one day only, and how he had himself helped her into the phaeton when she left it with a friend of the Colonel's.

'Who was this man?' asked Ernestine.

Fenton looked for one moment at the clear eyes that were turned anxiously towards him, and answered shortly, 'Mr. Brown, ma'am.'

'Mr. Brown!' repeated Ernestine thoughtfully. She could not recollect ever having heard George speak of a friend of that name; but he might have many friends she knew nothing about, especially such as were beneath his own rank in society, as she inferred from the name this Brown probably was. It was rather a relief to her to conclude that such was the case. If, in her search for Annie, she were forced, even in the remotest degree, to come in contact with this man, it would at least be a comfort to know she would not risk meeting him again afterwards in her ordinary routine of life.

'Do you know where the girl went to?' she continued, forcing herself to conclude the task of questioning the servant, which became each moment more repugnant to her.

'Not at first,' he replied; 'but I know that afterwards she was at Greyburgh, for the Colonel's girl, Lois, sent a box to her which had been left behind.'

'Do you suppose she is still there?'

'I cannot say, ma'am. I know Mr. Brown is not, for I saw him in London not long since; but it is very likely the girl is. Greyburgh is just the place for such as—'

'That will do,' interrupted Ernestine, in a manner which made Fenton close his lips suddenly and turn to the door. 'Of course you know Mr. Brown's address,' said Ernestine hastily, as he was going out.

'I do not, ma'am,' he answered with sudden energy; 'I have not the least idea where Mr. Brown is to be found.'

'Very well, you can go;' and, as he finally vanished, Ernestine threw herself into a seat and hid her face in her hands.

'It is sickening,' she murmured to herself; 'but oh! if I can but save that one immortal life, what will it all signify! if I can only bring one ransomed soul to plead for George at the bar of judgment, because for his sake she was sought and found. No—nothing I may have to bear shall stop me; I will find her, so help me God, though I have to spend my life in the search.'

Then she proceeded quietly to mature her plans on the information she had received. She was very glad to find that Greyburgh was the place to which in all probability she would have to go in pursuit of Annie; for her brother Reginald was at college there, and she had already been intending to go and see him, as there had been a tone of hopeless despondency in his letters for some time past which had filled her with anxiety. His health had been delicate ever since the severe illness through which she had nursed him, and it was plain that he was far from well, although it was chiefly the evidence of mental pain and unrest which had alarmed her. Ernestine could not help hoping, however, that Annie Brook might be found before she went to Greyburgh. If the man who had stolen her from her God and her home were no longer there, it seemed improbable that she would remain. Surely, in the misery of her desertion, she would fly back to the friends of her childhood, and at once be found under the shelter of her father's roof; but Ernestine little knew what temptations surround such helpless children as the girl she sought to save, and that Matthew Brook's cottage was the last place where she should expect to find her. There she resolved to go first of all, trusting that if she did not actually meet her, she should at least hear where she might be found. Before she took even this step, however, in the task which lay before her, there were certain formidable preliminaries to be gone through.

Ernestine knew, as we have said, that she could not commence a search for one whose very existence would be ignored in the society she frequented, without departing very far from the conventionalities of a well-born lady's ordinary routine of life; and to do so even in the smallest degree would be to commit a heinous offence in the eyes of Lady Beaufort,—the aunt with whom she had lived previous to Colonel Courtenay's return from India. But Ernestine was five-and-twenty, and at that age she did not hold herself bound to her aunt's views, if even five-and-twenty years out of one short life were not enough to have sacrificed to the stereotyped uselessness of a fashionable young lady's career. The tremendous realities of life and death, of sin and of judgment, which had been brought so vividly before her in the last few days, had given form and distinctness to many misgivings on those points which had been vaguely stirring in her mind for some time past. She was anxious, however, to do what she could to conciliate her aunt; and as she knew Lady Beaufort would expect her niece after Colonel Courtenay's departure, she determined to go to her in London for a day or two, and endeavour to allay her virtuous indignation at plans she would consider so eccentric, by assuring her that she meant in all her future wanderings, wherever they might lead her, to be accompanied by her former governess, Mrs. Tompson, whose devoted religion to the proprieties of life might satisfy possibly even the refined worldliness of Lady Beaufort.

Her aunt, however, was not the only person to be consulted, nor the one whose approbation was the most dear to her. Ernestine knew that she had given Hugh Lingard a full right to take cognisance of all her actions, and she was far too true and loyal to the engagement which bound her to him, to wish to take any step without his sanction; but she had not the slightest fear that he would withhold it. Not only did he love her so well, that her lightest fancy was sure to meet with entire and tender indulgence from him, but one of the most striking peculiarities of his character was an unbounded liberality and tolerance for the opinions and feelings of others, however various and contradictory they might be. It was a characteristic which gave a singular charm to this man in all social intercourse; but Ernestine had not as yet thought deeply enough on the mysteries of the hidden and inner human life to perceive from how poisoned a source it sprung.

It had fared with Hugh Lingard as with many thousands of men at the present day, who, like himself, are clever, without being deep thinkers. The misty theological atmosphere of the intellectual society with which his tastes led him to mix, had obscured for him the foundations of the old faith to which in his careless youth he had given a superficial assent; and it suited well with the mental indolence and love of pleasure, which were his greatest failings, to make it his only creed, that it was vain to seek the truth amongst so many conflicting theories and contradictory opinions, and that there was nothing to be done but to make the best of life in its visible aspect, and leave the problem of the grave to be solved by that sure death which had alone the key to it. He thought himself sincere in this negative belief, which left him free to make a god of his own unlicensed will; and he would think and talk with a gentle melancholy of those who rested in surer and brighter hopes, and fancied he envied them. But he deceived himself; for the real obstacle to his seeking and finding—as men of purer souls have done in similar circumstances, the sure ground-work of an intelligent faith—was his distaste to the mental labour of extracting the truth from the mass of sophistries in which his false teachers had submerged it, and a still greater unwillingness to give up the pleasant vices which he felt could not co-exist with a true religion. For deep in his soul, beneath all his shallow reasonings and many-sided doubts, there was an underlying consciousness of that great principle which has its being in the very nature of the Creator, that by the way of personal holiness all men may arrive at a knowledge of God, and of His truth. 'If any man will do His will, he shall know of the doctrine whether it be of God.'

Lingard did not find it very difficult to stifle this conviction, however, which only at rare intervals sent up a flash of unwelcome light into his self-chosen darkness, and he compounded with his conscience by an extensive charity to all forms of belief and error alike, and by indulging the natural kindliness of his disposition, in the relief of suffering so far as he could, whenever it happened to cross his path. He was not one to glorify himself in his want of definite principle, as men of shallower natures are apt to do; on the contrary, he kept his negation of faith, it could hardly be called active unbelief, as much as possible in the back-ground, and the same indolence which rendered him unwilling to probe

THE LAST RESTING-PLACE. 121

the questions modern scepticism had raised, made him ever seek, in his intercourse with others, to ignore the subject of religion altogether.

Ernestine had been won by his generous disposition, his abhorrence of everything mean and petty; his sweet temper and kindly impulses, as well as by the brilliant talents which promised one day to bring him both fame and fortune, and she had taken it for granted that these fair qualities sprung from as pure a creed as that which governed her own existence. She had not then thought so deeply on such matters as circumstances were likely now to make her do, and she was content with that half of his life which was displayed before her; the other half with its deadly vices, its degrading pleasures, its calm selfishness, sacrificing mortal lives and immortal souls at random, for personal gratification, was kept as a spectacle for the eyes of the pure God alone.

Ernestine expected to see Lingard in London, but she felt that she could more easily write than speak on such a subject as that which now engrossed her; and she sat down forthwith to tell him of her future plans. She did not find it very easy to do so, because she could not tell all the circumstances which had led her to her present resolution. Not even to Lingard, her brother's most intimate friend, and her own future husband, could she bear to betray the hidden guilt of George Courtenay, or the fatal result to his helpless victim; but she told Lingard that circumstances of a most painful nature had brought to her knowledge the history of a young girl, who had been allured from her home and her innocence, and now must in all probability be utterly lost, if no friendly hand were stretched out to save her, and further, that one just dead had indirectly, but yet most positively, imposed upon her the mission of seeking out and rescuing this unhappy child from ultimate destruction. She trusted to be able to accomplish her task quickly and easily, without exciting observation; but if it should take the labour of years, and force her to measures that would be thought unbecoming to her station in life, she still must carry it out to the end, though all the world should blame her,—if only he did not withhold his consent, and this she besought him not to do if he valued her peace of mind. There would not be time for him to answer by letter, as she intended to remain only one day more in Seamouth, but she trusted she should see him at her aunt's, soon after her arrival there.

To Lady Beaufort she merely wrote that she was coming to town for one day, and reserved all explanations till they met; and this done she turned her thoughts to the arrangements for Lois Brook's funeral, which was to take place the next day. Ernestine was resolved to be present at it herself. It was but a barren act of kindness to show to one who had had reason to curse the name she bore; but she could not let her be thrust into her dishonoured grave without a human being to stand by in sorrow for the young life quenched in such fatal darkness; and since by George Courtenay's deed, no kindred of her own could show her that last charity. Ernestine, as his representative, would do all that might yet be done to prove that the guilty suicide had once been loved and honoured. The man to whom she intrusted the arrangements for the burial, told her that it could not take place till the evening of the next day; and it was settled that she was to meet the funeral at the churchyard, where it was to be privately brought from the fisherman's cottage, in order to avoid the crowd who were very likely to assemble, under the circumstances, if the hour of interment were known. A long and dreary night followed for poor Ernestine, and a still more dreary day, till in the lingering twilight of a soft spring evening, she made her way to the last resting-place of Lois Brook.

The precautions taken had been quite effectual, and the churchyard was deserted when Ernestine reached it, by all but the sexton, who, having finished his task, was now lazily tolling the bell at long intervals, bent on getting his accustomed fee, even on an occasion so much beneath his notice as the present. There was no other living being among the countless dead, lying all around in their mysterious sleep, excepting two little children, who were playing on the brink of the open grave, with the falling leaves which the night breeze scattered round them.

Ernestine sat down in the shade of a tree to wait the coming of her who should go forth from those walls no more till the death-day of the world itself arrived.

Strange thoughts went surging through her heart as she sat there, thoughts that had never visited her in her existence of calm refinement heretofore. She thought how this young life over which she mourned, this soul, the dread of whose eternal loss burned into her heart with agony, was, after all, but *one*, one of the many thousands who in like manner met with wrong, and ruin, and everlasting perdition at the hands of their fellow-men, hunted down to the grave, and thence to hell, by those who shared their nature and their capacity for suffering and for joy; and then she thought of the no less countless numbers who sat by in careless ease, and watched this game of life and death as the Romans of old looked on while the gladiators tore each other limb by limb; who, if they did not of deliberate purpose deal guilt or misery on those who crossed their path, yet lifted not a hand to save them from more brutal natures, and indirectly preyed on many by following out their one purpose of personal gratification, heedless how far it were attained at the expense of others. She thought how each of these many thousands had but one life given them for a prey in the midst of this evil and suffering world, one life with all its capacity to bless, to curse, or superciliously to ignore the fellow-creatures, like themselves rushing down the steep of time to the unchangeable eternity.

Surely if they but looked on the awful mass of sin and anguish seething round them, the one life given them to use or waste would seem all too little to spend in lessening, in ever so small a degree, that mountain of evil, still rising higher and higher to fill up the measure of iniquity against the day of vengeance. Would the cry of accusation against those who might have saved and did not, be less piercing or less powerful than that which would denounce the very ministers of sin? Yet how in truth was that one precious life disposed of by the majority of those who deemed themselves righteous, because not actively malevolent in their sphere of influence?

Ernestine lifted her eyes to where the little children played by the open grave; their merry laughter mingling with the deep tolling of the funeral-bell; and it seemed to her that in them she saw the type of those who toyed with life and its passing pleasures on the brink of open graves,—the graves not of mortal ashes but of living souls, buried by cruel hands in a spiritual corruption, from which there may be no resurrection in all eternity; and who could tell but that, unheard by human ears, though echoing mournfully in the courts of heaven, the air was even now full of knells rung out by sorrowing angels for the perishing creatures of the most high God, whose happier children answered the funeral tones with sounds of careless mirth?

Ernestine felt the weight of her own past years of thoughtless ease lie heavy at her heart as she pondered on these things, and she turned with a sense of relief to the thought that she was now about to do her best to rescue one at least of that vast multitude, whose everlasting ruin would be charged on their fellow-men. It was to be with Ernestine, as with all who in any way are roused to definite action with reference solely to the unseen life; the one earnest purpose, the positive recognition of eternal results from temporal deeds, the true unselfish care for an immortal soul was to develop in her own mind truths but dimly apprehended before, to deepen all that was great and noble in her character, and rouse latent powers within her, which would lead her to such a height of self-devoted love to God and man, as would have made her shrink and tremble now, could she have seen the full revelation of all that was before her.

But the future was hid, and the present only was there, and that present the darkest moment of her life; for at the churchyard-gate the corpse of her brother's victim was entering slowly, slowly—coming to lie down in the grave his hands had surely dug for her.

The curate, summoned from an adjacent house by the sexton, came hurrying up, fastening his surplice with one hand, while he opened his book with the other. He turned and preceded the coffin, reading the opening sentences of the Burial Office. The men who bore it followed with careless haste, stumbling over the graves, and jostling their poor helpless burden as they walked. The sexton stood waiting, idly kicking stones into the grave. The little children laughed and shouted as the spectacle for which they had been looking, at last drew near; but not all the indifference or irreverence of the human beings round could destroy the wondrous beauty of the glorious hope, that age after age has blessed the world, in these words, 'I AM THE RESURRECTION AND THE LIFE,'—words that bind the dying race of man with chains of love to the very Throne of God. They fell on Ernestine's heart that night like fragrant dew on parched and thirsty ground. Yet not without tremor could she hear them; for she knew that to George and to Lois He who spoke them would indeed be the Resurrection, but to which—to either—would He be the Life?

As the coffin was laid by the side of the grave, Ernestine saw that there was one follower at that sad funeral. She could not call him a mourner; for he looked much more as if he would fain have been the avenger; dealing justice on him who had brought the dead to this early doom. It was the fisherman, who stood doggedly at the foot of the grave through the whole service; his hat slouched over his eyes and his hands clenched. As the sexton flung the earth on the coffin, while the curate gabbled over the solemn formula, 'Dust to dust, ashes to ashes,' the fisherman suddenly flung out his hand towards the corpse, and exclaimed, with stern vehemence, 'And may he who wronged and

THE LAST RESTING-PLACE.

murdered an innocent girl soon lie rotting in the dust himself.' Ernestine half shrieked, and joined her hands in a voiceless prayer that the curse might be averted; the curate frowned; the sexton angrily ordered him to leave the place, and not interrupt the service; and the fisherman quietly obeyed. But as he turned to go, he pointed to heaven, and said, 'My words 'll come true: the Lord does not sleep when men act like devils.'

The last prayers were said; the curate having, to his no small astonishment, recognised a lady in the solitary mourner at a fallen woman's funeral, bowed to her as he turned away. The undertaker's men gathered up their goods and hurried out of the churchyard. The sexton carelessly shovelled in the earth over the coffin, stamped it down with his feet, and having received from Ernestine a gratuity which made him heartily wish such peculiar funerals took place every day, he hastened home to his supper, driving the little children before him. So finished the closing scene on earth. For the last act of the tragedy we must wait till the curtain rises on the one tremendous spectacle, which every soul that ever lived shall witness.

Life had been very bright to Ernestine Courtenay hitherto; for it had been full of the sweetest joy this world can give, in the love of him most dear to her on earth. But on this night the weight of its mere responsibility lay upon her heart like lead, as she turned back to the living world, where in every human soul that struggle was still going on, which had terminated in such tremendous loss for the buried corpse at her feet. One last act of duty Ernestine performed before she left. She was anxious that the position of the grave should be recognisable at any future time; for she could not help hoping that a day might come when George Courtenay, sorrow-stricken for the sins of his youth, might learn at that tomb how heavy an accusation was written against him in its mouldering ashes, and make restitution at least in penitence,—since tears of blood, if wept for endless ages, could never give back to the dead the innocence—the life he had destroyed. Ernestine gave orders, therefore, that a simple stone cross should be placed at the head of the grave, with only these words marked on it,—

L. B.

Veniam supplicat.

No expression of hope, no holy words from the Book of God dared she write over the grave of the suicide; but surely she spoke an awful truth when she said that the ever-living soul, whether hopeful or despairing, implored forgiveness!

CHAPTER VIII.

THE OPINION OF THE WORLD.

'ERNESTINE, this is too much!' said Lady Beaufort, her lips quivering with indignation, as she flung down the last new book and turned to face her niece. 'A certain amount of eccentricity is rather *piquant* than otherwise in these days; it is, at all events, safe, as you are already *fiancée;* but the line you are striking out is perfectly unheard of. Anything which trenches on the *convenances* of society is quite out of the question; you are much mistaken if you think it will succeed.'

'Do you mean as regards pleasing the world in general?' said Ernestine, looking up with an amused smile.

'Of course I do,' replied Lady Beaufort.

'But that did not enter into my calculations at all,' said Ernestine; 'I had no intention of taking up any particular line, I assure you. I have but one purpose, which is to save, if I can, this poor lost child.'

'Lost child! what absurd sentimentality, to talk in

that way. Society would give a very different name to your extraordinary *protégée*.'

'It does not much matter what name they would give her,' said Ernestine wearily; 'she is too surely a perishing soul.'

'A soul, indeed! much she cares whether she has a soul or not; and if she has, pray what have you to do with it? I cannot imagine how you ever heard of such a creature.'

'If you knew how I did hear of her, aunt, I am sure you would excuse my determination to do what I can for her.'

'I can never excuse your lowering yourself to a pursuit which might perhaps be fitting for the matron of a gaol. The daughter of General and Lady Mary Courtenay scouring the country in search of a—! Really, Ernestine, you ought not to force me even to name such a being.'

'Then don't let us speak of her any more,' said Ernestine.

'Do I understand, then, that you give up this preposterous scheme?'

'I cannot; indeed I cannot; you do not know by what a heavy responsibility I am bound to it,' said Ernestine pleadingly. Lady Beaufort started impatiently from her seat, but at this moment the door opened and

Hugh Lingard entered the room. She turned to him with an expression of relief.

'I was on the point of sending for you, Mr. Lingard, to see if your greater influence would bring Ernestine to reason. I have failed to shake her obstinacy, but you may succeed better. She tells me she has written her intention to you; a singular communication certainly for a lady to make to a gentleman,' added Lady Beaufort, with a vindictive side glance at her niece, which made poor Ernestine grow crimson to the temples; 'but since she has not shrunk from introducing the subject, pray do your best to induce her to abstain from shocking her friends and degrading herself in such an extraordinary manner.' And having successfully fired this last shot, the lady gracefully sailed from the room and disappeared. The first result of her parting speech was that Ernestine, having impulsively held out her hands to Lingard, hid her face on his arm as he sat down beside her, and burst into tears.

'What, Ernie, darling,' he said, 'has a trial at single combat with Lady Beaufort proved too much for you? Well, I am not surprised; I should decline the encounter myself.'

'It was a combination of painful feelings overcame me for a moment; but I am very glad you came in, Hugh.'

'So am I; only you must not wish me away again, if I tell you that I think Lady Beaufort has reason on her side notwithstanding. This Quixotic scheme is really not a fitting thing for you, Ernestine; I came fully resolved to tell you so.'

Ernestine started up, and dashed the tears from her eyes. 'Oh, Hugh, don't say so,' she exclaimed, her grasp tightening on his hand with convulsive energy; 'you can never know how much is bound up for me in this matter, or what a terrible necessity is laid upon me to rescue this girl. She must be saved—she must!'

'Let her be saved, by all means, if she desires it, which is probably doubtful,' said Lingard; 'but why should you have anything to do with such an one as she is? Send a policeman after her, or a grim old matron out of a Refuge; only don't you mix yourself up with an affair of this kind.'

'Hugh,' said Ernestine, lifting her clear earnest eyes to his face, 'it is I who have been commissioned to do it; commissioned by one now lying cold in her grave; destroyed by her own hand, because none ever sought to save her, as she bids me save this child. I will tell you this much, and I know you will not ask me more: He through whose means destruction and misery has come upon the girl I seek, is very near and dear to me.

He can do nothing now to check the results of his evil deeds spreading far and wide, where he little dreamt they would extend; and on me it has fallen, by a solemn retribution, to represent him in the effort to make what little atonement may yet be possible, for all the ruin and wretchedness he has caused.' Her voice became choked with sobs as the cold white face of the drowned girl seemed to pass before her; and she remembered how, in the very death-agony, Lois's one prayer had been, that George Courtenay would save her sister. Struggling to retain composure, she went on: 'I think, perhaps, you imagine I am going to act in a much more unusual manner than I really am. I will tell you just what I mean to do: I am going into the country to see the girl's father first, and if I do not find her with him, which is possible, I have reason to think she may be at Greyburgh. Now, you know I had been intending to go there to see Reginald at all events; so there will be nothing strange in my doing so, although, when there, I shall do my very utmost to find this unhappy child.'

When Ernestine had said this much, Lingard imagined that he understood the whole story. One 'near and dear to her' could only, he felt sure, be one of her brothers. Reginald was at Greyburgh, and it was there

she was going to look for the girl, therefore there was
no question that it was to him she alluded. Lingard
knew that he was very ill, and that he was of a sensitive, gentle disposition, so that it was very likely some
sudden remorse had seized him, which was reacting
upon his equally sensitive sister. The suicide of which
she spoke was no doubt that of some companion of
Reginald's *protégée* which had deepened the impression
on both their minds. It seemed all very clear to him,
and having settled the facts to his own satisfaction, he
proceeded to deal with them after the fashion of the
society which was his world.

'Ernestine,' he said, ' I can quite understand how all
this appears to you; but your ideas are far too high-
flown and ecstatic for this practical world. Such cases
are more common than you think, and no one but yourself would imagine that the circumstances laid any responsibility on you. If every one, whose friends were
implicated in an affair of this kind considered it their
duty to act as you propose, there would be occupation
of a curious description for very many persons as little
suited to it as you are. There is a substratum of this
sort of thing underlying society everywhere, and it is
only because this case has chanced to crop up to the
surface that you give it such undue importance. You

must consider, my darling, that this girl is, in the first place, probably quite satisfied with her mode of life, and unwilling to leave it; and that even if she were not, she is but one of many thousands in exactly the same position. You are not going to carry a crusade through the whole of them, and why should you compromise yourself for one only, out of a tribe better ignored altogether?'

'One only,' said Ernestine, a light as from a purer world shining in her eyes as she spoke; 'but that one an immortal soul that never in all the eternal ages can cease to live, and living to suffer, if in the whole world there is not enough of compassion found to save her from a doom of such unimagined horror; one only, but that one so unspeakably precious in the sight of the God who made her for Himself, that we know His beloved Son would have come down from heaven to die in His awful agony for her alone, had she only of all the human race been perishing and sinful. You speak of thousands like her. Is it not enough to crush one's very soul with horror to think of what they are in the sight of the Righteous Heaven, and shall be, too probably, for ever? And the thought that it is their own fellow-creatures who have thus blasted their souls with eternal ruin, makes one wonder that God should still withhold the fire which one day must justly burn to ashes a world so cruel and so polluted. And can you think, Hugh, that apart from the judgment which will fall on the active agents in the ruin of the thousands of whom you speak, there will be no account demanded of their blood from those who were passive instruments in their destruction, who might have helped, who might have saved them, and *would not?*—on such as I am, who ought to be ready to give my whole life to win all and any I could? Am I to abstain from rescuing one, one actually given into my hand, because some painful humiliation, some bitter censure, may come to wound my vanity, from those who make this world's approval the idol of their worship? Oh, what will all that world be to me when I am lying cold and stiff in the grave, whence there is no return! How more than worthless in that time of silent waiting will be its praise or blame, —the praise or blame of those who will be dust and ashes like myself. But will not the doom of that one lost soul be everything to me,—the soul that will meet me at the bar of judgment, and cry out against me, " You might have saved me, and you did not; therefore you are my condemnation, you my sentence, you my everlasting despair?"'

Ernestine paused, her whole frame trembling with

strong feeling; then she went on with a quiet sadness, which was very touching—

'Hugh, I am to be your wife, and I will not now do anything which you could afterwards regret your wife had done. If you absolutely require me to give up the effort to save this most unhappy child, I will do so; and I will not vex you with any expressions of regret when the matter is once settled; but just now, while it is still an open question, while her fate still hangs in the balance, I cannot keep back from you, that I do so strongly feel the obligation laid upon me in her behalf, that if I now abandon her, I shall bring a lasting grief and remorse upon myself, which not all the happiness I look for in my life with you, will have power to banish. I shall never be able to forget her going down to the grave and to her terrible eternity, without one voice to warn her, one hand stretched out to save her from uttermost destruction. Hugh, you may think me absurd and romantic if you will, but I know too surely that at the very altar by your side I shall seem to hear the cry of that perishing soul. I shall ever hear it in all the bright days we hope to spend together, and oh, most of all, I shall hear it on my bed of death, when my own life is finished, written down to the last line, and sealed up against the great account, with but one record of her in all its pages, " I knew that she was perishing, and I left her to perish when I might have saved her." '

As Ernestine finished speaking, and bent down her head waiting for his decision, Lingard suddenly started up and went to the window, where he stood for a few minutes silent, struggling with thoughts that were altogether unaccountable to himself. That Ernestine, so good, so innocent—faultless, indeed, in his eyes,—should thus accuse herself of heavy guilt, and expect a life-long remorse because she believed herself a passive agent in the wide-spread evil, wherein he held the most active instrumentality to be but a trifling folly not worth remembering or regretting,—had aroused a tumult in his mind which he could neither comprehend nor resist. For one moment it was as though some lightning flash had revealed a glimpse of the dazzling purity, the awful, uncompromising holiness of that Fount and Essence of all goodness, in which he did not, and even in that hour would not, believe,—while in the same light the true nature of sin in its foul blackness darkened visibly on his sight. For a brief space his soul was in the grasp of truth, and cowered down well-nigh overwhelmed; but the impression was transient. Soon a rush of habitual thoughts and feelings swarmed on his mind; again the shadows closed over the transient gleam; the ground which for a moment had appeared steady beneath his feet seemed once more to rock to and fro on its insecure foundation, and his mind drifted helplessly back into its wonted chaos of doubts, misgivings, and sophistries, mingled with evil desires and dim aspirations. He was himself again very speedily; but when he turned to come back to Ernestine there was an unusually grave and gentle expression on his face; and the half playful, half bitter sarcasm with which he had treated the matter at first had quite disappeared.

'Ernestine, I will thwart you no more,' he said softly; 'do what good you can in your generation and in your own way, you shall never be hindered by me. What am I that I should stand between your pity and any poor wretch, however degraded she may be?' and as Ernestine thanked him, with a warmth of gratitude which showed how greatly she was relieved, he bent down to catch every tone of her low sweet voice, seeming to thirst for the assurance that he was thus indirectly associated with her in her loving charity.

'There is one condition, Ernie, dearest, which I must make with you for your own sake,' he continued, after a moment's silence, 'and that is, that you keep me to a certain extent *au courant* of your proceedings in this matter; it is very possible that you may find yourself in some position where you will really require help and advice; and I shall not be easy about you unless I have the certainty that you will always at least tell me where you are.'

'I will, gladly,' said Ernestine; 'it will be a great comfort to me; and you know, Hugh,' she added laughingly, 'I am to have Mrs. Tompson with me. Don't you think there is some chance of the *convenances* being attended to pretty well?'

'I should think so, indeed. What agonies she will be in as to what the railway porters and cabmen may think of your proceedings, Ernie! She certainly carries her deference to the world's opinion to the utmost limits of civilisation.'

'Her whole life consists of a representation of her own and her friends' greatness to the vulgar humanity outside,' said Ernestine; 'but happily she is much too timid and nervous to think of opposing me, so I shall get my own way, Hugh, all the same.'

'And so you ought, my dearest, considering what you are; but Ernestine,' he added, with a playfulness which veiled a real earnestness, 'don't go and become too good for me; I am very far from your level now, and I don't wish to find the distance widened between us. I have a horrible dread that I shall see wings growing out on your shoulders some day, and that you will soar away above me, Heaven knows where.'

'Oh, no fear,' said Ernestine, laughing merrily. 'I think, on the contrary, when I am out in the world on my adventures, I shall always be longing to rush back and hide in a corner beside you; and that is just what I shall do when my quest is over, if only I am successful.'

'Well, now, I want to tell you that I expect to be ready for you sooner than we thought,' said Lingard; and he proceeded to explain to her that his prospects of a more lucrative appointment than that he now held were much nearer their fulfilment than he had supposed, and that he believed their marriage might take place before many months were over.

CHAPTER IX.

THE SEARCH AT CARLETON HALL.

THE next afternoon saw Ernestine Courtenay in a railway carriage speeding away to the pretty village near which Annie Brook's father lived, as lodge-keeper to Lord Carleton. Opposite to her sat Mrs. Tompson, a lady with drab-coloured hair, pinched features, and a thin figure, attired in good taste, but with the most minute attention to the prevailing fashion on all points; there was not a fold out of place in her silk dress or a wrinkle in her irreproachable kid gloves, yet she looked as if made of inferior clay beside her quiet charge, who in her simple garments and unobtrusive demeanour was singularly attractive even to strangers, from the touching sweetness of expression which gave such a charm to her delicate features and soft brown eyes. Ernestine would have valued this gift of winning insensibly on all who saw her, had she known how useful it would prove to her in her future career, but she was too unconscious of self to be aware

THE SEARCH AT CARLETON HALL.

of it, and only wondered how it was that even strangers were so kind to her wherever she went. The twilight was stealing over the earth when they reached their destination, and Mrs. Tompson experienced the first of many shocks she was destined to receive in her attendance on Ernestine, when she found her quite resolved to pass the night at the village inn, in spite of the fact that below the really pleasant rooms assigned to them, there was a very undisguised tap.

'My dear,' said Mrs. Tompson, clasping the well-gloved hands, 'this is quite unheard-of, and most unnecessary. You are acquainted with Lord and Lady Carleton, and their house is, of course, the only suitable abode for you in this place; you have only to write a note to Lady Carleton, saying you are accidentally passing through the neighbourhood, and would have much pleasure in spending a day or two with her, and you will find her delighted to receive you.'

'But I am not passing accidentally, and it would not give me any pleasure at all to spend a day with her,' said Ernestine; 'so you see I must not say that; and besides, I could not possibly stay at their house under the circumstances. Now, let me beg you to order tea, and make yourself quite comfortable, and I shall soon come back to you.' And before Mrs. Tompson had time to prepare another speech, Ernestine had closed the door behind her, and soon she was to be seen from the window walking lightly down the village street. Mrs. Tompson did not attempt to follow. She knew perfectly well that Miss Courtenay would not be deterred from doing what she thought right; and a secret instinct seemed to tell her also that her actions were regulated by a somewhat higher code than her own. So she proceeded to establish what she was pleased to term her 'weak frame' on the horse-hair sofa; and in a painful combat between the angularities of the 'frame' and those of the sofa, she found enough to occupy her till Ernestine's return.

Meanwhile Ernestine Courtenay was walking quickly along the pleasant country road which led to Carleton Hall. She had no difficulty in finding her way, according to the directions given to her, and soon came in sight of the pretty rustic lodge, with its trim garden, where the gatekeeper lived. It stood almost in a nest of bright spring flowers, the walls covered with trailing plants; in front of it lay the park, where the deer were browsing quietly; behind it rose noble trees and luxuriant shrubberies, glowing with the beautiful but evanescent hues of the opening year, and over all was the tender light of the sunset sky, where the evening star shone

THE SEARCH AT CARLETON HALL. 147

pure and pale in its ethereal solitude. Ernestine leant against the gate for a few moments, looking round on the sweet peaceful scene; and she thought sadly how, but a few years before, Lois and Annie had dwelt there as innocent children, and how they played in their careless glee upon that fair green grass, and slept the sleep of guileless hearts beneath that cottage roof; but now!— by her brother's evil deeds the one was laid in the dust of death, and the other buried in a corruption worse than that of the grave. The mournful recollection nerved her to proceed with her task, which she felt was, even in this first step, very difficult.

Matthew Brook must be aware of Lois's fate by this time, as she had been told that the coroner had written to him with full particulars. He knew now, therefore, even if he had not known it before, that Colonel Courtenay was the cause of her death; and Ernestine felt that she could not venture to cross Brook's threshold if there was any chance of her being known as that man's sister; but this did not seem likely; while, on the other hand, she feared he might resent an entire stranger speaking to him of the disgrace of his children. Ernestine had been very little amongst the poor, or she would have known that there was small chance of their having such refined and sensitive feelings as she would have had in a matter of this kind. There was enough, however, to make the visit really formidable to one of her sympathetic nature, and her courage would almost have failed her had she not thoroughly counted the cost when she undertook her mission, and prepared herself for many a painful moment in the course of it.

She went up to the door and knocked gently. It was opened by a woman, with a child in her arms and another clinging to her skirts. She had a pleasant, but somewhat expressionless face, with a worn, fatigued look, as if she had found the cares of matrimony rather too oppressive.

'Can I speak to Matthew Brook?' said Ernestine, addressing her.

'Surely, ma'am,' said the woman, curtseying as she recognised 'one of the gentlefolk' in her visitor; 'he is just a-sitting down to his supper; please to walk in;' and she ushered her into a neat tidy cottage, where, at a little round table, placed before a blazing fire, her husband sat with a plate of bread and cheese beside him, and two or three children clustering round him. He rose as Ernestine entered, and turned towards her a hard weather-beaten face, with strongly marked features, and considerable sternness of expression; but he bowed respectfully, and begged her to sit down. His wife, who seemed at least twenty years younger than he was, brought forward a chair, told the children to mind their manners and stand out of the way, and in another moment Ernestine found herself placed in front of Lois Brook's father, who sat silently waiting for her to speak.

'I must ask you to excuse my intruding upon you,' said Ernestine, with the gentle courtesy which is too often considered an unnecessary luxury for the poor, even in their own houses, 'but I have come on a very painful errand.'

Brook looked up keenly at her.

'You have heard, doubtless,' she went on to say, her voice trembling, 'of the sad death of your child, your daughter Lois?'

The man's face darkened like a thunder-cloud. 'I have heard of the death of Lois Brook,' he answered, 'but she is no child of mine. From the day that she crossed that door-step to go to her disgrace, I have counted her a stranger to me, and so she is now when her shame has been made public. She is no child of mine.'

'Oh, surely still your child!' said Ernestine. 'She has done very wrong, and she has suffered cruelly for it, but she is what God made her—your own child?'

'No,' he said, striking his clenched fist on the table beside him, 'I won't have her called so! She was told what she had to expect if she ever disgraced herself, and she knew I would never go back from my word. I gave my children a good home, and brought them up respectable. I taught them their duty, and took them to church, and stinted myself that they might have the best of schooling, and they knew that so long as they did well they'd share every bit I'd got; but I told them, ay, and swore it to them, times on times, that so surely as they took to evil ways, and brought disgrace on themselves and me, they'd have to tramp for it, and they might seek a home and a father where they pleased, for they'd find none in my house never no more. So I said then, and so I says now to these children here,' he added, stretching out his hand towards two pretty little fair-haired girls, 'the same as I said it to them as is gone, and I'll keep my word to one and the whole of them, they may depend on it.'

'You have just reason to be angry,' said Ernestine 'but the fault was not all Lois's. She was deceived and cruelly deserted; the treatment she met with drove her to her dreadful death.'

'No doubt,' said Brook grimly, 'and the fine gentleman as ruined her will have to pay for it in kingdom come, if all is true as the parsons tell us. But that is no excuse for Lois. I taught her her place, and she knew she had no business to go looking after any grand gentleman, or to let him come swaggering here to play with an honest girl's good name when her father's back was turned. I told her what stuff such as he were made of, and what fine sport it is to them to take a decent man's daughter and make her only fit, as they think, to be trampled under their feet, and then flung away to die in a ditch. Yes, yes, I know, and I warned Lois of them; what she did, she did with her eyes open, and she must e'en abide by it.'

'She must indeed,' said Ernestine; 'for we can neither help the dead, nor speak forgiveness to them, however sorely they may need it. But I only mentioned Lois, because I wished to tell you what her last desire and prayer in this world were.'

'I beg your pardon, ma'am,' said Brook's wife; 'but were you with the poor wench when she died?'

'O no,' said Ernestine sadly; 'God alone saw her last agony.'

'Stupid! how could she be,' said Brook angrily, 'when you know the girl went and drownded herself in the night,'—and Ernestine could see that there was strong agitation working under his apparent harshness.

'But if I guesses right, ma'am,' he continued, turning to Ernestine, 'you are the lady that put her in the ground, and saved her a work'us funeral?'

'Yes,' said Ernestine; 'it was the only thing I could do for her, and I was very pleased to do it.'

'And I thank you for it, I will say that; bad as Lois has behaved to me, I am glad that she who was once known as my daughter was not buried like a work'us tramp. I do thank you for that, ma'am; and I am bound to listen to anything you may have to say, though what's the good of talking or thinking of such a black business, I can't tell, I'm sure,' and he writhed uneasily from side to side as he spoke.

'But it is of the living, not the dead, I have come to speak to you now,' said Ernestine. 'Lois left a letter, which fell into my hands, in which she made the most earnest entreaty that her sister Annie might be sought for and saved from such a fate as hers had been.'

Brook started at the name, and clenched his fist violently.

'Annie!' he thundered. 'She is as dead to me as the other is, and more so, for the grave where Lois lies can tell no tales, but while Annie lives, her shame

THE SEARCH AT CARLETON HALL.

would fall back on me if I still owned her for my child. I would not so much as hear her name from any but yourself, ma'am, and it is not a bit of good your talking of her; better not, far better not.' There was an appealing look under all the fierce anger of his eyes, as he turned them on Ernestine, which convinced her that this child had a firmer hold on his heart than ever Lois had, and that the struggle with his own feelings obliged him to take refuge in greater violence.

'Just let me tell you what I have to say, and I will trouble you no more,' said Ernestine gently. 'I resolved, when I read the heart-breaking letter poor Lois wrote on behalf of her sister, that I would never rest till I had fulfilled her last dying wish, and rescued Annie from a life of sin, and a death of misery. I gave her my promise that I would do so, as I held her cold hand in mine, and I will keep my word, though it was given to a silent corpse. Let it cost me what it may, I will never cease my efforts for your poor lost child till I have brought her back, if I can, to her Father in heaven, with whom is all mercy and forgiveness. It is for this purpose I have come to you. I thought I might have found her here, or that you might know where she is.'

'Here!' exclaimed Brook. 'She shall never enter this

house till I am carried out of it feet foremost. I know nothing of her, nor I don't want to.'

'O do not say so,' exclaimed Ernestine. 'If only I can find her and bring her back to penitence, where should she come but to her father's house? and indeed, from all I have heard, I feel sure she was far less to blame than Lois was: she quite believed her sister was married, when she went to her, and had no idea of the evils and temptations that awaited her.'

'Then she believed Lois's false words more than my true ones,' said Brook. 'I told her plain enough what Lois was, and she knew I had disowned her, and would serve her the same if she followed in her sister's steps. She knew this well, and she left my house unbeknown to me and without my leave, and went to her worthless sister; and now as she has made her bed, so she may lie on it.'

'I do not mean to excuse her,' said Ernestine; 'but she was young and unsuspicious, and her sister, whom she loved so much, persuaded her to come. At all events, whatever may have been her fault in the past, don't say you will refuse to take her in, if I can bring her back to you repentant.'

'But I do say it, and I will,' he replied, smiting the table fiercely. 'Find her if you can, and do your best with her. It is good of you to trouble yourself for such a one as she is, and I won't say but what I am thankful to you for it, but never let me hear her name, or see her with the sight of my eyes inside of this house. She shall not come while I am alive to bar the door against her.'

'Your own child!' said Ernestine. 'Will you not show mercy, as you hope for it yourself? What would become of any one of us if our Father in heaven so took vengeance on our sins?'

'I have other children to consider besides her,' said Brook doggedly.

'But they are so young they could not suffer any harm from intercourse with her.'

'They are not too young to suffer the loss of their home and their livelihood, and that is what it would come to if I brought a fallen woman into this house, be she twenty times my daughter.'

'How is that possible?' exclaimed Ernestine. 'Who could have the right to prevent you doing as you like in your own house, and with your own child?'

'Those to whom the house belongs, and whose money buys my children's bread,' said Brook. 'I must do what pleases my Lord and my Lady, or leave the house and the money to another lodge-keeper. There's many a one would be glad to step into my shoes—ay, and many a one watches to see me make a false move, that they may get into them.'

'But Lord and Lady Carleton would never object to your receiving your daughter, if she were really penitent, and came to your house only to seek a shelter from sin and temptation.'

'Would they not? Did they not send and tell me when Lois went, and again when Annie left, that if ever one or the other of them was seen within the park-gates I should be turned out without a day's notice? Did not Mrs. Brace, the housekeeper, in her silks and satins, bring me the message herself, and sit there as proud as a peacock, tossing her head and speaking of my girls as if she would not touch them with a pair of tongs, let alone my Lady? And I'd like you to tell me, ma'am,' continued Brook, turning round and putting his elbows on the table, while he looked full at Ernestine with a strangely sinister expression,—' I'd like you just to tell me how it is, that among you gentlefolks what is thought a shameful sin in a poor girl is neither a sin nor yet a shame in a fine gentleman? At the very time Mrs. Brace brought me my Lord's and my Lady's message, Colonel Courtenay, the grand swaggering Colonel that ruined my pretty Lois, was staying at the Hall courting my Lady's niece, Miss Julia Talbot; and who so civil to him as my Lord, and who so pleased to see him as my Lady? And they knew just as well as I did that my child's ruin lay at his door, and that his sin was the same as hers, to say the least of it,—for I take it his was something the blackest of the two,—anyhow, the one was as bad as the other; but she was not to dare to show her face within her father's door, at the risk of bringing us all to the work'us, while he was to ride with my Lady in her carriage, and sit with my Lord at his table, and have the whole house at his beck and call like master and more.' Brook paused a moment, still looking fixedly at Ernestine, and then said, ' Ma'am, our parson tells us that God Almighty knows all things: I should just like to know whether He knows these things, and if He does, what HE thinks of them?'

Ernestine bent down her head, unable for the moment to make him any answer, so keenly did the truth of his words strike home to her sense of right. She had felt her brother's guilt heavily enough, as her present conduct testified, and the general injustice of the world in the matter had struck her, as she stood by Lois's dead body; but the whole dreadful subject was of course entirely new to her, and it was the first time that her eyes had been opened to the practical working of the conventional law which visits sins of this description without mercy on the woman, the weaker sinner, while it leaves honoured and unscathed the man who has destroyed her. Ernestine shuddered as she thought how these things would appear when weighed in the balance of immaculate justice, but she had too much conscientious courage to gloss over the truth now, even to the hard man before her. She looked up at him with her candid eyes, and said, ' It is a most cruel injustice; but you may be sure it is one which is hateful in the sight of the righteous God, and for which He will surely require us to give account in our final trial. I still think, however, that Lady Carleton would not refuse to let you give your daughter Annie a shelter, if she were really penitent; now especially, when poor Lois can claim no more pity from either her or you. At all events I will see her to-morrow and try to gain her consent, provided you will promise me that if she does agree, you will not persist in your refusal to give the poor child a home.'

' It is of no use to ask her, ma'am; you may save yourself the trouble.'

' Still I may succeed; only say that if I do, and if I can bring Annie back to you, you will receive her.'

' Well, if you would take her by the hand, so that folk should not think she was altogether lost, I won't say but what I might,' said Brook; 'but there—it is no use thinking of it. I know well enough what your answer will be at the Hall.'

'Still I have your promise,' said Ernestine, rising, 'and I thank you sincerely for it, as indeed for your patience in listening to all I had to say. One question more I must ask: can you give me any idea where Annie is now?'

'None at all; I know nothing of her,' said Brook, relapsing into his sullen manner.

'Then she has never written to any of you?' asked Ernestine.

'She knew better than to do that,' said Brook. 'She'd have had her letter back just as she sent it. No, the last I can tell you of her is this: she stood there the night afore she left us, as pretty and innocent a little maid as ever you'd wish to see. She stood there looking at me, and I could see tears in her eyes, and I thought she were fretting because I had spoken a bit sharp to her for loitering about the gate; but I little thought she was giving just these few tears to the father and the home she would never see again.'

'Oh, don't say never!' exclaimed Ernestine. 'I must hope she may yet return to be a comfort to you, and all the more dutiful, because she has once fallen so far. If I succeed with Lady Carleton, I will come and tell you; if you do not see me, you will know I have failed.'

'I shall not see you,' said Brook determinedly.

'In that case I must do the best I can for Annie without your help; but I hope better things from Lady Carleton.'

Ernestine then took her leave, bending so tenderly over the children as she bade them farewell, that both Brook and his wife seemed touched. He took off his hat as he opened the gate for her, with a degree of genuine respect, which was very different from the conventional civility he usually showed to visitors at the Hall. Ernestine had gone some way down the road, when she heard a rapid step behind her, and turning she saw Brook's wife hastening after her. She came up breathless.

'I beg your pardon, ma'am, but I think this may help you to find our Annie,' she said, holding out a water-colour portrait of a young girl. 'A lady who was staying at the Hall once, thought her so pretty that she made this likeness of her, and her father can't a-bear to see it, so I hid it away, and never thought of it till you was gone.'

'Oh, thank you,' said Ernestine, taking it; 'it will help me very much indeed. Is it really like her?'

'It is just her very self,' said Mrs. Brook, 'only it was the lady dressed her up with flowers that way; her father would never have let her wear them so,' and taking leave once more, the woman went back to her cottage.

Ernestine stood looking at the drawing in the fast failing light; it was skilfully executed, and represented a girl not more than sixteen, with a sweet childish face, lovely in its look of happiness. Large eyes, of that limpid blue we see only in the early morning sky, sunny hair falling in bright waves from under a wreath of lilies of the valley, and lips parted in a smile of playful archness, combined to represent the very type of light-hearted innocence, and of girlish beauty undimmed by blight or shadow. As Ernestine gazed sadly on it, she felt her very soul rise up in indignation against the man who, in his selfish wickedness, had for ever marred this fair creation of the God of goodness, and darkened all that guileless loveliness with the ineffaceable stains of guilt and shame. That face, so bright with the sunshine of a soul unawakened yet to sorrow or to evil, was indeed blotted out from the very universe; since the best she could now hope for was to see one day those clear blue eyes looking sorrowfully out through penitential tears, and those smiling lips quivering with anguish, as they confessed the sin, repented bitterly, but never to be undone. It seemed to her a very marvel, that even the world's code of justice should impose on society so cruel a wrong as that which Brook's words had brought home so forcibly to her mind. If there were to be any distinction in the sin, the punishment, and the degradation of Annie Brook and her betrayer, surely the heaviest burden should fall on the mature man of the world, and not on the frail ignorant child, who knew neither trial nor temptation till he lured her from the shelter of her father's roof.

CHAPTER X.

LADY CARLETON'S DECISION.

IT was with ineffable satisfaction that Mrs. Tompson heard next morning of Ernestine's intention to visit Lady Carleton, although assured that she did not intend to spend more than an hour at the Hall. This was sufficient to enable the anxious chaperon to mention the fact before the innkeeper, in such terms as should convince that functionary that Miss Courtenay's proper abode had been in the aristocratic mansion, and not in his own ignominious dwelling.

'So distressing to reflect on what he must have thought of us!' she said to Ernestine.

'Who?—the innkeeper?' Ernestine answered, laughing, 'I cannot say I have reflected about him at all; but now I shall go at once to Lady Carleton, as I am anxious we should start for Greyburgh in time to reach it to-night. I have not heard from Reginald this morning as I expected, and I begin to fear he is seriously ill.'

Ernestine found Lady Carleton at home, and to her

great relief there was no one with her but her sister, Miss Verney, a lady *d'un certain âge*, who was reported, according to the phraseology of her set, to have become 'serious,' since the fatal lapse of years had caused her matrimonial ambition to descend from the marquises and earls of her earlier hopes, to the rectors and widowers, who were now, so far as she was concerned, the only game in season.

Lady Carleton received Ernestine with the utmost cordiality. Their previous acquaintance had been slight, but Colonel Courtenay had been very intimate at the Hall, where he had first met his wife; and it would have been music to Mrs. Tompson's ears to have heard Lady Carleton's pressing invitation to Ernestine to stay and spend a few days with them.

'Thank you very much,' said Ernestine, 'but I have only an hour to spare. I must hasten on to Greyburgh to see my brother Reginald, who is ill. My object in coming here to-day was to ask you a great favour,' she added, looking up into the calm expressionless face that was turned towards her.

'I trust I may be able to do anything you wish,' said Lady Carleton.

'I am afraid the subject is one which may be disagreeable to you,' said Ernestine, colouring painfully,

LADY CARLETON'S DECISION. 165

'but my request may really involve the whole future welfare of a very unhappy person.'

'Going to ask for a subscription,' thought Miss Verney; 'she need not come to me, while the dear Vicar of Dulton's new aisle is unfinished.'

'I have heard,' Ernestine went on, 'through some very painful circumstances, of a young girl named Annie Brook, the daughter of one of your lodge-keepers, and it is on her behalf I have come to speak to you.'

Lady Carleton's face grew rigid. 'My dear Miss Courtenay, you cannot be in the least aware what sort of a person this individual is, or you would certainly not wish to mention her to me or to any one.'

'I know too well what she is,' replied Ernestine; 'and it is because the strongest efforts are about to be made to rescue her out of her dreadful life, that I come with a request to you. If these efforts should succeed,' she went on hurriedly, 'if she should become truly repentant, and only anxious to hide from those who have known her otherwise, will you allow her father to give her a shelter in his house again? He is quite willing to take her, if you do not object.'

'If Brook leaves my service, he will naturally do as he pleases. I shall have no control over him. Of course, you do not propose a person of bad character venturing within a lodge on our property?' said Lady Carleton, with the utmost stiffness.

'Only if she were altogether penitent and changed, wishing nothing but to live a humble, unnoticed life. Brook cannot give up his situation without bringing his other children to want and misery; so that if he received her at all, it must be here; and it would seem too cruel to refuse her the shelter of her father's roof, if she were seeking to fly from a life and a future so dreadful as hers is now.'

'Are you aware, Miss Courtenay, that Brook's lodge is actually within our own gates, inside the park, and that my sister and I and our guests sometimes take shelter there from a shower of rain?'

'But you need hold no intercourse with this poor child,' said Ernestine eagerly; 'and, after all, how many there are whom we meet in society, at least among men, whom we have far more reason to shun than a miserable girl who has been the victim of such as they are.'

It was with something more than coldness that Lady Carleton answered now: 'Miss Courtenay, I am really totally unaccustomed to discussions on subjects of this nature.'

'Had I not better leave the room?' interrupted Miss Verney, rising with an air of injured innocence.

'Pray do nothing of the kind, Lorina,' said Lady Carleton hastily; 'Miss Courtenay will not, I am sure, continue so very unpleasant a conversation. I do not know from what theories you may draw your ideas,' she added, addressing Ernestine, 'but mine are those which have been always received in society, and I can in no way depart from them; allow me to decline pursuing the subject further.'

There was nothing more to be said, and after a few constrained speeches on indifferent subjects, Ernestine rose to go.

The cold politeness with which the ladies who had received her so cordially now took leave of her, was the first indication of the truth which was to meet her at every turn, that she could not unscathed run counter to the opinion of the world, however false and godless that opinion might be. Ernestine was not indifferent to the painful knowledge thus acquired. No one, especially no woman, can brave the censure of the class to which she belongs, without being made to feel it keenly; nor does the righteousness of the cause which has made her depart from received opinion, prevent her from growing daily more sensitive to the blame she has provoked. She may be, as Ernestine was, too unselfish to forsake the truth and the right, because her defence of it brings the world's contumely on her head; but the harsh judgment that will assail her, the unworthy motives that will be attributed to her, the misconceptions and exaggerations which her every action will call forth, must gradually make her shrink more and more into herself, till she finds herself happiest in the isolation to which she has involuntarily exiled herself. As yet Ernestine anticipated nothing of this, nor of far deeper pangs which her present course was one day to cost her; and she tried to shake off the feeling of humiliation and wounded pride which her interview with Lady Carleton had left on her mind. The sight of Brook's lodge was efficacious at once in chasing away all thoughts of self. As she drew near it she could see that he was standing, hidden, as he thought, by the muslin curtain of the lattice-window, watching her eagerly as she came down the avenue. She felt he was waiting to see if her errand had been successful, and if he might take home the lost child towards whom his indifference had been so much more assumed than real. She knew well she had not a hope to offer him, and she passed his door with her head bowed sadly down, and her heart aching with that strong sense of the injustice of men's dealings one with another which strikes us sometimes with such painful acuteness.

Mrs. Brook came out to open the gate for her, and looked inquiringly in her face,—

'I suppose the poor wench is not to come home, ma'am?'

'I am very sorry I have failed to get leave for her; but will you tell your husband that if only I can find her, I will take care that she finds a shelter in some safe home, where I hope he will come and see her?'

'God bless you, ma'am. I am right glad Annie has found a friend in you; she is no child of mine, but she were as sweet a little maid as ever you see, and I can't help fretting over her when I mind her merry ways, and how she used to go singing about the house like a bird. There was never a bit of harm in her, ma'am. She were a thought too frolicsome, perhaps; but she was light of heart, poor dear.'

'I will tell her how kindly you speak of her, if I can find her,' said Ernestine, pressing the woman's hand as she turned away to go forward in her search.

CHAPTER XI.

GREYBURGH.

ERNESTINE COURTENAY had never seen Greyburgh before, and she now saw it under the circumstances most favourable both to its beauty of outward aspect, and to the teeming associations which gave life and charm to every step within its walls. Its beautiful gardens, its fair meadows, and shady walks, were in all the glory of their fresh spring loveliness; the stately trees that arched over its finest avenue, till it looked like the nave of a glorious cathedral, or dipped their branches in the graceful winding river, were all bright with the luxuriant green that had renewed their youth; and the sparkling waters, covered with gay boats, that went shooting to and fro with their merry crews, glanced along under blossoming shrubberies and violet-covered banks. Side by side with this living nature, this freshness of youth and beauty, rose up in sombre stateliness the dark old colleges, like petrifactions of the thoughts and hopes and aspirations of the long-buried dead,—the glittering sunlight serving only to bring out in stronger relief the deep shadows cast by their massive proportions.

A more striking representation of past and present could scarcely have been imagined. The smiling gardens and sunny river-side were teeming, not with the life of nature only, but with the young life of the present generation in all the promise of early manhood; while, within the solemn colleges, beneath the chapel altars and the sombre corridors, the dead of ages past, the strength and sinews of the nation once, lay mouldering in their forgotten graves. And with this contrast,—the sure knowledge that all the life and brightness of the one must soon dissolve into the gloom and silence of the other, would have been strangely mournful, had it not been that there was a revelation of the future also in the clear blue sky, with its infinite depths of fathomless ether, that arched over living and dead alike, and spoke of an eternity for both.

It was in the radiance of the early morning that Ernestine thus saw Greyburgh for the first time, as she took her way to the college to which Reginald belonged. They had reached the hotel too late the night before to visit him then, but Ernestine had written to tell him of her arrival, and to ask when she could see him, either at the hotel where she was staying, or in his rooms, and the tone of his answer heightened her anxiety on his account. He wrote thus :—

'DEAREST ERNIE,—I am very sorry you have come here, and yet I shall be only too delighted to see you. You must come to me,—I cannot leave my rooms. Since you are here, do not delay letting me have you with me a moment longer than you can help. I shall expect to see you as soon as the college gates are open to-morrow morning.—R. C.'

This was all, and Ernestine was greatly perplexed by it. She knew it was no want of affection for herself which made him regret her coming, and she waited with anxiety for the moment when she should be able to ascertain the meaning of the strange state of mind in which he seemed to be. She was at the gate of the college, one of the oldest in Greyburgh, at the hour he had named, and, as she turned into the deep shadows of the quadrangle, with its dark walls and time-worn statues, she felt as if she had stepped from the living world into the realms of the past. Having mastered, by the help of a passing servant, the meaning of the cabalistic direction given her by the porter as to the position of Mr. Courtenay's rooms—'two five to the right'—she made her way up the steep stone staircase to his door.

'Mr. Courtenay sports oak most days,' said the servant, hastening up before her; 'but I can get in, and I will tell him you are here, ma'am.' In another moment he returned, flung open the door, and closed it again upon Ernestine, as she entered a sitting-room, arranged after the fashion of most undergraduates' rooms, though with abundant indication, in the books and papers which strewed the tables, and in the engravings on the walls, that Reginald Courtenay was not one of the fast men of his college. The room was empty, but a half-open door led into another, and Ernestine went in at once. On the threshold, however, she stopped, startled to the last degree at the sight which presented itself. The room was small, like most college bedrooms, and contained little besides the bed and a table covered with books, where a lamp, which Reginald had apparently forgotten to extinguish, still burned with a sickly flame, scarce visible in the bright sunshine that filled the room. Reginald himself sat in a low easy-chair at the open window, gazing out into the clear sky, which alone was visible from it. He did not hear his sister's light step, and she had time to scan the familiar face, so changed, that she scarcely recognised it, before he turned. It was nearly a year since she had seen him. In the previous long vacation he had gone with a reading-party to Wales, and had, much to her regret, avoided, on some slight pretext, coming to London to see her before returning to Greyburgh in October. When they last met, he had been delicate-looking, as he always was; but the indications of weakness of the chest, which had often alarmed her about him, had been less apparent than formerly. In the interval, he had never said a word about failing health, and had indeed written rarely and briefly, although his letters, short as they were, had betrayed a *malaise,* either mental or bodily, which had caused her a vague uneasiness. And now, as she looked at him, the conviction came upon her, sudden and irresistible, that he was not only dangerously ill, but that he had scarce a few days to live. The shock of this overwhelming impression was so great that she stood transfixed to the spot, scanning in dismay the wasted features, with their unmistakable symptoms of decaying life, and the attenuated figure, lying motionless in the languor of utter weakness. He was but one-and-twenty, and had been remarkable for the refined beauty of his face. It was now white and sharp of outline as if cut in marble, and all that remained to him of life seemed gathered in his dark eyes, which looked, from his extreme emaciation, unnaturally large, and were glowing with a restless feverish light, that spoke of intense unrest. The heavy masses of his dark hair, damp with the dews of weakness, were pushed back from his hollow temples, as if their weight were too much for him. His parched lips were perfectly colourless, and the thin transparent hands, hanging listlessly down, seemed moulded in wax. He was fully dressed, but the clothes hung loosely on his wasted limbs, and there was a hopeless decay written on every line of the sinking, feeble frame.

An involuntary sob broke from Ernestine, and Reginald turned his eyes upon her. In another instant she was at his side, his dry feverish hands in hers, and her warm kiss pressed on his cold white cheek.

'Reginald, dearest, surely you are fearfully ill?'

'Sick unto death, dear Ernie,' he answered, in a weak, hollow voice. His breath came quick and fast.

'Oh, why did you not tell me?' she said, bowing her face on his hands in an agony of grief.

'Because I did not want to cause you needless pain. Ernie, don't cry,' he continued, breathing hurriedly; 'I cannot bear it; my load is heavy enough already. I have had to look my wretchedness in the face night and day, and it has been as much as I can endure; if

I have to see your misery too, it will drive me distracted.'

He spoke with a feverish excitement, which was evidently too much for him, and Ernestine felt it was absolutely necessary she should control herself. She rose from his side and went into the other room, where she bathed her tearful face in cold water, struggled determinately to regain composure, and, coming back to him with a smile, she took a chair quietly, and sat down beside him.

'There,' she said, 'you shall see no more weakness, Reggie. I am going to be your nurse, and you know a nurse has no business to be hysterical.'

He smiled faintly, as he stroked the soft hair from her face with his wasted hand.

'That is right,' he said. 'I want to see your face calm and sweet as I remember it, when I was ill before. It used often to make me think of a clear, quiet lake reflecting the light of heaven. How the sight of you soothed and refreshed me then, and how I have longed for you since!'

'But then, why not send for me, darling?' said Ernestine. 'Could you suppose it possible that it would not be far more pain to me to know that you had been ill and suffering without me, than to be with you, and try my best to help you?'

'Yes, because at a distance you would only have known that I was dead—dead of rapid consumption,—and you would have grieved for me, I know, but there would have been no sting in your grief; and now, I fear—I fear,' he continued, clasping his hands painfully, 'you will learn all that makes death terrible in my case. I am too weak to control myself; I know that I shall tell you all in some moment of agony. I have cried out to these bare walls sometimes, when the horror of my fate was strong upon me.'

'I hope indeed you will tell me all,' said Ernestine, flinging her arms round him; 'whatever you have to suffer, it must be best that I should share it with you.'

'Ernestine, you do not know what you are saying,' said Reginald, with a vehemence which brought on a fit of coughing. When it was over he leant back exhausted. After a few minutes, he said feebly, 'Ernie, promise me you will never question me. If I am driven to confide in you by my own misery, you must bear the evil; but in the meantime I want to find comfort, if it be possible, in your presence. I don't want to be always struggling with you. Promise to ask me nothing.'

'I will promise, dearest,' said Ernestine soothingly. 'I have but one wish, and that is to be a comfort to you, if I can, and it shall be in the way that suits you best.'

He looked up to her with a grateful smile. 'Let us talk of something else, then,' he said.

'Well, tell me who is your doctor,' said Ernestine.

'Dr. Compton, the best physician, and one of the most scientific men in the University. So I have all the help that skill can give me, but he has owned long ago that he can do nothing except to give a passing relief. He will be here presently, and you can see him. I have a nurse too, whom he sent me; the best old woman in the world. You must not send her away, Ernie; she has quite devoted herself to me, and she does everything for me which I am too weak to do for myself.'

'I am glad you have got her, but I do not think she ought to have let you get up to-day; I am sure you should have been in bed.'

'My dear Ernie, I have not been in bed all night!'

'Not been in bed!'

'No; it is one of the things I cannot do,' he said, with a shudder; 'it is like lying down in my coffin; it will be soon enough when the time comes; doctor and nurse have both given up trying to make me do it. I asked Dr. Compton if he could logically prove it would signify one atom to myself, or to anything in the universe, if I died a week sooner in consequence of keeping out of bed, and he could not. Besides, he knows that the horrors which overtake me when I lie down are more injurious to me than the fatigue of sitting up.'

Ernestine was silent from mingled astonishment and distress.

'It seems to me very strange, Reginald,' she said at last, 'that the college authorities did not let some of us know how ill you were. Whether you wished it or not, they certainly ought to have done so.'

'And so they would, if I had not prevented them by a *ruse*, which you would no doubt have thought very wrong. A few falsehoods did it. I told them you and Lady Beaufort were on the Continent, and that I did not know your address, but that I told you myself how ill I was, and you would come as soon as you could. George I represented as being perpetually on his voyage from India,—a pretty little string of lies, was it not?'

Reginald telling falsehoods! Ernestine was utterly amazed. Not only had he been from childhood singularly truthful and honourable, but he had since his illness, a few years before, become deeply religious,—his strong impressions in that respect being very remarkable in so young a man, while the excessive sensitiveness of his conscience had reached a pitch that was almost morbid. He had fully intended to take holy orders and many a dream of missionary enterprise, of high devotedness and self-denial, had he told to Ernestine, in the days when they had been together. She had already noted that not a word of faith or resignation had passed his lips in speaking of his precarious state; and each moment convinced her more and more that some fearful change had passed over his spirit which was unaccountable to her. They were interrupted by the arrival of the doctor. He came in, a tall fair-haired man, with an intellectual face, and the unmistakable air of a gentleman.

'I am very glad you are come, Miss Courtenay,' he said, as Reginald introduced him to her; 'your brother will tell you it has not been my fault that some of his relations have not been here long ago.'

Ernestine went into the other room to wait till his examination of Reginald was over, and when he joined her there, and closed the door, she looked up at him with tears in her eyes: 'Dr. Compton, I cannot tell you how shocked and surprised I am at the condition in which I find my brother. I had no idea he was even seriously ill, and I come to find him dying: it is so, is it not?' she added, with a wistful look, in which a faint hope yet lingered.

'I fear so, indeed; it would be no kindness to conceal

it. He cannot last many days. He never told his friends of his condition, then?'

'Never. His letters gave me the impression that he was out of health, or low-spirited, but there was not a word to indicate serious illness.'

'I feared as much.'

'Dr. Compton, what can have brought him to this pass?' said Ernestine anxiously. 'He was always subject to delicacy of the chest, but such a sudden decline, such total prostration, seems to prove that his malady must have been aggravated by some unusual circumstances. He is in a very unhappy state of mind, I can see plainly, though I do not know the cause of it. Do you think that mental disquiet can have increased his illness?'

'No doubt it has,' said Dr. Compton; 'I have seen it with pain, but I could do nothing to prevent it.'

'But what can have caused it?' said Ernestine. 'I can see that his ideas, and even his principles, are completely changed, and his peace of mind is altogether overthrown. What can be the reason of it?'

A smile, half sad, half amused, passed over Dr. Compton's face.

'His is not the only unsettled mind in the university, Miss Courtenay; but you know that is not my province;

I only deal with physical difficulties. Mental disturbance has not, however, been the only evil influence in your brother's malady. He lived too fast last term; a strong man could hardly have stood the life he led, far less a youth so delicate as he was.'

'Do you mean that he was dissipated?' said Ernestine, unable in her painful surprise to find a word less crude to express her meaning.

'I fear so,' said the doctor gravely; 'your brother is young, and Greyburgh is a place of great temptation; but the whole circumstances of his case have been very sad, and much to be regretted.'

This put the finishing-stroke to Ernestine's astonishment and dismay. Of course, she had not lived so many years in the world without knowing that of many young men such a report would have been nothing surprising; but that Reginald, only one year before so high-souled, so pure-minded, so full of noble desires and holy aspirations, should have fallen into the low dissipation of coarse animal natures, was indeed an overwhelming astonishment to her.

She was roused by Dr. Compton's voice. 'Here is Nurse Berry,' he said; 'she has been very attentive to your brother; I should advise your leaving him with her for a few hours. I have given him a composing-draught, and I trust he will sleep. He never shut his eyes last night, and the duration of his life now mainly depends on the amount of rest he can get.'

A tidy motherly-looking woman came curtseying forward as the doctor left the room. She had a pleasant face, with kind, soft eyes, which took Ernestine's fancy at once. She held out her hand to her, as she said warmly—

'Thank you for your kindness to my poor brother, nurse; he is terribly ill, is he not?'

'As ill as he can be, ma'am,' said the nurse, tears filling her eyes, 'and nothing to comfort him no way. My heart has ached for him many a time. I am very glad you are come to him, ma'am.'

'If I had only known he was ill, I should have been here long ago, but there is no help for that now. I must do the best I can for him while he is left to me. The doctor says I must leave him to sleep for the present, but I will come back in a very few hours.'

'The evenings are his worst time, ma'am; if you would come to him then it would be best; he mostly dozes through the day, but his evenings and nights are awful; it is a wonder to me he has not been worn out long before; and so I think he would have been if it were not for the heavy sleeping-draughts the doctor gives him; they keep him quiet, in the afternoons at least.'

'I shall come early in the evening, and stay all night with him. I do not like leaving him now, but I must, as the doctor wishes it.'

She went back to Reginald's room. He was lying quiet, with his eyes closed, but slowly raised the heavy lids as she drew near. She bent down and kissed him.

'Dr. Compton tells me I must leave you to sleep for a few hours, darling. I cannot bear to be away from you, but I am coming in the evening to stay all night.'

'Yes, I shall sleep now,' said Reginald, 'and sleep is the one only blessing this life can give me; but come back, Ernie, come at night, it is then I shall need you. Save me from myself if you can.'

'My Reggie, I would save you from every shadow of evil if I could,' said Ernestine, struggling with her tears. He opened his lips as if to reply, then a spasm of mental pain contracted his features; he gave an impatient sigh, turned his face to the wall, and closed his eyes. Ernestine slowly left the room, and the nurse, closing the shutters, sat down for her patient watch, which she enlivened by knitting in the dark with marvellous speed.

CHAPTER XII.

DR. GRANBY.

IT would have been easy for Ernestine to have spent the remainder of that day in bitter lamentations over her brother's untimely fate, and in wearying herself with speculations as to the cause of his evident distress of mind; but she saw that her attendance on him would leave her little time for the search which had been her chief object in coming to Greyburgh, and that she must each day make use of the few hours when she would not be with Reginald for that purpose, or she would have little chance of success, so far as the lost girl was concerned. Indeed, if anything had been required to make her more earnest in her purpose, it would have been the sight of her brother's young life fleeting away so swiftly into the unknown deep of eternity. Of late she felt the mysteries of death and the unseen had been crowding strangely round her. What if that other soul which had seemed committed to her hands were even now, like Reginald's, trembling on the brink of its eternal destiny? Surely there is no time in this swift, sudden life, with its startling changes and its terrific power over that which is to come, to sit down and idly weep for the dying or the dead. In the future of the dead is the true existence. There are the countless generations gathered of all that ever breathed, living one and all to God, whether for weal or woe! and those yet abiding in the flesh on earth are but as a handful to that mighty multitude, like the gleaning-grapes left upon the vines when the vintage is over, like the autumn leaves lingering on the boughs when the summer wealth has passed away. Soon the rushing wings of time shall sweep them on to join their fellows in the unchangeable and everlasting state. What does aught signify for them, save the seal wherewith their brief probation shall stamp them for that enduring being,— whether reflecting the image of Christ, till the radiance of the Morning Star has been caught in the dim waters of their soul, they pass into the unimagined glory of His presence; or blackening into the likeness of a nature fallen below humanity, they go out to the desolation of that darkness which is exile from Him? This alone is matter of import to any who yet breathe the atmosphere of earth; and is it then a time to waste the hours in mourning for those whose little day has hastened to its close a few short moments, as it were, swifter than the rest ? Oh! to stay the ultimate perishing of souls ! to prevent the eternal death, the irremediable destruction,—surely this is the only worthy end, the only momentous object, to which time and thought, and life and energy should be given, while we walk our brief course to the grave !

So at least thought Ernestine Courtenay, as, resisting the impulse to relieve her heavy heart with unavailing tears, she roused herself at once to action on behalf of Annie Brook. The first step to be taken in so wide a search cost her no little thought; finally, she decided on applying to the only person she knew at Greyburgh who would be likely to assist her. One of the largest parishes in the town was under the care of a certain Dr. Granby, who, with his wife, had some time previously spent a few days at a country house where Ernestine was visiting. There had been a large party assembled, Hugh Lingard amongst others, and various of Ernestine's intimate friends, so that she had but a dim recollection of the rector of St. Gregory's and his wife, whom she had never met before. She remembered, however, that they had been exceedingly marked in their attentions to her, and had warmly invited her to visit them if she ever came to Greyburgh; and she thought it very possible, that Dr. Granby might be able amongst the poor of his own large parish to find some clue to the lost girl she was seeking.

Having left Mrs. Tompson lionizing Greyburgh in the manner she thought most aristocratic, by assuring the guide that the colleges were poor indeed compared to the buildings she had seen abroad. Ernestine therefore started off to enlist Dr. Granby in her service. She passed through the whole extent of St. Gregory's parish, and found that he did not live anywhere near it, but in a villa some little distance from the town. Entering through an iron gate, with two ambitious-looking griffins perched in painful attitudes on the side-posts, she passed up a gravel walk to the house, in front of which was a well-kept lawn. Here two young ladies were engaged in playing croquet, dressed in the most improved costume for that amusement, with impertinent little hats perched on a mass of hair, dresses looped up over full-blown crinolines, like sails reefed for a gale of wind, and high-heeled boots, which were not alone visible under their very short petticoats. A weak-looking curate and a vivacious undergraduate shared in their game, and Ernestine passed into the well-furnished drawing-room, preceded by a footman in livery, where

Mrs. Granby, rustling in the stiffest of silks, rose to receive her. A foreboding took possession of her that this was not an abode where lost or wandering outcasts were likely to be known.

Mrs. Granby received her with the greatest *empressement*, and had very soon informed herself anxiously of the health of every one of Ernestine's relations whose name had a place in the Peerage. Ernestine inquired for Dr. Granby.

'He is well, and will be so delighted to see you,' and Mrs. Granby, ringing the bell, desired that Dr. Granby and the young ladies might be told of Miss Courtenay's visit. Ernestine would thankfully have dispensed with the young ladies, who forthwith arrived through the window, accompanied by the mild curate and the fast undergraduate. More slowly, it may even be said majestically, the rector approached, a large, heavy man, conveying irresistibly the impression of a lifetime of excellent dinners, with a smooth face, a shining bald head, a good-tempered expression, and an elaborately courteous manner. He was profuse in his delight at seeing Miss Courtenay, and the list of titled relations was gone over again; then the conversation turned on the news of the day, with an occasional question from the Misses Granby on the prospects of the London season, and Ernestine saw that her only hope was to ask the polite rector for a private interview when he went with her to the door. Making her visit very short, therefore, she soon found herself passing through the hall with Dr. Granby.

'Can I speak to you for a moment alone, Dr. Granby?' she said hastily, as she saw the footman proceeding to open the door. 'I want to ask your help in a matter of some difficulty to me.'

'Undoubtedly, my dear Miss Courtenay, I shall be most happy if I can be of any assistance to you. Allow me'—and, opening the door of a luxuriously-furnished study, he ushered her in, placed a seat for her, and sat down himself in a huge easy-chair, which seemed to enshrine his portly form with the most sympathetic softness. Taking out his white cambric pocket-handkerchief, as if in readiness for any emotion that might arise, he bent forward in an attitude of polite attention, his bald head shining in the sunlight, and his gold-rimmed spectacles beaming with a mild effulgence as he turned them inquiringly on his visitor. Ernestine felt as if she could more easily have faced a colonel of dragoons than this bland ecclesiastic, who looked, in his irreproachable costume and perfect *bien-être*, as if he could never have even heard of such a thing as misery or sin;

but there was no help for it, so with a sort of desperation she plunged into her subject.

'Dr. Granby, I came to Greyburgh chiefly to try and find a poor young girl, in whom I am much interested, and I do not at all know where to look for her. I have thought that amongst the poor of your large parish you might be able to find some clue to her.'

'It would depend on any circumstance having brought her under my notice,' said the rector. 'Do you suppose she might be one of the pupil-teachers at the school, or amongst the young persons preparing for a confirmation to be held in this church—I mean, in my church—on the twenty-sixth of next month, by the Lord Bishop of the diocese?'

'O no!' said Ernestine, colouring painfully; 'she is not good, not respectable. She was taken from her father's house by a man—I believe he calls himself a gentleman—who has left her, I fear, to utter ruin.' The rector of St. Gregory's drew in his lips in a manner which caused him to give an involuntary whistle, while the gold-rimmed spectacles rapidly mounted up his round forehead, in consequence of the elevation of his eyebrows.

'My dear Miss Courtenay, if you are quite aware of the style of person you have described, you cannot possibly suppose I could know her. Of course, I have intercourse with none but respectable characters.'

'But you seek out the lost and erring among your people to try and reclaim them, do you not?' said Ernestine, raising her clear eyes to his face.

'Ahem! within proper limits, certainly; wherever there appears any reasonable hope of my ministrations being successful, and where there is no risk of my sacred person—I mean, my sacred office—being treated with irreverence; but disreputable creatures such as the individual you mention may be said to be sunk beneath the level of reclaimable humanity. It would be most incongruous that I should seek them out, or permit of their approaching me.'

'But I do not believe this case to be beyond hope,' said Ernestine eagerly; 'at least there is the possibility of trying what can be done for her. I only want to find her. I hoped you might have helped me in this, and as it would not be well for her to come to me at the hotel, I thought I might have met her here.'

'In my house!' shrieked the rector. 'My——dear Miss Courtenay,' he added, making a descent upon the affectionate term, to save himself from an exclamation of a different description, which had nearly escaped him. 'Impossible; utterly impossible. Pray, consider what is due to myself, my position,—Mrs. Granby,—my daughters. Why, only conceive, those sweet girls might actually see that wretched creature when they are taking their healthful exercise on the lawn! It is wholly out of the question that I should permit such a thing; and allow me to suggest, Miss Courtenay, with all due deference, that you are really making a mistake—a sad mistake, I may say—in allowing yourself to be occupied, in the smallest degree, about an individual of whose very existence, with that of all her class, you should properly be supposed to be ignorant.'

'But the fact of her existence has been forced upon me in a way I cannot escape, Dr. Granby, even if I wished it, and with that, also, the certainty that she has an immortal soul, which is but too likely to perish for ever, if no one will even try to save her.'

'Yes, I suppose—doubtless she has a soul,' said Dr. Granby, as if giving a reluctant assent to a logical fact; 'but it cannot be your concern, Miss Courtenay. Felons and murderers have souls, but you would not wish to interfere with their damnation—I mean, with their salvation—would you?' Ernestine thought she should be only too glad if she could get the chance of trying. 'No, no,' continued the rector, 'we must leave these things to the proper authorities.'

'But who are the proper authorities in this case, Dr. Granby?' said Ernestine, looking up quietly into his face. He shifted about uneasily in his chair.

'Why, the—the Board of Guardians, or the Church Penitentiary Association, or, stay,' he added, brightening up, 'did you not say the girl had a father?'

'Yes, but—'

'Then he is the proper authority,' exclaimed Dr. Granby, cutting her short triumphantly. 'Let him be informed of his daughter's disreputable proceedings, and let no one else interfere, far less a lady of your age and station in life, Miss Courtenay.'

Ernestine saw she need not waste any more time with the rector of St. Gregory, and she rose to go. Dr. Granby rose with alacrity also, but as she held out her hand to take leave, he took it in both his own, in the most paternal manner, and proceeded to expound a few more of his sentiments:—

'I trust I need not assure you, my dear Miss Courtenay, that although I have permitted myself to give you a little advice, becoming, I may say, to my pastoral office and my friendly feeling towards yourself, I have no desire whatever to discourage your amiable philanthropy. Far from it. I only wish to direct your too ardent, too liberal zeal into proper channels. My own daughters engage, at my desire, in works of charity, piety, and necessity. My sweet Louisa visits the infant-school once a week, and it is most cheering to see how she has taught the innocent little ones to clap their hands in unison; while Maria, who is strikingly talented, and has a powerful voice, always leads our little choir in Term time, when several of the collegians assist at our services, and can appreciate our musical efforts. In works such as these, my dear Miss Courtenay, let me advise you to exercise your benevolent disposition, and you will find yourself benefiting your fellow-creatures without departing from the station in which Providence has placed you, and the usages of that society which you are so well fitted to adorn.' He finished off with a low bow and a wave of the white pocket-handkerchief, as if it had been a flag of truce, and Ernestine, quietly wishing him good morning, without attempting any further reply, left the house.

'And this man,' she thought, as she walked away—'this man is the representative and messenger of Him who came to seek and save the lost,—who took upon Him the form of a servant, who had not where to lay His head, who sat with publicans and sinners, who suffered the sinful woman to wash His feet with her tears and wipe them with the hairs of her head!' Then she began to think of the clergyman of the church to which Lady Beaufort had always taken her in London, and she felt that his opinion of her mission to Annie Brook would be very much the same as Dr. Granby's, and she wondered how it was that it had never before struck her, these were strange interpreters of the gospel that was to be preached to the poor and needy—the gospel of that Immaculate Love who came 'to heal the broken-hearted, to preach deliverance to the captives and recovery of sight to the blind, and to set at liberty them that are bruised.' The fact was, that Ernestine was now, unknown to herself, touching on the outskirts of the deep comprehensive truth—the lack of which had caused Lingard to make shipwreck of his faith—contained in these words, 'If any man will do His will, he shall know of the doctrine whether it be of God;'—a truth underlying the very foundations of all real religion, and without which the loftiest creed, the fairest theories, are, and ever shall be, hollow and lifeless. The one impulse of loving pity, of active, unselfish charity, which had led her into this search for a lost sinner, was doing more to teach her the knowledge of God, and the truth of God, and the real nature of that atonement once made for the sins of the world, than all the theological instruction she had received from external sources in the whole course of her life.

Meantime, however, she went on to her hotel greatly disheartened. She was quite at a loss what to do next in her endeavour to find Annie Brook; but the very fact that all to whom she so much as mentioned the unhappy girl seemed straightway to harden their hearts against her, made her the more determined that she would never cease her efforts on her behalf, cost what it might.

Dinner with Mrs. Tompson was not enlivening. This aristocratically-minded lady, having completed her survey of the colleges for the day, was of opinion that Greyburgh was a very poor place indéed, dull and unfashionable. Why, it was nothing compared even to such towns as Bath or Leamington; there, one could at least find tolerable shops, and it was possible to meet one's friends on the parades; but the principal street of Greyburgh, which the guide pretended was worth seeing, why, really it was no promenade at all. There was hardly an elegant toilette to be seen. Perhaps if Mrs. Tompson had owned all the truth, she would have admitted that the most lady-like person she had observed, in her opinion, was a certain Don sailing down the street in his scarlet gown.

Ernestine went back early in the evening to her brother. She found him asleep. The nurse thought either that his composing-draught had been more potent than usual, or that Ernestine's visit in the morning had soothed him to a certain extent, as he seldom slept so long or so quietly. Ernestine stood looking at him in silence for some moments. It was a sleep so like to death! He lay perfectly motionless, the marble whiteness of his face brought out in strong relief, by the heavy masses of dark hair that hung round it, and the black eyelashes lying without a quiver on his wan cheek. She could almost have believed, as she gazed on him, that the mighty change had passed over him, and that his closed eyes had already looked into the tremendous mysteries which all the generations that have ever lived have sought in vain to penetrate on this side of the grave; his lips seemed locked in that inexorable silence which has ever baffled the living, and held back from them the knowledge that endues with awful wisdom each little babe that has sighed its feeble breath away ere well it has learned to live; while each line of the exhausted form seemed to imply that it only waited now to sink into the earth, with the cold insensibility to all that is most repugnant to it, which so surely marks the lifeless clay. If it were so—then were the ultimate state of that pale sleeper fixed irrevocably—the soul stamped with the seal that through the incomprehensible For Ever was to define unchangingly the conditions of his being. But, no! that faint, scarce perceptible, heaving of the breast, that little tremor of breath moving over the white lips, was the barrier, immovable as the laws which guide the stars in their courses, that shut from him the teeming immensity of the unseen, and held him bound to this visible life of brief probation. How frail a barrier! How tremendous the step beyond! Yet not one faint gleam of the coming revelation dawned with ever so pale a light upon those living eyes; that and that alone which he had made himself in his twenty little years of transient existence, he still must be till the last faint sigh of that gasping breath goes forth, and then—God face to face! all mystery, all doubt, all shadow destroyed in the light of His presence—the illimitable universe disclosed—death and the world behind him—infinity above, below, around—and immortality, fixed in the mould which he himself prepared for it in the life of earth, settling down upon his being, in its changeless power. Long did Ernestine stand watching him, as she thought on these things; but at last, with a sigh of disquietude and unrest, she turned away to seek some change from thoughts that seemed too weighty for her soul.

Nurse Berry had taken her knitting into the other room, where the waning light still lingered, and sat near the open door, so that she might perceive at once if her patient awoke. Ernestine went and sat down on a low stool at her side, looking up with a sense of rest into the kind motherly face, and listened gratefully to the homely tones which asked if she had had 'a good time' out of doors. The necessity for independent action, and for an unwonted degree of exposure to the rough ways of the world, had given Ernestine that longing for some sort of loving protection and shelter, which usually overtakes a woman thus situated, and she felt as if she should have liked to lay down her tired head on the good woman's lap, as she used to do when her own old nurse still lived to make her childhood safe and happy.

'Indeed, I have not had a good time at all,' she said, 'for I have been very much disappointed.'

'And how was that, my dear lady?'

It occurred to Ernestine that it was possible the nurse might be able to advise her how to proceed in the task that seemed to grow every hour more difficult. Looking up eagerly, she said—

'I was disappointed because I could get no help where I hoped for it; but, nurse, now I think of it, perhaps you yourself could help me.'

'I shall be very pleased, ma'am,' said the nurse,

smiling down upon the sweet eyes which had quite won her heart already, 'what be I to do?'

'I will tell you,' said Ernestine. 'I want so much to find a poor young girl, who has been deserted in Greyburgh, and I do not know in the least where to find her.'

'Is she one of them unfortunates?' said the nurse, making use of the technical phrase, which to the more inexperienced of that unhappy class has too often afforded a palliation for undeniable sin.

'Yes, unfortunate indeed; because she is so guilty,' said Ernestine.

'Ah! there be a many such in this here place,' said the nurse, shaking her head sadly. 'It often gives me a sore heart to see young things, no better than children, starting in their gay dresses of a winter night; but, ma'am, if you'll excuse me for saying it, bad as they are, I do think those university gentlemen that encourage them are worse. They ought to know better, with their learning, and their money, and their fine manners. It do seem a shocking thing that they should go ruining simple young girls, body and soul, just for their own wicked pleasure.'

'It is shocking beyond all words, nurse; you cannot think worse of these men than I do.'

'And to see how grand and proud they hold themselves all the time, counting even respectable poor people as dust under their feet; and as to the poor girls they ruin—why, when once they've cast them off, they'd dare them so much as to look near them, or make game of them for being what they've made them! I remember a poor child I knew about—she was but fourteen—a pretty, modest little maid, and she was servant at a lodging-house, where one of these fine college gentlemen had rooms. Well, he set himself to ruin her, and she too young and silly to know what she was about. So, when it was found out, she was turned off from her place at once, though they kept the fine gentleman in his rooms. She went home to her mother, but her stepfather shut the door in her face, and would not suffer her mother so much as to know what became of her. She wandered about starving for a few days, and then one of these wicked women who keep disreputable lodging-houses in the town got hold of her, and drove her out on the streets to get her bread by wickedness. Well, ma'am, one evening I was walking down the street, and I saw her coming along—looking so childish and simple, even in her flaunting dress—and I saw her meet this gentleman. She had not seen him since she had got turned out of doors for his sake. She stood stock-still, grew white as death, and then gazed up in his face with such a beseeching look; as if she wanted him to save her out of the life he had brought her to. He just half-stopt for a moment, and looked at her from head to foot, and then burst out into such a wicked, mocking laugh—I think the devil himself must have taught it to him—and said in a jeering tone: "So that's what you have come to, is it?" He pointed her out to the gentleman he was walking with, and then pushed past her; and they went down the street together laughing and sneering. The child looked after them for a moment, and then dashed up her hands, and began running as fast as she could towards the bridge. I was afraid she might mean to do as too many of them does; and perhaps she did mean it, and was scared when she saw the water; but, when I got up to her as fast as I could, she was standing at the parapet, leaning her face down on the stone, and beating her hands against it, as if she wanted to hurt them. I put my arm round her, and said,—"What is it, my dear?" and she seemed as if she must tell out her trouble, though she never saw me in her life before; for she cried out, "O ma'am! I met him, and he laughed at me! He laughed at me for being what I am; and who but he brought me to it—who but he brought me to it?"'

'And what became of the poor thing?' said Ernestine, with tears in her eyes.

'A clergyman I knew got her into a penitentiary, when I told him about her, and she is burying her days there still, and she not sixteen yet.'

'It is too dreadful,' said Ernestine; 'how it makes one think of the great God looking down on such deeds!'

'Ah! that's true, ma'am! I think of that many a time; we shall know the rights of these things when we go to stand before Him;' and involuntarily Ernestine shuddered. 'But about this girl you want to find, ma'am; do you know her name?'

'Yes; her name is Annie Brook. I know that much, and no more. I have never even seen her.'

'Indeed. Then I fear it won't be easy for you to find her among so many; but I'll tell you what to do, ma'am: you ask Mr. Thorold to help you, and he'll find her for you if any one can.'

'And who is Mr. Thorold?'

'The clergyman who got the poor child I told you of into the penitentiary. He is sure to find her out if she is in the town. He is always among thieves and lost women.'

'Always among thieves?' said Ernestine, looking up surprised.

'Yes, to try and do them good. He is at it night and day in all the most blackguard places in the town. I said to him once—for you see, ma'am, I nursed him through a fever he caught from a poor beggar who died of it, so I makes free with him—I said I did wonder he spent himself among these awful bad characters, that seemed as if nothing could make them any better—convicts, and drunkards, and tramps going to gaol with canvas bags on.'

'With canvas bags on!' said Ernestine, looking bewildered.

'Yes, ma'am. When they tear up their rags in the work'us to get new ones, the master just cuts a hole in a sack, and puts their heads through it, and they are sent off to prison in it. Well, it is these, and others like them, both men and women, that Mr. Thorold is always trying to teach and to help; and when I said to him I thought there was such little chance of ever getting one of them out of their bad ways, it seemed a pity he should wear himself out on them, he said, says he: "That's the very reason why I do it, nurse. Every one else has given them up, and I like to be the friend of those who have got no other in this world. People say they are hopeless characters, and there is nothing more to be done for them but to leave them to take their own course to hell; but you may depend on it," says he, "that's not the way the Father in heaven deals with us. He never gives any one up, be they ever so bad, to the very last moment of their lives; there is never a soul so lost or so dead but His grace can reach it; nor a heart so cold in despair but His pity can comfort it."'

'Oh, I like that!' exclaimed Ernestine, her eyes kindling.

'Ah, I have thought of his words many times,' said the nurse, 'when I have heard folks talking of those they thought hardened in vice.'

'And you think Mr. Thorold would help me?'

'He'd be more than glad, ma'am; it is just meat and drink to him to help those that are friendless and lost, like the girl you are looking for.'

'And how can I see him?'

'Well, if you did not mind, you might see him now; for I know where he is at this hour. He holds a night-school for boys down a lane not far from here; and he would speak to you there in a moment, if you liked to go. My daughter is down stairs waiting for me, and she shall show you the way if you like.'

'Do you think I might? Is it not too late?' said Ernestine, looking doubtfully at the window, where the shades of evening were gathering, though it was by no means dark.

'Well, ma'am, that's as you think. As for Mr. Thorold, he never thinks what hour it is. I don't believe he knows day from night, for he seems to me always at work; he is as often as not up at night with the dying, and I am sure he never rests by day.'

'While I am letting some wretched fear of infringing conventionalities stand in the way of saving a soul!' thought Ernestine. 'I will go at once,' she said, starting up. 'I hope my brother will not wake till I return.'

'I don't think he will, ma'am,' said the nurse; 'he is very still, poor lamb.'

And in another moment Ernestine found herself traversing some small narrow streets, with old-fashioned houses rising on either side, which grew more and more crowded with wretched-looking people, till she reached a parish school-house. This building, her guide told her, was lent to Mr. Thorold every evening for his 'wild boys;' and wild enough they certainly seemed, as the open door of a large room revealed a throng of such street Arabs as had never met her eyes before. Uncombed and unwashed, they seemed to Ernestine the most absolutely hopeless of possible recipients of learning; yet all were busy under the superintendence of Mr. Thorold, who came forward at once after receiving a whispered communication from the nurse's daughter. He was a tall man, apparently about five-and-thirty, wearing a rough great-coat, which had seen its best days, with bushy black hair pushed carelessly back from his forehead, strongly marked eyebrows, which almost hid his keen dark eyes, a sallow complexion, and an expression of great firmness and determination. Ernestine was both surprised and pleased to see that it was a young man in an undergraduate's gown whom he called to take his place while he left the room; her impression of the younger university men had not been such as to lead her to expect any of them to take an interest in a night-school for ragged boys.

Mr. Thorold came up to her, and bowing, without a word he opened the door of a small room, which was unoccupied, and placed a chair for her. He did not sit down himself, but stood leaning against the wall, waiting for her to speak. Ernestine remembered her interview with Dr. Granby, and thought that never in her life had she seen a greater contrast than between those two ecclesiastics; but she felt no difficulty in stating her wishes to this business-like cleric. He heard her to the end, then asked a few rapid questions as to the extent of her knowledge of the girl, with the somewhat brusque manner which seemed habitual to him; and after a moment's thought, said decisively—

'I believe your only chance of finding her is in the gaol.' Ernestine gave a start of surprise. 'Does that alarm you?' he said, a smile lighting up his dark face.

'Not for myself; but I have no reason to think Annie Brook dishonest, or anything of that sort.'

'That has nothing to do with it,' he said quickly. 'There is a peculiar sort of police-discipline in this place, which enables the college authorities to commit women of this unhappy class to gaol for certain short periods. We have that much of real Christianity in the universities, that the deadly crime which the law does not recognise as such at all, is at least punishable here.'

'And do you think it does these miserable women any good to be sent to prison?' asked Ernestine.

'Not as a punishment; the periods for which they are imprisoned are too short, and no care is taken to make it morally beneficial to them; they are all herded together, with every incitement to try and emulate one another in recklessness and bravado. But it is of incalculable use, as being the one only opportunity which their lives afford of bringing good influences to bear upon them, and offering them the means of reformation, if they can be induced to accept them. They are so guarded by the wretches who keep the houses where they congregate, that it is next to impossible to gain a hearing from them outside, but in the gaol they cannot escape; they must see the chaplain, or any one else who may try to benefit them; and this imprisonment has been the means of saving many.'

'One would think it ought to save all,' said Ernestine eagerly. 'Surely when they are actually there, in the very hands of those who would help them, not one should be allowed to go back to their dreadful life.'

Mr. Thorold shook his head. 'You little know the trammels that bind them, and besides, it is not easy to find persons who have both the will and the capacity for such a mission as that. It has been found that the chaplain alone cannot do it, for many reasons. It requires the help of a woman, at once wise and gentle, and there is no lady at present who is able to undertake it.'

'And are there many imprisoned?'

'In Term time there are often from twenty to thirty. I only wish,' he added, clenching his hand, 'that the university police would administer a somewhat more even justice, and imprison the men, who are a hundred-fold more guilty than these wretched women.'

'I am very glad to hear you say so,' said Ernestine, 'for I cannot understand the received code of opinion on that subject at all. You think, then, that I may find Annie Brook in the prison?'

'It is possible,—in any case, you are likely to get some clue to her. You say you have a portrait of her; I advise you to take it with you, and show it to the governor of the gaol; it is very possible he may recognise it; if not, ask him to show it to the women imprisoned there, and if he is careful not to say for what purpose he does so, they will be sure at least to betray the name by which she goes at present; these girls scarcely ever retain their own name.'

'But would they not be glad to tell all they knew of her to those who wished to help her?'

'Not if they thought there was any intention of persuading her to reform.'

'How very strange! I should have thought that, however lost and wretched they might be, they would retain enough of humanity to be glad that a companion should be saved out of misery like their own.'

'I fear it is a principle of human nature to feel it a relief to have companions in guilt, and to dread repentance in others, lest it awaken personal uneasiness of conscience. But there is a stronger motive in the case of these poor girls: the good people who have established "Refuges" and "Homes" for those who repent, have succeeded in making them so repellent and intolerable to them, that I believe they consider themselves to be performing an act of common humanity when they try to prevent any from being persuaded to enter them.'

At this moment a considerable degree of noise was heard from the next room, and Mr. Thorold went hurriedly to the door.

'My populace is becoming clamorous,' he said; 'I must go.'

'But pray tell me,' said Ernestine, 'how am I to gain admission to the gaol?'

'You must have an order from a magistrate. I will get one for you, if you will tell me your name.'

'You do not know my name?' said Ernestine, looking up with a smile of amusement.

'How should I?'

'True; I was only thinking how surprised my aunt, who regulates most of my proceedings, would be if she knew I had been talking to you as I have done, without your so much as knowing my name.'

He shrugged his shoulders. 'These abstruse etiquettes of society are quite beyond me—I cannot away with them. Life is too short and too solemn to be clogged with such trammels as these. If you want to save a soul, and I am willing to help you, what can it signify to me whether you are a duchess or a dairymaid, or to you who I am, if you have reason to believe I am neither a ruffian nor an impostor?'

'I quite agree with you,' said Ernestine, laughing; 'and my aunt is not here to argue the point with you. My name is Ernestine Courtenay; and I am so much obliged to you for your kindness.' He smiled as he looked keenly and searchingly at her for a moment, and then, having arranged that he was to bring the order to her brother's rooms next day, he opened the door for her, and she passed out into the dark streets with her guide.

CHAPTER XIII.

REGINALD.

REGINALD still lay in his deathlike sleep. Ernestine had decided to watch by him herself, at least for this night, that she might judge of his state more fully; and Mrs. Berry, after hearing, with great satisfaction, that Mr. Thorold had proved quite as helpful as she had prophesied, took her leave, promising to return early in the morning. Ernestine sat down by her brother's side, feeling that she could with a free heart give him her undivided attention, now that a hopeful step had at last been taken on behalf of Annie Brook. But while he slept, her thoughts flew away to the one who was dearer to her than even the dying brother, or than all the world beside,—the one to whom she had given the love that can be felt but once in a lifetime, and which it is a terrible thing to feel on this earth at all; for the exceeding preciousness with which it invests one perishable human being, to whom each day brings the chance of sickness and death, sorrow and danger, makes such a love an agony rather than a blessing. They who so love must ever drink deeply of the cup of trembling; but at times there will arise in their hearts a nameless terror, a sickening anxiety for the future, whose brightness all depends on this one cherished treasure, which often proves a foreboding of some real anguish looming in the distant hours. It was so on this night with Ernestine Courtenay. She did not wonder that, in the darkness of the quiet sick-room, her heart seemed to go out to Hugh Lingard with a tenderness almost mournful in its depth; it was often so when she was parted from him, but on this occasion she was oppressed by a vague yet most painful feeling that she had somehow separated herself from him to a certain degree,—that she had begun to raise a barrier between them which would ultimately shut him out from her for ever. She argued with herself on the unreasonableness of such shadowy fears. It was with his full consent that she had come to Greyburgh. She was going to write to him the next day, as she had promised, with a detail of all she had done as yet in her mission. The very last words they had said to each other had been to arrange that their marriage should take place in the course of a few months. Yet, do what she would, her spirits sunk under the weight of an undefined conviction, that she had entered on a path which by some means would lead her far away from the one being to whom she clung with all a woman's passionate devotion.

She was roused from her dark thoughts by Reginald, who suddenly started out of his heavy sleep with a cry of indescribable terror. He flung out his arms, beating the air with his helpless hands, while his large black eyes opened to their fullest extent, and gazed into the darkness with a vacant stare.

'Not yet—not yet,' he shrieked out. 'No! I cannot go—I cannot. Help, O help me!'

In a moment Ernestine was kneeling at his side with her arms clasped round him. 'Reginald, darling, what is it? There is no one here but me, Ernestine, your sister. Look at me, dearest; don't be afraid.'

His hands fell on her shoulders, the wildness passed from his eyes, and he looked down at her with returning consciousness; but she could feel his whole frame trembling from head to foot. 'Ernie,' he said, in a hoarse whisper, 'is the dreadful hour come? Must I go? Is this death?' and he literally shuddered.

'No, my darling,' she said soothingly, 'you are only faint; let me give you some wine; you will be better presently.'

She made him swallow some wine and then bathed his hands and temples with eau-de-cologne, till gradually the spasm of terror passed from his blanched face, and, falling back in his chair, he gave a heavy sigh, half of relief and half of remembered agony.

'Then it is still to come?' he murmured. 'Almost I could wish that first bitterness of death at least were past; yet no,' he continued, his features contracting with pain, 'anything—anything rather than that; better life, though it be torture, than the blackness of eternal night.'

It was on Ernestine's lips to ask why death was so dreadful to him. It was not so to her, though the love that brightened earth for her might make her sad to leave it yet awhile; and why should this boy, who once had loved to lose himself in glowing dreams of the consummation of bliss, now so shrink from that which was but the gate of immortality? But she remembered her promise to ask no questions, and, besides, he was still too much agitated to risk further disturbance, so she soothed him gently for a time, talking to him on indifferent subjects till gradually he became calm, and his eyes brightened as he turned them on her sweet face.

'You are a good nurse, my darling Ernie,' he said. 'I feel now as if I could almost enjoy this night, with you sitting at my side. Your voice is just like music.'

'I am so glad you are more comfortable,' she said, laying her head on the pillow beside him. 'We shall have such a nice quiet time. Now, you must tell me what you would like to talk about.'

'Shall I really?' he said, caressingly. 'May I choose the subject?'

'Of course. What am I here for but to be your slave?'

'Well, you remember how you used to tell me stories long ago, when we were children, though I used to consider you almost a grown-up lady, because you were four years older. I want you to do the same for me to-night. I want you to tell me all the histories you can remember of those who have gone to death calmly and fearlessly, though they had been compelled to face it in all its horrible certainty for some time previously.'

'What! beginning with Socrates and his poison-cup?'

'If you will; and tell me about that criminal, I forget his name, who, on the scaffold, thought neither of the shame nor the agony, but said only, " Now I shall learn the great secret."'

'And Julian the Apostate, who died saying, " O

Galilean, thou hast conquered,"' said Ernestine, lifting her head that she might look into her brother's eyes as she spoke.

A sudden flush dyed his pale face. 'As you please,' he answered shortly, and then went on: 'Who was it that said, "Death cannot be an evil, because it is universal"?'

'That was Goethe. But, darling,' said Ernestine softly, ' would it not be happiest of all to speak of the only true Conqueror over death—the One who took its sting away, and made the grave no strange place for any one of us since HE has lain in it ?'

'No, no!' exclaimed Reginald, starting up with a vehemence which seemed greater than his feeble frame could bear, ' Ernie, do not speak to me of Him. I cannot bear it—I cannot. I tell you I will not. You will kill me if you speak of Him; rather go and leave me quite alone.'

' My dearest Reggie, I will not touch on any subject you do not like. Lie down again, and trust me I will only tell you what you ask,—the histories, so far as I remember them, of brave men dying calmly and without fear;' and in a low gentle tone, as she would have soothed a wearied child, she spoke to him of those who have been seen to go down with fearless steps into the valley of the shadow of death; and of others, who being rescued from it, had spoken of a lovely pure light into which they seemed to sink, with echoes of softest music in their ears; and Reginald listened with her hand clasped in his, and grew very calm and still; and so the night wore peacefully on for both, till the faint glimmer of the far-off dawn stole into the sky, and the cool breath of the morning passed lightly over the wearied eyelids of the dying man, while, half-sleeping, half-waking, he lay gazing dreamily out upon the shifting shadows of the heavens. Then Ernestine relapsed into silence, and, with her head still laid beside her brother's, followed unconsciously the train of thought which that strange unearthly night suggested to her. The actual life of the present seemed so intangible, so fleeting, with all its briefness and uncertainty, that she felt as if no soul could ever seek in it to slake its thirst for joy and for existence, and in spirit she passed over the dark valley of which she had been speaking, into the realms of changeless light, where there is no shadow, no perplexity, no fear; and she thought what glorious bliss, what sweetest rest, it would be to dwell in that deathless land with him, her dearest loved,—with this poor wayward brother also, and with that other one for whom her heart still yearned,—gathered all together at the feet of Infinite Compassion. And so she lost herself in those sweet visions, till, with a smile, she woke to see that what appeared to her but the baseless fancies of her own deep longing, was, after all, the very reality which God has prepared for those that love Him.

At last the first sunbeam smote on the wan face of Reginald, and another day had begun for him who had so few to number now, and soon all unearthly thoughts were put to flight for both of them by the arrival of Nurse Berry, with all her homely arrangements for their comfort. She insisted especially that Ernestine should now go to the hotel to take a few hours' rest, and Reginald urged her to do so, with many loving thanks for the comfort she had been to him that night; so that she agreed to their wishes, promising to return in the course of the afternoon.

When Ernestine woke up later in the day from her needful rest, she found Mrs. Tompson in a state of considerable excitement. Dr. and Mrs. Granby had come to call on Miss Courtenay, and, finding that she could not be disturbed, had paid their visit to the chaperon. In the course of it they dropped various mysterious hints, that they feared Miss Courtenay's charitable zeal was carrying her beyond the *convenances* of society, and that they wished much she would place herself under their protection and guidance during her stay in a place where reticence of all sorts was so much required as in Greyburgh. These remarks Mrs. Tompson repeated with much unction, beseeching Ernestine to take them into serious consideration; but she, inwardly shuddering at the thought of placing herself under Dr. Granby's care, and of the aristocratic uselessness which would be the result, assured Mrs. Tompson she was quite satisfied with her chaperonage; and added, that in Reginald's precarious state she did not intend to see the Granbys, or any other acquaintance at all. She begged her chaperon, however, to accept all Mrs. Granby's invitations to dinner, etc., for herself, and finally reminding her that there was only one person to whom she owed any account of her actions, she pointed to the letter ready sealed for the post, which lay on the table, addressed to Mr. Lingard, and assured her it contained a detail of all her proceedings since she left him. With this Mrs. Tompson was fain to be content, and Ernestine hurried back as soon as she could to Reginald, for her uneasiness with regard to his mental condition increased every hour, and her great fear now was lest he should die with this dark burden, whatever it might be, unrevealed and unrelieved.

She had not long been in her place by his side when the nurse came to tell her that Mr. Thorold was waiting for her in the next room. She went in, and found him walking up and down, somewhat after the fashion of a wild beast in a cage, but he turned to meet Ernestine with a frankness and simplicity which set her at ease at once.

'I have brought your order,' he said, 'and I have persuaded the magistrate to give you one containing a general permission to visit the female prisoners, as it would not have answered your purpose to have it made out to any person in particular. I have had to fight a small battle on your behalf,' he added, with a smile; 'the conscientious magistrate would not grant you the order till he could satisfy himself that you had no intention of teaching these poor women Popery, or Puritanism, or various other distinctive forms of religion which he enumerated. I told him I knew little of you, but a great deal of the wretched prisoners; and that, whilst I had no reason to suppose the study of doctrinal theology formed any part of your intentions towards them, I was so certain that they, for the most part, did not realize the existence of a God or a future state, that I doubted its taking any serious effect on them if you did.'

'But do you mean that he would actually have refused me entrance to the gaol on such a ground as that? I could understand a fear of erroneous doctrine being introduced into the minds of high-principled, well-educated persons, but surely, in the case of women living, as you say, in utter ignorance of the very foundations of religion, and in gross violation of the plainest laws of God, it is not possible that he would let them miss any practical good I might be able to do them for so chimerical a fear?'

'It is not only possible,' said Thorold, 'but it is this same senseless fear which has shut the doors of our gaols and workhouses all over the country to the only persons who would care to try and help the unhappy inmates; it would be inconceivable, if it were not true; but the pig-headedness of British magistrates and guardians of the poor is something wonderful!' He said this with such hearty vehemence, that Ernestine could not help laughing.

'And are the poor convicts and paupers never allowed to see any one, then?' she asked.

'O yes! any ill-conditioned, disreputable person of their own rank, who chooses to call himself a friend, is quite welcome, at least in the workhouses, to go and revive all their associations with evil, and their longing to return to former bad habits. I will give you a true case in point, which came under my own notice: A poor girl was dying in one of the most infamous houses in the town. A lady whom she had herself sent for, and who had won her love most completely by her gentle kindness, was very anxious that her last hours should not be spent in a place where she heard and saw nothing but the worst of evil night and day. The only shelter to which she could be removed was the workhouse, and the lady begged her for her soul's sake to consent to go there. The girl had the usual horror of this last home of the poor, but she could not resist the loving counsels of the first person who had ever told her of a Saviour. She agreed to go, but on the one condition, that the lady should promise faithfully to visit her there as often as possible. This she gladly did, never dreaming of any difficulty which could stand in her way; and the poor creature, to whom her pure influence was bringing light and peace, was carried off to the workhouse. The next day she went to see her, and was refused admission at the gate; the porter roughly telling her it was the guardians' order that no lady should be admitted. You may imagine her distress, knowing the girl must suppose she had forgotten her promise. The lady had powerful friends, however, and she set them to work to obtain a special order of admission for her, which, after a fortnight of tedious delays she obtained. She went to the gate, and was told the poor girl had died the day before.'

'O how sad!' exclaimed Ernestine.

'Yes, but you have not heard the sting of the story yet. During the whole of that fortnight the wretched woman who kept the house whence the girl had been rescued was allowed to visit her daily, and to amuse her dying hours with such conversation as you have never dreamt of.'

'That is indeed inconceivable,' said Ernestine; 'I could not have believed it.'

'You see the lady might have been a High Churchwoman or an Evangelical, whereas the woman they admitted was only one of the vilest reprobates that ever disgraced her sex, and slew her thousands and ten thousands of living souls; but this is a subject which makes me rabid, so I must not go on. Here is your order, and you will not teach the prisoners Zuinglianism or Universalism, or any other "ism," will you?'

'No, I think not,' said Ernestine, laughing; 'I don't feel very competent to teach them anything; it will all be very strange to me at the gaol; I hope I shall not make any blunders. Is the governor a very fierce individual?'

'He is sharp enough to the prisoners, but he is likely to be very amiable to you, I should think. He is an old man, who has been thirty years a "servant of the city," as he terms it, and is probably the last remaining specimen of a race of gaolers that is almost obsolete. He is as different as well can be from the cold, stern, gentlemanlike officials who are to be found in such positions now. He has no pretensions to being a gentleman. He is very talkative; speaks with the broad Greyburgh accent, and gives his views on all subjects with the most uncompromising plainness; but he does his practical duties so well that the authorities cannot find an excuse for considering him superannuated, as they wish.'

'And is there a matron for the women?' asked Ernestine.

'His wife, old Mrs. Bolton, acts as such. She has all his roughness, without his sound good sense.'

'Ernestine, can you come to me for a moment?' said the faint voice of Reginald from the next room. She started up, and begged Mr. Thorold to wait a few minutes, while she hastily obeyed the call. The door stood wide open, so that Thorold could see and hear all that passed. Reginald, it seemed, wished to be moved nearer to the window. He wanted air, he said, and, leaning heavily on Ernestine, he began to walk feebly towards it. But her strength was not equal to the weight of his almost helpless frame, and seeing her begin to totter under it, Thorold started up, and, without a word, lifted Reginald in his strong arms, and placed him on the couch, near the window. Then, as both brother and sister thanked him, he answered in a low, soft tone, which sounded peculiarly soothing, and proceeded to smooth Reginald's pillows, and make various little arrangements for his comfort, with a tenderness which astonished Ernestine, who had thought him somewhat rough and brusque in manner previously. Reginald looked up with a grateful smile, and as Thorold shook hands with him before leaving the room, began a sentence, 'Will you—' then suddenly checked himself and said no more. Thorold took no notice of the half-formed speech, but with a few words of sympathy for his evident illness, made way for the nurse, who had just come in, and went into the outer room with Ernestine.

'You have a great sorrow there,' he said in a low tone.

'Oh, you cannot think how great,' replied Ernestine, her eyes filling with tears. 'It is not only that he is dying, as you perceive, but it is such a sad passing from this world. He gives me no clue to his state of mind, yet I see that these his last days are one long unrest, and I hardly know whether he hates life or dreads death most.'

The gravity of Thorold's face deepened almost to sternness. 'Were his associates among the reading men or those of the wilder set?' he asked.

'Always among the reading men, till lately. He intended to take holy orders, and gave himself up almost entirely to the study of divinity, but Dr. Compton tells me that he altered very much last term, and led a kind of life I should have thought impossible for Reginald. I never had dreaded the ordinary temptations of this place for him.'

'There are intellectual as well as moral dangers in Greyburgh now, and it is more than likely it is to these he has succumbed. But I must not stay. If I can be of use to you in any way, let me know, and I will come at once.'

He did not wait for her thanks, but went hurriedly away.

'How do you come to know Thorold, Ernestine?' said Reginald, when she went back to him.

She explained that she had gone to ask his assistance respecting a poor person in whom she was interested. 'And do you know him?' she asked in return.

'Not personally; but I have often been at his church. He is not an attractive man to most people, but I had, and indeed still have, the greatest admiration for his character. I never knew any one with such indomitable faith, such stern self-denial, and such entire devotion of heart and soul to the one cause in which he believes. Thorold has stood like a rock through all the whirlwinds and storms that have been raging through the university of late, casting men's minds into chaos, and making shipwreck of their peace.'

'Is he a man of influence here?' asked Ernestine.

'With all who really know him; but he is excessively quiet and unobtrusive. He lives entirely in and for his work, at which he toils like a slave; but if ever any one seeks his help in difficulties, of whatever nature, he is ready at once with the most fearless counsels. I have several times been on the point of going to him myself, and then I have thought better, or worse of it. And now, Ernie, I must try to sleep, for I am tired;' and he lay back with so evident a wish to stop the conversation, that she made no attempt to continue it.

END OF VOL. I.

EDINBURGH: T. CONSTABLE,
PRINTER TO THE QUEEN, AND TO THE UNIVERSITY.

HIDDEN DEPTHS.

EDINBURGH : PRINTED BY THOMAS CONSTABLE,

FOR

EDMONSTON AND DOUGLAS.

LONDON,	. . . . . .	HAMILTON, ADAMS, AND CO.
CAMBRIDGE,	. . . . .	MACMILLAN AND CO.
DUBLIN,	. . . . . .	M'GLASHAN AND GILL.
GLASGOW,	. . . . . .	JAMES MACLEHOSE.

HIDDEN DEPTHS

'VERITAS EST MAJOR CHARITAS'

VOLUME SECOND

EDINBURGH
EDMONSTON AND DOUGLAS
1866.

CONTENTS OF VOL. II.

I.
THE GAOL, ... 7

II.
REGINALD'S HISTORY, ... 22

III.
THE VALLEY OF THE SHADOW OF DEATH, . . 47

IV.
ANNIE BROOK, ... 62

V.
THE REFUGE, ... 79

VI.
THE CLOUDS BEGIN TO GATHER, ... 110

VII.

MRS. DORRELL, ... 122

VIII.

THE LOST FOUND, ... 156

IX.

THE LAST STRUGGLE, ... 177

X.

CHARITY SUFFERETH LONG, AND IS KIND, . . 202

CHAPTER I.

THE GAOL.

ERNESTINE COURTENAY stood that same afternoon at the gate of the gaol, waiting an answer to her summons. She looked up to the high massive walls which hid the building, and the ponderous door, with its ominous bolts and bars, and the grated loophole through which the turnkey inspected her before he opened it; and she smiled involuntarily as she thought of Lady Beaufort's horror and indignation could she have seen her niece in such a position. Her order at once gained her admission, and walking through an enclosure laid out as a garden, where a few sickly flowers strove to blossom in the perpetual shade of the high walls, she was ushered into the governor's room. He was seated writing at a table,—a tall rough-looking old man, with a keen eye, which had scanned her from head to foot before she had been two minutes in his presence. Her appearance seemed to propitiate him, for he very graciously asked her to sit down, and proceeded to read her order. He looked up sharply at her when he had done so.

'This is not a common order,' he said. 'You don't want to see one of those gals in particular, and you can't be come just to look at the whole lot, as if they were wild beasts in a show; so if you'll just tell me what you're up to, ma'am, we shall get on a deal better and quicker.'

'I will, gladly. Mr. Thorold told me you would help me in a matter I am anxious about.'

'Mr. Thorold advised you to come here, did he? then it's all right. He is a trump, he is; not one of your stuck-up parsons, talking out of a book, as stiff as a poker. Would you like to know what Mr. Thorold did once?' he continued, veering round on his chair so as to face Ernestine. 'There was a thundering blackguard here committed for manslaughter; he had hit a publican such a knock on the head that he killed his man then and there. Well, he was just like a devil when we got him in here. He knocked down one of the turnkeys, and squared up at me; only I had the handcuffs on him before he knew where he was, and it took the lot on us to get him into the black-hole.'

'The black-hole?' said Ernestine inquiringly.

THE GAOL.

'That's where we locks them up when they're rampagious; 'taint a pleasant place, I can tell you. Well, he was a-howling there like a hippopotamus' (it struck Ernestine that a howling hippopotamus was a curiosity in natural history, but she made no comment), 'and banging the door as if he'd have had it down; and Mr. Thorold, he had come in to see one of the other prisoners. "What's that?" says he to me, when he heard the row. I told him. "Now, Bolton," says he, "I'll tell you what: you're going to let me into the black-hole to speak to that man." "Lord bless you, sir," says I, "you must not think of such a thing; why, he'll fell you like an ox." "Not a bit of it," says he; "come, you take and open the door for me." "Just as you please," says I, for I could not help liking his pluck; "but if you once goes in, you'll have to stay there an hour, for I've got to go out, and I can't give the key of the black-hole to no one." "All right," says he; "I'll stay." "But I must lock you up," says I. "Lock me up," says he; and so I did; and whatever he did to the fellow, I can't tell you, but I went back in an hour's time, and the prisoner was sitting on the floor, crying like a baby, and Mr. Thorold was leaning over him, comforting him as tender as might be.'

'I am very glad you have told me that, Mr. Bolton,'

said Ernestine, 'for I like to think there are such people in the world.'

'There's not too many of them,' said the gaoler, nodding his head sententiously. 'Well now, your business, ma'am?'

'It is just this: I want to find a young girl who has gone astray in Greyburgh. Her name is Annie Brook. I have never seen her, but I have her picture; and Mr. Thorold said that even if she were not amongst the prisoners here, you, or some of the women, might recognise it.'

'It's very likely; let's have a look at it.'

Ernestine gave him the sketch of the pretty smiling face, with the waving hair and the wreath of flowers. The old man looked at it long and earnestly.

'I have seen this face,' he said at last; 'but not in here. I have seen it in the streets. She is new to the trade most probably, and has not been took up yet.'

'And do you think you can help me to find her?' said Ernestine eagerly.

'We'll find her if she is in Greyburgh, ma'am, I'll be bound. They all find their way here sooner or later; but we'll try if the girls know her; it's pretty sure they do, if she is one of their sort.'

'I fear there is little doubt she is,' said Ernestine.

'Then you'll not expect to see her look like this?' he said, pointing to the sweet innocent face in the sketch. 'She'll have got a bit more brazen before now, you may depend. Here, missus,' he shouted, and a fat old woman came waddling into the room at his call. 'This here lady wants to go and see the gals; give me your keys, and I'll take her in myself.'

'Going to see the gals, are you, ma'am?' said Mrs. Bolton. 'Ah! you'd not take a step to see them, if you had as much of them as I have. I am a'most out of my mind with their cantrips.'

'A val-ay-ble woman that, ma'am,' said the gaoler, drawing himself up, and flourishing his hand towards his wife; 'five years older than I am, and I'm no chicken, and to see how she cuts about after these vixens, it is a beautiful sight, ma'am, beautiful! The experience I have had in the female sex since I came within these walls is wonderful; you wouldn't credit it. I thought when I came here that women were all made of cheeny and glass; but, bless you! I have had reason to change my opinion. There's some of them it would be worse to meet than a roaring lion, when their blood's up. Why, I had a woman here, six feet in her stocking-soles, committed for trying to ram a red-hot poker down her husband's throat, and he a corporal six feet two. She said she had warned him of her sentiments about his staying out after dark, and she made his tea every blessed night, with the poker heating in the fire for him, till she caught him tripping, and then she was at him like a Philistine. But here are the keys, ma'am. This way.'

He rose, keys in hand, and marched in front of her, while Ernestine followed, thinking, with no small amusement, how Hugh Lingard would laugh at the new lights she was gaining in her present adventures. They passed through a heavy door, turning on a pivot, into a dreary stone passage, and having traversed various parts of the building, all gloomier and colder than anything Ernestine had ever imagined, they reached a small paved courtyard surrounded by high walls, where the female prisoners had just been turned out to exercise. The governor told Ernestine as they went on that the women who were sent there by the university authorities were always kept apart from those committed for theft or other offences, and therefore that all now before her were of that doomed class. For a moment Ernestine shrank from raising her eyes to any one of them, but, conquering the painful feeling which oppressed her, she turned towards them with a gentle imploring look, which would have told them, could they have read it aright, how much she hoped they would not suppose she had come there to scorn and humble them, and compare the honour and purity which shielded her own life, with the unspeakable degradation of theirs. Some eighteen or twenty women were before her, of all ages, from the hard callous-looking woman of more than thirty, to the mere child of fourteen. All possessed at least some trace of the beauty which had been at once their treasure and their curse, but in not one, even the youngest, was there the least remains of the freshness, the innocence, the frankness of youth and girlhood. It seemed to Ernestine as if they belonged not only to a distinct class, but to a separate race. Gathered as they were from different parts of the country, there was in one and all of them the same restless, unsatisfied expression, the same quick impulsiveness, with a bright keenness of look like that of some wild animal whose life depends on the winning of difficult prey; nor had she been long in their presence before she saw that sudden bursts of wild gaiety, diversified by intervals of sullen misery, characterized them all alike. Some there were, however, in whose eyes the lurking agony was more clearly visible than in others, while the younger girls seemed capable of keeping up, even amongst themselves, a reckless, mirthful excitement which compelled oblivion of the darker thoughts that would one day overwhelm them altogether. Ernestine felt heart-sick as she gazed at them, for these were all human beings, whom even the world called 'lost,' and were they indeed to be lost for ever? She was trying with her whole heart to save one of them, but were all these to be allowed to go their way without a hand stretched out to stay their perishing?

The appearance of a lady was evidently an unwonted sight, and the smallest event an excitement in their dreary imprisonment. They crowded together, gazing at Ernestine with eager looks. She soon found she was expected to play her part in a small drama, which the astute governor originated for the occasion.

'Yes, ma'am, this is our exercise-ground,' he said, with a wave of his hand. 'Male prisoners walk here at one, female prisoners at two o'clock. We are careful of their health, ma'am; you shall go through their cells presently.'

'I am glad they have a little fresh air,' said Ernestine.

'O yes, ma'am, and I gives them every indulgence in my power, when they behaves steady and does their oakum properly. Have you all picked your full quantity this morning?' he added, turning to the women.

'Yes, sir,' they answered in chorus.

'Then I'll give you a treat, and let you see this pretty picture,' and he held out Annie's portrait. With a shriek of delight they rushed forward, and crowded round him to look at it. For a moment there was a silence, then a shout from two or three, 'Why, it's Rosie Brown!'

'Well, to be sure, and so it is,' said another.

'It's Rosie, only prettier,' said a fourth.

'Ah, that's the flowers sets her off,' said another; and so on, one and all agreeing on the identity of the portrait. Ernestine remembered Thorold had told her of the probable change of name. Brown was just what Annie might have been expected to choose, and very likely Mr. Brown himself had given the name of Rose to the sweet blushing face represented in the sketch.

'Yes, it is Rosie Brown,' said the gaoler. 'I thought you would know it. It's like her, ain't it? But this was done before she came to Greyburgh.'

'Any one may see that,' said a girl; 'Rosie looks ever so much older now.'

'Oh, can you tell me where she is at present,' exclaimed Ernestine eagerly.

'There! you've been and spoiled all,' muttered the gaoler.

'Yes, sure,' said one of the younger girls, 'she is at Mother Dor—'

She was interrupted before she completed the name by a companion, who twitched her sleeve, while a sharp glance towards Ernestine, and a look of intelligence among themselves passed round the circle.

'Rosie Brown,' said the woman who had stopped the other; 'oh, she is gone away; been gone ever so long; don't live anywhere near Greyburgh now.'

'Polly Smith, if you've got nothing but lies to tell, you'll be pleased to hold your tongue,' said the gaoler.

'Law bless you, Mr. Bolton,' said a slim black-eyed girl, springing half across the yard towards him, 'don't you know as Rosie went off in a coach and six, quite grand and respectable? There was a gentleman inside, with a cocked-hat, and I think it must have been the Mayor.'

'Lydia Merrit, if you dares to give me any of your chaff, you'll be locked up, that's all. Ma'am, I'll show you over the rest of the gaol, if you please now; there's nothing more to see here.'

He held the door open for Ernestine, and she could not choose but go towards it, her expressive face shadowed by sorrow at the thought that her own indiscretion had defeated her object. A sad-eyed girl, who had remained silent from the first, was watching

THE GAOL.

Ernestine intently. Suddenly she went towards her, and whispered in a low voice—

'You mean nothing but good to Rosie, don't you?'

'Nothing, nothing but good,' said Ernestine anxiously.

'Then you'll find her at Mother Dorrell's in Priory Lane.'

Oh, thank you,' said Ernestine, pressing the girl's hand. A look of astonishment passed into the careworn faded face as the woman felt the touch of that soft white hand. She watched Ernestine till the last fold of her dress disappeared through the door, and then went and sat down in a corner, with her face buried in her hands.

The gaoler conducted Ernestine back to his room, and then turned round and looked at her.

'*You* was never made for a detective officer,' he said.

'I don't suppose I was,' said Ernestine, laughing. 'I saw how foolish I had been the moment I asked that question.'

'It was a green thing to go and do,' said the gaoler pensively.

'But did you hear what that girl said to me as we came out?' exclaimed Ernestine. 'She said Rosie Brown was at Mother Dorrell's in Priory Lane. It is such an odd address that I remember it well.'

'Yes, yes, and it was right enough, no doubt. It was Nell Lewis told you that, and there's a deal of good in that gal. I know all about her from the first, and a bigger rascal than the young fellow that ruined her does not live, for all he is a lord with a fine estate at his back.'

'Then if you know where this place is, had I not better go at once?' said Ernestine eagerly.

The gaoler sat down deliberately, put his hands on his knees, and looked steadily at her.

'Be you a-going to take my advice,' he said, 'or be you a-going to take your own way?'

'Oh, I shall certainly take your advice,' said Ernestine. 'You must know much better than I can do what is best. I only want so much to find this poor girl.'

'And you shall find her if you are guided by me, for I'll help you. I'll help you for two reasons: first and foremost, because I like to help those that are trying to do good. Though I've lived among a blessed lot of blackguards all my days, I still believe it's possible to do them good when folks goes at it with a will as you do. They've got the Lord on their side, and the devil's no match for them; and, secondly, I'll do what I can for you, because you are a real lady every inch of you; and I can tell you, I know a lady when I see her, from a make-believe, dressed up in silks and satins.'

THE GAOL. 19

'Thank you very much,' said Ernestine; 'I am sure we shall succeed, if you are kind enough to help me.'

'We shall succeed; but first, I'll tell you what would happen if you went yourself to Mother Dorrell's. You would knock at the door, and some one would take a look at you through a hole in the shutter of a closed window. You'd be kept waiting a bit; then the door would open, and you would see a most respectable-looking widow, who would say she was sorry to keep you waiting, but she had been lying down, her nerves was so bad ever since her poor dear husband died. Then you would ask for Rosie Brown, and she would say she never heard of no such person; and you would say, Wasn't she one of the gals lodging there? Then she'd hold up her hands, and say, Gals lodging there! what ever did you mean? And you'd say, Wasn't she Mrs. Dorrell? Yes, sure, she was Mrs. Dorrell, a lone widow, getting an honest livelihood; and who ever had dared to say she took in gals to lodge there? O the wickedness of this world! They wouldn't have ventured to say such a thing if her poor dear husband had been alive to purtect her. And she'd ask you to inspeck the premises, and see if she had any room for lodgers there; and you'd see a tidy parlour, with a Bible on the table, and a picture of the Bishop on the wall, and a little kitchen, and nothing more; and you'd pass a little door to the back as you went out again, and take no notice of it. But if you could have opened it, which you couldn't, for the old hypocrite would have the key in her pocket, you'd have seen a court with twenty or thirty rooms round it, and two or three gals in each of them; and there's nothing much more like hell upon earth than that is, so far as sin and wickedness is concerned.'

Ernestine shuddered. 'I could indeed do no good there, but how then shall I ever see this girl?'

'Well, I shall just speak a word to the university marshal, and tell him all about it; and I'll ask him to get the proctor to go past the place for a night or two with his bull-dogs.'

'Bull-dogs!' interrupted Ernestine, astonished.

That's half a dozen of the university police that follow the proctor on his rounds. I'll get them to walk near Mrs. Dorrell's when the gals are coming out, and I'll let them see this picture. Then they'll keep Rosie in sight till they see some gownsman speak to her, and they'll have her took up in a trice, and soon get her sent off to gaol. So you go home, ma'am, and take it easy. Leave it all to me, and in two or three days' time at furthest, I'll send and tell you to come and see her here.'

'That will indeed be helping me,' said Ernestine; 'I am very much obliged to you. I will go and wait quietly as you say; I shall be so thankful to find her at last.' Her cheek glowed, and her eyes brightened at the thought; and the gaoler, looking at her with evident approval, as she rose to go, held out a huge hand, with which he solemnly shook hers, looking as if he were celebrating a compact of eternal friendship; and this ceremony over, the turnkey appeared with his keys, and conducted her to the gate, whence she hurried home to the unsuspecting Mrs. Tompson, who little thought from what species of society her charge had come.

CHAPTER II.

REGINALD'S HISTORY.

REGINALD was worse next day. All night the nurse said his cough had racked him, and the morning found him exhausted and yet feverish, and so he continued through the whole day. Dr. Compton stood musingly by the window of the sitting-room, after he had left him in the evening; and at last turning round, he met Ernestine's anxious eyes.

'Of course,' he said, 'you understand that I can say nothing comforting of your brother's state. I was only thinking just now what a wonderful tenacity of life he displays.'

'I daresay you will think me fanciful,' said Ernestine, 'but it really seems to me as if he could not die, so long as this terrible disquiet and unrest is upon him. His horror of death, whatever may be its cause, appears to chain his very soul back to earth, and his whole will is centred in the struggle to cling to life with all his strength.'

'No, I do not think you fanciful,' said Dr. Compton,

in the slow, thoughtful manner habitual to him. 'The termination of life is of course the result of physical causes; but there is no doubt that the bright, willing acceptance of death I have seen in some cases, does smooth the dark passage to the grave most wonderfully; persons certainly die more easily, and it may be, at the last, more swiftly, when they have fully resigned their place in this world, and turned their thoughts and hopes to the unseen future. I wish your brother would do so; but—' he said no more, and again stood thoughtfully looking out.

Presently there came a light knock at the door, and the visitor, without waiting for an answer, opened it and walked in. He was a man apparently of middle age, although his hair, which was cut close on his small head, was quite grey. He had a clever face, but with a gentle, quiet expression; and his voice when he spoke was peculiarly low and pleasant. He wore the gown of an M.A., and came in, cap in hand, when he perceived Ernestine in the room. Dr. Compton turned round—

'Ah, Vincent, is it you? I am glad you are better. I heard you were laid up in town.'

'Yes, I have been ill for six weeks.'

'Miss Courtenay,' said Dr. Compton, 'perhaps you have not met with Mr. Vincent before. Let me introduce him,—one of our college tutors, with whom I believe your brother is a special favourite.

Ernestine remembered the name as that of a man for whom Reginald had a great affection and admiration, and whose lectures he had attended assiduously.

'Yes,' he said; 'there are few young men for whom I have felt a greater interest than for Courtenay. I am deeply grieved to hear of his illness. I had no idea it was serious when I left Greyburgh. What do you think of him, Compton?'

'I may tell you the truth,' said the doctor, 'for I have not deceived Miss Courtenay. He cannot recover; there is extensive disease of the lungs, and the progress of the complaint is rapid.'

'I am shocked to hear it,' said Vincent, who looked sincerely distressed. 'I hope I may see him. It will not hurt him, will it?'

'Certainly not; I should think it would do him good to see you,' said Compton. 'At least, anything that gives him pleasure is good for him.'

Vincent smiled, as if there could be no doubt of Reginald's pleasure in seeing him; and as the doctor now took his leave, Ernestine asked him to sit down while she went to tell her brother of his arrival. As she opened the door of the bedroom, she saw Reginald leaning forward with a look of intense anxiety on his face. He beckoned to her hastily to shut the door and come near to him. Then he seized both her hands with convulsive energy, and said in a hoarse whisper—

'Is it Vincent who is there? Is it Vincent?'

'Yes,' said Ernestine; 'he wishes to see you; he seems so kind, and so distressed at your illness.'

A moment before, she could not have thought it possible for Reginald's face to become paler than it was; but now every shade of colour receded even from his lips, and left him ghastly.

'Ernestine, if ever you have loved me, help me now. Don't let Vincent come near me. To see him would be to recall every moment of agony I have suffered in these last dreadful weeks, and make me live them over again all in one. It is more than I can bear. It would rouse up all the demons of thought with which I have struggled so long. I hoped he would not have returned till my little time of life was past. Don't let me be tortured more than I can bear. Ernie, save me—save me!'

'My dearest,' said Ernestine soothingly, 'you shall not see him unless you like. I will go and tell him so. Don't tremble, Reggie; no one shall come near you.'

'The thought of the agony it would be to see him is enough to make me tremble; but don't let him think I have lost my affection for him, or that I am ungrateful for his past kindness. Say what you like; only save me from seeing him.'

Ernestine went slowly back. She hardly knew how to word the refusal, for she was aware that Reginald had been constantly with Vincent, and had greatly enjoyed his society. Ernestine was, however, of too truthful a nature to have learnt the habit of equivocation in her former fashionable life; so, when she met Mr. Vincent's inquiring look, she lifted her candid eyes to his face, and said—

'I am very sorry that my brother does not feel able to see you. I do not know why. He begs you will not think him ungrateful for your former kindness, or that he has lost his attachment to you; but he is unequal to seeing you.'

Vincent bent his keen eyes inquiringly on Ernestine.

'This is very strange,' he said, in his low soft voice, 'and, I may say, very painful to me, for Courtenay and I have been great friends. I felt for him as I might have done for a son or a younger brother of my own, and I should have thought that in this his hour of trial it would have been a comfort to him to see me. Is it, perhaps, that he is acting in accordance with advice from others?'

Ernestine looked up astonished. 'There is no one to advise him but Dr. Compton and myself, and we should both have been glad if he could have seen you, and found pleasure in doing so; but the truth is, there is so much in my brother's state of mind which is wholly inexplicable, that he seems to me, mentally, like a man covered with secret wounds, who shrinks from the slightest touch. I am sure you will understand, however, that I must do all I can to avoid his being agitated in his present weak state.'

'Surely; and I should be the last to wish to cause him any disturbance, if, indeed, to see me could agitate him. I can hardly think it, and I must hope this is only a passing fancy. Perhaps he is afraid that the sight of me might recall happier times; at all events, I will call to-morrow, and I trust he may be then able to receive me.'

'I hope he may,' said Ernestine. 'I will tell him how kindly you speak of him,' and as Vincent took his leave, she opened the door, and went softly into Reginald's room. She stopped a moment, in surprise at his position. Through the shadows of the twilight she could see him, leaning forward, gathered almost into a heap, his hands clasped convulsively on the arm of the chair, and his face bent down upon them, while deep gasping sobs shook his whole frame. Ernestine flew to his side. 'Reggie, dearest, what is the matter?' She knelt down, and tenderly lifted up his head. He turned towards her his ghastly face, tearless, but convulsed with the hysterical sobs, which he could not control, and stretched out his hands to her.

'Oh, Ernie, that I had never seen him! O that I could go back to the days before I knew him, when all was bright and clear in the eternal future! What if it were a dream,—it still was life! it was hope; it was rest and peace; oh, Ernie, it was heaven!' He fell back exhausted. Ernestine sat down quietly beside him, passed her arm under his head, so that he could lean against her, in which position he always rested more easily, and said to him, very gently—

'My darling, you made me promise not to ask you any questions, and I have not done so; but I cannot be blind to the fact that the mental agony you have been enduring lately is caused by a loss of hope in the future beyond the grave. I do not know what has produced it, or in what form it has come upon you, but I am sure that nothing else could make the prospect of death so terrible to you. I do wish now, Reginald, that you would unburden your heart to me, and give me back the confidence which never failed between us before. I think it would be a relief to you, and it could not make me sadder than I am to see you so far from peace and hope.' He gave a heavy sigh.

'Yes, if I have failed to deceive you, I may as well let you know all. It can make little difference now to you, or to myself; and you, Ernestine, who have been my life's friend, have a right to my confidence. It will be a relief to me to trace back the slow, mysterious steps of the evil that has overwhelmed me at last. But is there no one within hearing? Shall we be quite undisturbed?'

'Quite. Nurse Berry has gone home for the night, and it is too late now for visitors either to you or me.'

'Draw down the blind then. I do not want to see that starlit sky; it has been one of the tests of my wretchedness that I can no longer look on it without despair.' He paused a moment, and then resting his head on Ernestine's shoulder, began in a low quiet voice to tell her all she so longed to know.

'I first knew that I was dying, Ernie, about a year ago. I had had a cough and pain in the chest for some time previously, but one day I felt a choking sensation, and when I put my handkerchief to my lips it was stained with blood. I thought I knew what that meant, but I determined to ascertain the truth, without hinting at my illness to any one here. I went to London, and saw Sir ——-, the great consumption doctor. I did not tell him who I was, or anything about myself, but I told him I had come to him for an honest opinion. I wished to know if my lungs were fatally affected, and if so, how long I had to live. He was very frank indeed with me. He said the disease had already reached a stage when human aid and skill could no longer check it, and that, indeed, mine was a case which had probably been hopeless from the first. He said that in a warm climate—Madeira, or some such place—I might live two years or so ; in England, scarce half that time. My mind was soon made up to be content with the shorter term. A last year of life, in suffering and weakness, would have been dearly purchased by the loss of my friends among the thinking men of Greyburgh, and the opportunities I had here of testing and deepening my knowledge of the only subject that could be of any importance to me from that hour for evermore. I came back with the determination to devote the brief remainder of my life entirely to the study of divinity.'

'And you never let me know you were so ill,' said Ernestine sorrowfully.

' I know it seems as if I had been unkind, Ernie, but I did not mean it so. I loved you truly all the time; don't blame me now. I knew no care, no tenderness, could prolong my life one hour, and I did not wish my last precious days to be wasted upon fruitless efforts, moving from place to place, consulting doctors, and all the rest of the useless medical machinery which is such a mockery in a case like mine. The great event that was before me occupied my whole heart and soul,—I had so much to do!' He paused a moment, as if a flood of recollections were coming over him, and then went on: ' At that time, Ernie, the thought of death was sweet to me beyond what words can at all express. You know that my delicate health had precluded me from entering with much zest into the pleasures of either childhood or youth, and, in fact, I never knew what it was to have any love for this life. From the first moment when I could reason on the uses of existence it failed to satisfy me. I saw in every one of its varied phases its utter incompleteness. Men seemed to me to spend the whole of their allotted time on earth in acquiring, in some shape or other, that which was to perish with them— learning, fame, riches, happiness: which of these things could pass the portal of the tomb? " There is no work, nor device, nor knowledge in the grave, whither thou goest." These words seemed to me the bitter commentary written on all the occupations and desires of men; and if there was little in life that I could love, there was much that I could hate and shrink from. Like others who have been destined to an early death, many things were pain and grief to me which caused no pang to sterner and stronger natures. The sight of oppression and cruelty, even when practised only on poor helpless animals, has made me long to die many a time. Falsehood and injustice, with all the suffering they caused to others, wore my very soul with fruitless indignation; low degrading vices, and the coarse sensuality which brutalizes human nature, literally sickened me, and I turned with loathing from the many forms of evil and wretchedness in this world, to long with unspeakable desire for the hour when the Vision of Peace should dawn upon my eyes, the heavenly new Jerusalem in which I believed, even as I believed in Him who was its light, and joy, and glory; for, Ernestine,' and his voice became trembling and broken as he spoke, 'this was the master principle of my whole being at that time, the source of every thought and feeling, every hope and wish, the centre round which all my aspirations revolved. I believed in the marvellous revelation of a Love, unearthly, sure, eternal, which is involved in the doctrine of the Incarnation; and that love,—the love of the Incarnate God, seemed to draw me to Himself with an ineffable sweetness and fascination. In it I found the full satisfaction of my whole immortal being. Yes, every faculty, every affection of heart, and soul, and mind, could find expression and rest in a love which combined the perfect sympathy of a heart, human and yet pure, with the perfect protection and wisdom of a God. To know then, that a few months only separated me from the free and full enjoyment of this the only really Good, was simply rapture to me. The thought of the probable previous suffering, of the pang of soul and body parting, were as nothing in comparison with the inexpressible blessedness of passing into the immediate presence of Him, who had loved me even unto the death, and would love me still, for ever and for ever. Had I died in the day I first heard my malady was fatal, I had gone to the grave with rapturous joy; and the change that has passed upon me, the change which makes me now, with unspeakable horror, shrink from the death which I believe to be annihilation, or a worse form of life, because unpurified and hopeless, is the work of the man whom I have just refused to see. You must not mistake me; he did not injure me wilfully. It was with no deliberate intention that he brought this curse of unbelief and darkness upon me. Far from it. His desire was to serve me; but it was the inevitable result of his teaching, on a speculative mind like mine, the irresistible deduction from the principles he laid down as the foundation of all religious argument.

'Some time before I knew that my malady was hopeless, I had attended his lectures; and he had enforced upon me strongly what he considered the duty, as well as the privilege, of "free inquiry" as to matters of faith. He said it was unworthy of the reason with which God had endowed us, that we should rest, in what he called the hereditary belief we derived from parents or instructors, and quietly accept the teaching of others, without testing its truth for ourselves. Ah! Ernestine, how well I can see the miserable sophistry of such words now! But I did not then. I had not, however, up to that time, followed his leading in this respect. The love of Christ in the atonement was a reality to me; it was in truth all in all!—but when I saw death staring me in the face, when I saw that the time given me to make sure of eternal life was drawing with fearful rapidity to a close, then many words, many casual expressions uttered by Vincent, awoke in me an uncertainty as to whether my faith were right, and not a mere traditionary creed, whose foundations I had in no way tested, while the very fact that this faith was now so terribly precious to me, as the one hope of the eternity already opening at my feet, made me tremble lest I were in any measure resting in delusions. I felt that I must make sure of the ground on which I was to take my first step beyond the grave; and, in my arrogance, I thought that Vincent was right when he called it a duty to inquire, without fear of sacrilege or presumption, into the deepest mysteries of God, and to demand proofs of them which should be agreeable to human reason. It seemed to me that there could not be a more fitting occupation for my last few months of earthly existence; and I never for a moment doubted that the result would only be to give me firmer confidence, and more entire security, at least in the greater principles of that religion which was my life. And so, indeed, it might have been, but that, for my unutterable loss and misery, I determined to place myself under Vincent's teaching for this inquiry. I believed I could not have a more able guide, and he had always been kind to me; ever ready to help me in any intellectual difficulties. He gladly met my wishes then; and for the remainder of the term, I spent the most of my time at his rooms; while for the long vacation I joined a reading-party which went with him to Wales. I resumed the same practices for a few weeks after our return here; but by the time the early winter came I needed his help no more, and the sight of him was very agony to me; for his work was done; the blackness of darkness had fallen over my soul, and my whole being was given up to that awful desolation, which those alone can realize for whom God is yet unrevealed; and existing creeds, the baseless fabrics of a dream.'

Reginald paused, his white lips quivering, and the cold dews standing on his forehead. Ernestine gave him some wine, and kissed many times the thin, waxen hand she held, but she did not speak, and in a few moments he went on :—

'What Vincent's belief was and is, I cannot tell. He is a good man; nominally he holds the religion of Christ, and in that Name ministers to others, and specially to the poor, by whom he is much beloved. Never in so many words, at least in my hearing, has he denied the great truths on which that religion hangs but he cast more than doubt on the means whereby they are revealed to us; and, by denying certain facts, he left it an open question whether others were true,— by overthrowing the authority of one portion of an indivisible system, he cut away the foundations of the whole. The essence of his own belief seemed to be in a progress of the human race, analogous to that which takes place in the individual man from infancy to age; and, though he never said so openly, yet I could see, and others saw it as well, that he held what he called the traditionary belief, to be but the undeveloped conclusions of the world in its infancy, which could no longer suffice to its growing maturity. Of course, the deduction was obvious, that if, at the point to which he had arrived, so much was to be cut off, it would, in a generation or two, be deemed wise to give up the whole. Ernestine, you know it was a peculiarity of my mind that I could never rest satisfied with the primary and partial results of any theory or principle newly brought before me. I always felt that I could not truly or reasonably, either accept or reject a new proposition, till I had sounded the depths of every ultimate possibility involved in it. It was thus that I was compelled to act with every position Vincent took in our many conversations on religion, and the inevitable result was that I arrived at conclusions which he neither intended nor taught; and which it would probably have shocked him to know I had reached. He seemed himself to have the power to stop short at a given point in the false and dangerous line of thought he pursued; but he could not check the course of another's mind. He could not set a man on a steep, downward path, with impetus violent enough to carry him into the abyss at the bottom; and say, " Thus far shalt thou go, and no further." Gradually, it became plain to me, though he would never have admitted it himself, that the whole course of his teaching, and the ultimate conclusions to be deduced from them, tended to the practical denial of the one glorious doctrine on which the whole of Christianity hinges. The thought was utter agony to me. I fought with it, as with the deadliest foe. I held back from it with a desperate horror of the result; for his great intellect had overborne my weaker powers. Mentally, I was his slave; and, Ernie, my wretched, helpless struggle was in vain. On, on swept the darkness that was to steep my soul in everlasting night; and the hour came when at last it overwhelmed me, and I could no longer pretend to myself that I believed. I remember that hour! and, if there be an eternity, I shall remember it with anguish in every instant of the illimitable ages.

'I had been reading with Vincent, and in his low quiet voice he had been commenting on certain passages of Scripture, in a manner to give a dark confirmation to the worst conclusions, which his whole course of teaching could possibly lead to. He had done this in answer to an objection I had raised to some of his arguments,—an objection on which depended the last hold I yet had on the faith in which all my hopes had been centred; and he had overthrown this my final chance with the same calm unconsciousness, which from first to last had seemed to characterize his gradual destruction of my belief. I knew that he had done it; and I knew that the worst was come. I could no longer deceive myself. The time had indeed arrived when I must face the truth, and understand what my position really was. I muttered something about feeling ill, and without waiting to hear Vincent's gentle regrets, I rushed from his room, never to enter it again. My brain seemed on fire, while my heart lay like lead in my breast, and I was only conscious of one feeling,—the wish to be alone where none could interrupt me. I dashed away through the streets, crowded with men coming back from their afternoon walk, laughing and talking in careless mirth. I never stopped till I reached the farthest point of the meadow,—your favourite walk, Ernestine, but which in that cold winter evening was completely deserted, and as dreary a spot as could well be found. I flung myself down on the seat under the old oak, whose skeleton branches could not shut out the grey lowering sky. At my feet the dark river went its way, silent and cheerless. All around me the dead leaves lay soaking into the earth, wet with recent rains; the wind moaned and sighed like a spirit in pain, and the bare leafless trees tossed wildly to and fro as it passed shuddering through them. It seemed the uttermost desolation of nature; but oh, Ernestine, what was it to the desolation of the soul which had lost Christ and His love for ever!' He gasped for a moment, and then went on: 'As I sat there, feeling at first stupified and incapable of thought, the last gleam of red light which the dying day had left like a streak of blood on the horizon, disappeared suddenly in the heavy bank of cloud that rose up to meet the descending shadows, and night fell black and hopeless, as it had already fallen on my living spirit. Then I roused myself, and gathered up such energy of thought as yet remained to me to look my destiny in the face, as it was now and ever must be. Night without morning; death without resurrection; eternity without God: this was what I saw as my only future—for the intervening space of mortal existence was I knew passing from me swift as the flight of the night-bird that just then rose with a plaintive cry over my head and vanished into the darkness. Death! I could imagine the sobbing breath growing faint and ever fainter till it ceased—the familiar faces fading into the dimness shadowing the closing eyes—the heart growing slowly cold and still—the last choking pang of parting life; and then the motionless clay stretched out before the loving eyes of watchers; but when I went further, and tried to realize the annihilation which I believed would follow, I could not. Did you ever try, Ernie, to compass in actual mental reality the thought of a total cessation of being for yourself, the complete loss of identity, the extinction of consciousness? You will find you cannot do it; at least I could not. Still the ever-living Ego in myself rose rampant, and refused to recognise or believe in any real sense the possibility of its future non-existence. It seemed to me that the deathlessness of that vital consciousness within, was an indestructible conviction born with life, an innate idea which no strength of argument could kill. Reason assured me that annihilation must be my doom, that I had no more right to expect an immortality than the crushed insect at my feet, but the living principle within me rose up in mockery at the thought; it could not, would not perish! When I found this I turned to look at the alternative, and the very blood seemed to freeze in my veins, as I saw how far more horrible it was than even an extinction of being would have been. Ernestine,' and he grasped her wrist with his thin fingers, 'think of the soul cast out from the body which housed and sheltered it, and placed it in communication with human affections and capacities, with the sources at least of comfort and rest,—think of it, flung, a helpless breath of indestructible life, an isolated principle of being, of identity, of consciousness, upon the desolate wilderness of illimitable space, like a feather tossed upon the boundless ocean, like a mote wandering on the boundless air,— no God, no Christ, no stay, no rest—no refuge, where it might hope to flee in the most distant immensity— no help, no protection, no love—no possible aim, no imaginable hope—alone, and alone for ever, in the most awful of conceivable solitudes, the desert of infinity! This is the doom I had learnt to expect beyond the grave, and, Ernestine, can you wonder that from the indescribable horror to which I am hastening, I shrink with an agony of dread, abhorrence, and repulsion, to which no human words can give expression? Doubtless it is a pitiable sight to see a dying wretch like me clinging to his diseased decaying life, with an abject terror of its loss. What a coward I must seem, shuddering through my worn frame at the thought of the dissolution which is the universal law of all mankind,— the death which feeble women and tender children have met with smiles of joy! But oh, Ernestine, the blackness and coldness of that eternal solitude beyond, who could endure it one instant, even in thought?—a spark of life alone in the abyss of infinite space!'

'This is too much for you, Reginald,' said Ernestine tenderly, as he remained silent for a moment, under the influence of a strong fit of shivering. 'Say no more now, you can tell me the rest to-morrow.'

He did not answer or seem to hear her. His dark eyes, wild and dilated, were fixed on vacancy, then gradually a softer light stole into them, shining through the dew of unshed tears, and he spoke again, not in the hoarse, excited voice with which he had up to this time given out his rapid utterance, but in a low dreamy tone, which fell softly on the ear:—

'I remember, as I lay upon the ground, crushed under the weight of this awful anticipation, from which I knew I could never escape till the reality swallowed me up, there rose upon my soul a vision of what death would have been if the love of Christ had still been truth to me. I saw myself passing from a life where all was incomplete, where human joys and loves proved to be but the mocking shadows of the divine reality; where an ever unsatisfied longing, an ever enduring restlessness, consumed the living soul, whose eternal rest and satisfaction could be in ONE alone; and through the grave and gate of death I seemed to float into the serene deep, the pure ecstatic calm of that Love, revealed in living Presence. As a bird flying back to its nest through storms and gloom, I seemed to dart towards that Fount and Centre of all peace and consolation, till, clinging with adoring thankfulness to the holy pierced Feet, I looked up into the Eyes once closed for me in mortal death, and met the infinite tenderness, the unfathomable love of their pitying gaze, and learned in that one look to know that He was the aim and object of my being, the desire of my immortality, the full contentment of every aspiration, the very consummation and perfection of all bliss. Oh, fairest, purest dream! Oh, heavenly light of boundless hope! Oh, blessed vision of rapturous peace! If but one instant it might visit me again, with its sweet soothing promise; if but once more I might imagine I could meet the compassionate eyes of the one True Love, stronger than death and deep as eternity! But in vain, in vain—never, never more—lost, all lost! Ernestine, I am faint; is this death?' and the broken words died on his lips, as he sank into a deep swoon. In great alarm Ernestine raised his head, and used strong restoratives, till the feeble pulse slowly beat again, and a tinge of colour dyed the white lips. As consciousness returned, he drew her face close to his, and whispered faintly : 'One more word I must say that you may know the worst, Ernie.' With a great effort he seemed to gather up all his strength to speak, and went on: 'The idea of living out my life with that awful prospect beyond it was too intolerable. I determined to lose all thought of the future in that which men call pleasure, but which the God in whom I once believed calls sin. What did it matter if I stained myself with deadly vice, if there were no loving Father, no compassionate Saviour, no sanctifying Spirit, to call for honour and purity from my deathless soul ? If there were no God, then was there no law, no righteousness, no distinction between good and evil. To make the most of life, such as it is, by sensual indulgence, is the religion of men who have no faith, and into this I plunged—loathing it, loathing myself, and ruining the souls of others with my own, till death came near enough to grasp me by the hand and drag me out of it, with but this certainty for fruit of sin, detested in its very commission, that if the religion in which I formerly believed was true, then had I, by my wanton defilement, cut myself off for ever from the Holy God.' As he spoke his form seemed to collapse, and his head sank on his breast, till he lay huddled into a heap in his chair. The nurse had been for some time in the next room, and Ernestine called her anxiously to come to him. She shook her head when she saw Reginald.

'Miss Courtenay,' she said, 'we must lay him in his bed now. He is too weak to refuse, and he cannot support himself any more in his chair, I am sure.' Ernestine agreed, and together they lifted the light burden and laid him down on the bed from which he was never to rise again. Then the nurse gave him a strong stimulant, which roused him from his stupor, and the mournful dark eyes opened slowly, and fixed themselves on Ernestine, with a look which seemed to bring tears from her very heart. She knelt down beside him, and whispered—

'My darling, the love you have so longed for is not and never can be lost. It is with you, it is round you still. You cannot see it, as a blind man cannot see the sun, but it is surely there, for the love of Christ is the charity that never faileth.'

He could not speak, but his eyes remained fixed on her with a piteous hungering look, till they gradually closed in utter weariness, and he slept the sleep of exhaustion.

CHAPTER III.

THE VALLEY OF THE SHADOW OF DEATH.

ERNESTINE had been in a measure prepared for the revelation made to her by her unhappy brother; nor did his complete subservience to the master-mind of another surprise her, for his reasoning powers had never been strong, and his susceptible temperament and ardent imagination laid him peculiarly open to any intellectual influence which might be brought to bear on him. But she remained in sore perplexity and distress about him during the long sleepless hours of that sad night. Was she to let him die in this utter darkness and despair? Yet what could she do: he would certainly refuse to see any one more able than herself to help him, and how was she to reach this wandering soul, from which the very light of life had been stolen? When she returned from the hotel, where she had vainly tried to obtain a few hours' rest, it was plain that a great change for the worse had taken place in Reginald since the night before. He lay now perfectly still, because too weak to move, saying nothing, but showing, by the restless eyes, which spoke volumes to his sister whenever she came near him, that the poor wearied spirit within was still keenly alive to its unabated torture. The doctor came early, and Ernestine saw by his manner that he believed Reginald to have gone down many steps into the valley of the shadow of death since he had seen him last; but he could do nothing beyond insisting on perfect quiet, and administering the usual composing-draught, which kept him half dozing through the first part of the day.

Ernestine had gone into the sitting-room to write a few lines to Lingard, when the door opened softly, and Vincent appeared. The hot blood rushed to her face with the sudden fiery indignation, most unusual to her gentle temperament, which the sight of him produced. She rose up, and remained standing;—unable, with all her habitual courtesy, to ask him to sit down in that room, while, with a quick glance, she satisfied herself that Reginald's door was close shut, so that no sound of the too familiar voice could meet his ear. Vincent came forward, and asked with tender anxiety how Courtenay was.

'He is dying,' answered Ernestine, with involuntary abruptness.

Vincent looked keenly at her. 'You shock me, Miss Courtenay; this is sad news: is he worse than he was yesterday?'

'Much, much worse.'

'Then I trust I shall have the comfort of seeing him to-day, as I fear from what you say it might be too late another time.'

'It is quite impossible,' exclaimed Ernestine.

'Does Compton forbid it?'

'I have not asked him.'

'You are acting, then, on your own responsibility in refusing me admission?'

'Yes, and I know that I am right,' she answered sadly.

'Miss Courtenay, may I ask you to consider that, notwithstanding the difference of age, I have been your brother's most intimate friend here; and I have some right to demand the opportunity of bidding him a last farewell.'

Ernestine turned impetuously towards him: 'You can call yourself his friend!' she exclaimed, 'when to you he owes it that he is dying the most miserable death it is possible for a mortal man to suffer!' The passionate tears burst from her eyes as she spoke, and, flinging herself down in a chair, she hid her face in her hands. Vincent stood before her quite silent for a moment, and then, in a cold calm voice, he said—

'This is a very grave charge, Miss Courtenay. I think you will admit that you are bound to substantiate it; to me it is quite inexplicable.'

Making a great effort to regain composure, she lifted her head and looked at him.

'My brother came to you in the ordinary course of his studies, full of the deepest peace, and the brightest hope in the Faith, which he had never doubted one hour. You told him that he was trusting to false securities, when he listened to the voice of God speaking to him through the channels of His own Divine appointment. You told him that a "free inquiry" was his duty; that he must seek the truth for himself, with no other guide but his reason; that he must demand to be initiated into the counsels of the Most High, and refuse to believe what he could not understand. His mind is not strong, his reasoning powers are not great: he followed your advice, under your own guidance, and the result has been that all faith, all light, have been obscured for him by the blackness of an utter infidelity, which is surrounding his deathbed now with the horrors of the most complete despair it is possible to imagine.'

Vincent was resting his head on his hand as he leant on the mantel-shelf. He looked down at Ernestine as she spoke, and when her eyes met his, the natural gentleness of her nature reasserted itself within her. 'Mr. Vincent,' she said, 'I feel that I have no right thus to seem to call you to account, though it is hard to watch such a death in silence; but when Reginald told me last night that there were many others on whom your influence had worked as fatally as on himself, I felt the longing wish that you could know the effect of your teaching as I know it now, who have witnessed my brother's agony. It would be some consolation even for his bitter misery and ruin,' she continued, her voice choked with emotion, 'if his cruel sufferings might save others from the risk of such a doom. I think it would, if you could see—'

She stopped, unable to proceed; and after a moment of painful silence Vincent said: 'Did your brother tell you that *I* had taught him infidelity?'

'Not in so many words, but you threw discredit on the sources whence his faith was derived. You cut away the old foundations from beneath his feet, and opened the way to dangerous speculations; you led him to a given point in theories whose ultimate conclusions could be none other than a denial of the truths he held;

and however little you may have intended such a result as has arisen, you first enforced this free inquiry upon him, which has been his ruin.'

'But,' said Vincent, 'unless men are to accept with a blind senseless submission the creed which comes to them by inheritance, without ever investigating its truth for themselves, what other guide can they have but the reason their Creator has given them?'

'They have the Word of God, the witness of the Church, and the voice of Him who redeemed them, speaking to their souls, if they will but hear Him.'

'These are the very points on which we require proof; and how are they to be tested but by reason?'

'The Redeemer of the world gave a very different test,' said Ernestine, lifting her clear eyes to his face. He said we were to learn the truth by personal holiness: "Whosoever will do the will of my Father which is in heaven, he shall know of the doctrine whether it be of God." He has once for all proclaimed Himself to be the Light of the world, and called on men to prove His truth by following Him, for in so doing they should not walk in darkness, but have the Light of life; and this is but the echo of more ancient teaching, when, long before Christ came, His Father had announced to men of old: "If with all your hearts ye truly seek Me, ye shall ever surely find Me." But, Mr. Vincent,' said Ernestine, checking the words which seemed to burst almost involuntarily from her lips, 'I feel that it is not for me to talk on such subjects with you: it is not a woman's province; and I have no wish to step beyond that, even if I were competent to argue with you. But one thing only I think I have a right to say, after witnessing the anguish of such a deathbed as my brother's. Whatever your own opinions may be, you have of course undoubted liberty to hold them free from questioning by any human being, but why,—why will you tamper with the faith of others? This is what I cannot understand in you, and teachers like you. Why risk a calamity so terrible as the loss of faith to any living soul, knowing, as you do, how subtle, how delicate is the hold we have on truth in this imperfect life, and how dreadful is the agony of doubt, the utter void and darkness of unbelief? Is it not enough that men have sin and temptation, and a thousand perils, to beset them on the path of eternal life? Why loosen their grasp on the only support on which they can lean with hope of safety? Why seek to make others share opinions of whose truth you can never be certain on this side of the grave, when in so doing you must disturb the calm which they believe has come to them from God? What if you imagine this to be delusion, death alone can prove if you are right or wrong,—too late for reparation to undying souls. Mr. Vincent, have you never thought what it is you are doing if the ancient faith you are undermining in these souls be indeed the very truth of God? Is it not their very life, their eternal life, which you are taking from them? Oh, surely it were better and safer to hide for ever in your own mind the doubts and speculations which may work such fearful ruin. Your own life is given you as a prey, but the souls of others are in the hand of God. Oh, why not leave them safe with Him!' She was almost sobbing before she ceased, and Vincent looked at her with an expression of deep pain.

'Miss Courtenay, believe me I would rather die than consciously injure the souls of others. But is there not a duty to the truth itself? Are we not bound by this free inquiry, against which you protest so warmly, to secure that truth from being falsified, or misrepresented, or overlaid with human traditions?'

'Cannot God defend His own truth, the true faith once given to the world? And is it likely that all the endless varieties of human intellect and reason, swayed by the impulses and motives of individual temperament, could meet in acknowledgment of the only truth? Mr.

Vincent, I pretend to no logical power of argument, or to learning a hundredth part as great as yours, but this I know, your teaching has wrecked the soul of him who lies there dying in despair; and I cannot believe that the utmost good you could ever have hoped from the avowal of your opinions, could weigh for a moment in comparison with the inestimable value of one deathless soul.'

He listened, his eyes fixed on her face, and, without waiting for an answer, she held out her hand and said, 'I must go to Reginald now; forgive me if I have spoken too freely.'

He held her hand tightly for a moment, and then spoke in a low voice, 'If indeed I have caused your brother the pain you speak of, it is I who need forgiveness; and in any case I deeply grieve for his distress and yours; but I find it hard to believe my teaching has caused a result so different to my wishes.' He seemed as if he would have said more, but, checking himself, he loosened his hold, and turned slowly away.

Ernestine went at once to her brother. He was lying quite still upon his bed, but there was an unusual brightness on his face, and all physical pain seemed to have ceased. The nurse had seen too many deathbeds not to know what these indications meant; but seeing no alarm in Ernestine's expression, she did not like to speak too freely.

'He is a little revived, ma'am,' she said, 'and has been asking for you very often. He can speak without coughing now, but I don't quite like his look,' she added in a whisper, as she passed out of the room.

To Ernestine it seemed, however, as if, for the time at least, he were better. His voice was stronger, and his mind evidently quite clear. As she came and sat down beside his bed, he drew her close to him, and asked, with a look of intense eagerness, 'Ernestine, on what ground did you make that assertion last night? What is the evidence on which you found your strong faith in Christ and His love?'

'The evidence of my own soul,' she answered. 'I *know Him* in the inmost depths of my spirit, not as a mere object of faith, but as a living Person, whose presence I can recognise to be a vivid reality, as clearly as if I saw Him with my bodily eyes. It is a faith not only in the historical Christ of eighteen centuries back, but in the Being, truly existent now, so surely as I live myself, who this day hears me when I speak to Him, who this day is conscious of every thought and feeling of my heart.'

'Internal evidence!' said Reginald; 'that is not a

ground on which logicians or scientific men would consider that any principle of faith could be established.'

'That may be; but there are some truths known as realities to the soul, which neither science nor logic may be able to discover. Reginald, I find it difficult to explain my convictions in words, but I will try. My trust, my whole confidence, is given irresistibly to the actual personal Christ, who is known and admitted by all to have existed once upon this earth. It is not the outward manifestations of His divinity which chiefly satisfy me, but the perfection, the unearthly loveliness of His character and life, which are unquestionable facts. My belief is in the Being, whom historical truth makes known to us in the incomprehensible greatness of His love, His justice, His purity, His utter abnegation of self. Nothing in the whole wide universe would induce me to believe that He, such as He was, could have come into this world to deceive, or even to have let that human race, whom He loved unto the death, deceive themselves concerning Him; nor could I for one moment look back upon the Mount of Calvary, and see Him in His calm, willing suffering, His majesty of forgiveness, His tenderness, His pity, the Omnipotent dispossessing Himself of life, and believe that He was mistaken. My faith is in His own individual truth, and, therefore, apart from all external evidences, I know that He of a surety is that which He represented Himself to be. For all mysteries, for all difficulties, for all apparent incompleteness even in His manifestation of Himself, I rest upon His own solemn assurance, "What I do thou knowest not now, but thou shalt know hereafter;" and oh, Reginald, there are other words of His, which, because of His incontrovertible holiness and love, might well have power to lay the whole unquiet world to rest,—" *If it were not so, I would have told you.*" If He were not the incarnate God, He would have told us; He would never have let us rest in false hopes of Himself. If He could not have saved us, He would have told us; if His sacrifice upon the cross were not indeed the atonement for the sins of the whole human race, He would have told us. Oh, Reginald, He, such as He was, such as all admit Him to have been, would never have bidden the hungering, thirsting generations of the dying world to come to Him, if He could not indeed have given them life.'

She remained silent, feeling the convulsive grasp of Reginald's hand tightening on hers, and his breathing growing more rapid with emotion as she spoke; but she was unable to divine what thoughts were passing through his mind, and he did not speak. Suddenly a slight noise at the open door attracted her attention, and, looking up, she saw Thorold standing on the threshold. Reginald perceived him too, and instantly, with a great effort, he raised himself on his pillow, and held out both hands towards him in silence, but with an appealing look which could not be mistaken. Thorold was at his side in a moment, and Ernestine went softly out of the room and closed the door, leaving them together. She felt thoroughly exhausted, and, sitting down, she let her head fall on the table before her, and remained a long time in that position, hardly knowing where she was, as her thoughts wandered far into the world beyond the grave.

At last, when a period much beyond what she imagined had elapsed, and unconscious that her name had been called several times without her hearing it, she felt a gentle touch on her shoulder. She started, and turned round to meet Thorold's grave, calm look.

'You must come at once to your brother,' he said, 'but be prepared.'

'For what?' she said, with a sudden gasp.

'For the end, which is come. He is sinking fast.'

She flew into Reginald's room, and flung herself on her knees beside him, but no word or glance told that he knew her. He had reached that awful, mysterious moment, when the boundaries of mortal sense are past, though life is not yet extinct. The spirit hovered already on the confines of the Unseen, and the eyes, wide open, were fixed upward in that look of fascinated awe and amazement, which those who have once seen it in the eyes of the dying can never forget. The sight checked the cry of love and anguish on Ernestine's lips, as appalled, she saw that, from the midst of his doubt, and darkness, and error, Reginald was passing to the inexorable truths of the changeless eternity. She would fain have called him back, if by any means he might yet have been armed and strengthened for the dread realities opening before him, but she dared not speak.

Thorold's voice, uttering the solemn words of the commendation of souls, alone thrilled through the death-chamber, as the dark, unmistakable shade stole over the wan face, and the breath gasped out at longer and ever longer intervals, ceased at last to stir the white lips with even the faintest motion. Silently, secretly, the mighty mystery was accomplished. The living, sentient soul was gone to know God in His justice and in His love, where no human speculations or error could dim the glory of His everlasting truth; and the wasted form, in which it had sinned and suffered, lay cold and motionless beneath the burning tears of that poor human love, which is ever so helpless in the face of death.

Yes, he was gone! And whether in that last hour the ineffable pity of the Lord he had denied restored him faith and gave forgiveness, or whether he passed away in his awful darkness, could never be known till the day when the secrets of all hearts shall be revealed, and the dread uncertainty must remain as a shadow on Ernestine's life for evermore. What passed between Thorold and Reginald in that supreme hour she never knew. No word on the subject ever escaped Thorold's lips, and she respected his silence too much to seek from him even the expression of an opinion which might have quieted her painful anxiety. Only once, a few days later, as she and Thorold stood one on each side of the coffin, looking down for the last time on the white still face before it was hid away for ever, her intense anxiety with regard to Reginald found expression in the earnest pleading look of her eyes as she raised them on Thorold. He understood and answered, ' It is not for man to judge. Only remember this, that while the justice of God is immaculate, His mercy is beyond what the human heart can ever in this world conceive. " God is love."'

CHAPTER IV.

ANNIE BROOK.

IT was well for Ernestine Courtenay, at this period, that her unselfish interest in Annie Brook made it impossible for her to dwell too exclusively on her brother's death, and the painful circumstances attending it. When Thorold had appeared so opportunely in Reginald's room, he had come to tell her that Rosie Brown had been arrested the night before, and committed to gaol for a fortnight. He told Ernestine he thought it would be as well that she should not see her for the first few days, that the girl might have time to realize the additional disgrace and wretchedness which her position had acquired by this first imprisonment; and it was not until a day or two after Reginald's funeral that Ernestine, exhausted by her grief, felt able for her visit to the object of her long search. She looked forward to this interview with intense anxiety. What if, having found the lost child, she should fail to win her from the deadly evil that enthralled her? She felt that she never could endure to let her go again. Yet legally she had no power to detain her, if Annie should refuse to leave her accursed life and her bad companions, and Thorold warned her that she must not be too sanguine.

The old gaoler received her with immense cordiality. He came himself to the second gate to meet her, and, without saying a word, held out his capacious hand, and took hers with an air which implied that their sworn friendship was a fact which he defied the world to disprove. He conducted her to his own room, and begging her with a majestic wave of the arm to be seated, he took his usual place opposite to her.

'Well, ma'am, we've been and caged your bird for you,' he said.

'Yes,' said Ernestine, 'I am so very glad, and I should have been here before to see her, only—' She glanced at her black dress.

'I know,' he said; 'there's not much goes on in this here town without my knowing of it. I'd like to see the man as would go and get buried in Greyburgh without telling me first,—leastways his friends. Well, ma'am, Rosie Brown's here, and she's a bright bit of a thing, that it is a sin and a shame to see driven to such a trade as this. Now, I'll tell you what I've done to help you. The gals that were here when you were so uncommon green in letting them see you wanted her had only three days of their term to make out when she came, so for that time I kept her down in the kitchen with my missus, and would not let her see one of them, except when some of us was there to prevent them speaking to her. They are so awful set against Penitentiaries, since one or two of them have tried them, they'd have persuaded her on no account to hear a word you said for fear you sent her to one. However, you'll find I have kept the road clear for you; neither she nor the gals we've got in now have ever heard of you.'

'I am so glad to hear that,' said Ernestine; 'it would have been hard indeed to have lost her before I had even spoken to her. Has the chaplain seen her?'

'Well, he has seen her in the chapel at prayers, and he has said a word or two to her along with the rest; but bless you! he has not time to lay a finger on the souls of one of these poor wretches. He is a good man, and he'd like to do his best for them, but he can't be in four places at once, and he had need to be if he was to be of any real use as a parson; for I don't count just putting on his white gown and saying the prayers, or giving them a Bible-class altogether, as the parson's real work. I want to see him drag their souls back from hell, and fight it out with the devil for each one of them; and how is he to do that when he is chaplain of the workhouse at Burton as well as here at the prison, and when he has a church and a parish besides, and when he's got to take the chaplain's work at the other gaol when he happens to be ill, which that chaplain do happen to be pretty often; and if that's not enough, this poor parson of ours has got private pupils at home, besides a wife and children to see to.'

'How strange!' said Ernestine; 'I thought there would have been a chaplain entirely devoted to the gaol. There must be quite work enough for one clergyman among so many prisoners.'

'Work enough and to spare; but you see, ma'am, our great people here who manage these things, they looks to the money, and, judging by the salary they gives the chaplain, they must count the souls of these prisoners to be dear at half-a-crown apiece; for he don't get so much, by a good deal, as you'd give your butler, ma'am. Well, he's got a wife and children, worse luck for him, and he must feed them; and as he don't get much more at the workhouse than he does at the gaol, he has to try it on with a few more things to get enough for their food and clothing. These matters want looking into by some one who would have the power to set them right.

But it will soon be locking-up time, so if you please, ma'am, I'll tell my missus to bring Rosie Brown to you.' He rose and went out.

Ernestine almost trembled when she found herself waiting at last for the child whose fate had lain so heavy on her heart. The white still face of Lois seemed to rise up before her with its mute, mournful entreaty, and her heart thrilled with the earnest longing, that by any means she might have power to win the yet living soul of that dead girl's sister to repentance.

'There, gal, you go in there; there's a lady wants to see you, and mind now how you behave, or you'll have a double lot of oakum-picking.' And Mrs. Bolton, who had not had time to perform a sufficiently elaborate toilette, opened the door, pushed in her charge, and closed it again without appearing.

Ernestine Courtenay was alone with Annie Brook. A young girl, in whom she at once recognised the original of the portrait, stood before her, and dropped a little curtsey as she met her gaze. She wore the prison dress, which, uncouth as it was, gave her an appearance of modesty and propriety she most probably would not have possessed in her own gay clothing. Her face had still much of the childish loveliness which her likeness had so well represented. The wealth of sunny hair was there, escaping from under the coarse white cap, and the large blue eyes yet shone beneath it,—bright, though restless; but the sweet look of candour and innocence was gone, and the face was very pale and haggard, while an expression, half defiant and half sullen, had replaced the smiling gladness which was so characteristic in the sketch. Yes! she was the same;—yet how changed, deeper than the change from mortal life to death; for over her undying soul had passed the darkness of that great mystery which changed the Eden of God's creation to a world of chaotic sin and sorrow, whose mournful beauty ill contrasts with the moral evil that taints it everywhere. In this fair child's lingering loveliness there were yet dim traces of the Image in which she was first created; but on her spiritual being had fallen the dreadful desolation of unrepented sin.

Never before had Ernestine Courtenay thus stood face to face with one on whom the brand of social disgrace was indelibly marked, who, in addition to the secret stings of conscience, had the consciousness of that public degradation which entailed upon her the scorn or avoidance of all whose good name was yet untarnished; and she would have been expected, not only in her own caste, but even by those whose charity made them seek to reclaim such sinners, to consider herself bound, for the sake of principle and the girl's own moral good, to hold her at an immeasurable distance, and teach her, by word and look and manner, the gulf which lies between the fallen and the pure. But, happily for Annie Brook, Ernestine followed the instincts of that inner sense with which the love of Christ had gifted her, and there was, though she knew it not, the deepest wisdom, as well as the truest charity, in her mode of action; for if ever human agency is to work for good upon the erring, it must be by the faint but true reflection of the one Love which alone gives hope of life and restoration to a ruined world; and, so far as regards the special class to which Annie Brook belonged, it is a short-sighted policy indeed which would suppose they require coldness and haughtiness on the part of the unfallen to teach the awful distance which lies between them. They know it already, these poor lost women. God help them! they know it with a bitterness of knowledge which brings keener anguish to their souls than the direst insult their fellow-creatures could inflict. Seldom, doubtless, does one of them, however hardened, look in the face of those who have not known their temptation or their sin, without a maddening sense of their own unspeakable loss, and an anguish of envy, almost akin to that which the spirits of the lost might feel when gazing across the gulf to Paradise. It is not the religious aspect of their state which moves them. Most often they do not know of religion, even the name; but it is the innate instinct implanted in them by God, which makes them feel to their heart's core that purity is the one priceless treasure which marks the boundary between the soul's own inmost heaven and hell.

Ernestine Courtenay stretched out both hands to the fallen girl before her, and, clasping hers with a warm pressure, exclaimed, 'Dear Annie, I am so thankful to have found you!'

The girl looked up at her with a glance of surprise. 'Do you know me?' she said.

'Yes, Annie, though I have never seen you before I know you well, and I am your true friend. Sit down here beside me, and I will tell you why I have come to you.'

With evident reluctance, and shunning Ernestine's eyes, Annie did as she was told; but the sound of her real name, so long unheard, seemed to fill her with vague apprehensions that her conduct was about to undergo a scrutiny it could ill bear, and that the liberty of action she had so long misused would now be assailed. There was a good deal of sullen rebellion in her expression as she sat beside Ernestine, rolling her apron-strings in her fingers, and looking determinately down at them. Ernestine was fully resolved to tell her Lois's whole history, as the surest mode of leading her to hate and dread her own wretched life, but she feared to shock her by too abrupt an announcement of her sister's death.

'Annie, I have come to you from one who loved you well,' she said.

A flood of crimson colour dyed the girl's fair face at these words. Her lips parted, and she turned to Ernestine with a half-uttered question. It was plain that her thoughts had flown to the man whose love had been her curse; but a dark remembrance seemed to come upon her; the glow died out, and was replaced by a look of dogged despair.

'There was few that ever loved me, and there are none now,' she said.

'You are mistaken there, my child; but the one who caused me to come here to look for you was your own sister, Lois.'

'Lois!' she said, with a sad bitterness; 'she has been my worst enemy; she and her fine make-believe husband. I would never have left father but for her, and then—I should never have been here.' She covered her face with her hands, a flood of bitter memories coming over her.

'I know,' said Ernestine, 'it was very cruel to take you from your home; but poor Lois bitterly repented it, and you must not think unkindly of her now; indeed you must not.'

Something in her tone struck the girl. She turned round—

'Is anything wrong with Lois? I left her gay enough, I am sure.'

'It was a wretched gaiety, and had a wretched ending. Annie, you will never see Lois again in this world.'

'Is she dead?' almost screamed the girl.

'She is indeed; poor Lois is already lying in her lonely grave.'

In an instant tears were bursting from the bright blue eyes, and a convulsion of grief, as brief as it was violent, passed over the impulsive girl. As she rocked to and fro in her wild sobbing, Ernestine gently held her hand, and smoothed the fair hair, till the soft tender touch unconsciously soothed her. After a few minutes her passionate agitation subsided; she wiped her eyes, and, speaking in a gentle, humble tone, said—

'Please to tell me all about her, ma'am.'

'I will, my dear child,' said Ernestine; 'but it will be very sad for you to hear it.' Then, conquering her repugnance to speak of her brother, she began: 'You know the—the gentleman with whom Lois was living was not her husband?'

'I know it—I know it; no more was he my husband who drew me from home with his fine promises, and then flung me on the streets to get my living.'

Ernestine sighed heavily as she thought of the countless similar victims whom selfish wickedness had driven to hopeless misery. She went on sadly—

'Lois was deserted at last by this gentleman. After a time she heard he was going to India.'

'Oh, that must have gone nigh to break her heart, she did love him so. Was that what killed her, ma'am?'

'No,' said Ernestine; 'it would have been happier for her if she had died of a broken heart. She unwisely thought she could go to India with him, and came on board the ship where he was, and then she found he was married, and she had to go on shore and leave him.'

'That would put Lois almost wild. What did she do, ma'am?'

'The worst, the saddest thing she could do, Annie: she took away her own life; she drowned herself.'

'Drowned herself! O poor Lois! O my poor darling sister! It's too sad—it's too hard. Oh, to think of her lying in the cold, cold water, all wet and cold and dead! And we used to sleep together, she and I; and she would cover me up so warm, and kiss me always first and last thing, night and morning. O it's cruel—it's cruel! Why did that bad man take her from her home to ruin her—and me? O it's all so miserable. I wish I were dead, like her, and lying with her in the grave!' And the sobs, which had been bursting from her through all her incoherent words, now fairly choked her; in a paroxysm of agony she flung herself on the floor; but Ernestine lifted her up, so that the poor sunny head, now brought so low, might rest upon her knees, and then she let her weep out there the grief that would have vent. Gradually she became more calm, and, quite exhausted, she lay like a tired child in Ernestine's compassionate arms.

'Annie,' she said gently, after a time, 'I think you will like to know that Lois's last thought was for you, and the very last words she ever wrote were all for you alone. It is because of what she wrote then, that I am here.'

'What did she say, ma'am? I should like to know,' and she lifted up her head and listened anxiously.

'She said that in the last most awful hour, when she was going to try and escape, by a guilty death, the sin and misery that seemed more than she could bear, her only wish, her only prayer was for you, that you might be rescued out of the life you were living, and saved from such a death as she was dying. She knew it was through her fault you had fallen away, and this was the bitterest thought in all the bitter grief that weighed her down. Annie, when Lois wrote that about you, she was very near the other world, where she would see face to face the God she had offended, and the Saviour she had forgotten; and she saw things then as they really are, and not as they appear to us when death seems far away, and this world everything. She saw how very short life is, and how quickly all its pains and pleasures pass, whether they be for good or evil. She saw and knew what a terrible madness, as well as sin, it is in us so to spend our little time on earth doing the devil's will, not God's, that when we come to die we have nothing but eternal punishment before us, instead of trying to lead good and holy lives, that we may be happy with the dear Lord Christ for ever. Annie, poor Lois had no hope for herself. She was going to die a sinful death, as she had lived a sinful life, but she thought there might still be hope for you; so she spent her last moments upon earth in writing to the man who first led you both to evil, entreating him to find some means to save you out of your wretched life, and give you a chance of coming back to the blessed Lord who died for you, and still loves you, Annie, deeply as you have sinned against Him. The letter your poor sister wrote was given to me, and I only waited to see her laid in the grave, before I came to look for you, my child, and save you from your misery, if you will let me.'

The girl's face was bowed upon Ernestine's hands, which were wet with the tears she seemed to shed in silent hopelessness; and now she neither moved nor spoke, but only breathed long shuddering sighs, which shook her whole frame.

'Dear Annie,' said Ernestine, after a few moments' silence, 'will you not listen to Lois pleading with you from her very grave? and still more,' she added, in a low tone, 'will you not hear the voice of your departed Lord speaking to you from the blessed heaven, where He longs to have you with Himself?' And then, in words too solemn for these pages, she spoke to the lost child of the Love that suffered for her sin, and even now watched and waited for her in realms of deathless light. She spoke of the eternal desolation of the soul cut off from Him, and of the ineffable sweetness of pardon that might yet be hers, if she sought the grace of true repentance, and washed the sin-stained garments of her soul in the precious Blood, which alone could make them white as snow. Long and earnestly, with glistening eyes and trembling voice, Ernestine spoke of the home beyond the grave, and the rest it gave from sin and temptation, from pain and weariness, and cruelty of man,—of the blessedness of laying down the tired head upon the Feet once pierced for us, in safety and in peace for evermore; and, with her whole heart in each word she uttered, she implored the fallen girl to break away from the hideous, loathsome evil that encompassed her, and fly for refuge to the Deathless Pity that never failed the repentant soul, how dark soever all past sin might be. 'Annie, Annie, say that you will turn and repent,' she added. 'I cannot leave you till you have promised me to save your soul from living death.'

Then the girl flung out her hands passionately, and exclaimed—

'What shall I do? Oh what shall I do? I know it's a wicked and wretched life; and I thought at first I'd rather die than join in it; but he drove me to it—he, the only one I ever loved. Yes! he forced me to it, and told me it was all I was fit for now; he who ruined me;

and oh, when I heard that—when I knew that he thought me lost and degraded already—I did not care what came of me, and I tried to believe it was a gay life, as others said, and to forget everything, or I should have gone mad altogether; but oh! I have been wretched, and I am wretched now, and yet I can't leave it—I can't. He who took me away has deserted me for ever, and father will never look on me again; and Lois is dead, and I can never, never go back to what I was. Oh, why was I born? why was I born?' and she rocked herself from side to side in uncontrollable emotion.

That agony was upon her—the fiercest that human nature can ever know—the agony of regret for dark deeds done in the irrevocable past, which never, in all the everlasting ages, can be undone again! God help those who have known, and yet may know, the burning fire of that intolerable anguish!

Ernestine's intense power of sympathy made her thoroughly comprehend the living torture embodied in that writhing frame, and she let the girl's misery have its way for a time; then she gently took her hand, and said—

'Annie, my child, if you will only trust me, I will find you a home where you will be safe and peaceful, if not happy as you once were; and where, in a good and useful life, you may win your way back to our blessed Lord, who is our only consolation and our only real joy. Say that you will trust me, dear child, and I will come for you the day you leave the gaol, and take you with me. You will come to me, will you not?'

Annie lifted her head and looked at Ernestine; and as she met the sweet eyes which were so full of pitying, pleading love, her heart seemed to melt within her. She let her head fall down again on the delicate hands which held her own, and said—

'You are so kind and good, I must do what you wish. I will go with you wherever you like.'

CHAPTER V.

THE REFUGE.

THUS far the victory was gained, and Ernestine was very thankful; but her interview with Annie Brook had roused her gentle nature to a degree of indignation against the man who had destroyed her, of which she could hardly have believed herself capable. When she wrote that evening to tell Lingard that she had really found the unhappy girl she had sought so long, she gave vent involuntarily to some of the strong feelings which moved her :—

'Apart from the actual wickedness of his conduct,' she wrote, 'which lies of course between himself and his God alone, I could not have believed it possible that any man could have been, not only so cruel, but so cowardly and so mean as to rid himself of his victim when she became a burden to him, by forcing her into the last depths of sin and degradation, because his own treachery had made her, as he thought, fit for nothing else! And this pitiful selfish being is, no doubt, received by his acquaintance as if he were good and honourable, instead of really deserving to be branded with a thousand times more of infamy and disgrace, than the poor child for whom he has prepared a life of misery here and eternal death hereafter. I hope this man will never cross my path in the course of my lifelong care of his victim, for I feel as if I could not breathe the same air with him; nor would I consent to the smallest intercourse with such an one; for I can no longer abide by the world's code of morals on this subject. It seems to me simply a mockery of the God of truth, and purity, and justice, whom we profess to worship, to visit the poor weak victim with the heaviest punishment, casting her out like the leper of old, while we allow the greater criminal to come amongst us not only unscathed, but welcomed and honoured.'

Ernestine received no direct answer to this letter; but a day or two later, Lingard wrote, urging her most warmly, now that her object was accomplished, to come to London, and let arrangements at once be made for their marriage. He was now certain of the appointment he had been expecting, and there was no further reason for delay, excepting her brother's recent death; and he trusted she would not think it necessary to wait till the period of her mourning had quite expired. Ernestine answered by promising to come to town the following week, so soon as she had placed her charge in some safe refuge; and as it was now early in May, she agreed that their marriage should take place in the course of the summer.

In the meantime, her great anxiety was to provide a safe home for poor Annie, before the time when her term of imprisonment expired, which would be in the course of a few days. She knew that there were now, happily, various 'Homes' and Penitentiaries where such an one could be received; but she had no idea where it would be best to apply. She therefore wrote a line to Thorold, telling him she had been thus far successful in persuading Annie to begin the work of repentance, and begging him to tell her where it would be wisest to place the poor child. He came to her that same evening on his way to the night-school, just as Mrs. Tompson, attired in elaborate slight mourning, was starting for a dinner-party at the Granbys'. Ernestine inwardly rejoiced at the fortunate circumstance which prevented her chaperon from assisting at a conversation which was likely to make her hair stand on end; for poor Ernestine's interest in Annie Brook had not in the slightest degree shaken Mrs. Tompson's allegiance to the orthodox theory, that such individuals, and the Homes that shelter them, should be simply ignored, and considered non-existent by all persons of 'good society.' Whether the privileges of good society were to extend into the other world, when the proscribed class, and those who might have saved them, met face to face, was not a question into which this well-bred lady thought it necessary to enter. Mrs. Tompson was, however, by no means satisfied to forego her proper duties as Ernestine's chaperon.

'A most extraordinary hour for a morning call!' she exclaimed, as she heard Thorold coming up the stair. 'Introduce me, my dear,' she added in a whisper, as he appeared.

This ceremony Ernestine performed with a smile lurking on her lips, which Thorold quickly detected.

'I have much pleasure in making your acquaintance, Mr. Thorold,' said Mrs. Tompson, with a sweeping salutation, to which he responded with the utmost gravity; 'but unhappily it is rather late: I am on the point of going to dine with Dr. and Mrs. Granby. Miss Courtenay does not go out in consequence of her recent bereavement, and is, I think, fatigued; but if you could give us the pleasure of seeing you to-morrow, instead of this evening, we should then both be able to receive you.'

'I am afraid I cannot at all answer for what I may be doing to-morrow,' he answered quietly ; ' but I think Miss Courtenay can spare me a few minutes now. Will you allow me to conduct you to your carriage, which I see is waiting?' and he offered his arm with such exquisite politeness, that Mrs. Tompson was fain to accept it, and allow her silks to rustle down stairs in company with his rough great-coat, as if they were most congenial companions. He placed her in the carriage, told the coachman to drive on, and having satisfactorily despatched her, came up the stairs two or three steps at a time.

'You have asked me a difficult question,' he said, plunging into his subject at once, as he sat down. ' I doubt if I can recommend any Penitentiary to you, which would be likely to suit a girl of so impulsive a temperament as Annie Brook.'

'Do you not approve of the system on which they are conducted?' asked Ernestine.

'I approve of their theory, but not of their practice. The state of the case is just this:—Some years ago, a strong impetus was given to the exercise of charity on behalf of that unhappy class. It was shown to be a black stigma on our country, that they should be left to perish by thousands, with scarce an effort made for their rescue; and it was further demonstrated, with great truth, that the only persons who could undertake their reformation, with any chance of success, would be earnest, religious women of the upper ranks, who would be willing, for the love of Christ, to devote themselves to so painful task. Thus far, nothing could be better. The principles on which they started were sound in themselves, and their fruits were the same up to a certain point. Many Homes for the Fallen were established all over the country, and good women were found to conduct them, whose saintly self-denial, and true devotion of heart and soul, are beyond praise. So far as they themselves and their honesty of purpose are concerned, not a disparaging word can be said; they are living for others in the true abnegation of self, which is the sure test of Christ's people; and I doubt not that they will be of those who, in the day of His glory, will be astonished at the greatness of their salvation, so far beyond what they looked for; but all this does not prevent the fact that they have, as I believe, started on a mistaken system, so far as the treatment of these poor sinners is concerned, which has greatly marred their success. They begin with the fatal error of dealing with those unhappy girls, as if they were, what they are called—*penitents;* whereas not one in a hundred has even such knowledge of God, and of a future state, as would enable them to understand what penitence means. And, building on this erroneous foundation, they fix for them a rule of life, which none but persons not only heart-broken with remorseful sorrow for sin, but possessing also cultivated minds and highly-wrought religious feelings, could endure for any length of time. I cannot enter into details; but, generally speaking, the system in our Penitentiaries is one of great over-legislation; of unchanging conventual strictness; of iron rule binding on the corporate body without relaxation for individual temperament or circumstances; of monotonous duties, irksome punishments, religious services too often, which they do not understand; and an almost total deprivation of open air and exercise. Add to this, that the exemplary ladies who guard them have conceived the unfortunate idea, that instead of working on their affections, they are to teach them the difference between the holy and the fallen, by treating them with distance and coldness, and by rigorously demanding, and enforcing by penalties, the highest respect to themselves as their superiors,— and you will have some of the causes which have rendered these Homes more repugnant to their inmates than the gaol, as they themselves say, and which makes them, with few exceptions, so unwilling to remain, or to return to them a second time. And this brings me to my difficulty: I cannot tell you of any one of those Refuges where I think you can place Annie Brook, with any hope that she will be able to endure the rigid discipline long enough to work a real reform.'

'I am sure Annie is not a girl who could stand severity,' said Ernestine, 'especially after the lawless independence of her present life; but have none of these Homes profited by their non-success, so far as to see the necessity of a change? Have none of the more recently formed been induced by the experience of others to alter their system?'

Thorold shrugged his shoulders. 'We human beings are strangely gregarious,' he said, 'after the manner of sheep, who will all, one after another, press through the gap the first has made in the hedge, though there is an open gate a little way beyond. These excellent people have religiously followed in each other's steps; each newly established Refuge receiving its "Rules" and form of discipline from one of the elder Homes. I cannot tell you the vexation with which I hear, whenever a new Penitentiary is about to be commenced, that a lady from one of the other Refuges has been sent to teach the persons engaged to work in it, the "proper" system of management, so that each one is firmly planted in the mistakes of its predecessors. However, there is such true love for souls, and such unselfish zeal in those who thus devote themselves to the fallen, that I feel sure in time they will learn a happier mode of dealing with them, and I do not mean to say that even now they are uniformly unsuccessful; far from it. The earnestness and holiness of the workers cannot fail to bring a blessing on the work, and although the souls they have saved are, as I believe, few in comparison with the numbers they might have rescued on a different system, yet the salvation of even one soul is more than worth all that the Home could ever cost; so you must not suppose I would discourage any one from giving them the utmost sympathy and assistance in their power. Whenever one of these unhappy women enters a Penitentiary from any motive sufficiently strong to induce her to bear the irksome rules, the confinement, and severity, long enough to let the good teaching she receives awaken some spark of real repentance in her heart, it becomes then possible for her to submit to all that is so galling and depressing as a needful chastisement for her sin, and we must hope that this may be the case with Annie Brook. If you can win her personal love to yourself, you will have done a great deal towards her ultimate rescue: for where the love of God does not exist, human affection is the only other impulse that can work for good within the soul, though in a feeble and uncertain way. It is often allowed to serve as a guide to the higher, purer love, and it can at least accomplish what haughtiness and severity could never effect.'

'You do not think then that there is any preference to be given to one of these Homes above another?'

'I think not; they have all the same advantages, and the same defects. I will give you the names of several, and you had better take your charge to the first which has a vacancy. I trust you may not find that in some particular, she is not eligible for reception there, according to the rules of admission, which seem to be generally framed with the peculiar property of frustrating the object of the charity, by rendering it scarcely possible for the poor creatures to effect an entrance to the Home built expressly for them. They are very generous in taking them in free of charge, but you will like, no doubt, to offer some payment for Annie, and you will do well, as the funds of all these Refuges are scanty enough, I fear.'

Ernestine thought it only right that the girl should be supported at her expense, and having somewhat magnificent notions in such respects, she offered a sum sufficiently large to be of great use to the 'Home' where they agreed to take Annie Brook on her application. There was, however, one absolute condition made to her reception, besides various hints as to what would be expected of her, and this was that she should be able to bring with her a certificate of perfect health—about the last thing which one of her class would be likely to find possible. In this emergency Ernestine applied to Dr. Compton, who went at once to the gaol to see the girl, and on his return he told Ernestine he considered her in a very feeble and precarious state of health.

'There is no organic complaint at present,' he said, 'and nothing certainly which need prevent her being received at the refuge, so that I can give her a certificate; but there is extreme debility and exhaustion of the system, and, like too many of her class, she will die a premature death on the first occasion when her powers are in any way unusually taxed.'

'And can nothing be done to restore her, or prevent such a result?' said Ernestine.

'You can only use preventive means. Quiet, good food, and plenty of fresh air in fine weather, will give her the best chance for life. She must guard against exposure to cold. Whatever happens, you can have the comfort of feeling that if you had not taken her out of her present life, she would not have lived six months longer in it.'

If anything could have deepened Ernestine's anxiety about the unhappy child, it would have been this opinion. Her time for repentance was likely to be short; how earnestly she trusted nothing would occur to mar it.

The day of Annie's release from prison came at last, and at seven in the morning Ernestine was at the gaol to receive her into her own safe keeping. This was the gaoler's wise arrangement, for Ernestine, in her ignorance, had been quite ready to let Annie go to her lodgings first, for the various effects she had left there.

'Bless my heart,' said old Bolton, when he heard this proposal, 'how precious innocent these ladies be, to be sure! Miss Courtenay, if you want to make very sure that you'll never set eyes on Rosie Brown again, you'll just let her go off to Mother Dorrell's when she goes out from here.'

'They would not keep her by force, would they?' asked Ernestine.

'They wouldn't need to, for they could soon persuade her to stop; and if so be they couldn't, though that ain't likely, they would just give her a neat little glass of gin to keep her spirits up, and a drop of something besides in it, and she'd be asleep in five minutes, and then, when she woke up, they'd say you had never come for her, and a blessed thing too, for they had found out you were going to shut her up in a place worse than the black-hole; and then they'd say there was a fine new hat some one had brought for her; and see if you or any one else could ever lay a finger on her after that.'

'What had I better do then?' said Ernestine.

'Well, I'm bound to let her out by seven in the morning; it's against the law to keep her longer, and you had best be here to take care of her as soon as she is out of my hands. If you take my advice, you'll have her off by the train as fast as ever you can; it's pretty sure there'll be some bad 'un sneaking about outside the gaol waiting for her, but they'll not venture to show themselves if she's with you. I'll send a policeman to Mother Dorrell's for her clothes, and he'll take the bundle straight to the railway station, so you'll be all right, if she does not make off on the road.'

The Refuge where Annie was to be received was at some distance from Greyburgh, so that Ernestine was well pleased to start early; and having persuaded Mrs. Tompson to go on to London by a later train, she found herself at the gaol before seven on a glorious summer morning.

The gaoler told her that Rosie Brown was exchanging her prison-dress for her own clothes, and as Ernestine preferred waiting among the flower-beds, with which the court-yard of the prison was embellished, he gallantly plucked some lily of the valley, which grew under the shade of the high wall, and presented it to her. Then he went in to complete the formularies of Annie Brook's release. Ernestine remained looking at the flowers he had given her, the lovely little snow white bells showing spotless against the fresh green leaves, still glittering with the early dew; then she gazed up to the cloudless morning sky—one bright expanse of limpid blue—and felt around the cool untainted air, which scarce that day had met the breath of man, and saw in them all but faint reflections of the eternal beauty and purity of the Creative Mind; and there awoke in her soul that intense longing which sometimes overpowers us, for the coming of the sinless kingdom, when the Divine One, who alone passed holy and stainless through this world's pollutions, shall reign in righteousness; when over all the glorious renewed creation there shall not be a blot or shadow, and when through the myriad hosts that then shall live eternally to love Him, there shall not be one who bears upon the soul a taint of evil. 'O Lord, how long?' she could have asked, with the souls that were bid to wait in their white robes beneath the heavenly altar till their brethren should be fulfilled; but far off in the inscrutable mystery of the Divine Will that radiant vision lies, and she had only meantime her one brief life wherewith to struggle through her little part, in the accomplishment of its desired fulfilment.

The gaoler's voice, telling her that his prisoner was delivered over to her, woke her rudely from these thoughts; and she started in complete astonishment at the sight which presented itself when she looked round. Annie Brook stood in the doorway of the prison, as if in a picture-frame, dressed in a costume, in which there could be no doubt she looked strikingly beautiful, but which was much more fitted for the stage than for a walk through the streets to the railway station. A little white hat with a scarlet feather rested lightly on her sunny hair, which fell its whole length in waving masses almost to her waist; and she wore a red cloak of somewhat fantastic shape, over a dress of silver grey. The excitement of the moment had brightened her large blue eyes, and brought a vivid colour into her cheeks, contrasting with the waxen white which was now apparently her habitual complexion. Lovely she certainly looked, but strangely out of keeping with the place and the purpose for which she was equipped; and Ernestine, willing as she was to undergo pain and annoyance on Annie's account, thought with no small dismay of the observation she would excite walking through the streets with such a companion, and there was no longer time to send for a carriage. Mrs. Bolton, however, who came out with the girl, was equal to the occasion. 'Ah! I see what you are thinking of, Miss Courtenay. She looks more fit to go and dance as Columbine with Harlequin, than to walk through the streets with a lady like you. Here, gal, you just pull that red feather out of your hat, and put it in your pocket; and take off that flashy cloak, fit to set a bull crazy, and I'll lend you a decent black shawl, which the lady'll send safe back to me, I make no doubt.'

'That I certainly will, and thank you very much,' said Ernestine; and Annie, flushing crimson, began with feverish haste to obey Mrs. Bolton's direction.

'Here,' said the old woman, 'give me the cloak, and I'll wrap it in a bundle for you to take with you, and then you'll have it at hand if so be you should want it where you be agoing;" and she winked to Ernestine, with a significance which showed she thought this a piece of exquisite sarcasm. Annie was soon more suitably attired, and walked beside Ernestine down to the gate, which the gaoler himself held open for them.

'Good-bye, my gal,' he said to Annie. 'I hope I may never see you here again; and that's about the best wish I can make for you; for I've turned the key on some of your sort as good as a hundred times. You go and do whatever that lady tells you first and last, and you may be a bright woman yet. And as to you, ma'am,' he added, turning to Ernestine, 'if so be I don't happen to see you here again, I'll see you in heaven as sure as I'm alive, for you're as safe to get there as ever was Moses and Aaron, or any of these fine Bible fellows. Bless you, you'll go up as straight as a sky-rocket, you will.' With which favourable prediction he closed the gate, and left Ernestine alone with her charge.

So long as they were traversing the square in which the gaol stood, Annie walked quietly by her side, never looking up, and seeming scarcely to breathe; but when they got into the streets, she began to gaze from side to side, with a quick, restless movement of the eyes, like those of a startled fawn, when it comes suddenly from a wood to the open country. Her cheek was flushed, her breathing hurried, and she seemed hardly able to control her nervous excitement. Occasionally, she gave a sudden glance towards Ernestine, which, if the latter had had a little more experience, might have alarmed her considerably for the safe conduct of her charge, but Ernestine knew nothing of the impulsive, irritable temperament, which is induced by such a life as Annie had been leading. As they proceeded on their way to the station, they passed out of the streets, and came to a road where the green fields were to be seen on either side, and Annie's excitement seemed to increase.

'Oh! I wish I were out running in those fields,' she exclaimed. 'Ma'am, I hope you are not going to shut me up, where you're taking me; I couldn't bear it—indeed I couldn't. There was this good in my life before,' she added, 'I could do just as I liked, with no one to stop me, whatever I fancied.'

'But you see, Annie dear, you did very badly for yourself, when you did as you liked. Where you are going now, you will learn to lead a better life, and you will wonder you could ever bear to do as you have done.' Annie seemed scarcely to hear her, so anxiously was she looking round. The station had now appeared in sight.

'We shall be just in time,' said Ernestine. 'There

is the train almost ready to start.' At these words the girl made a sudden movement; but at the same moment the little terrier Fury, who was trotting quietly on in front, turned right round and ran furiously at Annie, barking with such violence that she screamed aloud, and flew back to Ernestine, catching hold of her arm in her terror. Ernestine took her hand and quieted the dog, wondering much at his strange violence; and so long as Annie remained close to her side, he made no further demonstration beyond a watchful glance of his eloquent brown eyes; but if she moved even a step forward, he barked angrily again, till Annie fairly clung to Ernestine in great trepidation; and so they reached the station, just in time to take their places in the train before it started. Long afterwards, Annie told Ernestine that at the moment the dog barked at her, she had, in her longing for freedom, finally made up her mind to run away from her, and hide in a house not far off, where she knew Ernestine could never have obtained access to her. By what instinct the dog divined her purpose, and by what mysterious ray of light he knew that he must save her from the dark temptation which assailed her, none can say; but the fact that a little Skye terrier did, by his sudden barking, stop the flight of a reckless soul to its destruction, is no fiction, but a very truth, to which the poor sinner herself bore witness.

From the moment they entered the railway carriage Annie seemed to resign herself. She sat beside Ernestine, with her hands listlessly folded on her lap, and her head drooping, as if she cared little what became of her. After a time, when they were alone in the carriage, she said—

'Miss Courtenay, does father know poor Lois is dead?'

'Yes, the coroner wrote to him about her, and I saw him myself afterwards.'

'And was he sorry?'

'I am sure he was, but he did not like to speak of her.'

'No, because she had disgraced him, as I have done;' and tears gathered in her eyes as she spoke. 'Father was often sharp to Lois, because she was so high-spirited, but he was always kind to me. When Lois wrote and bid me come to her, I left a letter, telling him I had only gone to see her. I was a bad girl to go, for I knew father would be vexed; but I never meant to stay; and next day father sent me a letter to say if I'd come back then and there, he'd take me in before my Lady knew I was gone, and look over it; but that he'd never see me again if I went and did as Lois had done. And oh, Miss Courtenay! I did so want to go back to him; and I would have gone, if Mr. Brown would have let me, for all I loved him better than any one else in the world.'

'You had known him before, then?' said Ernestine.

'Yes, he was staying at the Hall, and when I went walking he used to come and talk to me, and be so kind to me, and he gave me such a many pretty things, and I loved him with all my heart; but I knew he was a gentleman, far above me, and I tried so hard to forget him; and oh, Miss Courtenay, it was very sweet to see him again at Lois's house: but still, when I got father's letter I said I would go back; and I knew poor Lois wished it, for she told me she would never have brought me there if she could have helped it; and Mr. Brown over-persuaded me not to go, and said if I'd come with him I should have everything in the world I wished. But still I said I'd go home, ma'am, for I had heard the names Lois had been called in the village, and then Mr. Brown said, Well, I should go then, but he'd drive me himself to the station, and go part of the way with me, and I was pleased at that, for I loved him so it half broke my heart to part with him; and he fetched such a beautiful carriage and horses,—I so enjoyed going out in it with him! But I remember so well—oh, so well!—as I stood on the doorstep looking at the carriage, Lois came and took tight hold of my hand, and whispered, " Annie, don't go with him; for the love of God don't go; I'll send and get a cab to take you to the train, and see you off myself!" And I stood thinking what I should do, when Mr. Brown turned round and held out his hand, looking so smiling and bright, and bid me come, for it was all ready, and we should have such a nice drive to the station; and I went; but oh, Miss Courtenay, I've thought of that moment over and over again, till I have been almost mad, for it was my last chance. If I'd refused to go with him, and let Lois take me to the train, I'd have gone straight home, and father would have taken me in, and I'd never have brought disgrace on him and ruin on myself; and I might have been good and happy, and held up my head with the best of them. Oh, if only I could get that moment back again, if only I could!' and she literally writhed on her seat, in the impotent longing for that which could never be hers again while the universe lasted. Poor child, she thought perhaps that none could suffer as she did then; but there are probably few amongst us who do not know what it is to look back to some point in our own life, when our destinies in this world, and perhaps in the next, were yet in our hands for good or for ill, and when, in our blindness and madness, we chose the fair-seeming evil, and let the good slip through our fingers for ever and for ever. Earth has no anguish greater than the hopeless passionate yearning for such a moment to return. It would have been so easy then to have taken a different course—yes, even if it cost a pang; but now, not tears of blood, not the rending of soul and body, not the bringing down of heaven with prayers, could give that one omnipotent moment back again! Ernestine saw what she was suffering, and tried gently to soothe her.

'And did Mr. Brown take you to the train?' she said, wishing to draw her thoughts away from the one recollection which seemed to madden her.

'Yes, but not to take me,—oh, not to take me home! When we got to the station he said he'd go a bit of the way with me, and I was very, very glad to have him a little longer, but I never doubted I was going straight to father's till I saw the towers of Greyburgh; then he told me he had brought me there because he could not bear to part with me, and he said I couldn't go back now, for father would never take me in, after I had gone off like that alone with a gentleman, and Lois couldn't, for he knew she was not going to stay where she was, and that I had not a friend in the world but him now, and I must trust him, for he loved me well; and he said he'd give me a pretty house to live in; and when I still cried, and said I must go to father, he said perhaps some day he'd marry me, and so I stayed with him; and the end of all his love and all his promises has been that now I am in the railway train again, going from a gaol to a penitentiary;' and without saying another word she remained silent, shedding hopeless tears, which seemed to give no relief to her aching heart; and Ernestine thought, mournfully, of the awful guilt, that surely must one day call for vengeance, on the man who could with such dark treachery compass a fellow-creature's ruin. In this world he would walk unchallenged among his equals—respected, it might be—and happy as those can be whom selfishness and worldliness have hardened into enjoyment of the pleasures of life, even though their existence is weighted with the murder of an immortal soul. That is a crime which on this earth is neither recognised nor punished; but how will it be when its black hideousness is exposed before the face of Him who sits upon the great white throne?

Once only Annie spoke again as they went on their way. She lifted up her head, and said to Ernestine, 'Miss Courtenay, will you tell father that I have never been called by my own name, so at least I have not brought disgrace on his? Lois said, when I went there,

I should never be called by it, for she had heard how mad it made father to have her spoken of as she was in our village; so when Mr. Brown asked her my name, for he had not heard it at the Hall, she said he might call me what he pleased, for he should never know my true name any more than hers. She called herself Mrs. George, so he said then he'd call me Rosie, for I was just like a rose; and I had on a brown dress, so he said I should be Rosie Brown, and he'd be Mr. Brown. I don't know now what his own name was, but he never knew mine.'

'I will tell your father, dear Annie; I am sure he will be glad to know that you are going to a safe home now.'

At length the painful journey was over, and Ernestine and her charge had reached the door of the Refuge.

'Oh, Miss Courtenay, if only you were going to stay with me!' said Annie, clinging to her as they stood waiting. 'I love you, and I'd do anything for you, but I am afraid of being shut up here.'

The door was opened by a lady, who locked it again so soon as they were inside; and as Ernestine gave her name she glanced at Annie, saying, 'The penitent, I suppose?' Then she opened the door of a small room, and told Annie to wait there till she could attend to her. The girl did as she was told, and was locked in; and Ernestine was then conducted through various long and somewhat gloomy corridors to a large comfortable sitting-room. Here her guide left her to call the lady who superintended the establishment; and this latter soon made her appearance. She was very courteous and kind to Ernestine herself, but she listened to her account of Annie Brook with a certain sternness, and did not seem to think there was so much excuse for her as Ernestine was disposed to find in the circumstances of her ruin. It was evident, too, that she gave not the slightest weight to Miss Courtenay's anxious explanations of Annie's impulsive and sensitive disposition, which would make her so easily led by any appeal to her affections, and so fatally repelled by harshness.

'We treat all our penitents alike, of course,' she said calmly; 'I cannot undertake to show any special favour to this girl.'

'I should not think of asking you to do so,' said Ernestine, 'only, individual temperament must surely be considered in the manner in which they are spoken to, and in their treatment in all that concerns themselves separately?'

'Our rules embrace the whole course of their management, and to them we adhere.'

'But your object is to save individual souls. Surely you leave yourselves the power of such relaxation as may sometimes be required by special circumstances?'

'Our first consideration must be the general good of the penitents and the peace of the house, which can only be attained by strict conformity to rule; also,' she added, with a smile which was gently disdainful, 'from what you tell me of your wishes with regard to this penitent, I am not disposed to think that our views would be the same as to the most fitting mode of treatment for her.'

'You have experience and I have none,' said Ernestine courteously. 'In any case, I am sure you will do your best for this poor child. Circumstances have caused me to take a deep interest in her, and I feel very anxious for her future. I am afraid I must go now, however, leaving her in your safe keeping, for I must travel to town by the express.'

'I am sorry to detain you, but I must beg you to wait a few minutes. I have sent one of the ladies to read the rules to Annie Brook; and it must depend, of course, on her promising to abide by them whether I can retain her in the house.'

'Oh, I trust they are not very formidable!' exclaimed Ernestine; 'she is so timid and excitable that she is very likely to be dismayed at first by what might afterwards seem easy to her.'

'No penitent is admitted who does not promise to comply with the rules,' was the inflexible answer. Presently there came a light knock at the door, and the lady went out. In a few minutes she returned—

'I am very sorry to distress you, Miss Courtenay, but I fear you must take this young woman back with you. She has refused to give the necessary promise that she will stay two years.'

'Oh, surely she is not obliged to promise that at present?' exclaimed Ernestine. 'Of course, it is all new and strange to her. She cannot possibly tell whether she would be content to remain two years. I do not think any one could do so on first entering upon a life of which they knew nothing.'

'It is our rule,' was the lady's answer.

Ernestine was in despair. 'Will you let me talk to her, and perhaps I can persuade her to say what you would wish?'

'Certainly,' said the lady, and she was conducted back through the long corridors to the little room where Annie was sitting in a corner, crying as if her heart would break. She flew to Ernestine the moment she saw her—

THE REFUGE.

'Oh, Miss Courtenay, take me away from here. I shall never be able to bear it. They say I must promise to stay two whole years, and that's just like a lifetime. I can't promise to let myself be shut up among strangers all that while; and there's such a many things I am to do and I am not to do, I am frightened to death at it all. Tell them to let me out. I must go away.'

'But, Annie dear,' said Ernestine soothingly, 'where would you go to? I am sure you don't want to go back to your wickedness, and it is impossible for you to get an honest living anywhere without a character. I am sure you could not bring yourself to go to the workhouse if you went out from here, could you?'

'O no, no!' said Annie, shuddering.

'Well, that is the only other place where you could be safe from the sin that is bringing you to destruction. Surely you will say that you will try and stay two years, rather than let yourself be drawn away again from the merciful God who is calling you to repentance?'

'I don't want to do wrong again,' said Annie; 'but I can't promise to stay in this place two years.'

'Annie, it would be better to die than do wrong. Yes,' she continued, as the girl looked up surprised, 'it would be better to die in any tortures than to sin against our Father in heaven, for our Saviour tells us Himself not to fear those who can only kill the body, and then have nothing more that they can do, but to fear Him who has power to cast both soul and body into hell. Annie, think of Lois. Her body is lying in the cold grave, and her soul is gone to wait the dreadful judgment-day. If she could come back to earth again, do you not think she would be only too thankful to have two years, or twenty, or a thousand given her in this house for repentance? Oh my dear child, what need it matter to any of us what we have to bear in our short lives here, if only we find mercy with our dear Lord at the last? He died to save you: will you not suffer a little to go to Him?'

'Oh, Miss Courtenay, I could bear anything if you were going to stay with me.'

'But I will come and see you often, Annie dear, and I will write to you. Now, you will let me tell the ladies you will try and stay two years, will you not?'

'I would do anything to please you,' said Annie, and Ernestine went at once for the lady, who was in the next room, and having returned with her to Annie, she told her the girl would try and stay two years.

'You must not only try, you must do it,' said the lady very decidedly, and then Ernestine took leave of Annie, with a warm pressure of the hand and a few words of kind encouragement, to which the poor girl's sobs prevented her from making any answer. Ernestine caught the last look of her blue eyes wistfully turned towards her as the door closed, and she could not resist a final entreaty to the lady, to treat with as much indulgence as she could, one of so impressible and affectionate a disposition. 'I forgot too to tell you that the doctor who wrote her certificate considers her in a very feeble state. He does not think she can live long.'

'That is very likely,' said the lady. 'It has been proved by statistics that the average length of these girls' career is from four to five years; but the good food and quiet of this house may do much for her.'

Ernestine then quitted the Refuge, knowing that she left Annie in safety for the present, and it was with a feeling of intense thankfulness that she looked back over all the difficulties she had surmounted, and felt that she had been thus far able to keep the pledge she had given to the dead.

CHAPTER VI.

THE CLOUDS BEGIN TO GATHER.

THE month which followed this day of anxiety was one of such deep happiness to Ernestine Courtenay that the memory of it haunted her to the very hour of her death. She tasted then to the full the sweetness which the human heart can sometimes know even in this perishing world. Long after, when all the sunshine had faded out of her life, and existence lay around her like a dim landscape at eventide, where the shadows fall heavily on earth, and the only brightness is in the sunset gleam which seems to open a vista to the purer land, the thought of that little time of exquisite joy would come back to her, as in the gloom of a northern winter the recollection returns of the perfumes and beauty of a southern clime. She had no misgivings while the bright weeks were passing that it was happiness too great to last, nor did she seem to hear, as some have done, the footsteps of the coming sorrow echoing down the long dim aisles of the future. She gave herself up to the trusting love which filled her heart, and let it flood her whole being with its ineffable joys. There was not a shadow on the radiance with which it surrounded her; not a doubt, not a fear. The undercurrent of sadness which the thought of both her brothers would ever leave for her beneath all the enjoyments of this world, had not power to mar the intense personal happiness which she found in Hugh Lingard's love. He had from the first been passionately attached to her, but there was an inexplicable change in his bearing towards her, which was calculated to have the deepest charm for one so gentle and warm-hearted as Ernestine Courtenay. There was a tender reverence in his manner now, a loving devotion which was unwearied in seeking how to please her. He seemed to hang on every word she spoke, as if he longed to learn from her on all points, and to bring his very thoughts into accordance with hers, if that were possible. He did not now, any more than formerly, make professions of religious faith, and Ernestine's own convictions on that subject had greatly deepened since she had of late been brought so near to some of the great mysteries of the soul, in life and in death; but she had ever believed Hugh Lingard to be good, and pure, and chivalrous, as the knights of old, and she hoped now more than ever, that he did hold a true religion in the hidden depths of his spirit, though he mistrusted himself too much to show it openly, and that it yet would find its full development in the life they hoped to lead together. In this she was deceived. Whatever change there was in Hugh Lingard had not sprung from any clearer perception of the truth of God than that to which he had attained when she first became engaged to him.

Very little was said between them on the subject of Annie Brook. Ernestine had fulfilled her promise of keeping Lingard *au courant* of her proceedings at Grey-burgh, but of course the subject was one on which it was painful to her to speak; and after having told him that her mind was now at rest in the knowledge that the poor child was safe in the Refuge, she said no more, and Hugh Lingard himself never alluded to the subject. Her account of Reginald's state of mind before his death confirmed him in his original belief, that it was as a victim of this young brother Ernestine had felt bound to find the girl out. Ernestine had purposely avoided ever giving Mr. Brown's name in any of her letters, as she thought it not unlikely, since he had been her brother George's friend, that Hugh might also have some slight acquaintance with him; and she was too honourable to reveal the dark secrets of a man's hidden life, acquired in such a

THE CLOUDS BEGIN TO GATHER.

manner. There was a vein of sadness in all Hugh Lingard said which touched her very much, and which she had never known in him before; but she only laboured the more earnestly to show, how entirely she would care for his happiness when it became her first earthly duty. The preparations for their marriage were now going on rapidly, and it had been fixed to take place in three months from the time of Ernestine's return to London. And so the golden hours floated on for Ernestine, brightened with sweetest hope, and precious already by the human sympathy which has so marvellous a charm for every living heart. Then suddenly came the first mutterings of the gathering storm, though she failed to perceive their import.

One day, when she was sitting alone in the drawing-room, her aunt having gone out, the mid-day post brought her a letter from the Refuge. It contained the news that Annie Brook had the evening before made her escape from the Home. She had, the writer stated, been gradually growing more and more restless, and had shown symptoms of rebellion against some of the rules, especially the 'silence times.' These, the writer explained, were periods during the day when entire silence was enforced on the penitents, as a form of discipline, and when they were required to perform their various duties in each other's society without the utterance of a single word. To this Annie had objected, on what the lady termed the 'unreasonable ground' that 'she could not bear her own thoughts.' The half-hour between 1 and 1:30 was divided between ' mid-day prayers and recreation,' —the only recreation allowed during the day, and on having been summoned from this brief respite to enter upon the afternoon ' silence time,' Annie had refused to obey. For this act of disobedience she was locked up in the ' punishment-room,' and sentenced to remain there, on a diet of bread and water, till she was properly humbled. When visited in the evening it was found that she had made her escape through the window, at the risk of breaking her neck. Nothing had been heard of her since, and the letter concluded with the announcement that even if she were found, she could never again be received at the Home, as Miss Courtenay no doubt would easily understand.

Ernestine's first impulse was to fling the letter from her, and clasp her hands in dismay, while something like a groan escaped her. Had it then all been in vain? Had all her efforts, her longings, her endurance, been useless after all? Was the unhappy child lost whom she had so struggled to save from destruction? A pang of keen remorse shot through her heart : was it perhaps

THE CLOUDS BEGIN TO GATHER. 115

her own fault after all? She knew that Annie loved her, and she remembered how Thorold had warned her, that a human affection was almost the only influence which could be brought to bear on a heart still dead to the love of God: had she not too long neglected to use her power over that wayward soul? She had promised to go and see her; Annie had depended upon it; and she had let a whole month slip by in the golden light of her own deep happiness, which had seemed to hide from her charmed eyes all the darkness and sorrow of the world without. She had written to the girl, it was true, but it was one of the rules of the Home that the penitents were to write letters only once a month, so that Annie had never yet had the opportunity of telling her whether she were contented with her position or not.

There are few, probably, of those who think deeply, who have not known at times a feeling of overwhelming dismay and almost terror, at the thought of the whole world lying in wickedness round them, while they are living in quiet and comfort, full of their own hopes and fears, and lifting not so much as a finger to stem the awful tide of woe and sin, which is for ever engulfing so many deathless spirits in its fatal depths. Such a feeling, fraught with keenest remorse, plunged Ernestine's very soul in anguish now, for it came with the special sting which the thought of Annie Brook's fatal disappearance had power to give it. Here had been one, but one soul, out of the myriads daily perishing, given for its salvation into her own hands by the marked providence of God, and she had carelessly let it slip from her grasp. She had neglected, she had lost it! She had been wrapped in her own selfish love, intoxicated with her own selfish happiness. She had been revelling in hours of joy, in all that makes this world most dear. She had left that poor, weak, fainting soul to battle alone in the bitter waters of repentance, till she made shipwreck among them, while the only friend she loved was not at hand to save her. Oh, how Ernestine hated and despised herself as she thought of it,—she who had let her own sweet moments of earthly bliss weigh heavier in the balance than the eternal safety of that immortal soul! Probably she blamed herself too severely, and the fault did not in actual fact lie with her in this particular instance, but it is in truth a problem whose solution we well may dread, how far the souls that have perished round us may not rise up in judgment against us at the last for the doom which, but for supineness and easy selfishness, we might perhaps have averted. Ernestine could not, however, long endure the thoughts that pierced her heart; they

THE CLOUDS BEGIN TO GATHER.

goaded her to immediate action. Annie Brook at least still lived, and find her she must, though all her own life were spent in the search. She concluded that the girl would return to Greyburgh, and she determined to seek her there without an hour's delay. She knew that her doing so would be even more violently opposed by her aunt than on the former occasion, for Mrs. Tompson's account of her proceedings there had been by no means palatable to that lady, and therefore she resolved to start before Lady Beaufort's return home; while much as she would have wished to have seen Lingard before leaving him for an indefinite period, she dreaded, if she stayed to tell him of her plans, meeting the look of sadness in the eyes which followed her so lovingly wherever she went. She knew that he would not oppose any wish of hers, however much he might regret her departure, so she decided to leave a letter for him, without waiting for the hour of his daily visit.

In a short time, therefore, Ernestine was in the train, taking with her only her maid; but from the station she telegraphed to Mrs. Berry, the nurse who had attended Reginald in his last illness, and told her to take lodgings for her, as she did not wish to go to an hotel alone. Poor Ernestine carried an aching heart with her on her journey. It had cost her a bitter pang to break up her present happiness, and separate herself from her future husband, who seemed to grow each day more dear to her; and who in this changing life can ever part with a time of joy, without dreading that such another may never dawn for them again? The loss of Annie Brook, too, weighed heavily on her spirit: the search for her had been a bitter and a painful task, and if the poor girl had gone back to her evil life, it had all been worse than useless. Then, as the fair towers of Greyburgh came in sight, glistening in the evening sun, the remembrance of Reginald's unhappy death seemed to shroud it for her in sudden darkness, so fatal had this place, his so-called *Alma Mater*, been to him.

It was a comfort to see at the station, the kind motherly face of Mrs. Berry, who was waiting to conduct her to her lodgings, but even she had her tale of sadness on this occasion. The good woman was, as she expressed it, very 'down-hearted.' She had strained herself in the last case of illness she had attended, and was for the present, and probably for the rest of her life, incapacitated from continuing her employment as sick-nurse. As it was all she had to depend on for a livelihood, this was a serious calamity for her, and her delight and gratitude knew no bounds when Ernestine told her

THE CLOUDS BEGIN TO GATHER.

she should remain with her till she was better, and that she would find means to make her useful in some light work. Ernestine's gentleness and sweetness had won on the nurse unspeakably during the time of Reginald's illness, and the idea of being with her or near her in any way was the greatest happiness she could have known. Having made Mrs. Berry happy was, however, the only gleam of comfort poor Ernestine had for the next few days. Her first thought was to take counsel with Thorold as to the best means of once more finding Annie, but to her dismay she heard from Mrs. Berry that he was in London, having undertaken a six weeks' duty for an overworked perpetual curate, in one of the most crowded districts. Mrs. Berry affirmed that he had done this solely that he might 'work himself a bit harder' than he could do in Greyburgh just at present, when all the schools had holidays, and most of the people of the poorest class were out at work in the fields. He was not to return for some time, so Ernestine's next resource was to go to the old gaoler for advice, and early next morning she was once more at the gaol. Bolton was very glad to see her, but he shook his head when he heard her errand.

'It's a cruel pity they could not keep her when they had got her, for I doubt you'll not soon set eyes on her again. They should have coaxed her a bit. Rosie Brown would do anything on earth for a kind word, but she was scared in a moment if you were anyways harsh to her. However, she's gone, and the job now is to find her, and that won't be easy. She'd never come back here, you may depend. She'd be too much afraid of being took up and sent back to the 'tentiary.'

'But where can she be then?'

'Most likely in London; she was nearer there than here, and it's where most of them makes their way to sooner or later.'

'London!' Ernestine's heart sank within her. How hopeless any search would be in London she knew well. 'Oh, I must hope she is here,' she said; 'is there no way of finding out?'

'Oh, I'll find out for you right enough,' said the gaoler; 'Rosie's known now, and I'll send one of our police to look for her. He is as 'cute a chap as you'd wish to see, and he'll soon find out if she is in Greyburgh. If you'll come round here to-morrow, Miss Courtenay, I'll undertake to tell you whether she's in this town or no.'

There was nothing to be done but to wait through the dreary day, and dreary enough it was to poor Ernestine. She went to look at Reginald's grave, on which the grass was already green. Truly his place

THE CLOUDS BEGIN TO GATHER.

knew him no more; his name was but a memory, his life as a tale that is told. But where was the deathless soul, that had shivered so long in its darkness, without hope or stay, on the brink of the eternity that held him now? As she thought upon him her whole heart rose up in one earnest supplication, that even yet the love of Christ, higher than the highest heaven, and deeper than the deepest hell, might reach him wheresoever he might be,—and therein she obeyed the irresistible instinct which burns in the heart of every one, be their creed what it may, who have seen their beloved pass into the mystery of the unseen life.

CHAPTER VII.

MRS. DORRELL.

ERNESTINE COURTENAY was at the prison next day before the appointed time, in her anxiety to know the result of the policeman's search. The consequence of her early arrival was, that she found Mr. Bolton performing some occult ceremonies as the conclusion to his toilette, which it seemed always took place in the sitting-room, and during which Mrs. Bolton ministered to him with great assiduity. He was in no wise disconcerted, however, by Ernestine's entrance, but seemed on the contrary to think his appearance rather imposing, as he sat with a huge napkin suspended round his neck. He had redeemed his promise of ascertaining whether Annie Brook were in the town or not, and had discovered that she positively was not in Greyburgh, and had not been there since the day she left it with a 'lady.' Ernestine sat in mute despair. What was she to do next?

'I doubt you'll have a tough job looking for her now,

Miss Courtenay,' said Bolton; 'but the policeman told me one thing which may help you: it's more than likely that some one at Mother Dorrell's knows where she is, for the postman delivered a letter there which had the post-mark of Layton.' This was the village where the Home was situated, and Ernestine caught eagerly at the chance it afforded of finding out where Annie had gone.

'Oh, how do you think I could induce them to tell me about her?'

'There's only one chance, and that is, if you choose to pay them down a good round sum for the information.'

'I will pay them anything they please,' exclaimed Ernestine.

'Bless me! don't you go for to tell them that,' said Bolton; 'they'd please to ruin you, if they could; it's a shame that a penny of honest money should ever get into their hands, let alone your giving them their choice of the quantity.'

'Well, do tell me how to proceed,' said Ernestine, rather impatiently. 'I only want to find the girl, and I don't care what it costs to learn where she is.'

'I don't say as you will be able to learn,' said Bolton gravely, 'and certainly not unless you are uncommon sharp, for they'll do their best to deceive you for the sake of their trade in the long-run. But as the girl is positively not at Mother Dorrell's, it cannot make any real difference to her that you should know where she is; and if she finds she can't get your money otherwise, perhaps she may tell you.'

'Was the letter written to her?' asked Ernestine.

'No, it was to one of the gals, but the postman could not remember the name. It's Mother Dorrell you'll have to deal with, however. She's a regular tyrant among them, and she's sure to have read the letter before the girl got it. She would only let her have it if it contained what pleased her.'

'Then I suppose I had better go to her at once,' said Ernestine. The intense repugnance she felt to the idea of seeing this woman prompted her to nerve herself to the task without delay.

'I think it is your only chance, Miss Courtenay. You had better just offer her a sum down to tell you where the gal is; but you must make her understand she'll not get it unless you have proof positive that she's telling you the truth. She'll take you in if she can, you may depend.'

With this consolatory assurance Ernestine left the gaol to go at once on her errand. It was by far the most painful effort she had yet made for Annie Brook. Her regret for what her sensitive conscience considered her neglect of her, made her feel as if she ought to rejoice in any pain which she could now endure for her sake; but her whole being revolted at the thought of being brought in contact with the wretched woman, who was so infinitely more vile and guilty than the unhappy girls she harboured in her home. Ernestine took Mrs. Berry with her, feeling that she really could not approach this den of wickedness alone, and she was forcibly reminded of the governor's description of her probable reception on arriving there.

There was nothing externally to indicate that the house was otherwise than respectable, but she knocked a long time at the door before she was admitted, while the sound of a window closing rapidly showed that she had been reconnoitred from above. At last the door was opened, and the woman in widow's dress, whom she had been told to expect, appeared. Ernestine looked upon her face, and actually shivered with the intense repulsion it caused her, though it was not in the least the villanous sort of face she expected to see. The forehead was broad and high, surmounted by false braids, from under which a few white hairs straggled out; the eyes were small, keen, and light in colour;

the nose high and pinched; the lips so thin that they formed a mere snaky line across her face. Her complexion was a dead white, in spite of her being, as Ernestine was afterwards told, about the hardest drinker in Greyburgh, and her expression was one of extreme meekness and suavity. Yet, in some indefinable way, this face conveyed an impression of wickedness, treachery, and cruelty, far beyond what words can describe. Were it the account of some fictitious character which was being given, doubtless invention would have sought for some more marked features of evil in the outward aspect, to convey the idea of subtle malignant iniquity, which that white hypocritical face betrayed. But it is the face of a woman probably still living which has been described, and the simple truth has been told as to the impression it conveyed to those who looked on it. The subsequent acts of this wretched woman are also true, almost impossible as they may appear; unless voluntary witnesses have lied needlessly against her. Conquering the shrinking horror she felt, Ernestine said—

'Mrs. Dorrell, I wish to speak to you for a few minutes on a matter about which I am anxious.' The woman did not move out of the doorway. She dropped a slow profound curtsey, and, speaking in a soft, smooth voice, with an accent and a choice of words which seemed far above her station, said, 'I think, madam, you must be mistaken; I do not think you can have any business with me; perhaps you wish to see the person next door.'

'No, it is yourself I wish to speak to. I think you can give me some information for which I am willing to pay highly.'

'Oh! pray come in then, madam,' she said at once, and making way for Ernestine and Mrs. Berry to enter, she closed the door carefully behind her, and led the way into a small parlour, furnished in a gaudy style, with some prints on the wall, which were not of the most edifying description. Two little children, one almost an infant, sat huddled together in a corner. They looked haggard and wasted, and when Mrs. Dorrell came in they hid their faces as if in an agony of terror. Mrs. Berry had her eyes on them at once, and the look was instantly observed by the woman.

'Pretty dears,' she said; 'I hope they will not disturb you, madam. They are the children of a young friend of mine, a most respectable married woman, who is unable at present to have them at home on account of her weak health. I am so doatingly fond of children, I was pleased to take care of them for her.'

'They will not disturb me,' said Ernestine, looking compassionately on the poor terrified children, whom Mrs. Berry was already coaxing to come near her. 'Now, Mrs. Dorrell,' she said, going straight to her subject, ' I am anxious to know where a young girl is, known by the name of Rosie Brown. She lodged here at one time, but she is not in Greyburgh now. She has written, however, within the last two days, to some one in this house, and I will pay any one well who will bring me correct information as to where she is.'

'Rosie Brown!' said Mrs. Dorrell, putting on a reflective air. 'Ah! I remember now—a poor, friendless young girl, whom I allowed to take shelter here for a few days until I should be able to find a situation for her. I grieve to say, madam, she turned out very worthless; in fact, so loose a character that I could not retain her in my respectable house. I was obliged to dismiss her. I regretted doing it, but I had my reputation to consider. The humblest among us, madam, prizes a good name.'

This was more than Ernestine could endure. 'It is quite useless to speak to me in this way, Mrs. Dorrell. The point is, will you tell me where the girl is, or not?'

'I think you mentioned a reward for the trouble of ascertaining?' she said, in a cringing tone.

'I will give you five pounds at once, if you can bring me proof positive that your information is correct.'

The woman's eyes glistened. 'Well, madam, I am sure I will gladly assist you in any work of charity. I will endeavour to ascertain where the girl is, and, if you will allow me to call upon you this evening, I will give you her correct address.'

'Can I not have it now?' asked Ernestine.

'Unfortunately I do not know it. You are mistaken in supposing any letter came to this house. I live here alone with these sweet children; but I will endeavour to ascertain for you, though it will cost me no doubt some hours' toil.'

Ernestine felt certain that the woman knew the address at the moment she spoke perfectly well; but her smooth lying face was quite imperturbable, and feeling thankful to escape from so odious a presence, she hurriedly wrote down the address of her own lodging, and rose to go.

Mrs. Berry meanwhile had been fondling the two poor little children, and as she got up they clung to her with their puny hands, and seemed unwilling to let her go. Ernestine saw Mrs. Dorrell give them a look so vindictive, that she wished she could have carried away the unhappy infants then and there; but she was learning daily more and more the bitter lesson, that we must ever in this life walk amidst sorrow and pain we have no power to alleviate. As Ernestine came out into the little passage, she saw a door at the end of it partly open, and a young woman, who was standing behind it, looked eagerly round to catch a glimpse of her as she passed. Ernestine half-stopped, feeling convinced she had seen that handsome, mournful face before, though she could not recall it at first. The quick glance of recognition from the girl's dark eyes, however, reminded her that she was the one among the band of prisoners at the gaol who had whispered to her where Annie Brook really was, and whose name the gaoler had told her afterwards was Nellie Lewis. Before she had time to say a word, however, Mrs. Dorrell had detected the girl's presence, and pushed the door back upon her so violently, that Ernestine heard her give a cry as if hurt.

'My servant girl, madam,' said Mrs. Dorrell. 'I am shocked at her impertinence to stand staring at you in that way.'

Ernestine felt it was in vain to contradict the woman's incessant lies, and she went out in silence. Mrs. Berry was still looking wistfully at the poor little children, who, at a glance from Mrs. Dorrell, had cowered down in their corner, and Ernestine and she had not walked many steps down the street when they heard a shriek of pain from a childish voice in the house they had left.

'Oh, Miss Courtenay, that's a wicked woman!' said Mrs. Berry.

'Indeed, I am sure she is,' said Ernestine. 'Whose children do you suppose them to be?'

'Ah! there's little doubt what they are, poor babes. They are the children of some of these unfortunate girls, who pay Mrs. Dorrell for taking care of them; but I'm sure she cruelly ill-uses them, and indeed I've heard that the children left in these houses always die.'

'For want of food and care, no doubt,' said Ernestine.

Mrs. Berry looked as if she could have told more, but shrank from doing so. Presently, however, she said: 'It passes me to understand, Miss Courtenay, how it is that the people who make laws and govern the country can allow such places as Mrs. Dorrell's to be kept openly in the town. They are perfect nests of wickedness, such as the heathen lands I have read about might be ashamed of; and I am sure of this, they're the ruin of thousands of souls, for they lure every young girl they can catch into them; and many a one, if they've lost their character or their place anyhow, would turn and do better, if they had no such house as that to fly to.'

'I thought there was some law against them,' said Ernestine, ' but it does not seem to be enforced.'

' Bless you! it's a law that's of no sort of use,' said Mrs. Berry. ' It's just this: If any of the neighbours chooses to go and accuse such people as Mrs. Dorrell of keeping a riotous house that's a nuisance to the street, some notice would be taken of it, but there's not one would dare to do such a thing. It would be as much as their life's worth. It's the police should have the power to go and rout them out; and it's just a mystery to me why they, or the magistrates, or some one don't take it in hand.'

This is no less a mystery to wiser people than good Mrs. Berry. These houses are notorious, carried on openly in the face of day; and how is it that in this Christian country they are allowed thus to exist untouched, poisoning the whole community with the propagation of the deadliest evil?

Ernestine could give no solution to a question which seemed to her inexplicable; and she asked Mrs. Berry if she thought it likely Mrs. Dorrell would really tell her where Annie Brook was to be found.

' I am sure she won't tell you the truth if she can help it, Miss Courtenay. These wretches always consider it a loss to their trade when a girl goes into a

Penitentiary. But if she can't get your money otherwise, perhaps she will.'

It was just what the gaoler said, and Ernestine waited impatiently for nine o'clock, the hour fixed by Mrs. Dorrell for her visit. It was then almost dark, and punctually to the time the woman's knock was heard at the door. She came stealing into the room with a noiseless step. Ernestine was alone; and she bade her sit down, and asked eagerly if she could now tell her where Rosie Brown was.

'Yes, madam, I am happy to say I have been successful in my search, on which I have been employed all day, and I feel much exhausted. Madam, my strength is not what it was.'

Ernestine did not in the least understand that this was a hint for the offer of a glass of spirits, and if she had, she would not have given it, so she only said somewhat impatiently, ' Let me have the address, then.'

'I will, madam. Of course, I know I can depend upon receiving the reward so soon as it is in your possession?'

'Provided there is sufficient proof that you are giving me correct information.'

'I am grieved that you should doubt me, madam; but you will see that there is no occasion. Here is the address;' and she read it from a piece of paper: ' Rosie

Brown, or, more properly, Annie Brook, is at the house of Matthew Brook, lodge-keeper to Lord Carleton, Carleton Park, Garsley.'

Ernestine started in extreme surprise. That was unquestionably the address of Annie's father, and no invention of Mrs. Dorrell's. Nor was it at all unlikely that Annie had longed to return to her father when she left the Penitentiary. Ernestine felt sure that she hated her former life, and that her position at Mrs. Dorrell's had really been one of galling bondage, to which she would not now be willing to return if she could find a shelter anywhere else. She had dreaded the confinement and discipline of the Penitentiary, and had proved unable to bear it; and therefore Ernestine did not look on her escape from it as any proof that she wished to return to her evil ways. If, indeed, she desired to lead a better life, her father's house was the most natural place to which she could go; but it did astonish her that she should have attempted it, knowing how completely he had disowned her. It was possible, however, that she had made a desperate venture, and gone actually to his door, in the hope that he would not turn her away; and it was also possible that he might take some steps to place her in safety, even if he dared not himself brave Lady Carleton's anger, by receiving her into his house. In any case, the address was a true one; and therefore Mrs. Dorrell was entitled to her reward, which Ernestine forthwith gave her. She naturally expected the woman to go so soon as she had received the money, and certainly she did not desire to breathe the same air with her a moment longer than was necessary; but Mrs. Dorrell lingered, evidently for some set purpose of her own, although she talked of nothing more important than the weather and the crops. Out of patience at last, Ernestine rose and called Mrs. Berry to show her out; but even then she remained in the passage, endeavouring to keep up a conversation with the good old nurse, who gave her the sulkiest of answers, and tried several times to get her out at the door in vain. At length, however, the clock struck ten; and then, as if she had been only waiting for this, she instantly left the house and hastened away.

Ernestine at once sat down and wrote to Matthew Brook, begging him to let her know where Annie was, and saying everything she thought likely to soften him towards the poor forlorn child. She thought it best to wait for the answer in Greyburgh; in case Annie, repulsed from her home, might yet return there.

In the course of the next afternoon, Ernestine was sitting in her room, writing her daily letter to Hugh

Lingard, when Mrs. Berry, who had been out on some business of her own, burst in, in a state of the greatest agitation, her eyes full of tears, and her hands trembling—'O Miss Courtenay! such a dreadful thing has happened; it makes my flesh creep, it do! Poor little dears! Only to think—it is too shocking!'

'What do you mean, dear Mrs. Berry?' said Ernestine, unable to comprehend these incoherent expressions. Mrs. Berry's only answer was to sit down and cry. 'Do tell me,' said Ernestine, taking her hand soothingly. With an effort, the good old woman composed herself and said, drying her eyes: 'It is these two poor little children we saw at Mrs. Dorrell's yesterday, ma'am; they were burnt alive in their beds last night.'

'Burnt! Do you mean that they are dead?'

'Indeed they are, ma'am; quite dead. They had an inquest on them this forenoon; and I saw one of the jury; he told me all about it.' Ernestine sat down, trembling from head to foot. A horror for which she could hardly account took possession of her.

'Tell me the particulars, Mrs. Berry,' she said.

'Ma'am, I am afraid it will shock you very much; but it was while that vile woman was here that it happened. She said in her evidence that she was here from nine o'clock to ten; that she could bring you and me as witnesses of it; that she left them alive, and came back to find them dead.'

'Did she mean that it happened in consequence of her having left them to come here?' said Ernestine, growing very pale.

'That's what she says, ma'am; but it seems a strange story altogether. She says she put them to bed before she went, and that the eldest of them must have got up and taken the matches off the mantel-shelf to play with, and so set fire to the bed.'

'How was it the house did not take fire if the bed was burnt?' said Ernestine.

'It was only a straw mattress laid on the middle of the stone floor in the back kitchen, and there was no other furniture in the room at all, so when the mattress burnt out the fire died away; but it killed the children first, poor little lambs!'

'But they must have screamed, poor things!—did no one hear them?'

'There was only one of the girls at home, at the back part of the house. She did hear them, and went to the door, but it was locked, and she could not get in; and the poor innocents did not cry long; I daresay they were soon dead!' and Mrs. Berry's tears began to flow again.

'It is the most dreadful thing I ever heard of,' said Ernestine, with quivering lips. 'What was the verdict of the coroner's jury?'

'Accidental death, ma'am; but I think it's a dark business altogether. I can't abide the looks of that woman, and it seems strange her making so much of being here with you; and as to the poor little thing getting up to fetch matches, I believe he was too scared to have moved an inch from where she put him.'

'Then how do you suppose it happened, Mrs. Berry?' said Ernestine.

Before she could answer there was a hurried knock at the outer door; presently the servant came to say that a young person wished to speak to Miss Courtenay; and forthwith ushered in a tall woman, somewhat gaudily dressed, but with a thick black veil over her face. Ernestine at once recognised the girl who had looked so wistfully at her the day before at Mrs. Dorrell's.

'May I speak with you alone, ma'am?' she said, in a low voice.

'Certainly,' said Ernestine; and Mrs. Berry, taking the hint, left the room. The girl threw back her veil, and showed a pale worn face, still singularly handsome, and eyes swollen with tears.

'Ma'am, may I ask you to promise never to tell any

one what I am going to say? I want to speak freely to you if I may.'

'Indeed you may,' said Ernestine, and never doubting that her visitor's confidence would be about herself alone she willingly gave the promise she asked. The girl thanked her, and then in a low sad tone went on: 'I wished to tell you, ma'am, first, that Mrs. Dorrell has deceived you about Rosie Brown: she is not at her father's.'

'Is it possible?' said Ernestine. 'But how then could Mrs. Dorrell have known the address? She was correct as to that.'

'She saw it in a letter Rosie had received when she was at home, and which Mrs. Dorrell took out of her box when she went to gaol. She made sure you would believe her, and give her the money, if she said Rosie had gone to her father; and she boasted to us all how she had taken you in last night.'

'But where is the poor child then, can you tell me?'

'Yes, ma'am, I can; for the letter she wrote when she left the Penitentiary was to me. Mrs. Dorrell read it before she would let me have it; but I got it at last. I brought it with me, that you might read it yourself, and see I have no wish to deceive you.'

'I am sure you have not,' said Ernestine, who was

much struck by the sorrowful, subdued manner in which the poor girl spoke. She anxiously took the letter, which was dated the day of Annie's flight from the Home, from whence she had probably taken the paper and envelope. It ran thus:—

'Dear Nell,— I write you these few lines to tell you that I have left the Penitentiary. You would hear Miss Courtenay took me there from the gaol. She was such a dear lady. I did love her. I tried to stay in that place to please her, for I knew she would grieve if I left; but I could not bear it, not another day. I am going now to London to try and get work, for I won't do as I have done, never no more. I hate to think as ever I lived a gay life. You know I never was happy in it, and I would not go back to it now for all the world. I would go to that dear lady, if I were not afraid she would want me to go to a Penitentiary again, and I couldn't do that. So I must do the best I can. Surely in such a big place as London there will be some work for me. I write this to ask you, Nell, to take a letter out of my box, which was sent me when I was at home, and keep it safe for me; for I am afraid Mrs. Dorrell will sell all my things when she finds I don't mean to come back, and I don't want to lose that letter. It is the last my sister Lois ever wrote to me; and she's dead now—poor Lois! I often wish I were dead too. So no more at present from your friend,

'ROSIE BROWN.'

'But there is no address given here,' said Ernestine in alarm. 'She only says she is going to London. Do you know no more than this?'.

'No, ma'am; I only had that one letter, and I know nothing of her but what she tells me in it.'

'She must have written it immediately on leaving the Home, and posted it at the village, for I see it has that post-mark; and then I suppose she went on to London. But how shall I ever find her there? Poor Annie, I fear she is lost to me indeed,' and tears rose to Ernestine's eyes as she spoke. The girl was gazing intently at her, and as she saw how deeply she felt for Annie, her chest heaved with strong emotion. She pressed her hands tightly together in the effort to control her agitation, and at last exclaimed, the words bursting from her lips with a sob—

'O ma'am! if you can feel so much for Rosie, will you not show a little pity too for me?'

'Indeed I will,' said Ernestine, rising from her seat and coming to sit down beside her. 'I should not have let you go till I had found out if I could help you in any way. Tell me what I can do for you. Your name is Nellie Lewis, is it not?'

'Ellen Lucas is my real name,' and then, looking up imploringly, she said, 'O ma'am, I want to leave this wicked life. I've always hated it from first to last. I would have left it long ago if there had been any way of doing so except by going to a Penitentiary; but the girls all advised me not to think of that, in such a way that I was frightened at the thought of it; and if only you would help me out of it now, ma'am, I could never thank you enough. I think I'd rather die than go back to Mrs. Dorrell's after what happened last night.'

'You mean the accident to the two poor little children?'

'It was not an accident,' she answered, with a shudder.

'Not an accident! What do you mean?'

'Ma'am, you promised me you would tell no one what I had to say,' said Ellen, lifting her dark eyes to her face. 'I may be quite sure you will not, may I?'

'Certainly,' said Ernestine; 'I have promised, and that is enough.'

'Then it will seem a comfort to tell you what I know, ma'am; for I can get no rest for thinking of it, and it would be as much as my life is worth, I'm sure, to tell it to any one else, in case it got round to Mrs. Dorrell's ears. These poor children, ma'am,' she continued, lowering her voice, 'were not burnt by accident; they were murdered!'

Ernestine almost shrieked with horror. 'Oh! can this be true?'

'It is too true, ma'am. The girls whose children they were, had gone off to Aldershot when the long vacation began, and never paid Mrs. Dorrell for keeping them all that time. I don't suppose they cared what became of the poor babies; for most of them know Mrs. Dorrell always puts away the children that are not paid for,—though I never knew it till last night.'

'Puts them away?' said Ernestine, not understanding.

'Puts them to death, ma'am! Polly Smith, who is almost an old woman now, and has lived half her life between Mrs. Dorrell's and the gaol, said she knew she had got rid of several since she had been there. She had mostly smothered them, and then dropped them into the canal, with a stone round their neck, in the middle of the night. But the body of the last one floated, and she was afraid of being found out, so Polly said she thought she had hit on a clever dodge last night, because she could call on your servants to prove she had been with you at the time of their death. So she laid them down on a straw mattress, on the stone floor of the kitchen, and made a hole in it, and put two or three lighted matches in, and then she went out, and locked the door, and came off to you. She stayed out a whole hour, to make sure they should be dead when she came back; and so they were, poor dears, sure enough.'

Ernestine grew so faint at this horrible account, that it was some minutes before she recovered herself sufficiently to speak. 'Did no one try to save them?' she gasped out at last.

'There was no one at home but Polly Smith. Mrs. Dorrell took good care all the rest should be out; and Polly has helped her to put the others in the water before now. But she told me when she heard the screams last night it did make her flesh creep; for burning seemed worse than anything, and she did go to the door and try to open it, but she could not.'

'Oh, why did she not go for the police, or get some neighbour to burst the door open?'

'O ma'am!' exclaimed Ellen, almost trembling at the idea, 'she would not have dared to do that for fear of Mrs. Dorrell. I would not have any one but you know what I've told you for all the world. It would do no good to tell it; for it could not be proved against her. Polly was the only one who knew anything about it, and she would swear just as Mrs. Dorrell pleased. She said this morning at the inquest it was all an accident, for she knew there were no matches near the children, and they must have got up and taken them to play with. The jury quite believed her.'

'Were you called as a witness?'

'No, ma'am; I had been out of the house some hours before it happened, and I knew nothing of it till this morning, when Polly told me, and then I felt that, come what would, I could not stay in that house another day. I thought I would come and ask you to take me away, and that if you would not I would go and lie down in some lonely place and die; for I can't bear it any longer—I can't,' and she burst into a passion of tears; 'it's like being in hell to be in the midst of all that wickedness, and to feel that I am lost for ever!'

'Not for ever,' said Ernestine compassionately; 'the deep mercy of our Saviour never fails. I will help you with all my heart. You do not look to me like one who could ever willingly have entered on such a life.'

'Willingly! O ma'am, if you knew all,—how I was driven to it, and how wretched I've been times and times. I would have made away with myself, only I was afraid of God. I did not dare to go before Him so wicked as I have been. I have longed for some way to get out of my sin and misery, and I could find none. I was so lonely, without a friend in the world; and when I saw you at the gaol, ma'am, and you let me touch your hand, and seemed so sweet and good, I felt just for a moment as if I were not quite alone on the earth, and that perhaps you'd help me; but I never saw you more till yesterday, and then I seemed more lost than ever; for Mrs. Dorrell threatened me so when you were gone, that if it had not been for this cruel murder, I don't think I should have had courage to come to you.'

'You need fear nothing now, my poor child,' said Ernestine; 'but I hardly know how best to help you; you seem to shrink from going to a Penitentiary?'

'I do indeed, ma'am,' said Ellen, with a palpable shiver. 'I would rather go there than stay at Mrs. Dorrell's; but oh! if you would help me out of this life in any other way I should be so thankful. I don't care how hard I work, or what I do, just to get bread to eat. I have been used to service; but I know I must not hope for that now,' and she hung her head down, as tears fell from her eyes.

'What sort of service were you in?' said Ernestine.

'I was never but in one situation, ma'am; and it was such a happy one! I waited on a lady who was an invalid, and could not leave her sofa; but she was such a dear, good lady; it was a pleasure to do anything for her; and she was so kind to me. My father was a small farmer near where she lived, and he failed, and died of a broken heart when I was about sixteen. Mother had been dead a year, and I was left alone, without a friend or a penny in the world; and this dear lady took me on trial, and soon taught me all her ways, and I lived three years with her, and was so happy. I used to read to her, and stay with her in the drawing-room most of the day, and she would often say I must never leave her as long as she lived; and I never would, if it had not been for—' her sobs choked her for a moment.

'And how did you come to leave her?' said Ernestine gently.

She had a nephew, young Lord Sedley, heir to a grand castle and estate not far from where his aunt lived, and he used to come and stay with her often. He was such a handsome, dashing gentleman, and had such a winning way with him,—and of course I often saw him; for I was always with my lady, even when he was there, and he found plenty ways of seeing me alone. He would saunter into the garden with his cigar when my lady sent me to gather flowers, and he would come to the room where I sat almost every evening after she was gone to bed. He was the master and I was the servant, and I could not tell him to go away, as I might with another. I should have told his aunt, I know, but she would hardly have believed anything against him; and then I loved him—I loved him,' and again the passionate tears forced their way from her eyes. 'At last the end of it all was that I saw nothing but misery and shame before me, and I waited till he came next time, in such an agony lest I should be found out, and told him, and he was so vexed and angry. It did seem so hard. I thought my heart would break when I found how he took it all. At last he said I was to tell his aunt I was ill, and wished to go and stay with a friend. I had no friend in all the world, ma'am; but I told the lie to my dear lady; for he taught me to lie; I had never done it before. Well, she was so kind, and let me go, and said I was to come back as soon as ever I could; and then he gave me money to go and take a lodging somewhere; and I came here because I knew he was at college, and I thought I should see him. But he never once came near me; and before my boy was born he had left Greyburgh for good, and never came back. I wrote to tell him of the baby's birth, and he sent me a ten-pound note, with such a cruel letter, asking how I dared write to him, and that I was never to presume to take such a liberty again, and that I was mad to suppose he was going to keep up any acquaintance with such an one as I was. He said he sent me some money now, and there was to be an end to it. When I got that letter I think I must have died, if it had not been for my baby. I lived quietly till the money was all spent, and then I tried to work for my living, but my character was gone, and no one would employ me. I was weak and ill, and half-broken-hearted, and had no strength to do rough field work, or anything of that kind. Then I began to sell my clothes to get food for me and my boy, and they were soon all gone. If I had been alone, I think I would have tried to make up my mind to go to the workhouse then, but they would have separated me from my child, and I could not stand that; and besides, I could only have remained there a short time, and then they'd have passed me on to my own parish; and I never could have borne to go back to my native place as a workhouse pauper, and something worse. Well, ma'am, when both the baby and I were half-starved, I thought I would try to see him who had brought me to this misery; so I set off to walk to the beautiful place where he lived. It took me days and days, carrying the child, but at last

I got there; and when I came to the gate, the lodge-keeper would not let me in. I told him I wanted to speak to the young lord, and he jeered at me, and said it was just likely he'd speak to such an one as I was; and then, when I still persisted, he said if I chose to wait outside the gate, I could see him when he came home from his ride. So I sat down by the roadside and waited. Oh, Miss Courtenay, I wish I had died then! I wish his horse's hoofs had kicked me to death; it would have been better than to have been trampled on by the man who had ruined me, body and soul. I sat there, on that hot summer day, thirsty and weary, with the sun beating down on my head, and the baby lying asleep on my lap, till I felt ready to faint with fatigue and hunger; and I thought if I could but get sight of his dear face again, it would be like new life. Then there came the clatter of horses swiftly towards me; the sound of gay laughing and talking; and in a moment, more a large party swept past me, and cantered up to the gate. They stopped close to the place where I sat, and he was the last, with a beautiful young lady riding close by his side. I never saw her but that once, for a moment, and yet I remember her as distinctly as if she were standing before me now: her bright laughing face, and her pretty hat and feather, with her fair hair all in confusion below it. I seem still to see the look, half shy, half saucy, that she turned on my lord. Somehow it stirred my blood, and made me forget to be prudent. I felt as if I must show I had a right to him—I, the mother of his child; and I walked straight up to him, put my hand on his horse's mane, and called him by his name. I said I had come to see him, as I had not heard from him, and I wanted help for his child. Oh, ma'am, if you had seen his face when he saw and heard me; it grew just like the face of a devil. He struck me with his riding-switch on the wrist to make me loose my hold, and he spurred his horse, so that the beast reared and threw me back against the bank. The young lady screamed, and I saw him stoop to her so tenderly, and bid her not be afraid; it was only an impudent beggar, he said; and he took her horse by the bridle and led him in at the gate, talking to her all the while, till her face grew bright again, and she looked up into his eyes with a smile and a blush. I saw it all, though my heart had stopped beating, and I felt like to die. I leant there against the bank, not knowing where I was, or what I was doing, till suddenly I saw him coming striding down the avenue on foot from the house. I felt nothing but terror then. I thought he was coming to kill me, and I would have run away, but my feet failed under me. He came on and on through the gate and past me, making a sign to me to follow him; and I dared not disobey, for he looked as if he were almost mad with fury and rage. He struck into a bypath, and, as soon as we were out of sight of the road, he turned round and took hold of me by the shoulder with such a grip that I screamed with the pain. "Be still, you devil," he said, and shook me, and then, when I cowered down, frightened to death, he poured out such a volley of oaths and abuse, that I thought I must be dreaming to think he was the same who once spoke to me all the loving words that worked my destruction. He asked me how I dared to come near him, and swore if ever I tried either to see him, or write to him again, he would have me put in gaol for a vagrant and impostor. All I could do was to gasp out that his child was starving, and I held it towards him; but he pushed it back, so as nearly to knock it out of my arms; and he laughed—yes, he laughed,—and asked if I expected him to believe it was his child. He called me the worst name, and said he knew it was all a trick to get money out of him; but I had had too much already, and he would not give me a penny more than enough to take me out of the place. He pointed to the station, which was close at hand, and ordered me to go there at once, and he would send some one to pay my fare, and see me off. I was too frightened and broken-hearted to resist; so I said never a word, but crept away to the station, and presently the village policeman came after me, and took my ticket, and sent me away in the train, threatening me with all manner of things, if ever I came begging about the place again. I suppose my lord told him I was a common tramp. I never contradicted him. I did not care what any one thought; and when I got back here, homeless and penniless, what could I do but go to Mother Dorrell's, to get food for myself and the child? I suppose God wanted to punish me, for He soon took my baby; it died; and then it did not matter what happened. I was quite ready to be what my lord had called me. What did it signify?'

A look of wild desperation was gradually wakening in Ellen's eyes as she spoke, and she began nervously drawing her cloak around her, as if she were about to rise and go away; but Ernestine took her hand—

'It has been dreadful for you, my poor child, and that man was very cruel; but you see God has not forgotten you. He has sent me to help you, and now I am going to take care of you. You shall never go back to that life of sin and wretchedness any more.'

The sweet, kind words fell on the wretched woman's

heart like soft summer raindrops on the parched ground. She clasped the soft hand she held in both of hers, and burst into tears.

Ernestine whispered to her to remain quiet for a few minutes, and she would return to her; and then went to confer with Mrs. Berry as to a plan she had already conceived on behalf of this unhappy girl.

She had promised Mrs. Berry that she would give her a home, at least until her health were somewhat restored; and the idea at once suggested itself, that she might take a small house for the nurse somewhere in the suburbs of London, and establish her in it, on condition that she received Ellen Lucas as an inmate, and undertook the care of her; and that in the event of Annie Brook being found, she would afford her an asylum also. There was an additional advantage in the plan, that Ellen would find ample employment in nursing Mrs. Berry, who required constant attendance; and the occupation of soothing the sufferings of another, was calculated more than anything to soften and humanize her, after the dreadful demoralization she had undergone.

This plan approved itself to Mrs. Berry most entirely. She was an honest, conscientious woman, and was very unwilling to be dependent on Miss Courtenay, without giving her services in return, which, in her enfeebled state, was not an easy matter; but she felt that by affording an asylum to those unhappy girls, she would be really of essential use to her, while her own kind-hearted wish to help these, the most wretched and forlorn of human beings, would likewise be gratified.

She therefore eagerly undertook to do all Ernestine wished, and told her, to the lady's great delight, that she could provide a home for Ellen Lucas that very night, as she had a sister living in London who would, she knew, gladly take them both in till she could find a house for herself. It was at once settled, therefore, that they should go up to town by the next train; and as Ernestine had now no motive for remaining in Greyburgh, beyond receiving Matthew Brook's answer, which could be forwarded to her, she herself followed that same evening. She arrived in London to find her aunt, Lady Beaufort, 'in a state of high displeasure' at what she termed her extraordinary proceedings; for which *désagrément*, however, the warmth and tenderness of Hugh Lingard's welcome amply compensated.

CHAPTER VIII.

THE LOST FOUND.

ERNESTINE had the comfort of feeling that her journey to Greyburgh, though unavailing so far as Annie was concerned, had not been in vain, since it had resulted in the rescue of Ellen Lucas; yet a strange depression hung about her after her return to London, for which, she felt, her anxiety about the lost girl was not sufficient to account. The deeper revelation of evil which these last events had brought to her filled her with an indescribable terror of this world's wickedness, which had its rise in the strong spiritual instinct, common to all human beings, though in the great majority of them it is stifled and obscured till it becomes almost non-existent—that instinct which gives intuitive knowledge of the great truth, that in the perfection of God alone the immortal soul can find its real joy, its one repose, its ultimate and eternal satisfaction; and, forasmuch as union with Him in His infinite holiness is the aim and end of our being, it follows that in proportion as a soul recognises this its true destiny, the more it will shrink from the antagonistic principle of evil, and cling to such faint reflections of the Infinite Goodness as may be found in the creatures once made in their Creator's image. Faith, and Truth, and Love were all deepening in Ernestine's soul at this time day by day, for in seeking Christ's lost little one she had found at every step the sinless Christ Himself; she shrunk with ever increasing sensitiveness from evil external to herself, and struggled more and more vehemently with that which lurked in her own being, her whole spirit going out in ardent love and longing to the only Holy, whom she recognised as her true and eternal Life, while the human affections, which shared in her growing sanctification, strove anxiously to rest on the one human being, whom her short-sighted partiality endowed with so bright a ray from the Divine Perfection.

Ernestine believed with all a woman's blind, unreasoning faith, in Hugh Lingard's goodness. She was aware at the time of her first engagement to him that such views on religion as he possessed were more negative than positive, but she knew nothing then of the immutable principle which a deeper knowledge of life was rapidly teaching her, that true virtue can have no existence except on a foundation of dogmatic truth

Now, when all things pertaining to the kingdom of God were ever looming larger and more distinct upon her view, she grasped at the hope that Lingard was also awakening to the realities of a more clearly defined creed, and that the tender reverence he showed to her, the consideration with which he treated all her ideas, was the result of his adoption of her faith, and not of his love to herself; and so it came to pass that the nearer insight into the hidden depths that underlie the surface of society, which had filled her with such horror and dismay, drove her to fling herself, so far as this world was concerned, far more entirely than ever before upon the love of Hugh Lingard, and on the tie which bound her to him.

Thoughts of this description had been stirring in her mind one morning, as she sat on a low seat at his side, while he showed her some plans for the improvement of the old manor-house he had inherited from his impoverished father, without an acre of land to render the place of any value. When they had fully discussed the plans, and laid them aside, Ernestine leant her head on the arm of his chair, with a wistful sigh.

'Do you know, Hugh, it makes me tremble to think what it would be to me to live in this terrible world, if I had not you. You cannot think how full of dread it has grown for me since I have seen some of its dark realities, or how thankful I am to have you to rest on, safe and sure.'

'Dearest,' he said, 'I can only be rejoiced at anything which binds you more closely to me; but I trust it is not because you think well of me that you can find this comfort in me?'

'But it is because I do think well of you,' she answered, clinging to him. 'Oh, what would become of me if I did not? What a black, horrible wilderness this world would be to me if I were compelled to think of you as of some—cruel, degraded, selfish, mean! Oh, I could not bear it! I think I could not live; but, thank Heaven, it is not so. You are my own—noble, and good, and true—whom I may love as such to all eternity.'

'Ernestine, don't. I cannot bear it,' said Lingard, almost writhing in the soft clasp of her clinging hands. 'You do not know what you are saying. To you, I hope, I always shall be true and stainless; but I am not good—not better than others. Don't think it, child.'

'And now I love you better than ever after that speech,' said Ernestine, looking up laughingly; 'for of all things in the world a vain man is what I most despise; and you are only proving that you are not vain.

No, it is of no use; you shall not beat me out of my position. I must and will honour and admire as well as love you, even before the Church makes me vow to do so.' He bent down over her and kissed her hands, without speaking, and with the rapid change of expression so characteristic of her mobile countenance, the smile faded from her face, and her eyes filled with tears, as she said: 'I do not know how I could laugh about it, even for a moment, for it is a terrible thing to rest on the goodness of one human being so completely as I do on yours. If anything could ever obscure this faith in you, the whole world would grow dark for me—all earthly hope and joy would pass away for ever, and life become only a toilsome passage to the grave.'

'Ernestine, these are words which might terrify any man,' said Lingard gravely. 'I conclude then, that if you were to find me such an one as those of whom you heard at Greyburgh it would have this effect upon you?'

'Can you doubt it?' she said, crimsoning all over her fair face. 'But don't speak of such dreadful impossibilities. I should like to forget the very existence of such beings. There cannot surely be many like them in the world?'

Lingard made no answer. He sat deep in thought for a few minutes, and then suddenly asked her why so much time was necessary before their marriage could take place.

'Your aunt talks of six weeks, even now, from this time, while it seems to me we have already waited needlessly long.'

'But, you see, it is to be at Beaufort Court. My aunt will require a week or two after her arrival there before she can fill the house with guests, and we are still to be three weeks in town.'

'It seems to me all very unnecessary,' he said impatiently. 'Why cannot we just go out to-morrow morning, and be married quietly in the nearest church, without all these senseless preliminaries? You would become quite as securely my wife in that plain black silk, as in all the white satin and lace Lady Beaufort no doubt means to heap upon you.'

'That is very true,' said Ernestine, laughing; 'and there is nothing I should like better than a wedding of that description; but I am afraid you would find Aunt Beaufort rather impracticable on the subject.'

'I suppose I should,' he answered moodily, and the subject dropped.

About a fortnight after this conversation Ernestine came home one day from driving with her aunt, and found a letter waiting her, in a strange handwriting.

She opened it, and straightway uttered such a sudden exclamation that Lady Beaufort declared she had shaken her nerves for the remainder of the day. It was from the matron of one of the London workhouses, stating that a young woman had been brought in the night before by a policeman, who had found her lying near the door in a fainting-fit, which appeared to have been caused by want of food and exhaustion. She had gradually revived, and, having taken a little nourishment, had been able to speak; but the doctor, who had seen her that morning, had pronounced her in a dying state, from fatal disease of the lungs and other organs, and said that the utmost care and attention could only prolong her life a few days. She had stated her name to be Rosie Brown, and when they asked her if she had any friend who ought to be made acquainted with her hopeless condition, she took from within her dress a paper on which Miss Courtenay's name and address were written, and begged them to send for her—in accordance with which request the matron now wrote.

Found once more! dying indeed, but still found, so that a last effort might be made to bring the immortal soul to God, before it passed for ever from the world which had worked its cruel woe. Ernestine remembered having given Annie her address when she left her at the Penitentiary, and she augured well of the feeling which had made the poor child wear this scrap of paper next her heart, even in the midst of all her wilful wanderings.

Without a moment's delay she sent for a hired conveyance, knowing that Lady Beaufort would not at all approve of her aristocratic carriage being used for the purposes contemplated by her, for it was her full intention, if it could be done without risk, to take Annie at once to Mrs. Berry's, where she could attend to her herself, and where also Thorold could visit her; as Mrs. Berry, firm in her allegiance, had managed to get a house in the district where he was working for the present. Ernestine took her maid with her, in case she might require help, and started at once. After a drive which seemed interminable, through streets and lanes such as she had never even imagined in their squalor and misery, she at length reached a dingy, dismal-looking building, which proved to be the workhouse in question. It struck Ernestine that the gaol she had thought so terrible at Greyburgh, was quite a cheerful residence compared to this, and certainly old Bolton contrasted favourably with the surly porter who now opened the door about two inches, and informed her that ladies were not allowed to see the paupers. He was about to close it, when she hurriedly told him that she had come at the matron's request, and showed him the letter, which she had fortunately brought with her. He gruffly told her to wait, and went apparently to inquire the truth of her statement. When at last he came back and let her in, it was with the aggrieved look of a man who is being imposed upon.

Ernestine was shown into the matron's room, where she found that functionary sitting over a fire, in spite of the warm weather, and discussing some tea and buttered toast with remarkable gusto. It was with no good grace that she got up to show Ernestine the way to the sick ward.

'The young woman is dying,' she said; 'and I shouldn't have troubled for no one to come to see her, if the doctor hadn't said if she went off sudden to-day, and she unbeknown to any one, there might 'ave to be a 'quest; and these coroners and magistrates have got that bumptious and interfering with the way we does for the paupers here, that we're obliged to make as much of these tramps as if they were worth their keep, which they ain't. Here's the ward, ma'am, and the nurse will show you the bed;' and pushing open the door of a narrow, dark, ill-ventilated room, she went back in all haste to her tea.

Ernestine went in, and stood for a moment, almost overcome with the close, disagreeable air of the ward. It was filled with beds on either side, and all were occupied by suffering women. Nearly every fatal disease was represented there, for the poor creatures had not come to this, the last home of despair, till the long lingering hopes which life could give in any shape had wholly died away. Cancer, dropsy, consumption, and many another malady were there, and, worse than all, insanity and idiocy had their place beside those whose physical sufferings were greatly aggravated by their presence. Stretched on small hard beds, under scanty covering, lay those helpless sufferers, and over all presided one wretched old woman, herself a pauper, dignified with the name of a nurse, and receiving, for what may simply be termed the non-discharge of her duties, a payment sufficient to enable her to procure surreptitiously the bottle of gin, which she thrust under the nearest bed when Ernestine came in, her flushed face and indistinct speech, however, implying that she had already been regaling to a considerable extent. She was bent nearly double with rheumatism, and walked with a stick, of which her unfortunate patients seemed to stand in great awe. Her expression was that of habitual ill-temper, aggravated, no doubt, by the pain and weakness resulting from her malady, and which rendered her, independently of everything else, wholly unfit for her post.

'Now, then,' she exclaimed, in a harsh grating voice, knocking with her stick furiously on the floor, as the poor patients turned round to look at Ernestine, 'now, then, what are you a-staring and a-gaping for like that? what business is it of yours who comes here: lie down, every one of you, or I'll find a way to make you. What was you wanting, ma'am?' she added, to Ernestine, with an attempt at civility, inspired by the hope that sundry shillings might be forthcoming from the pocket of so well-dressed a lady.

'I have come to see Rosie Brown: where is she?'

'Rosie Brown: don't know such a name; there's none such here.'

'Yes, there is,' said a miserable-looking woman, who, unable to lie down from her difficulty of breathing, and having nothing to support her back, was trying to rest her head against the wall; 'she was brought in last night, but you didn't notice her, nurse, you was so drowsy-like,' she added tremulously, afraid of the nurse's wrath, who had simply been dead drunk. 'I don't think you've seen her this morning, but I heard her tell her name. That's her over there, ma'am,' she added, pointing to a distant bed.

'See if I don't stop your tea for this, you—.' We forbear to give the horrible oath with which the nurse closed her speech; and as the poor dying woman heard that her tea, her one little comfort, was to be taken away, tears rolled silently over her faded cheeks. She watched Ernestine, however, who with gentle step, that she might not disturb the sufferers, was making her way to the bed she had indicated; and the poor creature murmured to herself, ' I am glad I told her, for all I've lost my tea; for she'll bring a bit of comfort to that poor wench dying there, and she's younger nor I, and less used to rough it.'

Annie was lying with her head turned from the direction in which Ernestine was coming, and she did not hear or see her, so that she was able to stand and look at her for a few moments without being observed. It was Annie indeed, but changed to a degree that Ernestine·could hardly have believed possible, in the course of the few weeks since she had escaped from the Penitentiary. She was wasted almost to a skeleton; her wan face, with its bloodless lips and sharpened features, speaking of terrible suffering from want and destitution. The only traces of her former beauty were the blue eyes, looking preternaturally large from her excessive thinness, and the bright hair, far too profuse to be confined in the workhouse cap, flowing all in confusion over the hard pillow. She lay in a heap on the bed, the sharp outline of her limbs showing distinctly under the scanty covering, as if she had just been flung there by some rude hand, and was too exhausted to move from the position in which she had been placed. Her breathing was hurried and oppressed, and the burning spot on the cheek showed that she was parched with fever. 'Oh,' thought Ernestine, 'if her destroyer could but see the mournful wreck he has made!' Hearing a step, but not looking round, Annie feebly murmured, 'Some drink, please, some drink, for the love of heaven!'

'What can I give her to drink?' said Ernestine, turning round to the nurse, who had followed her.

'Hang me if I know,' said the woman; 'I've got nothing for her, not so much as for myself—worse luck. Here, give her this fine cold water,' she added, snatching up a mug of water that stood by the bedside of another patient, who looked wistfully after it.

'I will bring it to you again,' said Ernestine to the sufferer, 'if you will kindly let me have just a little for this poor girl;' and the patient, brightening into a smile, begged her to take it. She went back to Annie's bedside. As she came close to her the girl looked up, and, seeing who it was, uttered a stifled cry, and buried her face on the pillow. It was evident that the recollection of her ingratitude in leaving the Home where the lady had placed her made her afraid to meet her again. Ernestine stooped down and kissed her forehead. 'Annie, dear Annie,' she said, 'I am thankful to have found you again. I am so sorry for all you seem to have suffered.'

Then Annie lifted up her head, and looked with an intense gaze into Ernestine's face. As she met the pitying eyes looking down so lovingly upon her, she suddenly flung her wasted arms round Ernestine, and, laying her head on her breast, exclaimed, 'Oh, my dear lady, you are like an angel from heaven to me!' Then, with something of her old impulsiveness, even in the midst of her great weakness, she started from Ernestine's gentle hold, and said, 'Miss Courtenay, I have not done wrong since I saw you last,—indeed, indeed I have not. I could not stay at the Penitentiary, but I felt that I'd starve rather than do wrong, and I have starved, but I've not sinned. Oh, I hope you'll believe me!'

'I do believe you, Annie, my child: don't doubt it, and I am thankful for it. It was better to suffer, as I can see you have done, than to sin.'

'I don't know, I'm sure,' said Annie wearily; 'it was the one thought of you, and all you told me, kept me from it, but it has been an awful time. I tried to work and get an honest living when I came from the Penitentiary, but the whole world was turned against me: they could all see what I was, and no one would employ me; so I sold my clothes, bit by bit, for food, till I had nothing left but my gown, and I slept under the arches of the bridge at night, but the water looked so black and cold I could not drown myself, as Lois did. I got ill, and my cough was dreadful, and at last I fell down on the pavement, and I thought I was dying, and so I am, I suppose, and then there's hell—' Her voice, which had been growing feebler as she spoke, died away, and she sank back on the bed half-fainting. Ernestine bathed her face and hands with water, and slowly the dim blue eyes opened again, and a smile flickered over the wan face, but she did not speak, and lay seemingly quite content to hold Ernestine's hand and look at her.

'Has the doctor seen her to-day?' asked Ernestine.

'That he han't,' said the nurse; 'where's he to get the time to see folk every half-hour?'

'He saw her last night when she was brought in,' said an old woman in the next bed, 'and he said she was a-dying, and it was no use doing anything.'

'And the chaplain, has he been to visit her yet, or will he come to-day ?'

'Bless you, he'll see her in his regular rounds; and her turn ain't like to come for a week or two yet.'

Ernestine looked at Annie's deathlike face, and thought of the answer made a few years ago by a Bishop's chaplain to a prison official, who intimated to him that a condemned criminal awaiting his execution was desirous of receiving the rite of confirmation: 'His Lordship would make his biennial confirmation tour in the course of a year and a half, and would be happy then to receive any candidates who might be presented to him.'

'She is very low and faint,' said Ernestine, feeling the poor girl's scarcely perceptible pulse. 'What nourishment has she had?'

'The doctor gave her some beef-tea hisself last night,' said the old woman in the next bed; 'and she han't had nothing since.'

'She ought to have something immediately,' exclaimed Ernestine, much shocked at the neglect, which in this case was likely to be fatal.

'Oh, it's all very fine to say ought this and ought that,' said the nurse; 'but she can't have anything if there is nothing to have. We keeps regular hours here and it ain't dinner-time now, nor yet supper-time. She'll have her rations with the rest when the proper hour comes.'

To leave Annie in this place was certainly not to be thought of, and Ernestine determined to lose no time in taking her away.

'I shall take this patient home,' she said to the nurse. 'Do you know if there is anything to prevent my doing so?'

'Nothing at all as I knows on. A good riddance, I should say. Leastways, not unless the doctor were to say it would kill her to move her.'

'Can I hear what he says now, then?' said Ernestine. 'Is he in the house?'

'Sure to be at this hour; for it's his time for going through the men's ward.'

'Would you be so kind as to go and ask him, then?' said Ernestine, putting some money into the nurse's hand; 'and if he does not object to my removing her, will you tell the matron I shall do so at once?'

The old woman hobbled off willingly enough after the receipt of such a gratuity; and Ernestine went to tell her maid, who was waiting at the door, to go to the nearest shop, and buy some blankets to wrap round the dying girl. As she came back through the room, the poor woman who had pointed out Annie's bed to her, said, in a sad voice—

'Be you a-going to take her away, ma'am? It's a blessed thing for her, poor wench; but I wish I was a-going too.'

'And so do I, and so do I,' was echoed from all the beds near her.

'I am sure I wish I could take you all away,' said Ernestine, looking sorrowfully round on the forlorn faces which met her on every side. 'I wish indeed I could help you in any way; but I do not know how. I fear it is against the rules to give money.'

'Ah, that it is,' said the woman; 'and it would be no use, for they never let us keep it. That nurse would find it out, I do believe, if we hid it in our coffins.'

'I am very sorry for you all,' said Ernestine; 'and I will try if I can get leave to come and visit you, and bring you some little comforts. I will do all I can.'

'God bless you,' resounded on all sides, and the poor woman said gratefully, 'You have done something for us already, ma'am, for you have given us kind words; and that's what we don't get many days in the year.' She heard the nurse's step, and shrunk back.

'The doctor says you may take her and welcome,' said the old woman as she came in. 'She's got to die anyhow, he says, and it won't make a bit of difference what you do with her. And the matron, she says you can please yourself; but she's very particular engaged just now, and can't be disturbed. She's engaged a-having of her tea,' continued the nurse savagely, 'a-frying her bacon, and a-bolting on it like anything. It is a shame, it is, she as has nothing to do but to sit with her hands across like a fine lady, feeding on the best; and me, that am toiling and moiling among them worrying sick folk all the day long, getting nothing much better nor the pauper's rations;' and so she went grumbling on, till Ernestine stopped her to ask if she could get one of the men to carry poor Annie down stairs to the carriage. This she did for a further 'consideration,' and the blankets having been brought, Annie was borne through the midst of her fellow-sufferers, who looked wistfully after her, and placed in the carriage, which was ordered to drive at once to Mrs. Berry's.

Annie lay half insensible in Ernestine's arms the whole way; but she opened her eyes and smiled faintly at the cry of passionate delight with which Ellen Lucas recognised her, as she was carried into the house.

'Oh, I am so glad Annie's found, and safe with me in this happy home. You will let me nurse her, Miss Courtenay, won't you?'

'Gladly,' said Ernestine, smiling. 'You and Mrs. Berry together will, I know, take good care of her.'

'That we will, poor lamb,' said Mrs. Berry, looking compassionately on the wasted form that lay in the coachman's arms, with the face of marble whiteness, and the long bright hair streaming over his rough coat-sleeve. And they certainly did their best for her. That evening, placed in a clean comfortable bed, after having a little soup and wine, Annie fell into so quiet a slumber that Ernestine was able to leave her without anxiety.

Next day, when the physician, whom Ernestine sent for, saw her, he said, that although the workhouse doctor had been quite right in saying the case was entirely hopeless, and the end very near, yet he thought the great care and good nursing she was likely to have, might prolong her life two or three weeks at least.

And so it proved. The frequent nourishment she took, and the perfect rest and quiet she enjoyed, enabled her to rally considerably, and a last little wave of life seemed to bear her up once more on the mortal shore, from which she was so soon to pass away, and be no more seen.

Ernestine was very thankful for this respite. Poor Annie's earthly life had been so mercilessly blighted, that it would indeed have been a mistaken compassion to have wished it ultimately prolonged; but she did desire earnestly that time might be given her to make her peace with God, in whom alone could be her true and eternal rest. This anxiety Thorold shared to the full; and he undertook, with his usual quiet energy, to do all he could for the dying girl. Ernestine wrote to Annie's father, to tell him of her hopeless state; and also, that it had been induced entirely by the sufferings she had endured, in consequence of her determination to keep from evil. In his reply he thanked Miss Courtenay heartily for all her kindness, and said the only comfort he could know about his wretched child, was the fact of her being saved from dying in the workhouse. He sent her his love and free forgiveness; but he said he could not bring himself to see her, and he felt sure it was happiest for them both not to meet; and as Annie shared in this opinion, Ernestine made no opposition to his decision.

CHAPTER IX.

THE LAST STRUGGLE.

AND now commenced within that narrow room another phase of the awful and mysterious struggle, which, from the highest heaven, when angels fell from their first estate, in ages inconceivably remote, down to the feeblest child that this day wakes to personal consciousness, has still rent the universe with dreadful combat, dying into stillness by every open grave, but reproduced again at every human birth; and never ceasing where living breath is drawn, to make earth ghastly with the 'confused noise of battle, and garments rolled in blood.'

'There was war in heaven: Michael and his angels fought against the dragon, and the dragon fought, and his angels.' What affinity could there be between the stupendous scene of mystery and terror opened to us in these words, and the deathbed of that lost degraded child, seeming in her dishonour and weakness the most despicable and insignificant of God's creatures? Yet were they but links of the one great chain, whose beginning and end are alike hid in the Omniscient hand,—the chain forged by the electric shock of the antagonistic principles of good and evil. What though in the one case it might be the destinies of the universe to all eternity which were involved, and in the other but one immortal soul which trembled in the balance of everlasting life or death ?—who shall say which seemed most momentous in the impartial judgments of Perfection ; for has not the Cross on Calvary taught us that the fate of a single soul could have moved the Throne of God Himself to the very centre, since He who became incarnate to save the human race, would have done no less had but one out of all their millions stood in risk of perishing !

The struggle in this instance was very fierce. The course it took in the deathless soul of this young girl, opened up strange vistas as to the far-spreading and indestructible consequences of one evil act, such as that of the man who had lured her to her ruin ; and showed how, in the ages to come, it might live to meet him, in such forms of hideousness as would appal him in his hour of final judgment.

Annie Brook's mental state, when told by Thorold that her life's probation was wearing to its close, was simply one of entire despair; but it was a condition which resulted not from her own sin, but from that of her betrayer. For her own guilt, dark and dreadful as it was, she knew that sacred blood had been shed, from a Heart so spotlessly pure that it had power to wash away even the black stain that defiled her soul; but she felt that, if he, who with words of sweetest promise had won her innocent love, had but left her as he found her, a safe and happy child in her father's home, she might even now have been traversing life with honour and affection round her, and blessed years in store, which the holy ties of wife and mother would fill with tranquil joy. She knew that he had deceived her with the cruellest deceit one human being can practise on another, —he, the experienced man of the world, she, the ignorant girl of sixteen. She knew that he had demanded, and by false words obtained, the sacrifice of her whole being for time and for eternity, in order to give himself a passing pleasure. And when he desired to rid himself of a burden which had lost its charm, he had consigned her to depths of guilt and degradation unknown to her before even by name; while he himself, whose words had ever been law to her, had told her that, because of what he had made her, no other resource but that remained to her in all the earth,—except a grave. He had told her this; he had lashed her with words which stung like scourges of fire, till he had driven her on to set the seal on her infamy, and then turned away to enter on his fair honourable life again—his life of pleasure, sensual and intellectual, of refinement, of high ambition, of glowing hopes, and bright reality;—and the thought of these things crushed hope and trust utterly out of her soul, and cursed her with the fatal conviction, that one doomed to such a fate could never have had a share in the love of God.

'If God loves sinners, I am too great a sinner for Him to love,' she said; 'if He had loved me He would have killed me when I stepped out of father's house to go to my ruin. No; it seems as if the one He loves is the man who has been my curse; for I saw him, Mr. Thorold, I saw him, a few nights ago, driving to the theatre in a carriage, with some of his fine friends, looking so well and so handsome, laughing and talking, with livery-servants waiting on him, and the people making way to let him into the bright beautiful place, with its lights and its music. Yes, and he flung money to a beggar standing near; and I, what do you think I was doing? crouching on the wet pavement, soaked through and through, for it was pouring of rain, faint and like to die; for not a bit had I had to eat that day, and with no other place to sleep that night but the stones at my feet; and because I leant forward to look at the face I had loved too well, a policeman gave me a push that sent me reeling against a door-step, and then called me a bad name, and said none of my sort should stand among respectable folk; so I was frightened, and I turned into a dark court, where nobody would pass, and lay down on the stones for the night; and was I to lie there thinking God loved me and not rather him, who sat in the bright warm theatre listening to the music and taking his pleasure?'

It was not easy to convince an unreasoning and un-intellectual mind like Annie's, that in the very fact of the success of the wicked, and the sufferings their sin inflicts often alike on the innocent and guilty, lies the strongest natural argument for the immortality of the soul and the future retribution of God, 'the righteous Judge, strong and patient.' In all ages, in all places, the human instinct has responded to this truth. David of old, in his grief and dismay at sight of the ungodly in such prosperity, exclaimed: 'Then thought I to understand this, but it was too hard for me, until I went into the sanctuary of God, then understood I the end of these men. Oh how suddenly do they consume away, perish, and come to a fearful end! Yea; even like as a dream when one awaketh.' And from his day to the present, the consideration of this great mystery of evil has led every honest mind to see, in the existence of these deep and hidden things of God, the certain promise that His immutable justice shall yet shine forth as the sun of all eternity in the death-day of the world; when the clamorous instinct of right and wrong that cries aloud in every living soul, shall find perfect satisfaction in His most pure judgment, and His final adjustment of the moral creation.[1]

Strongly as those arguments commend themselves to those whose reasoning powers have been cultivated, Thorold knew they would not be understood by Annie Brook; but for her, as for all, there was one most potent and infallible proof, which lay open and glorious in its truth as the clear light of day in the face of heaven. In the charity that clothed the Immaculate God with the humility of the Incarnation, and won from Him voluntary endurance of death and sufferings, whose bitterness exceeded the world's accumulated woe, there is a revelation of the Divine Love which swallows up in its fulness and completeness all seeming mysteries of evil, and stamps with the seal of eternal tenderness, and the

---

[1] An able exposition of this argument will be found in a work entitled *Some Words for God*, under the heading IMMORTALITY (published by Messrs. Rivington, London).

promise of ultimate good, every incident in the life of individual souls, as in the history of the world at large. Whatever may be the darkness, and confusion, and injustice that seems to plunge the earth in chaos, none who have realized, so far as human comprehension may, the meaning of the awful '*It is finished*' which has echoed down the vanished ages to thrill in the heart of every one of us, can doubt that at the last, love, immaculate, illimitable, all-enduring, will be found the one governing principle that has ruled the world, and shall be the deathless life of man's eternity.

To awaken Annie Brook therefore to a perception of the love manifest on the Cross was the work to which Thorold now set himself with his whole might. How difficult a task it was, those only can know who have attempted to teach this simplest yet sublimest truth to an uneducated mind. Perhaps not one in a thousand of the lower orders does in reality discern the motive power which made the Son of God obedient unto death; they repeat by rote words which imply it, and they have a vague knowledge of the actual event of the crucifixion; but that they are to see in it not only an evidence of love, but of a love which is personal to themselves, and of the deepest moment to them, is what most of them go from the cradle to the grave without ever realizing.

Their teachers imagine that the words 'He died for me,' repeated by every Sunday-school child, prove their acquaintance with the glorious truth it involves, but there is in reality no idea connected with the sentence in their minds. The fact is that the religious teaching of the lower class is superficial and hollow to the last degree, and so it will continue to be, till the whole of their instruction is brought to bear on their realization of these two great truths—the Divinity of our Lord, and His personal and living interest in themselves.

Annie Brook had received what would be considered a good religious education for a girl of her rank. She knew most of the facts contained in the Pentateuch, and could repeat the names of the Patriarchs, and of some of the Kings of Israel and Judah; and she knew also of the birth of One whom angels worshipped, and Herod sought to slay, and who at length was killed by wicked men, and yet arose the third day, and went up to heaven; but to her it was all just a 'Bible story,' which had no more reality for her than the 'pretty tales,' as she expressed it, which her grandmother used to tell her by the winter hearth.

When at length Thorold brought her to realize the true meaning of the words she had so often repeated, 'He died for me,' it broke her down completely; the bold unbelief, the rebellious complaint, the angry cry of injustice, were stilled for ever, and replaced by the one weary passionate longing to find a shelter for evermore in the Divine compassion of that love, from which she feared she was too fatally shut out. Thorold taught her to trace the evidences of it even in her own past life. The care of her earthly father, type of the Heavenly, which would have shielded her from all evil had she not abandoned it;—the very desertion of her destroyer, which else had let her sin remain too dear to be relinquished;—the remembrance of her by Lois in her last dark hour;—the pity which had tracked her steps from the first day that Ernestine received her mission from the dead;—the providence which had discovered her to her true friend in her last extremity : all these tokens from God, shining like rays of light in the hideous darkness of her sinful past, now but woke in her a deeper pining for Him who can alone be perfect satisfaction to the undying soul; and she implored of Thorold to teach her, the guilty wanderer, how she might seek the crucified Lord, and so feel after Him and find Him, that even she, like happy Magdalene, might yet rest her weary head beneath His blessed feet.

One less experienced than Thorold might have thought the work was done when so much was gained, but he too surely presaged the next difficulty which would assail this victim of a fellow-creature. He told her she must forgive ere she could ask to be forgiven, and with a cry of passionate indignation she exclaimed it was impossible! Thorold must know it was impossible for her to forgive the merciless betrayer who had made such havoc of her life and soul; he was cruel to ask her; and she writhed on her bed, and clenched her wasted hands convulsively, as if the very remembrance of this man ate into her heart like fire. It has been well said that the deepest hate is that which springs from a dead affection; it was the bitterness of her outraged love which brought this frenzy on Annie Brook's feeble frame, and made her blue eyes, dim already with the shades of death, gleam with the impotent fury of some wild beast at bay.

Thorold waited till the paroxysm was spent, and then he began, in a low, sad voice, to speak of the inconceivable sufferings of the Passion, in all its awful details of insult, blasphemy, and torture. He spoke of the Perfect Innocence thus punished, the Perfect Love thus cruelly rewarded and betrayed, of the awful agonies, mocked by those for whom they were endured; and as he went on with this history, which has broken harder hearts than Annie's, the angry fire died out of her eyes, her lip quivered with strong feeling; and when at last he reminded her how, in return for all this brutal cruelty, this wanton pain and humiliation, the Divine Sufferer lifted up His dying voice and uttered that holiest prayer, with which He still pleads at God's right hand for the pardon of every living soul that, sinning, crucifies Him afresh, and puts Him to open shame, '*Father, forgive them,*'—she suddenly hid her face in her hands, while tears burst through the thin white fingers, and exclaimed—

'Oh, wicked, wretched that I am, what are all my sufferings, my injuries to His? And I say I will not forgive, while He forgave the cruel men that mocked and tortured Him. Blessed Jesus, I will, I do forgive him! Oh, pity and pardon us both!'

Again, it might have been thought that from this point, all would have been easy and peaceful in the progress of this departing soul; but there was yet another struggle almost inevitably before her, which Thorold well knew would prove harder than any other. The keen sense of the love and goodness of her Lord, which seemed at last to take possession of Annie's whole being, brought with it such an overwhelming conviction of her own sin, that a time came when she utterly despaired of any possible pardon for herself. That, after all the blessed Saviour had endured and done for her, she should have turned away from Him to give herself to the sins which

He abhorred, seemed to the heart-broken girl to place her beyond the pale of possible forgiveness. She made a full confession of all her guilt to Thorold. She prayed constantly that she might be allowed once again to see the man who had been her enemy, that she might forgive him in words as well as in heart; but still she could not lift her weeping eyes to heaven, and see aught but justice in the dreadful doom which she anticipated. She refused the Last Sacrament, which Thorold would not now have withheld from her, because she thought that to receive it would but increase her condemnation; and so she passed through some days and nights in an agony such as no earthly trial or sorrow could ever bring on a living soul. It was plain that, if it continued, it would soon consume the little life still left to her, and both Thorold and Ernestine were greatly concerned about her.

Ernestine spent every moment with her which she could spare from Lingard; but he seemed now as if he could not endure her to be absent from his sight; and the wistful tenderness with which his eyes followed when she left the room, often filled her with a strange sadness, which haunted her even at the deathbed of the dying girl. One evening there was a large dinner-party at Lady Beaufort's, and Lingard had come early that he might have a few minutes with Ernestine before the guests

THE LAST STRUGGLE. 189

arrived. They were alone in the drawing-room; she was examining some lovely flowers in a vase near her, and he was watching the unconscious grace of her movements, and thinking that she was the very type of all that was gentle and pure and womanly, with her sweet thoughtful face, and soft brown hair, and the flowing white draperies that seemed to create a light around her, when a servant came in with a note for her. It was written in haste by Mrs. Berry, to say that Annie had suddenly become very much worse; that, indeed, in the expressive phraseology of the nurse, she was 'taken for death.' The doctor had been sent for, and pronounced it impossible she could live through the night, and her exhaustion and breathlessness were so great that Mrs. Berry almost feared she would not last till Ernestine could reach her. The nurse had sent for Thorold, but he was out, and she had desired that he might be told of the girl's dying state immediately on his return. Finally, Mrs. Berry entreated Ernestine not to delay an instant in coming, for Annie was waiting her arrival with all the feverish anxiety of one whose moments were numbered. Ernestine put the note into Lingard's hand.

'I must go,' she exclaimed; 'I will not wait, even to change my dress. You will explain my absence to my aunt, and make peace for me, will you not, dearest Hugh?'

She had already rung the bell and ordered a cab, and desired that her maid should be sent with a shawl.

'Must you go, darling?' said Lingard, holding both her hands fast.

She looked up to him in surprise.

'You see nurse says she is dying, and fears I can scarce be in time. I must not delay a moment.'

Still he would not lose his hold.

'She may be dead before you get there,' he said, 'then your drive at this untoward hour will be useless.

'Oh, I hope not,' exclaimed Ernestine, tears starting to her eyes. 'I promised poor Annie to be with her at the last; you know she has not a friend in the world but me. Don't hold me, dearest Hugh; there is Benson at the door with my shawl, and I grudge every moment.'

Still he held her.

'I never was so unwilling to part with you in my life, Ernestine.'

'But why, dearest?' she said, looking at him anxiously. 'I shall only be a few hours away from you, and soon we shall be always together, Hugh.'

'Heaven grant it,' he said, and for a moment clasped her passionately in his arms, then he let her go, and she hurried to the door. Her maid was standing on the stair, ready to go with her, and with a thick shawl on her arm. Lingard took it from her, and wrapped it round Ernestine with the utmost care. Then he went down with her, and helped her into the carriage, holding her hand fast as he did so, and whispering, 'Come back soon, my darling, or I shall come and fetch you.'

She turned round her face and smiled at him,— a sweet, bright smile, which was never again to pass from his memory. Lingard returned to the house, with its lights and its flowers, its luxury and its aristocratic guests, while Ernestine, after a long drive through the dark streets, entered the little humble room where the fallen girl was dying in her shame,—a common sight enough in this land of Christian faith and vaunted civilisation, yet one—how awful and mysterious!—a deathless soul about to go forth into the dread unknown, with all the stains and wounds of its mortal life upon it, and with eternity rising up before it, dark in despair, because of the sin wherewith one human being had quenched the light of heaven on its path.

As Ernestine entered the room she stopped, almost startled at Annie's wonderful beauty, which at that moment far exceeded even the loveliness she must have possessed when her portrait was taken. It is often thus in the last hours of human existence. The poor people call it the 'lightening before death;' and those who have once seen the peculiar brilliancy of the eyes, and the intensely spiritualized expression of the countenance, during that last and brightest flash of life, can never forget it. Annie's breathing was so short and difficult that she could not lie down, and she was propped up in bed, her head supported by several cushions, that she might have as much air as possible. The delicate white of her complexion was relieved by the crimson tinge of fever in her cheeks; her blue eyes, wide open, and shining with unnatural light, flashed from side to side in unceasing restlessness; her wealth of fair hair lay scattered on the pillow round her, and as she gasped, with the heaving of her chest painfully evident, she clutched the bed-clothes convulsively, or pushed back the heavy curls from her face, and glanced round constantly with an eager famishing look, as if she were hungering for some new source of life. As her bright restless eyes fell on Ernestine, she held out her arms passionately, and exclaimed, in a voice pitched high with feverish excitement and exhaustion—

'Oh, Miss Courtenay, come to me, come and help me! What shall I do? Oh what shall I do? I am dying. I am going to see the face of Christ, and how shall I bear it? My sin, my sin; it has crucified Him again and again

—the Scripture says it; crucified Him afresh, after the blood He shed, after all He suffered to save me—yes, me! I turned my back on Him, and would have none of Him; I wanted to do the things He hated. He offered me life, and I chose death; He offered me heaven, and I chose hell. Oh, what shall I do, what shall I do?' and she clasped Ernestine's hands in her convulsive agony, and gazed into her eyes as if she would have wrung some hope from her answer; then, before Ernestine could speak, she had flung herself back again, and was staring upward, almost with a prophetic look.

'The face of Christ, shining as the sun in its strength; Christ, who never sinned, the Judge of all the earth. And I to stand before Him with all my wickedness black upon me! Mercy, mercy; but there is no time; the minutes are flying; I am growing faint; death is cold at my heart. Oh that I could live again! Oh Lord, that I could live again. I can't, I can't! My soul is lost; yes, my wretched soul is lost!' and, breathless, she sank back again. How impotent all human agency was in that hour! Ernestine, trembling from head to foot, would have given worlds to have helped her; but how? She felt that it was in truth a soul alone with its God, struggling under an awful revelation of His purity and its own iniquity, and that she at least was powerless in such a conflict.

'Is there no chance of Mr. Thorold's coming?' she said, turning anxiously to Mrs. Berry, who was standing near, with tears streaming down her cheeks.

'He's sure to come, my dear lady, the moment he goes home and gets the message; but he's out among the sick and poor somewhere, and no one can tell where to find him, or when he will be back.'

'Well, you must not stay here, dear nurse, at all events,' said Ernestine, who saw that the good woman was feeling faint and ill. 'I shall not leave Annie now, and you must go and lie down. I will call you if I want you.'

'I'll go to poor Ellen, then, for she is wonderful timid at the thought of death in the house. She says she's been such a sinner, it scares her; and she can't bring herself to come near the room, for all she's so fond of Annie.'

'Yes, go and make her take care of you;' but as she went to the door to close it after Mrs. Berry, Annie thought she was going away, and shrieked out—

'Miss Courtenay, are you going to leave me to die alone, and go out before God with all my sins upon my head? Oh why won't you help me? Don't you see I am dying; and every wicked thing I've ever done is written on the wall there in letters all of fire; and I'm obliged to see it; I'm obliged to read it. I tell you it's dreadful. And then, there's the Lord Christ dying on His cross, and me flaunting past Him, laughing and mocking. What did I care? I took my pleasure, and let Him suffer in vain for me. O Miss Courtenay, you have done your best for me; but I'm lost, I'm lost!' Only exhaustion made her pause for a moment, but the restless glancing of her eyes never ceased for an instant, or the convulsive clenching of her hands. She was beginning to cry out again with her despairing words, but Ernestine forcibly took the trembling hands in hers, and compelled her to turn her glance on her.

'Annie, listen to me,' she said; 'I have one word to say, which you must hear. Listen to me quietly now for a moment.' Annie's eyes rested on hers, and she saw that, for the time at least, she was giving her full attention, and slowly and solemnly Ernestine said—
'The Lord Jesus Christ declared, "I am come into the world to seek and to save that which was lost." Do you hear me, Annie? He came to save that which was LOST.'

'Lost!' repeated Annie slowly. 'Lost! and who so lost as I am?' She remained silent a moment; then over the bright flashing eyes there gathered a mist of tears.

'Oh, is it possible, that me, even me! so lost, He would seek and save?' She drew her hands out of Ernestine's grasp, and folded them together as she had been taught to do when a little child she repeated her evening prayers, and in a trembling voice she said—

'Lord Jesus, I am lost indeed; O seek and save me, even me, Lord Jesus!' Then she remained perfectly still, her eyes closed, and tears slowly coursing down her cheeks, now grown deadly pale. Ernestine remained kneeling at her side in perfect silence. At last Annie whispered softly—

'Do you think the Lord Jesus would like to save me?'

'I am sure he would, my child.'

'But so bad as I have been?'

'His love is greater even than your sin, Annie.'

Then there was silence again for a long time. The terrible restlessness was gone. The feverish flush had died away. The calm which often precedes death had set in; and, but for her laboured breathing, it would have seemed as if the struggle were already over, so like a marble statue did she seem, with her closed eyes and her unearthly whiteness. Once only she spoke during this interval—

'Do you think Mr. Thorold will come and give me the Sacrament now?'

'I hope so, dear Annie; we have sent for him; he was out, but he will come the moment he gets the message.'

'Too late!' she said, with a quiet movement of the head. 'He will be too late. But it is only just I should not have it now; I refused it so often.'

Then she relapsed into silence. So passed some hours. Sometimes Ernestine thought she slept; at other times her lips moved as if in prayer; but her breathing was growing perceptibly fainter, and it was plain that death was very near. Ernestine knelt, with her back to the door, looking sorrowfully on the white, sad face, and feeling as if she ought to be speaking some words of comfort to her: while at the same time she dared not break in upon a silence in which the departing soul might be listening to the very voice of God. Suddenly she saw Annie start as if she had received an electric shock. Her eyes opened wide, clear and bright as in her fairest days, and fixed themselves intently on the door, which had opened a moment previously, though Ernestine had been too much absorbed to hear it. The powers of the girl's failing life seemed to rush over her sinking frame once more. She gazed towards that spot with a smile of ecstasy, and stretching out her arms, exclaimed—

'You are come! Oh, God be praised, who has heard my prayer. You are come, that I may tell you I forgive you with all my heart, with all my soul, as I pray the dear Lord may forgive me too. Come to me; come to me quick. I have but a moment, and I want to take back the bitter words I have said against you; let us part in peace, though you wronged me so cruelly, who loved you so well.'

Ernestine was utterly astonished at this sudden outburst, and at the strange words Annie uttered, and for a moment she almost thought her delirious; but it was evident from her look that she was indeed addressing some one actually present, and turning quickly round to see who it was, she gave a suppressed shriek, while her heart seemed to stop beating, and she felt as if turned to stone. It was Hugh Lingard who was standing there in the door-way, with a look of horror and dismay on his face such as no words could paint, while his eyes were fixed on the dying girl with unmistakable recognition; his arms fell slowly to his sides, and the one word, 'Rosie!' escaped involuntarily from his lips. In a moment

Ernestine saw it all. The truth flashed upon her soul in all its details, with that irresistible conviction which seems almost like an inspiration from heaven. She knew in that moment, with a terrible knowledge which could never pass away from her, that the destroyer of this child, whom God had sent her to seek throughout the world, was that very man who was dearer to her than life itself, and in whom her whole earthly happiness was bound up only too fatally. It was like the shock of an earthquake to her thus to learn that the truth and goodness, in which she had believed so fondly as being his special characteristic, had in fact never existed. Kneeling as she was, she had to catch hold of the bed to keep herself from falling, for there was a mist before her eyes, and a roaring as of thunder in her ears; but through it all, she caught the tones of Annie's voice, fainter far than before—

'Oh, why will you not come to me? I am going fast. Why do you look at me so? Are you sorry I am dying? It is best. I could not live any more in this world. But come quick. I want to ask God to forgive you. I want to part friends. My breath is failing. Come.'

Her faltering words died away. Her breathing came in long gasps, and Ernestine, forcing herself to look up, saw that an awful change was passing over her features. There was no time to be lost. No earthly thoughts or human feelings must stay the work of charity in that supreme moment. She rose up and went towards Lingard, who had staggered against the wall, and covered his face with his hands.

'Is this true?' she said, in her low sweet voice, which trembled as she spoke. 'Is it indeed you who have need to ask her forgiveness?'

He let his hands fall and turned towards her—

'It is true, Ernestine. God, in whom you believe, has brought this judgment on me.'

'Then come as she wishes—come quickly—she is expiring.'

He looked towards Annie, and saw that it was so indeed. Her head had fallen back, her shadowy blue eyes were partly hidden beneath the white lids, and over her parted lips the breath was coming each moment fainter, like the heaving tide falling ever lower and lower on the shore it is deserting. Lingard rushed to the bedside, and, sinking on his knees, exclaimed,

Rosie, forgive me—forgive!'

Slowly she turned her dim eyes with a last look of life towards him, and, with great difficulty, lifting one thin white hand, she let it fall on his head as if in token of pardon and blessing. It rested there for a few more awful moments, during which her dying breath still sighed into the silence; then suddenly a light broke over her face like morning on the distant hills; with one low sob the spirit passed away from the worn and weary frame, and Annie Brook was beyond the reach of mortal ill.

CHAPTER X.

CHARITY SUFFERETH LONG, AND IS KIND.

YES! Annie Brook was beyond the reach of mortal ill, but not so Ernestine Courtenay. The scorn of the world could never more bring the flush of shame to that cold white cheek, nor could its cruel hate or deadly love rend the poor heart that lay so still beneath the hand of death; but life, with its terrible capacity for suffering, was strong in the sensitive palpitating frame of her who now beside that quiet corpse was entering on a silent agony which could only terminate with actual existence on the earth.

Thorold came hurriedly into the room, almost immediately after Annie breathed her last, and Lingard, hearing his step, rose up at once from his kneeling posture by the bed, and walked quickly to the door; but there he paused for a moment, and, turning round, he looked on Ernestine. Their gaze met, and though not a word was spoken, both knew that it was an eternal farewell which was passing between them; yet he saw there was not one shade of reproach in the sweet eyes that were looking their last on all that made life dear, —only mournful regret and anguish, which he rightly judged was far more for his sin than her own sorrow. He could not bear the sight; a spasm of pain contracted his features; and hastily turning from the room, he rushed down stairs, and Ernestine knew she would never look upon his face again. Thorold was astonished at his abrupt departure, for he had heard from Mrs. Berry that Mr. Lingard, finding Miss Courtenay was detained to so late an hour, had come to escort her home; but when he turned and caught a glimpse of the dumb agony on Ernestine's face as she flung herself down by the dead body, with her hands clasped above her head, he understood it all. Very gently he asked her a few questions as to Annie's last moments, and she lifted up her head and answered him in a strange half-stifled voice; then he bid her take comfort in the thought that she had been able to carry out her mission to the last; and that she might hope the poor lost wanderer, now lying before them with so quiet a smile on her pale face, was even then at peace at her pitying Saviour's feet.

A faint light stole into Ernestine's mournful eyes, as he thus said the only words which could have given her comfort at that moment, and she looked up gratefully to him, but did not speak. Then he asked her if she wished any one to assist her in performing the last offices for Annie. She softly answered, 'No.' He saw that indeed it was best for her at that moment to be alone with the dead, so he quietly withdrew, giving Mrs. Berry many directions for her comfort, when she should have finished the last act of charity to her whom she had so long sought, and found at last, at the cost of all her own happiness on earth.

The glad sunshine of the early summer morning was pouring into the room when Ernestine began to compose the limbs of the dead, and spread over them the fair white linen, type of the wedding-garment, which she trusted even this poor erring child might win from the tender mercy of the sinless Lord; and, as she saw that a new day had begun, a strange feeling took possession of her, as if she herself had died with Annie—died for ever to the sweet life of the past, with its love and hope and joy, and as if the whole earth would henceforth be for her cold and dark as the grave, whither that dead form must descend. She seemed to be acting out in a mournful drama her own future existence, as she performed her last duties to the corpse. When she closed the eyes she felt that her own also could look no more on all that had been beauty and brightness to her in this world; and as she crossed the hands, in token of meek submission, on the lifeless breast, so she felt must she, in calm resignation, accept the death of hope and gladness in her heart, and only wait with Annie for the blessed resurrection, when the sorrows of earth would vanish like fleeting vapours in the light of the eternal day.

Very quietly she went through her task; only at times the bitter pain at her heart found vent in a choking sob. With a lingering tenderness she combed out Annie's fair hair till it fell like a golden shroud over the lifeless form, then she took a lovely white camellia from her dress, which Lingard had given her the night before, when, radiant with happiness, she had hurried to meet him, and laid it upon Annie's breast. She knew she had done with the flowers of life for ever. When all was finished she kissed the marble brow, and, kneeling down, lifted up her whole soul in one earnest supplication, that she might be able to turn the love she still must feel for Lingard, while life lasted, into one long unwearied prayer for him, that when he too should be a silent corpse upon the bed of death, his soul might win forgiveness from his God, as she trusted this his victim had; then she bowed her head on her hands, and said in a low, calm voice, 'Now, Lord, I am thine alone!' and so remained motionless, as if her spirit too had passed away to the land of perfect rest.

She found Mrs. Berry waiting anxiously for her appearance, when at last she left the death-chamber. Thorold had desired that Miss Courtenay should not be disturbed, and the nurse had not ventured to disobey; but now, as she came forward to meet the lady, she started back, as much appalled as if, to use her own words, she had seen a ghost. And truly Ernestine might almost have passed for one, with her white dress shining in the morning light, her face perfectly colourless, and a shadowy look in her eyes, as if they saw nothing near, but were gazing into some far-distant realm, unseen by others. When Mrs. Berry spoke to her there was a peculiar quietude in her manner, which never again left her; it was as though nothing which could now befall her would have power to wound her any more, and she were merely passing through the world, with her hopes and heart elsewhere.

'My dear, dear lady, you do look so ill! what ever can I do for you?' said Mrs. Berry. 'The carriage is waiting for you; but I am sure you are not fit to go home.'

'I am quite well, dear nurse. Don't distress yourself

about me. But I must go; I have nothing more to do here now.'

'But you have had no rest, my dear lady, and not a morsel of food.'

'It will not hurt me.' What indeed could hurt her now! 'I do not want anything, dear nurse. Mr. Thorold will help you with all arrangements for the funeral. I shall be present at it myself.'

'Indeed, ma'am, you are not able for it; you don't know how ill you look.'

'It will not hurt me,' she still repeated, and quietly, though with a feeble step, she went into the carriage, and drove through the streets as if all were unreal around her, and the people whom she saw but moving shadows in a dream.

That same day, as Ernestine expected, a packet was brought to her from Hugh Lingard. It contained her letters, and a few little things she had given him, all arranged with a degree of tender care, which touched her very much, and there was a note which contained only these words:—

'I know that I must never look upon your face again. I know that my presence would henceforth be utterly insupportable to you; nor could I now myself endure to link my guilty life with yours, so innocent and holy. Ernestine, you will believe me that I never for one moment guessed the truth, or dreamt of the horrible vengeance that was pursuing me, while you, in your guileless charity, were tracking out the unhappy girl who, best in all the world, could teach you what I was. You always spoke of Annie Brook, and I knew only Rosie Brown. But I did know, from the first moment that your intense desire to save her revealed to me the depths of your pure soul, that I was totally unfit to be your life's companion; that you would have shrunk from me with horror had you known my previous history; and that I was in truth cruelly deceiving you in suffering you to bind yourself to such an one as I am. The honourable course would have been to have given you up, even if I could not have brought myself to tell you the hateful cause of so dreadful a necessity; but, Ernestine, my one, my only love, you were dearer to me than words can ever tell; the very light of my life. I could not part with you; rather every word you said, which showed how mistaken you were in your opinion of me, made me long to hasten the time when no such discovery as this could have torn you from me, though it might have broken your heart. But your God has taken care of you. My own deeds have risen

CHARITY SUFFERETH LONG, AND IS KIND. 209

up between us, and thrust us asunder for ever. I acknowledge the retribution to be just. My only love, farewell! HUGH LINGARD.'

A postscript merely stated that by the time Ernestine received this letter he would have left England. And so terminated her life's bright dream, in a darkness which had no ray of light, save in the hope that by the wreck of her own mortal happiness, she had secured eternal peace for Annie Brook.

For the next few days Ernestine moved about at her usual occupations, calm and still, speaking very little, and seeming to hear and see nothing of what was passing round her. She told Lady Beaufort quietly, that the engagement between herself and Hugh Lingard was broken off by mutual consent, and bore without a word the storm of indignant and astonished remarks with which the various members of the family met her announcement; still less did she heed the varying reports as to the cause of the rupture which were circulated in society. In her late experience she had gone far above and beyond all that the world could do, either for or against her. But her physical strength was not proof against the shock she had undergone, and the long mental strain which had preceded it. She came home from Annie Brook's funeral chilled and shivering, though it was a warm summer day. In the night, fever came on, and for some weeks she was too ill to be conscious of anything that had befallen her, or was yet to come.

In the long hours of convalescence, however, all the past came back upon her, with the deep lessons it had to teach as to the true use and meaning of the life which, for so brief a time, is intrusted to each one of us, to make it in its fruits, an eternal blessing or a curse.

Slowly she turned her wearied eyes to the future that might yet stretch out before her many years, and forced herself to consider how she meant to spend it. It was now about the time when her marriage would have been over, and Lady Beaufort had always intended after that event to take her two daughters to spend the winter in Rome; and she still adhered to her plan, though she would have been quite willing to let her niece accompany her. This, however, was what Ernestine felt she could not do. She knew that if she went with her aunt and cousins she would have to enter on a round of gaieties, for which the events of the last few months had totally unfitted her; and, besides, she felt she had arrived at a turning-point in her life, which had changed the aspect of the whole world, and her own

CHARITY SUFFERETH LONG, AND IS KIND. 211

position in it altogether. The natural happiness to which a woman looks in the ties of wife and mother could never now be hers. Hugh Lingard had alone possessed her love, and she knew that she could love none other while existence lasted. The life of mere society and amusement had always failed to satisfy her, and now the very thought of it was utter weariness to her; for her recent experiences had opened up to her a glimpse of the vast universe of sin and sorrow round her, and she longed with all her heart to make her life of some use to those who so sorely needed help, feeling that it would be only too short for all she should like to do for others in her course through the world. She thought of what she had seen in the gaol and the workhouse, and of the terrible necessities of that unhappy class to whom Lois and Annie had belonged; and it seemed to her as if her difficulty lay only in a choice among so many, who needed all that she or any one could do for them. She had a sufficient income to live independently in any way she pleased; but, while she was revolving many different plans in her mind, she found the whole matter suddenly taken out of her hands, and a claim of so urgent a nature made upon her, that she could have no hesitation in giving up all else to it.

Tidings arrived from India of a terrible accident which had befallen Colonel Courtenay and his wife.

The very day after their arrival at Calcutta, he had been driving her out in an open phaeton, with a pair of fiery horses, little used to harness. Something had frightened them at the top of a steep ascent. They had run off at a tremendous pace, and had dashed the carriage against a stone wall at the bottom. It had been smashed to pieces, and both Colonel and Mrs. Courtenay were thrown out to a considerable distance. When persons came to their assistance, it was found that the young and beautiful Mrs. Courtenay was quite dead; she had fallen with great violence on a heap of stones, in such a manner as to cause instant death, while her husband had received a blow on the head which rendered him completely insensible. He had after a time regained consciousness; but there had been some fatal injury to the brain, and though his life was in no danger, he had subsided into a state of hopeless imbecility. Of course, all that his friends in India could do for him, was to send him home at once to England, under the care of a doctor; and at the time when the letter reached Ernestine, her brother might be expected to arrive any day.

She was almost overwhelmed at the tidings. The thought of her proud, handsome brother, stricken down in the very prime of life and strength, and changed into a helpless idiot, was very terrible; but more dreadful far was the recognition of the awful judgment of God, which had taken from him the power to repent of the evil deeds which had made him a murderer, while life was still spared to drag on perhaps for many hopeless years. And Julia, the gay, brilliant girl, for whose sake he had driven Lois to her death—a few short weeks only had he been allowed to look on her with pride and pleasure as his wife, and then she was suddenly withdrawn into the Unseen, while the world was still all in all to her. Ernestine bowed her head before the justice of God, as she remembered the words, —'When Thy judgments are in the earth, the inhabitants of the world will learn righteousness.'

Her own course was plain. Woman-like, her deep love for her brother had never faltered, even when she knew him to be least worthy of it; and now her whole heart yearned towards him in his hopeless imbecility. She was his nearest living relation, and none cared to dispute her claim to take the sole care of him; and so it came to pass that Ernestine Courtenay once more took her way to Seamouth, feeling as if a lifetime of bitter experience had passed over her head since last she looked upon its quiet waters.

She was only just in time to go on board the steamer to meet her brother, before the passengers disembarked, and, sad as her anticipations had been, she almost reeled beneath the shock of his first appearance, as he was led up to her by the doctor and a servant: a broken-down, prematurely old man, with the tremor of a sort of palsy in all his limbs, and a face from which every spark of intelligence had fled; the eyes weak and glazed; the under lip drooping, and the helpless, useless hands hanging down on either side, as his attendants held him up by the arms. When Ernestine had recovered herself sufficiently to call him by his name, and try to attract his attention, he stared vacantly at her, without the smallest recognition in his eyes, and began in a querulous feeble voice to ask for his dinner; he wanted his dinner—why could he not have it?

'He has just dined,' said the doctor; but ceaselessly he continued to mumble out the same request while they conveyed him on shore, and the last word Ernestine heard, when she had seen him laid comfortably in bed, was the repetition of the same demand.

They had put him to bed early, as eating and sleeping were his sole occupations, and Ernestine, being thus left at liberty, went out in the twilight to visit the grave of Lois Brook. All was unchanged since she stood there last, save that a few pale autumn flowers had sprung up over the last resting-place of the suicide. But what centuries of mental life for her and for others had passed away since then! The doom of eternity itself had been fixed for most of those who were dear to her. With a deep sigh she looked at the inscription she had placed on the headstone to mark the grave,

L. B.
Veniam supplicat,

in the hope that her unhappy brother might one day himself awake to penitence, and come to that spot to seek forgiveness over the ashes of his victim. And now, was he not already as much beyond the power of repentance as if he too lay cold and still beneath the turf with Lois? He was dead now, even as she was, to moral responsibility and consciousness; and not till the last day of awful revelation could he know the dread results of his sin in the fate of Lois Brook. And this was the brother who had been her pride and joy so long; to whom she had been wont to look up with such love and admiration! Then she thought of Reginald, no less dear, her dead mother's darling, the refined, intellectual, enthusiastic boy, who used to confide to her his dreams of exalted goodness and noble service in the cause of Christ. Gone was his brief life as the memory of a dream; and over his grave too there hung a gloom which never would have rested on it but for one man's presumptuous tampering with that faith, in others, which he had lost for himself. Reginald too was the victim of a fellow-creature.

With the remembrance of Annie came the never-dying anguish of the thought, that the hand which had driven her to her dishonoured grave, was the one on which she herself had hoped to lean, throughout the life that now must pass away uncheered by human love or joy. And Lingard,—how did her heart die within her as she thought of him, and of her own false faith in the goodness and holiness which he had never possessed!

Her head drooped lower and lower as these dark images rose one by one before her; and her soul quailed beneath the mournful mystery of that unnatural cruelty, which makes human beings prey one upon another like wild beasts thirsting for each other's blood. The same life given to each, so brief, so momentous, so full of peril and temptation and suffering; the same eternity, with the awful uncertainty of its blessedness or woe; the same death, hastening with swift feet down the path which each must tread; and yet the horrible spectacle is hourly seen of men driving one another down to hell, —corrupting, torturing each other! Who would not sink beneath the weight of such dark truths, were it not for the One Vision on which the saddest, most bewildered eyes, may yet ever rest in peace,—the Cross of Calvary, where hangs the Light of the world, shining through all the gloom and tempests of the ages as they pass, and where all who have been wounded by sin or treachery may find their healing, if they will.

On Ernestine's soul that vision rose like the sun on the blackness of night, and to the inexhaustible love that there burns on for ever and ever, she felt she could leave the living and the dead alike.

In the course of a fortnight, Ernestine was established with her brother George in a country-house she had taken for him, and her long attendance began on the clouded existence which was to outlive her own. She soon found, however, that the care she bestowed on him, though absolutely essential to prevent his being neglected or ill-used by his attendants, could not fill up either her time or her thoughts; and she was very thankful to be enabled now to carry out a plan which had been in her mind ever since Annie Brook had escaped from the Penitentiary. Her interest in that miserable class of outcasts had been far too strongly excited ever to die away, and she had greatly longed to try the experiment of providing a refuge for them, on a different system from that which prevailed in most Homes, and which might at least serve as a preparatory shelter for them, until they were sufficiently advanced in real repentance to be able to accept the corrective discipline already in use. She gave up the whole of her fortune, except the small sum necessary for her personal expenses, to this object, and had soon prepared a suitable house near her brother's, which she took care should be surrounded with large gardens and grounds, so as to afford the means for ample out-door exercise and amusement. A kind-hearted, gentle lady, who had been left a childless widow, without the means of living, was, by Thorold's advice, placed in charge of it, with Mrs. Berry to assist her, and one or two other simple, kindly women, who had no theories as to rigid discipline or rule, but willingly agreed to take, for their one principle of action, the endeavour, by love and gentleness, to lead the wanderers they sheltered, to a perception of that everlasting love of which they knew absolutely nothing.

Ernestine had learnt from Thorold to believe that the chief mistake made in most other Refuges, was the treatment of these lawless impulsive beings as if they were already in reality penitents, which it is not too much to say they never are. Many motives may lead them to seek a shelter, which have no foundation in sorrow for sin, or even in resignation of it; and when, therefore, they are placed under a system of conventual strictness and high moral pressure, which could only be advisable for persons deeply remorseful for a shameless life, it is inevitable that in many cases the result should be a failure, which leaves them to fall back into their guilt.

To grant these poor outcasts a simple shelter from evil, unencumbered by needless rules and constraints, and to strive to show them the goodness of their Father in heaven reflected in the love and compassion of His creatures, was Ernestine's first object; and when their health and spirits had improved under a few months' care and kindness, she tried gently to influence for good each individual separately, dealing with every one according to her special temperament, instead of placing the whole number *en masse* under a machinery of discipline, enforced by punishments, as is too often done elsewhere. She received all who came or were sent to her, without requiring certificates of health, or otherwise raising obstacles to their admission; indeed, it seemed to her, that to take them when they were ill, and nurse them through their sickness, was one of the best means of gaining an influence over them. If an application was made when the house was full, she found a home for them elsewhere till she could take them in; but she would rather have sacrificed anything than let one be refused a refuge who could be induced to seek for it. She provided work for them; but when their shattered nerves or hysterical tendencies made a monotonous employment impossible or irksome, they were free to roam, without constraint, through the grounds; and a considerable part of their ordinary occupation was the care of the garden, which afforded them both fresh air and amusement. Often they were taken a walk over the breezy common at the back of the house, which was too far from any town to render this liberty dangerous as an inducement to escape; but Ernestine would have thought it a less evil to lose one or two in this way, than to subject the whole of them to the feeling of confinement and imprisonment, which they are so unable to bear. With Thorold's help she was able to make arrangements for the emigration of some of them every year to a distant colony, where situations were found for them, and where, in many cases, they married respectably. Not a few of them found their last home under her care, and met the early death, which

CHARITY SUFFERETH LONG, AND IS KIND. 221

so often overtakes them, with her arms round them, and her prayers ascending for them. She was able to spend a great part of every day at the Home, where her appearance always made a general festival; and though she had many disappointments and sorrows, as the inevitable result of thus charging herself with the care of beings so wayward and so demoralized, yet did the work often bring to her, in the course of her patient life, the sweetest, purest joy which ever can be known on earth,— the hope that she had saved a deathless soul, and brought back to the feet of her dear Lord the wandering and the lost, for whom He died.

. . . . . .

Lois and Annie Brook lie cold and silent in the grave. That which man has made them they must remain, till the voice of the archangel calls them to meet their destroyers before the throne of God. But there are thousands like unto them in this land of ours,—a multitude such as no man can number, in whom the breath of life yet lingers, for whom the immutable fiat has not yet been spoken; and there are others scattered thick on the earth as flowers in the spring, children young and pure, sent into this world to be made fit for the Paradise of saints, who we know shall all too swiftly be made like unto the lost in their dishonoured graves, if justice and mercy continue to veil their faces in sight of this deadly plague as now they do.

Shall it be ever thus? Shall this dread evil slay its thousands and ten thousands yearly, unheeded by those to whom legislative power is given, or by the no less influential rulers of public opinion, while still it ever cries to God for the vengeance that shall surely come at last? Shall its hideous wickedness still be ignored, glossed over, or made light of, as regards the destroyers, while the destroyed are branded with dishonour, and driven to deeper evil, by the blackest injustice that ever disgraced a Christian land? Is it to be always so, that in the realm which calls Christ, master, the crime He denounced in awful terms is to be held by men, and *for men*, as scarce a sin? Are the haunts and centres of infamy always to be suffered to exist openly, and still allure souls to destruction in the face of day? Will a time never come when this matter shall be tried by God's estimate of right and wrong, and not by man's; when the measure of HIS justice shall alone regulate the balance of comparative guilt; when His standard of holiness shall fix the place it is to hold for all alike, in the world's code of moral and spiritual evil? Would that such a

time might be foreseen even in hope alone! for till that day comes, this great Empire may advance in knowledge, in wisdom, in power, and in science, but it can never really become that which even now it claims to be—
THE KINGDOM OF GOD, AND OF HIS CHRIST.

THE END.

EDINBURGH : T. CONSTABLE,
PRINTER TO THE QUEEN, AND TO THE UNIVERSITY.